THE WEAP

1: ECHOES OF CHAOS

Ralston squarely faced the alien . . . He tried to get past the P'torra again. The alien had wedged himself firmly into the narrow doorway, making escape almost impossible.

Ralston stepped back and quickly sized up the alien. He had fought enough of them in the Nex-P'torra war to have an appreciation for how strong and hardy they were. Once, he had blasted off both legs of a P'torra field officer. That hadn't killed him. He had followed the officer for almost twenty kilometers; along the way the P'torra had killed four different varieties of creature with his bare hands.

Ralston might respect them for their toughness, but he despised them for what they had done to the Nex — and what they continued to do on a half dozen other worlds.

"You think to slay me?" asked the P'torra . . .

THE WEAPONS OF CHAOS

2: EQUATIONS OF CHAOS

The animal looked up. One emerald eye blazed with hatred. The other had been malformed, only a patch of fur where the socket should have been. Forepaws with glistening talons raked the air to hold Ralston at bay.

"Here, over here!" yelled Bernssen, waving his arms and trying to distract the creature.

Ralston saw his chance and acted. The spear flashed forward once more, finding a vulnerable throat. Blood spurting, the creature spun back to face Ralston. He closed the contacts once more. The electrical surge flopped the creature onto its side. It lay there, feebly pawing the air. Bernssen came up, breathing hard, and said, "Never saw anything like it."

"Look at its claws. They're metallic — naturally metallic. And the musculature. Such a powerful creature, but twisted out of shape."

"What spawned such a monster?" asked Bernssen.

"It's a mutant," said Ralston. "A mutant spawned by chaos."

THE WEAPONS OF CHAOS

3: COLORS OF CHAOS

"P'torra must not possess secret of randomness," said Slenth.

The reptile's talons clicked on the floor to emphasize his concern. "Must *never* learn of its nature."

Ralston struggled to find the words to tell his friend when a soft click alerted him. In the shadows at the far end of the hall he saw a darker figure. A glint of light caught the focusing muzzle of an energy weopon.

Without thinking, Ralston threw his arms around Slenth and drove forward. The two of them smashed hard into the wall just as a sizzling blue torrent of energy ripped through the space where Ralston had been. The Nex dropped to the floor and had his weapon in action before Ralston could recover his senses.

The computer console blinked slowly, numbers still solemnly marching across the screen. Whoever had put the spy devices in his office now alerted campus security about the firefight in progress. Would this save them — or doom them?

WEAPONS OF CHAOS

**Echoes of Chaos
Equations of Chaos
Colors of Chaos**

ROBERT E. VARDEMAN

NEW ENGLISH LIBRARY
Hodder and Stoughton

First published in the United States of
America as three separate volumes:

ECHOES OF CHAOS © 1986 by Robert E.
Vardeman
Published by Berkley Books in 1986

EQUATIONS OF CHAOS © 1987 by
Robert E. Vardeman
Published by Berkley Books in 1987

COLORS OF CHAOS © 1988 by Robert E.
Vardeman
Published by Berkley Books

New English Library paperback edition
1989

British Library C.I.P.

Vardeman, Robert E.
  The weapons of chaos.
  I. Title
  813'.54[F]

ISBN 0–450–42854–0

Printed and bound in Great Britain
for Hodder and Stoughton
Paperbacks, a division of Hodder and
Stoughton Ltd., Mill Road,
Dunton Green, Sevenoaks, Kent
TN13 2YA (Editorial Office:
47 Bedford Square, London
WC1B 3DP) by Cox & Wyman Ltd.,
Reading.

1: ECHOES OF CHAOS

To Roy Tackett

ONE

"WE ARE DYING." The gaunt, trembling figure turned and looked away from the others gathered around the long rectangular Table of Rules. Fordyne, advisor to the Council of State, statistician without peer, had never felt older and less able to deal with destiny. His burning amethyst eyes stared out the window of the towering Aerie and swept across the city stretched below him. From this height the chaos wasn't visible, but Fordyne knew it existed.

"You exaggerate," came the Chief of Rules' mocking voice. Fordyne's exhaustion vanished in a heady mixture of anger and frustration with such stubbornness. He spun, his embroidered chamber robes swirling around his lean frame.

"I do not." The fire in his reply took the Chief aback. Never had anyone spoken to the ruler of all civilization in such a manner. Politeness, if not duty, dictated only serene responses, measured tones, orderly emotions.

Fordyne had passed beyond accepted behavior. His world was dying around him and none of these fools believed!

"The facts are incontrovertible. Examine them. Have others you trust more do so. You will see." Anger faded, leaving only exhaustion—exhaustion and distress. He had worked hard for over three years, accumulating the evidence to support what his heart already had told him. The beige folders containing the results of the correlational study lay untouched in the center of the Table of Rules. No one at this meeting even dared open one and scan the first page abstract.

In their hearts they, too, knew what Fordyne had feared and had now shown true.

"Societal dynamics is a confusing issue, Fordyne," the Chief of Rules said, lounging back to nest in his feather-encrusted chair. He stared at the Council statistician. "You of all people know this. These . . . disturbances. They're random. No organized attempt is being made to overthrow us." The Chief snorted derisively. He laid one finger alongside his thick, hard nose to accentuate the point. "The last attempt to subvert a government is almost two hundred years in the past. Memo is stable. The country is stable." The Chief leaned forward, four-fingered hands gripping the edge of the table until the yellow-taloned tips turned white. "We are *all* stable."

"This madness has nothing to do with the toppling of governments by an organization," said Fordyne. "It—its only characteristic is disorganization."

"Talk sense. You're a scholar, not some giddy doomster on a park perch prophesying the return of feathered Larn, bringing his vengeance for our sins."

Fordyne noted several Councilors around the table stiffen at the mention of the mythical god. While the Chief of Rules scoffed at the ancient religion, Fordyne had learned that many— some in that room—had again embraced the old ways. They were less able than he to articulate their fears, and they reached out for solace, for explanations of why their secure nest/world was falling to pieces around them.

"Very well," Fordyne said, determination again rising within him. "A brief presentation. I trust its dryness will not unduly bore you."

Before the Chief could either approve or dismiss him, Fordyne reached into his robe and pulled forth a small projector. He aimed it at the far wall, and then stroked along its control surface. The window shutters closed, blocking off the deceptive serenity of Memo, the room lights dimmed, and a pale ruby beam stretched out over the surface of the wall. Tiny speckles set there burst into amorphous, colored life. To the eye came no scene; Fordyne's picture formed within the minds of all present.

"Fact: Accidental deaths have risen forty-six percent in the past seven years." The charts burned hotly into their brains. Many stirred uneasily but Fordyne had trapped them. They had to stay and witness the progression of evidence.

"Faulty control systems at General Guidance," muttered the Chief.

"Fact: Less than half of these deaths occurred during machine operation. Those that do have this profile indicate high probability, to the ninety-five percent confidence level, of operator error rather than machine malfunction."

"You're saying that all of these accidents are just that, accidents," pointed out the Chief. The others at the Table of Rules remained silent. They couldn't evade the numbers marching like a burning army through their brains, but they might dull their impact by concentrating on other, less disturbing ideas.

"The only malfunction, according to extensive autopsy evidence, is with the people." When the Chief said nothing to this, Fordyne pressed on. "Fact: Epilepsy has become epidemic among certain sectors of our population. It is my contention that the rise in accidental death is strongly linked to this factor."

"All these . . . freaks caused their own deaths? That makes them murderers," blurted out a Councilor.

Fordyne felt revulsion at this. Epileptics were not spoken of in polite society. This, in part, made it even more difficult to force the others to believe in the seriousness of the matter. They refused to stroke the pinfeather because of the proscribed affliction.

"It has become an epidemic," Fordyne repeated. He closed his eyes and calmed his rampaging emotions. To lose control, to clack your dental ridges wildly, insanely, to twitch and thrash about, to lose all civilized behavior seemed a fate worse than death. The stark embarrassment of such a seizure had, no doubt, caused hundreds—or by his numbers, thousands— of the afflicted to tread the only honorable path and kill themselves.

"Epidemics can be blunted, the disease cured. Such unsightly behavior is not induced like a viral infection," scoffed another of the Councilors. "To say that such disgusting behavior is induced—contagious!—denigrates all our medical science."

"I realize that it is difficult to speak of such things." Fordyne squeezed his projector so tightly that the plastic began to warp. He controlled himself and relaxed his grip. "But the facts will not go away simply because we wish for some other cause."

"Wheeze!" The Chief whistled derisively through his dental plate. "There's nothing wrong with this country, this world! We've never been so prosperous, our people so at peace with themselves and with their neighbors."

"Fact: Our population is in decline. The absolute number of our people is beginning to drop."

"A mere anomaly," said the Chief.

"The birthrate fell to less than replacement fourteen years ago. The latest flash figures from the medical division show that the replacement figure has dropped below one." The projected image rustling through their brains contained sorrow, funeral processions, infinite cold untouched by the pure flame of rebirth.

"Explain."

"For every two deaths, there is less than one born to take their place. The actual numbers." Fordyne stroked the side of the controller. The ruby beam brightened as the images Fordyne desired insinuated themselves into the others' heads. "For every thousand deaths, there are only four hundred and eighty-nine births."

"As I said, an anomaly. Time will ease this."

"There is more than an accelerating death rate, a declining birth rate, and the . . . seizure numbers." Fordyne found himself unable to even mention epilepsy. His hand shook harder and fear rose within him, fear of personal shame. Nothing controlled his trembling, not even the illicit drugs he had been using. "These are to be considered restricted data." The murmur around the Table of Rules showed the Councilors' disapproval. Secrecy solved nothing. And from whom would they keep such knowledge? They had been at peace for well over a hundred years, war only a vague, disturbing memory.

Fordyne pressed on. "Innovation and scientific discovery are on the wane."

"Really, Fordyne, don't be absurd. You've carried this distasteful folly of yours far enough." The Chief of Rules rose and leaned forward on the table, knuckles bent under and supporting his weight. "I want to hear nothing more from you on this."

"Denying our trouble will not erase it," Fordyne said. "Look! Examine the figures. In the folders. Here!" He almost crushed the projector as he squeezed down hard on it. Columns of numbers, the correlational coefficients, the matrices laden with proof raced across the surface of their unwilling minds.

"Begone. We have other matters to deal with."

"As you will it, Chief." Fordyne bowed his head, both in deference to his leader's command and in defeat. He stroked the projector and a sigh of relief went around the Table of Rules. Once more they could deny without the interference of truth.

"They refused to listen?" Young Jerad stood staring at his instructor. Fordyne could only nod. "But the facts! The numbers! The high correlations!"

"They meant nothing to the Chief. Or to the others." Fordyne collapsed into an amorphous cloth cushion that threatened to swallow him whole. He almost wished that it would and put him out of his inner torment.

"But can't they *see* what is happening all around us?" Jerad hadn't learned patience. Fordyne closed his hot eyes and felt the welling wetness at the corners. Jerad would never learn. There wouldn't be enough time. Not for Jerad, not for anyone.

"They dismiss it all as anomaly, an unexpected singularity in the data. Such turnings in the number patterns have happened previously," Fordyne explained, more for the comfort of hearing his own voice than for any other reason. More softly he added, "But never with such impressive force."

"The results of my research," Jerad said, kneeling beside Fordyne. "Look!" The young statistician thrust out the folder. Fordyne laid his hand on the first page. Images flashed through his mind. He pulled his hand back and stared at his assistant.

"Yes," Jerad said, anticipating Fordyne's words. "One reason our research has deteriorated over the past few decades is irreproducibility. A classic experiment, even one as well-documented as the light-speed determinators, give varying results with each new test. Even when the same instruments are used."

This shocked even Fordyne, who had thought himself beyond surprise. "How?"

Jerad shook his head. Bright purple eyes blazed and his lipless mouth pulled into a thin, determined line. "Cossia thinks it might have something to do with the pass-by."

Fordyne frowned. What had been hailed fifty years earlier as the greatest event in scientific history had proven to be anticlimactic. Worse, the astronomers who had focused their telescopes on the cometary object had been ridiculed when the promised cosmic display of winter-sky-brightening coma had failed to appear. It had set space research back a hundred years and had, in Fordyne's mind, been responsible for the Council canceling all attempts to reach either of the nearby planets. Since those days, research funds had gone into geophysical research, not astronomical. A race that had once soared on wings doomed itself to remaining planetbound.

Fordyne sighed as he thought of missed opportunities. The data to be accumulated upon reaching a near orbit of the planet would have been immense. Even the geologists would have benefited. He sighed again. It wasn't to be. The bulk of data accumulated by the specialists in volcanoes defied mathematical analysis, being of a subjective nature. Lost opportunities. So many. Too many.

He shook himself from the sad reverie, and asked of Jerad, "What effect could the comet have had on us?"

"Cossia is unsure. She says it may have been a potent force field, not unlike this electromagnetic field Illfon and the others speak of. The comet may have cast its unseen net in front of the planet, and we may have passed through it."

Fordyne did not call the theory far-fetched. What he had presented to the Chief of Rules and the other Councilors counted as far-fetched. Jerad merely theorized. A hypothesis and nothing more that might explain their data.

"Fordyne, your pallor ... " Jerad stood, flapping his arms futilely as if to take wing, as their ancient ancestors had done at the first hint of confusion.

Fordyne tried to answer. He bit his tongue, felt the dental plate severing the rock-hard appendage, drawing blood, choking him. He reached out and found himself trembling uncontrollably. Panic seized him. Fordyne flopped forward, thrashing about, knocking over tables laden with folders and drinking saucers.

"Help me," he croaked. Froth coated his lips and caked on his chin, hardening with dried blood. The world exploded in vivid, crazy colors and his eyes rolled up. Back arching, limbs beyond command, Fordyne dissolved into misery as the seizure fully possessed him.

"I am so ashamed," Jerad said, his head hanging low between his thin shoulders. Cossia's hand fluttered along a quaking arm. She stroked and soothed, as if Jerad were a fledgling who had fallen from his birthing nest.

"Fordyne is at peace. He counts numbers in a land beyond our understanding. He is happy."

Jerad turned stricken eyes to his friend. "You don't understand. He did not simply *die*. He was . . . taken."

Cossia pulled away.

"Yes," Jerad cried. "Like the others. He died in an"—he fought down his revulsion—"epileptic seizure."

"How awful! Such a great mathematician to be so dishonored."

"I did nothing for him." Jerad pleaded with Cossia for absolution. He did not find it in her amber eyes.

"You were his friend. While he lived, he conducted himself honorably. None can do more than Fordyne."

"I'd just told him of your theory concerning the pass-by."

They gazed at the funeral tree, now ablaze and consuming Fordyne's remains. They backed from the heat, waiting for the flames to die. In older times the trees had been real, but with the need to deal with thousands of deaths every year in the city alone, the funeral pyres had become increasingly symbolic. The trees were now of steel, and gas jets fueled the cleansing fires.

Jerad spun and stalked off, hardly trusting himself. His nose spasmed with the smell of Fordyne's cremation. Did that nose twitch signal the onset of a seizure? Or did he merely react to the odor of his mentor and friend's funeral? How could anyone tell in time to avoid dishonor?

Jerad shuddered.

Cossia's strides lengthened. She matched his bobbing gait perfectly. "We have no evidence, but much became confusing when the comet passed so close."

"Close?" Jerad shook his head. "It didn't even come near enough to the sun to leave a tail. What sort of comet is that?"

"My point, Jerad," she said, gripping his arm. "What if it left a gas in space and the planet swept through it? We might have been poisoned. The"—she swallowed and avoided naming their friend's affliction—"unfortunate disease might be curable, as many have suggested. We might find an antidote to this poison."

Jerad sucked in a deep lungful of air. Only the taint of Fordyne's passing marred the perfect spring day. Cool breezes blew off the ocean and pure rain would fall before sunset. He had always cherished the rain, enjoying its wetness against his thick hide. Jerad flexed one yellow hand, pushed back the sleeve of his robe and let the strong radiation from the sun bathe him.

"Why has no one detected this poison?" He didn't put into words his feeling that such a fine day put the lie to Cossia's claim. It felt *good* in the sun. She caught the sense of his emotions.

"We are dealing with problems beyond our understanding," she said. "Fordyne believed that nothing could be known unless it could be quantified. He failed. And from that we learn a valuable lesson. We must trust our instincts. Not in science but in emotion." She thumped her rounded chest. "Here lies the answer, not here." Cossia tapped her skull.

Jerad shrugged. Fordyne's death had left him stunned and peculiarly hollow within. Such dishonor for a researcher he had so admired.

"We must try. We must solve this problem or we will all end up stripped of life and dignity." Cossia glanced over one of her sloping shoulders. The heavenly flight crews had already prepared the death tree for another funeral. They had developed an efficient system for their task; too many left this world for the promise of clear skies and limitless flight.

"We must try," Jerad repeated listlessly. "Perhaps Dial's project is the answer."

Jerad doubted any answer to their problems existed, especially such a feather-headed one as Dial pursued.

• • •

The riots raged only a few blocks down the street. Cossia and Jerad peered out through a slit cut in the thatched wall of their refuge.

"It's no use, Cossia. They are caught in the throes of hysteria. The mob will destroy all Merno before dawn."

"If only we could understand. The answer is so close. I *feel* it!"

Jerad nodded. He, too, sensed their nearness to understanding. They had taken Fordyne's folders and gone over them, the numbers burning into their brains throughout long nights until they saw the clean, neat columns intruding into their dreams—and their nightmares. But they had studied these past two years since Fordyne had died in disgrace. To no avail.

The Chief of Rules had been assassinated. The Council's attempts to restore order had failed with the rise of one demagogue after another. Each subsequent fanatical leader brought civilization closer to the brink of dishonor. Any would-be leader who attempted to preserve discipline in the capital was not a leader for long. The mobs usually rebelled and destroyed them, as everything of worth was being destroyed.

Worst of all, even those such as Dial with his strange notion of escaping the planet had vanished in the ensuing years. All that remained to them was preserving what they could of their culture in hopes of a reborn society at some later, less chaotic, time.

A much later time.

"The fires burn closer," Jerad said, all emotion gone from his voice. Death no longer held the fascination and fear for him that it once had. To be gone from this world of illogic seemed a worthier goal than continued life.

"We can escape through the back," said Cossia, always the more tenacious of the two. "The vaults are still months away from completion. We need to work harder if we . . ." Her voice trailed off. Her large, mobile ears rotated. Cossia frowned. The sounds carried on the hot summer winds were confusing.

Then she *felt* what she feared most. Cossia spun and faced Jerad. Her friend, her lover, the most precious of all those left on this declining world jerked and twitched as if someone had attached wires to his limbs and sent electric charges surging. Jerad smashed hard against the thatched wall and fell to the

floor, arms windmilling out of control, purple eyes wide and
showing yellow sclera as vivid as his hide. Cossia ran to him,
but his strength startled her. With the ease of someone ten times
stronger, Jerad batted her away—and did not know that he did
so.

Cossia watched in horror as Jerad died from the epileptic
seizure, as so many others before him had done,

"The virulence," she said, her voice low and choked. She
had *felt* the onslaught, but it had taken Jerad so fast! Less than
a dozen frenzied heartbeats had passed from beginning until
death.

Jerad gave another death jerk, snapping his spine like a
dried twig. From past experiences, Cossia knew the twitchings
would continue for some time. Jerad had died following the
first seizure, but his body's resilience persisted.

Cossia looked at her own hands. They shook. Fear rose and
died within her. "Reaction," she said aloud. "Shock. Nothing
more." But Cossia knew she lied to herself. The epileptic convulsions that had killed Fordyne and Jerad would soon claim
her.

She *felt* it.

With the rioters only a dozen paces from the door of the
thatched house, Cossia burst into the street. She saw the de-
monic stares on the faces of the crowd, the expressions of lost
hope. Cossia almost despaired enough to join them in their fear
and frustration in burning down the city's most magnificent
edifices.

Cossia turned her misted eyes aloft to the majestic spire of
the Aerie where the Chief of Rules and his Council had once
met around the Table of Rules to decide the proper path for all
to tread. No longer. They had died in the riots, and now licking
tongues of orange flame sampled the base of the mighty building.

Cossia watched as the symbol of her world began to burn.
At first only the lower levels filled with bright oranges and
yellows. Then upper levels began belching black plumes of
smoke. As the fire quickly spread, the top floors crumbled and
the entire building's integrity was compromised.

The Aerie died, as did Cossia's world.

She let herself be carried away by the vortex of the crowd.
Slowly, Cossia worked her way into eddies and backwaters,

finally finding a deserted street leading into the countryside. Arms flapping in mock flight, she hurried along to the vaults. The others worked feverishly to complete the last of the accumulated displays, to seal them before the mobs thought about this final legacy and rebelled against informing future generations of their shame. But Cossia allowed herself a gut-wrenching doubt about the effectiveness of what she and Jerad and the others had done.

For whom were the vaults constructed? Cossia had seen the statistics compiled by Fordyne and his successors. This world died. There would be no survivors, no successors to carry on civilization.

Cossia *felt* it.

TWO

MICHAEL RALSTON FLOATED in the center of the University starship's main cabin, oblivious to all that went on around him, isolated by the sound-deadening effect of the lowered atmospheric pressure aboard ship. The trip to Alpha 3 hadn't been a long one by current standards, but it had worn on him. He didn't look forward to this dig; he expressed open hostility even to being assigned such a minor find when real work went begging on Vega 14 and Nuevo Seguro and Proteus 4.

He inhaled deeply, then exhaled slowly at the thought of Proteus. That should have been his. He'd been on the initial planetary survey that had located the ruins. A civilization older than mankind, only the second ever discovered that had possessed space travel—and possibly a stardrive—and waiting for the careful analysis and loving care he could lavish on it.

But it wasn't his. Alpha 3 was his while Velasquez got Proteus 4.

Ralston opened his eyes and noticed that the air currents caused him to drift slowly toward the wall section with the chipped blue enamel. He extended arms and legs, slowing the small amount of rotation he'd developed. He started when he realized he wasn't alone in the cabin as he'd thought. Ralston faced a trim, small woman barely ten years younger.

He stared at her as if a million years separated them. He might be Leonore Disa's graduate advisor on this dig, but they had nothing in common. Ralston closed his eyes and went back into a self-pitying world. None of the students accompanying him shared his devotion to the field. Dilettantes, all of them. He had started on the flight with high hopes. He always did.

Nothing had come of them. The students were lackluster at best. All knew this wasn't the best expedition the University of Ilium had in space. That was Proteus. They were all second-rate students sent to a second-rate planet without sufficient equipment.

Or drive or skill, Ralston mentally added. His early attempts to establish any kind of rapport with the students had failed, and the professor had not been sufficiently motivated to pursue the matter. Better to drift off, lost in his own thoughts, his own pity.

Proteus should have been his! Damn campus politics!

Faint gabbling noises reached him, words altered by the lower than Novo Terra norm air pressure. Leonore Disa gestured for him to come closer. Ralston pulled in his arms and legs, increased rotation, and grabbed an elastic band stretched around the cabin. He collided hard, and then felt the band tighten and send him back across the room. With contemptuous ease, he came to a total stop beside the woman. She floundered a bit while turning simply. He took some small vindictive pleasure at her clumsiness. They had been in space for seven weeks, and the graduate student still hadn't mastered weightlessness.

"What is it?" Ralston asked.

"The pilot says we're about ready to shift out of stardrive." Leonore spoke louder than necessary. She also still misjudged hearing distances in the low pressure.

"Any guesses about how close to Alpha 3 we'll be?"

The incomprehension on her face told Ralston she had scant idea what he meant.

"How much longer till we get into orbit around Alpha 3?"

Leonore shrugged. Her brown eyes left Ralston's pale gray ones and focused somewhere behind the professor. He pulled in his legs and spun to see another graduate student enter. Ralston had even less respect for this one. If Leonore Disa, with her expensive implanted glowing jewelry plates and perfect coiffure seemed a dilettante, Yago de la Cruz proved even more of a dabbler. Ralston had no idea why the son of one of the wealthiest men on Novo Terra bothered pursuing a profession of dubious social standing, with few creature comforts and no promise for riches.

"What is it, Citizen de la Cruz?" he asked.

"The pilot says we're within a local A.U. of Alpha 3, *Doctor* Ralston. Shouldn't be more than another ten hours before orbit." Ralston watched Leonore Disa's face go from confusion to understanding as de la Cruz reported. She wasn't stupid, just ignorant, Ralston decided. Of de la Cruz, all he could say was that he didn't like the man or the sarcastic emphasis de la Cruz always placed on *Doctor* when addressing him.

"Good. Check out the equipment. Make certain we've got the monitoring station ready for grounding. While we're in parking orbit, we'll kick out the survey satellites." Caught up in enthusiasm over being able to work again, Ralston forgot his distaste for his assigned students and the paltry results likely on Alpha 3.

"At once, *Doctor* Ralston." De la Cruz misjudged his trajectory, bounced off the wall in an inept move, turned and glowered at Ralston, then shot through the door.

"He'll have a bruise off that," Ralston said, finding that he enjoyed the idea of de la Cruz battering himself.

"Doctor, may I ask a question?" Leonore's cheeks glowed a soft purple in counter to the lush pinks and flashing greens marching in strict geometric patterns along her hands and arms. He wondered if the implanted jewelry plates responded to the woman's emotions—some did—or if they could be programmed for random color display.

"Of course. That's why you're here. Consider this a giant classroom."

She frowned. He realized his bitter tone mirrored Yago de la Cruz's too closely.

"Sorry," he said, softer. "What is it?"

"We didn't come out of the shift very close to Alpha 3, did we? That's why we have to spend another ten hours getting into orbit."

"Actually, the pilot is to be commended on his navigation. Some commercial flights do a lot worse." Ralston looked around. The University of Ilium starship was hardly more than a space-going waste can. Reduced air pressure saved the cost of transporting expensive mass. Even the exterior walls were a light boron fiber composite hardly a centimeter thick—Ralston repressed a shudder at being so close to infinite space—and the cramped quarters had made him think that the University hadn't gone to any great expense hiring a pilot. In that, at least, he'd been wrong.

Traditionally and from preference, pilots interacted very little with their passengers. This one had proven no different, but Ralston had spoken to him twice in the seven weeks and had been impressed with his attention to detail and general knowledge of spacing. Ralston gave one over to the University for having the sense not to send out a novice pilot, even if this expedition accounted for little.

Coming within a local A.U. of their destination amounted to damned good navigation. While some might call it luck, Ralston knew better. The lesser pilots always erred on the side of increased distance. Shifting out of stardrive at less than this might indicate foolhardiness. One A.U. showed true skill, being neither too close nor too far from the planetary target.

"I've never been off Novo Terra before," she said. It hadn't been necessary for her to reveal this.

"There's not going to be much excitement," he told her.

"Not like there'd be on Proteus," Leonore said. He looked at her sharply. "Really, Dr. Ralston, we all know you wanted that dig."

"Alpha 3's not bad."

"It's going to be hard getting a good dissertation out of it," she said. Her frankness startled him. Ralston had maintained an aloofness from Leonore Disa and the others throughout the trip, contenting himself with the book he pretended to write. Whenever he had a few spare minutes he worked on it, but during seven weeks of unrelieved "spare minutes" he had done little more than jot down notes.

"That's one of the hazards in archaeology. You can't know what you'll find until you start digging."

"Where'd you do your dissertation?"

He smiled as he remembered. "A sweet find on Archænor

2. I was Benjamin Uzoma's student. Great instincts, he had. Great. One look at a site and he knew where the real stuff was. We spent seven standard months there."

"What did your research cover?" Leonore seemed genuinely interested. Ralston reflected briefly on the difference when he'd gone to school a mere ten years ago and the students now. He'd scoured the university library for every publication Uzoma had written, studied them, evaluated the quality of the work and decided he could learn much from such a man before even applying to the department. Leonore had just admitted she knew nothing of his background; Ralston doubted de la Cruz or any of the others had bothered to check into his publications, either.

That annoyed Ralston. The dissertation and the subsequent fourteen papers were his *life*.

"The natives had evolved into a 'social insect' culture. My paper dealt with the relationship between such a communal existence and its effect on architecture."

Leonore looked dreamy, as if thinking about the Novo Terra Gala Ball rather than archaeology. Then she surprised Ralston by saying, "Something like the Earth termite." Ralston waited for her to continue, to explain. "A few seem to have no function, but a dozen or more begin organizing into platoons and stacking pellets to the proper height and angle to make keystone arches."

"They manage to build very elaborate structures," Ralston said. "One or two can't, but a larger group seems to instinctively grasp complex relationships and know how to build in such a way to control the humidity and temperature."

"I remember reading that the termites worked together using chemical signals. I doubt the Archænor natives did, though. Too much acid in that atmosphere."

"You've read my dissertation," Ralston said. "That was my finding. They constructed on the basis of visual cues, being very sensitive to subtle changes in wavelength." He watched in growing appreciation as Leonore's jewelry plates flashed pastels. Someone with a good eye had programmed her plates; they heightened shadows on her cheeks, turning her face into something exotic rather than plain.

"I called it up from University files," Leonore admitted. "I was interested in seeing what your field of specialty was. We seemed to be stuck with one another."

"'Stuck' is a bit harsh." He wondered why he had withdrawn so on the trip. He might have been disappointed—crushed—that he'd been assigned to Alpha 3, but that didn't relieve him of his obligations as an instructor. He ought to have found out more about his students. As he had done with Uzoma, he should have investigated the strengths and weaknesses of his graduate assistants. It was, after all, what the University paid him to do.

"We're the lowest ranking students in the department," Leonore said without rancor. "And you haven't gotten tenure because of your involvement with the Nex."

Ralston stiffened. He hadn't realized anyone outside the department staff knew of his youthful windmill tilting.

"It must have been fascinating, being so close to a truly alien race. Is that what sparked your interest in archaeology?" Leonore's question came out innocent and almost ingenuous, but Ralston sensed a sharp intellect hiding behind the façade.

"Not really."

"They seem so . . . repulsive. The Nex, I mean." Her brown eyes speared him, demanding a substantive reply.

"I enlisted in their forces. I fought against the P'torra rather than for the Nex."

"Why?"

Ralston had asked himself the same question repeatedly. The humanoid P'torra had commanded human sympathy and aid. The reptilian, virtually boneless, formless Nex triggered only fear.

"If you don't understand it, oppose it," he said with a bleak smile. "That's the way most people responded to the Nex. I saw firsthand the atrocities done by the P'torra, though. Complete planets devastated. They used chemical and biological agents to depopulate four Nex-inhabited worlds."

"The war was started by the Nex," Leonore said. "They attacked the P'torra homeworld."

Ralston snorted. "I won't get into the politics of it. The Nex are alien in many ways and their views of both human and P'torra are skewed. They thought a quick strike at the homeworld would end the conflict. Instead, it only rallied support for the P'torra."

"They destroyed four worlds? The P'torra? I never heard that."

"Before war was declared, the P'torra killed two more. Six worlds turned into bacterial jungles. After the declaration of war, the Nex stopped them from harming any more of the planets, but the damage had been done."

"What did the P'torra gain? If the worlds are uninhabitable, they can't use them, either."

"A good point. Like most wars, this was fought for economic gain. The Nex were becoming too efficient in markets the P'torra coveted. The racial overtones came into play only after the P'torra saw how we could be manipulated by it. Societal shame over our own beginnings on Earth still run deep."

"After what happened on Earth, why didn't we rally around the Nex? A world destroyed is an awful loss, even if only the temperate zones on Earth are gone."

"Again, it's the Nex failure to understand warm-blooded psychology. I doubt one in a thousand citizens even know of the P'torra world killings." Ralston unconsciously distanced himself from Leonore, letting the lowered pressure isolate him again. Then he forced himself back within distance for easy hearing. Drifting in weightlessness and letting the bubble of silence formed a retreat to the womb. He might not like this dig or the promise held out by Alpha 3 or the students, but he had to make the best of it.

"I don't want to talk about that anymore. Get the others. We'll meet for a quick conference in, say, fifteen minutes."

"Very well, Doctor." Leonore Disa turned inexpertly, aimed herself for the door, and arrowed out, wobbling slightly around her major axis. All things considered, she did much better than de la Cruz had. And Ralston found himself glad for this, too.

Ralston smiled. He remembered his first time in weightlessness. He hadn't been able to eat and keep it down longer than a few minutes. But then the Nex food hadn't been palatable, either. Only when they shifted to a supply planet and he had the chance to buy four cases of peanut butter, a few chocolate bars and coffee from a black marketeer had he found adequate sustenance.

He made a wry face. To this day, he couldn't stand the sight of peanut butter. It had been all he'd lived on for over two months—that and the vile-tasting Nex supplements that gave nourishment and damned little else.

But Michael Ralston didn't regret his decision to fight with the Nex and against the more popular P'torra. Humankind hadn't been involved directly with the war—and had played an insignificant role in the final peace negotiations—but sympathies had been against any allying with the Nex.

He had been lucky Benjamin Uzoma hadn't carried such prejudices and had accepted him as a student. But even having such a noted archaeologist as an advisor and attending a school as prestigious as the University of Novo Terra did nothing to erase the resentment among his peers at Ilium. Velasquez got Proteus 4 and the first real chance at a spacefaring culture granted anyone in the department.

That should have been his! Ralston calmed himself as the seven graduate students began filtering into the room. What Leonore Disa had said about these being the lowliest in the department carried more than a hint of truth. Two of them Ralston suspected to be felons placed in a rehabilitation program. They spent their time huddled together, whispering behind cupped hands and furtively studying the others. He vowed to inventory his equipment before leaving the ship and after uncrating on Alpha 3.

Three more drifted in. He almost laughed aloud at that. Not only did they simply hang like sacks of dirty laundry, they went through their studies in the same lackluster fashion—they existed and little else.

De la Cruz and Leonore followed the others in.

Ralston studied both of them more closely, damning himself for not paying more attention earlier in the trip. Seven weeks had been wasted, as far as he was concerned. Of the pair, Leonore seemed the more enigmatic and promising as a student. He believed she had studied his dissertation closely but hadn't wanted to admit it. Some students asked questions to which they already knew the answers, thinking they could curry favor by looking bright. Leonore didn't seem that type. But what did drive her? While she was far from the top of the graduate crop, she wasn't simply squeaking by on the bottom like Asan and Lantalman.

He had to face the possibility that it had been his own aloofness that kept her from speaking up sooner.

Yago de la Cruz went hand-over-hand along one of the elastic ropes and positioned himself at the nominal "top" of the room. From this lofty perch, he glowered at the others.

Ralston had seen de la Cruz's type before. Spoiled rich bastard thrust into a world where money no longer bought his slightest whim. Ralston wondered how long it would be before de la Cruz offered him a bribe in return for his vote of approval before a dissertation committee.

Ralston slumped and folded himself into a loose sphere. Considering the probity of others in the archaeology department at Ilium, they might be amenable to a little extra money under the table. Even the department head might be bought for a substantial contribution in the form of unrestricted research grants. Ralston had to face the possibility that he alone in the department couldn't be bribed, that academic honesty meant something to him alone.

Always the rebel, Uzoma had said.

"Citizens," Ralston said, almost shouting to be heard, and pulling out from his comfortable position and pressing himself against a far wall, legs entwined in the elastic. "You've heard of the excellent navigation done by the pilot." Heads bobbed. He doubted many had heard or cared. For them this was little more than a vacation. In spite of his classes on field procedures he doubted any truly understood the work involved with a dig. That would change. Soon.

"We will orbit Alpha 3, launch our survey satellites and— yes, Citizen de la Cruz?"

"Why bother with new satellite recon?" the man demanded, his chin thrust out truculently. He reminded Ralston of a dog refusing to release an innocent victim. "We already have the preliminary ones. Their photos are better than we can take."

"I disagree. The exploration team that found Alpha 3 launched six satellites, most of them designed to detect life. Not the remnants of life," Ralston said. He shoved himself into the center of the room. He knew how a spider felt when it left the security of its web. With a quick grab, he caught a rope and found the appropriate spot to address his students. De la Cruz hung behind him, but Ralston ignored this. The other six floated where he could see them.

"An archaeologist has to be as much an electronics expert as a good scientist. We will be cut off from support and will need to repair our equipment. Who's taken the computer archaeology course?" All indicated that they had, but Ralston discounted any expertise since Pieter Nordon taught the course.

Nordon's technical abilities ran more to shovel than ultrasonic digger. Ralston knew Nordon hadn't wanted the course but had been forced into teaching it when it had come up on the seniority rotation. Nordon had been low man on the totem pole.

"The satellite will get us a better look at the ruins we're to explore." Ralston experienced a rush of enthusiasm. Back in the field! To be on a dig again, even an insignificant one, was a world better than lecturing or listening to dull seminars given by tenured members of the department. "Alpha 3's population died off approximately ten thousand standard years ago. That, hmmm, makes it close to ninety-two hundred local years ago."

"What killed the geeks off?" de la Cruz asked.

"The *population*, Citizen de la Cruz," Ralston said pointedly. "We will refer to the natives in the proper fashion. There wasn't any indication of the cause of decline by prelim reconnaissance. That's part of our job. The Alpha 3 natives weren't spacefaring, even to nearby planets, but their level of development might be very close. There will be enough information to go around," he finished.

No one looked excited, Ralston thought. Except—maybe— Leonore Disa. She was holding in her emotions, and only small muscle twitches were betraying her.

Leonore shifted when she noticed his direct gaze. She spoke up. "How do we go about choosing a topic for our dissertations?"

"Whatever interests you," Ralston said, surprised. Even such an uninspiring group of students ought to know better.

"Some of the other professors assign topics."

That didn't come as a shock. "I don't believe in such practices. Choose a topic of interest—and significant importance to the field of archaeology. You are expected to demonstrate imagination, innovation, and technical ability in how you pursue your research. I see no way to dictate a topic and then expect what must be the finest work of your career. Only when you're personally motivated, excited, can you possibly do this."

He looked around the small sphere of faces and shook his head. No excitement at being in the field. No thrill for potential discovery. Even worse, he detected no commitment to archaeology among his group. Why did any of them bother coming on the dig? Why bother putting in the long years needed to get a degree? They had guaranteed themselves a safe future when they had passed the tests and legally became citizens. Most of the students at Ilium came from wealthy families. What prestige did they find in a doctorate of archaeology? He hadn't found any.

"I can't say what we'll discover on the planet, but it won't conform to any preconceived notions. Each culture is distinct, with points of interest and real opportunity for advancing knowledge." Ralston wound down his pep talk. He found it hard to get too enthused over a pre-spaceflight planetary culture that had slipped into oblivion. Better to study a post-spaceflight world such as Proteus 4.

Damn Velasquez and his political maneuvers!

"You each have your duties. Go and get ready. We'll launch the survey satellites in four hours. By the time we're ready to ground, they ought to have good photos."

"How long will it take to analyze the photos and choose a site?" asked Leonore.

"With luck, we can get the largest city's ruins spotted and begin there within a day." His tone told them this conference had come to an end. They left awkwardly.

Ralston said nothing as Yago de la Cruz shot by, giving him a sour expression. Michael Ralston retreated to the isolation afforded by the center of the room and simply hung, lost in his own irresolute thoughts. Alpha 3 had to reveal something. He refused to waste precious time on a worthless planet.

His own mood darkened, though. No one at the University of Ilium was likely to give him a choice assignment, even if he did his best here. On Alpha 3 he'd be lucky to find anything worthy of a publication, anything more advanced than mud and firehardened sticks.

Damn!

THREE

MICHAEL RALSTON CRANED his head back until his neck developed a muscle spasm. He rubbed the spot but kept scanning the pitch black sky of Alpha 3 for the tiny, moving dots of his satellites.

The landing had gone smoothly, the shuttle setting them down less than a kilometer from the spot with the most prominent ruins. He had noticed Leonore Disa had been excited by the nearness to the solar physics research station, even if he hadn't been. The University facilities there were less than five kilometers away. But she hadn't allowed this to interfere with her work. She and Ralston had ended up doing most of the work while the others flittered about ineffectually. Since time had been a factor and the pilot had badgered them constantly from orbit for the return of the robot shuttle, Ralston hadn't driven the others as he might have.

Simply being grounded gave him renewed energy.

"There's one, Doctor," Leonore Disa said. He tried to follow the direction of her pointing finger. All he could look at was the pale orange and blue glow from the jewelry plates flashing just below the surface of her skin.

"Can you turn those damned things off?" he asked querulously. "Any light at all kills my night vision."

Ralston didn't see what the woman did but the plates blinked once before fading.

"Thank you. Now where did you spot it? Oh, that one." He frowned, his mind working over the orbits of the six satellites. "That's not one of ours. Too low in the sky."

"Might be one of the solar physics satellites," Leonore said.

Ralston controlled his anger at the mere mention of the University's solar physics station. No one had told him that another department had been on planet for three months. Something about the Alpha primary interested them. All he knew was that the physicist in charge had stopped by shortly after they'd grounded to warn him about higher than normal levels of solar radiation.

Ralston rubbed sunburned cheeks and brushed away the flaking skin. Their supplies hadn't included much in the way of sun screen, and he had let the students use most of what had been brought—the preliminary survey hadn't indicated it would be needed on a planet circling a G5 yellow-orange star. Even with a perigee of 0.82 standard A.U., Alpha Prime appeared less than four-fifths as large as the Earth's sun.

Ralston looked around the night-shrouded muddy plains where he and Leonore had come to pick up the latest intelligence from their photo satellite. In a way, Alpha 3 reminded him of Earth. It had been too many years since he'd been home—and for him, Earth would always be home. Novo Terra had become the center of human-dominated space after the wars had wiped out most of Earth's temperate zones, relegating it to a minor role among the stars, but Ralston felt that special bond between a man and his birthplace.

His only real regrets, other than the stupidity of the four-day nuclear exchange, were the losses of Catal Huyuk, the Ming Tombs, Puye and Chaco and Mesa Verde, and the entire Olduvai Gorge. This latter hadn't gone up in a radioactive cloud but had been destroyed by the huge numbers of people fleeing the higher latitudes. Ralston shifted from one foot to the other. The lewd sucking noise brought him back to the reality of Alpha 3 and the persistent rainstorms.

"Going to rain again," he muttered. Heavy, lead-bottomed clouds dotted the night sky, blocking off many of the almost-familiar constellations.

"Doesn't it ever stop? Why can't some of those hotshots over at Solar Base 1 do a better job of predicting the showers?" asked Leonore Disa. "That's supposed to be their field."

"Didn't know that," said Ralston, distracted. No one had told him anything about the solar physics research being done, and he didn't really care. That was out of his area of expertise. He had come to Alpha 3 to dig, and that's all he intended to do. Fraternizing with physicists didn't strike him as decent. They were too strange and would only divert him. When Justine Rasmussen had stopped by to greet them, it had wasted an hour.

"There! That's it." He swung around the hand-held half-meter parabolic dish, sighted through the axis optics, and placed the satellite on the cross hairs. A tiny red light flashed when he successfully locked on and received the recognition signal. Ralston flipped a tiny switch; a microburst went to the satellite and convinced the block circuits to release their precious information. In less than ten seconds Ralston had received two days' recon data.

He switched off the equipment and reslung it on his back. "That ought to do it. Wind and rain patterns as well as the radar images. Want to help me analyze it?"

"Sure, if you don't mind."

"Mind? You're out here to learn." Ralston smiled. "You're also along to do all the chores I detest. I *hate* poring over this type of data. I'd rather be at the bottom of a trench with an ultrasonic."

"That seems too dreary for words," Leonore said.

They sloughed their way across the plain and down into the lowlands, near a river where the largest ruins had been detected. Few walls extended above ground level, having been eroded away by centuries of wind and the incessant downpour. Every dig held its challenges. Alpha 3's seemed to be one of endurance. The rains ruined most carbon dating, forcing them to use other means to date the artifacts found.

"I read something once about Chinese water torture," Leonore said. "I think Muckup is it. All the time dripping on the top of my head. I swear, my brain cavity sounds like a drum."

Ralston sighed at the name the students had given the planet, tightening his own collar against the burgeoning rain. While picking up the satellite signal, it had been almost clear. Less than halfway back to camp a light mist had formed. Now gravid drops splattered heavily on them and gave birth to wet misery. Before they would reach shelter, they'd be drenched.

"Wear a hat," was all the advice he gave her.

Ralston and Leonore ducked under the low overhang and into his shelter. Rain beat a heavy tattoo against the plastic before running off to trenches he'd dug along the edges of the slope-roofed shelter. Ralston unslung the pack with the electronics and pulled out the small block circuit holding the data. He popped it into a viewer and focused against the back wall.

They studied frame after frame in silence, each taking notes and cross-referring what they saw. The computer automatically plotted isanemones and isotherms and detailed the information in a miniature map being developed at the lower side of the display. From this they might be able to determine the effects of erosion and better date the ruins. Ralston finished with one and flipped to the next, frowned, then reversed to bring the prior picture into sharper focus.

"What is it, Doctor?"

"Can't say for sure. Look at this. A good view of the city. Here's where we started with the cleaners. The computer's this dot. But what's all this? The lines and boxes?" He indicated the spot in the lower corner.

"That'd be about two kilometers away," Leonore said, working on the scaler. "How'd you take these shots?"

"Synthetic aperture radar. These aren't surface striations. It shows up off the major isanemones. They're just *under* the mud."

"Some structure that got buried. It could happen easily here." Leonore's tone indicated she saw nothing unusual in this discovery. Ralston had to admit the rains lent credence to such a theory.

But something that wouldn't go away kept flitting at the corners of his mind. Ralston finally pushed it aside and went on. In less than an hour, they had finished their mapping.

Leonore tapped her field computer and said, "Time to let it all digest."

"Time to get some sleep. I want to be up early in the morning to check out how the dig's going."

Leonore laughed lightly, the sound of silver chimes muffled by the patter of falling rain. "You'd work eighteen hours a day, if you could."

"Local day's only seventeen and a half," he said without thinking.

"I rest my case. Good night, Dr. Ralston."

"Good night, Citizen."

She left, a sudden rush of humid air entering to mark her passage. Ralston hardly noticed. He turned on the projector again and just stared at the patterns as if they might come alive and explain themselves to him. He fell asleep at the table, head on folded arms, dreaming of those hidden shapes.

"No, that's not the way!" he shouted. Ralston jumped down into the trench beside Asan. The graduate student backed off as if he'd been caught robbing the chancellor's wife of her family tiara. "Look. You've got to do this carefully, gently, as if you were making love to a sensitive woman."

His fingers stroked lovingly over the controls. The ultrasonic digger's pitch lowered, mellowed. Ralston guided the device forward millimeter by slow millimeter. Mud and grime vanished and a concrete foundation appeared. More quick touches produced a neat line of five green lights indicating that the machine had been programmed successfully and now worked at removing caked on grime and recording all data without destroying the object of study.

"There's no rush. If you had to do this by hand, it'd take months. The digger lets you go off and grab a nap now and again. You *do* have the alarm on it set?" Ralston saw Asan's furtive eye movements. That could mean only that the man knew nothing of what he did. Ralston shook his head and dropped into the mud-filled trench beside the digger. The graduate student hadn't bothered to set the alarm.

"How do you expect to find anything important?" Ralston asked. "You've got to use the equipment to the fullest."

"There's nothing of importance to find," came de la Cruz's sour words.

Ralston left Asan to ponder the error of his ways and vaulted out of the trench. His boots sank only a centimeter into the muck; they'd had a lucky two days without rain. He might have sunk in over the top of his boot, otherwise.

"Are you one of those rarities we see mentioned on the evening vidnews, Citizen de la Cruz?"

"What do you mean?" De la Cruz gave Ralston a suspicious look.

"A telepath. More precisely, a precognitive or a psychometrician, I believe the term is. You have a sense the rest of us poor mortals don't have?"

De la Cruz didn't answer.

"Can you tell us without equivocation that there's nothing worth finding at this site?"

"Nothing but foundations."

"But they are *big* foundations. This building towered, Citizen de la Cruz. It might have been the largest building on the planet. Surely that indicates the natives placed great importance on it. Maybe it was a governmental headquarters or a cathedral. What purpose did the building serve?"

De la Cruz shrugged.

"You don't know, Citizen de la Cruz?" Ralston asked with mock surprise. "Neither do I. But we're going to find out." Ralston studied the younger man, then motioned. "Come over here for a moment." He led de la Cruz away from the work site where the ultrasonic digger shook away more and more mud to reveal an interesting, but hardly unique, foundation.

"What is it, Doctor?"

"Your attitude, Citizen de la Cruz. Why are you on this dig? You barely do your share of the work. You display no interest at all concerning the natives that once lived here."

"Why should I?" de la Cruz blurted. "They're not important. There's nothing important on this mudball. Muckup's not going to get any of us the recognition we deserve."

"And what recognition is that?" asked Ralston. "What have you done to deserve any notice?"

"You don't like me because my family is rich. Richer than you'll ever be." A sneer crossed de la Cruz's swarthy face like a dark wave. "Admit it, Ralston, you hate me because you envy all the money I control."

"I may never be rich, but I have something you never will: satisfaction in my work. Even more to the point, I'm willing to work. You are lazy and willful and . . ."

De la Cruz's face darkened even more. Ralston saw he had

pushed the student beyond his limit. Something about being judged worthless had touched off intense anger. Ralston barely ducked and backed away when the student swung a hard fist at his face.

De la Cruz recovered and came at Ralston—a mistake. Ralston felt descend over him the curious calm that he'd experienced each time before battle. Gone were the automated Nex weapons he'd become so expert with. But their intense hypnotic training remained. He deflected de la Cruz's fist, stepped inside, and slammed his fist down hard on the graduate assistant's neck. In the same motion, his knee came up to jolt into de la Cruz's groin.

Ralston blinked and came out of fighting mode. He hadn't realized the training still held such power over him. The last thing he'd wanted was to strike his student. His breath returned to normal. Ralston knelt, helping de la Cruz to sit upright.

"Sorry. Don't ever try anything like that again." De la Cruz jerked away and got to shaky feet. Ralston let the man go. He hadn't expected de la Cruz to physically assault him; he certainly hadn't expected his own quick reactions to produce such an outcome.

He turned to see Asan staring at him with appreciation. The man's eyes told Ralston that he approved.

"Why are *you* here?" Ralston asked, too loudly.

Asan shrugged. "Same as most of the others. Nowhere else to go."

Ralston started to snap back that he hadn't meant that. Before he spoke, he caught hold of his emotions, forced calm upon himself, and regained control.

"You are in a rehab program, aren't you?"

Asan nodded. Ralston knew he violated Novo Terra law and ethics; he asked what crime Asan had committed.

"Killed a few people who got in my way during a robbery."

Ralston barely understood. Killing for reasons of passion had never died out in any human culture, but thefts had become more and more automated over the centuries. To physically steal from another struck him as alien as the Nex. More so. They were supposed to be alien.

"Keep after the digger. Check to see if it hits anything its dig frequency might damage."

"Got an estimate on the building's height," Asan said.

"Must've been damn near ten stories tall. A lot for the way the rest were built: low, near the ground."

Ralston sat on the edge of the trench, feet dangling just above the muddy bottom. "That's strange," he said. "The natives were of avian descent. Flightless, possibly for most of their history, but very birdlike. Comes from the low gravity."

"You find a photo of the natives? Haven't found statues or any paintings. How do you know what they looked like?"

"Guesswork, right now. In a few weeks, we'll know for certain. Leonore found a skeleton—the first, actually. The natives were taller than we are. I suspect they had larger ears to compensate for the thinner atmosphere. Their bones were more fragile, more birdlike. Shoulders lead me to think they were birdlike, at any rate."

Asan gave his shrug and turned to clear the digger's sonic head of small twigs and rocky debris. Ralston heaved himself erect and began pacing through the city. Here and there the automated diggers worked to reveal the ruins of what must have been the largest city on Alpha 3. But it seemed wrong. Ralston had spent a good deal of his life wandering through burned-out cities, across plains hiding the secrets of the ages, and never had he gotten the feeling of such *wrongness*.

"Getting crazy," he said to himself. "Muckup's dead." He considered this. Archaeologists were hardly more than grave robbers, inspecting the dead and the belongings of the dead. Such a feeling of being surrounded by natives long gone ought to be normal.

It *was* natural to him after ten years of intense training as a scientist.

Alpha 3 held something more than a deceased race. Eyes unfocused, Ralston returned to his shelter, hardly noticing the rain pelting down harder and harder.

"Are you all right?" Leonore Disa asked.

"Hmm? What?" Ralston turned to stare at her. He hadn't heard the woman enter his shelter. Ralston looked past her and saw that the rain had stopped. For the time being, at least. He took a long drink from a flask, then silently offered her some.

Leonore made a face when she sampled it. She handed it back, asking, "What is that? Liquid lithium?"

"Bourbon."

"Why do you drink it? Tastes terrible."

"Maybe that's why. You must have some vices of your own. If not alcohol, then something else. It gives some limit to your existence, lets you put things into perspective. When you're stuck on a mudball like we are for at least a couple more months, this helps." He tipped the flask back and took another burning drink.

She pulled back her poncho and unfastened her blouse, exposing her midriff. A small silver plate gleamed.

"Oh," said Ralston, disappointed. "You're one of those."

"There's nothing wrong with recreational drugs," she said primly. "And the med-port makes it easier for a doctor if anything happens to me. I *hate* the idea of putting a needle into my arm."

"Use the air injectors."

"And leave a bruise?"

Ralston smiled at this. Bruises for someone with subcutaneously implanted jewelry plates would be an anathema.

"So you leak drugs into your system through that thing." He reached out and tapped the med-port. Leonore pulled away. "What do you use?"

"My privilege to use anything I want. I've been a citizen since I was eleven years old."

While this was several years younger than most who became full members of society—those that did at all—Ralston didn't think she was lying. There wasn't any reason to.

"You're hovering near the edge of ethanol poisoning for some reason," Leonore said. "Self-pity? You have a full measure of it. At least, when I 'port my drugs, I don't wallow in hating myself. They make me feel happy."

"*Feel* happy, not *be* happy," he said. Ralston knew better than to argue. Especially since she came too close to describing his state of mind. "I don't like being shunted off to this mudball—Muckup's such a fine name for it—but I intend to do the best I can."

Ralston frowned and took another drink. The bourbon burned his throat and puddled warmly in his belly, but he didn't taste it.

"Something's wrong with Alpha 3's archaeology," he said. "Just a sense. Everything we've uncovered so far indicates this city was destroyed by fires. Civil disorder is my guess. Riots.

To see an entire city of almost a million in flames!"

"You wish you'd been there?"

"Of course I do!" Ralston dropped the flask to the table and paced, hands locked behind his back. He studied her on every return of his nervous orbit. "There's no other way we can determine what really happened. All we do now is guess. We have only our intellect to piece the puzzle together."

"What do you think caused the rioting? War?"

"Not war," he said. "The destruction isn't organized enough. There's no systematic pattern as if an army marched through or aerial assaults took place. There didn't even seem to be an effort to bury the dead. That indicates . . ."

"Mass hysteria," cut in Leonore. "Or universal insanity."

"Yes," Ralston said, his mind abuzz with possibilities. "Mass insanity. As if they all went quite mad simultaneously."

"What could cause it?" the brunette woman asked. "There's never been a culture that declined worldwide for such a fantastic reason."

Ralston didn't answer. He turned back to the photo projected on the wall. The computer analysis had turned up nothing substantive, but his instincts told him that the neat rectangular patterns underground two kilometers south were important.

But why? What were they?

Muckup might provide a decent paper or two after all.

FOUR

"WE DO IT," Michael Ralston said. Leonore Disa looked up from the computer console, where she ran cross-checks on the architectural data they had uncovered using the ultrasonic digger.

"Do what?" The woman leaned back and pushed a vagrant strand of brown hair from her eyes. She hadn't activated the jewelry plates in Ralston's presence in almost a week. For his taste, that improved her looks, but he knew this was only a whimsical notion. They had all been in Alpha 3's rain too long. Leonore might have been a drowned rat with her damp hair and completely formless, soaked clothing.

"It's never good practice to jump about. Once you start excavation on one site, you make certain there's nothing more to be found before you move on." Ralston paced now, hands locked behind him. Every step he took rearranged the mud that had been tracked onto the floor of his shelter. A scant meter above his head, the fierce afternoon rain pounded harshly against the plastic roof and muffled his words. He might as well have been back aboard the University starship for the freedom of movement this planet afforded.

"You're thinking about the ruins to the south. You don't want to totally abandon this, do you?" She pointed to the photos with the superimposed grid pattern laid atop them. Each square carried its own identifying number. At the end of the day's excavation, one of them would remove the memory block from the ultrasonic digger and directly transfer the data into their main computer. The smallest item registered; nothing was overlooked.

While the excavation of the primary site had gone well enough, it hadn't revealed anything of real interest. Asan's earliest estimates of the building's original height had proven very accurate. Since then, only routine discoveries had been made.

Nothing worthy of a publication, much less a doctoral dissertation. No one in the camp had been happy over this, least of all Ralston.

"Never quit a project," he said, more to himself than to his graduate assistant. "That's when you're likeliest to miss the one important clue to a culture."

"But it wouldn't be out of the question to do a quick survey. Maybe using a couple EM probes? We don't have a proton magnetometer, but I might be able to juryrig something."

"Not that way," he said, settling into a chair. He faced the woman. Only with Leonore did he feel any need to explain his thoughts. The others did their jobs in a desultory fashion—automatons putting in their hours and nothing more. Even Yago de la Cruz had become more machine than human. Ralston almost wished he would show that spark of anger again that had caused the outburst and the abortive fight. Anything out of the ordinary broke the monotony—and Muckup's weather and former civilization had proven extremely tedious.

"Yeah, you're right. It might interfere with the solar physics equipment."

"What? Oh, them. I didn't even think of that. You're right."

"Some other reason?" Leonore's eyes unfocused as she thought. Ralston didn't interrupt her. Given a thread, she had proven herself able to follow it toward a logical conclusion. "The electromagnetic pulses might interfere with whatever's buried there. What do you think it is, Doctor?"

"I'm hoping it's a burial ground. We don't have any other spot marked off that is a more likely candidate for a cemetery. Hell, we've uncovered only a few decent skeletons. Most have decomposed badly, or were pretty much destroyed in death. Can't figure out how the planet's managed to keep up such steady rainstorms for so long. What analysis we've done doesn't show this recurring wet pattern prior to the decline."

"Sudden decline," Leonore said. "Less than two hundred years is the best estimate so far."

Ralston frowned. "Just a quick look at the southern site. A hand-held sonic cleaner, maybe some non-intrusive devices, a camera. Also an IR scanner to determine the boundaries and some of the walls, and to see if there're actually graves or not." He reached over and began rummaging through his equipment, getting what he needed for the short trip.

"Are you going to wait for the rain to stop?"

"It never stops. Or hadn't you noticed?" He smiled. "When's there going to be a better time? Want to come along?"

"Verd." Ralston winced at the slang. Leonore usually avoided such verbal bastardizations. She powered down the computer and peripherals, and then grabbed her poncho. With it on, she seemed even more formless. Ralston found himself wondering what she looked like when she went all out, dressed for a formal ball on Novo Terra.

He ducked out of the shelter and instantly regretted his decision to go exploring. The rain hammered at him with liquid, hard fists. Ralston blamed only himself for not being better prepared. The initial survey hadn't said anything about the incessant rains; they might stop during some other season. He had been unlucky enough to land with his seven students in the midst of a wet season when he had been expecting less rain and more sun.

If there was a dry season, he thought. He wasn't sure the original survey had been accurate. Even with the clouds, they were treated to more than expected solar radiation.

He and Leonore tramped southward for some time without conversation. Ralston finally asked, "Why are you here?"

"You said we were going to check out the ruins to the south." She stopped and peered at him through the curtain of rain. "Or did you have something more in mind? If you did, why didn't we stay in your shelter? It's not as wet there."

"That's not what I meant. Not at all." Ralston found himself tongue-tied in his confusion. His question had been directed toward an entirely different end, and Leonore had misinterpreted badly. Intentionally? He stopped, got his wits about him, then said, "Why did you come on the dig? What is it about this glamorous, fun-filled life that makes you want to be an archaeologist?" He wiped his forehead and sent a stream of cool water fanning out into the downpour. Droplet hit falling droplet, merged and tumbled to the muddy ground.

"Sorry, Doctor," Leonore said, not in the least contrite. "I mistook your intentions."

Had she? Ralston wondered. He pushed such thoughts from his mind. It was bad policy for a professor to become involved sexually with a student under any circumstance. That they had been away from Novo Terra for almost nine standard weeks only added to his frustration. Leonore Disa wasn't especially pretty, or even the type of woman he usually found attractive. But she was a woman. The only one on this ridiculous expedition.

"This isn't the life a socialite enjoys," he said.

"What makes you think I'm a socialite? The jewelry?" She shook her head. "I should have turned it off before the trip. Didn't even think about it since it's so much a part of me." They splashed through another fifty meters of mud puddles before Leonore continued. "I wanted away from my family."

"That's all? A vacation off planet could have achieved the same end—and much more comfortably."

"That'd be a temporary solution. I want something more permanent, a reason never to have to go back unless I choose."

"That upsetting being around your family? I don't have any. My parents died when I was young. They always told me to avoid the radiation zones. I did, they didn't."

"I'm sorry."

"So you're running away. Happy to run away to this?" Ralston made a sweeping motion. Rain fell in a steady stream off his arm. He quickly lowered it and shook free the water before it started soaking through. Even waterproofed, the material succeeded in becoming engorged with the rain.

"Actually, yes. I know the others don't enjoy this much, but I do."

"Asan and Lantalman are both rehabs. They've been so

heavily hypno'd there's no telling where they think they are—
or maybe they can't care."

"I heard about them being with us before we left Novo
Terra," the woman said. "A shame to send them out like this.
A shame to brain-burn anyone."

"That's the heart of the program, get felons into useful
professions."

Leonore snorted. In the humid weather, this sent tiny silvered plumes of steam from her nostrils. "There's no spark of
humanity left in them. They can go through the motions, do
everything by rote, but how can they possibly be more than
average? All their initiative has been stripped away by drugs
and hypnosis."

"My feelings, too," Ralston admitted. "But the other students aren't that much different, and nobody's been tightening
the bolts in their skulls."

"For them, I can't speak. I want to establish a solid reputation for myself," Leonore said. "My mother says I'll come
running back, that I'll never be able to do anything she or my
father haven't plotted out in minute detail for me."

"I think she's wrong." Ralston stopped and looked at his
wristcom. It provided a distance estimate as well as an inertial
tracking fix if needed to return to camp. The tiny red arrow
pointed almost directly backward to show the location of the
main site. Ralston touched a stud on the side and got a green
arrow pointing obliquely left. "That direction, about fifty meters or so to the edge."

The rain diminished by the time the green arrow turned to
a small dot in the center of the wristcom display.

"This is it," Ralston said. The muddy flats appeared no
different from any other stretch they'd passed, but the imaging
radar had found the distinct outlines under the surface.

Ralston turned his small ultrasonic cleaner toward the ground
and pressed the switch. It hummed for ten seconds, then shut
down automatically. The mud had been blasted away in a small
trench, but nothing of importance lay at the bottom. Methodically Ralston began a crisscrossing until he found a rectangular
block.

"The corner?" asked Leonore. She had been following Ralston with the camera, ready to take a photo of anything uncovered. She trained the camera on the stone block.

"Maybe." Ralston took the camera from her and flipped on the IR viewfinder. Using this makeshift infrared detector to trace the buried wall for several meters, Ralston mapped out the buried structure. Then a large hotspot showed. He used the sonic whiskbroom again and unearthed a metal door.

"Looks copper-clad," Leonore said, running her fingernail along the edge and scraping away part of the green corrosion. He silently handed the camera back to Leonore, and she took pictures from several angles. "There's the lock." Her brown eyes turned questioningly to Ralston. Procedure dictated that they be more thorough with exterior investigation before opening any tomb. If sealed, they might have to pump out a few liters of trapped air for analysis before opening. A fiber optic probe would then be put into the chamber for a complete photo scan before they tried to open the door. Any number of methods might be employed. Ralston considered building an airtight room, evacuating it, and then opening the door so that no new gases would be introduced. Great care had to be taken to avoid introducing unwanted variables.

And then the real job would start. No datum could be taken for granted.

"It's been opened. Not too long ago, either," Ralston said, examining the lock. He gusted out pent-up breath in relief. Several days of tedious work could now be avoided. The air within the find would be the same as that outside. "The scratches around the catch—it's a simple one—aren't corroded as heavily. I find it hard to believe this dates back to the decline. Certainly, there've been natives opening it since then." His wristcom worked on the information gathered by a tiny probe Ralston passed close to the scratches and the lock.

Leonore peered over his shoulder. "Opened less than a thousand years ago?"

"Took a while for them to all die off, maybe. This might be a shelter."

"It might hold the reason for their sudden disappearance."

Neither spoke for long minutes, each lost in thought. Ralston knew that this tomb held their future on Alpha 3. Publications? Seldom did a solid reason for a culture's passing present itself. Mostly, archaeologists guessed, made up fanciful theories, spent long hours debating what no one could ever know for sure. This tomb might hold the definitive answer to Alpha 3's abrupt descent from pre-spaceflight civilization to complete oblivion.

Several good, solid papers could result because he'd followed his instincts. Ralston knew the same thought ran through Leonore's mind. A dissertation topic that would have the journals begging to publish it came along all too infrequently.

But the procedures for opening such a tomb had been worked out a thousand years back. The earliest archaeologists on Earth had known what to do. Schliemann. Mouhot.

"We can't open it," he said simply. "To spoil whatever's inside is too great a risk. We've got to do it carefully, recording every step of the way." Leonore nodded. Ralston smiled and added, "But we *can* make a few preliminary checks."

He pulled the probe, mounted at the tip of a slender fiber optic, from the side of his wristcom. Lowering the probe through the lock, working it around, he got a good view of the lock's innards. All the while, the wristcom recorded.

"Michael, look out!" cried Leonore.

Ralston jerked the probe back, but the tip caught just inside the rim of the lock. The mechanism had activated at even this innocuous touch. The door let out a moan like a dying man and began sliding sideways. A blast of fetid air struck Ralston in the face. He choked and turned from it. When he looked back, he saw only a dark, yawning cavity. The door had opened fully. Leonore took pictures, switching to an IR light and lens.

"I didn't think this would happen," Ralston said.

"But it did. Should we? I mean, nothing seems to have happened. No demons from the pits of hell have rushed up to devour us." Even as she spoke, she instinctively crossed herself. Ralston doubted she knew that she fell back on the comfort it gave her.

Ralston considered the possibility that Alpha 3 had died from a plague and that this, as a refuge for the few survivors, might be contaminated. Even now millions of viruses or berserk bacteria might be gnawing their way into his blood, taunting his T-cells and daring the leukocytes to resist. He shook that notion off as paranoid. Never had such a naturally occurring disease been found on another planet; even if they had become exposed, their bodies were ecologies where a disease had to find a niche. If too foreign, it wouldn't survive. If it fit in too well, their bodies, bolstered by the arm-numbing series of vaccinations they'd all taken prior to leaving Novo Terra, would fight successfully against intruders. For the first time, Ralston actually envied Leonore her med-port. He rubbed his arm and thought how painless it would be having the serum injected into the computer-driven box, then slowly pumped into the bloodstream.

Only on the Nex worlds had biological disasters happened— and this because of the P'torra meddling with one bacterium in the food chain. The planet deaths had taken years.

But the slim chance still existed: he and Leonore might have been exposed to a lethal disease. And he hadn't brought along an analyzer to check.

"Think your wristcom's good enough to gather the info we need?" the woman asked. Leonore peered down the steps into the vault, eager to go farther.

"We'd better close up and get back right away."

"I don't see how the mechanism operated," she said. She ran her fingers along the edge. "The probe inside the lock acted as a key. What mechanism lasts for ten thousand years? They must have been serious about whatever was placed here."

"It might not be that old. And if they wanted to protect whatever's below, why design the door to open so easily?"

"Didn't want to protect it from people, just the elements," Leonore guessed.

"Go back to camp," he said. "Get an analyzer and bring it here right away."

"Disease?" she asked. Ralston shrugged. Leonore backed from the opening, reluctant to abandon such a find. "I'll be back as fast as I can run."

"Don't slip and kill yourself in the mud," Ralston cautioned. "The analyzer would be hard to replace."

"But . . ." Leonore's sudden flare of temper faded when she saw he only joked. "I'll carry it back on a satin pillow. What service, right? Remember me in your paper."

"Co-authors," Ralston promised. He adjusted the wristcom to check on his body temperature and pulse rate. While his heart beat more rapidly than normal, no other vital sign appeared out of the ordinary. This meant nothing, but Ralston took it as a good sign that he hadn't gotten a faceful of exotic alien microbes. Only a complete blood chemistry would verify his gut-level feeling, though.

"It's starting to rain again," he said. "Better get going."

"It's always raining. Never stopped. Not really." Leonore paused and looked directly into his gray eyes. "Be careful." She held out the camera.

"I won't enter until we get the analyzer running."

Leonore's lips curled into what was almost a sneer. Her head bobbed up and down, then she turned and vanished through the gray wall of rain.

Ralston heaved a deep sigh. She knew him better than he knew himself. The lure of that black square proved too much. "Only a step or two," he said aloud.

He peered through the IR range finder on the camera and saw a long hallway extending due south from the foot of the stairs. At twenty meters the corridor T-branched, hinting at an extensive subterranean facility. Ralston pulled the fiber optic probe out as far as it would go, then descended another few steps until the door frame came level with his eyes. To one side he saw the mechanism, an elaborately encased set of mechanical gears and weights. This alone might tell much about the culture and its development.

But the corridor. That branching both left and right. No magnet pulled iron more strongly than this mystery drew Michael Ralston.

His wristcom beeped loudly, startling him. He glanced down and saw that he still had the body scan activated. His pulse rate had climbed well past norms from the excitement. Ralston turned off this function and let the full capacity of its tiny block circuit fill with data.

"This is wrong," he said softly, but he couldn't help himself. Ralston went down to the lowest step and peered into the darkness. The Stygian black thwarted his eyes, but through the IR lens he saw walls covered with intricately painted murals. If he'd left the wristcom monitoring his pulse, it would have beeped again. Ralston forced himself to calm.

He looked back up the stairs. Rain pelted through the door and dribbled down into the corridor. He shucked off his coat, used it to meticulously clean his boots of all the mud caked on them, and went back up the short stairway. A few minutes tinkering with the door mechanism permitted him to half close the door. The narrow opening he shielded with his coat to keep out the worst of the water.

"IR goggles. We'll need to get out the IR goggles," he

muttered. Dropping to hands and knees, Ralston began using the ultrasonic whiskbroom to brush the dust on the floor to one side. He made sure that the wristcom and sonic cleaner both recorded the depth of the dust before he moved it. Analysis of the dust could come later.

Centimeter by agonizing centimeter he cleaned a narrow path the length of the corridor to the juncture. Most of the work Ralston had done in semidarkness, using only the wan light entering the door. Now, to both right and left, he saw absolute darkness. Using the IR camera viewfinder, Ralston studied the floor, walls—and beyond.

"Eat your goddamned heart out, Velasquez!" Ralston crowed. "Proteus 4 is shit compared with this!"

Ralston hurriedly whisked a path along the right-hand corridor for a distance of ten meters, then stopped and stood. He cursed volubly, wishing for visible light. He peered through the IR viewfinder in stark amazement at what he saw. Slowly, he took one picture after another, knowing the visible spectrum would reveal even more when they got down into these catacombs with the proper photographic and recording equipment.

"I don't believe this!" he exclaimed, turning to his left. The corridor stretched far beyond the limited range of the IR camera. He took a few more pictures before retracing his path to the juncture, then going down the left-hand branch.

Ralston had to stop several times and control himself. He shook with excitement. He had always wondered how Howard Carter and Lord Carnarvon had felt on entering Tut's tomb. Or the sense of wonder Griegos had experienced seeing lofty, delicate spires of Vegan spider steel for the first time.

"Dr. Michael Lewis Ralston, explorer," he said proudly. Ralston had always thought he had a firm, pragmatic opinion of himself and his abilities. Now he found himself more than a bit awed by the discovery he'd made. "Damn, but this is *great!*" he exclaimed.

Another corridor, again vanishing beyond the limits of his infrared viewfinder, stretched to the right. This vault might extend for untold kilometers. This might be only the top level!

A scratching noise sounded behind him. Ralston didn't turn. He was too intent on taking in everything before him.

"Bring the analyzer over here, Leonore," he called. "And I hope you brought a couple more film blocks for the camera.

I don't think a thousand pictures will scratch the surface. This
is great!"

The footsteps became more distinct now. The squishing
sounds drew Ralston's attention. Leonore shouldn't be tracking
in water and mud. Not into the find of the century.

"Leonore, clean off your—"

Ralston got no further. Blackness filled blackness as a heavy
object smashed into the side of his head. He reeled, then slumped
to the floor, unconscious.

FIVE

WAR DRUMS SOUNDED. It took Michael Ralston several seconds to realize that he hadn't been mysteriously transported back to a Nex war vessel, that the only pounding lay within his throbbing head. Ralston opened his eyes and thought he'd gone blind, then realized he still lay on the vault floor. Rolling over produced a new constellation of flaring stars in his head, but the pain subsided. To his relief, dim light shone from the direction of the opened door. The wet odor of fresh rain and the gentle *pat-pat-pat* as it fell reassured him he hadn't been trapped in this alien subterranean vault.

"Dr. Ralston? Are you there?"

"Leonore, inside. Be careful," he called. He instantly regretted the effort. Ralston reached back and touched the large, tender knot on his head. His fingers came away sticky with blood.

"You said you wouldn't go in," came the woman's disembodied voice. Ralston tried to understand what had happened to him. Someone had hit him from behind, but it wasn't Leonore.

At least he doubted it. She sounded both envious and disapproving. Nothing in her tone indicated anger—and not to the extent of physical assault.

Soft shuffling steps neared. Ralston heaved himself erect and swayed slightly. The dizziness and nausea passed before Leonore Disa rounded the corner. In one hand she held a small light. In the other she carried the analyzer.

"Are you all right?" she asked. Ralston thought the concern in her voice sounded too real to be feigned. He decided not to mention the attack.

"Of course. No reason to think otherwise, is there? Just because," he rushed on, not giving her a chance to speak, "your professor showed his moral and intellectual weakness doesn't mean anything's wrong. I don't think I disturbed anything."

"You tracked in mud," she said disapprovingly. Ralston peered at the large chunks of drying mud on the floor between them. Either Leonore had entered, hit him, retreated and then cleaned her boots before re-entering, or she hadn't been responsible.

"Thanks for not doing the same," he said. Her boots were spotlessly clean. The woman frowned and Ralston knew why. He, too, had cleaned his boots. She had to wonder who *had* been tracking in the mud.

Ralston wondered, too.

"We'll do a quick check, then seal up and evaluate the prelim data," he said. "After we get a better idea of what we've uncovered, then we can bring in the real equipment." His enthusiasm soared again. The knot on the side of his head still throbbed, but curiosity over their find erased any discomfort.

"Any need to analyze the dirt on the floor?" Leonore asked.

"Later. I want a good set of photos for these." He took the hand light from her and gave the lens a twist. The narrow cylinder of light expanded into a cone five meters wide at its base. One of the small side chambers lit up.

Leonore gasped. Even Ralston had to restrain his impulse to cry out. The scene in the first diorama looked *real*.

"Them. The natives of Alpha 3," Leonore said in a voice cracking with emotion. "They preserved themselves in a museum."

"Are they replicas? It doesn't look like they're embalmed," Ralston said, peering intently into the scene. Unlike most dioramas he was familiar with, this one had no restraining rail or glass partition. Two natives stood, a full head taller than Ralston's 190 centimeters. Their heads lacked hair or covering of any sort other than a close-cropped down; the most prominent features were the ears. They stuck out like radar dish horns.

"Mobile ears capable of independent movement, just as you surmised," Ralston said to Leonore. "Good work. You guessed a lot from the moldy corpses we've found."

"They look so . . . so peaceful," she said. She started to enter the diorama for a closer examination but Ralston restrained her. "Sorry," Leonore said. "Got too involved."

She took out the analyzer and turned it on. The various indicator lights flashed, and tiny beeps came from the guts of the machine as it began photographing, running tests of a dozen different kinds, recording everything, missing nothing.

"This must be the start of the exhibit," Ralston said. "These two are reaching out in greeting."

"Or the end of the exhibit," Leonore said. "They might be waving good-bye."

Ralston laughed. "It never pays to jump to conclusions. We are scientists and must follow strict procedure, even if we've done such a good job of ignoring it so far. Study everything, learn what we can, *then* come up with theories to explain it all."

"Do you think this is representative of the terrain?" Leonore asked. The ground under the natives' taloned feet looked nothing like the mud flats that covered so much of Alpha 3. "They don't appear to be products of a wet world—not like Muckup is now."

Ralston reluctantly pulled his attention from the first scene. He wanted it all—now! But there was so much to examine. He had to pick and choose. And be more alert than he had been earlier. Down the length of the corridor he saw particles of mud. Whoever had struck him had rushed on, perhaps performing a cursory examination of his own.

"Do a quick survey. Don't let the analyzer do more than take visual, IR and UV shots. We'll be more thorough later." Ralston left Leonore and went back down the corridor to the juncture. As he'd guessed, bits of mud marked where his assailant had moved down the other corridor. Ralston itched to do a full, immediate investigation of this wondrous find. Never had an intact museum been found, much less one depicting scenes of everyday life.

The scientific papers he'd get out of this would turn Velasquez green with envy!

"How many of these scenes do you want done?" Leonore asked, her voice distracted. She walked slowly down the center of the corridor, shining her hand flash into each tiny diorama to study it visually before using the analyzer.

"Let's break now. We can spend years giving this the study it deserves."

"Each one is more intricate than the prior one," she said, her mind obviously working over the ramifications of what they'd found. "Might give a complete picture of Alpha 3. A complete history!"

"They were definitely of avian ancestry," Ralston said. Then he tugged on Leonore's arm. "Come on. Let's seal up the door again to keep the water out. We'll want to build an entry portal, a small office to store our equipment and clean our boots. The last thing we want is to contaminate a major find."

"They're statues," Leonore said. Then she understood what Ralston had said. "Sorry. Just getting too involved."

"I know the feeling." He ushered her out, almost having to shove the graduate student ahead of him. They managed to get the copper-clad door pulled shut, but didn't allow the locking mechanism to operate. Ralston crammed his dirty jacket in the small crack to keep most of the moisture out. Loss of the jacket seemed a minuscule price to pay for such a tremendous find.

He tapped his wristcom, set the inertial mark so he could return directly to this spot, then started back to the primary camp site. With cold rainwater drenching him, the hammering storm isolating him with his own thoughts, he wondered why he'd been attacked.

"Leonore?"

"Yes?"

"Don't mention this to anyone else. Not yet. I want it to be a surprise."

She peered at him questioningly through the driving rain, but bobbed her head in agreement. The longer they kept this to themselves, the longer she had to think and formulate her own theories.

• • •

The rain slamming incessantly into the plastic roof of his shelter threatened Ralston's sanity. He had almost enjoyed the long, boring trip to Alpha 3 because of the isolation it afforded. He had always wondered about this seeming anomaly. The cramped conditions aboard a starship—any starship, not just the tiny bucket the University used—did not promote friendships. Rather, crew and passengers withdrew into themselves.

He'd heard it said that there were more mystics among starship crews than in any other segment of human population. That might not be so, but all the Buddhists he knew were spacers. They'd spend long hours in deep meditation rather than speak to one another.

Ralston wished for time and quiet and isolation for that kind of inner looking, for self-examination.

Perhaps he held within him the clue to the person who had assaulted him. Yago de la Cruz kept rising to the top of the possible list, but Ralston couldn't definitely eliminate Asan and Lantalman, both hypno-burned and drugged to eliminate their violent tendencies. He had no respect for the rehab psychologists and their always-changing techniques. A new grant sent them off meddling and hypothesizing into different corridors of a person's mind. During the war, he'd seen how the P'torra turned captives into mindless, drooling beasts before reimprinting them into loyal soldiers.

Ralston shuddered. He had to admit that he feared the mind tinkerings as much as he disapproved of removing a personality and remolding it, even for the dubious benefit it afforded society. And he had no idea how to judge if either Asan or Lantalman had managed to slip out of the bonds of their rehabilitation.

Ralston began to pace furiously like a caged animal. The sound of rain added a frenzied quality to his movements. Why did it have to be de la Cruz or either of the two rehabs? The remaining three—he still discounted Leonore—might have a grudge against him. He'd made it clear that none of them would be handed their degrees, that they'd have to work hard for them, that he expected only the highest quality work. The University of Ilium had a reputation as being the school for the indolent rich. Ralston equated this with laziness, both physical and mental. It still surprised him that none of the students had approached him with a bribe.

A lavish grant, from a parent's company, in exchange for favorable treatment. He knew it happened all the time. Ralston's anger mounted. He had been cheated out of the Proteus 4 expedition because of such underhanded dealings.

He snorted in disgust. Proteus 4 would be nothing compared to this find. Nothing!

Ralston began viewing the photos taken by the analyzer using IR. He had tramped through mud and rain, been hit on the head and it had been a full planetary day—seventeen and a half standard hours—since he'd slept. Ralston ought to have been dead on his feet.

He wasn't. His eyes shone as he studied the photos. Adrenaline pumped through his veins, and he knew he could go another planetary day before he slowed and his mind dulled with fatigue. The excitement of this find was worth that much.

At least.

Leonore Disa peered out into the storm raging across the plains. Jagged bolts of vivid green lightning leaped from cloud to cloud to produce a constant rolling of thunder. The rain drove down so hard that it caused mud to splash up waist high.

She pulled her poncho closer and stepped into the full force of the wind blowing in from the distant ocean. The only redeeming quality, as Leonore saw it, was the new warmth of changing seasons. They had landed on Muckup during early spring. The early rains after they had landed had been frigid, but no longer. The temperature hovered at a very warm 305 degrees K.

Leonore tightened the headband on her IR goggles and peered myopically into the storm. What had been the road to the main excavation site had vanished in the torrential downpour, but wavering red lines shown through the goggles gave her some idea where the road had been. She doggedly walked until she reached the spot where the ultrasonic digger continued on, oblivious to the weather.

Instinctively, Leonore checked it and made certain it functioned properly. Then she kept walking, past the ancient center of government, past the boundaries of the city, and farther into the muddy countryside. Only when she saw the heat shimmers of an approaching ground crawler did she stop.

She knew Nels drove using IR, too. The low-slung, track-driven transport ground to a noisy halt just a few meters away. The hatch opened, and she saw Nels Bernssen waving. Leonore hurried inside the vehicle, slamming the heavy metal door behind.

"Stop dripping on the rug," the big-boned, blond man said jokingly. Oblivious to her soaked clothing or his own injunction against getting the interior wet, he took her in his arms and kissed her.

"Whew," Leonore said, finally breaking off for air. "You'd think we hadn't seen each other in four months."

"Four months, three weeks, four days, and a few assorted seconds, each longer than a century."

Leonore held back a girlish giggle. She leaned over and kissed Nels Bernssen again.

"Stop that," she said, batting away his thick-fingered hand as it worked on her clothing fasteners. He stepped back and stared at her in surprise. "Unless you mean it."

"The crawler's got living quarters," Nels said. "Nice for one person, a bit cramped for two."

"How cramped?"

Nels guided Leonore around until they landed on the bed. He showed her how nice it could be in the compact machine.

Afterward, Leonore half lay atop Nels. She kissed him, then said, "I couldn't get away any sooner."

"A likely story. I know you, girl. The only woman in a camp of men. Horny graduate assistants. A lusty professor. You just couldn't find time for a poor, lonely post-doc trapped on the barren plains, staring forlornly at the stars, pining away for the woman he loves."

"Nels!"

"Sounded good while I was saying it," the man said, smiling broadly. They kissed again. "But I *did* miss you. You don't know how glad I was when you managed to get assigned here to Muckup instead of with—what was his name?"

"Velasquez," she said, sighing. "That was a hard decision for me, too."

"I know. He's supposed to be archaeology's shining star, isn't he? Turning down a spot with his expedition to come to a nothing planet like this had to be a disaster for your career." Nels stared into her brown eyes. Softly, he said, "Thank you."

"I love you," Leonore said.

Nels heaved a sigh and sat up in the tiny bunk. "We've got to get moving. I promised the boss lady I'd check up on the latest data collection. Supposed to be beamed down in less than an hour."

"In this weather?"

"Why not? We've got the antenna array working just fine. Outer ring of sleeve monopoles, inner ring of folded monopoles with a low band reflector screen."

"I'm sure you've got a nice antenna," Leonore said, "but I meant that the rain would kill your signal from the satellite."

"That's why we used an omnidirectional antenna array. The damned absorption from the water is too much for us around 14 gigahertz without a lot of fancy massaging."

Leonore nodded. "We use a hand-held transceiver and have to wait for clear nights."

"Nights," mumbled Nels. "Radiation is too much in the day and the rain kills the signal most other times. Hell of a planet." Nels Bernssen smiled and pulled Leonore close once more. "But even hell looks more bearable with you in it."

"Thanks a lot," Leonore said sarcastically. "This is the first time anyone's ever told me I'd decorate even a miserable place like Muckup." She tipped her head to one side and studied the physicist. "I guess that's as much of a compliment as I'm going to get from you."

"You know how us post-doc types are. All the time with our head in the clouds."

"*Everyone's* in the clouds here." The rain's hammering against the outside of the crawler didn't diminish its tempo. If anything, the storm worsened. The teravolt discharges of lightning cast an eerie light throughout the crawler's interior.

"And Justine will have my ass for lunch if I don't get moving. Got to collect. But you know I love it. Otherwise, why come to such a wonderful vacation spot?"

"Dr. Ralston met her when we landed. I don't think he likes her."

"Who does? But from what Justine said about your prof, he's the one with his head in the clouds. Or his nose is going that way. Is he always such a snob or was it Justine's charmingly obnoxious manner that burned him off?"

"He wasn't mad at her," Leonore said. "He's just not an easy man to know."

"Can't be much of a researcher," said Nels, getting dressed

in the cramped space. "He wouldn't have been sent to Muckup if he was. This is Satan's left asscheek for an archaeologist."

"That's not so!" Leonore flared, surprising herself. She had no real feeling for Michael Ralston, one way or the other. He tended to be aloof, churlish, self-centered and, even worse, self-pitying. But, dammit, he was *her* churlish advisor. She had seen flashes of true dedication to archaeology. Maybe even brilliance. The way he had been unable to restrain his enthusiasm over entering the vaults definitely showed more fire burned under his cold exterior than anyone thought.

"This isn't such a bad place," Leonore went on. "We've made what might be a major find."

"Sure. I saw the imaging radar pix. We took detailed shots before picking the spot for our base." Bernssen got the crawler in gear. They lurched off, mud flying in all directions. He flipped on the electrostatic shield to keep the worst off the forward window. When that didn't work, he cursed and started the mechanical wipers, which were only slightly more effective. The IR was good for finding warm bodies—like Leonore's—but impossible for driving in a storm. Bernssen preferred visual.

"You did? You should have offered them to us. It'd've saved us putting up our own satellites. The University has really slashed our budget to the bone. One landing pod—and the starship we came out in was ancient twenty years ago."

"It's a matter of funding. We've got a good chance at something *important*," Bernssen said. "The physics department had to fight off sponsors for us."

"Is that your antenna?" In spite of herself, Leonore felt anger rising. She was happy that Nels and the solar physics researchers got adequate funding. At the same time, it annoyed her that the archaeology department was tossed only well-gnawed bones for its projects, especially one as exciting as Ralston's find.

The omnidirectional antenna spread out over a full sixty meters of the muddy terrain. Leonore knew only the rudiments of com theory, but guessed that this array would pick up a dozen satellites simultaneously and multiplex the data into a station better equipped than anything her expedition had been offered.

She held back cold anger. They hadn't even been given some of the rudimentary devices like a proton magnetometer or a supervisor.

"Nice, isn't it?" Bernssen said proudly. He helped her from

the crawler. Together, sharing her poncho, they rushed to the door of the computer station. Once inside, Leonore's suspicions were realized. More had been spent on this single setup than for Ralston's entire expedition. Everywhere she looked rose large banks of state-of-the-art field computer gear.

"The room's air-conditioned," she said.

"Has to be. For the computers. We took the biggest available." Nels didn't seem to realize that all the University had provided Ralston were plastic huts and a single sanitary station. No heat, no air-conditioning, barely watertight shelters.

Leonore also saw that she'd lost Nels. His eyes locked on one terminal and he homed in as if on inertial guidance. He dropped heavily into a chair and began working on the data coming in from seven different satellites.

"We've got four in polar orbits, ten others in a variety of west-to-east configurations and three in geosynch orbits," he explained as he checked the flashing figures spit out by the computer. "The primary's never out of sight for us."

"Why so many satellites? The cost . . ."

"Cost doesn't count. I told you sponsors were tripping over each other's asses to fund us. We need all this and more if we want to monitor continuously."

Nels Bernssen's voice trailed off as another satellite spat out its data in a quick burst; the screen flashed and his attention centered on the work. Feeling neglected, but understanding his need to follow the experiments, Leonore wandered about. Most of the equipment performed functions totally alien to her. She'd never been especially good at physics, which was how she'd met Nels. He had offered to tutor her until she passed her basic courses in the subject.

She had passed, and his tutoring had turned to other, more intimate subjects.

"Glad you arranged to come out to Alpha, Leonore," the man said, not looking up from the terminal. "Not many women'd do that just to be with me."

"I'm glad now. More than just being with you, Nels. I thought I'd passed by a real chance on Proteus 4, but now I'm not so sure. We've got a big find. Maybe the biggest ever. It'll make a great dissertation. If I do it right, it'll establish me up there with Velasquez and maybe even Griegos."

"Damn!" Bernssen exclaimed, rocking back in his chair.

"What's wrong?"

"Things are moving faster than Justine expected. When was the starship supposed to be back for you?"

"Not for five months local."

"Damn," Nels repeated. He reached over and thumbed the communications unit mounted on the wall. "Justine, you there?"

"What is it, Nels?" came the project leader's voice.

"Just harvested the current crop from on high. Rayleigh-Taylor instability detected on the solar surface. Alternating hot and cold spots. Coronal activity mounting. The whole ball of wax. The computer's still working on it, but I'd say less than a hundred planetary days before burn-off."

Garbled static came from the speaker.

"Been talking to one of the grave robbers from over at the city," Nels went on. "Their relief's not due for a half year standard. Better send out a message packet to Novo Terra asking for an evac ship and get them the hell off before then."

"What!" cried Leonore. Bernssen motioned her to silence.

". . . damn radiation levels are rising, too. Cutting apart communication," came Justine's voice.

"You'll have to ask Rodrigo about that. He's the rad-man. All I do is solar hydrofluidics."

"Document everything. I'll get the packet starred off immediately, and I'll tell Stoneface he's got to vacate." Justine chuckled. "It's going to be fun kicking Ralston off planet. Teach him to be civil to his betters in the future."

"Nels, what's going on? We can't leave. We . . . we just found a site that'll turn the archaeology department around. It's a once-in-a-lifetime find!"

"Sorry, darling. Justine'll send the message back to the University. Ought to arrive in, oh, a week."

"A week!"

"Superdrive. Damned near nothing but stardrive engine, a tad of fuel, and a marble-sized compartment for the message. Doesn't take much to tell what's happening since the powers that be already know. Anyway, they'll dispatch another starship for you, and you'll be off planet in about two months." Bernssen's expression turned grim. "Even that might be cutting it fine."

"What's going on?" Leonore demanded.

"Darling, I'm sorry now that you came. Wait, don't get

mad. This isn't my doing." Nels smiled. "But what a chance! The primary's going nova."

Leonore had passed beyond anger. She simply stood and stared at him in disbelief.

"Really strange, too. This is a G5 yellow-orange. Shouldn't go nova, but everything's indicating it will. Soon."

"You knew the star was going to blow up?"

"We suspected, not knew. I've been mapping the surface of the star. The latest conformal mapping showed an oddity usually found only in rising magma plumes."

"The Rayleigh-whatever?"

"Rayleigh-Taylor instability. A density inversion. Heavier matter has come to the surface. Same phenomenon shows up in gas fingers escaping black holes."

"Your dissertation," Leonore said.

"Right. That's why they wanted me on this expedition. We're looking at a sun going nova. Up close, for the first time with full instrumentation, everything!"

"The radiation," Leonore said. "That's why we've all been sunburning so badly."

"You don't look too good with a peeling nose," said Nels. "Didn't Justine tell your prof to keep you out of the direct sunlight?" Nels shrugged it off. "That's just part of it. The instabilities are increasing. The solar mechanism is becoming increasingly upset. It started out following a familiar Bessel function, a zeroth order one. Simple stuff. The perturbations started creating flow pathways between the density layers. Now the oscillations in the corona are—" Words failed the physicist.

"We can't leave, Nels," pleaded Leonore. "Our discovery. What about it? The University wouldn't send us all the way to Alpha 3 unless they expected us to do our work to completion."

"They probably sent Ralston here to get him out of the way."

Leonore went cold inside. That carried the ring of truth. It was no secret that Michael Ralston was an embarrassment for the archaeology department. She had seen the others treat him as a pariah. Even she had been guilty of believing the stories before she'd gotten to know him better.

"Shouldn't have allowed anyone to come at all," Nels finished. "Especially you."

"What's the risk in staying?" Leonore asked.

Nels Bernssen looked as if she'd put the electrodes on his

ears and then turned on the current. "You're not thinking this through, Leonore. The primary in this system is going to explode, go nova, go *pop!* Nothing but superheated plasma will be left of Muckup and all the other planets. Nothing. Not a twig, not a pebble, not one single drop of that damned rain."

"We can't possibly get all our data in two months."

"Leonore," he said, taking her arms and shaking her, as if this might change her mind. She pulled away. "No one has ever witnessed a nova before. We've seen the after-effects— centuries later. We're dealing with a completely new set of data. G5s aren't supposed to blow up like this one's threatening to do. When I say the primary's going off in six months, I might be wrong. It might be half that."

"Or twice?"

"Stop it," Nels said angrily. "You and Ralston and the others are going to have to leave when the evac ship arrives. Staying any longer is stupid. Suicidal."

Leonore Diṣa had come all this way to be with her lover, but she'd found more on Alpha 3 than she'd intended. She took it as a personal affront that she wouldn't be allowed to study the vault and pry loose the answers to this planet's mysteries locked within.

"Get me back to the dig right now," she said. "We've got a lot of work to do."

SIX

MICHAEL RALSTON DIDN'T even hear Leonore enter his shelter. He bent over the hardcopy of a photo taken within the diorama, studying one segment with a magnifier.

"What happened to you?" the woman asked, startled at the size of the knot on the back of the professor's head. In the light, it showed as an ugly purple and green mountain of tender flesh.

Ralston jerked upright, knocking the magnifier to the floor. It lay there buzzing in protest. He switched it off before asking angrily, "Don't you ever knock before entering?"

"Sorry, Doctor," she said. "But what happened to your head? It looks as if you gave yourself a good rap." She reached out hesitantly. Ralston flinched away when her fingers brushed over the edge of the wound. "Let me tend to it."

"I'm all right. What do you want?"

Leonore dropped onto an uncomfortable plastic folding chair, and pulled it closer to the table. She hunched forward, hands clenching and unclenching.

"I've just been over at the solar physics site," she said.

Ralston's mind shifted from how to best investigate the intricacies of the problem posed by the dioramas to another type of problem. "Who'd you go over there to see?"

A hot flush rose in Leonore's cheeks. She hadn't thought her motives were that transparent, but why else would she willingly associate with researchers in the physics camp? They weren't archaeologists.

"Nels Bernssen. He's a post-doctoral worker for the University. We met about a year ago and . . ."

"Spare me the details," Ralston said impatiently. "I'm happy for you. May the two of you be happy forever and ever." The words came abruptly, a clear dismissal.

"Dr. Ralston, please. We've got to talk about this. What Nels found out tonight is important."

"All research is important."

His attitude began to annoy her. Ralston saw her mounting anger and added, "I'm sure Dr. Bernssen is very good at what he does. I'm also sure you are very proud of his accomplishments. It's just that our find today is foremost in my mind."

"It has a bearing on the find," she said. "Nels reported to his project leader . . ."

"Justine Rasmussen? She's the one I met when we first grounded. A garrulous person. All she wanted to do was talk. Didn't seem to notice we had a considerable amount of work to do then."

"Yes, her," Leonore rushed on. "Dr. Rasmussen has starred back a com packet requesting our immediate evacuation. Nels doesn't think it'll take more than two months for the starship to arrive."

"Ridiculous," snorted Ralston. "The ship just left. It'll be another few weeks before it'll even arrive back at Novo Terra. You know there's no way of communicating while a ship is shifting. Besides, it's too expensive to retrieve us this quickly."

"Nels said the University would send another immediately and damn the cost when they read Dr. Rasmussen's message. This system's primary is going nova."

Ralston sat and stared. The coldness within him spread, frosty fingers gripping at throat and heart and belly.

"No," he said. "You didn't understand this Nels. Physicists always talk in riddles and you simply missed his meaning. I read the survey reports. Alpha Prime is a G5, not too dissimilar from Earth's sun. They don't blow up, they collapse into white dwarves. I checked everything out about Muckup, too." Desperation entered his voice. He would *not* be denied his find! "I showed the planetary data to Estevez. He's the top-ranked xeno man at Ilium."

"The radiation levels are rising," said Leonore. "Nels found some sort of disturbance both in the star's corona and on the surface. He can't say exactly when Alpha Prime will explode, but he knows that it will eventually."

"That's it," said Ralston, a flood of relief washing over him. "He's talking in astronomical terms. That's like speaking with a geologist. They say 'soon' and they mean 'soon geologically' or 'soon in astronomical terms.' It might be a million years. For a star's evolution, that's fast."

"Nels means months. Maybe only days. Please, Doctor, call him. Or com Dr. Rasmussen and talk to her. I might have misunderstood, but I don't think so. Nels was too emphatic. We're going to lose not only the find but the entire planet."

"You told this Nels about the find?"

"I didn't describe it in any detail. He wouldn't have appreciated its importance even if I had. He's always been more interested in stability criteria." Leonore smiled wryly. "Sometimes, he's more interested in that than he is in me."

"Now I know you're exaggerating," said Ralston. Leonore's soft brown eyes shot wide open at the unexpected compliment. He smiled and pushed the hardcopy photos into an accordion folder. "I'll call Justine Rasmussen and see what's happening. It might not be as bad as your friend made it sound."

Ralston dragged out the small, battered com unit and fussed with it several minutes. Hissing and popping almost drowned out Rasmussen's reedy voice.

"Wanted to talk with you, Dr. Ralston," came the physicist's cracked reply.

"Why is the communication so bad?" Ralston shouted into the unit. "Shouldn't be this broken. Getting crosstalk from one of the other bands, too."

"We're being uplinked. I'm in orbit to align one of our optical telescopes." Hisses drowned out a sentence, then, "...Nels Bernssen is the expert. All I've seen substantiates his theory—his certainty now. I've already starred back the packet with a request for your evacuation. They'll have a starship here within two months to get you and your students off."

"What about your own researchers?"

"We've made plans to stay a bit longer. Our evac ship will follow yours by about a week, if all stays on schedule."

"When do you star back to Novo Terra, then?"

More static. Justine Rasmussen repeated. "We stay as long as radiation levels allow. We're hoping for as long as a year— but we're keeping the starship in orbit in case we have to run for it. Nels thinks we'll be close behind you on the way back to Novo Terra."

"We can do the same," insisted Ralston. "We can stay here, then leave when you do." Precious days might be all it would require to better examine the unique dioramas and the culture and history locked within their descriptive scenes.

"That's between you and University officials. We made our plans before we left Novo Terra. They might not want to go to the expense of leaving one of their starships in orbit for you."

"But they will for you?" Ralston's anger rose now. A career hung in the balance—careers, if he counted the dissertations his seven students could write on the Alpha 3 find. The responsibility Ralston felt for his students wasn't as great as it might have been, but it still existed. And he wouldn't be denied his chance at the greatest find since the Rosetta Stone. "There's no way they can force us to go back."

Ralston didn't have to hear Rasmussen's reply. Even though static tore apart her words, the sentiment came through clearly. The physicist told him in clipped, precise words he'd be destroyed professionally if he knowingly allowed any of his students to remain on a planet marked for vaporization.

But the find!

". . . talk in person," came the woman's parting words. A metallic click sounded, and all Ralston received was solar interference. He turned off the com unit.

"If we abandon the city site and concentrate on the dioramas," said Leonore, "we might be able to get a great deal done in two months. Not a complete workup, of course, but enough to save something. We'll be able to study the photos at leisure back at school."

Ralston hesitated telling her about being attacked within the alien museum. He thought it was one of the seven archaeology students, but new possibilities entered now. He couldn't restrict his suspicions to only the graduate students. It might be someone connected with Rasmussen's solar physics group, though this seemed farfetched.

The other possibility, as remote as it was, couldn't be discounted. An Alpha 3 native might still survive and stalk the ruins of its once lofty civilization.

"Let me consider our options," he said. "We'll keep working on the city until further notice. A day or two won't make a great deal of difference."

"But it might!" protested Leonore. "There's no way to estimate the extent of the displays without going down and mapping every turn in the tunnels. Just photographing it all might take months!"

"Don't mention this to anyone," Ralston said. "To anyone."

"But . . ."

Leonore Disa subsided when she saw her professor's determination in this matter. She spun and stomped from the shelter, vanishing into the curtain of rain plummeting from a treacherously clouded sky.

Ralston watched his graduate student leave, then turned back to the photos. Somehow, his concentration had fled. The more he stared into the magnifier, the less he saw.

Ralston wiped rain droplets from the lenses of the IR goggles. Stalking about to spy on his students struck him as absurd, yet he had to do it. To protect the sanctity of the find was important, but not of as great an importance as finding who had attacked him.

The rain prevented anyone not similarly equipped from seeing him. A quick scan of the compound showed no one else braving the elements. He moved quickly to the nearest shelter, the large one he had designated as a conference room. The pounding of rain destroyed all but the most muffled of words coming through the thin plastic walls. Ralston moved stealthily until he came to the back wall and a punchout spot where air conditioners were supposed to be mounted.

The University hadn't sent air conditioners or any other type of climate modifier. They'd sent nothing but the barest equipment necessary for survival. In a way, Ralston approved. This dig was supposed to provide experience for the seven graduate students. Living in shelters more suitable for a billionaire would do little to instill in them the need for innovation and the appreciation for detail.

Even if they failed in their attempt to gain their degrees, they would go out into Novo Terran society with a more acute appreciation of the luxuries afforded them.

Ralston pressed the IR goggles firmly against the thin plastic panel. Dim, wavering red shapes moved within. He made out three separate bodies before turning to press one ear against the wall.

The three students, Abeyta y Conejo, Fernandez and Butz, had been staying close together, and Ralston had spoken infrequently to them. On the starship he had ignored them totally after his feeble efforts to involve them in some sort of communication. Once grounded, he had given them their instructions and let them work unhindered. Now he wished he'd learned more about them—other than that they, too, were department rejects. The lowliest students were selected to accompany the Nex-loving Dr. Michael Lewis Ralston, he thought bitterly. While these three hadn't made any major mistakes on the dig, they hadn't distinguished themselves for brilliance or even great attention to detail, either. The best that might be said about them was that they put in their time and didn't complain too much.

Ralston shook his head. That sounded like an ancient prison sentence being fulfilled.

". . . it's verd, I tell you," said Fernandez.

"She and that cloud of space gas?" scoffed Abeyta y Conejo. "She's too bonita for him."

"She's the only one who'll get a good topic, wait and see," insisted Fernandez. Ralston didn't have to guess at the topic being bandied about. "Just 'cause she's chinging him, she'll get the prize. That's the way it works. Verd."

"Who cares?" Ralston decided this had to be the third student, Butz, responding. "I'm here because my father said I gotta do something besides lying around Veral Beach and chinging all the good-looking muchas. Let them have their fun, as long as I get a degree. Then I can get back to the beaches where *I* can enjoy myself again."

After listening to the three curse Muckup's mud and perpetual rain, Ralston drifted away, heavy rain drowning the sounds of his boots sucking in the mud. Those three only verified what he'd suspected. Three rich kids forced into the University to get a degree and become "respectable." Too many of the rich on Novo Terra had fought and clawed their way to the top. Getting away from a burned-out cinder of an Earth had made them a hard breed. But that had been a generation back. For their children they wanted only the finest, the easiest, all that they'd lacked when growing up on Earth.

Novo Terra provided warm sun, soft breezes, temperate climate, fabulous beaches stretching for kilometers with eye-dazzling white sand. If anything, life on Novo Terra was too easy. Those who had fought so hard found their children drifting. That explained why so many pushed their offspring into graduate schools. Getting a doctorate was easier than cutting them off without any credit and forcing them to fend for themselves.

It did nothing to improve the quality of student work. Too many bought their degrees and appeased their parents that way.

Ralston knew that if he simply gave all three within that shelter a degree they'd be satisfied. None would care that it hadn't been earned legitimately. The professor smiled, water running away from the corners of his mouth, when he thought of Leonore Disa. In one respect, Abeyta y Conejo and the others were right. She *would* get the choicest project. He'd personally see to that.

Not because he was sleeping with her but because she of all the group shared some measure of his excitement for archaeology. Ralston believed that she would be in the field digging, struggling, sweating over shards and bits of steel to reconstruct entire civilizations whether she received her advanced degree or had to work as a technician. The work, the ineffable thrill of discovery, took precedence over status, real or imagined.

Ralston frowned. He knew Leonore came from a wealthy background like the others; what made her different? A pang of doubt assailed him. Were the three students right in thinking he harbored sexual fantasies about her?

Ralston pushed it from his mind. She wasn't that attractive a woman. What he felt might go beyond simple liking for a student—but it didn't go *that* much past.

The heavy rain and his lack of attention almost made him walk into the side of Asan's shelter. Ralston wiped the infrared lenses clear again. Through the thin plastic wall he could not make out whether there was one very warm body or two sitting side by side. Spying allowed him to hear Asan and Lantalman talking in their subdued, paranoid tones. They always spoke with protective hands over their mouths. He guessed this derived from time spent in a rehabilitation clinic where infractions of the rules merited far more punishment than did poor grades.

Ralston couldn't hear clearly anything that passed between the two rehabs.

He made his way through the sucking mud to Yago de la Cruz's shelter. One body inside. No sound. He moved on, hesitated when he saw Leonore's shelter, then continued into the night, strides lengthening until the ground seemed to evaporate beneath him. Ralston checked the inertial tracker in his wristcom until the green arrow turned into a dot and began blinking.

Through the IR goggles he saw the warm outline of the copper-clad door leading down to the alien museum. Carefully, he pulled out the jacket still stuffed in the crack between door and frame, pushed open the door, and went down into the corridor. Again using his coat, he cleaned his boots. He closed the door to keep out the rain and, satisfied that he didn't do undue harm to the hallway, turned and went deeper into the catacombs.

Ralston stopped and simply stared down the row of dioramas. Each held a slightly different scene. Each promised to give a clue to a different aspect of an alien culture.

Ralston swallowed hard as he mentally pictured the Alpha primary glowing whiter and hotter, expanding, the limits of its photosphere reaching out hungry tongues of plasma that eventually engulfed Alpha 3. The water began boiling off the planet's surface, then the atmosphere exploded into space. Before many more microseconds the planet itself began boiling—or would it simply sublimate? One second it spun through space as a muddy chunk, the next it was only superheated gas, a plasma cooling as it expanded to infinity. No matter how it occurred, boiling or sublimating, all this would be gone in the wink of an eye. The heritage of a lost race snuffed out by a berserk star.

"No!" he shouted. His single cry of negation echoed along the halls and finally died in the bowels of the exhibit.

He wouldn't let it happen. It couldn't! Such knowledge couldn't be lost forever. Ralston walked slowly down the corridor, came to a juncture, then reluctantly turned and retraced his steps. With his decision made to exploit this as vigorously as possible, using all seven of the graduate students, Ralston opened the copper door, exited into the driving rain, closed the door securely behind him, and followed the green arrow on the face of his wristcom back to camp. There'd be plenty of work to do in the morning.

Cold eyes filled with hate watched Ralston vanish into the downpour. With the archaeologist gone, he had nothing to stop him now. It proved only a matter of seconds to reopen the door leading to the treasure trove below.

SEVEN

DR. MICHAEL RALSTON DISAPPEARED into the heavily falling rain. Yago de la Cruz let his anger smolder as he waited several minutes before going to the copper door leading underground. He pulled out his professor's jacket and carelessly tossed it aside. De la Cruz descended into the alien museum again, smiling in grim recollection of how he had stalked Ralston here and struck him.

"Served the fool right," he muttered. De la Cruz made no attempt to be careful with his entry; his every step left behind a fresh cake of mud on the floor. All de la Cruz wanted was the big find, the discovery that would establish him in the field of archaeology. All his life he had been ridiculed by his family.

"Why don't you go into business?" they demanded. "Your father will finance it. Or your uncle. Or your aunt." Always they dunned him with becoming a success. *Their* success.

Everything Yago de la Cruz touched turned to dust. Three businesses had failed because of bad luck. How was he to know of so many laws governing import-export? That business had to fail when the government seized it. And who but his family could blame him when the orchid importer stupidly allowed the Terran rust blight to destroy the entire nursery? So what if de la Cruz hadn't kept the orchids in quarantine for the prescribed time? It had been the importer who had allowed tainted flowers to be starred to Novo Terra.

Of the third attempt, de la Cruz couldn't even bring himself to remember it. But the crushing failure hadn't been his fault, either. None of the chinging business disasters had been his fault.

The University of Ilium seemed his only refuge, his only chance for prominence and acceptance in his family's eyes.

"I can never be like my brother and sisters," de la Cruz said. The words echoed hollowly down the corridors. The sound finally died in one of the dioramas, swallowed by a distance both physical and temporal. "Arturo and Constance and Angelina are all in business. I'm not."

Anger grew within him again, a burning, ugly seed blossoming into hatred. How dare Ralston hide this discovery? It meant more than a simple paper to Yago de la Cruz. It meant freedom, it meant becoming his own man.

"If he won't give it to us, I'll *take* it," de la Cruz said, smirking now. He strutted up and down the narrow corridors, shining a small hand flash into each diorama. The slow progression in the scenes went unnoticed by the man. All he saw was opportunity and acceptance. A dissertation, yes, but more!

The University of Ilium officials might have rejected his application to assist Valasquez on Proteus, but after he delivered this find to them on a silver platter like Herod presenting the head of John the Baptist to Salome, they'd never deny him anything in the future.

De la Cruz crossed himself and muttered a quick prayer for success. What alien technology lay hidden here, waiting to be exploited? He might not have the business sense of his siblings, but a good, solid piece of hardware didn't require business.

Madre de Dios, he'd *hire* his family to market what he found!

De la Cruz turned a corner and explored deeper into the catacombs. Some corridors intersected while others ran a distance and came to a dead end. The graduate student frowned. Some sense ought to be made from the patterns. Only in that way would he know where to look first for the highest probability of finding something like Vegan spider steel or the fabulous refractory Lars Stormgren found in the devastated city on airless Prolix 11.

"Should be recording all this. Got to get it documented before Ralston." De la Cruz's smile turned even broader now. For whatever reason, Ralston hadn't done more than shoot a few photos and run the analyzer on the first strange scene set in its alcove. He hadn't ventured deep into the guts of this museum. The fool! Ralston might not have properly dated his photos or analysis, either.

"If he did, so what?" de la Cruz said to himself. "Photos can be lost. Analyzer findings can be erased." He rubbed a hand across his sunburned nose. With the high UV on this planet, a good case might be made for the destruction of many records by radiation. De la Cruz thought it would be a shame if Ralston carelessly pulled out the block circuits from his analyzer and left them out in the sunlight where irradiation destroyed the electronically encrypted data.

Stranger incidents had occurred on digs. De la Cruz knew. He'd studied the reports, seeking ways for a smart, ambitious man like himself to get ahead. After the boring seven weeks as they starred to Muckup, he counted himself an expert in all those methods. Not a single report in the starship's small library had gone unread.

For a moment, indecision struck de la Cruz. He shouldn't wander alone in the catacombs. Danger never entered his fantasies; de la Cruz worried that he might need a witness to "his" find. But which of the other graduate students would be the most amenable?

Certainly not that bitch Leonore Disa. She was chinging Ralston for her chance to study this underground museum— and it worked. *Doctor* Ralston had allowed her inside to use the analyzer. She would not suit de la Cruz's purposes. But he couldn't trust either of the rehabs. Who did? Their brains had been picked apart chemically, electrically, and mechanically and restructured in patterns known only to their rehabilitation psychologist. The other three graduate students seemed no better choices for what de la Cruz intended. Abeyta y Conejo had no ambition; he wouldn't fight his professor when Ralston challenged the validity—and priority—of de la Cruz's claim to this museum. Fernandez and Butz had no strength, no *coraje*.

De la Cruz resigned himself to working alone on this project. No other course presented itself. He thrust out his chest and strutted back and forth. With the proper altered records, he could claim all this for his own, even down to the last speck of the precious dust that Ralston seemed so solicitous of.

But the figures in the dioramas were the true find. Somewhere within them lay his future, his ticket to accolades!

He unslung a pack and pulled forth the cameras and portable analyzer he'd taken from the storage shelter. De la Cruz set up a few battery-powered xenon lights and turned the impenetrable murk day-bright. He switched off his handflash and slipped it into his pocket. Working as accurately as his eagerness allowed, de la Cruz set up the analyzer, slid in a fresh recording block and tapped a spurious date and time on the input keys. His claim now lay recorded a full two days prior to Ralston's blundering onto the doorway. Without diurnal light cycles, who was to say that this wasn't nine in the morning, local time? The analyzer, once started, ran continuously and no alteration of the start date was permitted without destroying the entire block circuit.

But de la Cruz had learned well. He need only fill up a block or two and his claim would be firmly established.

"This is the first diorama," he said, speaking so that the recorder built into the analyzer picked up his words. De la Cruz ignored it for further investigation. It had been the one Ralston had studied. Better to choose other, more interesting ones. That diorama held only two figures, both avian and neither posed in a dramatic fashion.

De la Cruz desired force in his photos, drive, drama. And, of course, the solid discovery of an alien technological gadget to exploit.

"The tenth diorama along the corridor holds several figures of interest." De la Cruz almost chortled when he saw one figure holding what might be a weapon. What would the Novo Terra Defense League pay for an alien weapon that couldn't be shielded against or circumvented?

De la Cruz placed the camera atop the analyzer and turned both to cover the diorama. He wanted his every move documented when he took the weapon from the birdman's hands. Stepping into the picture, the graduate student said, "I am now examining the artifact held by the ge—by the leftmost native."

De la Cruz took two quick steps into the diorama. For an instant, he felt as if he'd been returned to the freefall of a starship. The curious weightless sensation passed, not even leaving him with residual dizziness. But de la Cruz noted something peculiar.

"I . . . I smell burning organics," he said. "It might be tree leaves. Or hemp. And a small breeze blows warmly across my face. I . . . the sun is so bright. Not a cloud to be seen anywhere in the sky. Where did the rainstorms go?"

Confused, de la Cruz stood and stared. It had been night— and a storm had hurled downward its rain—when he'd entered the catacombs. Now he stood on a small rise looking out over a burning city. Flames licked upward to a brilliant sky, marring its azure perfection with greasy black plumes of smoke.

"You, traitor, halt!"

Startled, de la Cruz spun. He faced the native clutching the long-barreled weapon. The avian lifted the *sear* rifle. Tiny blue sparks marched along the top and sides of the barrel to sputter and spark at the muzzle.

"You, Wennord of Lost Aerie, have been convicted of crimes against the Nest. No more will we tolerate your rebellion. You might have destroyed our capital, but we, the rightful authority for this country, have caught and condemned you to death."

"Wait!" de la Cruz cried. He raised his hands to show he carried no weapons. The avian native aimed the *sear* rifle. De la Cruz stared into its black maw and saw tiny specks of red and white forming. The sparks coalesced into a miniature tornado that erupted from the muzzle. He felt himself thrown into the air, carried on gossamer wings, then dropped heavily.

De la Cruz screamed. He didn't want to die. It wasn't his fault! He knew nothing of this traitor Wennord. On hands and knees, de la Cruz pleaded with the native for mercy, to reconsider his dastardly crimes. But it had held such satisfaction for him to ignite the fuses that ultimately burned all of the capital.

He had conquered. Even in death, he, Wennord of Lost Aerie, had conquered by destroying what the tyrants held dearest!

De la Cruz slammed hard against a wall and fell prone. Sweating, heart pounding, he opened his eyes. It took several seconds for him to realize that he wasn't dead. The native hadn't fired the strange energy weapon.

And he wasn't Wennord of Lost Aerie.

The graduate student wiped the fear-sweat from his contorted face and sat trembling on the diorama floor. It had seemed so real. It *had* been real. He had walked into this chinging diorama and the natives had come alive and he'd been transported to a different world in the first rush of spring.

"Where'd it go?" he asked, his voice grating and cracked with emotion. He crossed himself twice and prayed for mercy from the aliens stalking him in the catacombs.

Where had they come from? He'd seen no trace of any bird-geek in the corridors.

On shaking legs, he stood and faced the figure with the weapon. He turned and looked at the companion figure, the one obviously being held prisoner by the armed avian. De la Cruz reached out to touch the energy rifle—the *sear* rifle the birdman had called it.

He jerked his hand back along the barrel, its static charge biting him.

"You might kill me," Wennord told him, angrily clacking his dental plates, "but that won't stop the rebellion. Look! Your precious capital city is in flames. *We* did that. You cannot halt the tides of progress. We will soar above your petty nestings!"

"Wennord," de la Cruz said, grinding his teeth and feeling the nervous tension along his forearms as fingers tightened on the energy weapon's trigger, "you are a traitor. It gives me great enjoyment to carry out my duty."

"May all your eggs break!" Wennord tried to bolt and run. De la Cruz whirled, lifted the cumbersome *sear* rifle and fired. The energy discharge rocked him back. Wennord blasted apart into a million burning fragments. Little enough punishment for defying the Chief of Rules and Council, de la Cruz thought.

He looked over his capital and knew that civilization had triumphed over the powers of anarchy this day. And he had been an important part of defending the Nest. His duty had been clear, and he would be given the highest honors in front of the Table of Rules.

He preened and began walking toward the inferno that was his capital . . . and stumbled over his analyzer, falling heavily to the corridor floor. De la Cruz jerked spastically, as if he'd awakened suddenly from a nightmare.

Hands trembling, de la Cruz grabbed the analyzer and used its familiar, comforting bulk to support himself in an attempt to sit upright. He looked back into the diorama; nothing within it had changed. One alien figure still clutched the rifle and menaced the other. Neither had shifted position by even a millimeter.

"Wennord the usurper," de la Cruz said. He licked his lips and swallowed hard. Moisture returned to his mouth. De la Cruz stood and stared. He knew what this scene depicted. No, he mentally corrected himself, he didn't know, he *knew*. As if every nuance had been burned into his brain, he *knew* the story of the last of the great insurrectionists and the man who had stopped him.

"I was there," de la Cruz said in awe. "I lived through it. I saw the pain, the destruction Wennord caused. But I know why he did it. He thought he was right. But he wasn't. I see it all!"

Awed by the impact of such knowledge, de la Cruz stared at the diorama's figures. He was galvanized into action by the sudden clutching fear that the analyzer hadn't been properly adjusted, that the camera had failed to record the bizarre scene. De la Cruz ripped off the protective plate on the analyzer and studied the red flashing numbers revealed on an interior instrumentation panel.

He heaved a sigh of relief. The analyzer had been running during his stint within the diorama. It had faithfully recorded everything, every whisper of radiation, every flash of light, the entire spectrum from UV to IR, and had sampled other frequencies along the way. Even com frequencies for microwave and shortwave had been monitored intermittently. He had it all locked with the block circuits of the analyzer! And the automatically recorded date made this discovery his and his alone!

De la Cruz almost re-entered the diorama to take the energy weapon from the avian's hand. Disorientation struck him again as he passed the plane formed by the front walls. He backed out, shaking like a leaf caught in a whirlwind. De la Cruz stood and stared until the tremors passed. He hefted the camera and analyzer and moved them along to the next diorama and the next and the next. He wanted to choose another which might give him the financially profitable discovery that would free

him from familial guilt at not achieving all that they expected
from a de la Cruz scion.

"The scenes show a definite progression in complexity," he
recorded as he walked to another scene. "The first ones in this
hall contained one or two figures, mostly without props. Later
ones are packed with them. I am going to enter another diorama
and take a sample of the material used to construct the statues."

De la Cruz experienced a thrill of possible victory in his
search as he considered how these figures had endured at least
ten thousand years. What material made up their bones and
skin and turned them impervious to the passing eons?

De la Cruz entered an alcove with only four figures. He
braced himself for the dizziness, but it didn't occur. Sure of
himself, de la Cruz quickly stepped into the center of the figures
and reached out with the analyzer's mobile probe. Using the
device, he scanned the surfaces of the mannequin.

He jumped as an odd odor pervaded the scene. His nose
wrinkled. He said, "I smell something. A cross between roses
. . . and frying onions."

De la Cruz looked over his shoulder and caught a cold blast
of air in the face. He blinked back tears and rubbed his eyes
as he crossed himself.

"It's the event of the decade, I tell you," Blan said. "Think
of it. When else in our history has a cometary object swept
this close? If you fail to take full advantage of this opportunity,
Zonnerg, all our grants will dry up. Believe it."

"Grants?" he asked stupidly.

"The Table of Rules frowns on missed chances to publicize
their efforts as much as they do wasted funds," Blan said. His
excitement obvious, the tall avian flapped his arms as if to take
wing. "We can launch a platform, set it into orbit, and have a
telescope on it to observe as the comet passes. It'll be so close
the coma will stretch halfway out of the solar system."

De la Cruz nodded, slowly coming into agreement with his
trusted colleague.

"You won't regret this, Zonnerg, you won't! The information from this comet will place us on the top perch for years."

"Launch it?" de la Cruz asked.

"Yes, launch it," Blan said, irritation entering his voice.
"That funny thing the astro group has cobbled together will
serve us well."

"We can go on from that," de la Cruz said, entering into the spirit of the discussion. "Why stop with a simple orbiting telescope? We can launch probes for the other planets. This comet can capture both the public's and the Council's imagination. Funds will pour into our nest."

"Yes, Zonnerg, yes!" cried Blan.

De la Cruz existed, his personality split between the avian astronomer Zonnerg and his own. As de la Cruz, he rejoiced. He had discovered spaceflight in this culture! Proteus 4 wasn't the only newly discovered post-spaceflight race. And this one was his discovery. He'd rank beside Velasquez before he'd finished.

Waves of staggering dizziness struck de la Cruz, but he recovered swiftly. He had expected it but still felt confusion and giddy disorientation after it passed. He heard himself—as Zonnerg—saying, "What went wrong?"

"The coma. It never developed. All our theories are as feathers on the wind," answered Blan.

"Comets are composed of frozen ammonia and other gases. It had to develop a tail," de la Cruz/Zonnerg protested. "We must have spectrographic readings to confirm this. We must!"

"The Council is angry at what they call a waste. The entire program has been canceled."

"But the planetary probe?"

"It, too," answered Blan, shaking his narrow head and blinking eyes of liquid amber, "has succumbed to public opinion. It will be many years before we can recover. Damn that comet! Why didn't it live up to our expectations?"

"We asked too much of it," de la Cruz answered. "There must be more to research than a single goal. We gained knowledge. The telescope is still in orbit. We can turn it on other objects. The stars! We can study them with Predario's new spectrum analyzer."

"My friend, it's not to be," Blan said sadly. "The Council has ordered the platform dismantled and returned to our southern hemisphere observatory. Space research is forbidden."

"But they can't. Not because of one comet!"

De la Cruz staggered from the diorama, still incensed at the failings of bureaucratic thinking. He stared directly into the lens of his camera; he heard the baleful *whir-whir-whir* as it took a photo every ten seconds. The analyzer continued to record on a wide variety of frequencies, missing nothing.

The student sat on the floor and cried. The entire planet's first tentative reach into space had been thwarted because of faulty theories concerning a comet. It was unfair!

De la Cruz shook himself free of Zonnerg's memories. For long minutes he simply stood and stared sightlessly. Then his own thoughts forced upward and replaced the void in his skull.

"Their history. It's all here," he said, jolted by the immensity of the discovery. There wasn't any need for a Rosetta Stone to decipher meaningless scribbles. He had only to walk into one of the dioramas and he'd be given a history lesson. He *knew* the lesson intimately after leaving. De la Cruz's experience carried far more weight than a simple book, too.

Their emotions, their motivations, all were his for the asking—for the living!

The audacity of the avians also impressed de la Cruz. "They have no fear in showing both sides. I was both the rebel Wennord *and* his executioner. I knew the reasons both acted as they did."

Never in all of human history had such a find been made. And it was his, his, all his!

De la Cruz could hardly restrain himself as he prowled the corridors. He guessed that a new student might enter the first diorama—the one Ralston had examined—and then progress to the next and the next and the next, learning as he went. By the time each diorama had been visited and fully experienced, a complete knowledge, both intellectual and emotional, of the planet would have been imparted.

De la Cruz stopped in front of a diorama near the end of the corridor. Only two figures crouched within. Without hesitation, de la Cruz stepped inside. He had learned to position himself in the same fashion as one of the avian mannequins—and he became Cossia.

"Are you all right, Jerad?" he heard himself asking. His body twitched and trembled oddly. It took several seconds for him to realize he was now a female in anguish over her lover.

"It's seized me again. I can't stop it. Oh, I love you, Cossia. I do!"

De la Cruz reflected on the strangeness of this diorama. The others had been scenes of obvious historical importance. A dying lover hardly qualified as being in the same rank as the death of a major space research program dooming the avians forever to a landlocked existence or the execution of the last traitor trying to overturn the planet's governing authority.

"Fordyne is gone. I follow in his distinguished steps." Jerad jerked about, his dental plates snapping shut so hard that pieces broke off.

De la Cruz/Cossia knelt beside her lover and stroked over a fleecy skull. "Don't worry, my love. The project is done. Dial is away on his star journey. And the vaults are filled. We will not perish without our memory wafting along the ages."

"This is the final record?" Jerad asked. His eyes had turned to dull orbs, fogged as if by cataracts.

"The final warning is being recorded now," Cossia said. Anger and frustration filled her. The unfairness to rob an entire planet of life filled de la Cruz/Cossia until he/she shook. "Zonnerg and Blan ought to have fought harder. We had to leave this planet. The comet. It caused our destruction."

"There's no other possibility," Jerad said. A massive convulsion struck him. The avian arched his back and jerked spastically, obviously dying. Cossia heard fragile bones snapping as the seizure took control of her lover.

Cossia stood. "Good-bye, dear Jerad. Good-bye, Fordyne and all the precious others. The end has come upon us. and we'll never know the reason. Only that the comet has brought the wrath of the ages upon us. But how?"

Cossia turned and straightened as courage firmed within her breast. De la Cruz was vaguely aware that he now faced the analyzer and camera, an actor performing for an unseen audience.

"The comet," he/she said, voice booming. "We are dead, but you, the finder of this vault containing our entire racial history, still have a chance. Use wisely what you have found here to solve the mystery of our death." He/she held out an imploring hand, then stumbled and fell to his/her knees.

De la Cruz recovered from the grip of the mental communication. His legs proved even weaker than before as he staggered out and braced himself against a wall. Within the diorama Cossia and Jerad still stood as they had for ten thousand years.

"They fled a riot-torn city—the capital," de la Cruz said, more to himself than for the analyzer. "The tall central building, the one we're scraping out the foundations on. That was the Aerie. The Table of Rules convened there. How magnificent it was! And their rulers. The Council and its Chief of Rules. They met on the uppermost floor of the Aerie to view the entire city."

The shakes hit de la Cruz—hard.

"Reaction," he panted when the quaking had passed. Yago de la Cruz stood on rubbery legs but smiled broadly. He had just gained an insight. There were things transcending mere wealth. His momentous discoveries in the dioramas would burn forever in the history and archaeology texts. Fame would be his!

All his!

EIGHT

MICHAEL RALSTON ASSEMBLED his small band of graduate students. He took a deep breath as if preparing for a lecture, then forced himself to relax. This wasn't a classroom on Novo Terra. They were in the field, and he'd made a discovery that would assure them all of a good professional future in archaeology.

Ralston only wished that more of them deserved what he was about to drop into their laps.

"Citizens, we're going to cease all attended digging on the city site. I want the automated data collection to proceed, but no longer will we stand and watch for the smallest artifact to be spat up by the ultrasonic digger."

Ralston paused for dramatic effect. It was lost on everyone. Leonore knew what he was going to announce, and the others didn't care.

"I've made what might be conservatively termed the discovery of the century." Ralston couldn't keep from grinning broadly now. He didn't care if they felt the same excitement that he did. He had enough for them all!

"And if you're not conservative, you might want to call it the premier find of all time. I've uncovered an intact alien museum not two kilometers south of this site. The buried outlines showed up on the synthetic aperture radar photos taken right after we grounded, and Citizen Disa and I went out a few days ago to examine the site more closely. We opened a copper-clad door and found an extensive underground complex. While I've not explored it except to take a few preliminary photos, I'm sure these will excite you as much as they do me."

Ralston turned on the projector and began flashing the visual spectrum photos he and Leonore had taken of the dioramas.

He turned when Yago de la Cruz began chuckling.

"Citizen de la Cruz, is there something amusing about this? Do you find detailed depictions of the former inhabitants of Alpha 3 funny? Or are you so damned stupid that you don't understand what this means?" Ralston wouldn't let anyone belittle this find. It was big, it was *great*.

"Dr. Ralston, this isn't *your* discovery."

De la Cruz's mocking tone turned Ralston cold inside. "Explain yourself."

"Run this through the projector. And note the dates imprinted on each frame." De la Cruz dropped a block of ceramic film on the table. Ralston took it and held it in the palm of his hand. To Ralston, it felt colder than it actually was. He pulled out his ceramic photo block and inserted de la Cruz's.

Leonore Disa gasped when she saw the scenes that Ralston had just projected duplicated—and with earlier establishing dates. They showed that de la Cruz had taken the photos fully a week prior to her and Ralston's accidentally opening the copper-clad door.

"Dr. Ralston, we . . . " Ralston cut off her protests with an impatient gesture. His unwavering gray eyes locked squarely on Yago de la Cruz.

"Citizen de la Cruz, I want a word with you in private." Ralston fought to hold his anger in check. A single glance at the dates told him what de la Cruz had done to alter the time sequence. He had been the first human to enter the catacombs, not Yago de la Cruz.

And he now knew who had struck him.

"Doctor?" Leonore looked at him, worry lines wrinkling her forehead.

"I'll speak with you when I'm done with Citizen de la Cruz."

The others left, not comprehending the scene being played out before them. Ralston watched them go, wondering why the University hadn't sent along a flock of sheep. Those animals' genetic predisposition was to mindless behavior—and they were good at cropping grass and for providing mutton. These students showed the same wide-eyed stupidity and had none of a sheep's other redeeming values.

Leonore was the last to leave. She'd barely closed the plastic door behind her when Ralston swung around and faced de la Cruz. "You're not smart enough to doctor the records in such a way that they'll stand up if anyone really examines them."

"The analyzer I used is all the evidence I need that *I* found the geeks' museum." De la Cruz's smugness angered Ralston even more. He stepped back to keep from striking his student.

"It's not that easy. I'm sure you aren't smart enough to think of this on your own. What you weren't told, those aren't legal documents without the secondary time stamp."

"There's no such thing."

Ralston nodded grimly. "When the analyzer is constructed, an internal cesium clock is activated marking the planet of origin and time. It runs continuously, and the other clock, the one you set with a false date, is checked against it as an error-preventing service. It also provides protection against students cheating by date alteration, as you've done, Citizen de la Cruz."

"The trip here," de la Cruz cried. Sweat beaded his face. With sudden insight, Ralston understood that the panic he read came not from fear of being caught stealing another's rightful project, but from the impact of losing the accolades that would gain his family's respect. "We shifted in a starship. Starring here would destroy the reliability of any time stamping. General relativity. Space tensors."

Ralston shook his head. "Every shift is duly recorded—all automatic."

"It might not be working."

"The analyzer functioned properly, didn't it? Unless the cesium clock is running, nothing works. Some archaeologists have complained that their clocks were damaged and that they had to record everything in notebooks—by hand."

"That must have happened," de la Cruz blurted.

"Such documents are only valid when done holographically—and witnessed by two others."

"You're trying to steal my find!"

"No, Citizen de la Cruz, you're the thief."

"We'll let the head of the department decide." De la Cruz's dark eyes darted about, making him look more like a trapped animal than a serious scholar. "He'll decide in my favor."

"He won't. He can't. Not with the analyzer data showing that you misentered the date and presumably violated most of the tenets of careful archaeology with your meddling." Ralston's voice lowered. "You made another big mistake by revealing this ridiculous piracy. I know you entered the catacombs immediately after I did that first time and then attacked me."

"You'll never be able to prove it. You . . ." De la Cruz's words trailed off. His eyes widened and his mouth moved but only choked sounds issued forth. De la Cruz dropped to his knees and jerked violently, one arm flying out from his body so hard that he smashed into the table and sent it scooting across the shelter.

"What's wrong?" Ralston thought de la Cruz was faking this bizarre behavior. Insanity pleas were almost always accepted, especially from those who had starred from their home world only once. Something about dimension shifting adversely affected some people in a fashion similar to an allergy. De la Cruz might attempt such a ploy to preserve what little standing he had in the academic community.

Then Ralston changed his mind. De la Cruz was frothing at the mouth. No amount of acting could duplicate an epileptic seizure. The student's eyes rolled up until only the whites showed. Blood trickled from his lips; he had bitten his tongue.

"Leonore!" Ralston bellowed. He grabbed de la Cruz's shoulders, but the powerful convulsions threw the man free. Using hand-to-hand fighting grips he had learned during the war, Ralston succeeded in getting de la Cruz flat on the floor, face down and immobile.

"Michael, what are you doing to him?" Leonore stood in the doorway. All she could see was her professor pinning a struggling student to the floor.

"Get over here. Get something between his teeth. He's having a seizure of some kind. Damn!" As strong as he was and with as much skill as he'd applied the immobilizing hold, de la Cruz jerked free. Ralston had to release the grip or the graduate student would have ripped ligaments in both shoulders.

Ralston wrestled the writhing de la Cruz to immobility again. With one hand he grabbed a handful of hair and pulled back. This opened de la Cruz's jaws enough for Leonore to thrust a scrap of plastic between his teeth.

"His mouth is a mess," she said. "His tongue's all bloody. My lord!"

"Don't get sick on me," warned Ralston. "He needs attention right now. Get the automedic. I think de la Cruz's got a med-port. Find out what to inject and *do it!*"

De la Cruz's struggles had diminished until they were little more than powerful twitches. Ralston had no trouble holding the student down until Leonore returned with the portable medical unit. Putting a half nelson on de la Cruz, Ralston flipped the graduate student over onto his side. Leonore fumbled and opened de la Cruz's shirt to reveal the tiny silver plate in his belly.

"Attach it. Full analysis."

"That'll take too long. I . . . I started it reading Yago's med record. That'll be faster. This didn't just happen. God, why didn't they warn us?"

"My sentiments exactly," Ralston grated between clenched teeth. His own muscles ached from the strain of holding de la Cruz down. How did one fleshy, out-of-shape student generate so much power? Ralston had never seen an epileptic seizure before; such things were a rarity on Novo Terra. But he remembered his father talking about several seizure-prone friends back on Earth. Only this dim recollection had served him— and Yago de la Cruz—now.

"No history of seizures of any sort," Leonore said. Her voice rose to a shrillness that hinted panic.

"Start the automedic's analyzer. Not full scan, just emergency. Plug it in. Good," said Ralston, soothing her. Seeing a medical emergency of any sort lay far beyond everyday existence on Novo Terra and most other planets. "You do that a lot better than I could." His simple compliment steadied her. She flashed him a wan smile, then fumbled about to insert the connector into de la Cruz's med-port.

The automedic hummed and whirred. The hose that Leonore had connected began to buck and swing about when the machine decided on the proper type and dosage of medication and began pumping it into de la Cruz's bloodstream.

"Whew," Ralston said, lowering de la Cruz flat onto his

back. The student had gone limp with the influx of the drug. Ralston guessed the automedic had injected a tranquilizer.

He jumped when a siren went off and a bright red light flashed atop the machine.

"What's that?" asked Leonore.

"De la Cruz just died."

They stood and stared at the motionless body. Before dying, Yago de la Cruz had broken several bones. One compound fracture gleamed whitely where bone protruded from the flesh of his left arm. De la Cruz's face showed no peace in death, either. The seizure had ripped him apart, inside and out, physically and emotionally.

Ralston took a blanket out of a supply box and covered de la Cruz's face. It hid the graduate student's features, but somehow the formless mound mocked Ralston more than the contorted face.

"It's verd," Asan said with more fervor than Ralston had seen in the rehabilitated felon before. "They're going to brainwipe you for certain. You'll end up a rehab." He didn't need to add "just like me" to scare Ralston.

"I didn't kill him. The automedic's report will verify that." Ralston tried not to sound too defensive. He hadn't done anything wrong, but he knew that appearances were more important in academic circles than actions.

Yago de la Cruz had been his graduate student during this expedition. His ward had died under mysterious circumstances. It hadn't been anyone's fault, but the archaeology department investigation committee and the chairman wouldn't care about that. They'd see this as a simple way of ridding themselves of Ralston. He had questioned policy one too many times, had tried to gain tenure in a system designed to reward obedience rather than brilliance, and had made damned few allies because of his stand for the Nex.

"He's right, Asan," Leonore spoke up. "The automedic shows some sort of massive neurological failure. It's too complicated for its simple programming, but Michael didn't cause de la Cruz's death. We all saw what happened."

Even a rehab like Asan caught the way Leonore now referred to her professor by his first name. Asan gave his neutral shrug that might mean anything. He turned and left.

"We've got to keep his body intact. Get it back to Novo Terra for an autopsy," said Ralston.

"We don't have the facilities," Leonore pointed out. "What's the usual procedure when someone dies in the field?"

"I don't know," Ralston admitted. "It's never happened to me—or anyone I've even heard of." The University of Ilium medical requirements for admission to a field program were as strict as any Ralston had ever seen; this was one of the few things done by the school that he approved of. Scanning the data on de la Cruz showed nothing to indicate why he had died in such agony.

"Do we bury him? Here?" The woman's voice threatened to break with emotion. None of them cared for Muckup. The constant rains, the thin atmosphere, the slight gravity and the muddy desolation all wore on them. Even if they hadn't liked de la Cruz, burying one of their own here seemed a travesty.

The war years came back to Ralston. The Nex hadn't been interested in retrieving their dead, but they had developed extensive battle zone facilities for recovering wounded. One of their pickup methods might be worthwhile to try. He had nothing to lose, after all—and de la Cruz wouldn't care.

Ralston went to the com unit and switched it on. The static wasn't as bad as it had been during earlier calls to the solar physics site.

"Dr. Justine Rasmussen, come in. This is Ralston, over."

Justine Rasmussen's voice barked out, loud and clear and annoyed. "What is it, Ralston? I'm very busy right now."

"We've had a medical emergency."

"Need our doctor?"

"Automated?" he asked.

"Automedic Model 23."

"That's the same as ours. University standard issue."

A long pause, then Rasmussen's worried question crackled over the speaker. "That unit'll handle just about anything. What's the problem? Did your unit break down?"

"One of my students died."

"You're not distilling your own, are you? You are serious about a fatality?"

"Quite serious. I need a large dewar flask and liquid nitrogen for cooling it."

"Corpse-sized dewar?" Justine Rasmussen caught on to Ralston's idea quickly. "Will fly it over to you within the hour. Need more than, say, fifty liters of liquid nitrogen?"

"That will be adequate until the starship comes. The body will be starred back to the University."

"You'll be going with it, won't you? Please remember what we spoke of earlier."

"I know, I know," Ralston said. "But it'll take almost two months for the starship to arrive. Plenty of time to make a decision about the rest of the expedition returning."

"The decision's been made," Rasmussen barked. "Alpha Prime *is* going nova. Our indications for it mount every day. There is no arguing with an exploding star, Doctor."

"Keep us posted. And thanks for the dewar."

Ralston flipped off the unit, then sat heavily in a sagging plastic chair. He wished he had a decent, comfortable one to sit in. He wished a lot of things. He hurt all over. Worst of all, a headache started behind his eyes. It felt as if someone kicked him with spiked boots.

"Michael?" came Leonore's hesitant voice. He opened his eyes and stared at her. "I . . . I went through Yago's things." She held out an analyzer block circuit. "I think this is his recording of all he did within the catacombs."

"He showed the camera shots," Ralston said, more tired than ever. "He really panicked when I mentioned the analyzer, so I knew he had one running. Go on, put that in. Let's see what the chinging son of a bitch did."

Together they watched. With every subsequent shot, their puzzlement grew. The analyzer showed de la Cruz walking into a diorama, then freeze in a pose for several minutes before shivering as if cold, then collapsing.

"Check the radiation readings," ordered Ralston.

"Nothing out of the ordinary. High static electricity readings, though. But that's nothing unusual. We've fought them ever since we landed."

"He shot these last night during the storm," Ralston said. "Static electricity levels aren't that high and might be caused by the lightning." He punched the rapid advance sequencer. They watched silently as de la Cruz invaded one after another of the dioramas. Each time he emerged, his smile broadened. But Ralston clearly saw de la Cruz's physical deterioration. At the end of the block's recording, de la Cruz trembled with an intensity just short of an outright epileptic event.

"Do you think he caught something by going into the dioramas? Some alien disease?" Leonore's voice had firmed. She was a scientist with a problem, and that precluded panic.

Ralston let her lean on that crutch—or whatever it was she depended on now to keep from screaming.

"You're thinking I might have loosed something ominous that had been penned up in the catacombs," he said.

"We, Michael. We were both there and we took the first photos."

"That's verd," he said, hating the slang even as he used it. "Our analyzer will verify that." He slammed his fist down hard against the table. The projector bounced and the picture shimmered. "Dammit, what happened to de la Cruz?"

"Poison?"

"Nothing I've come across indicates poison. Besides, the automedic would have found it quickly enough. It compared his current blood chemistry with his records. No, de la Cruz went into a diorama and something happened to him while he was inside. It wasn't poison or disease."

"Whatever occurred happened to him in each one," added Leonore. "The expression on his face when he left the first diorama changed from fear to . . . to triumph."

"Run a comparison of his block and ours." Ralston waited while the two blocks were checked by the computer. He punched in a request for only radiation and chemical comparisons. In less than a minute the negative answer flashed on the readout screen.

"Nothing unusual on either block. Both readings matched within a half percent."

"Nothing unusual at all, then," said Ralston. "I've been over our data several times. Nothing lethal indicated in it."

He rocked back in the chair and stared at the last image from de la Cruz's data as it shone against the far wall. De la Cruz stood with that shit-eating grin on his face, as if he had just conquered the universe. Behind him stood a pair of the avian native figures. Ralston's sharp eyes discerned minute differences in their bodies and faces. One might be male and the other female.

Other than this, he found nothing amiss. Certainly, he saw nothing fatal.

What had he loosed on this world? And did it matter, if Alpha Prime went nova?

Ralston had less than two months to discover the answer. Somehow, the thrill of his discovery had faded considerably. It had been replaced by a cold fear clutching at his guts.

NINE

"CAN YOU BLAME them, Michael?" asked Leonore Disa.

He could. But Ralston held down his temper. The past six weeks had been nothing less than hell. The students, except for Leonore, had refused to enter the underground museum, fearing a fate similar to de la Cruz's. Ralston stared out the shelter door at the bright silver dewar the solar physics group had given them. Plumes of condensation wreathed the large flask; inside lay Yago de la Cruz's frozen body. When the University starship arrived in a few days, the dewar and corpse would be the first items to go up.

Then Ralston and the students would follow. And his discovery would be lost for all time.

"I suppose it's only human nature," he said after a long pause. "They don't want to die like he did."

"They should have realized it was only a fluke, an accident of nature. Something made Yago susceptible to the messages. As long as they don't enter the dioramas, they'd be safe. If they'd only think it through!"

Ralston didn't argue with her. He wasn't as sure about the cause of de la Cruz's death as Leonore seemed. They had explored the dioramas far more carefully than de la Cruz. Starting with the first scene, they had spent a full week doing nothing but monitoring radiation from all frequencies. Along with this they had run a special analyzer with a surface acoustic wave sensor designed to pick up the most minute odors. Nothing unexpected had been found. No sign of danger.

That made the student's death all the more frustrating to explain.

A full seven days of observation—and no clue as to what had happened to de la Cruz. Ralston had then entered the diorama as they'd witnessed de la Cruz do. The surprise he'd felt at the telepathic communication, the sense of being transported back to a culture and time far beyond his wildest dreams at first had almost overcome the history lesson slipping across the edges of his mind. He had left the diorama quickly, Leonore recording everything.

Their most sensitive instruments detected no trace of the telepathic message. The analyzer, however, picked up the pheromones denoting Ralston's sudden fear, the sound of his heart hammering away, every physiological change he experienced as a result of the unexpected world forming within his head.

But the most careful examination by the automedic turned up no substantive neurological change.

Why had de la Cruz died when Ralston seemed unaffected?

Ralston had re-entered the first diorama and fully experienced the lesson. A change in orientation had produced a new and complementary version of the same lesson. And none of it impinged on their analyzer's block circuits.

He had been extremely careful and had denied Leonore her wish to experience the dioramas personally. If anyone took the risk of death, it would be Michael Ralston. But their slow progress down the corridor of dioramas, each scene taking a full three days to experience and for Ralston to record all that had happened, produced no physiological changes in the archaeologist.

Working steadily, doing two dioramas a week and using the seventh day to go over their data, he and Leonore had finished examining only ten. Dozens more lay ahead—and the final ones which might hold the secret to de la Cruz's death were more than a year away, if they continued on their current time-table.

"Nels called today," Leonore said. Ralston pulled out of his introspection.

"What did he have to say?"

"The surface disturbances on the sun have quieted."

Hope flared. "Then Alpha Prime isn't going to blow? We can stay and finish our work?"

Leonore shook her head. Ralston's hope died stillborn. "Nels doesn't understand the dynamics of the nova process, but he says their current theory is that it doesn't proceed in a linear fashion. There are odd spurts and surges, then a falling back into normal stellar behavior. But each leveling off comes at a higher and higher level, which makes new instabilities even worse. When they reach some unknown threshold, the star explodes."

"But this tailing off in instability gives us more time?" Ralston clutched at the slimmest hope now. The dioramas constituted a major discovery that must be exploited fully. Without the graduate students helping him and Leonore, recording the pertinent data had gone much too slowly. Any additional time allotted by the capricious star could be put to good use.

"Maybe. I don't know." Leonore smiled wryly. "Remember, I met Nels when he was a tutor—a tutor I needed to get through elementary physics. Why not ask him what this means? Or Dr. Rasmussen?"

Ralston hadn't gotten along well at all with Justine Rasmussen. Each subsequent call had become more brusque, colder. When she learned of de la Cruz's death and its possible cause, she had prohibited any social contact between the two groups. Of all the people affected, Nels Bernssen and Leonore Disa felt this the most, but they had felt compelled to obey the order, even though no sign of disease, poison, or radiation had been detected since the deadly tragedy.

Ralston considered all his options. He had too few. He might stay and work alone, but if he did so, Rasmussen might refuse to allow him to leave the planet with her researchers when Alpha Prime reached nova stage. The fear of alien disease still struck at the hearts of many otherwise sane people. Even though expert xenobiologists had shown it was impossible for an alien virus or bacterium not based on DNA to do any real damage to a human, primitive fears still persisted. And those races that shared DNA with mankind had produced no disease that didn't have an already existing—and known—counterpart. The human body was an ecology of living flora, microbes, and viruses. If an alien invader somehow found a niche and began growing, the body provided a natural defense to check it.

"Even though I wish there were a way of staying, I'll return with the rest of you, I suppose," he said. "The University will want to know firsthand the details of de la Cruz's death." Ralston laughed mirthlessly. "What I'll be able to tell them isn't going to be very enlightening, though."

"There hasn't been any hint of an answer in the dioramas?" Leonore asked.

"No, and you're to stay away from them. Understand me? That is a direct order."

"You're not being affected. The constant med monitoring shows you within norms." Leonore looked at her professor carefully. "But the last few readings have shown increased stress levels."

"Really?" Ralston said sarcastically. "The find of all time lies under my feet, a student dies exploring it, and the damned star will go nova before I can do more than photograph lifeless figures. Stress? Whatever might cause stress?"

"Michael, please. You know what I mean. You're taking this all on yourself."

"I'm in charge. The excavations in the city have shown nothing we haven't already guessed." He stared at the dewar with de la Cruz's body and then past it to the direction of the copper door leading to fame and something even headier: knowledge.

"The answer is down there. I know it. And I won't have time to find it!"

Frustration boiled over. Ralston stalked from the shelter just as the com unit beeped for his attention. He almost didn't return to answer. Let Leonore talk to Justine Rasmussen. But duty drew him just as Leonore reached for the signal button.

"I'll take it. Thanks."

"Dr. Ralston?" came the physicist's voice. "You still there?"

"Yes, Dr. Rasmussen, I'm still here. The alien slime monsters haven't devoured me yet."

"Your ship just shifted in. It'll be in orbit the day after tomorrow, E.T.A. noon."

He silently cursed. The damned pilot had come in exactly on target. A small error of just a microsecond of arc would have given an extra few days' intra-system travel. And even worse, the starship would enter orbit at precisely the best time for transfer. The pilot wasted not a single nanosecond.

"When will you leave?" asked Ralston.

"Our ship starred a few days after yours," she answered. "We'll stay as long as possible, but there's some discussion among my staff members about when that might be. The space-time tensors become distorted near a nova, and no one's sure what this might mean to the starship's engines."

Ralston didn't pretend to understand their concern, but it afforded him a chance. He mustered his courage, then almost blurted, "Could I stay behind and work, then leave with your group? I'm sure you'd have enough room aboard."

"I don't think that would be wise, Dr. Ralston," came Justine Rasmussen's cold voice. "There is still concern among my colleagues concerning the Pandora's box you seem to have opened."

"But—"

"Two days, Dr. Ralston. Be ready. The pilot told us he is anxious to return to Novo Terra as quickly as possible. And the University administration will want to discuss your student's death in some detail, I'm sure."

"Thank you." Ralston disconsolately flipped off the com unit. The absence of Rasmussen's voice and the static surrounding it made Ralston feel as if he'd stepped into a vacuum.

"There it is!" Asan cried with genuine animation. He pointed into Muckup's unusually clear sky at the bright silver spot. The starship had come for them.

"Is everything packed and ready?" Ralston asked needlessly. Since receiving Rasmussen's message two days ago, the entire camp had been ready for instant departure. Ralston had only haphazardly supervised, letting each student attend to his own belongings. The shelters and most of the equipment would be left. All Ralston personally packed were a few hardcopy photos and the analyzer block circuits that had recorded what had happened within the alien dioramas.

"It's not the end of the world," Leonore comforted.

Ralston laughed harshly. "It is. For Muckup. He looked around at the muddy plains and scraggly, off-green trees that reminded him of Earthly bonsai with their stunted height and contorted limbs. The biome had been devastated by the incessant rains, changing the face of the planet into not-quite-sea, not-quite-prairie. Whatever had caused the avian society's demise ten thousand years ago had also altered the weather patterns. His time spent in those few dioramas convinced him of that. Not a single scene showed the towering black thunderheads, the intense lightning storms, the incessant rain that had threatened to drive them all crazy.

"I'm sorry, Michael," Leonore said softly.

"About what?"

"Everything, I guess. Most of all about the dioramas."

They had attempted dismantling one to ship back to Novo Terra. While the figures moved easily enough, Ralston had been unable to preserve the telepathic messages after repositioning. Search as he might, he'd found no transmitter or other instrument projecting the thought lessons. Though he would bring back one figure, he could not transport the essence of the dioramas.

"We've got the photos and all the data from the analyzer. I can testify to the dioramas' effect. We recorded everything I said after leaving."

Leonore said nothing. They both knew that this meant little. Without analyzer readings to substantiate the claim of telepathic transfer, Ralston might have been inventing everything learned within the dioramas.

"It's not the end of my career," Ralston said. "But there's no future for me at the University of Ilium. After the hearings on de la Cruz's death, I'll be marked as a real pariah there. Every request for tenure will be disregarded." He shook his head. "That's nothing new, though. But even dead-end digs like Alpha 3 will be denied me. I'll end up like poor Pieter Nordon, doing nothing but classroom work, trapped in pointless lectures. Academe is the only place I know where they retire you to the primary business of the University."

Leonore said nothing. Research counted the most in the archaeology department—in any research-oriented department. Without the field trips, without choice selections for digs, a professor's career came to a slow halt. The department put those they wished to punish into the classroom to take the teaching burden off those on their way up in the hierarchy.

Fame and prominence came not from being a good professor but from being a good field researcher.

Michael Ralston's career was over, and they both knew it.

"A flare," called out Lantalman. "The pod's jets!"

Ralston squinted into the sun and saw the long orange flame from the transfer pod's engine. With an uncanny knack, the pilot landed almost precisely on the spot best suited for it. A solid rock foundation supported the landing gear; a dozen meters in any direction would have placed the pod on muddier, less stable ground.

Ralston ought to have counted this as a good sign. All he could think of was abandoning the find.

They trudged stolidly toward the grounded shuttle pod. Already the pilot and two crewmen swung out a loading crane. Contrary to Ralston's wishes, the first platform up contained the students' belongings. The second carried the eager students. Only then did Ralston convince the pilot to retrieve the dewar holding Yago de la Cruz's cryogenically frozen body.

"So you got him iced down, huh, Doc?" asked the pilot. He wrinkled his nose in distaste at the sight. "Damnedest thing I ever saw. How'd you come to think of it?"

"During the Nex-P'torra war the Nex preserved their wounded this way. They'd quick-freeze by dipping into liquid nitrogen, then thaw them out when they returned to a hospital."

The pilot fell silent. Ralston knew the starman had heard rumors of the crazy professor fighting for the Nex. Mention of the aliens' medical procedures had brought back the faint memories in the pilot and put them foremost in his mind. For Ralston's part, he was content not to bandy words with the pilot.

All he wanted was an end to this. To be off planet. To be away from Muckup. To be back on Novo Terra and hunting for a new position. He felt as if his life had come to an ignominious end.

And all because of Yago de la Cruz's greed in wanting to steal the find.

Ralston grunted when the pilot kicked in the jets and sent them skyward. Four hours later they docked with the starship. Seven hours after that, they starred for Novo Terra.

• • •

Michael Ralston walked under clear blue skies caught in the middle of a seasonally warm summer. While a heavier gravity than the one he had grown used to on Alpha 3 tugged at him, he didn't mind. Any gravity, great or small, was preferable to the weightlessness of star travel. He looked around the University campus and smiled. Students walked rapidly to and from classes, usually in small groups passionately arguing or quietly gossiping. A few lay beneath the trees or under the warm sun, catching up on needed sleep.

But the energy of the school transmitted itself to him. Ralston came more alive, renewed and eager. These students wanted to learn what he had to teach. They ... they weren't his students, he corrected mentally. Not a single one was. The University Committee on Academics had relieved him of all duties—and pay—pending their investigation into de la Cruz's death.

Ralston stopped and stared at the green-domed building holding the committee offices. Few people entered and left this structure. Even fewer had business with the U.C.A. The classrooms were crowded, the student building overflowed onto the grounds, but the committee offices stayed virtually empty. Here decisions affecting a professor's academic life were made.

No one treaded those hallways lightly. Not when the slightest misstep produced a blighted future.

One or two of the passing students recognized him, but they quickly averted their eyes and walked faster. Ralston tried to blame them but couldn't. Who knowingly associates with a damned sinner summoned by the Inquisition?

His steps came slower now as he neared the building. He stared up at the green dome glistening in the sunlight. It ought to have been a beacon of hope. This was, after all, part of the University, an institution devoted to the pursuit of knowledge. All Ralston could picture was that dome falling to trap him. Beneath it he'd slowly suffocate, trapped like a bug in a bell jar, lost forever.

He looked for ways to avoid entering. To one side stood a news kiosk. He wandered over and saw that it had been tuned to the University station. The newsers were all students learning their trade.

Ralston shook his head. They didn't report news, not like their forerunners on Earth. He had studied how propaganda is written and recognized nothing but loaded phrases, subtle body movements, and clever distortions in the students' vidnewscast. A written text of their broadcast would reveal nothing but objective reporting.

As he watched, one slowly shook his head to indicate disapproval. So much for objectivity. But Ralston knew they trained for a hard market that had little to do with unbiased reporting. The newsers had become vid stars, actors editorializing.

"Bonita stuff, don't you agree?" came a voice so slick it must have been oiled.

It took Ralston a few seconds to recognize the woman as one of the newsers.

"Murra Tranton," she said, supplying the name that eluded Ralston.

"I've seen you on the vid kiosk," he said in as neutral a tone as possible. He knew what he faced inside this building—and what Murra Tranton wanted.

"Any comments, Dr. Ralston?" The woman's expression had been carefully rehearsed, he thought. She looked intelligent and concerned, interested and ready to aid him however she could.

He also thought she looked like a predatory beast, and no amount of acting could disguise that avarice.

He started to speak, then saw the vid pickup on her lapel. Anything he said would be transmitted back to the campus studio. Once there, he had no idea what they'd do with his words. Edit? Definitely. Change the question to any answer he might give? Possibly. Make him look like a bloody-handed butcher? If it served Murra Tranton's purpose. A story like this might get her recognized by the larger vidnews organizations.

Making a noncommittal gesture and saying nothing, he pushed past the newser. How had he gotten himself into such straits? It hardly seemed fair.

Ralston shook off the self-pity and went inside. The long marble halls were lined with wood-paneled doors. At precisely the hour when the cathedral clock chimed four, he entered the second door on the right without knocking. The inquisitors had gathered. Ralston looked around, expecting to see a black-hooded man standing beside a medieval Earth torture rack.

"Sit down, Dr. Ralston." The chairman of the U.C.A. pointed to a solitary seat in the center of the room. They isolated him as if he carried a virulent plague.

He sat.

"We have studied your report. Frankly, Doctor, we find it incomplete in all respects."

"Dr. Salazar, there wasn't adequate time to finish a report."

"You had a little over six weeks while starring back," another of the committee said. "Isn't that time enough?"

"The matter is complex," said Ralston, knowing they wouldn't listen to anything he said. They needed a scapegoat for de la Cruz's death. Since he'd been on the scene, he'd been elected already. "The alien museum with its dioramas is unique. Nothing like it has been—"

"Doctor," cut in Salazar, distaste altering his face into a mask of evil. Ralston tried to shake off that satanic image and found he couldn't. "We aren't here to discuss archaeology. Citizen de la Cruz's death is the only topic to be considered."

"But they tie together. I am sure that de la Cruz, by entering the dioramas without authorization or adequate precaution, triggered a telepathic projector and—"

"You're saying that Citizen de la Cruz caused his own demise? There's no evidence to support that, Dr. Ralston. You have produced not one shred of evidence for the existence of this so-called telepathic projector. No mechanism, no recording, nothing."

"As stated in the report, sir, the analyzer failed to detect it because I believe it is strictly a communication between biological entities."

"The last native of Alpha 3 died ten thousand years ago. No evidence has been given to show they still survive."

"The dioramas are unique," Ralston repeated. "And unknown. Their functioning is a mystery. I didn't have enough time to—"

"We're getting off the subject of Citizen de la Cruz's untimely death," interrupted Salazar. "Two of our late student's family have consented to appear today. Arturo and Constance de la Cruz, brother and sister of the deceased."

Ralston sat upright. He had been prohibited from speaking with any of de la Cruz's family. Now the committee brought two of them forward? For what purpose?

"He is the one?" came a voice from behind Ralston. He turned to see a man younger than Yago de la Cruz behind the chair. The family resemblance was obvious. Arturo de la Cruz shared his brother's insufferable arrogance.

"Citizens de la Cruz, thank you for coming," said Dr. Salazar.

"He even looks like a murderer," said Constance de la Cruz.

"Dr. Salazar, I protest!" Ralston shot to his feet. "This was supposed to be a closed hearing. Detailed minutes are being taken. I demand that Citizen de la Cruz's slanderous comment be deleted. I did *not* kill her brother nor did I allow him to die through any fault on my part."

"Liar," hissed the woman.

"Dr. Ralston, your protest is noted, but it is out of order. We are not assembled today to pass judgment. Rather, we gather information to decide whether to convene full hearings on this matter. Since we only investigate, the usual rules for conduct are suspended." Salazar made a brushing motion in Ralston's direction. "Do sit down and hold your tongue until you're addressed, Doctor."

"We will sue the University," promised Arturo de la Cruz. "My family will not rest until justice is served."

Ralston ignored Salazar's order and faced Yago de la Cruz's brother and sister. "I feel very deeply saddened by your brother's death. It is a fact, however, that field work is dangerous. Yago died advancing our knowledge of a newly discovered race with unknown powers. I did all I could to save him when the seizure struck. The automedic records will bear this out."

"You stole his discovery. The block circuits bear *that* out," shot back Arturo de la Cruz. "You killed him to take the discovery for yourself. That is apparent!"

"Citizens, please," called out Salazar. "We have gone over the records submitted by Dr. Ralston, we have conferred with medical authorities who are still conducting their autopsy of Citizen de la Cruz's body, and we have discussed the matter with University attorneys. In one week, formal hearings will be convened to decide on what actions, if any, should be taken in this matter. Until then, please accept the University of Ilium's condolences on the death of your brother."

The two de la Cruzes left without another word, both visibly furious and doing nothing to conceal it. Ralston simply sat in the chair and stared. Salazar hadn't addressed the decision to him—it had been for the de la Cruzes' benefit. The formal hearing would be a farce—any evidence he might present would be disallowed or ignored.

He had already been judged and found guilty.

Ralston didn't know which was worse, being placed in disgrace by his peers and possibly accused of murder, or losing the Alpha 3 dioramas for all time.

Without a word, Dr. Michael Ralston rose and marched from the room. The summer day outside the building no longer seemed so warm and cheerful.

TEN

"I'M NOT GOING to let them do this to me!" Michael Ralston raged. He paced back and forth in his tiny cubicle office and felt like bouncing from the walls. Caged. They had caged him like an animal, and he didn't like it.

"Really, Michael, it might not be that bad," Leonore Disa said without any conviction.

"Why hadn't you told me you'd turned down a chance to go with Velasquez to Proteus?" he asked, stopping to stare at her. She pushed a strand of brunette hair back to reveal the flashing plates on her forehead. They winked in soft pastel, Leonore's favorite, Ralston decided.

"It had no bearing on going to Alpha 3," she said simply.

"You wanted to be with Nels Bernssen."

"I'd be lying if I denied that. I love him."

"Does he love you?"

"That's none of your business." She sighed and folded her hands chastely in her lap. "In his way he does. He's so wrapped up in his project right now. No one's ever been this close to a pre-nova star. It'll make his career."

"The sort of discovery that wins awards," muttered Ralston, remembering his own find on Muckup. Muckup? Mucked up came closer to the truth. He cursed what seemed to be a cosmic balance. Bernssen had found his accolades in Alpha Prime's instability. That very same instability ruined Ralston's chances for a find equally as important.

"He's very good, Nels is."

"Who else at the University knows about his project? Someone I could talk to about novas. I always avoided the heavier science courses during my student years. All I cared about were archaeology and a bit of anthropology."

"Michael, please. The committee has suspended you until the hearing."

"They're going to flay me alive at the hearing," he said with some bitterness. "This is their chance to get rid of the professor who didn't kiss enough ass, who valued knowledge over politics. And they can do it ever so neatly. The de la Cruzes will ask for my head, and the University will give it to them. Simple."

"There's no way you could have prevented Yago's death."

"What's truth got to do with it?" Self-pity flooded him again, then burned away with a flame of determination. "Muckup's *my* discovery. I'm not going to let it go up in a flash of superheated plasma." He ignored his graduate student totally now, as if Leonore didn't even exist. "I can get back to Alpha 3. It won't be easy but I can do it. With a bit of additional, sophisticated equipment—most of what I'll need was left there—I can get enough for a paper. Automation. A supervisor-controller would be useful."

"But that's for controlling major robotic equipment," Leonore said, her head tipped to one side as she studied him.

"I can't ask anyone to risk their lives for this. I'll have to automate as much as I can."

"I can get a supervisor," Leonore said.

"How much?" he snapped, gray eyes sharp and hard.

"For free. My father owns Interstellar Computronics."

Ralston sank to the edge of his desk and simply stared. IC was one of the largest suppliers of automated equipment on Novo Terra. Leonore came from a family so wealthy that Ralston couldn't even guess within an order of magnitude what their worth must be.

"You'd do that for me?"

"No one else around here seems to recognize the importance of this find. I do."

"I can arrange to star back in a week."

"How? Not on any of the University starships."

Ralston smiled. "I've still got contacts. Don't worry about that. You *can* get a supervisor?"

Leonore nodded. "What else would you need? I'm afraid Daddy's company doesn't manufacture much else in the way of robotic research equipment."

"I can get the rest. Most of it," he amended. Ralston's enthusiasm died a little when logic reclaimed him. He looked at Leonore suspiciously and asked, "What do you want in return for this? Your name's already on the paper as co-author. You know that."

"I don't have nearly enough data to do an adequate dissertation," she said, not angry that he accused her of motives other than altruism. "I want to go back with you."

"No Leonore, no supervisor?"

"That's putting it so harshly, Dr. Ralston," Leonore said.

"But it's accurate." Ralston frowned, then let a smile dawn. "I don't care if it's the diorama find or Nels Bernssen that's drawing you back to Muckup. When we're finished with that planet, we'll both be famous."

"I'll be content with a good thesis," she said. Leonore rose and left Ralston's office.

Ralston sat and stared out a tiny window across the Quad. A statue of Bacon gleamed in Novo Terra's warm sunlight. Even though Ralston couldn't read the inscription from this distance, he knew it by heart: "For knowledge, too, is itself a power."

"Verd, I know Nels Bernssen," the research assistant said. He looked up from the terminal where he'd scattered papers and block readers. "Good instincts. And a damn fine mathematician. Wish I had his skill there. Might have done better on my comps. But you're not here to offer me some tutoring, are you? What can I do for you, Dr. Ralston?"

Ralston glanced at the nameplate above the terminal. "You're Liu Chen?"

"Chen Liu, but don't worry about getting my name wrong.

Even the University computer gets confused. Call me Chen."

Ralston pulled a chair up and leaned on Chen's small, cluttered desk, his elbows resting on a thick mat of paper covered with intricate doodlings.

"Here, let me take some of that," Chen said, obviously distraught over Ralston's disturbing the order of his mess. "Not too many use paper for their calculations. Never could get the feel of looking at it on a screen."

"I need some information about novas."

"Since Nels is off on Alpha 3, damn his bones, you've come to the right place. Simply put, a nova is a star that goes *bang!*"

"You don't like Nels?"

"I *love* the man. And I envy him. Being right up there to witness the early stages. While my interests lie more in what happens after the bang, I'd still like to be there nudging Nels' elbow, getting him to take readings on parameters that count."

"What makes Alpha Prime so unusual? I don't know much about the H-R star classes but I gather it's the wrong type to go nova."

"Verd," Chen agreed. "Take a look at my big project." He punched in a few long code words. A nebula leaped into focus on the screen. "I've sent a couple probes to the 1054 'guest star' to study the accretion disk."

"The gaseous disk around it?"

Chen looked at Ralston, then nodded. "We call it the 1054 because that's when it was seen on Earth. They call it the Crab Nebula, but it doesn't look like one from here." He brightened even more. "In China it was well documented. They called any nova a 'guest star' because it grew brighter and brighter, then faded away. A guest.

"My work is coming to a chinging dead end and I don't know why." Chen thumped a pile of papers to one side of his terminal. "My first automated probe just broke down."

"No more telemetry?"

Chen nodded glumly. "Can't figure out what went wrong, either. The best I can determine from the readings I got, some flaw in the block circuitry caused the failure."

"That's a bit unusual, isn't it?"

"Verd," Chen agreed. "We always check those babies out to a zillionth of a decimal place. Cost too damn much to have them go wrong five hundred light years from the nearest screwdriver. But random electronics failures *do* happen. But why to me?"

"Your other probe's still sending back information, isn't it?"

"I guess so." Chen turned even gloomier. "The data I expected aren't showing up. Nothing matches. Some of it is so far off beam I'm beginning to think that I'm looking at a second electronics failure. Won't be able to get the University to spring for any more probes, either. Too chinging expensive. When everything's getting confusing and we have a chance to learn something really deep, they cut off our funding."

Chen shook his head and stared at the star field on his screen.

"But Alpha," urged Ralston. "Is it interesting because you can put observers close by?"

"That's part of it. The rest is as perplexing on the good side as my probe failures are on the bad. Alpha is the wrong spectral type. It's a G5, not a B7 like my 'guest star.'" Chen shook his head. "Do envy Nels, that son of a bitch. A real chance to shake up all our theories about stellar evolution. The spectrographic readings alone are worth a dozen papers. Nels is seeing iron sublimations in the photosphere. Hope he loosens up and shares some of it with me. I can do a lot for him after the primary goes." Chen's face lit like the nova he discussed. "There's got to be an accretion disk. I can watch it forming. Be a novel idea to co-author with him. The dynamic instability leading to formation of accretion."

"Do you have any idea how long before Muckup—Alpha 3—becomes dangerous?"

"Dangerous now," Chen said. "Oh, you mean how long before the radiation from the primary fries everything on the planet?" He shook his head. "No way of telling. There'll be an initial intense burst of x-rays, if our theories are accurate, followed by a powerful solar wind composed mostly of highly energetic protons. Heavy ionizing radiation," he said, more to himself than to Ralston. "Then?" Chen shrugged.

"The planet is vaporized?"

"Verd. But the timetable for it is murky. We just can't predict to the nanosecond. I'd say that it's less than six months away."

"No more?"

"Might be less. A lot less."

Ralston left. At first he walked with shoulders bowed. Then he began to straighten. Resolve hardened within him. There could be no hesitation, he realized. To vacillate now meant lost opportunity. The civilization on Alpha 3 must not die unexamined.

And it wouldn't. Even if Michael Ralston had to die along with the planet.

"I can't do it, Doc. No way I can get a chinging starship on such short notice." The man looked around nervously, as if expecting police to arrest him. "You sure it's safe here?"

"The Quad's as safe as any place I know," Ralston told him. "I didn't want to risk my office."

"Got it eared?"

Ralston solemnly nodded, playing the paranoid game. "There's no way to know who might be listening," he agreed. "Out here, there's open spaces and enough noise and people going by to cover whatever we say."

"They got good circuits. They can pick up a feather dropping in the middle of a rocket test. Hell, the student newsers got snoops able to do better'n that."

"That's why we've got to keep moving. We dare not let them catch up." Ralston wondered who the man feared—or if anyone truly sought him. He had seen others like this man after the war. They had turned inward, examining themselves and finding only a hollow shell. To give meaning to their emptiness they had fantasized cabals and plots and persecution.

Ralston knew the man needed psychologic aid, but he couldn't bring himself to suggest it, not with the radical chemical and electronic techniques used by those in the field.

"Cost you a chinging fortune, Doc. You know it."

"I can pay. For the cause," he added, almost as an afterthought. This sealed the deal.

"Two days. Take a shuttle pod up and follow the beacon. Two whites and a red. No other contact."

The man slipped away, mingled in the crowd of students watching a news kiosk, and vanished as if he'd never existed. Ralston sat under a large cryptomeria, his back against the rough bark. In a way, the man he'd just dealt with didn't exist. At least, not officially. Somehow, he had managed to expunge his name from all computer records. Ralston had never heard a name mentioned, nor did he ask. That would violate a trust.

He briefly considered a life at the fringes of society, providing contraband, smuggling, shipping that which no one else dared ship. Ralston laughed ruefully. That wasn't the kind of life he wanted for himself. The University of Ilium stretched out in front of him, living greens mingling with artificial browns, the soft scents of summer wrinkling his nose, students hurrying to classes, discussing their lives and newfound knowledge, a tranquil oasis of learning.

For all the students who only put in their time, he knew there were others who sought to learn, really learn. For those cherished students, he'd gladly devote his life.

Ralston found himself missing the classroom work, the fostering of education. Sometimes he felt like pounding heads to get an idea into an especially dense skull, but the rewards, for the most part, were worth the effort. The sight of a face brightening as a concept penetrated, the student who clearly stood out as exceptional, the rush of new knowledge, new discoveries, new methods of work.

He lived for this. The University sheltered Ralston from the pressures that drove the man he'd just spoken with past the bounds of accepted behavior. In return, Ralston performed the generally pleasurable chore of educating students. And writing his research papers.

All this was worth fighting for. Ralston wouldn't lightly surrender it because of the unfortunate accident that had taken Yago de la Cruz's life.

"We triumph without glory when we triumph without danger," he said softly. "Knowledge is dangerous to gain and dangerous to use. But we need it. Oh, yes, how we need it. How *I* need it." Ralston couldn't conceive of an existence without progress, without the promise of new and wondrous revelations and the chance to explore them fully.

A chanting from across the Quadrangle disturbed his thoughts. He leaned over and peered past the statue of Bacon in the center. A tight knot of students—not more than thirty—shouted something he didn't hear clearly and thrust their fists at the azure sky.

Such vehemence surprised Ralston. He didn't think he'd been away from the University so long that he had missed out on the formation of new campus action groups. Apparently, he had.

Ralston plucked a blade of grass and sucked at the juices,

trying to channel his thoughts to Muckup and the equipment he needed. It was nothing short of a miracle that Leonore Disa could supply the supervisor. That would insure a dozen times more work being done than he might achieve alone.

He frowned when he thought of her demand to be allowed to accompany him. While Ralston hated to deceive her, he couldn't allow her to return with him to Alpha 3. The danger outweighed keeping his word. All he had to do was drop a word to his mysterious friend that Leonore was one of "them" and she'd be led astray.

In two days he'd be aboard the starship bound for Alpha 3—and she'd be in the middle of the Quad staring up at the empty sky.

The chanting again disturbed his concentration. The students had begun moving toward the statue. Ralston went cold inside when he heard their chants.

"Kill the Nex-lover!" the small crowd roared.

Michael Ralston had no trouble deciding they meant him. No one else in the University fit that description so well.

One student climbed onto Bacon's statue and held on to the precarious perch with one hand. The other waved vigorously to emphasize his obviously popular words.

"He is a menace! We cannot allow such warmongers and traitors to exist among us. Bigotry must be cut out and destroyed to make a better society!"

"And he killed Yago!" came the bull-throated cry from the crowd. The others picked up on de la Cruz's first name. "Yago, Yago, Yago!" the crowd chanted.

"For that alone Ralston should be barred from the University."

Raucous shouts of agreement and encouragement rose from the growing crowd. Ralston didn't stir. Movement might attract unwanted attention. He looked over those assembled, trying to find students he recognized. Sometimes, students disgruntled with low grades formed into such groups to take out their frustrations. He saw no one who'd ever been in any of his classes.

What he did see angered him. A gray-skinned, thick-fleshed P'torra stood to one side as an observer rather than as an active participant. Short, bulbous fingers worked at the tiny keyboard of a hand-held electronic device. Ralston had often seen the

P'torra use these "impulse drivers" to devastating advantage. A P'torra entered human psychological parameters and, with the intensity of responses to key words from whoever harangued the crowd, got out a detailed blueprint of how to more effectively manipulate behavior.

The P'torra signaled to his human co-conspirator, who shifted from the bigotry theme to one of praise for Yago de la Cruz. The crowd's reaction mounted exponentially. They had been angry before. Now they reached a peak where murder wasn't inconceivable.

The P'torra's blubbery lips pulled back to reveal twin rows of needle-sharp teeth. He had found the crowd's resonance frequency with this topic. His impulse driver had again proven its worth in controlling human behavior.

Ralston slowly rose, the tree guarding his back. He slowly circled the tree and placed it between him and the crowd. He walked quickly toward his office, trying not to draw attention.

He failed.

Ralston heard the impassioned cries go up from the crowd as the man haranguing from the statue sighted him. Decorum dictated that he not change his pace. Common sense told him he'd be torn apart if the crowd caught him on the Quad. Ralston ran as if all the demons of hell nipped at his heels.

And, as far as he was concerned, at least one did: the P'torra.

A large rock whirled past his head and smashed into the office building. He ducked and got through the door. Another rock crashed against the clear plastic pane. Ralston vainly sought some way of locking the door. A magnetic key was required; only the night patrol was likely to have one properly coded.

Ralston thought about barring himself in his office, then discarded the idea as suicidal. If the crowd trapped him there, they could do any number of things. While most University buildings were relatively fireproof, papers still burned and plastics melted. The fumes from the plastic might not be deadly, but they'd certainly be dangerous if the crowd held him prisoner within his office.

He hurried toward the far end of the building. An exit there would allow him to slip out the back way and elude the crowd. Sooner or later, even the lethargic campus security squad would arrive to contain the students.

Ralston skidded to a halt. "Damn!" Somehow they had

already circled the building and cut off his escape. "The P'torra plotted this out. He had to!" Crowds did not operate with such foresight. Ralston saw no other explanation for the students' coordinated efforts to capture him.

He ducked through a door leading into the cellar. Ralston slammed it behind him and leaned against it, heart pounding. He slowly regained his breath. In the corridor he heard the harsh footsteps of a dozen or more pursuers.

"Where'd he go? Where did that chinging son of a bitch go?"

"Check the offices!" another shouted.

"Coolness," came a soft voice. "Composure. Examine the lower reaches of this edifice."

The P'torra!

Ralston ran down the stairs, new knowledge bursting on him in that instant.

He knew how a trapped rat felt.

The door opened and the students rushed after him.

ELEVEN

"KILL HIM!"

The echoes reverberated down the long hallway and through the dusty crates stored in the cellar. The sound of pursuit gave Michael Ralston the added speed he needed to find a small storage room, slip inside, then close the door and block it the best he could.

He stared in horror at the tiny box he'd shoved in front of the door. It wouldn't hold back a crowd spurred on by the P'torra's psychological needlings. It'd hardly hold back a stiff breeze. Ralston's fear rose, then slowly faded as reason regained a hold. If he acted like a hunted animal, that was the way he'd die.

Only thinking this through afforded him any hope for escape. Forcing himself to breathe deeply, he calmed more and more. He closed his eyes and found the Nex-embedded hypnotic commands deep within. They hadn't understood how humans entered battles keyed and nervous. A few deft lessons with their combat psychologists had given Ralston the control needed to keep an edge but not be pushed into panic.

He shook his head. He had tried to deny that training because of the war and the way his peers reacted to the Nex. No more. He needed every advantage possible if he wanted to get away from the mob and leave Novo Terra for Alpha 3.

Gray eyes darted around the small storage room, checking, evaluating, hypothesizing, discarding. The window out of the room was far too small for him to squeeze through—and freedom tantalized him on the other side. The bright blue sky shone with the glow of a new lover, and Novo Terra's summer winds promised life eternal.

Ralston pulled a crate under the window and jumped atop its sagging wood surface. A desperate jerk tore the window's lock from the wall. He flung it open so hard that the plastic window popped out of its frame and clattered to the floor. Ralston jumped and cut both arms on the sides of the window. With trembling fingers, he pulled threads from his shirt and stuck them onto the frame. Only then did he jump to one side and crawl into an empty box barely large enough to contain him. He pulled his makeshift blind in close, leaving only a crack through which to peer into the room.

Barely had he hidden when the door burst inward. A rush of confused colors passed his narrow cone of vision. At least five students had entered the room.

Ralston's nose wrinkled. The P'torra with his distinctive body odor had also entered.

"He got away!" cried one of the men.

"A moment," came the P'torra's sharp command. Ralston heard the crate on which he'd stood creak under the alien's ponderous weight. He imagined the P'torra running a stubby finger along the window frame, finding the blood, bringing it to his slit-nostriled nose, then lightly sampling it with the tip of his tongue. Then the P'torra would bend closer, check the fibers. The alien's mind would make odd leaps of intuition not shared by humans.

"In this, you find surety. He got away," the P'torra announced, finally convinced. "Please to seek him out. Dr. Ralston is a danger to all spirited beings."

Footsteps shuffled from the room. Ralston waited. He knew the P'torra mind—and his nose still wrinkled. After long minutes, Ralston heard a slight creaking sound. The alien shifted position on the crate on which he sat. Ralston's mind raced. If he emerged to confront the P'torra, he knew he could physically overpower the alien. He had met enough in single combat to learn their weaknesses. For all their bulk and muscle, they moved slowly to achieve certain positions. He might lure the P'torra to bend slightly from the waist; this constrained motion around their hips. A quick turn to the side, a blow to the side of the neck, death.

Ralston pictured it all clearly in his mind.

But he waited. After another five minutes, the creaking noises sounded once more, this time accompanied by soft footsteps. What had the P'torra thought about while he waited? The same things that Ralston had? Vulnerability and advantage? Or something so totally bizarre no human could share it?

Ralston waited a few more minutes, then slowly pushed aside the box and peered into the room. Warm afternoon sunlight slanted through the destroyed window. Ralston straightened stiffened joints and cautiously looked out into the cellar's central corridor. Empty. He jumped atop the crate again and looked out across a grassy area leading down to the University's athletic fields. In the distance he saw the cathedral's tall central spire and heard the chimes sounding the hour.

"Now they come," he grumbled when he saw six uniformed men trotting along the walkways. The University security police had arrived to disperse the crowd. More than a hundred students protested. As he watched, the security force used sleep gas against the more violent protestors, but Ralston knew that the P'torra wouldn't be among them. Always the alien would hold back, stay at the periphery, incite but never participate. That was the P'torra way.

Ralston retraced his path through the cellar and back up to the ground level. He considered going to his second-floor office, then discarded the notion. If the P'torra really wanted his blood, students would be posted there to alert the mob. Ralston walked briskly down the hall, found the westernmost door and left through an arboretum. The overhanging limbs of the trees and large shrubs gave him a sense of security. Away from prying eyes and masked by the cloying floral perfumes from the nose slits of the P'torra, Ralston walked aimlessly until he circled around to face the athletic fields.

The crowd had vanished. The security force no doubt breathed a sigh of relief at their day's work. And this brief interruption of the University's tranquillity had passed. Ralston went to one of the outlying buildings and slipped inside, taking care not to be seen. He found a shadowy corner in a balcony overlooking the gymnasium floor. With a sigh, he sank into a chair and once again forced himself to relax. The effort this time proved more successful than before.

The danger had passed. Temporarily.

On the floor two teams played mag ball, shuttling a light, metal-encased cork ball back and forth using electromagnetic wands. Each side was allowed only so much charge. The mag ball might be passed back and forth between team members a dozen times or more, as long as each used only a fraction of their allotted energy, or one player might use all the team's charge in getting the mag ball over the net. If the ball touched ground, a point was scored. As with most games, it required skill and teamwork—and was a game Ralston never appreciated.

"Did you come to play or just ogle all the sweet young girls strutting about in their shorts?"

Ralston whirled at the voice, banging his elbow against the wall.

"My, aren't you the jumpy one? I've *got* to fence with you today. I really do. This is my best chance in months and months to win. You'll be a real sucker for even my lousy feints if you keep overreacting like that, Michael."

"Sorry, Druanna," he said, settling back into the chair and rubbing his elbow. "You startled me."

"Hiding out, eh?"

"Nothing gets by you, does it?" He stared at Druanna Thorkkin, wondering how much she knew and how much she'd only guessed. The woman was sharp, he'd have to grant her that. He sighed. She looked so much like another he'd known. The same light brown hair falling in soft waves, the same flush to the cheeks from being perpetually excited by life, the same vitality and imagination and piercing intelligence.

So much like Marta.

Ralston had never gotten it clear in his own mind whether he enjoyed Druanna's company because of the resemblance to that love long lost, or if he actually appreciated her for herself.

"I was down in the office when the call came for the security force. Those fools came blundering back after they'd so valiantly defended the University's honor. The P'torra, wasn't it?"

Druanna Thorkkin didn't share his dislike of the blubbery aliens, nor did she much appreciate the reptilian aspect of the Nex. But she was a friend.

"I think so."

"You've really stirred up a fuss around here. Makes a staid old University like Ilium sit up and take notice. I think you're good for the creeping lethargy I see around here." Druanna looked at Ralston for a moment, then said, "You're not here for a match, are you?"

"No. Hiding out is closer to it."

"A pity. I could use a good workout. Foil? Saber? You sure?"

Ralston shook his head. Druanna Thorkkin was the only one at the University who shared his enthusiasm for fencing. The others considered it an anachronism, as they did his passion for other Earthly skills and pursuits. After the brief nuclear exchange, Earth had become little more than a backwater in human affairs. Novo Terra had assumed the role of leadership in political and economic matters, but Ralston still felt a kinship to the planet of his birth. Fencing was just one of the arts that he considered worthy of remembering.

"Grave-robbing isn't what it used to be," Druanna said sadly. "You used to be more alive. Just the hint of me besting you at foil sent you into a spiraling orbit."

"You're quicker than I am," he admitted, "but what makes you think I've given up the sport?"

"I can't taunt you into a match," she said. "Or is it more than stark, shuddering fear of being beaten that stays your mighty sword?" Druanna cocked her head to one side and peered at him. "The P'torra's not doing this? Are you afraid of Salazar?"

"Verd. I'm afraid of what Salazar and the committee will do to me."

"Green shit from a purple cow, Ralston! You're not even lying so's I believe you."

"I'd better be going."

"I think that's exactly what you're going to do," she said firmly. "You're going back to Alpha 3, aren't you? Without University sanction, unless I missed all the clues."

"You're speculating. I can't do anything until the hearing.

Maybe I can't do anything after it."

Druanna went on, as if she hadn't heard a word he said. "That funny man with no name you find so interesting. You know the one I mean. The one who's sure everyone's spying on him. He's got the connections to smuggle you back, doesn't he? You're going to star out to your dig. You left the equipment on Alpha 3, so to hell with the primary going nova. Is that it, Michael?"

"You've been reading those quaint mysteries I loaned you," Ralston said.

"The Doyles were good, but I liked the Blocks and Ulfbloms better. And I can read you just like I do them. Better, since I don't have to turn your pages."

Ralston stared at her. He liked Druanna for her wit and intelligence, but this time she pushed into territory he wanted left unexplored.

"You," she said, eyes narrowing and finger pointing, "are going to be in more trouble than you can handle if you go back."

"Do I have a choice?"

"I suppose not," Druanna said. "The find's that important, is it?"

Ralston smiled broadly. "Thank you. I appreciate it."

"What?"

"That you knew the only thing drawing me to Alpha 3 was the museum, that I wasn't running away from the hearing because of what happened to de la Cruz."

"Never occurred to me. I know you grave robbers. All wrapped up in your work like a mummy. If de la Cruz had been one of your graduate students instead of one who caught the consolation prize in the grades lottery, I'd've thought you worked him to death."

"It was accidental. I've been thinking about it. A lot. And some other things, too. Those I can't quite put into words, but the de la Cruz death is a part of it." Ralston leaned forward, looking at the mag ball players without really seeing them. "De la Cruz entered one of the last dioramas. Something happened there that killed him. Something that didn't show up in earlier scenes."

"You believe it might give a clue to the culture's decline?"

"It might not be the cause, but it has to be significant. I

experienced nothing but the telepathic communication in the first few dioramas."

"Handy gadget," mused Druanna. "I wish I could teach my students mind to mind. Those that have minds would benefit, and I'd find out quicker about the others."

"I'd like to get the mind projector, too," Ralston admitted. "The notes I found in de la Cruz's belongings showed he was interested only in the commercial exploitation of the gadget. But there's so much more, even if I can't bring away a working projector to tear apart and reverse engineer."

"The society?"

"Dead. And the decline came so quickly. Their capital city had been razed. It's as if the dioramas were their last real effort to pass along their history."

"You think the last ones show what happened and that de la Cruz died from it. Interesting conjecture."

Druanna Thorkkin leaned back and hiked her feet to the balcony guard rail. She laced strong fingers behind her head and looked at Ralston out of the corner of her eye.

"It's a mean job for anyone to help you find out what happened to de la Cruz—and the folks on Alpha 3."

"I don't want you to get involved."

"I didn't volunteer. I just pointed out what Salazar would say."

In silence they watched as the far team won the mag ball game. Sweaty, laughing students laid down their playing electrodes and left for the showers.

"I've got so much money I hardly know what to do with it," Druanna said.

"I can't take it."

"I didn't offer it. Just talking. Don't think Salazar would consider it collusion on my part, either, if some of that money just happened to vanish from my account and show up in yours. You're going to need a great deal, Michael."

"If that star goes nova, you may never see any of your money back."

"My loss is going to be bigger than a few months' wages lost," she said. "Hell, Michael, I'll have lost the only fool on this campus I can out-fence."

Ralston turned, reached out and laid his fingertips on the line of Druanna's jaw. He bent over, lightly kissed her on the lips, and said, "Thank you."

Druanna snorted and pulled away. "What's got into me, consorting with known grave robbers?" She rose and walked off, never looking back. Ralston sank into the chair and let his mind race ahead. He had so much to plan, so much to do.

But first he had to make one last visit. Ralston wasn't sure he wanted to see Westcott. Some people were just too strange for him to bear, and Westcott was one of them.

"Something Chen said bothered me," he told Westcott. Ralston stared at the mathematician and wondered if the man heard or not. Westcott had shaved his head to better accommodate the remote IR interface mounted there. Ralston shivered. No matter that Westcott had all the permits and authorizations required to connect himself directly into his beloved computers, the sight of a man with the flesh-mounted plugs and remote IR devices made him uneasy.

Ralston wasn't overly religious but he understood the Church's injunction against such meddling with the human spirit. It seemed sacrilegious.

Westcott leaned back, eyes hooded and a dreamy expression on his face. He reached up and made some minute adjustment to the infrared remote control device atop his head. He smiled, but Ralston shivered even more at it. The smile wasn't human.

"I'm so slow," Westcott murmured, almost a croon to put a baby to sleep. "So slow, but my loving friends, they're so fast, so wondrously fast."

Ralston looked away from the man, if Westcott could be called that. Even the Nex seemed more human than the mathematician. A single framed diploma decorated the walls of Westcott's laboratory. Ralston looked at it more closely. As he'd thought, this wasn't a diploma in the strictest sense. It was Westcott's license to direct-connect with a computer. Only a few ever applied and less than one in a thousand of those applying were granted what Ralston considered a dubious privilege.

Westcott spoke directly to his computer's block circuits, saw with the computer's laser probes, felt with piezoelectric plates, heard with amplifiers, smelled with surface acoustic wave sensors—what truly human function remained in the mathematician? Not emotions, of that Ralston was certain.

He wished that the planetary licensing authorities had totally outlawed such human-computer connection instead of severely restricting it.

From the contented expression on Westcott's hatchet-thin face, however, Ralston knew where to find one dissenting vote to his gut-level reaction.

"Not brilliant, but sound," Westcott said.

"What?"

"Chen. You mentioned Chen Liu. Or has it already been erased from your memory?"

"Something Chen said disturbed me."

"Emotion," cut in Westcott, "has no place in science."

"He mentioned a nova seen on Earth in 1054. He mentioned losing a robot probe, possibly two, that he'd recently started out to investigate the accretion disk."

"Interesting dynamics in the disk," whispered Westcott, eyes closed now. The light on his interface unit blinked a baleful red. Across the room, the IR beam impinged on a sensor plate and transferred Westcott's thoughts directly into the computer. Another IR unit broadcast back the computer's results.

"The Alpha primary is going nova."

"Much of interest mathematically," said Westcott. "The tensors for the region are showing..." His voice trailed off to nothing.

Ralston rushed on, wanting only to state his case, see if Westcott would help, and then get the hell out of the lab. "I know the 1054 'guest star' and Alpha Prime represent only two points and thus can be connected with a straight line—" Ralston waited for comment. None came. "I tried to extrapolate along that line to see if there were other novas occurring. I didn't find anything. But the *feel* is there. Something else ought to be found from this data."

"A straight line?" scoffed Westcott, showing that he had, indeed, been listening. "You naively assumed a linear trajectory?"

Westcott did nothing, but an entire wall screen glowed a pale blue. Tiny points began appearing. To Ralston's eye, they were randomly distributed. But then the display began to change, to turn, to give a new perspective. A dotted red line ran smoothly from one point to the next, forming a distinct nonlinear curve.

"This takes into account not only appropriate novas, but

also proper motion of the stars, drag from gas clouds and other variations in gravity wells."

Ralston stared at the dozen or so points. "What are they? All novas?"

"You asked for that, didn't you?" The scorn in Westcott's voice irritated Ralston. "Here is a different view of the same data. A time variable has been added."

This confused him. The points along the curve appeared at random—but all the points eventually showed on the graph. The point that interested him most eventually winked into being: Alpha 3 lay in the path. With the 1054 star the last point, and the Alpha primary two points in the past by ten thousand years, Ralston began getting a sense of inevitability to what he witnessed.

"Something following this trajectory might be causing the stars to go nova," he said. "But there seems to be a time delay from point to point. One star might go nova long before stars on either side along the trajectory."

Westcott sat as still as any granite statue. His gaunt face seemed to shrink and the red light indicating computer access blinked faster and faster until it shone constantly.

Ralston went to Westcott and placed a hand against the man's throat. The flesh felt dry and leathery; no pulse throbbed in the arteries. He moved his hand under Westcott's nose. The faintest of warm breath issued forth. Ralston jerked away when the red indicator light began to blink at a speed detectable by the human eye. When it flashed only once every second, Westcott opened his eyes.

"A problem of great interest." For the first time, Westcott's expression showed some humanity. "Curious that one of your type would stumble across this problem and have the intelligence to recognize it for what it is."

"Then something might follow that dotted line and be causing the suns to explode?"

"A high probability exists. That is not the question. Rather, how is this accomplished? The mathematics of chaos has not been properly examined for"—the red light flashed once on his interface—"since the twenty-first century on Earth. On Earth." Westcott snickered, as if this were the dirtiest joke he'd ever heard.

"What does this moving *thing* do?" asked Ralston.

"The mathematical intricacy of the problem is worthy of my time."

With that, Westcott closed his eyes. The interface indicator light began pulsating once more. Ralston stopped and considered running his hand through the IR beam connecting cortex with computer.

"Don't," came Westcott's warning. "It gives me a headache."

Ralston started, then forced calm on himself. It was as if a corpse had risen from the grave to speak. He quickly left Westcott's laboratory without breaking the IR remote sensor beam. Ralston wasn't certain what he'd learned, other than Alpha 3's civilization had died because of something that had passed by.

Now the star was going nova.

How did all this tie in with Yago de la Cruz's death and the dioramas? Ralston had to know.

TWELVE

MICHAEL RALSTON LEFT the mathematician's office feeling unclean. He had nothing against Westcott as a researcher; it was generally admitted that Westcott had few peers in the abstract geometries where he lived. Nor did Ralston fault Westcott for his undeniable dedication to his work. He shuddered involuntarily at the thought of being so closely tied to a computer. While Ralston depended heavily on their use in the field—and in the classroom—the concept of oneness with a machine troubled him deeply.

Ralston stopped at the door leading from the laboratory and quickly scanned the University's spacious grounds. The sylvan setting had always soothed him—it had been one of the reasons he had accepted the University's niggardly offer to teach archaeology. When the pressures of too many students, too much politics, too little time all came crushing in on him, Ralston had walked through the grounds and retreated to a better time.

For him, that time was more fantasy than reality. Earth had never been like this, even before the quick war. His earliest childhood memories were of smog-filled skies, acid rains that stung the skin and burned the eyes, snow that fell black with soot, yellowish plumes of sulfur dioxide rising into the air, and his father talking of radon gas from fossil fuel combustion shortening their lives. The dinosaurs' revenge, his father had always said with a cynical laugh.

Ralston didn't think of the Earth war as positive, but it seemed only a faster version of death to him. Choke on noxious fumes and glow blue from burning coal and heavy industry, or go up in a swift radioactive cloud.

Slow or fast. He wasn't sure which was the better death.

But he didn't have that to worry about on Novo Terra. All on-planet manufacturing had been banned soon after colonization two hundred years ago. What needed to be built was done in orbit where the detritus of industry could be disposed of safely. Most of the electricity on the planet came from orbiting genosynchronous solar power stations. The high-intensity beams to the ground afforded some leakage of microwave radiation, but it was a small price to pay for not sucking in flyash with every breath. The surface of Novo Terra had been transformed into a garden with strict laws to maintain it.

Ralston inhaled deeply and caught the subtle fragrances wafting on the gentle breeze. But when he closed his eyes he saw only the mud flats of Muckup, the copper door and the museum of death beneath Alpha 3's surface. Ralston screwed his eyes shut all the tighter and winced at his mental image of the planet vanishing in a sudden flare of a nova.

He knew such a sight would be impossible. The highest speed framing cameras, or even electronic block cameras, would be incapable of capturing the final instant of Alpha 3's life. If such things were possible, a human observer would see only a purple flash as the speed-of-light radiation burned out optic nerves.

Even this was fantasy. The slowness of impulse transmission along nerve paths would prevent any sight of the nova at all. Ten thousand centimeters a second versus thirty billion centimeters a second. His body and brain wouldn't respond fast enough to the stimulus, not by a factor of three million.

Ralston shook himself free of such morbid thoughts. He cared nothing for the destruction of Alpha 3; he wanted its preservation. More precisely, he wanted to preserve whatever might be uncovered about the populace that had lived on the planet. Knowledge of this magnitude should not be lost.

Even in Nature's fierce, cleansing nova fire.

Ralston looked around to Novo Terra's primary. The sun quietly slipped behind a row of greenery to the west and cast long, distorted shadows across the grounds. To think that Alpha 3's sun looked so much like this one. Ralston didn't want to think that whatever caused that nova might also be capable of triggering another.

The main room of the library stretched before him, virtually deserted for the evening meal. One or two librarians sat hunched over their glowing consoles, rearranging their databases for the hundredth time that month, seeking new ways of making searches more esoteric, thus protecting their jobs for another pay period. They knew that their positions were tolerated, long since unnecessary because of easy access to their information from any point on campus. But old traditions died hard, especially in academic circles.

Ralston tried to imagine a university without a library and failed. It might be an anachronism, but symbols usually were. He had never seen a promotional advertising for a school that didn't include at least one zoomshot of the library, a quiet spot for reflection and study, a quick and still meaningful representation of the entire higher educational system in one location.

He settled into one of the saddles and thumbed on the terminal. At the prompt, he typed in his departmental billing code number. Ralston frowned when it took a dozen seconds to respond. The authorization finally blinked on the screen.

His fingers flew over the keys, demanding information, ordering it sent to the hardcopy room, asking for more. In less than five minutes he had finished. Ralston looked over his right shoulder toward the door. No one. Over his left he saw a solitary librarian behind a desk digging out a sandwich for dinner.

The feeling of being watched had halted his work. And now that sensation forced him away from the console and toward the hardcopy room at a pace only slightly less than a run.

The imprinter had spat out a stack of plastic sheets for him. He was one of the few who bothered with hardcopy. Most had the information placed in their computer files or had it burned onto a block for viewing later. But as an archaeologist, Ralston lived for the past. Some even accused him of living *in* the past.

He pulled the sheets from the imprinter and began riffling through them, but his eyes weren't focused on the pages. His nose wrinkled from an unexpected odor. Hairs rose on the back of his neck, as if he'd touched a high-voltage electrode. He didn't have to turn to know who blocked his exit from the room.

"Did you bring your mob with you?" Ralston asked.

"Dr. Ralston, what fine coincidences this is meeting you," came the P'torra's voice.

The rear door from the room was securely locked and alarmed. If Ralston managed to batter it down, he'd alert everyone. Better to fight his way past the P'torra, if that proved necessary.

"Do not think so to do this unmentionable act," the P'torra cautioned. Ralston squarely faced the alien. Clutched in one of the well-fleshed, stubby-fingered hands the P'torra held a small box with two protruding wires.

"Not a lethal device, is it?" Ralston asked.

"I wish no harm to come to you, Doctor. Why for do you think so ill of me?"

Ralston tried to push past. He encountered blubbery P'torra flesh that didn't yield.

"I've got to get back to teach a class. Let me by."

"Your wondrous duties in teaching classrooms are suspended," answered the P'torra, unperturbed by Ralston's more aggressive attempts to push past and escape. "I mean you none harm."

"You manipulated the crowd well. I saw you with your impulse driver."

"I mean nothing against you personally," explained the P'torra. It smiled, revealing the twin rows of needle-sharp teeth. Without a decent nose, with the heavy folds of flesh on his face, the P'torra looked like something out of Ralston's worst nightmare.

Ralston tried to get past the P'torra again. The alien had wedged himself firmly into the narrow doorway, making escape almost impossible. Ralston stepped back and quickly sized up the alien. He had fought enough of them in the Nex-P'torra war to have an appreciation for how strong and hardy they were. Once, he had blasted off both legs of a P'torra field officer. That hadn't killed him. He had followed the officer for almost twenty kilometers; along the way the P'torra had killed four different varieties of creature with his bare hands. One of them, Ralston had heard, couldn't be killed with any armament short of a land-based energy cannon. When he'd finally found the P'torra officer, it took another five minutes of intense combat before the last whisper of life fled the fleshy alien body.

Ralston might respect them for their toughness, but he despised them for what they had done to the Nex—and what they continued to do on a half dozen other worlds.

"You think to slay me?" asked the P'torra.

"The thought never crossed my mind." Ralston knew how difficult such an act would be. He'd content himself with a disabling kick to the knees, a feint to one side and a quick escape in the opposite direction.

"I mean you none harm." The P'torra vented what Ralston knew to be laugh. He felt as if someone had scratched his soul with a diamond. "You are more much valuable to me as a symbol of the administration at Ilium University."

From outside the library, Ralston heard a student haranguing a crowd. He looked at the P'torra, who smiled even more wickedly.

"How did you know where to find me?" Ralston asked. Even as he asked, he knew. The answer burned brightly within him. He wanted verification, however.

"You are a popularly wanted professor, Dr. Ralston. All computer billings show their importance at some point in the University."

"You sidetracked the request at the comptroller's office," he said. This told Ralston more than he wanted to know. Not only did Salazar and the committee want to keep track of him, the University officials didn't care who was privy to that information. They wanted to write him off as quickly and quietly as possible. If the P'torra provided additional aid, so much the better.

"Such paranoia that is yours." The P'torra chuckled. "Many humans want to be sought out. Are you unlike them?"

Ralston kicked without any tensing of his muscles. The blow lacked real power but he'd aimed it accurately. He caught the P'torra on the side of his knee and brought the bulky alien down. A second, harder kick disabled the P'torra. Ralston lithely jumped over his victim and landed outside the hardcopy room.

"Don't," Ralston said, such menace in his voice that the P'torra stopped trying to reach out and grab his leg. Ralston stepped away, out of any possible reach. "You say you don't bear me any malice. It's not true for me. Remember that."

"There is no need for to remember such a memory, Dr. Ralston," said the P'torra. "You will not long be at this University."

Ralston didn't want to blunder into the crowd gathering in front of the library. He found a side exit, glanced around and saw nothing but shadows and the insectlike winklights floating along the paths and providing gentle illumination. Ralston avoided the paths and kept to the darker areas. As he got to the top of a small rise, he looked back down at the library where the crowd gathered.

The words were lost in the distance, but not their intent. The student leader on the steps made all the gestures appropriate to a lynch mob. Ralston kept walking, wanting to find Druanna Thorkkin and talk with her. But he knew that wasn't possible. As much as he needed her, it wouldn't be fair for him to involve her with the P'torra and his campaign of campus unrest. The P'torra had made it quite clear that Ralston's every move was being closely watched.

Ralston would have to do without a friend and consolation this night. He spent many long hours studying the information he had pulled from the University computer banks, integrating this with what Westcott had told him.

After he had finished, Ralston needed a friend to confide in even more. Never had he felt so alone.

"I've got to see Dr. Salazar right away. This is important," Ralston said, almost shouting. He'd gotten little sleep the night before and his nerves were frayed from dodging the P'torra-incited students around campus. He didn't want to deal with underlings.

"I'm sure you think it is, Dr. Ralston," said Salazar's secretary, "but he is in conference."

Ralston chafed at the delay but saw no way to circumvent the officious secretary. Few at the University had human secretaries; most bureaucrats made do with automated systems. Salazar proved more status conscious, and flaunted his importance by hiring the man sitting and glaring at Ralston.

Ralston had to admit a human buffer proved more effective in most cases. Most people had been well enough trained to obey a mechanical command. Those few—like him—who hadn't, only a human barrier could stop.

After twenty minutes, three people left Salazar's office. Two of them Ralston recognized as Constance and Arturo de la Cruz. The third, a neatly dressed woman carrying a small legal case, had to be their attorney. The two de la Cruzes glared at Ralston but made no comment. The attorney didn't even notice him.

"You wanted something, Doctor?" called out Salazar.

"Something vital, Dr. Salazar."

"Very well," the man said tiredly. "But I can only give you a few minutes. This has been a busy day and it looks as if I'll be here until well past midnight. I'm to meet with University legal counsel at eleven hours."

Ralston glanced at the wall chronometer. That gave him less than ten minutes. He hurried into Salazar's office.

"What is it, Ralston? I've had about enough of you these past few days. I assume you recognized the brother and sister of the student you killed."

"I killed no one," Ralston said, hardly expecting more from Salazar. The man had already made up his mind on the matter. Ralston pushed aside such concerns for one he considered even greater. "Look at this."

Ralston dropped a block into Salazar's desk projector. Without asking permission, he turned it on. One wall filled with decorations faded away as the projection dominated.

"Westcott plotted this. A trajectory of some device past Alpha 3, past these other points—all novas. I believe that this device caused the decline of Alpha 3's civilization and was responsible for its eventual demise. And that it also caused these stars to go nova."

Ralston paused, then amended, "At least some of them might have gone nova. I haven't had time to check on the possibility that some are naturally occurring. This one—the one in orange—seems to be of a type to naturally evolve into a nova." He pointed out Chen's 1054 "guest star." "The others might have been triggered."

"What is all this rubbish?" demanded Salazar. "Are you totally insane?"

"Consider this, Dr. Salazar. An object passes by a solar system. Somehow it causes instabilities to occur, in societies, in the stellar processes, in individuals."

"You're trying to tell me this imagined device of yours is responsible for de la Cruz's death?"

"I don't know," Ralston said honestly, "but it's possible that, by entering one of the dioramas depicting the final days of Alpha 3, he absorbed part of the madness that destroyed their culture."

"Absurd."

"I thought so, too, but this all fits together."

"What produced this alleged device?"

"Maybe not *what* but *who*. It might be a messenger from some other race trying to contact intelligences. Back in pre-space days, Earth sent out satellites with messages."

"Preposterous. Both that and your theory."

"This might not be a friendly warning. It might be a weapon. Or it might be a naturally occurring field somehow orbiting through the plane of the galaxy. I don't know what it is or its possible origin, but its results are obvious."

"Not to me."

"Here," Ralston said, moving to a new projection. "Something Westcott said to me sent me off on a search of University records. Three centuries ago on Earth mathematicians formulated what they called the equations of chaos." Ralston cut off Salazar's angry response. "These equations were supposed to predict what appears to be random behavior. The formation of weather patterns, radioactive decay, electronic component failure."

"And?" Salazar said sarcastically. "What else?"

"They also worked to predict the course of epilepsy in humans. That and computer component failure have much in common."

Salazar rocked back in his chair and stared at Ralston for a few seconds, then said, "You want me to believe this mythical device, artificial or naturally occurring, went speeding by Alpha 3 more than ten thousand years ago and left as its legacy seizures of the sort that claimed Citizen de la Cruz?"

"It's possible."

"It's ridiculous."

"There might be another problem, Dr. Salazar. The legacy, as you called it, might not be limited to humans. I strongly believe that it has caused the Alpha primary to become pre-nova."

"People go crazy, stars blow up, is there anything else this mythical machine of yours does?"

"What other natural processes might be destabilized?" asked Ralston. "Can it cause war? Devastating weather patterns?" He spoke off the top of his head. Even as he mentioned the weather patterns, he remembered the diorama pictures of Alpha 3 and the current mudball. This change, too, might have been caused by the device's passing.

"This leap of faith on your part is incredible, Ralston. You have not one shred of evidence for your wild claims, and I don't believe them for an instant. I must assume that you seek a scapegoat for your own negligence. Why de la Cruz died, I can't say. But I can and do say that you are responsible."

"What if I'm right? This device is still roving through the galaxy. We have no way of determining which direction along the trajectory Westcott plotted it might be traveling."

"Correlate with time of occurrence," snapped Salazar.

"We are talking about *random* events. This thing might interfere with what we think of as random, spontaneous events. Think of the power, Dr. Salazar! To be able to control radio-active decay—or to predict it. To predict weather exactly."

Salazar stared out his window. An unexpected rain shower dampened the campus. Even with extensive weather satellite forecasts, mistakes were made, usually on a daily basis.

Ralston saw how the man weakened at the notion of something financially beneficial for the University of Ilium.

"If nothing else, if I can't unlock the secret, there is always the thought projector inside the dioramas. The later ones might be tainted with this uncertainty, this randomness or forced order—call it what you will—but the earlier ones aren't."

"The University could certainly use an influx of fresh funds," mused Salazar.

"I need permission to return to Alpha 3 immediately."

"Out of the question. There are preliminary hearings in the de la Cruz matter. And we cannot afford funding for such a venture on your part."

"We dare not wait. The Alpha primary might go nova at any instant. Seconds might be vital."

"No," Salazar said firmly. "I will present your request to the full committee, but under no circumstance could we authorize your return until after the de la Cruz situation is satisfactorily resolved."

"Time is running out," said Ralston. He pulled the block from the projector and slid it across Salazar's desk. "Study this more carefully. And think what might happen if we don't find out what caused an entire civilization to self-destruct." Ralston paused, then said, "Can you imagine not learning what controls such chaos, what gives it order and uses it for destructive purposes?" He glanced dramatically out the window. Warm, syrupy sunlight broke through the cloud cover.

"Can you imagine *our* sun exploding?"

Ralston turned and left Salazar's office. He didn't know if the administrator had been convinced of the seriousness of the problem, but Ralston knew one thing: He had certainly convinced himself.

THIRTEEN

"I'M BEING FOLLOWED," the seedy man said, nervously looking around for pursuers.

"Don't worry," Michael Ralston assured the man. "You're safe. It's me they want."

"The P'torra?"

Ralston nodded. He hadn't had an instant's rest since the abortive riot in front of the office building. Students came to the University of Ilium for many reasons. Some fled here to be away from their family for the first time in their lives. Others genuinely sought education. A few wanted something to do and had nothing better to occupy their time. And then Ralston considered the P'torra in this quagmire of half-realized dreams and frustrations. The alien seemed interested in learning—but what he studied!

Everywhere Ralston turned, the P'torra stood with his impulse driver in hand, tallying up human responses, suggesting alternatives to his pawns, finding new tactics to drive the crowd to a frenzy. By the time the alien left Novo Terra and returned to his home world, he would be expert in psychological techniques.

That he might be one of the select few who had learned what he'd come to the University of Ilium to learn didn't keep Ralston from cursing him.

"He finds me convenient because of my beliefs," Ralston said. "I need to know your progress." The sudden shift in topic took the nervous man by surprise.

"What? Oh, the starship. It's ready. In orbit. But it'll cost you dearly. Pilot's got expenses. Have to avoid the authorized traffic. A lot is going into orbit now. Manufacturing season for the orbiting factories. And the patrols might think you're smuggling something, too. Dangerous."

Ralston had withdrawn his life savings. It barely covered this man's finder's fee for the starship. But Ralston wasn't above using his University account to the maximum. He hadn't been shut off completely—apparently Salazar hadn't considered Ralston's drawing on funds a possibility. Even with this and Druanna's loan, Ralston found himself short.

Leonore Disa covered that and furnished the master supervisor he so desperately needed on Muckup.

It paid to have rich, committed graduate students willing to take risks. Ralston smiled. It didn't hurt to have the hottest discovery of all time, either—and Leonore Disa separated from her lover on that planet.

"Take the shuttle pod up at half past midnight. You'll star out an hour later. If you don't show, everything's off. No second chances, no refunds."

"I understand," Ralston said. "Is everything on board now?"

A quick nod was the only answer.

"And Leonore? Is she already aboard?" Ralston still had reservations about allowing her to accompany him, but the need for skilled hands at the machinery outweighed the danger. He was gambling everything. Leonore Disa might die, but if she did, Ralston wouldn't be in any worse trouble than he was now—he'd be dead alongside her.

Ralston snorted. He doubted that was the proper way of looking at their situation. Their atoms would be intermixed with the superheated gases of the outer edge of an expanding nova. No bodies, no remains, no trace except for a few energetic protons, neutrons and electrons. All his worries would be over in a flash.

But that wouldn't happen. A better conclusion to this reck-lessness would be proof of his theories concerning Alpha 3.

Again came the quick jerking movement of the head Ralston interpreted to mean the man assented. Leonore and the equip-ment spun in orbit above Novo Terra. He had to join them by half past midnight or the entire mad venture came to an end.

Ralston said nothing to the man as he turned and walked off. To have spoken even a simple good-bye would have trig-gered paranoias best left untouched. The friendly environment of the University campus spread around Ralston like a green ocean wave, interrupted here and there by buildings. But what-ever serenity he'd felt here before had evaporated. He walked quickly toward the administration building. With luck he could catch Salazar and the committee before they got down to serious discussion of how best to remove him from their school.

"Dr. Ralston, wait!" cried the secretary as he hurried past. Ralston didn't slow down. He got through the door and had it closed before the secretary could stop him. Inside the room, a half dozen heads swiveled to see who intruded on their delib-erations.

"Dr. Ralston, this is a closed meeting," said Salazar in an icy tone that meant they'd been discussing the termination of a professor: Dr. Michael Lewis Ralston.

Ralston held on to the door handle and prevented the sec-retary from entering. Muscles stood out in thick cords on his arms as he applied more and more pressure to keep the door shut.

"I only need a few minutes of your time, Doctor."

"Very well." Though Salazar seemed resigned to such in-trusions, he didn't appear to be receptive to anything Ralston might say.

Ralston released the door handle and abruptly stepped to one side. The secretary slammed through the suddenly unre-sisting door and fell facedown on the floor. The sheepish expres-sion and mumbled apology covered Ralston's move across the room to seat himself before the committee that would decide his fate. Salazar waved the secretary back to his post outside.

"I'm not here to plead my case," said Ralston. "Rather, I'd like a firm commitment from you to exploit the valuable tech-nology we found on Alpha 3."

"What?" Salazar frowned.

"After the de la Cruz matter is settled, and I am certain it will be terminated in my favor, I'd like permission to return to Alpha 3 to expedite removal of the technology."

"This is premature, Ralston."

"Not really, Dr. Salazar. It takes time to get even a skeleton expedition put together." One of the committee snickered at the small joke. Ralston gratefully acknowledged and rushed on. "It'll have to be done quickly, in and out before the nova."

"I appreciate your eagerness, Doctor, but . . ."

"All I'm asking is for the committee to give a tentative agreement that, should I be cleared of all charges in the de la Cruz unpleasantness, that I be allowed to return to Alpha 3."

"The telepathic projection device might prove a boon," murmured one of the committee members Ralston didn't recognize. "A financial banquet from which the University might feed for many years."

"Remember the Vegan spider steel," another said. "We missed out on that entirely. We dare not permit another financial opportunity to pass us by."

"Exactly," Ralston gushed. "We owe it to the University to exploit this discovery to the fullest." He had their attention, and he knew what Salazar would say next. Ralston almost laughed when it came.

"Dr. Ralston, I'm sure you'll agree that this discovery is too, uh, significant to be bypassed, should you become mired down in litigation over Citizen de la Cruz's demise."

Ralston surprised Salazar by volunteering what the man hinted at. "If such occurs, I'd be willing to allow others to exploit my find. For the good of the University, of course."

Salazar sat speechless, taken back. Archaeologists, like all researchers, had insufferable egos when it came to protecting their discoveries. Ralston casually passed it over to another simply because he discounted any possible involvement in Yago de la Cruz's death. The wicked smile of triumph crossing Salazar's face couldn't be stopped.

Ralston didn't mind. He needed this agreement, no matter the price in emotional terms.

"Let it be so recorded," said Salazar. He punched a button hidden on the desktop. "There. If there's nothing else, Ralston, please excuse us. We have considerable business to attend to before the public hearing tomorrow." Salazar glanced at a screen out of Ralston's line of sight. "Be here for the opening recitation of preliminary statements at eight hours, sharp."

"Yes, sir." Ralston stood. "Thank you for your confidence. I'm sure we'll be free of this quickly."

He left, not caring that Salazar smirked and that the secretary shot daggers at him with his eyes. Ralston didn't slow until he came to a computer console down the hall in the administration building. While this sort of larceny required quiet for total concentration, Ralston knew he didn't have much time. And to return to his office and the console there might take too long.

One of his students had long ago showed him how minutes from all administration meetings were filed in the University data banks. Every five minutes the voice record dumped into memory. In this way, not more than that five minutes could be lost, should an equipment malfunction occur, yet unwanted or unacceptable testimony could be deleted before permanent entry.

Ralston intercepted the agreement as it went into a buffer. He worked quickly, perhaps too quickly. Sweat beaded his forehead. He might miss editing something significant, but he didn't have the benefit of infinite time to work.

Ralston leaned back and let out a pent-up breath. The effort looked crude to his eye, but then he had been present in the room and knew what really had been said. A deletion here, a changed word there and the computer record now authorized Ralston to leave for Alpha 3, with no mention made of the de la Cruz hearing or sending someone in his stead to the find. Ralston pushed the transmit key and the screen blinked clear, the altered record now a permanent part of University records.

Ralston tried to remember all his student had said about access to other files. He hadn't paid that much attention to what he had considered little more than a prank. Now he struggled to call up the University vidnews account and leave a message. Ralston failed, but he did find a way to send a memo to the reporter who had tried to interview him. He struggled to remember her name. He finally addressed it simply to Citizen Tranton, unable to call back her first name.

"Dr. Ralston," came the voice that dug into his consciousness like a nail pounded into wood.

"What do you want?" he asked harshly. The P'torra moved around to a point where he might view the screen. Ralston hastily punched the transmit button again; the text of the falsified interview now went into the reporter's file. The University vidnews would pick up the story since anything dealing with Ralston constituted front-page news. And Ralston believed that it would be a banner headline because he had emphasized the financial returns possible to the University from the telepathic projector he'd supposedly promised to bring back.

Fail and he might be the butt of jokes. Ralston vowed that wouldn't happen, either—he wouldn't go up in a puff of plasma nor would he let one tidbit of knowledge slip through his fingers.

"You call up to the others of your department of archaeology?" the P'torra asked.

"I've been leaving dirty notes for all the female students." Ralston swung away from the computer console and tried to get past the P'torra. The alien blocked him.

"This I do not understand. How can computer memos be soiled?"

Ralston glanced past the P'torra, expecting to see another mob forming. Wherever the alien went, trouble followed. But not this time. If anything, this worried Ralston even more.

"Excuse me. I've got business elsewhere." When the alien didn't move, Ralston took a half step back. Seeing that the professor might unleash another attack, the P'torra moved. Ralston thought he noticed a slight jerkiness to the movement in the alien's knee. He hoped so. But they were tough. It'd take more than a swift kick to a joint to disable the P'torra.

"Dr. Ralston, we should gather for food-eating and speak to each other."

Ralston almost vomited. The idea of eating with a P'torra nauseated him. He walked out the side door of the administration building, then wandered aimlessly through the campus, no destination in mind. All he wanted to do was walk off the nervousness that had accumulated while he altered the computer files.

The soft green of the grass, the blue skies, and caressing breezes took the edge off his tension, but Ralston knew that he couldn't linger to savor them. If Salazar called back the minutes of the meeting, he'd notice immediately how they had been falsified. Since the only one with a motive for such a crime was Ralston, it wouldn't be hard finding the guilty party.

Ralston couldn't miss the late-night deadline for starring back to Alpha 3. He looked up into the morning sky and saw nothing, but somewhere in a low parking orbit spun the starship that meant his future.

He turned and retraced his steps, then made a sudden right angle turn. Shielded by a row of shrubs Ralston waited. The P'torra came waddling along, head swiveling back and forth on the thick neck as he vainly sought his quarry. Ralston had no idea what the alien wanted, but it wasn't likely to be beneficial.

He considered removing the alien permanently, then immediately discarded the notion. Killing the P'torra might be gratifying, but it only raised the ugly specter of police intervention. They might close down all his possible escape routes, especially if the University vidnews released the story on how Salazar authorized Ralston to return to Alpha 3 immediately.

While he couldn't read it at this distance, he stared across the Quad at one of the vidnews kiosks. All he saw was the slow march of lines up and off the screen top; the words weren't distinct. Ralston hurried on until he topped a rise and looked down at the gymnasium. He hated to involve Druanna Thorkkin but had no other choice now.

Trying not to appear as if he thought everyone on Novo Terra chased him, Ralston went down the hill toward the large building.

"I suppose that will have to keep me happy until you get back," Druanna Thorkkin said. She rolled over in bed and stared at Ralston. He paced to and fro, then stopped and smiled at her. Ralston bent over and lightly kissed her.

"I don't know what I'd do without you, Dru," he said. "You and your optimism."

"What optimism?" she said, sitting up. "I'm a realist. I look at you and what do I see? Someone whose drive won't let him stop until he wins. It comes out when you fence. You're relentless."

"Is that another way of telling me I'm a better fencer than you are?"

"It's *why* you are. I'm quicker, but it doesn't matter. You don't give in. Besides, you owe me money."

Ralston peered out the window of Druanna's small, quaintly

furnished home and saw the sun setting. Less than four hours until the deadline for reaching the starship. By early morning, Novo Terra reckoning, he'd be returning to Alpha 3.

"You set goals well and you've got the tenacity to carry through. This isn't ego-building on my part. It's just the way you are. Don't get me wrong. I like it."

"You don't think Alpha Prime will go nova and turn me into a cinder?" Ralston only half joked.

"It wouldn't dare. Not until you've stripped everything you want from that muddy planet." Druanna rose and began rummaging through her closet. "Can't find a thing. Maybe I ought to get that robot valet I saw advertised on the vid."

"You'd hate it. I tried one and it organized me out of my home. Everything was in its place. Awful," said Ralston.

"For you, that must be purest hell. Your place always looks as if you intend for it to be the primary dig site for archaeologists a thousand years from now. You people do revel in debris, don't you?" She selected and quickly dressed. Ralston watched with appreciation and a little sadness.

Accepting. That summed up Druanna Thorkkin's attitude well. She made no demands, yet she gave willingly. And in that giving lay the true strength of their relationship. Ralston never—quite—dared deny her anything. It wasn't—quite—freely given on his part, but he owed it to her. That always struck him as unfair. Dru deserved more from him. But it wasn't in him to give it.

She accepted that, too.

"You still have that night class?" he asked.

"The medieval lit course? Hardly. Registration for it has been falling off drastically. Who wants to read Hawthorne and Tolstoy and Unamuno when they can read the moderns?"

"You do."

"I'm weird. Just like you. We're of a kind, Michael. Both of us are mired in the past. Your past just happens to be further in the past than mine."

"If you don't have the class, mind taking me for a ride?"

"I'll take you for a ride anytime, bucko," she said.

"Might get nasty."

"I can handle it." From her joking response Ralston knew she didn't believe him. He had never been more serious, however. A hundred things might have betrayed him—a thousand.

He had no idea what sources of information the P'torra had. He didn't even know the alien's motives in making him the scapegoat for the campus unrest. It might go much deeper than trying to eliminate P'torra opposition.

Salazar might have discovered the tampering with the committee minutes. The University vidnews might have already run the story. If Salazar saw that, he'd definitely have the campus security force looking for Ralston.

"You did something pretty outrageous today, didn't you?" asked Druanna.

"You call what we did outrageous? Why, I've heard that on Elysium 2, they . . ."

"You know what I mean, Michael."

He told her how he'd tampered with the records. Druanna smiled broadly and asked, "How did you do it, now? I want to know. This can come in handy."

"I've put Salazar in a bad spot," he said. "It'll look as if he authorized my departure *before* the de la Cruz hearing. If I come back with the telepathy gadget, I'm a hero and they have to give me medals."

"And if you don't, your ass is grass, anyway. Nice move. You could have taught the ancient generals a thing or two, Michael."

"I've studied more than how to rob graves. *Vom Kriege* is one of my favorite books. Can we get going?" He glanced out the window again. Dusk had hardened into night. In the sky he saw a half-dozen slowly moving points. Some were information satellites, others starships in orbit waiting for cargos or passengers. He had no idea which was going to be his ticket back to Muckup.

A pounding on the door startled him.

"No, Michael, not that way," Druanna said when he tried to force open the window. "It's permanently sealed. This way."

"We're not going to be able to hide," he said. "They'll scan the place with IR sensors. Even a single wall between us won't . . ." His voice trailed off when he saw a staircase hidden in one closet and going below ground level. The woman impatiently gestured for him to be quiet. He hurried down the spiraling stairs. Druanna closed the closet door and rushed after him.

"That way. A tunnel out to my flyer."

"How'd you ever come to have this built?" he asked.

"I dug it myself. Pretty good work, eh? See the supports?"

"But why?"

"You pace. I need to be doing something more substantial and more private. So I dig. Got fed up with a garden that kept dying and thought this'd be a positively medieval touch for the house. Keeps me out of the rain, too."

Ralston quickly ascended another spiral staircase and came out in a small shed not five meters from Druanna's flyer. A man stood guard beside it.

"Now what?" she whispered.

Ralston never hesitated. All the combat training given him by the Nex rushed back. He strode out, planted his feet, and drove his fist only a few centimeters—into the man's left kidney. The guard gasped and fell face-forward onto the ground, unconscious before he hit.

"Who does he belong to?" asked Druanna. Ralston jerked her into the flyer. He didn't care. He had to reach the launch site or be left behind.

He seated himself at the controls, warmed up the engine, and complimented Druanna on how well she maintained the machine. He swung the flyer around and sent it quietly following the buried induction cable to the main road. He glanced behind and saw a half-dozen figures rushing from Druanna's home.

He turned the controls to max. The acceleration flattened them in their seats.

"You always were a dangerous one," she said.

"And this is getting too dangerous for you," he said. "Take the controls. Keep it at full speed. You know the Estrellita Launch Bay?"

"The tiny field outside the main port? I think so."

"I have a shuttle pod waiting for me there. When we get near it, I want you to slow down, I'll jump out, then you speed up and just drive around."

"You think they're following us?" She made a motion with her head indicating those who'd been in her home.

"Not a bad working hypothesis," he said. "You decoy them. I'll be off for Alpha 3."

"Some people have all the fun."

"I'll bring back lots of photos."

"How I spent my summer vacation," Druanna said sarcastically. "You never take me anywhere."

"You wouldn't like it on Muckup. Too wet." He leaned over and kissed her. Before she could say another word, he pointed. "There's the turn where I want off."

"This slow enough?"

"Have to do. See you in a few months." With that Ralston threw open the door and heaved himself out. He hit, rolled, and smashed hard against a tree. For several seconds all he heard was the ringing in his ears. He shook himself and got painfully to his feet.

Druanna's flyer had already vanished down the road. At top speed she might already be three or four kilometers distant. He oriented himself and started walking.

Before he'd gone two hundred meters he broke into a run. The resonant hum of at least two flyers broke the stillness of the night. If they had figured out what he was up to, they'd know he was headed for the shuttle launch site. He couldn't risk their continuing on after Druanna's flyer. He ran even faster when he saw the launch lights ahead.

Gasping for breath, Ralston leaned heavily against a shed. Through the pounding of his pulse in his head he heard the magnetic hum of flyers. They hadn't been decoyed away. That was all right with Ralston; that meant Druanna had gotten away cleanly.

Some wind regained, Ralston sprinted hard for the stubby cargo ship sitting in the middle of the launch apron. The gigantic laser beneath it hissed with escaping coolant gases and crackled with the ultrahigh voltages.

"Get it ready for launch," he shouted as he ran. Ralston took a second to look over his shoulder. The first flyer grounded and three men clambered out.

"What's going on?" asked the field tech. "Look, if you're running from the police, forget this launch. I'm not getting paid enough to get myself rehabbed."

"They're not police," gasped Ralston. "University prank. They're supposed to kidnap me as part of an initiation. I'm their archaeology professor."

"Yeah, he'd mentioned you were one of those." The man frowned as he worked through the possibilities. "Then we'll call the police. They shouldn't do that to you. Not unless you want to play along."

"Launch the damned thing!"

"All right, all right. We'll show them. You're going to be in orbit before they know what's happening."

A loud klaxon signaled all off the field. Ralston dived through the door and flopped onto an acceleration couch. The pilot silently waited in the cockpit for takeoff, oblivious to all that went on below.

Ralston screwed his eyes tightly shut, even though it was impossible for him to see the launcher light. The sudden takeoff crushed the air from his still straining lungs. The laser repeatedly fired, hammering against the ceramic refractory base of the shuttle pod. The only sounds Ralston heard were the rush of air past the hull, the pilot's monotone recitation of launch data, and the pounding of his own heart.

When the shuttle's guidance rockets cut in, Ralston knew he'd escaped. Novo Terra would be left behind and Alpha 3's secrets would be unlocked. He tried to relax but found himself too keyed up.

Alpha 3's secrets would be his!

FOURTEEN

"THIS ISN'T WHAT I thought he'd arrange," said Michael Ralston after he had boarded the starship. This vessel was easily twice the size of the one he had starred on previously to Alpha 3.

"A few additional arrangements were made," Leonore Disa told him, smiling. "I thought you might appreciate this more than the garbage can your mysterious friend had arranged."

"He's no friend," Ralston said. "But I paid him good money. You didn't spook him, did you? He's paranoid about anything out of the ordinary happening during a deal."

"Then he'll approve of the change in plans." Leonore gestured that Ralston was to follow her. They went to a lounge area—a lounge!—and peered up at a small vidscreen showing the cockpit where the pilot toiled in preflight checks.

"This isn't possible," Ralston said. "He couldn't have gotten a ship this large." Suspiciously, Ralston asked the woman, "Your father furnished it, didn't he? Does he know?"

"Daddy doesn't know any more than I told him. Which isn't

much. Relax, Michael. This is all legal, unlike that other starship." She pointed to an inset in the screen. A small cargo ship showed in it, hardly more than a dot, even with the electronic magnification.

Before Ralston could say anything, the pilot's voice came over a speaker. "Flight Control's just canceled the cargo ship's launch request. What do you think's on that monstrosity? Some members of that religious cult who go around blowing up churches?"

"That doesn't matter," Leonore said into a small microphone. "What's *not* on it matters more. Hurry with the shift."

"Even if FC tells us to wait?" The pilot's voice quivered with excitement.

"It might be best if you experienced some difficulty hearing such orders," Leonore said, skirting a direct answer. The pilot's face almost glowed at the intrigue and challenge.

"We'll be on Alpha 3 in three weeks," he promised. Ralston watched in fascination as the pilot's hands glided over the controls. A gentle nudge told of acceleration pulling them to a higher orbit.

"This is an Interstellar Computronics ship?" Ralston asked Leonore. "And your father doesn't know what his daughter's doing?"

"Something like that. Don't worry so. You're sounding as if it's not important to get back to Alpha 3."

"Three weeks?"

"This ship is faster than most. Daddy always wanted me to use my own initiative. What'll he do to me, anyway? Spank me? I own fifteen percent of IC, and he knows I'd give him a hard time at the next stockholders' meeting. So relax, Michael. It's all right."

Ralston didn't have it in his heart to complain. The less time in transit, the more time he could spend gathering information on Muckup. That muddy ball spinning through space had such a short lifetime now. He wanted to be its biographer, to find every secret of its people, to know it all!

If some small deceptions had to be made along the way, so be it. Hadn't he already altered University records, released a vidnews story to the effect that Salazar had authorized this return? What was it to him if Leonore lied her way into a faster, more luxurious starship than he could possibly afford through connections who survived at the very fringes of Novo Terran law?

"They've definitely impounded the cargo ship," the pilot said over the speaker. "Something about contraband? Maybe so, yeah, verd, definitely. This is hot. Prepare for preshift maneuvers. Starting sequencing . . . now!"

The ship had attained an orbit at six planetary diameters. Rockets cut in and slammed Ralston back onto his couch. The ship headed into emptiness where the pilot had marked an imaginary takeoff spot. Once there, they would star for Alpha 3.

"How long?" he asked Leonore.

"The pilot's the best. We'll shift within a few hours."

"Good," said Ralston, settling down, knowing this would be the last weight he'd feel for close to a month. But the trip would be a busy one this time. No work on an archaeology textbook that'd never see publication. He had equipment to prepare. And he and Leonore had to work out a schedule to maximize what they could accomplish.

Time pressed in on him. But Ralston smiled. He felt more alive than he had since finding the dioramas. The committee meetings were behind him, confronting de la Cruz's death something to be postponed, all that he hated most either deferred or finished. Everything that lay ahead was what he loved most: discovery.

"Can't he hurry?" Ralston asked. He floated through the lounge area, trailing equipment like a mechanical hydra. He needed several more weeks to finish programming the master supervisor, but he found himself even more anxious to land on Alpha 3's muddy surface.

"He came in on target," Leonore said. She seemed to be able to read the pilot's instruments. Ralston wondered if she might not be a starship pilot herself, but he didn't ask. Too many other things to know, too much else to do.

"Two days?" he pressed.

"I'm certain."

"Citizen Disa," came the pilot's voice. Throughout the three-week trip, the pilot had remained in his quarters. Only twice had Ralston seen him drifting through the ship—he counted these as the peculiar moments. Pilots tended to be clannish and reclusive, never dealing directly with their passengers. Even on the longest trips, those lasting several months, pilots segregated themselves from their passengers.

"Yes?"

"Got a Dr. Bernssen on the com. You want to talk to him?"

"Yes!" Ralston both heard the delighted excitement in Leonore's voice and saw the reaction. Her cheeks flushed and her space-induced paleness vanished.

"What are you doing back here?" came Nels Bernssen's querulous voice. "We're in the middle of a heavy-particle solar storm alert. Might come at any time."

Ralston saw the pilot stiffen at the warning and reach over to tap a detector. The dull amber glow on the instrument's face indicated only moderate danger, he guessed.

"We'll land within a day," Leonore said. "Aren't you glad that I'm back, Nels?"

"No! It's getting dangerous. Radiation levels are up. Solar instability is increasing again. There might be only days left."

Ralston cursed under his breath.

"You're not leaving, are you?"

"Not for a while. But it can't be much longer. Weeks, maybe, days are more likely. You were safe. Why'd you come back?"

"We have work to do, too," she said primly. Ralston saw how irritated Leonore was at the lack of warm reception on Bernssen's part.

"Let me," Ralston said, reaching to the microphone. "Dr. Bernssen, we can't let the discovery go up in a flash of nova, but we're not suicidal, either. If you can give me a guarantee that the star will explode before we can unload and work a few more days, we'll turn around and go back to Novo Terra."

"Do it," said Bernssen.

"You can guarantee we'll never get even a few days' further exploration done?"

"Hell, I can't *guarantee* that, but the star's going to blow soon. Why the hell else do you think *I'm* here?"

"Please let us know when you're preparing to leave. We'll depart then, too."

"Leonore's going to be in danger," Bernssen protested.

"So are you, Nels. Your work's important. Mine is, too!" the woman said angrily.

Bernssen mumbled something that got lost in the heavy solar storm—induced static. "Land, then," he said. "I've got to tell Dr. Rasmussen about it, though."

"Please do," said Ralston. "We'll want to keep in close communication." Ralston relinquished the microphone and kicked away a few feet.

The lowered air pressure robbed him of the words Leonore spoke, but he saw her lips moving. He read, "I love you, Nels." She then tossed the microphone away and went back to work on one of their ultrasonic cleaning heads, as if nothing had happened.

But Ralston saw that the glow in her cheeks remained.

"You're out of your chinging minds," complained Nels Bernssen. The burly solar physicist heaved one of the bulky instrument-laden crates aside where a small robot worked to pull off the sides and ready the equipment inside.

"Thanks for helping us, Nels. I appreciate it." Leonore stood on tiptoe and lightly kissed him on the cheek.

"You're going to get yourselves killed, and all for what? A few lousy pictures that wouldn't be of interest to anybody at the University, even in a tridee play."

"This isn't fiction. It's an entire culture. We can't let it be destroyed."

"It's all going up, no matter what we do."

"It's important," insisted Leonore, pausing to wipe sweat from her eyes. "Just as your work's important."

Ralston knew that line of logic would fail. To Bernssen, nothing could be as important. Ralston had to smile to himself. Each researcher thought their particular line of inquiry was the most vital. Ego entered into it, but often that fed genius and produced breakthroughs. Intuition as much as logic produced the important discoveries. He had been lucky with this one. Luck. Intuition. Logic. All elements of good research. And maybe the most important part, the researcher's absolute conviction in the project.

Ralston looked up at the sky. Through the fluffy clouds forming up for the afternoon's rainstorm, he saw shimmering veils that floated and vanished, darted about and formed thicker blankets in what ought to be clear sky.

"So you noticed it, eh?" asked Bernssen.

"What is it?"

"You've never seen an aurora?"

"In the middle of the day?"

"That," said Bernssen grimly, "is what worries all of us. The electrical activity in the atmosphere is growing more and more intense each day. At night, the sky's lit up like a neon sign. Pretty, when you can see it through the clouds."

"Did Dr. Rasmussen get the block I sent over this morning after we landed?"

Bernssen nodded. "The pilot delivered it. What's in it?"

"An explanation for all this, I think," Ralston said.

Bernssen didn't reply. He would hardly believe an archaeologist held such knowledge.

"It's all chaotic behavior," Ralston went on. "Induced, I think, by something that passed by Alpha 3 over ten thousand years ago. The weather's different now, the native populace died out, their sun's exploding."

Bernssen looked on all this as another proof that Ralston had become quite insane.

"Stay out of the direct sunlight, if you can," Bernssen advised. "The proton storms that hit now and again get through even the atmosphere and give quite a jolt. We'll give you warning on those so you can get underground. Justine thinks the atmosphere will boil off before too much longer."

"All the more reason to get to work," Ralston said. He stared at the master controller. The complex device could drive a thousand different machines. They had only a few dozen. He flipped the switch. Grinding noises from outside the plastic shelter told of the automated collector equipment beginning operation. Ralston glanced outside and saw the automated probes vanishing through the copper door.

But for all the spectroscopic analyses, for all the photos and probings, the real work lay with him and Leonore. The dioramas "spoke" only to the human mind.

Ralston waited for Leonore to bid her farewells to Bernssen in private before he went outside to join her. Bernssen's land crawler vanished behind a brown cloud of mud and spray and soon passed beyond limits of hearing.

Leonore sighed. "He's really upset with me for coming back. Nels said that the weather patterns are totally unpredictable now. No matter how much their meteorologist studies the satellite photos, he can't guess what'll happen for longer than a few hours."

"Chaos is accelerating," Ralston mused. "It's almost as if it were a virus that's finally spread throughout the body, destroying all systems."

"Or an echo that's finally returned," she said. "As much as your theory bothers me, it seems to fit what we know of Alpha 3. Their decline came too fast."

"The epilepsy epidemic is a strong argument that I'm right. Such an affliction couldn't have been caused by an ordinary disease and gone undetected. The evidence points to the natives as being fairly advanced in medicine."

"It's almost as if it were a capricious act of God," Leonore said. "He reached out His finger and touched the world, and its people died. And then its biome died. And then the sun."

"I think I interested Westcott enough in the problem to give it a few minutes' thought. He'll be trying to track the path of whatever it is that passed by. A device, I'm calling it. I refuse to believe such a chaotic field might exist naturally."

"Do you think it was a weapon that got away from the natives?"

"I think it's much older. The dioramas we've examined show them to be at peace for some time. I think the device came through on a more cosmic journey. I hope Westcott can pinpoint where it might have started—and where it went."

"Went?" Leonore's question hung in the air.

"I don't think it stayed here. It went on. Somewhere."

Leonore looked up into the overcast sky and shuddered. Lightning bolts of unimaginable proportions leaped from cloud to cloud and the first hints of rain began, virgas trailing down from the sky and drawing lacy fingers across the muddy terrain. She squinted at the sudden flashes, then turned to the supervisor and made a few minor adjustments.

"Static electricity's a problem," she said, not wanting to confront the idea of chaos forcing itself on any world she knew. "But we can compensate. Got it grounded pretty well."

Ralston nodded. They had set the data collection equipment in motion. Now they—he—had to do the rest. Ralston silently gestured for Leonore to pick up her camera and join him underground.

He'd have to selectively pick which dioramas to enter and

which to avoid. After all, Ralston wanted as much information as possible—and without ending up like the natives. Or Yago de la Cruz.

"The weather's driving me wild," Leonore Disa said. "How do you stand it?"

"I don't try," Ralston said. "I ignore it. He weaved from lack of sleep and from entering and experiencing twelve of the dioramas in the past planetary day. For a little over seventeen hours he had been swept back in time to an alien world, a world filled with birdlike natives and strange rituals and thought patterns—and he had *lived* their lives and learned the lessons they taught to their young. Ralston wobbled a bit, then sank down. One of the supervisor's data probes beeped. He moved out of its way. It hummed in contentment and entered the diorama he had just vacated.

"It's not getting any of the impressions I did, is it?" he asked. Ralston closed his eyes and wished for a month's sleep. But too much remained to be done. The threat of the nova hung over him like a sharp sword on a weakening thread.

Leonore didn't have to check the supervisor block circuits to know the answer. She shook her head.

Ralston looked along the corridor. Hundreds more of the dioramas remained. He increasingly felt the pressures of time. Justine Rasmussen had called twice to check on them, to urge them to leave. Nels Bernssen had called three more times. Ralston appreciated their solicitude but hated the interruptions.

The last call, however, had worn at him the most. Dr. Rasmussen claimed that the weather patterns had turned completely chaotic. Some sections between the solar physics site and the underground museum had been flooded to the point that travel might be impossible, even with the crawlers.

"There's so many to go," Leonore said, almost wistfully. "Can we make any progress at all?"

"You're still worried about lingering effects, aren't you?" he asked. Ralston thought his graduate assistant had summed it up well when she said that echoes of the cause had finally returned and were now being heard. Echoes of chaos, he mused. The primary cause of such disorder had passed ten thousand years ago, killing Alpha 3's populace, but the final result only now became apparent.

Ralston reached out and a static charge leaped from his finger to one of the IR probes. The robot flinched, as if it were human. He knew the master supervisor corrected current levels internally in the probe to keep the data uncompromised.

"I think that the natives carried the seeds of destruction within them. Whatever caused the epilepsy in de la Cruz must have been present in their population, also. Their telepathic projector transmitted it—can still transmit it."

"Pick the wrong scene to examine and you'll end up like de la Cruz. Not a cheerful notion," said Leonore.

"Any luck on removing the scenes and maintaining the projection?" The primary task, as he saw it, was not to personally examine as many of the dioramas as he could but to find a method of removing them intact and keeping them workable. The IC starship in orbit around Muckup had ample cargo space for dozens of the dioramas.

"Some," said Leonore. "The supervisor is still analyzing the strengths of various EM fields. Unusual intensity readings point to a possible mechanism being in the walls and in the figures themselves. We..."

The beeping of the com unit interrupted her. Almost angrily, Ralston grabbed it and snapped, "What is it?"

"Michael?" came Justine Rasmussen's voice. The interference caused by the lightning, the intense aurora, and the solar radiation bathing their com satellite made her sound weak, vulnerable. Ralston softened somewhat. The fatigue wore on him as much as his frustration at not making more progress.

"Yes, Justine?" Since she'd called on a first-name basis, he'd respond similarly.

"We have troubles here. Like that you found in the native population. Like the student's."

"Epilepsy?"

"Six of our techs are down. The automedic has them heavily sedated. One broke his thigh bone thrashing around."

"Did they come across another museum? Like the one here?" Ralston had visions of the physicists blundering about in the dioramas, experiencing the long-lost culture as Yago de la Cruz had done—and dying because of it.

"No." That answer chilled Ralston even more. The echoes from the past came back even stronger. He almost heard them creating chaos all around. "They tend to be the staff on planet the longest, however. Most of us are relative newcomers compared to them."

"I've been working on the assumption that the effects of the chaos device remained, even though the device itself went on," he explained. "The most obvious effects are the unpredictable weather and Alpha Prime going nova."

"It's a radiation rather than a poison? Can we shield against it?"

She approached the problem as a physicist. Block it out; keep working; study it later under controlled conditions. Chaos followed no rules.

"Is Bernssen all right?" Ralston asked, seeing Leonore's anguished face.

"Nels is as strong as a bull. Nothing stops him," came the gratifying answer. "But I have ordered a termination of all experiments over the next three days. Four days from now we lift for orbit. Conditions then will determine if we stay any longer or star for Novo Terra immediately. I thought you should know."

"Thank you, Justine. Is there anything we can do?"

"Our automedic isn't equipped to handle six at once. Can Nels bring three of the, uh, victims over so yours can care for them? You might have to shuttle them to your starship if things turn suddenly worse."

Ralston knew that conditions could only deteriorate.

"Bring them over. We can use Bernssen's help shutting down our own work."

"Michael, no!"

Ralston motioned Leonore to silence. The signal broke up continually and he strained to hear Justine Rasmussen.

". . . over right away. Look for him within a few hours. The mud plains are especially treacherous now."

"All right, Justine. Thank you again for the warning."

Ralston clicked off the com unit and sat, feeling curiously drained. All their work had been for nothing. The cloak of chaos had descended and hid knowledge from his eyes now.

"Michael, something's wrong."

"What?" He sat up, instantly alert. It took him several seconds to realize what it was. He relaxed again, as much as he could. "The rain's stopped. That's all."

"But the storm just started."

He tried to keep from screaming at her. What else did Leonore expect from chaotic behavior? It started, it stopped—at random. Their macroscopic world had become as indeterminate as the quantum mechanical domain. Anything might happen. Anything.

FIFTEEN

"THE SKY'S ON fire," Leonore Disa said in a hushed tone. She stood at the base of the stairs leading to the alien museum, staring up at the dancing veils of lacy, electrical aurora. "The last time it was only white. Now I see reds and even blues and greens."

"Heavy ionization," said Nels Bernssen. He moved beside her, one arm circling her waist.

"It's so beautiful. I can hardly believe that this is the final performance."

"Curtain's coming down," agreed Bernssen. "You and Ralston about got your equipment packed away?"

"I told him it'd be all right to leave the supervisor," she said. "Daddy'll never miss it, especially if he gets some cut of the profits off the find. Michael agreed that since it was, in a way, IC's grant that got us back here in time, the company ought to have a minority share in any profits."

"Does that mean you've figured out the telepathy gadget? That'll bring in a planet's ransom in licensing fees."

"The licensing fees belong to the University. The monetary split will get nasty before everyone's finished. And no, we're still no closer to figuring it out, but Michael thinks he has a way of getting the information. He won't say how."

Leonore looked out at the desolate mud flats where they had packed a half dozen of the dioramas. They had taken tridee photos, run the analyzer for precise locations, had put all their data through the supervisor, done everything within their power to record in the hope of reconstructing on Novo Terra. But Leonore held little hope for that. The natives of Alpha 3 had been more clever than they. If only a full-scale expedition had been possible!

Engineers might have torn apart the displays and found the answer. Or xenopsychologists skilled with alien thought. Or any of a score of other researchers. She and Ralston were experts at uncovering, not figuring out how these devices worked.

And always the specter of the nova hung over them like the angel of death. There simply hadn't been adequate time to explore, to think, to try theory after theory until truth became obvious. No good science would be done on Muckup.

"It's starting to rain again," she said, pulling away from the museum door as a gust of wind stung her face. "Let's go see if Michael needs us."

"I want to check on the others," Bernssen said, worry creeping into his voice. "The automed doesn't seem to do very much for them. It pumps in tranquilizers but little else."

"If they've come down with what affected de la Cruz, there'll be neurological damage that can't heal." Leonore swallowed hard. "If we don't leave Muckup, we might all end up that way."

"How cheerful," Bernssen said, worry giving a brittle edge to his voice.

"How much longer?" came Ralston's shouted question. "As much as an hour?"

"The shuttle pod's ready to go within the hour," said Bernssen. "The last of the diorama crates needs to be loaded. The robots are working on them now, but the rain might slow them down. Call it two hours until launch."

"Good. As soon as the robots are finished with the important stuff, get them all here. I want the supervisor's full attention directed on this single diorama." Ralston pointed to one with four figures huddled around a low table. All stared at a blank sheet on the table as if it contained the wisdom of the universe.

"What's so important about this one?" asked Bernssen.

"Maybe nothing, but I'm betting everything on it being pivotal. The later ones"—Ralston pointed down the corridor to his right—"were obviously constructed within a few years of their eventual collapse. I feel those hold the most danger for anyone entering."

"Like de la Cruz," Leonore said in a whisper so low only Bernssen heard.

"This one seems to have been constructed after the object— what I'm calling the chaos device—passed but before the decline became obvious to everyone."

"You make it sound as if the people in this sideshow knew what it was," said Bernssen.

"I think that's true."

"But there's not enough time to study it. There are four figures. That," said Leonore, mentally calculating, "might be as long as ten hours of telepathic lessons."

Robots clanked down the corridor, some dripping chunks of mud. Ralston no longer cared. Within weeks or even days, the entire planet would be superheated vapor. Preservation of his find no longer mattered in the face of such cosmic catastrophe.

"All here?" Ralston asked. His face paled as he considered the danger in what he was about to do. He wobbled slightly and caught himself against the wall.

"Ready for dismantling, Michael." Leonore looked up from the remote panel. "Are you feeling all right?"

"Yes. Now listen carefully and don't argue. I want the entire display removed intact. Blast a hole through the roof and lift it out in one piece. Load it onto the shuttle immediately. Then I want you to gather anything important—don't miss a single block circuit!—and then get yourself and Bernssen's colleagues onto the shuttle."

"We can start them right now, if you like," said Bernssen. "That'd speed up the transfer."

Ralston wasn't thinking straight. All he wanted was assurance that this particular diorama reached orbit and the IC starship cargo bay intact.

"Do it however you like."

Leonore made a single adjustment to the remote panel. Outside, robots began shifting the anesthetized victims of the chaos device to the shuttle.

"You make it sound as if you won't be able to supervise," said Leonore.

"I've left my notes in the analyzer, if anything happens. I'm sure they won't blame you."

"What are you going to do?" Leonore asked sharply.

"As soon as I enter the diorama, begin removal."

"With you in it? Are you crazy?" Bernssen's shock turned his face into a flowing putty mask of confusion.

"I don't want to kill myself, but this means too much not to make one last try. If I activate the telepathic projection circuit, then you move the entire diorama, perhaps we can keep it intact until we get back to Novo Terra."

"Michael, this is ridiculous."

Leonore's protest fell on deaf ears. Ralston stepped forward, chose his subject, turned and assumed that posture. He reeled a bit as the mental projection took hold. He sensed a substantial difference in the "texture" of the thoughts, a definite indication of change from the earliest dioramas. Then he became lost in arcane discussions and melted into his role.

"He's lost it," said Bernssen. "I'll get him out of there and . . ."

"No!"

"Leonore, we can't ship him back like this. It might kill him."

"What's he got to lose, Nels? His life? That's a small price to pay if he learns how this device works. And if he returns to Novo Terra without it, what are they going to do to him?"

"The psychologists would get him," Bernssen said in a choked voice. "If they find him guilty of de la Cruz's death, they'll wipe his mind and rehab him."

"Which would you want?" Leonore asked.

In answer, Bernssen turned, pushed her away from the remote control panel, and began changing the settings. "I'm better at this than you are. More practice. And I've been here longer to learn to really hate the mud."

His words were drowned out by the sound of ultrasonic diggers working their way through the roof of the alien museum. In less than five minutes the diggers had chewed away a hole large enough to lift the entire diorama onto the rainy surface.

"Shouldn't we protect it from the rain?" asked Leonore.

"Being done now. The electrostatic field is being scrambled by the lightning and upper atmosphere ionization, but it ought to repel most of the rain." Bernssen played the remote like an organ, producing whines and hisses and hums from the toiling robots.

The robots in the corridor had been working on the dioramas to either side of the one where Ralston stood frozen, his eyes wide and his throat trembling as if he subvocalized. Another ten minutes passed before the robots demolished the dioramas around their target. Leonore cringed at the wantonness of that work, but she knew it was necessary.

Ralston's life might depend on it.

"We're ready to lift it now," said Bernssen. Leonore couldn't tell if sweat beaded his forehead or if raindrops blew through the roof and ran down his face. "Here it goes."

Leonore clapped hands over her ears and twisted away. Torn metal screamed as the robots lifted the entire scene. Bernssen worked constantly now, adjusting, making certain that the robots did not apply torque to the floor of the diorama.

"Get to the surface," Bernssen yelled over the whine of machinery pushed to its limits. "Make certain the robots aren't getting mired down."

Leonore raced to the stairs and hurried to the surface. The rain had slowed, leaving veils of fog intermixed with the sporadically falling drops. She began working as hard as any of the metal servants. The mud caused them to slide and turn out of position. She used manual overrides to correct, shouted instructions to Bernssen, worked as hard as if she lifted Ralston's diorama on her own back.

It finally slid away from the hole. The shrieks of tortured metal died. One robot fell to its side, treads spinning in opposite directions. Leonore turned it off. She felt as if she buried a friend. Patting it on the side of its block circuit case, Leonore quietly said, "Thank you," then turned her attention to the others.

"I'll use the main panel now," came Bernssen's voice. He had shut down the remote and worked directly from the master supervisor. The entire diorama began sliding over the mud flats and toward the spot where the exhibit might be loaded into the shuttle.

Two hours later, Bernssen and Leonore hugged one another, their job finished. "He's still in the diorama," Leonore said. "I put an analyzer in with him to monitor heart rate and respiration."

"Ralston's alive?"

"So far he's not showing any different response than in the other dioramas."

Bernssen began laughing. And the laughter soared to heights beyond his imagining, out of control, past human redemption. He heard Leonore's shouts as if they came from the end of infinity. Then the world went dark around him.

Nels Bernssen screamed and thrashed about. Disoriented, he struck out and found nothing.

"Calm down, Nels. Please!" Leonore's anguished voice returned a semblance of control to the physicist, and convinced him he hadn't suddenly died. He forced open one eye, then the other. For a few seconds he didn't recognize his surroundings.

It slowly penetrated. Weightlessness. He was in orbit. In a starship. Not his expedition's—Leonore's. Webbing held him so that he couldn't float off and hurt himself.

"What happened?" he asked. His voice turned gravelly in his throat and his mouth felt like a desert, complete with rocks and sand and slithering reptiles.

"You went a little crazy."

"Am I all right?" Fear welled within him. He panicked as much as Ralston had at the idea of the psychologists rehabilitating him.

"The ship's automedic says so. Some evidence of synaptic disorder, but that's beyond its capacity to diagnose."

"The chaos?""

Leonore nodded.

Bernssen flexed his fingers and toes, moved slowly, and decided he had full control of his extremities. He unfastened the web restraints; Leonore didn't try to stop him. He took that as a good sign.

"What about Ralston?"

"Still in the hold. I didn't want to disturb him until you could help get him out."

"You trust me not to go spacy on you?" He only half joked. He saw her expression and knew she trusted him with her life.

"Got to check in with Justine. She'll think I ran out on her."

"No need to worry over that. Here's a com unit. The pilot's been talking with your expedition pilot." She handed it to Bernssen.

"Call through to Justine Rasmussen, please," he said. Heavy static caused Bernssen to jerk the unit away. His ears rang from the onslaught. "You there, Justine?"

"We're off planet, Nels. You get away?"

"Verd. What's happening with our star?"

"It's got indigestion bad," came the answer. "We've sent out probes toward Novo Terra via rocket with automatic trips to shift them back as soon as the first wavefront hits. Don't know if it'll work, but we've got no choice. Our pilot says leave now or not at all. His equipment is showing anomalous readings due to radiation levels."

"What of our probes?"

"The ones into the star have all failed. No reason. They died long before they should have."

"Like Chen's did on the 1054," mumbled Bernssen, remembering what Ralston had told him.

"What?"

"Never mind, Justine. I hate to leave, but I think you're right. Alpha 3's ready to go bang."

"See you back on Novo Terra," the project leader said.

"Good luck, yourself." Bernssen turned off the com unit, glad to be rid of the incessant background static. To the pilot he said, "Get us back to Novo Terra. We may not have much time."

"Got to boost for at least a day. You know that, Doc. We got the time?"

"We'd better. There's no way of outrunning the wavefront from a nova. It'll be coming at us at the speed of light."

The pilot began his preflight preparations.

"Can't we just shift from here?" asked Leonore. "I know you're not supposed to do it within a half-dozen planetary diameters, but this isn't going to hurt anyone below."

"We need the proper velocity to start the shift," said Bernssen. "If we hit shift speed but aren't aimed right, we'll end up in some out-of-the-way spot; if we aren't up to speed but are aimed right, we'll fall short. So velocity is very important."

"The latter sounds better than going out in a flash," said Leonore.

"Not if we ran out of air before we could recompute and shift a second time. These are precise calculations." He snorted. "That's why the pilots stay so aloof. They don't want to get involved with their passengers and maybe miss something. That's just superstition, of course, but they believe it—so it's true."

Bernssen felt better putting his arms around Leonore and holding her close.

"Let's get Dr. Ralston out of the diorama," she said finally. "I don't like the idea of just leaving him there. Something might happen when we star back."

"There's no telling where that projector's power comes from," agreed Bernssen. "Hate to permanently imprint him with the alien history lesson and burn out everything else in his head. That'd be as bad as rehabbing him."

They floated through a door and down the central axis to the cargo bays. At Leonore's request, the pilot had kept them at the same pressure as the rest of the ship. When they got Ralston out, the pilot could reduce pressure to only a fraction of a bar and give them that much more fresh air.

"Madre de Dios," murmured Bernssen. "He looks just like one of the statues."

Leonore moved around the hold, looking at Ralston from different angles. She hated to admit how close Bernssen's description came to reality. Ralston stood with that strange set to his jaw. His throat muscles still worked, as if he swallowed constantly, and his gray eyes were glassy and unfocused. But Leonore felt a sense of life within the man, as if he understood he had achieved all he'd hoped.

"How do we get him free?" asked Bernssen.

"I've never just walked in and pulled him out. I don't know if the field would affect me, too." She longed to try it, to experience what only Ralston—and Yago de la Cruz—had. The life of an alien unfolded for her intimate perusal pushed archaeology past the traditional boundaries and into unexplored territory. And Leonore wanted to be a part of that exciting pioneering effort, to feel the alien thoughts slide into her mind, take her back centuries, and instruct her as the young of Alpha 3 must have been.

"Let me try this." Bernssen swung a short length of rope and let it whip out to curl around Ralston's leg. A swift yank staggered Ralston, bringing him to his knees. For a moment his eyes failed to focus, but wonder slowly replaced the stupe-fied expression.

"I did it," he said softly. Louder, "I did it! The diorama is still functioning!"

Leonore helped her professor to his feet. His knees trembled and the paleness gave him the aspect of a corpse, but his triumph wasn't to be denied.

"We did it! Salazar will have to roll over and play dead now. The Alpha 3 find is the most significant ever!"

"Are you sure the sideshow gadget still works?" asked Bernssen. "You might have been a sort of human feedback circuit. Take you out and it dies."

"No, it can't be that way. I won't permit it to be that way!" Ralston jerked free of Leonore and stepped back into the dior-ama, taking another position. The familiar rictus took control and froze him into an attentive statue. Bernssen retrieved him once more using his makeshift lariat.

"Still works, eh?" Bernssen said.

Ralston's immense smile told the story. He grinned even more when he said, "I chose well. The history lesson in this diorama tells of—"

A raucous warning alarm cut him off. Over the cacophony came the pilot's anxious voice, "Get out of the cargo hold and into webbing. I'm depressurizing for immediate acceleration."

"What's going on?" demanded Ralston.

Neither Leonore nor Bernssen had any idea. As fast as they could, they pulled their way up the central shaft and into the lounge area. As they strapped down, Ralston flipped on the com unit. The datascreen showing the cockpit had already been turned on.

"What's wrong?" Ralston asked the pilot.

"Bad radiation surges. We're getting fried in orbit. If I try lifting us to a higher orbit before vectoring off for a shift, we'll be exposed even longer. We just passed behind the planet. Got to blast hard for our shift point. No time to talk."

Ralston watched the man working feverishly. Behind him he heard Leonore and Bernssen quietly talking.

Bernssen called forward, "I checked the remote probes I put outside on the ship. He's not exaggerating about radiation levels. The hull's protected us from a bad burn, but we can't last too long. The star's pre-nova. We may not have the time to get away."

"We will," Ralston said more confidently than he felt. "Do you have an analyzer working on the star now?"

"Of course. That supervisor getting left behind is a loss. Could have really used it, but we have enough analyzers around to gather the data I need. That Rayleigh-Taylor instability had worsened, over a fifty percent density difference in the inversion layer. That must be building up pressure internally. The sun's going to superheat, then explode past the denser material."

The pilot applied even more acceleration and slammed them back into their couches. Ralston changed the screen to show Alpha 3. A catch came to his throat as he looked down on the nightside of the planet. Brilliant auroral prominences arched outward, seemingly coming from Alpha 3's surface. Intense lightning flashes illuminated thousands of hectares of the normally dark landscape, turning it into momentary noon. Ralston imagined what the conditions must be on Muckup's surface now. Rain storms of unending intensity, winds strong enough to slash the flesh from human bones, the lightning that almost blinded, the very air coming alive with static discharge.

Alpha 3 died before his eyes. And along with it went virtually all of the avian civilization that had once flourished there.

Virtually all.

Ralston threw up his arms to shield his eyes when a hundred lightning flashes hit simultaneously.

"Put the damned filter on," came the pilot's querulous voice. "There. Mark 3 polarizer on. And don't try to get a view of the sun at all. Burn your optic nerves out all the way to your brainstem."

"I'll get good enough photos," came Bernssen's voice. "When we get back to Novo Terra, I'll show them to you."

Ralston nodded. He couldn't take his eyes off Alpha 3. The radiation storms smashing into the sunward side must have reached titanic proportions by now. And as soon as they passed from the planetary shield, they, too, would bear the full brunt of that mad burning.

"Keep arms and legs in tight. *Here we gooooo!*"

The acceleration caused Ralston to black out. When he fought back to consciousness, he thought he'd gone blind. It took several seconds to realize that the external camera viewing Alpha 3 had burned out. He switched back to the cockpit. The pilot strained against the invisible bonds he applied to them all.

"We're gonna make it. We are," the pilot said. Ralston thought he was trying to convince himself rather than his passengers. "That damned star's a goner." Muscles rippled across the visible portion of the pilot's arm as he reached out to touch another control.

The additional acceleration pinned Ralston as surely as if glasteel bonds had been applied. Through half-hooded eyes he saw the pilot cross himself. Ralston succumbed to the pressure against his chest. Mercifully, he blacked out again, his last thoughts on fierce fifty-thousand-degree Kelvin prominences from the star creeping up slowly on them.

SIXTEEN

MICHAEL RALSTON SCREAMED, his world locked in a nightmare of exploding light, searing heat, and infinite falling.

Falling?

He fought to regain his senses. The harder he struggled, the more tangled he became. Finally forcing himself to look, Ralston saw that the restraining webbing on the couch had come loose; he had become entangled to the point where circulation in his right arm had been cut off. He clumsily pulled himself free, then floated a few centimeters above the couch and marveled that he was still alive.

They had all survived.

Behind him, Leonore Disa tried to restore consciousness to Nels Bernssen. The physicist hadn't been properly strapped into his couch. From the unnatural angle of his right leg, Ralston guessed the man had one and perhaps several broken bones. Only weightlessness kept him from intense pain.

"I'll get the automedic," Ralston said.

"I sent a signal to it already," Leonore told him. "Wait a

few minutes. It's still tending the others. We didn't have them fastened down too well, either."

Ralston wiped the sweat from his forehead and his hand came away wet and red. He started, then relaxed. His head hurt like a son of a bitch, but the wounds were superficial. His vision wasn't blurred, no ringing in his ears, and he felt... alive.

"I've done what I can for Nels," the woman said. She kicked against one of the couches and arrowed forward to Ralston. "Let me take care of that gash on your head. Something must have come flying through the lounge. I picked up a few scratches myself. We should have tied things down better."

Ralston winced when she applied an astringent. Leonore frowned at the wound, took the tail of his shirt and placed it directly over the wound.

"Press hard. Good. The automed will be done soon enough."

Ralston decided it didn't matter if his shirt got any bloodier. It was ready for the disposal.

"What about the pilot?"

"He's all right. He was ready for the acceleration."

"Are we all right?"

Leonore laughed. "We must be. Wait a minute." She went to the com unit and turned it on. The pilot's off-key singing came through. Leonore arched one eyebrow, as if saying, "See? We're fine."

Ralston called out, "What's our status?"

"That you, Doc? We made it off, right on the point. Good work, if I do say so."

"The star went nova?"

"Can't say but it sure looked like it was trying hard. We got a few fried circuits but nothing dangerous. I evacuated the cargo hold. Hope you don't mind. Didn't want any radiation leaking in, then ionizing the atmosphere there. Cascades like hell, you know."

Ralston swallowed hard. Would the airlessness affect his diorama? He hoped not.

"We're on course for Novo Terra?"

"What's wrong? You didn't want to go there? Of *course* we're on course for Novo Terra. I'm the damnedest, best pilot that ever lifted from a planet." The pilot went back to singing his bawdy ballad about shoreleave on a pleasure planet. Ralston flipped off the unit, glad for the silence.

"We made it," he said. "We really did." He let the shock work its way through his body then. The danger had passed and they were on their way home.

Back to Novo Terra. Back to the University of Ilium. And Salazar's committee and the de la Cruz family.

Ralston wondered if he had only traded one danger for another.

"The automedic's working on Nels," said Leonore. "I'll have it check you out next."

"Uh, thanks."

"We succeeded, Michael," she said softly. "It's all over."

"Over," he repeated dully. All Ralston could think of was the reception he'd get from Salazar.

"Is it safe?" demanded Leonid Disa. The chief executive officer and chairman of the board of Interstellar Computronics peered at the display skeptically. He heaved his huge belly up and braced it against the edge of the conference table as if readying himself for flight. "I'm not killing myself when the vidnews cameras come in."

"It's safe," Dr. Salazar assured him. "I've personally tried it. The experience is . . . unique."

Disa looked at his daughter, who nodded, then at Ralston. The archaeology professor said, "I've entered dozens of the dioramas with no ill effect."

"What of this de la Cruz boy?"

"That was an unfortunate accident," spoke up Salazar. "We are going to be in litigation over it for some time, I'm afraid. That will, of course, slow development of this find, but . . ."

Leonid Disa snorted and boldly stepped into the diorama Ralston had retrieved from Alpha 3. The man's expression froze and his eyes glassed over. Forty minutes later, he sagged slightly and stumbled from the alien scene.

"That's the damnedest, most remarkable thing I've ever experienced. Think of the possibilities. Schools. Military training. My company can do a complicated briefing in a fraction of the time it takes now. IC is proud to have sponsored the expedition that brought this back, Dr. Salazar."

"But the University owns it, Citizen Disa." Salazar's smooth reply told Ralston that this had been well thought out and had been decided they owned it since Ralston was an employee.

"You're forgetting where the equipment and money came from. And that was my daughter out there risking her life to bring this back." Leonid Disa shook his head. "IC owns this, Doctor."

"The terms of Dr. Ralston's employment preclude such an arrangement," said Salazar.

"A shame." Disa shook his head.

"Yes," agreed Salazar, delighted that the IC chairman had relented so easily. "But your quitclaim of the process will provide both financial and technical support for the University."

"I didn't mean IC was giving up the telepathy transmitter," said Disa. "I meant it was a shame that IC has to retract all its funding for this school. What's that total this year, Dr. Salazar?"

From the way Salazar turned pale, Ralston guessed it amounted to a sizable sum.

"Of course," said Salazar, trembling, "the University needs a corporate partner to properly develop and market this machine. IC might be the appropriate company."

"We'll license it." Disa named a ridiculously small sum. Salazar started to protest, then changed his mind.

"The lawsuit over Citizen de la Cruz's unfortunate accident . . ." Salazar said.

"We'll see about settling that. I know the de la Cruzes. Money-hungry upstarts. They'd sell their immortal souls if it fattened their credit balance enough. IC wants this, Dr. Salazar. We want it badly."

"Doctor, the newsers," came the worried secretary's voice. "Should I allow them in?"

"At once. Don't keep the vidnews waiting," Salazar said with gusto, again in his element.

Ralston thought he might be sick. Since they'd returned to Novo Terra, everything had been taken from his control. Salazar had pounced on the working diorama like a carnivore hungry for a meal. Still, Ralston hadn't minded too much. Salazar had postponed the proceedings against him in the de la Cruz death—and Ralston saw that Leonid Disa might take care of that matter completely.

Ralston sighed. It'd be good to return to a more routine schedule—and to pursue what he had learned on Alpha 3.

"Citizens," spoke up Salazar, "we are here today to announce the discovery of a device that will revolutionize education." Salazar went on to briefly describe the telepathic projector's discovery, function, and potential.

"Dr. Salazar, is it true that this device was whisked away from Alpha 3 just minutes before its star went nova?" The newser motioned to bring cameras in closer for the reply.

"It is. One of our very own graduate students, Leonore Disa, was responsible. She is the daughter of the chairman of Interstellar Computronics, and, uh, co-sponsor of this expedition." In a voice almost too low to hear, Salazar added, "She worked under the tutelage of Michael Ralston of our University."

"Citizen Disa, comments?" The newser elbowed Salazar out of the way. Leonore tried to speak, to give Ralston the credit for the discovery. When her replies didn't jibe with what the newser wanted, he quickly turned to Leonid Disa. The crusty industrialist had dealt with the news before; he gave them curt, slightly belligerent answers. They focused fully on him.

Salazar cut in. "We have begun intensive investigation of the mechanisms. Our Dr. Binton, head of the University engineering department, will be in charge."

"Binton?" asked Ralston in a low voice. "How'd he get into this?"

Leonore shrugged. "Salazar must have thought Binton had better camera presence than you."

"He ought to. All he does is lecture at women's clubs and write articles on how microwaves are your friend."

"Don't, Michael. Being bitter isn't going to solve anything."

He saw that Leonore was right. He'd been let off the hook and ought to be happy, but the discovery of a lifetime had slipped through his fingers. The engineering department now took full credit for the telepathic projector—or as much as Leonid Disa would let them. The elder Disa wanted his daughter to receive full credit for the discovery.

Ralston wasn't inclined to argue that point. Leonore had furnished the starship, the expensive equipment supervisor, and the personal support that had made it possible to recover the diorama from Muckup. Without her and her father's money, Ralston would have been left with nothing except headaches.

"Can we get away from this?" he asked her.

She pointed to a side door in the conference room. No one noticed their leaving. Binton, Salazar, and Leonid Disa held the newsers' cameras and attention.

"No one's mentioned the most important thing," Ralston said as soon as they were in a quiet room. "The *message* in the diorama confirms what I'd thought. They called it a comet. Apparently it was supposed to be intensely brilliant, but it wasn't. No tail, no coma, nothing. An astronomical flop."

"You feel it was the chaos device?"

"What else?" Ralston said, enthusiasm burning brighter now. He began to pace, hands behind him. "The time frames are perfect. This diorama was constructed approximately a hundred years after the passage of their under-achieving comet. These scientists, the ones depicted in the diorama, are worried about the rise in civil disorder—and epilepsy. Their fears are truly paranoid, without much foundation, but they are worried. *Were* worried."

"Do you think there's any danger of catching the epileptic breakdown from the diorama?"

Ralston impatiently shook his head. "Not really. Maybe. How can I say? Some vestige of the field remains on the planet. De la Cruz is dead, and six of the solar physics scientists are disabled. The weather patterns are chaotic. The sun's going nova definitely shows that the field affected the stellar furnace mechanisms, even if it came slowly. It took almost ten thousand years for its regular fusion cycle to be disrupted."

"But Nels and the others..."

"They were on Alpha 3 almost three times as long as we were. The lingering effect might be more intense in some places than at others. Who can say? We're dealing with forces of unknown power."

"The medics say Nels will be all right. A tiny chemical neurotransmitter imbalance, they said. That was all they could come up with to explain the seizure." Leonore heaved a heart-felt sigh. "His brain scans are normal now."

Ralston knew that the others who had been struck down weren't as lucky. All of them would be slightly impaired in movement, but their health would not be affected further now that they were away from the insidious presence of the chaos field.

Ralston almost laughed at himself. He thought of it as a field. It might not be a radiation at all. Maybe the earliest guesses made by the avian natives were right. Poison. Or something totally beyond their—and the Alphans'—ability to understand. But until he had more data on the phenomenon, he'd continue thinking of it as a radiation device scattering chaos to and fro.

"That clears up a lot that had been worrying me," he said. "Nels and the others. Now we can concentrate on the real find."

"Real find? What's that? The diorama is being torn apart by the engineering department."

"They're interested only in the projector. No one has questioned the meaning of what was transmitted. Those alien scientists didn't say it outright, but they implied that they were beginning construction of a starship. I caught whispers of a scientist named Dial. They considered him a crackpot, but I believe he succeeded prior to the final decline."

"They didn't have the technology!" protested Leonore.

"Exactly. Without faster-than-light travel, they'd have to launch a sublight ship. I think this Dial built the ship and launched it. Maybe they left just a few years before their entire civilization collapsed. Maybe it was at the last possible instant."

"It might not have left at all."

Ralston smiled and motioned for Leonore to follow. They left the building and headed toward the laboratories.

"Where are we going?" Leonore turned and looked over her shoulder at the administration building. "I'm not sure we ought to leave yet. The newsers might . . ."

"They don't need us. The newsers have their story being spoon-fed to them by Salazar—and we're not a part of it any longer."

"Michael, I'm sorry about that."

"About what?" he said in surprise, his thoughts far distant.

"About their saying I'd discovered the dioramas. That was *your* discovery, but they didn't give me the chance to correct it. I know what it means to you."

Ralston shrugged it off. "Let them say what they want. After this, Salazar will leave me alone, and we can pursue this to the logical end. *That* will be a solution to rock them back."

"Finding the starship?"

He nodded.

They trooped up the stairs to the second floor. Ralston hesitated as he always did before the door to Westcott's lab. The idea of entering made him uneasier than experiencing alien thoughts blasted into his brain by the avians' telepathic projector. He heaved a quick breath, knocked, and entered.

Westcott sat in his chair, eyes half-closed, mouth slack.

"He's the one, isn't he?" said Leonore with some disgust. Her quick brown eyes darted to the authorization hanging on the wall. "He's plugged in directly to the computer."

"The only one allowed to do it at the University."

"So slow," murmured Westcott, drool running from the corner of his mouth. As a robot might, he reached up and methodically wiped it away. "I am so slow today. Can't integrate quickly enough."

"Westcott," Ralston said, too loudly. He moderated his voice. "Have you worked out the trajectories I gave you?"

"What? Oh, it's you." Westcott's rheumy eyes focused. No pleasure showed that he enjoyed their company. No displeasure came, either. He was a part of his machine. "An interesting problem. Where would a sublight spaceship go, given the astronomical parameters of the Alpha system ten thousand years ago?"

The entire wall at the back of the laboratory glowed a dull blue. Pinpoints appeared.

"This is the position of the stars ten thousand years ago. That," he said, indicating a flaming orange line, "is the vector of the chaos device."

Leonore started to speak, but Ralston silenced her.

"How did you determine its speed?" he asked the mathematician.

"Couldn't from the shoddy data given. But the information from the planet gave me several parallax sightings. From this I determined apparent motion. Coupled with distance estimates, I came out with the vector. Fast moving, not quite light speed but close."

"But the spaceship?" prompted Ralston.

"There." A single light flashed so intensely that Ralston and Leonore shielded their eyes. This was Westcott's moment of drama. The scene faded and he turned back to whatever imponderable problem he'd been working on when they entered his domain.

"But we need more," said Leonore. "Just a light on a datascreen doesn't—"

Ralston silenced her. He pointed to a hardcopy imprinter.

A single plastic sheet lay atop it. He picked it up, quickly scanned it, and then left Westcott's lab without even thanking the mathematician.

In the corridor outside the lab, Ralston leaned back against the wall and wiped away a sheen of sweat from his forehead.

"He bothers you, doesn't he?"

"He bothers everybody, but he's useful. No, more than that. He's a damned genius because he's linked to his computers. But that doesn't mean I have to like dealing with him. Let's get back to my office. I want to look this over more closely."

They walked out to the Quad, then stopped. Several demonstrations grew in intensity. One in particular caught Ralston's attention. He pointed.

"See the P'torra? And the gadget in his hand? That's an impulse driver. He's using it to gauge the mood of the crowd. Whatever it tells him, he passes along to the one haranguing the others." A woman stood on a small chair yelling incoherent phrases.

"She's saying something about God's will being ignored with the diorama," Leonore said, shocked.

"Come on. If the P'torra sees us, he'll focus the crowd on us."

"But the dioramas are such a potent hope for us. Just imagine! We can alleviate . . ."

"That's not the point. The P'torra wants only to hone his skill at rabble-rousing. Actually, I suspect he'd love to be able to steal the telepathic projector. He might be promoted all the way to the top of the military pyramid."

"He's a soldier? I thought that only their students were allowed on campus."

"What's the difference? To them there isn't one. Come on before they see us."

Ralston climbed the steps to his office in silence. The P'torra provided a constant source of irritation for him. But between the P'torra and the newsers, he wasn't sure who he hated more. The newsers sought only the momentary thrill, the brief scandal, whatever titillated. He had a solid story for them.

An entire race had been destroyed by a force—artificial or natural?—passing through space near their planet. The culture had collapsed, their solar system had been destroyed by their G-class sun going atypically nova. A single spaceship containing their leading scientists might have escaped almost ten thousand years ago—and he held their most probable destination in his hand.

Did the newsers care about that? No, they gobbled up the muck that Salazar fed them about a trinket. Granted the projector from the diorama might be a profitable and useful gadget, but it meant less than finding the remnants of an entire civilization.

Or the device that had destroyed it.

Ralston closed the door behind Leonore and dropped heavily into his own chair. He pressed the switch for the projector.

"There it is," he said. "I'm going to call it Beta, for lack of a better name. That's where they fled for sanctuary when they left Alpha 3. I know it."

Leonore stared at the datascreen, then said, "You sound so positive about what happened. You can't be, even with what you learned in the last diorama."

"All the data fit into a matrix. This is the answer. The only one that makes any sense. The avian natives fled their dying planet, and we're going to follow."

"Will the University let you?"

Ralston laughed harshly. "They'll be more than happy to get rid of me for however long it takes. Out of sight, out of mind. I disturb their neat, orderly society."

"You force your students to think," Leonore said.

"That's what I just said. I disturb the current order at Ilium." Ralston flipped over to another screen of data. "If the University won't fund this expedition, do you think your father might?"

"What? Why, I suppose so, if I ask him. But IC isn't known for such funding ventures. He'll be hard-pressed to justify it to the board of directors."

"No, he won't." Ralston smiled without any humor. "Not when you tell him we'll bring back someone who can construct one of those projectors. I don't think Binton will be able to reverse-engineer the device. Not soon."

Leonore laughed. She enjoyed the irony of this. "You really think we can find the survivors of Alpha 3, get them to license it, and return before anyone can build a duplicate?"

Ralston nodded.

"That's rich. And with them in the spotlight, they'll take the heat for it, too."

"Archaeology has its moments," Ralston said. "But I'm more concerned about one other problem."

"What's that?"

"The chaos device. It's still out there. And it might still be actively interfering with the natural processes of the universe. Can we afford to let such a weapon be held at our heads?"

"You're exaggerating, Michael."

He didn't think so.

"Things turned out well enough for us this time. What if the chaos device comes back? By Novo Terra? We're not immune. Yago de la Cruz showed that. The members of Justine Rasmussen's research team proved it, too. We've got to find it and destroy it."

Michael Ralston started planning the new expedition to Beta with Leonore, but the thought burned like a black flame inside his head: The chaos device might destroy them all. And only he believed enough in the danger it posed to attempt to stop it.

2: EQUATIONS OF CHAOS

For Dennis and Lou
and the brainstorming sessions

ONE

THE RAYS FROM the distant star cast wan shadows but provided no warmth to the planet. Nothing on this darkness-shrouded world had ever tasted the life-giving full warmth of a sun, but still life flourished. No chlorophyll worked its magic inside plants. Photosynthesis provided a curiosity for the laboratory, an intriguing speculation more philosophical than empirical or useful. No DNA dictated the patterns of life on the frigid world. But life did exist.

From the planet's inner fires came the spark for life, and because of a mindless tenacity that knew no bounds, the life forms not only grew, but flourished in this dark, freezing environment.

Beq slithered toward a pillar of warmth and wrapped long, wispy tendrils about the column of dark, razor-edged lava. The creature gave a sigh and snuggled closer, replenishing its energy, thanking the All Wise for providing such a fine dinner. After a decent pause, Beq reluctantly pulled free of the pillar and flowed on its way. As much as it wished to dawdle, the war effort required uncharacteristically swift motion and decisive action. Beq's tendrils elongated even more when a frigid gust blew past.

Liquid ammonia winds caught the tenuous body and lofted it. Beq sighed again, relishing the cold as much as it had the warmth of its energy meal. Each presented different stimuli, a commodity sadly lacking on such a barren home world.

Beq felt itself carried along faster and faster, until its body resembled a spider web caught in a hurricane. Consciousness began to fade as the body dissipated. Beq vaguely sensed the problem and pulled the vagrant body parts inward until a reasonable level of thought could be maintained. Beq, as did so many others of its spawn-time, enjoyed the peaceful nothingness of being pulled into vapor. The world leaders, however, discouraged such rash, dangerous activity in the younger generations.

The war required full effort. Everyone had to be coherent if the enemy was to be defeated.

But Beq had never seen the enemy. There had never been any attacks on the world. The same lava columns of its youth still provided sustenance. The ammonia winds still blew. Only the intense focusing of the entire planet's meager resources marked any noticeable change in policy over the past years.

Beq coalesced into a tight sphere, presented more resistance to the ammonia plumes, and fell heavily to the rocky surface. Body reforming into a new motile shape, it slithered into a tiny crevice. Volcanic warmth thrilled it once again. The only benefit Beq saw from this elusive war lay in frequent visits to the seat of power on the planet. The ruling committee always chose the most energetic spots for their meetings. And why not? Beq approved of the increased alertness in such surroundings. If the world had to be at war, why shouldn't some of the inhabitants enjoy heightened awareness?

Beq always reveled at the feel of warmth oozing through its body and bringing mentation to a higher level.

The creature sighed. Those higher planes of awareness always brought ineffable emotions, too. Beq preferred floating mindlessly on the winds until its energy level sank almost to death. But as the ruling committee decreed, each must contribute to the effort.

Beq contributed more than most, being the outstanding theoretical mathematician of its spawn-time.

"Report," came the crisp command from the creature chosen this day to head the ruling committee.

Another, clutching at a steamy lava rock, reluctantly freed itself and descended to the center of the chamber. "There is progress in our effort," the being stated in an overly theatrical manner.

Beq allowed its tendrils to snake forth and lightly brush several warm rocks. Energy flowed into its main body and elevated thought processes to the point where it saw truth and knew this creature lied. "Why do you say this?" Beq demanded. "What setbacks have there been for you to hide it so?"

The creature assumed a defensive form. "The enemy has destroyed every weapon we sent this past time increment."

To Beq this meant little. Time flowed in spurts, and often took on a fugue state where the universe halted. The ruling committee had been waging this war for . . . how long? Beq had no easy answer to this, nor did it matter. Its realm was almost entirely theoretical, and Beq experienced its greatest uneasiness and feelings of impatience when dealing with substantive events.

"What was the nature of our weapon? How was it destroyed?" Beq showed uncharacteristic impatience. Although it enjoyed the warmth, it preferred to spend time as it chose. The ruling committee insisted on these meetings every hundred revolutions of the star.

"The method of destruction is unknown. Our weapon induced a field that would disrupt the enemy's cellular structure."

"How odd," Beq said.

The being presiding interrupted. "The enemy is of a fixed form, comprised of living cells that use chemical energy rather than radiation, as is normal."

"How truly odd," Beq said. It had not known that the enemy's form differed so radically. It tightened tendrils around several black, craggy upjuts. The warmth heightened Beq's senses.

"You develop new thoughts?" demanded another on the ruling committee. "We must hear these ideas immediately."

Beq sighed. Such impatience would be their downfall. But it appreciated the ruling committee's dilemma. The war had raged for too long. These pesky enemy creatures did whatever it was they did, and annoyed everyone. To see so many of its spawn-time occupied with war tasks, provoked sympathy and even sorrow in Beq.

"I have been studying," Beq said. "The methods used for our attack are of an obvious nature. The enemy expects and counters such weapons with ease."

A creature elsewhere in the chamber snorted derisively at this. Beq ignored it.

"A more fundamental attack is required, one that the enemy will not understand and respond to." Beq gushed forth and assumed the central spot, so that all on the ruling committee might see it. Beq cared little for such attention but found it necessary if this war was to be ended. So many *interesting* questions remained unanswered. The war only absorbed energy better spent contemplating important problems.

"As the winds carried my body," Beq went on, "mathematical formulations came to me. And a question. Are the ammonia currents truly random?"

"Of course not," scoffed one of the ruling committee. "We have long since derived the physics of their motion. Uneven heating of the surface, mass differentials, the action of gravity, convection, all these play a role in causing the winds to blow."

"This is my thought," agreed Beq. "To know every variable, to place this data into the appropriate thermodynamic equation, add the differential equations of molecular motion, and we might know precisely the path of the winds." Beq paused to absorb more energy. "But the slightest deviation radically alters those state equations.

The most minute fluctuation alters the outcome of our most precise predictions."

"You speak of quantum mechanical fluctuations?"

"Grosser ones. The cracking of a rock. The passage of a cloud between star and surface. The wing motion of a single insect. These are adequate to turn an ordered system into chaos."

Another creature snorted derisively at Beq's idea. "An insect wing turns a breeze into a gale? Ridiculous."

"So?" Beq began a careful explanation of the set of coupled nonlinear differential equations it had derived while floating on the cold winds. For several slow planetary rotations it revealed all that had come to mind during the times of deliberate, slow, penetratingly precise thought.

"You can describe randomness," concluded one of the ruling committee. "But of what use is this to the war effort?"

"The enemy sensors are acute. They detect our most carefully shielded weapons." Beq waited for disagreement. None came. "I propose a weapon that is not a weapon. A field of disorder can be constructed and sent toward the enemy home planet."

It began sketching out the salient points of its plan. A full revolution of the planet around the distant star passed before Beq's mathematical proposal had been presented.

"This field will then confuse their bodies?" asked one of the ruling committee.

This garnered only scorn from its more attentive and astute colleagues. Beq had presented the material clearly and concisely. The creature only showed its lack of concentration and low energy level by such a query.

"It disrupts the most basic processes, not only in life, but of other physical events," Beq explained patiently. "Their chemical processes might take odd turns, some reactions proceeding normally while others produce random events. Weather patterns on their planet would shift. The physical movement of electrons would be disrupted, causing neural damage in their brains and malfunction in their equipment." Beq sighed. It seemed a perversion of a fine theory to use it in such a fashion.

"How did you happen to come upon this system of equations?"

Beq sighed once more. Tiny currents of ammonia drifted away from it. "I considered how inefficient it was to wait for thermal activity to rise to the surface for our consumption. The equations for predicting radioactive decay linked into those of chaos."

"You can create radiation?" The creature shifted about a large lava rock spire. The others of the ruling committee moved away from it. Such a display of ignorance reflected badly on all their number.

"There are many forms of radiation," said Beq. "I wanted to predict—and create—radioactive decay. These equations suggest a way of causing any substance to become radioactive. Even lead." Beq found itself lost in the labyrinth of wondrously complex equations. A cold gust of ammonia along one tendril brought it back to the necessity of speaking with the ruling committee.

"This will bring us much warmth for many years," said a committee member. "But your true accomplishment will be in the creation of a weapon to destroy our enemy. Their sensitive electronic sensing equipment will fail. Their planet becomes uninhabitable due to action of wind and wave. Their very bodies will rebel against them when their brains no longer produce reliable neural connections. Your name, Beq, will be revered throughout our long history."

Beq barely heard. Already, it followed different pathways through the multiple solutions to the chaos equations. They danced into imaginary realms and back into the physical world. Warmth! No longer dependent on the slow march of heat from the world's magma-laden center, Beq could generate more potent radiation for warming the body.

Beq sobered as it considered the ramifications. What would this do to society? If all had an abundant source of energy, would this destroy the simple pleasures? To never again drift almost comatose on the ammonia winds, because the whole surface glowed with energy, robbed all of a valuable intellectual retreat. Beq's finest ideas came when tendrils were cast forth and the gusty winds lofted its body in an aimless fashion. Thoughts barely possible, all contact with body gone, Beq managed its finest theoretical work in this desultory state.

It would vanish if it allowed unlimited generation of radioactive sources. The others, especially those of the ruling committee, showed such greed for energy. They weren't like Beq, who appreciated aloneness and an opportunity to meditate deeply.

Beq sighed. Its discovery of the equations governing randomness couldn't be hidden. Another would derive the necessary matrices, given a rotation or a revolution or a thousand. Beq had to content itself with the notion that the enemy would at last be removed, allowing everything to return to normal.

Compassion did not enter Beq's consciousness. Such an emotion had to be reserved for only the highest energy state. But Beq came close. To destroy another civilization with such an awesome—and awful—chaos field, bothered it.

But not for long. Beq found a weakly rising thermal, distended its body, and caught the feathery extensions on the ammonia as it evaporated and mingled with the atmosphere.

The chaos weapon had no substance. The mechanicians overseeing its construction worked with tools that were more theoretical than physical. But this disturbed none of them. Beq drifted nearby, thoughts on the equations holding the field in place. With the senses the creature possessed, it saw only blackness against blackness, an occluding rather than a hole. But Beq knew the field quivered with vibrant energy. Every oscillation caused Beq to shudder, as it disturbed the very fabric of both living body and inanimate matter.

"Are you finished?" Beq asked of the mechanicians.

Neither of the creatures attained a high enough energy level to be disturbed by the restrained chaos. Their bodies shimmered and distended with every pulsation in the randomness, but their minds were untouched. Beq wished it could attain that level and let itself drift aimlessly on the ammonia winds.

But now, with its knowledge of the chaos equations, nothing could ever prove truly random for it. Beq could calculate, solve, know. Such power robbed it of speculation about the universe.

Beq tightened and rolled over on the ground, sensory apparatus studying the planetary surface. Since they had allowed the chaos field to come into existence, the weather patterns had grown unstable. The ammonia thermals it so loved to ride had vanished, replaced with violent storm winds which ripped drifting tendrils asunder. Beq had cautioned the ruling committee about allowing the chaos field to come into existence on the surface; it had requested some point in space.

The vote had gone against Beq. The ruling committee felt that secrecy outweighed any danger to their planet. Even when Beq presented the equations governing the randomness and showed potential effects, the ruling committe had insisted. Beq had not argued. To do so would waste precious energy.

Even though the black-on-black field disrupted the planet, Beq felt a high energy surge of love for it. Seldom did any of its race see their theoretical, highly abstruse thoughts turned into something physical. Beq's chaos equations had proven themselves worthy of the highest praise. Mathematics bloomed into reality.

Beq curled a dozen tendrils around a pillar of fiercely radiating lead and allowed its energy level to soar. One of the first applications it had insisted on was the transmutation of inert substances into radioactive ones. The mere presence of the chaos field had worked its randomness on the particles within the lead atoms. Quantum level transitions took place more often than those from uranium, and provided energy for detailed thought.

"Beq, we must hurry. One of the enemy weapons approaches our planet. This device must halt the progress."

Beq curled into a tight sphere, then extended pseudopods to turn and face the member of the ruling committee. "What is the nature of their weapon?" it asked.

The ruling committee member rippled. "It is another of their puzzle weapons." Beq worked on understanding this statement. Their enemy, like them, fought not with explosives and nuclear devices, but with conceptual weapons. One such weapon had jumbled thought processes, but nothing more. Still another had blanked light from the distant star.

Beq had worried over this. Why had the enemy considered this a weapon? Beq had decided that enemy reconnaissance and intelligence had been faulty—or ethnocentric. Beq found it difficult to believe that any intelligent race could survive off chemical energy derived indirectly from sunlight; curling up around a rock post and absorbing the radiant warmth seemed much more direct and efficient. But if the enemy had the same trouble understanding, it made a twisted sort of sense that they might blank out the sunlight, thinking this would cripple those on the planet.

The ruling committee hadn't even noticed the attack for over three revolutions around the primary. One theoretical astronomer had commented that verifying its spectroscopic theories had become difficult. Only then had anyone become concerned.

"This weapon will tear at the fabric of space," declared the ruling committee member.

Beq sighed. Such drama ought to be reserved for the theatre. The chaos field performed according to the abstract equations Beq had derived and implemented. This weapon was a mathematical construct and nothing more. Beq predicted random events with the system of equations, then used conformal mappings of those same equations to cause the event they predicted.

"The field will disrupt their weapon, no matter what it is," said Beq. "I have chosen carefully the sets of equations governing this device. The nuclear adhesion force will weaken. We might be flooded with a radiant shower of leptons and baryons as their weapon comes apart, but this will be a minor event."

Inflicting intense uncertainty on the nuclear force appealed to Beq's intellectual curiosity. It wondered if the weaker forces might likewise be manipulated. To disrupt gravity, such a weak force, might allow indefinite soaring on even the most meager of breezes. Beq worked through the potential before it. Total removal of gravity would not do. It still needed convection currents for the proper lift and sensuous feel of moving cool vapor along its tendrils. But a major diminution in gravity might prove exciting, if in the proper low energy state.

Beq supervised the launching in the field, if launching was the proper word. The chaos field lacked extension, and retained existence only in abstract manner. The mechanicians maneuvered it about, using Beq's instructions, manipulating probability of the field's location. The blackness vanished in one spot, only to *be* in another. No distance seemed to be traversed. This didn't upset Beq. It had no clear idea as to the complete properties of the chaos field it had brought into this war. Beq merely observed and correlated. Later, on its wondrous thermals, energy levels sinking and mind operating at almost animalistic levels, Beq would consider all this.

"Allow it to meet the enemy weapon," Beq ordered. A shimmer of excitement passed through the thin tendrils wrapped about the pillar of radioactive lead. Beq forced itself to ever higher energy levels, straining to observe, keeping its mind on the chaos field.

The weapon vanished, leaving behind only dust.

"Stop!" barked Beq, halting a mechanician as it slid toward the launch area. "Be careful. My calculations show release of the binding energy for quarks in the planetary surface. There is no information on such radiation's effects."

The member of the ruling committee waved away the slowly drifting mechanicians. The entire rocky plain would be cordoned off until counteracting abstractions could be brought to erase the residual chaotic effects.

"There is little time before the enemy realizes something has gone awry with their weapon," said Beq. It floated just above the surface, mind turned to geometries of ever higher orders. These tensors thrilled Beq more than the chaos equations now. It had mastered one complex set of equations. Unless it wanted to risk boredom, it had to seek new diversions.

"Our orbiting sensors relay the battle at forty planetary diameters," said the member of the ruling committee. "The chaos field interacted with their puzzle weapon."

"So?" prompted Beq. The only thing it disliked more than the officiousness of the ruling committee was their strained sense of the dramatic.

"The fields mingled."

"An inexact phrase," murmured Beq. It drifted on a vagrant breeze of cool ammonia, wanting to be free of the ruling committee and this inexplicable war.

Beq allowed a few moments thought to cover the history of the conflict. It found no reason for it. The chemical burners had no interest in Beq's home; why should they? Paradise to one was purgatory to another. Beq found it impossible to believe the enemy, with its precise, ugly form and inefficient internal chemical combustion, would want to populate this world or live under rules of polite society formulated ten million years earlier. The ruling committee did not often allow more than carefully done thought experiments to be performed, unless some more physical tool was required for survival.

This suited Beq. Nothing aroused it so much as the solitude and lowered energy levels where it returned to a bestial state. Its best ideas developed unhindered by the coils of polite behavior in such a drifting, floating, soaring existence. But the war?

Beq found no purpose for it.

"The chaos field has disrupted the enemy weapon," said the ruling committee member. "It veers away from our home world."

"And the chaos field itself? What of it?" demanded Beq. A quick mental calculation had produced indeterminacy. The thought of the field returning to the planet meant disaster now that it had been launched. Beq held some curiosity about the chaos field's effect, but not enough to pursue it actively.

"It spins off through the void. Other mathematicians plot its trajectory. Do you wish to—"

"I wish nothing more to do with it," Beq stated flatly. "I find amusement now in higher geometries. The tensors deform strangely near the chaos field. It is puzzling and bears more examination." Beq exhaled strongly, lifted on an ammonia current, and blew toward the plain where the chaos field had been brought into existence.

Beq ignored the strangeness within its body. Residuals in the mathematical sense, it decided. Faint tuggings left from proximity to the chaos device. Nothing of importance. Beq slipped through the atmosphere and allowed its energy level to dip. New and dazzlingly complex geometries assaulted its brain and pleased it mightily.

The chaos device destroyed the enemy weapon, deflected from the puzzle field, and sailed off across the galaxy, leaving confusion and enforced randomness in its wake.

TWO

MICHAEL RALSTON LEANED back in his chair, letting the pneumatic cushion sigh as it worked to shift and adequately cradle his spine. Strong, stubby work-hardened fingers laced behind his dark-haired head and cold gray eyes, which were fixed on the student shifting nervously in front of the archaeology professor's desk.

"Verd, Dr. Ralston," the student said, eyes averted. "That's what I heard."

"Why are you telling me this, Citizen? There's nothing in it for you, is there?" His tone cut like a stainless steel blade. He was growing tired of the campus politics with its Machiavellian turnings and alliances and enmities.

"Doctor!" The student stiffened angrily. "I don't like the way they're convicting you without a hearing."

Ralston turned slightly and idly drummed fingers over his computer console. Set between two large stacks of dusty books, the palely glowing screen seemed out of place. Nowhere else on the campus of the University of Ilium did books appear the norm and the consoles unusual. Two walls of Ralston's tiny office were lined with books, while the large window in the outer wall had been cycled to total transmission, giving the impression of not existing at all. It wasn't unusual for dedicated archaeology students to come into his office and begin to sneeze from the accumulated dust. But Ralston had long since decided this was a fitting, if minor, lesson for any would-be archaeologist to learn.

Ralston didn't mind the jibes of "grave robber." That ancient epithet came into the profession and could even be tolerated with an air of amused superiority. But since he had returned from Alpha 3 with the intricate and potentially profitable alien technology that allowed telepathic transference of information, many on campus had begun calling him something more—and much worse.

"I see by your record, Citizen Karolli, that you're not much of a student. Is it possible you are currying favor with me by making this allegation?"

"I'm sorry I bothered you, Dr. Ralston." The student turned and started to leave. The lock on the door barred his way. "May I leave?" Karolli's hand nervously jiggled the door handle.

"In a moment." Ralston studied the student, wondering who had sent him. Considering the number of enemies Ralston had made since coming to Ilium, it might be any of them. In his younger days—not that long past—Ralston had fought in the Nex-P'torra war on the side of the reptilian Nex. He had seen how the humanoid P'torra had depopulated a half-dozen worlds with their biologic weapons, and had known instantly that such evil had to be opposed.

His stand had proven increasingly unpopular because of clever P'torra agitation on campus, relying on shape prejudices and the malleability of student opinions. The war was over some years back, but the P'torra carried it on, not with planet-shaking bombs and diabolical mutated viruses, but with propaganda. Ralston had seen a P'torra exchange student with his emotion gauging "impulse driver" at the periphery of more than one campus demonstration. The P'torra never overtly agitated. Their method was to direct from the sidelines, using the impulse driver to calculate the precise words, the proper tones, the correct images needed to whip a crowd to a frenzy.

Ralston had been the target of that psychological technology more than once because of his pro-Nex stand.

Karolli might be a P'torra pawn. Or he might represent more human but nonetheless inimical factions. The newly promoted Chancellor of the University had no love for Ralston. Dr. Salazar's animosity ran deep and knew no bounds. But Ralston didn't fear Salazar, not in the same way he did the P'torra. Academic infighting had always proved non-lethal, as far as life went. Ralston's tenure might be denied again, he might find it impossible to get research grants, he might be passed over for the choicest of the archaeological finds, he might even be evicted from his small, dusty office, but no physical harm would come from that.

Or were there other players in the game? Ralston sighed. Life had been much simpler, if less intellectually stimulating, before he had discovered the ruins on Alpha 3 and returned to Novo Terra and the University with the telepathic projector.

"You," Ralston said, "might be sincere. I'll operate on that assumption. What is it you want me to do about this threat against my continued good health?"

The student shrugged. "Just thought you should know what's being said."

"Where did you hear it?" The way Karolli blanched when Ralston asked, told the archaeology professor a great deal. And he didn't like it. From Karolli's records, Ralston had made a good guess as to the source. Another player *had* entered the game, and this one held power far beyond that of Chancellor Salazar or even the P'torra with his impulse driver and eager throngs of students.

"I . . . I just heard."

"From the Archbishop?" Ralston asked in a low voice. "Is he telling everyone that I'm tainted with evil, that Satan's imprint must linger on my forehead because I dig up ruins on other worlds?" Ralston saw that his guess hit the mark. He didn't need to detain Citizen Karolli any further. Ralston touched the button under the edge of his desk. A tiny click signaled the lock opening. The student bolted, and almost ran from the small office.

Ralston made certain the door had locked once more, then turned and hiked his feet to the windowsill. He, virtually alone in the entire department, had a glass window looking out over the central University quadrangle. The others preferred programmed pictures, scenes of distant worlds or of snow or oceans or of selected people. Ralston preferred the unplanned parade of students rushing to and fro, some on their way to class. That the University demanded their physical presence instead of viewing through computer screens, made the University of Ilium almost unique.

Ralston preferred it; this was one reason he'd chosen to come to Ilium as a professor. The personal contact meant more to him than having a thousand unseen, nameless, intermittently faceless students getting high grades. But he knew the winds of change blew constantly, even in such a conservative setting. Fewer and fewer classes required physical attendance. Some professors held out for lab courses to be held in central locations, but even their voices were drowned out by the convenience of remote classing, as they called it.

Lack of personal contact, Ralston called it.

"I *like* windows," Ralston said forcefully. And, he silently admitted to himself, he liked teaching. No matter what it became, how it mutated, he liked it.

But with the Archbishop leading the pack of hungry dogs nipping at his heels, what chance did he have? Salazar could put him into academic limbo. The Archbishop might consign him to a Hell of a more than spiritual nature.

Ralston had left behind the Earth of his childhood. Its northern temperate zones had been scorched by nuclear weapons, but civilization had hung on with grim tenacity. That the southern hemisphere remained virtually untouched had been a miracle—one the Church had played on heavily.

Ralston didn't waste time thinking about such things. That much of the Earth had survived seemed sufficient.

That war might never happen again was the miracle. But the hold of Churchmen spread from New Rome in Argentina and now brushed across Ralston.

They had held a convocation and deemed the Alpha 3 technology the work of Satan. Michael Ralston had publicly ridiculed such a notion, and drawn their notice and ire. Was Karolli the harbinger of damnation from the Archbishop? Ralston might find himself excommunicated at any instant for his temerity in opposing Church dictates.

Ralston shrugged it off. He preferred to sit and observe the students on the lovely campus Quad stretched out for his unique pleasure. No video display could ever replace the actual substance, depth, and feel of the real scene.

Mind turning to other topics, Ralston jumped when his door alarm sounded loudly. He turned in his chair and touched the key on his console.

"What is it?" he demanded harshly, thinking Karolli had returned with some further tidbit of gossip.

"Sorry to interrupt, Michael," came Leonore Disa's soft voice. "I can come back later."

"Come in." Ralston pressed the button to release the lock. When he'd insisted that one of his students wire the office, the student had laughed. No one but Ralston would request a lock operated independently of the computer. Through the main console any entry and exit could be checked by both the office's occupant and the campus security force. The student had told his professor that this would be convenient in case anyone broke in.

Ralston didn't care to have any illicit office intrusion in the main campus computer's memory, any more than he did his own comings and goings.

Leonore Disa came in and stood in front of his desk, nervously shifting from one foot to the other. It seemed that this was his day to discomfit students. He motioned for the small, dark woman to sit down in the only other chair in the cramped room. She perched on the edge, as if relaxing might be painful. Her surgically implanted jewelry plates had been reprogrammed, Ralston noted. The usual pastels had given way to more garish reds and blues, which highlighted Leonore's cheekbones and gave her a slightly menacing aspect.

He started to comment on this, then bit back the words. He didn't want to get the woman any more upset than she obviously was. Leonore and he had made the discovery on Alpha 3 that led to the alien projector being returned to Novo Terra.

"How's Nels?" he asked, inquiring after Leonore's lover. Nels Bernssen had presented a seminar on pre-nova conditions in stars, which had been well received in the astronomical community.

"He's all right. The talk went well," she said. Her brown eyes fixed on his cooler gray ones. "What are you doing, Michael?" Leonore asked bluntly.

"Not much," Ralston said. "Not much I can do. Salazar took the projector away from me and gave it to the engineering department. That doesn't matter, though, since I'm an archaeologist, not an engineer. With Alpha 3 gone up in the puff of smoke that made Nels' career, there's not much left for me."

"You never struck me as the suicidal type before. Good day, Dr. Ralston." Leonore spun lithely from the chair and almost gained the hallway before Ralston's finger touched the lock button and denied the woman exit.

"I'm not suicidal," he said. "But there's not much I can do right now about the find. Salazar hasn't assigned me a new teaching schedule. He might not next term, either. I'm a consultant, he says." Ralston snorted derisively. "More likely, this is his way of keeping me out of sight."

"To hell with Salazar!" raged Leonore. She slammed both palms flat on his desk and leaned forward, anger accentuated by the bright crimson of her intensely flashing jewelry plates. "So you lost Alpha 3 to the nova. So what?"

"The greatest discovery of this or any other century," sighed Ralston. "Gone in the wavefront from the nova."

"That sun wasn't the right class to go nova," she said.

"Nels is making quite a reputation based on that observation," admitted Ralston.

"And you know why the star blew up. You know why civilization on Alpha 3 declined so suddenly. You know! And you're not doing a damned thing about it!"

"No research money," Ralston said.

"You went back to Alpha 3 without Salazar's approval. You had the confidence in your instincts and you made him buy it. You *forced* him to. If he hadn't agreed that the funding came from the University, my father would have taken it all, telepathic projector included."

Ralston nodded. As it was, Leonid Disa, Leonore's father and chief executive officer of Interstellar Computronics, had claimed marketing rights to the projector. Both the University and IC stood to make billions off the device. Not even the Vegan spider-steel find a decade earlier had netted this much. Ralston decried the way research groups so eagerly sought and exploited the commercial finds, but he knew that he stood alone on this point. The money had to come from somewhere. Only the potential for big returns off alien ruins justified spending the grant money, or so thought the people controlling the funds.

He shook his head as he considered an historical parallel. Spain had pillaged the New World back on Earth, robbing the Incas, Aztecs, and Mayas to fill royal coffers. Yet it had been that plunder that fueled new exploration.

"Whatever happened to pure research?" he muttered.

"Daddy is willing to finance another expedition for you."

"Alpha 3's gone. Poof!" Ralston made an exploding gesture with his hands.

"You learned a great deal from that diorama we brought back. You were locked within it for hours." Leonore relaxed now, settling once more into the chair. But her brown eyes burned with almost religious fervor. Ralston

wondered if this was the way he looked when starting on a
new dig. Probably.

"The diorama held a great deal of information," he said
carefully. "I maintained the telepathic projection alignment by staying within the scene while you and Nels
moved it on board the starship." Ralston heaved a deep
sigh. While within the alien scene, he had done more than
experience the thoughts of the creatures depicted. He had
become a part of a history lesson, an active participant
complete with all the knowledge held by that creature. The
thoughts, emotions, needs, drives, and ambitions—he
understood them all while locked within the telepathic
projector's invisible grip.

And Michael Ralston knew more than any other human
about the last days of civilization on Alpha 3—and how
one of the alien scientists, Dial, had labored to save a
small number of colleagues from the deadly, lingering
effects of the chaos device that had passed by Alpha 3 two
hundred years earlier.

"We are in as much danger as those on Alpha 3,"
Leonore said. Whoever had programmed her jewelry plates
had added a skin temperature sensor. As her passion
mounted, the colors flashing just under her skin muted and
changed. Ralston found himself more interested in this
phenomenon than in pursuing the path of the chaos device
through space.

"You know where it went. You know where it came
from. We can find it!" the woman cried.

Ralston held back a rising tide of emotion. He wanted to
tell Leonore that he valued her as a researcher, that her
skills would lead her into prominence in archaeology one
day. But how could he also tell her that he didn't want her
tainted by his increasingly unsavory reputation? Everyone
worked against him because he lacked the desire—or the
disposition—to play campus politics.

Chancellor Salazar opposed him and denied every
tenure vote. The P'torra stirred up student activists against
him because of his alliance with and sympathy for the

Nex. Now even the Archbishop of Ilium found reason to publicly denounce him. Ralston *would* follow that device; he *would* learn its secrets; he *would* learn all he could about the race that fashioned such a horrendous weapon. But he didn't want to involve Leonore Disa.

That might end her burgeoning career.

"There's nothing much I can do," he said finally. "I need the money and—"

"My father will supply it—IC will. The chance for a repeat of the telepathic projector sways even the most flint-hearted of IC's miserly directors."

"What use would they put the chaos device to, if I happen to discover it and return with it?" he asked, genuinely curious. "We've seen its effects. It makes otherwise stable stars go nova. It causes epileptic seizures in humans. There's evidence that it creates computer equipment failures. I suppose it might be useful in manufacturing radioactive elements out of those not usually energetic, but . . ." He let his words trail off. Why did IC want to fund what seemed, even to him, a fool's errand?

"The mathematics of it intrigues Daddy," Leonore said. Ralston saw her expression change and become neutral, as if she'd started gambling and didn't want an opponent to know the cards she held. "He says IC can use it for societal predictions."

Ralston leaned back in his chair, his mind racing, trying to put aside his uneasiness that anyone, especially Leonore, might think of the cold, hard Leonid Disa as "Daddy."

"You mean he thinks IC can predict wars if they understand the equations governing the device?" The archaeology professor started to ask what use this might be, then went cold inside when the understanding dawned like a polar morning.

"No one ever accused Daddy of being a pleasant man," Leonore said, a touch of bleakness in her voice. "If the instabilities in a planet's culture that lead to war can be studied and known in advance, vast fortunes can be made."

"Supplying both sides the weapons of war," said Ralston.

"Oh, more than that." Leonore Disa swallowed hard. "Daddy believes it'd be possible to stockpile raw materials that might be in short supply. To know the most likely spots where destruction would occur gives any company an advantage, too. You don't build plants where a bomb will fall."

"And I thought I was a cynical son of a bitch." Ralston shook his head. He felt out of his league. "All I want to do is my research. Let me teach, let me get into the field to study dead civilizations. Is that so much to ask?"

"It is when you make a discovery like this projector. The security forces are already thinking of it as a propaganda device at worst and a brainwashing machine at best."

"I ought to blow up the engineering lab." Desolation washed over Ralston. He hadn't even thought of such applications. For education, for correcting mental disorders—those things he considered for the telepathic projector.

"They've moved it." Leonore saw his expression and hastily added, "I don't know where. I didn't ask, and Daddy wouldn't have told me. It's a joint project now, the University and Interstellar Computronics."

"I can't accept IC's funding for any such expedition. I think you understand why."

"You," said Leonore, "don't want me going along because you think it'd hurt my career."

"It would."

Leonore smiled, tenseness gone. Ralston believed he saw genuine emotion, not an act. "Thank you. I truly appreciate your concern. There aren't many who'd worry over things like that."

"Nels would."

"Yes."

For a few minutes they sat and said nothing. Ralston finally broke the silence. "This is too momentous a discovery for any single private company. I'm not sure I'd even want the government in control of the chaos device."

"Now that they know such a thing is possible, how long

will it be before someone stumbles across it on their own?''

"Nature is a blabbermouth," he admitted. "But it's possible that such work might take years, even centuries. That's beyond me. All I know how to do is poke around in ruins and hunt for garbage and anything else discarded by the people who lived there.''

"Michael," she said solemnly, "you're more than that." Leonore rose. "Daddy is a bastard, but he's an honest one. Whatever contract you sign with him, he'll honor. I think it's important to find that machine, or whatever it is, and see if it's still functioning. It might be dangerous to all of us if it is.''

Ralston pushed the lock button and opened the door for her. "It passed Alpha 3 more than ten thousand years ago. That's quite a while ago.''

Leonore nodded, but he read her thoughts perfectly: Not such a long time, astronomically speaking. The small woman left Ralston to his own musings.

He rocked back and forth in his chair, then launched himself and walked briskly from the office. He'd sat and thought long enough. Accepting Interstellar Computronic's offer to fund an expedition was out of the question. He'd never agree to be in Leonid Disa's debt. He had seen the man and the way he worked, and didn't like him. Leonore might be right in saying her father always observed scrupulously any contract he signed, but attorneys were paid well to find niches unthought of.

And Ralston had no doubt that Disa hired the best lawyers he could to find those unexpected crevices in any contract.

Ralston paused at the ground floor and peered into the Quadrangle. Bacon's statue stood a lonely sentinel outside. No students. Even more to Ralston's liking, no P'torra. He slipped out into the bright, warm summer afternoon, feeling more like a sneak thief than a professor. Ralston kept to shadows and only ventured across open areas when no other path afforded itself.

He walked briskly along shady paths in the arboretum until he came to the building containing many of the University's pure research laboratories. On the second floor was one lab in particular that always frightened Ralston. But it was that room where he had to go, for only there would he find out what he needed to learn of the chaos device that had destroyed Alpha 3's civilization and caused its G5-class sun to go nova.

Ralston heaved a deep sigh and tried to calm himself. Such apprehension on his part seemed silly. Westcott wasn't a mad butcher. Westcott didn't seek his eternal damnation like the Archbishop did. Westcott didn't even care what academic sanctions Salazar might impose against him. Westcott's work was paramount, and anything else in the universe counted as trivial.

It was how Westcoit pursued his researches that made Ralston so uneasy.

Ralston went up the stairs at one end of the building and hastened down the hall. At this time of afternoon, most of the researchers were in their labs. Only one or two idled in the hallway.

Ralston paused an instant before Westcott's door, then hurried in.

He screamed. He left solid floor and building to step into infinite space. Ralston tumbled and twisted in free fall, parsecs away from the nearest planet. Galaxies spiraled about in their eons-old dance and provided a ghostly light that showed how truly alone he was.

Michael Ralston fell and fell and fell.

THREE

FOR ALL ETERNITY Michael Ralston fell. He screamed but the words vanished in the hard vacuum of space, mutated and became hauntingly familiar notes that merged into oddly appealing chords and symphonies. Only slowly did he come to realize he hadn't died from internal rupturing, that the air hadn't gusted from his straining lungs, that he still lived.

Why?

"I'm a scientist," he murmured. "I will not be ruled by fear of the unknown." Easy words, and ones he accepted intellectually, but the fear still clutched his belly like a cold fist, and rational thought came only with great difficulty.

Ralston mentally retraced his path to figure out how he had come to this terrifying point. From his office, across the Quad, to the laboratory building, to Westcott's lab . . .

Westcott!

He called out the mathematician's name as if it were an ancient curse, an Earth voodoo incantation that would lift evil from him like shucking off a jacket.

"What?" came the querulous reply. "Who is it? I don't want anyone in my lab when I am . . . experimenting."

"Help me," Ralston called. Westcott's voice gave him an anchor, something to home in on. He didn't really drift aimlessly between the galaxies or hear the strange songs rattling about inside his head. Whatever happened had an explanation. Ralston knew that Westcott could supply it.

As suddenly as Michael Ralston had stepped into nothingness, an ordinary laboratory appeared around him. His knees buckled and he crashed to the floor, stunned. Ralston worked his way to hands and knees and tried to quell his rising gorge. He was partially successful. The acid burning stopped just under his Adam's apple.

"Can't you read?" came Westcott's cold question. "The sign said No Admittance."

"What sign? There wasn't one on the door."

"Idiot. Fool. *Hijo de* . . ."

Ralston twisted about and sat on the cool plastic floor, back against a primitive file cabinet as he watched Westcott stalk to the lab door and fling it open. The mathematician began cursing in earnest when he didn't find the warning sign.

"Damned students think it's funny to take the sign down and then let fools like you blunder in to disturb me."

"What were you doing? I . . . I thought I was falling through space. And there was a strange song. It sounded so familiar, but I didn't really recognize it."

Ralston spoke more from nervousness than any desire to find out what the bizarre mathematician had been doing. Westcott returned to his swivel chair. His shaved head glowed in the dimly lit lab, the infrared sensor surgically implanted on the bald pate looking like some evil weapon of war. Across the room, a matching unit sat atop the computer link. Westcott had been implanted with an electrode that entered his cortex and allowed him to communicate directly with his computer.

Ralston considered few acts to be sinful or blasphemous. Allowing this surgery was one that he wished to see outlawed. It repulsed him to such an extent that he wanted to turn and run from Westcott, but the mathematician had done nothing illegal. The government regulated the implantation, permitting less than five a decade to undergo the surgery. How Westcott had qualified, Ralston couldn't say; on one wall hung a simple license authorizing the Class IV human-computer connect.

That the government regulated it and had given permission in Westcott's case, didn't lessen Ralston's revulsion.

"So slow," Westcott muttered, eyes closed. The man's face screwed into a tight bunch until his red-veined nose twitched like a weasel's. "Input is too slow. My mind can't keep up with the computer, even when I reduce the transfer rates. And it's so hard to correlate. Too many dimensions, too many tide-dependent variables."

Ralston got to his feet. The computer into which the IR sensor linked acted as a buffer for Westcott. His organic brain proved a thousand times too slow for even the slowest of University computers. A special interface computer had been built to reduce the output speed from bigger computers for Westcott's consumption. After his feeble thoughts were accumulated in a buffer, they were then squirted to the larger computer in a microburst to prevent wasting precious computing time. Ralston had heard it said that Westcott used less than a millisecond of the University computer's runtime a month, even though the mathematician remained hooked into the interface for periods up to forty hours at a stretch.

"What were you doing?" asked Ralston, calmer now. He tried not to look directly at Westcott, but little else in the man's lab commanded his attention. The single license dangling from a hook on the wall constituted the only adornment. Tables were littered with remnants of half-eaten, then forgotten meals. Westcott's desk held a standard issue console, but Ralston saw dust on the keys. What computing Westcott needed, he asked for directly through his interconnect. The far wall of the room had been outfitted with a tri-vid screen; this gave Ralston some clue as to what might have happened.

He walked to the screen and studied the touch controls. The archaeology professor shook his head. They hadn't been used in months. Dust covered them.

As quickly as he came to this conclusion, he again found himself plunging through space, hearing the tune that had haunted him before. Ralston yelped and reached out. The painful contact with the wall helped him maintain a semblance of control.

"What's going on?" he asked in a choked voice.

"Helps me think. I visualize better when I am able to surround myself with the graph." Westcott's thin frame showed eerily in the light cast by his IR sensor. "I translate data points into musical notes."

"What? Why?"

"Sounds are more transient than a purely visual display," Westcott said. "They give added dimensions when I analyze data employing time-dependent variables." Westcott smiled; Ralston thought he looked like a death's head. "I sometimes find that the sounds turn into songs that are not totally independent. It provides new ways of looking at the data. Pitch, duration, loudness, even waveshape," said Westcott, "provide new clues for me. But the waveshape— now there's an interesting factor. I can vary the pure tone of a wave down to the buzz of random fluctuations. Information falls out when I do this. So interesting. No one else at the University analyzes data this way."

Ralston made his way along the wall, found Westcott's desk and settled onto it. The feel of solid material beneath him helped hold at bay the sensation of falling forever.

"The chaos device?" Ralston asked, pulse accelerating as he understood Westcott's objectives. "You're trying to study its effects, trace its trajectory?"

"No."

Ralston's heart sank. He'd hoped that Westcott, with his unique connection with the University's computer, would be able to plot exactly the device's course through space using Alpha 3 as a point, then assuming other novas were also caused by the device's passage.

"I succeeded in that some time ago. I informed you of that."

Ralston blinked. Dotted red lines began forming in midair around him. The perspective shifted, and he floated outside the galaxy, looking inward. The curving line showed where the chaos device had been—or gone.

"I cannot ascertain direction along the line," Westcott said. "The effects of the field's passage is randomly delayed. It probably came from the far rim of the galaxy and spiraled inward in this manner." The red line vanished, only to reappear in the way Westcott suggested. A low, bone-rattling hum rose. Westcott added sound to the display to emphasize the probable trajectory. Ralston had no idea what this signified, but to the mathematician it was obviously important.

"Its point of origin is on the other side of the galaxy?"

"Some eighty thousand light years distant," said Westcott.

"We won't be exploring for the civilization that built it, then," Ralston said with some sadness. He had hoped for a *real* find—the people who had built the device. Velasquez still promised big discoveries on Proteus, and all those in the University touted him as the next departmental chairman. While Ralston cared little for such a hollow honor and added burden, he knew Velasquez had the potential for making significant strides.

That mattered far more than a chairmanship.

Michael Ralston wanted to do more than bring back alien artifacts. He wanted to find the civilization responsible for igniting the nuclear furnaces of a dozen or more stable stars and causing them to go nova. Any race with knowledge so fundamental and profound had to be worth examining minutely.

That would be the discovery of all time!

"We share much," muttered Westcott.

"What?"

"The time it would take to star to the probable planet of origin is comparable to my feeble attempts to take input directly from a block computer."

Ralston shook his head. Westcott's view of the world filtered through the computer. The mathematician saw—

and heard—everything in terms of baud rates and how inept his flesh was in accepting block circuit output. Ralston had heard it said by some mathematicians on campus that Westcott was brilliant, and this brilliance depended on his linkage to the computer. Ralston would settle for merely bright—even moronic—rather than be a slave to a machine.

Westcott might argue this point. The man might even claim it freed him to do calculations vastly beyond the comprehension of unmodified scholars. Ralston couldn't deny this, but he could deny any semblance of humanity remaining in Westcott.

"Floating in space helps you think?" he asked.

"The tri-vid display? An amusement, nothing more. As long as the computer is running, I have no trouble concentrating. The flow is like . . ." Westcott's words trailed off, then returned louder, more forceful and confident. ". . . a shining river that flows forever. I'm a leaf tossed on the singing waves. I sense so much lurking beneath the pitifully small surface I' swim across, and I know it'll be closed to me for all time. But I don't mind. Not really, because most never even have the chance to ride that wondrous flow of infinite information, to get their feet wet in such incredible knowledge."

"The chaos device," pressed Ralston, not liking the fanatical light in Westcott's watery eyes. "What other information? Anything on the data I provided on possible escapes from Alpha 3?"

"Oh, that. Of course. The data proved sketchy."

Ralston's hopes sank.

"But I succeeded in pinpointing a most likely destination. Statistical confidence level ninety-five percent." On the vid screen glowed a bright orange point. "The planet is similar to Alpha 3. Only cursory survey work has been done."

"No living beings?" asked Ralston. His eagerness soared.

A preliminary survey often missed even gross planetary features. A satellite orbited a planet a few times, monitoring the usual frequencies for communications while the human scout searched geosynchronous points for satellites launched by any planet dwellers. If neither search proved positive, spectro readings were taken and a few space photos made, then the scout ship left. Space was too huge to lavish much attention on any given uninhabited planet. If for any reason a planet was needed, for research stations or even colonization, more detailed studies would be ordered as needed.

But a scout might miss a rudimentary society. The survivors from Alpha 3 might still flourish on this planet, especially if they had fallen on hard times and retreated into a more primitive culture without easily identifiable electronics.

"Call it Beta," said Westcott.

"What?" Ralston moved toward the door, upset at the way Westcott seemed to have read his thoughts. He'd wondered what they should call this system.

"Beta is appropriate, since you started with Alpha. Unless you are going to quit. Then call it Omega."

"I'm not going to quit. This Alphan named Dial left his planet without a stardrive."

"Took them almost forty years standard to arrive at Beta, then, if they succeeded in achieving eighty-seven percent light speed," said Westcott. The mathematician shrugged. "The distance between the primaries is about thirty-five light years, and I judge it difficult for a first effort to achieve velocities much in excess of 0.87c."

Ralston worked through the numbers. Forty years travel meant that almost eighty had transpired on Alpha, due to time dilation effects.

"That means they've had almost ten thousand years to colonize Beta."

"They died. High probability on that," said Westcott, almost smirking. "In that long a time, they'd have achieved planet-wide communication the scout would have intercepted. Cities large enough to see visually from space would be present, too."

Ralston sighed. Westcott was right. The more exhaus-

tive IR scans and synthetic aperture radar photos that
revealed artifacts buried under the planetary surface, were
done only if visible spectrum or ten-centimeter band communications were positive. Chances were excellent that the
refugees from Alpha 3 had died before reaching Beta, or
had perished soon after due to inimical conditions.

Their untried starship might have blown up, too. Ralston
didn't even know that Dial had reached Beta. But he could
hope that the Alphan scientist succeeded. He could hope.

As he considered the ramifications, Ralston shuddered.
They might even have carried with them the seeds of their
own destruction. It had taken ten thousand years for the
instabilities in the Alpha primary to reach nova point; the
natives had died from the effects of the chaos device much
sooner.

"It won't cost much," said Westcott.

"What are you talking about?" Ralston's uneasiness
with Westcott magnified when the man insisted on talking
in riddles. Something about communicating with the computer directly caused the mathematician to do this.

"You want to go to Beta. You need an expedition. It
won't cost much. And I want to go."

This surprised Ralston. He'd never known Westcott to
leave this laboratory. The man had to at some time, but the
IR link to the computers seemed more vital to Westcott
than any human contact. Ralston had never even heard of
Westcott having friends.

"I must gather data directly," explained the computer-
linked mathematician. "Nothing less than this will suffice
for me. The equations are so beguiling. There is an elegance
to them that doesn't exist in other systems of differential
equations. The solution to chaos will be . . . it will be
orgasmic!"

Ralston didn't argue. "When I get everything together,
you can come. Have you ever left Novo Terra before?"

"You need not worry about me. I know what to do. All
knowledge I require is locked away within the University's
computer circuitry. And it's mine, all mine!"

The IR sensor atop Westcott's shaved head began to glow more intensely, indicating harder linking to the computer. Ralston avoided breaking the beam, as Westcott had once warned him this gave the man headaches. With relief approaching release from stark terror, Ralston slipped into the corridor and shut the door to Westcott's lab behind him. The archaeologist leaned against a cool wall and took several deep, calming breaths.

"I didn't want that," he said to himself, realizing he had agreed to let Westcott accompany him when he went searching for the survivors of Alpha 3. But he had. Ralston shook his head as he went down the broad steps at the end of the hall.

He was lost in thought and didn't hear the angry voices until he exited the building. Ralston stopped and stared, then cursed his bad luck. He had walked into the center of a student demonstration. At that instant, he wished that the traditionalists had lost and the remote classing proponents had won their fight to get people off the campus and into cramped cubicles scattered about the planet.

". . . against the principles that made Novo Terra great!" bellowed a student standing on the steps of the building. Ralston didn't have to be a genius to know that they spoke about him. Many carried placards denouncing him and the menace posed by the telepathic projector. But two signs in particular hinted at the mood and composition of the crowd. "The wages of sin is death" and "Ye are fallen from grace" were scrawled with a ragged brush.

The Archbishop's displeasure with him had boiled over and taken the form of a steadily more violent crowd.

Ralston was shoved and jostled, but the students ignored him, caught up in the fiery sermon being preached by the orator. He allowed himself to bounce from one to another and diffuse like a gas molecule back to the edge of the gathering. Then he paused for a moment and saw what he'd feared—and expected.

The P'torra stood a few meters distant and worked diligently on a small device in his blubbery, stubby-fingered hand. The impulse driver recorded every word uttered, their tone and duration and the result. The small computer would return suggestions for increasing the crowd's wrath or quelling it.

Ralston had no doubt that the P'torra sought only to inflame the passions of those gathered.

The P'torra intently worked on the impulse driver and failed to see Ralston. The archaeology professor ducked behind a tall column and almost ran from the scene. The students had already been whipped into an ugly mood by the idea that Ralston had somehow committed acts against their God. The alien's gentle proddings would only push them over the edge of violence. Given such scientific meddlings, the Inquisition might appear mild in comparison. Ralston closed his eyes for a moment and pictured himself ripped apart, his parts scattered on the Quadrangle in front of Bacon's statue.

Not the end he intended. Better he die on the site of a new find, somewhere among the stars, tracking down the chaos device that had produced so much death and misery.

He knew better than to argue with the Archbishop on this point. The cleric had said that no such device could exist, that it ran counter to God's blueprint for the universe. Simply stating that it did exist put him at odds with the Church.

Ralston found one small tidbit to smile at. With luck, he could convince Chancellor Salazar that sending him on an expedition to the Beta system was better than allowing him to remain on campus. Out of sight, out of mind.

Ralston's steps turned from the narrow, rubber-paved path. He hurried toward another research building, this one untouched by a crowd's angry shouts. He wandered down the corridors until he came to an office door with three names scribbled on a piece of paper, then knocked and went in.

Nels Bernssen looked up from one of the four small desks in the room. For a moment, the astrophysicist didn't seem to recognize him. Then the man smiled.

"Dr. Ralston, good to see you. You caught me in the middle of some calculations."

Ralston knew how difficult it was to drop detailed work and cope with unexpected visitors, and the postdoctoral assistant had more than enough material to work on. Some already called the stellar instability they'd witnessed in the Alpha primary a Bernssen Condition in honor of the work done in describing it mathematically. With some additional work and a little luck, Bernssen's career would be assured.

"Sit down." Bernssen motioned vaguely toward two chairs covered with litter. Ralston didn't mind sweeping some of it off and placing it into a neat pile on the floor beside the chair. He, too, had other things to do besides housekeeping chores.

"I didn't want to disturb you but this is important," Ralston said without preamble.

"Is it about your chaos device? Leonore was telling me that you might have a good lead on its trajectory. I'd certainly like to get close enough to it for detailed examination."

"That's part of what I want to talk to you about. I think I know where refugees from Alpha 3 went."

Bernssen rocked back, his long legs curled around the chair's front legs. "For you, that'd be fine. Why come to me about it?"

"You can ask them what they saw, what they observed. A scientist—an astronomer—named Dial led a small group off Alpha 3 and toward a system we've called Beta."

"We? Who else knows about this? Leonore's father?"

Ralston shook his head. It almost pained him to admit that Westcott had done the calculations. He was heartened, though, when he saw that Bernssen's reaction to the mathematician and his mind-machine link was similar to his own.

"Brilliant, but not the sort I enjoy socially, if you track my meaning." Bernssen thought for a moment. "This Beta system was colonized by scientists who directly observed the chaos field passing by their planet? Such observations would be invaluable in determining the initial conditions in the nova.''

"We'd all benefit," said Ralston. "Westcott wants to study the mathematics of the chaos field, I want a chance to see their culture and match it with what I already know, you could get information on the chaos device. We all benefit," he repeated.

"I've got several seminars to give. Papers to write. A lifetime of work just processing the data accumulated," muttered Bernssen. "I'll be here forever." The blond smiled broadly. "When do you leave? I want to go with you. This is nothing more than dog work. I want to be where I can observe and do real science."

"I never thought of astronomy as an experimental science, but you're right." Ralston said, and frowned.

"What's the problem?" asked Bernssen. "There's something I missed. While I'm not too pleased with the idea of Leonore's father funding such an expedition—"

"He doesn't know."

Bernssen raised one eyebrow. "This is even better. Salazar has authorized your trip? I don't mind the University getting the glory, but I think IC is big enough."

"Salazar hasn't authorized it. I need your help in getting the funds."

"Blackmail, that's what this is. You don't tell me where your Beta system is unless I use my newfound leverage to get the money, transportation, and equipment."

"That's a bit blunt, and not the way I'd have phrased it."

"But it is accurate?"

Ralston nodded. The archaeology professor smiled slowly, saying, "I think Leonore might be interested in the expedition, even if her father has nothing to do with it. For her it'd be a risk having me organize the trip. But not if you did it."

"You make it sound more interesting by the second." Bernssen rocked forward and thrust out his meaty hand.

"Let's see how much the University of Ilium is willing to spend on Nels Bernssen's expedition to Beta."

Ralston shook the physicist's hand. Things were working out better than he'd hoped.

"But tell me, Dr. Ralston, if I hadn't agreed, would you have kept Beta's location a secret?"

Bernssen read the answer in Michael Ralston's cold gray eyes.

FOUR

"SO YOU AREN'T even going to say good-bye?"

The accusation came at Michael Ralston from deep shadows. His heart beat faster, and he tried to keep a quaver from his voice. He had walked through what should have been a quiet campus in a miasma of fear the past two weeks. Ralston had tried to speak with the Archbishop and been denied an audience. Seeing the P'torra quietly talking to the Archbishop's secretary a few hours later told the archaeology professor much about the reason for the prelate's rejection. He knew better than to be seen with the P'torra. The alien bore him no personal malice but would cherish the sight of Ralston being torn apart by an enraged crowd.

Ralston snorted. If anything, the P'torra was the most devoted student at the University of Ilium. He worked assiduously on perfecting his techniques using the impulse driver. By the time he graduated, he'd be expert in human manipulations.

"What do you want?" Ralston called, moving quickly to put his back to a wall.

"You've gotten paranoid in your old age." The shadow moved, changed, became a distinct figure.

"Druanna!"

"At least you recognize me." The small, sleek woman

moved closer and took Ralston's wrist, holding it expertly. Fingers probed until she found his pulse under the cords of muscle. "You were frightened! I'm sorry. I didn't mean to—"

"I'm all right. Things have been orbiting around me too fast lately. I thought you were—never mind. Sorry to have ignored you." Ralston was genuinely contrite. Druanna Thorkkin was a good friend, and occasionally more than just a friend. Their lives intertwined, sometimes with passion, other times with needed companionship or simple friendship. Druanna listened when he needed to talk; what he provided for her was something Ralston had never quite fathomed. Perhaps he gave her a taste of a change, a respite from their overly academic colleagues, a touch of uncertainty and wildness.

Druanna released his wrist. He didn't allow his hand to drop. Ralston reached out and lightly touched her cheek. The flesh felt warm, alive.

"I wouldn't leave without letting you know," he said. "I owe you too much."

"So you remembered, eh?" She shook her head in mock anger. "I doubt it. You're just telling me what you think I want to hear. And don't you dare stop!"

They laughed together. Ralston's arm slipped about her shoulders and he pulled her close. The comfort of her nearness turned him weak. He had been in a state of constant stress, worrying over Bernssen's expedition being grounded, not getting enough funding, a thousand details that might stop them from exploring the Beta system. Being with Druanna Thorkkin took him away from all that.

For a moment.

"How's medieval literature this term?" he asked.

"A year older, that's all. I tried out some of those authors you suggested. I'll never know where you dredged them up, but some are good. That Dupin, for instance. And Hillman. He's good."

"Hillerman," Ralston corrected. "I started reading his

work when I was an undergraduate at the University of Novo Terra. Interesting speculations on primitive migratory and farming cultures locked in those words.''

They argued over the value of the fictional work, whether a literature professor had more claim to them than did an archaeology professor. Ralston enjoyed the verbal sparring, not so much because Druanna was cleverer at it than he, but because it didn't matter. If he lost this debate, it meant nothing.

When they had wound down, the point unresolved, Ralston asked, "How did you know I was about ready to star out?''

"Rumors," said Druanna. "I guessed even more from not having seen you. What else would keep you from my bed for so long? You know I'm irresistible.''

"Not another woman," he said.

She turned and stared into his gray eyes as if to read truth there, then grunted and turned away. "Damn. You're not lying. That means I'm still stuck with you.''

"You're not angling for a spot with the expedition, are you?''

"Hardly. What would a lit prof do out among the stars?''

"I'm not sure what a lit prof does here, on campus," he said.

"It's a good thing," Druanna Thorkkin said sternly, "that you're joking." They walked, shoulders brushing lightly, into the deserted Quad. The last hint of summer warmth still clung tenaciously to the nighttime air, but autumn intruded with an occasional cool breeze that rippled sonorously through the leaves.

"In a way, you deserve a spot, if you wanted it," said Ralston. "There wouldn't have been a sliver of a chance for me if you hadn't helped me get back to Alpha 3.''

Druanna Thorkkin had hidden Ralston while campus security had sought him just prior to his return to the doomed planet. She had even driven him to the shuttle launch site and decoyed away pursuers so that he could rendezvous in near orbit. Ralston had succeeded in getting the mental-projection equipment off planet before the primary went nova and cindered the entire Alpha solar system.

"So name something after me," Druanna said. "My idea of roughing it is not finding anything on the tri-dee that interests me. Being in primitive dig sites on dirty planets doesn't seem to me to be very . . . academic."

In spite of Druanna's athletic prowess and slim figure, he knew she was right. Try as he might, Ralston couldn't picture her out grubbing among thousand-year-old ruins and chortling over the discovery of a single pot shard or a new alloy hunk of steel. He *could* see her poring over a musty book made from ancient paper and taking detailed notes on how an author achieved a precise effect.

"Does it bother you?" she asked. They settled down under a tree, completely encased in shadow. Here and there around the Quad a yellow light shone through a window. For the most part, the University had gone to sleep.

"What? That it's Bernssen's expedition and not mine?" Ralston shook his head. "Hardly. I'm going along. It doesn't matter what they call me. Just being able to follow along the thread and maybe find more recent evidence of the Alpha civilization is important. What does bother me is not being able to fully staff my research as a result of it being Bernssen's show."

"And the chaos device?"

"That, too." He took a deep breath, held it for a few seconds, then exhaled slowly. The rush of fear he'd experienced when Druanna had startled him was gone now. "I don't think it's any menace to us. It worked past Alpha 3 too many years ago, but it's out there somewhere." He lounged back and let the soft, dew-moist grass support him. Stars burned with blue-white ferocity in the clear sky arching above.

"Chen said something about his probe being destroyed. Is there anything to it?"

"You mean any connection to the chaos device? I think

there might be. That 1054 guest star of his blew into an entire nebula. While his probes might have been destroyed by debris or any number of other things, the way they failed seems too similar to be discounted. Also, the nebula lies on the trajectory Westcott plotted for the device.''

Ralston felt Druanna shiver beside him. He couldn't decide if it came from the mention of Westcott, whom she loathed for the same reasons he did, or from the cold. Ralston decided to pretend it was the cold. He put his arm around her. Druanna snuggled close, cheeks pressing into his shoulder. Warm breath gusted into his chest.

"Seems lonely out here," Druanna said. "No one in sight. You leaving. When?"

"Just before dawn."

"That's hours off," she said.

"Think we might scare anyone if we stayed here for a while longer?" Ralston asked.

Druanna kissed him. Later, he doubted they'd scared anyone at all with their activity under the stars, and it had been the send-off he needed to assure him that returning to the University might not be such a bad thing after all.

"Does he have to go up with us?" asked Leonore Disa. "He's already complaining."

Michael Ralston paced back and forth, not trying to hide his nervousness. It was always this way with him before a launch. When he had been a soldier with the Nex military forces, he'd received deep hypnotic commands to calm him. That conditioning seldom worked now, unless he concentrated hard on the patterns buried in his mind. At the moment, too many people bustled about for Ralston to do that.

"Westcott is an important member of the team," Ralston said, not bothering to look at the distraught woman.

"You mean his funding is important," she snapped.

"Nels certainly did his best to get what funding he could, but we both know it wasn't enough." Ralston didn't try to keep the bitterness from his voice. Bernssen wasn't happy, Leonore wasn't happy, and neither was he.

Leonid Disa had done his best to block Bernssen's obtaining permission for the expedition. At first Ralston had thought it was because the man didn't want his daughter risking her life in a new and unexplored system. Leonore had coldly informed Ralston that her father couldn't care less about such things. The chairman of Interstellar Computronics worried more about Ralston finding Alpha 3 survivors who could lay significant claim to the telepathic projector. Dealing with Chancellor Salazar was one thing, buying the rights to the device from aliens with unknown ideas of money and coercion bothered him.

Even worse, Ralston guessed, was the idea that these unknown aliens might be able to construct one of the devices that the best scientific minds at the University and at IC hadn't been able to reverse engineer. Such a blow to IC and the elder Disa's ego wasn't to be borne.

"Westcott had the funds from other grants," said Ralston. "He's willing to free it for us if he can go along. Your real objection is to him, not his money."

"He . . . he gives me the heart-hops. Just looking at him makes me queasy." Leonore folded her arms under her breasts and hugged herself. Ralston looked past her to where Westcott sat.

The archaeology professor had to admit Leonore had a point. Westcott sat with an unfocused expression, his jaw slack and a tiny rivulet of spittle trickling from the corner of his mouth. The IR sensor that linked the mathematician to his precious computer lay quiescent atop his shaved head. Not until they boarded the starship would Westcott again be able to direct-link.

"What's going through his mind, do you suppose?" Leonore asked. "He hardly looks human. Makes me want to deny I'm human, and claim to be . . . to be from Alpha 3."

"They were birdlike," said Ralston. "You, my dear, are definitely and delightfully apelike." On impulse, he kissed her. Leonore stepped back in surprise, unsure of herself.

"Dr. Ralston," she said, struggling for just the right way of protesting.

"There's Nels. Let's see if there's anything more that has to be loaded before they turn on the boost laser." Ralston ignored his graduate assistant and went to speak with Nels Bernssen. Leonore trailed after, still confused.

The cold, brisk dawn wind whipping across the plains forced Ralston to pull his coat tighter around his whipcord-muscled body. Huge, silvery plumes of carbon dioxide vented from beneath the paving near the shuttle. The powerful gas laser was being readied to fire repeatedly and hurl the stubby shuttle into low orbit. Ralston avoided one of the chilling gas vents and crossed the distance to where Bernssen oversaw last minute cargo loading.

"About ready to go, Nels?" Ralston asked.

"We've got everything. I just commed the ship upstairs, and the pilot said clearance to star for Beta has come through. We'd best not wait much longer before leaving."

"You have the feeling that Salazar will rescind permission?"

Bernssen turned to Ralston and smiled slowly. "Would it matter?" he asked.

"Hell, no."

"Let's get aboard. The ground crew is starting to grumble about the weather. Let 'em squirt us aloft and get free of Novo Terra." Bernssen took Leonore's hand and together they went up the steeply sloped gangway. Ralston followed, wondering if he should alert Westcott.

Let the mathematician be stranded, he thought. They could use his grant money and not have to put up with him in space.

But Ralston saw Westcott stir, as if some unheard command awoke him. He turned like an automaton and plodded toward the portal. Ralston made way for the mathematician, who passed him without saying a word. As if he'd been in space a hundred times before, Westcott found his way to a pneumatic acceleration couch and fastened himself in with deft, efficient motions.

Ralston sprang into the couch beside the mathematician when the strident launch alarm sounded. He'd barely fastened his safety webbing when the portal hissed shut, and less than thirty seconds later the launch warning light flashed red. The laser buried under the tarmac spewed forth prodigious amounts of energy, directing the full force of its coherent beam against the shuttle's splash plate.

The heavy vessel lurched aloft, seemed to pause, then the laser recharged and again smashed into the underside. Over and over the pulsed beam blasted at the shuttle, until the whining died down signaling that they were free of most of the atmosphere. In the two-hundred-kilometer-high orbit, more than ninety-nine percent of the atmosphere had been left behind. What tenuous fingers caressed the shuttle were insignificant as it angled farther aloft to rendezvous with the starship.

Ralston closed his eyes. In less than an hour the heavy jolt told him they had docked with the starship. In another hour they had transferred their final load of cargo to the larger ship's hold and were again in acceleration couches, awaiting launch.

This time it would be for a star system so distant the Beta primary wasn't even visible from Novo Terra.

"The pilot's not very communicative," observed Bernssen. "He shut off the screen showing the cockpit."

"There aren't many who socialize with their passengers," said Ralston. "They claim it keeps them from peak efficiency."

"Verd, but I like to watch the controls," said Bernssen. "Not that I could do anything, but I want to know if anything goes wrong."

Ralston turned and looked at Leonore, who shook her head. Ralston said nothing. If Bernssen's worst fears came true and something happened to the pilot, Ralston knew that Leonore could operate the complex computers that drove the starship. She might not be a licensed pilot, but she know enough to get them back to a planet. He wondered why Leonore hadn't told Bernssen about this particular skill of hers. Would it have annoyed the physicist?

"We're ready. He's got us lined up for the shift," she said. Her body tensed, then relaxed beneath its webbing.

It took no pilot to know that they were on their way. The starship gave a deep-throated rumble as the shift engines powered up. Rockets flared and pressed them gently into their couches. Before Ralston could even call out "good luck," the pilot ordered the shift.

Blackness grabbed at Michael Ralston, pushed him into the couch, shut off nose and mouth, hammered at his chest, then pulled him inside out before showing him all the colors of the spectrum. Every shift affected him differently, and this one combined pain with beauty.

But through it all, he exulted. The Beta system and answers lay ahead!

Ralston tucked his knees to his chest, performed a quick rotation, and straightened just in time to grab an elastic band to stop himself. He had adjusted to the free fall quickly, and spent the nineteen weeks starring to the Beta system going over all the material he and Leonore Disa had accumulated on Alpha 3. In addition, Bernssen had shared the information he had garnered from the Alpha primary's spectral analysis before it had gone nova.

Only Westcott had remained aloof and uncommunicative, floating in a cocoon of silence, the pale red light in his sensor flickering on and off as he presented problem after problem for the small on-board computer to solve.

"We know so little about this field causing the random behavior," said the astrophysicist in a voice loud enough to be heard by both Ralston and Leonore in the low pressure chamber. "At least the pilot starred us within a day's travel of the most likely planet."

"Beta 5," mused Leonore. "It looks so like Alpha 3. They might be twins."

"Dial might have known it would be similar," said

Ralston, "but I think he just guessed. The Alphans didn't seem adequately advanced to have sent out survey probes that could return with the information needed for colonization."

"What courage," the woman said. "To set off with a sublight drive, perhaps not even knowing what you'd find at the end."

"With the chaos wracking the populace on Alpha 3, did they have a choice?" asked Ralston. He remembered all too clearly the devastating problems the residual effects of chaos had caused. One of his graduate students had died from an epileptic seizure induced by the field, and several of Bernssen's fellow researchers had been similarly affected. The chaos effect distorted electrical transmission, turned chemical reactions into chance rather than energy-gradient-driven occurrences—and it had triggered instabilities in the star that, ten thousand years after passage, had caused it to explode.

"They had no choice," Ralston stated firmly, now sure of himself. "I know them as well as anyone since I've been through so many of their dioramas. The telepathic lessons might not have been perfect for me since I'm not of their race, but I learned enough to know that they had no choice."

"Still," murmured Leonore. "Such a long trip, possibly generations, depending on their speed."

"Westcott said it might have taken up to eighty years planet time for them to arrive here," said Bernssen. "I think his estimate is close for a sublight velocity starship."

"It's a pretty planet, but there's no EM emanations," said Ralston. "I checked my own equipment."

"We'll get a few satellites in orbit," said Bernssen. "Then we'll know for certain."

"Be sure to send out the radar-imaging satellite in the first launch," said Ralston. He heaved a deep sigh. "I expect we'll have to sift through ruins once more."

"Just because they didn't send a greeting party doesn't mean the planet's devoid of life," said Leonore. "They might be cautious. After all, for them it's only been about ten thousand years since all the trouble on Alpha 3.''

Ralston laughed without humor. He floated to the center of the chamber, legs slightly bent and arms loose at his sides, the most comfortable position in free fall. By distancing himself from the others, he floated into an eerie silence. The lowered air pressure made it more difficult for sound transmission and, as long as he stayed away from the metal struts supporting the boron-fiber composite walls, he got no vibration from the ship's massive shift engines. He might as well have been cast into that awesomely infinite well he'd experienced on blundering into Westcott's lab.

Leonore and Bernssen began going down their checklist. Much of the work had been done using automated equipment; this had allowed them to bring fewer human personnel and the requisite support material. Still, Bernssen had ten assistants—and Ralston had to rely on his own two hands and Leonore's. He needed Bernssen's ten scientists and a hundred more besides, but he knew better than to complain.

He was here! He had left behind the University and again starred to where real science could be done.

Bernssen gave the signal that he'd popped out the first of his recon satellites, then sent Ralston's synthetic-aperture radar satellite into polar orbit around the planet. Ralston stiffened a few minutes later when Bernssen's control panel blossomed red. The archaeology professor scissors-kicked and he got himself moving slowly, until he snared a line and pulled himself to where Bernssen and Leonore worked feverishly.

"What's wrong?"

"My probe's glitched on me. Signal turned thready, then winked out."

"What about mine?" Ralston demanded.

Bernssen shook his head. "Looks fine, so far. I missed the calculated orbit a bit. A bit too much eccentricity, and the other orbital parameter's wrong. Call it a hundred kilometers too high, but that's within equipment limits.''

"The second probe is ready, Nels," said Leonore.

The astrophysicist launched it. As with his first satellite, this one also sent back a continuous data feed that turned to inexplicable white noise before dying.

"I checked those myself. Zero defects on both. On all my equipment. Hell, what else was there for me to do for over three months while we were in stardrive?" Bernssen looked guiltily at Leonore, as if she might contradict him. But Ralston's graduate student was as absorbed over the loss as her lover.

"Try a third?" suggested Ralston.

"Not yet. We'll let yours relay back its data. That might give some idea what's happening. We're still a few hours from orbit ourselves. We might not want to stay."

"A radiation belt? Micrometeorites?"

Nels Bernssen looked at the archaeologist, a curious expression on his face. "There might be more," said Bernssen. "The residual effects of the chaos device on Alpha 3 might be stronger here. They might have brought it with them."

"Your calculations are inadequate, sloppy, and lacking in the necessary rigor," Westcott said, and all three jerked around. "I have analyzed the fleeing aliens' course to this system."

"So?" asked Ralston.

The mathematician smirked, and said, "The poor bastards failed to run away from the path of the chaos field. They followed it backward, possibly by accident or ignorance, but they ended up in this system."

"What are you saying, Westcott?"

"The chaos field had already passed through the Beta system twenty-three hundred years prior to their arrival. The Alphans didn't run away from it, they ran *into* it."

Michael Ralston's eyes turned to the probe control panel. A new red light winked on. His probe had just died of equipment failure, too. Chaos held Beta 5 firmly in its sway. There was no chance at all now that he would find any survivors of the Alpha system. None.

"DEFINITELY INSTABILITY IN weather patterns," said Michael Ralston, straining to move a crate containing excavation equipment. He blinked as heavy droplets pelted down into his face. He wiped the rain off and levered the crate to a spot where he could open it under a slanting plastic roof set up for this purpose.

They had grounded four days earlier, after a week in orbit. None of their probes had failed after the first three; retrieving those satellites had shown what Ralston had feared, however. The block circuits had simply ceased functioning. The only explanation for the massive solid state failure had to lie with the residual randomizing effects of the chaos device.

Ralston had repaired his radar-imaging probe and done a quick survey of Beta 5, finding only two widely separated sites likely to produce any results archaeologically. Of any survivors from Alpha 3 he found no trace at all.

The laborobots had toiled ceaselessly since grounding and produced a tiny village of plastic huts. Some were set aside as living quarters, but Bernssen had used the largest to set up his stellar-probe equipment. A few satellites orbited the planet, and from those the astrophysicist took constant readings.

"Michael, the ultrasonic digger's finally ready," said

Leonore Disa. "I've got the supervisor hooked into it. All we need to do is program the path, and the equipment will do the rest."

Ralston wiped more rain from his face, turned and perched on the side of the crate. He didn't like the prospect of letting the sophisticated guidance system do work he enjoyed. There was no personal thrill in having the ultrasonic diggers operating day and night. He *liked* grubbing about, eyes alert for any hint of a discovery. He *liked* the feel of dirt sifting through his fingers as he worked out the complex history of the society whose ruins he researched. But Ralston would be the first to admit that they were shorthanded and that the complex supervisor computer was more than adequate for the task of monitoring excavation. If anything of note appeared in the digger's maw, an alarm would sound and let him do what he liked doing.

Ralston snorted in disgust. He had to admit that the supervisor and the robots connected to it would do a better, more efficient job than the group of graduate students he'd had with him on Alpha 3. The machines wouldn't blunder about and destroy precious information through ignorance or carelessness or simply not caring.

That had been the point that troubled him the most.

The students—except for Leonore Disa—simply hadn't cared. Two had been rehabs—criminals whose brains had been chemically and electrically altered to the point of destroying any initiative or curiosity. The others had merely put in their time, hoping to complete the equation Physical Presence = Advanced Degree.

All except Yago de la Cruz. That student had been hungry for notoriety and honor in his family's eyes. It had robbed him of both caution and his life.

Ralston shuddered at the way de la Cruz had died. The student had been seized in an epileptic fit induced by the Alpha 3 telepathic projectors. The chaos-caused epidemic had ravaged the alien society near the end of their civilization, and somehow this seed of madness had been implanted in de la Cruz and cost him his life.

Ralston looked out over the gently rolling, verdant hills of Beta 5. A lovely world and one not as obviously being destroyed by the chaotic conditions inflicted on it by the passing device. Trees rose to admirable heights not ten kilometers away and formed a forest Ralston vowed to explore. The flora and fauna of this world seemed harmless enough. His eyes dropped to the neat lines marked out by the digger, the first of the ruins being revealed. Whatever had killed off the last of the Alpha 3 refugees, it wasn't inimical wildlife.

"Pretty, isn't it?" said Leonore.

She sat beside him on the crate. The rain had cooled the day considerably, but the woman wore only a halter top and shorts. A bright silver plate and injector connection just above her navel marked her medport. Ralston knew she used various recreational drugs and direct-injected them through the med-port, but an old-fashioned stubbornness clung to much of his own actions. He didn't like the idea of anything running through his bloodstream that didn't belong there. Out in the field it made life easier if he didn't "need" chemical recreation.

He knew most of the current faddish drugs favored by the students were non-addicting. On occasion he might partake himself. But having a medport installed in his belly struck him as a modification that went against all logic and good taste.

"Verd," Ralston agreed, looking across a tiny stream of crystal clear water. "It's hard to believe that the chaos device passed by this planet."

"The weather makes it easier to believe," said Leonore. "It's just as bad as on Alpha 3. Unpredictable. I've had the computer trying to formulate an accurate weather forecast for three days. No good. Random results over any period longer than a few minutes, even though the planet's only got a twenty-degree axial tilt that should moderate the climate."

"Maybe that's the way it should be. Don't you get a little bored with the weather on Novo Terra?"

"No. Why should I?"

"You know what it'll be at any given time. There's no surprise, no thrill of a sudden rainstorm or unexpected sunshine when you've braced yourself for clouds."

"Some surprises I can live without." Leonore peered out from under the plastic roof. The sun shone brightly, a few fleecy white clouds drifting through the azure sky before the faint outlines of both moons clung. Only minutes before it had been raining.

"The digger's started," said Ralston. The ultrasonic hum filled the warm afternoon air. The supervisor recorded every grain of dirt in its block circuits for future analysis. "We ought to get the other two running, also. Cuts down on the time before we find something."

"This was the only other ruin on the radar?"

"This was it," said Ralston. "That bothers me. If Dial reached Beta 5 and they had any success colonizing, there ought to have been more cities."

"You've verified the other ruin?" asked Leonore.

Ralston frowned. "Verd, and it's on the other side of the planet, almost antipodal to this ruin. That strikes me as odd, unless the refugees had a falling out. After forty years aboard their ship, maybe they couldn't stand each other and decided to split their forces. Otherwise, I'd think their best chance for survival would be to stay in as large a group as possible."

"The evidence from their culture shows how revolted they were by epileptics," said Leonore. "Perhaps they isolated those showing the symptoms of being touched by the chaos field."

"We'll find out soon enough."

Ralston looked up to see Nels Bernssen walking through the muddy area in front of the equipment shelter. He waved to them and came over.

"The poor stupid bastards," the physicist said.

"What are you talking about, Nels?" asked Leonore.

"The Alphans. They left their home to get away from the destruction going on in their society, and where did they come? Here. Beta 5 had already seen a pass-by from the chaos field."

"Westcott's sure of that?"

"It's definite." Something in the man's tone alerted Ralston.

"What do you mean?"

"I just finished a preliminary data analysis," said Bernssen. "This is going to make me damned famous, and I don't much like it."

"Nels, no!" Leonore's stricken cry matched the cold knot forming in Ralston's belly.

Bernssen nodded grimly. "The so-called Bernssen Condition is present in the Beta primary, too." He laughed without any humor. "Life is hell when you find yourself getting famous off something that will destroy any future research."

"How long do we have before the sun goes nova?" asked Ralston, seeing a repetition of his disaster on Alpha 3.

"Hard to get quantitative about it. There's nothing pressing. But we've definitely got a run of bad luck on it. I'd say within a planetary year."

Ralston had hoped for more. The rough estimates placed a Beta 5 year at a half standard year. From the planet, the G8 primary seemed only half as bright as normal, giving the impression of perpetual descending twilight.

How appropriate, he thought. Darkness always falling. The slightly heavier gravity wore on him almost as much as this new and unwanted information. He didn't ask Nels if he was certain. Ralston had enough confidence in the astrophysicist to know that the data had been analyzed properly. The 5600-degree Kelvin temperature of the sun's surface would begin to rise, hotter and hotter, cool slightly, then rise uncontrollably and beyond belief until the star exploded.

Perhaps a planetary year—six months—until this occurred, Nels had said. Ralston thanked the planet's slower rotation and thirty-three hour days. If he had little time to work, he could at least work most of it in the dim daylight.

This gave him enough time to poke about in the ruins, but probably not enough to completely exhaust all available data. Still, he wouldn't be under the pressure he'd experienced on Alpha 3.

"Looks like another storm moving up fast," said Leonore, pointing to the horizon. Clouds lead gray with moisture accumulated and rose in a terrifyingly immense thunderhead. Strong upper winds sheared the top into a familiar anvil pattern. Already tiny sparks of lightning formed to light the dark underbelly.

"There's not much the rain will harm." Ralston looked over the ruins where the digger had uncovered a neat masonry wall. "If anything, it might wash off the dirt and help us out."

The words were hardly out of his mouth when the ground began to quiver. Ralston felt as if he'd been on an all-night binge and his knees had turned to putty. He wobbled and grabbed for support, thinking perversely that the fault lay within him rather than outside. A stroke? Did he suffer momentary dizziness from working too hard?

"Quake!" bellowed Bernssen. "Get out from under the shelters and into the open. Where's that hijo Westcott?"

Ralston went limp and let the motion of the moving surface toss him about. He hit and rolled and tried vainly to stand. The best he succeeded in accomplishing was to balance himself on hands and knees. The world spun around him, and his gut felt as if it had turned to jelly.

"It's a bad one, the worst I've ever been through," called out Bernssen. The physicist had one arm around Leonore, but she pushed him away, preferring to weather the violent natural assault apart. Ralston watched the couple bounce together, then rebound and fall to the suddenly treacherous ground. They bobbed up and down before vanishing from his line of sight.

Ralston held back his nausea and a sense of helplessness. The quake seemed to go on forever. He looked about and saw crates being overturned by invisible hands, the supervisor blinking wildly that its mechanical minions had ceased operation, the plastic shelters tumbling down from unexpected stresses.

Then the rains hit with a fury that Ralston hadn't believed possible. It wasn't enough that the planet rattled his teeth. Now the skies had to open and drench him.

"Quake's about over," he heard Bernssen calling from some spot on the other side of their compound. "Reading has it at 5.9 Richter. Wasn't all that bad. Just a light temblor."

Ralston doubted this. The shaking had been severe enough to throw him off his feet. But when he peered through the curtain of rain all around, he saw minimal damage. The supervisor had restarted the ultrasonic diggers, and the parts of the shelters that had fallen wouldn't take more than a few minutes to snap back together.

The archaeology professor checked the instruments, satisfied himself that none of the programming had been altered by the quake, then went to see how Bernssen and Leonore fared. They grumbled at the rain but gamely worked to get the roof lifted back onto a shelter. Ralston walked on briskly to find Westcott.

"You in there?" he called out. Westcott's shelters had sustained minor damage. "Are you all right, Westcott?"

No answer. Ralston tugged open the sprung door and moved it to one side. Within the shelter he saw no light. The heavy clouds had cut off the feeble sunlight, but Westcott hadn't set his interior for automatic illumination. Or if he had, the quake had damaged the control circuits.

"Westcott?"

A pale red light winked balefully: Westcott's head-mounted sensor. Ralston entered the room and knelt beside the mathematician, taking a pulse. The beat of the man's heart proved strong. Ralston took Westcott by the shoulders and turned him so that he stretched out supine. As he did so, one accusing eye opened and speared him.

"What do you want? Interrupting me is not something I appreciate, especially when I am in the middle of such intricate and demanding calculations."

"Sorry," Ralston said without meaning it.

"Worst of all is breaking my direct-link beam with the computer. I told you that gives me a headache." Westcott fought to sit upright. He appeared weak.

"We had a quake. In case you didn't notice, it brought down most of the buildings in the compound. I worried that you might have been injured."

"You were worried about me?" asked Westcott, as if this were more complex a statement than even the most esoteric of the higher geometries he studied. "I was working out the mathematics governing your culture's death."

"The Alphans?" Ralston wondered at the mathematician. How could he have not noticed the world shaking all around him?

"Yes, yes, of course. Who else?" Westcott pushed past Ralston and stepped into the rain. He immediately returned, hands covering his sensor. "A hard failure in the planet's geologic structure," he said unexpectedly.

"The quake?"

"A product of topological dynamics. I must add that to my set of equations. You see," Westcott said, as if Ralston really cared, "there are two types of failure: hard and soft. The soft failures occur with some regularity. Small strokes in humans, minor memory lapse, that sort of thing. No real importance. The hard failures constitute the epilepsy you've found."

"You're saying the planet just had an epileptic fit?"

"Don't be ridiculous," scoffed Westcott. He seated himself in front of his computer console and made minute adjustments to the IR sensor pickup on it. Satisfied that his link had been fine-tuned, he went on. "Nonetheless, it is a hard failure, a solution only slightly different for the set of nonlinear differential equations governing crustal plate movement." Westcott's IR sensor blinked on and off slowly— the man "thought."

"Can you predict if there'll be more quakes? We might want to move to a safer area."

"You don't understand, do you? The model for weather is a complex set of equations in which even the smallest disturbance will cause chaotic behavior. A falling leaf will trigger instability. How can you avoid such minor movement?"

"I didn't mean the weather. I meant the . . ." Ralston swallowed hard when he realized that to Westcott weather and quakes were simply different manifestations of the same equation set. *Any* movement might trigger a new quake since the passage of the chaos device had forced randomness on the system.

"The time evolution of any system obeys strictly deterministic laws," said Westcott, "but your chaos field has caused the system to act as if it obeyed only its own free will." He chuckled. "I am sure the Archbishop would be tempted to say this is God's will at work, but it can't be. It is random. Enforced randomness."

"I've got to check my equipment for damage," Ralston said, wanting to be away from Westcott. The mathematician took away what little hope he had.

Ralston left, hardly noticing the rain hammering away at his face. He squinted and walked through the mud and murk to the excavation site. The quiet humming of the digger reassured him that not all in the universe fell prey to chaotic dynamics.

He dropped to his knees and looked at the debris produced by the digger, knowing he wouldn't find anything of consequence but wanting to make sure that neither the supervisor nor digger hadn't glitched for a moment during the quake and missed something. The archaeologist found only bits of rock and insignificant organic matter that had been caught in the digger's maw.

"Michael," came the faint cry. He looked up. The rain obscured his vision farther than a few meters. Again came the plaintive call. "I need you."

"Leonore?" Ralston stood, trying to decide the direction of the woman's voice. But it hadn't sounded like Leonore. Not exactly. He swallowed hard. It had sounded more like Druanna Thorkkin. He pushed such an absurd notion away, but uneasiness grew like some evil seed within him. "Druanna?" he called.

"Here, Michael. Here!"

He turned slowly, unable to pinpoint the source of the voice. He bent down and wiped off the casing atop the ultrasonic digger. Using his thumbnail, he pried back a lid to expose the programming console. He poked a few times until he hit the proper buttons.

"Michael? Come to me. Now!"

The digger let out a beep and slowly turned until it faced outward, in the direction of the copse he had noted earlier. Rain hid the trees—and whoever called to him. Ralston reprogrammed the digger to return to its mindless chewing away at the dirt around the ruins.

He set his inertial tracker to be sure he wouldn't get lost in the downpour, then started out across the grassy plains. Ralston knew it wasn't Leonore Disa who called. And he couldn't quite decide why he didn't return to find her and Bernssen to tell them what he'd just heard. It wasn't pride, or fear that they might laugh at him. Ralston had been scorned and ridiculed by the best and lived through it. Curiosity moved him—but what else?

He swallowed, tried to get enough spittle to spit, and failed. The voice sounded so much like Druanna, yes, but even more like Marta. There had never been another woman in his life like the vivacious Marta, now lost to him. It couldn't be her, not on Beta 5. But who was it?

What was it?

"Michael, hurry. Please!"

His pace across the meadow remained constant even though he wanted to break into a headlong run to discover who played such a cruel joke on him. Bernssen? The man seemed affable enough, but did he wrongly suspect anything between professor and student? Ralston felt only admiration for Leonore Disa—and nothing more intimate.

She had aided him when he needed it, and he'd seen that she received all the accolades due her for their discoveries.

But what if Nels Bernssen was jealous? Would he take the opportunity to kill the archaeology professor?

Ralston considered this ridiculous, but the voice did draw him.

He slipped once in the mud and stayed on one knee, listening intently. The rain slackened, but the weather continued its onslaught with fiercer winds. Cold and wet, he now had to fight against winds he guessed to be gusting to at least sixty kilometers an hour. Ralston shielded his eyes with his hand. The sun cast strange shadows through the clouds and rain, turning the landscape into something surreal.

Ralston checked his inertial tracker and found the green arrow pointing back to camp. He almost spun and followed it to safety. But the voice sang out again and drew him. He remembered one of Druanna's stories, an Earth folktale about creatures living on rocks along a river. Their voices called out and hypnotized sailors, drawing them and their vessels to the rocks where they wrecked and died.

"Michael! I need you!"

Ralston moved on, not bothering to wipe off the mud on his pants leg. He walked with a springy step, the heavier gravity of this world unnoticed now that he walked toward . . . who? He felt stronger and confident in his ability to handle anything. What could be in the small forest? Their sensors hadn't picked up any large animals.

He skirted the edge of the forest, moving to put the pale orange sun at his back. If he discovered something eager for dinner, Ralston wanted the feeble rays of sunlight slanting in under the storm clouds to work for him, not against him. Even a momentary blinding would allow him to escape, he was sure.

"Who's there?" he called out.

"It's been so long, Michael," came the hidden voice. Closer, Ralston noted a peculiar twang unlike either Marta or Druanna. Definitely female but not . . . quite . . . human. Too much bass undertone.

Leaves rustled. Ralston moved to put a tree trunk at his back. He peered in the direction of the noise. A flash of intuition told him that this was a ruse. He dropped to one knee just as a heavily taloned paw circled the tree and ripped away bark. That might have been his face if he'd reacted a nanosecond slower.

"Madre de Dios," he gasped, moving away. Ralston fumbled for the call button on his tracker. Once activated, Leonore would be able to home in on him. She might even come immediately.

Or she might not notice for hours, if she and Nels were together or if she worked to put the compound back in order after the quake.

"Michael," the creature called. "Come to me." It lumbered around the tree and gave Ralston a clear look at it. Almost as tall as the archaeologist, the beast was stockier, possessing muscles that rippled like an ocean's waves under a scraggly brown fur coat. Its mouth opened to reveal double rows of teeth. But it shut its mouth, and he again heard his name called.

Ralston feinted to the left and dived to the right. The creature followed him with contemptuous ease. He barely missed having an arm clawed off for his effort. Ralston grunted and kicked away, blood trickling from four narrow gashes in his shoulder.

"Michael, come closer."

The long snout opened, and heavily muscled jaws clacked shut. Ralston saw that it'd be impossible for this creature to speak in a human voice. He postponed any further speculation on the source of the voice when the creature dropped to all fours and rushed him. Ralston rolled away, picked up a fallen limb, and used it as a clumsy club to hold back the creature. The beast rolled itself into a ball, then exploded with claws lashing out. Ralston received another set of scratches on his right leg. More painful than dangerous, the wound bled freely.

Ralston cursed his hubris in not bringing a weapon. Then he laughed. What weapon would he have lugged with him? This was a physics-archaeology expedition. They hadn't brought any weapons with them. Mass had counted aboard the starship. Superfluous equipment had been left on Novo Terra. Never had Ralston heard of an expedition where a member had been attacked by indigenous wildlife.

It was his bad luck to be the first. All he had to do was live to write it into his research paper.

"Stay back," he shouted, hoping the sound of his voice would frighten the creature. If anything, it emboldened his attacker. Ralston managed to find another dried limb, this one devoid of smaller branches. He swung it like a bat and connected squarely with the beast's snout just as it opened its mouth.

Ralston felt teeth breaking. Claws raked just centimeters away from his stomach. He danced away, swinging his weapon.

"Michael, why is this?"

He swung again, putting all his strength into the blow. It crashed hard on the beast's sloping shoulder. Ralston couldn't kill it, but he hoped to drive it off. If it broke off its attack for just a few seconds, he could run. Even in the heavier gravity—with fear to lend speed to his retreat—he thought he could outdistance this predator.

The creature circled to put itself between him and the camp.

"Michael, I am hurt. You shouldn't do this to me."

Ralston blinked. He straightened and looked at Marta.

"I've changed," she said. "Please help me, Michael. You hurt me. Help me now."

"I—" he began.

Sharp talons tore with impossible speed at his vulnerable left side and drove him to the ground. The slender woman's body turned back into the heavy creature. It reared up over him, ready to make the death stroke across his throat.

SIX

"WHERE'S MICHAEL?" ASKED Leonore Disa. "I want to ask him about starting on a new area in the site. The ruins just to the north look more interesting from these photos than the one we're working on now."

Nels Bernssen didn't look up from his work as he shook his head and said, "Haven't seen him recently. He went to talk with Westcott after the quake. He might still be there."

"I just looked. Westcott's sitting in the corner of his shelter all glassy-eyed and thinking his computer thoughts."

"I don't like him, either," Bernssen said, finishing the adjustment, then straightening to pull Leonore into the circle of his arms, "but he's useful. Before we're finished with Beta 5, you'll see. We might have to use him as a paperweight, but he'll be useful."

"Michael said that Westcott is responsible for the calculations leading us here. That still doesn't make me like him any more. He . . . he's hardly human."

"You're the one who deals with alien cultures."

"I'm only a grave robber," Leonore joked. "I do awful things with their skeletons."

"Want to do wonderful things with mine?" asked the astrophysicist.

"Depends on what you had in mind." Leonore kissed

him. The sound of rain gently falling outside the plastic
shelter soothed her. The quake had come unexpectedly,
and she needed Nels' assurance that everything would be
all right. She received it.

The talons flashed downward in an arc, catching the
orange rays of the setting sun and turning them into bloody
spikes. Michael Ralston's combat experience saved him;
the Nex had hypno-trained him well to respond to attack.
He jerked to one side, then exploded past the deadly
talons. He slammed hard into the bole of a tree, rebounded, and pulled himself to a sitting position. He
kicked out at the creature and drove a foot into the back
leg, finding the knee joint.

The beast dropped forward on all fours, giving Ralston a
chance to get to his feet. He wobbled, and blood seeped
from the wounds he had already received, but fear had
been purged from him by the hypnotic commands. Cold,
clear thought showed him the precise location on the creature's neck.

Ralston swung the tree limb club, and the impact of
wood against flesh rocked him. Weakness assailed him—
but the beast broke off its attack. Whining, it lumbered
into the depths of the forest.

Ralston almost collapsed as the adrenaline flow subsided. He fell to his knees, breathing hard.

"Marta," he said softly, looking after the creature. But
the archaeology professor knew that he hadn't really seen
the woman he'd loved so long ago. Her image, her voice,
had been projected into his mind. He now saw how he had
supplied the details that had been missing. The voice
wasn't quite right, but it had been close enough. The
image wasn't perfect, but it had taken him aback.

Those were all the creature had intended—or needed. It
was a predator laying a complex trap.

Ralston held onto the tree trunk for support. What had
gone wrong with their survey? No large animals had been
detected. Another equipment failure? Or had he just been

in too big a hurry to get started on the excavation and ignored the evidence?

He hated to admit it but there hadn't been time to do a complete workup of the data collected from orbit. The IR scans might have shown a creature that size if he'd made the effort to find it. Carelessness had almost cost him his life.

"But what a fabulous creature," he said softly. "How did it come to learn to hunt like that?"

Ralston checked his wristcom. The alarm button had been depressed. He peered out in the fine mist and looked for Leonore or Nels or any of the others to come to his aid. No one. Nels' researchers wouldn't be monitoring his com frequency, he decided; Leonore and Nels were the only two he could reasonably expect to respond.

He heaved himself out into the open, following the green arrow that pointed the way back to the compound. As he walked, he felt better. The thicker air supplied needed oxygen to his laboring lungs, and strength returned after the initial surge of fear. Ralston held a bit of torn shirt over his shoulder wounds; the compress stanched the bleeding and helped the blood clot. By the time the plastic shelters came into view through the drizzle, he felt almost human.

He made his way to the shelter set up with the automedic. The small, mobile robot hummed and whistled to itself as Ralston sat on the floor in front of it. Tiny metal probes worked across the surface of the wound, checking for deeper and more serious injury. Finding none, the automed gently held the edges of the cleansed wound together and sprayed plastiskin over it.

"Thanks," Ralston said when the automed had finished the last of the scratches. "Take a blood sample to make certain the chemistry is normal. I don't want to pick up any strange infections." He winced as the automedic obeyed. Ten millimeters of blood came from a vein and another five from an artery for blood gas analysis.

Ralston pulled away and rubbed the two punctures. At

repairing humans, the robot was unparalleled, but it lacked much in the way of bedside manner. Ralston always vowed to check the automed's programming to make certain it hadn't been given a slight vindictiveness in drawing the blood.

A beep sounded. Ralston glanced at the readout on the main console. He heaved a sigh of relief. As far as the sophisticated mobile unit could tell, he hadn't been invaded by any alien microbes.

"Michael, what happened?" came Leonore's worried voice. "We were passing by and heard the automed's signal." She went to the console and studied the data still displayed. "What did this to you?"

"That's a good question," said Ralston. "I've been thinking about it while the robot worked on me—I'm all right. Don't worry about that." He quickly told of the attack, then said, "This might seem far-fetched, but we've never found any other creature that hunts telepathically. More to the point, it recognized me as prey."

"You're saying this might be an animal brought to the planet by the Alphans?"

"Could be," said Ralston. "Or it might be a native creature who learned to live off the Alphans. They looked a great deal like us—humanoid, bilaterally symmetrical, about the same height and build, if you ignore the details of our features."

"It might have been waiting a long time between meals," said Bernssen. "If the refugees died off very long ago—and it looks as if they did—what's this creature been living on?"

"That thought occurred to me, also. It seems possible that it isn't naturally a telepathic hunter. What if it blundered into one of the Alphans' dioramas and learned about them—and even became telepathic itself?"

"You may have hit your head. Did you have the automed check for concussion?" scoffed Leonore.

"The chaos device passed by this planet much longer ago. That had to affect the native wildlife in some way we can't even begin to guess at. What if the creature blundered into a diorama and the combined effects of chaos and the projection turned it telepathic?''

"A mutation?'' asked Bernssen.

"More like an adaptation. Call it a mental scarring. It might not be able to breed true—most mutations don't. But it might have made its nest in a diorama. Over the years, it not only learned that Alphans were acceptable food, but also how to project the images. It didn't find Alphans but it did find us—me.''

Leonore and Nels exchanged glances. "All right, all right,'' said Ralston. "I haven't the slightest idea what's happened with the beast. Maybe every creature on this world is telepathic.''

"Not likely,'' said Leonore. "The other creatures wouldn't fall prey to such mentally projected images. They'd adapt or learn to tell the difference.'' She cocked her head to one side and asked, "What image did it lure you with? You didn't say.''

Ralston ignored her, not wanting to dredge up memories best left untouched. He said, "Let's look for the creature and track it to its lair. I think we'll find another Alphan diorama.''

"Let's track it down, no matter what we're likely to find,'' said Nels. "This beast is dangerous to us all. What if it sent out a mental attack while we slept? It might lure us from camp one by one, and we'd never know until it was too late.''

"We don't have anything to kill it with,'' said Leonore. "No weapons.''

"Fix up a spear,'' said Ralston. "I'll put a small battery pack on it. If we can't stab it, we can shock it.''

"I'll have Melendez or one of the others start on a perimeter alarm, too,'' said Bernssen. "I want to know what comes and goes through the camp.''

Leonore glanced at Ralston, saw that her professor was well tended to by the robot, then hurried after Nels. Ralston sat on a hard chair and considered other explanations for the telepathic beast's presence. No matter how he twisted logic, he kept returning to a combination of chaos—Westcott's topological dynamics—and the Alphan refugees' thought projector.

He rose and left the shelter, the sun setting just over the horizon. The gusty winds had blown away the clouds, and once more the sky shone clear, clean, and perfect.

"I don't like this," said Leonore Disa. She looked apprehensive about stalking through the darkened woods hunting the beast that had attacked her professor. "What if it's a nocturnal animal? It'll be able to see us better than we can see it, even with the IR glasses."

Nels Bernssen tugged at the night goggles, trying to bring them into adjustment. He failed.

"I was out at twilight," said Ralston, checking the meter on the device he held. "That means it's crepuscular. We have the chance to track it down now, while it's gone to its burrow."

"It might live in the trees," said Leonore, glancing into the shadowy, leafy masses above them. "Arboreal."

"The limbs were wrong for that," said Ralston. "There. Got it. I've locked on to its trail."

"What is that thing?" Leonore asked irritably. She glanced around, visions of huge monsters leaping at her. "I hope it's better than your spear."

Ralston smiled. The spear had been a jury-rigged nightmare. The best they had been able to do was file down the sides of a piece of scrap steel and mount it at the end of a long plastic tube. Running down the inside of the tube were the wires Ralston had attached to the steel knife. By thumbing a contact at the far end, a sizable electrical jolt could be produced. He had no idea if it would kill the beast, or even stun it, but he knew it would produce some effect. And if it didn't, the spear itself would serve well.

Ralston had to grin at the thought of venturing out like savages with a primitive spear. All the tri-vid dramas had the mighty interstellar hunters equipped with power rifles capable of leveling cities and sonic devices that stunned through the sheer power of their pulsed shock waves. He thought they were carrying weapons more in line with the way it should be done. The more primitive you went out, the better chance you had of returning.

He didn't want to be any creature's dinner, and this kept his senses at their peak. Ralston knew that both Leonore and Nels were similarly on edge. They might jump at the slightest unusual sound, but they reacted rather than letting it pass by.

"This might not work in a city, but it's performing well out here where there's nothing to confuse it," he said, indicating the tracking device Leonore had mentioned. "The surface acoustic wave caused by its scent is picked up by a transducer. The internal block circuit then gives me a readout on the meter. Anything less than twenty-percent deflection is a lost signal. About eighty percent is strong."

"You're really able to track its scent using a sniffer?" Leonore shook her head in wonder. "I've used the damned things to scout out poison fumes in underground dig sites, but I never thought of using it like a bloodhound."

Ralston laughed. "You'd be surprised at some of the ways I've used sniffers. With the right block circuit inside, you can differentiate between male and female phero-mones and . . ." Ralston's voice trailed off. He didn't want to get into what he'd done while a graduate student at the University of Novo Terra.

"I don't see any hint of heat trail," said Bernssen, pulling off the bulky IR-powered goggles. He held them out to Leonore. "You want to use them?" The physicist wiped his forehead clear of the accumulated sweat and dust that had dammed up above the goggles' headband. Leonore shook her head.

They trooped through the forest, Ralston maintaining a sixty-percent deflection on the meter. Gradually, the read-ing mounted until it hit an optimal level. Ralston stopped and slowly turned to take in the entire area. Only in one direction did he pick up a strong reading indicating the beast's passage.

"There," he said, pointing toward a dark spot in the forest. He took the IR lenses from Bernssen and handed the sniffer to Leonore. The terrain jumped about until his eyes adjusted to the ghostly imaging created by the sensors. A heat vent glowed brightly in the night. Clutching the spear, Ralston advanced one slow step at a time until he stood at the mouth of the crevice leading down into the ground. A large boulder protected one side, and a fallen, rotting log the other. The creature had found itself a well-protected home.

"Different readings from below," said Leonore, frowning. "There's the creature, but I'm picking up something else. Looks familiar, but I can't place it." Ralston heard her fiddling with the sniffer.

"Well?" he asked. "Decided where you've seen similar readings?"

"No, except . . ."

"Except on Alpha 3," he finished for her. "In the dioramas."

"The Alphans?"

"Our beast might prove itself an ally. It just might have found a burrow in the very spot we've been looking for so hard." Ralston adjusted the ungainly goggles to a more comfortable position, then dropped to hands and knees and stuck his head into the crevice. "It'll be a tight squeeze, but I can make it."

"You're not going in there!" protested Leonore.

"She's right," spoke up Bernssen. "You need more than that pathetic spear if you're going to crawl into a monster's lap."

"It wasn't that much of a monster. Dangerous, verd, I'll agree with you there. It's strong and quick, but it thought it was safe hunting with the telepathic imaging. Finding its lair here explains how it came by its only real talent."

"So the creature did get it from the dioramas," mused Leonore, fascinated in spite of her uneasiness. "It sounded far-fetched before, but it looks as if you were right, Michael. The combination of the chaos device's residual effects and the Alphans' projector allowed it to develop usable telepathic talents.''

''We've got one way of finding out for certain. Any of those back in camp biologists?''

''No, just astrophysicists,'' said Bernssen. ''My department—and Westcott's—did fund this expedition, after all.'' He sounded apologetic.

''We can always put it on ice.'' Ralston trembled a little when he mentally finished, As I did with de la Cruz's body. He shook off the troubling thought. ''I'll leave my wristcom on to record everything. Track me with the sniffer. All my scent parameters are in its block memory.''

''Michael,'' said Leonore, touching his shoulder.

''Verd, I'll not take any foolish risks.'' He heaved a deep, calming breath. ''At least no more after this one.'' With that, the archaeology professor slid forward into the darkness.

Through the infrared lenses the tunnel took on a surreal, red, shimmering aspect. Ralston ignored this and pushed forward, keeping the tip of his makeshift electric-powered spear in front of him. If the creature had chosen that instant to attack, Ralston would have been helpless. He couldn't thrust well while wiggling on his belly, and he couldn't reach the contact that would send the charge into the electrified steel tip.

Ralston found the passageway dirty and littered with odd bits of debris—and no trace of the creature that had attacked him earlier in the woods.

''Whew,'' he said, as heavy animal musk assailed his nostrils. If he'd kept the surface acoustic wave detector, it would have overloaded. Ralston tumbled out onto a floor unnaturally smooth beneath the detritus. He held back a sneeze and carefully studied his surroundings. For the benefit of his wrist recorder, he said, ''I've entered a long, artificial corridor. The walls are bare—no, there are murals painted on them. Visual spectrum light is required for clearer reading. It appears to me as splotches of light and dark, with only a slight difference between pigmented and bare wall.''

Ralston walked slowly, glad that he could stand upright. The stench almost overwhelmed him when he rounded a right angle and came into the creature's lair.

He turned slowly and studied the larger, open area. No sound reached his ears. The odors were too overpowering for him to pinpoint the beast's whereabouts. And the IR goggles revealed no living heat source. What they did reveal, though, sent Ralston stumbling forward, oblivious to any danger that might be in hiding.

"Dioramas! I've found them!" He took a few deep breaths, regretted it when he choked, then forced himself to breathe in shallow pants. He reached out with the tip of his spear and traced over the faint outlines of the statues inside the first diorama. Carefully, trying to keep his voice level and at a slow, clear pace, he described all that was visible.

Ralston became enthralled by the little he could see— and how he wanted to enter those dioramas and learn the telepathic lessons he knew awaited there!

"I am staying in the central area," he said with more than a little sadness, "because of the lack of light. It was found on Alpha 3 that a general idea of the subject of each diorama could be formed on the basis of composition, number of characters and their relative positioning within the scene.''

Ralston continued to dictate as he wandered, oblivious now to the odors around him. Once he flipped off the IR goggles and found himself plunged into total darkness except for the brief More's secondary lightning flashing within his eyes. Ralston turned on the power once more to the IR goggles, relieved at the ghostly images that reappeared. The irrational fear always struck him that he'd become permanently blind when he experienced such darkness. It had never happened, but intellectually knowing his sight would still be there and emotionally knowing it proved two different things.

Ralston made a careful circuit of the large area from which all the dioramas appeared to radiate, then stopped at the end farthest from the hallway where he had entered. A circular hot spot showed at about waist level.

He probed gently with his long spear. The resulting heat surge in his goggles, and the force with which the spear was batted from his hand, took him by surprise. He'd unexpectedly found where the creature had holed up.

The beast exploded from the circular opening. The slight delay between the IR goggles sensing the heat and the small block circuit actually showing the image on the lenses worked against Ralston. He saw, but always a fraction of a second too late.

He grunted and stumbled in the detritus on the floor. Feet slipping from under him, Ralston fell heavily. Above, he saw the beast rearing. The slight pause before it made its attack saved him. He instantly jerked and rolled to one side. A talon raked his back, but the creature's death stroke had missed its target. Ralston kept rolling and came to hands and knees, gagging as he sucked in huge lungfuls of the fetid air.

He spun and kicked when he saw the heat-shimmered bulk come for him. The animal may prefer hunting at twilight, Ralston thought, but its night vision was incredibly acute. Or did it track him with another sense? Had it learned to stalk by its prey's thoughts?

His foot connected with a hairy leg, and the creature yelped in pain. Ralston had done it no significant damage, but he had forced it to break off its attack.

For a few seconds.

He took in a deep breath to shout for help. Bernssen and Leonore were less than a hundred meters away. The tiny crevice and corridors would funnel his cry.

Ralston gasped as the creature ran full tilt into him. One sloping, powerfully muscled shoulder drove into his midriff. He felt his diaphragm crushing under the impact and could do nothing about it. He smashed into a wall. Feeble kicks at the predator did little more than enrage it.

The archaeology professor spun to one side, sustaining deep gashes on his flank. He groaned at the pain. He couldn't outfight the beast. He had to retreat.

Ralston forced himself upright and looked around. The shining red blob had to be the creature. A rectangular glow in the other direction was the entry point. Ralston stumbled, righted himself, then ran as hard as he could for the opening. If he reached it, he might be able to slither back up to the forest.

Even as he ran, he discarded that idea. The beast was more agile—and it was the creature's tunnel. It hadn't dug a way in and out that would be hard for itself.

Ralston changed his plans as he reached the corridor. He'd yell. Bernssen and Leonore would come and help him. The creature wouldn't want to fight off three humans. It'd retreat. It'd go back into its small hidey hole.

A powerful blow to the back of his head sent Ralston sprawling. Stunned, he turned onto his side. All that the archaeology professor saw was the towering red heat outline of the beast. It prepared for the death stroke.

SEVEN

THE INFRARED GOGGLES tilted on Michael Ralston's head, giving him a skewed picture of the creature—but there could be no doubt that death was an instant away.

Ralston shrieked and tried to kick at the beast. His legs refused to obey. He'd fallen and gotten them twisted under him. His head rang like the University carillon. The outcry did nothing to stay the attacking beast. It reared and, for the first time, Ralston heard it growl deep in its throat.

It knew victory lay only a quick stroke away.

At the beast took a step forward to make the death slash, it grunted and slid to one side. Stepping on the shaft of the spear it had batted from Ralston's hands, the beast had stumbled. The brief pause in the attack allowed Ralston to drag himself a few centimeters farther away.

The enraged animal struck out at the spear—and gave Ralston his first real chance. The spear bounced from the animal's claws, rattled into the wall and fell at Ralston's side. The archaeology professor picked it up, touched the contact at the base, felt the electric surge along the shaft, then braced himself.

The creature snarled, rose and threw itself on him. A vivid electric spark blinded Ralston as the creature touched the electrified steel tip. Then the plastic shaft began warp-

ing as the weight of the creature bore down. Ralston
fought to gain his feet but dared not let loose of the spear.

It was all that kept death at bay.

Talons dripping with his blood slashed just millimeters
from his face. Ralston felt their passage as fetid air gusted
into his nostrils. He turned and twisted and worked the
spear deeper from the creature's heaving chest. The battery
continued to send galvanizing jolts into a primitive nervous
system. By the time Ralston pulled the spear free, then
thrust hard at the dim form outlined in the IR lenses, he
knew the animal was more dead than alive.

He finished the chore with three more weak stabs.

Gasping, Ralston reeled away, spear clutched in hand.
He reached out to brace himself against a wall but missed.
He yelped in surprise, then fell heavily into the first diorama.

Ralston tried to escape the scene before the telepathic
projector began its message. He was too weak; as he
straightened, the familiar tingling sensation at the fringes
of his mind began. Rather than struggle, he resigned himself to ride out the lesson programmed into this alien
diorama.

"Dial, we can't do it!" came Querno's sobbing words.
The tall, thin avian being held hands over his face to hide
his shame. Ralston-Dial's sympathy went out to his friend.
They had been through so much. And now they failed!

"No," said Ralston-Dial. "There is still hope. All our
world is in flame. Valiant comrades die in disgrace before
our eyes—" Ralston-Dial shuddered at the mere thought
of such dishonor as the epileptic fits brought to both victim
and observer—"but we will succeed. They laugh at my
theories, but I *know* we can do it." Ralston-Dial stroked
Querno's close-feathered scalp ridge.

Ralston-Dial gasped. The scene changed from a burned-
out hut to the oil-tang-scented hold of a large, clumsy
spaceship. A curious otherness assailed him. He knew this
ship lacked stardrive capacity. It looked wrong. But at the
same time, it looked right. It had been *his* dream brought
to fruition.

"We launch soon, Dial?" came the fledgling starship captain's timorous question. Captain Fennalt fussed about the cockpit, long, thin fingers stroking the controls as if they might come alive under his ministrations.

"There are others escaping the city," Dial said. "It isn't seemly hurrying away when our journey will take so long."

Fennalt nodded, stretched his long arms, then settled into the acceleration couch contoured to fit his body. He curled his feet around the perch bar and tried to relax. "You are sure of this star? It will take us away from all misery?"

Dial bobbed his head up and down several times in agreement, but he said nothing. He feared he might betray his uncertainty. This star showed a spectral pattern of bands and dark and bright lines similar to their sun. No astronomer had ventured a theory, at least in his hearing, about the chance of finding another planet, much less a planet capable of sustaining avian life circling a distant star.

But Dial saw no other possibility. They had to take the desperate gamble. If a pitiful few might flee the planet and escape the carnage and madness seizing the populace, their race might continue to thrive. Honor demanded that they try. Dial's curiosity also drove him, but mostly honor dictated his course.

This similar star lay the closest to home—and its distance was incomprehensible to him. His skills were in engineering, not in the wild imaginings of star travel. Hadn't the Council of Rules decreed that no space travel, even within the confines of the solar system, be attempted? It had been for the best, Dial knew. The comet that had so stirred the interest of an entire world had also betrayed them.

The dark comet had passed within a few planetary diameters but had produced no coma, no tail, no evidence of the spectacular gases boldly predicted by scientists and expected by the populace. This had been two hundred years before, but Dial had seen the disappointing pictures. Space travel had been dealt a death blow.

Dial prayed for those who had already died. In his mind, the connection between the dark comet and those slow, dishonorable deaths was firm. The dark wanderer through their system had sprayed poison gases into their atmosphere and doomed so many.

It must have. No other explanation came to him.

Dial kept his breathing shallow and slow, his chest barely moving. Through this he would escape, as had the others going with him on this desperate trip.

"It is difficult to believe," said Captain Fennalt, "that the first real expedition from our planet will be one of such tremendous duration and daring."

Dial silently signaled for Fennalt to begin preparation for the rocket blast. He tiredly went to quiet those already in their couches, especially Querno.

Ralston-Dial felt the acceleration. With the crushing pressure on his chest came a curious exaltation. The first star voyagers! They were rocketing for the stars!

Ralston coughed, stumbled, and braced himself against the wall of the diorama. The lesson had ended. Sweat beaded his forehead, and his side had turned stiff from his oozing wounds and the caked blood. Ralston kept one hand on the slick surface as he guided himself from the scene. To have done anything else might have proven dangerous for him. He knew each of the figures in the diorama carried a distinct telepathic lesson told from their individual point of view.

He could see the lift-off from Alpha 3 through the eyes of both Fennalt and Querno if he wanted.

All Michael Ralston wanted at the moment was to rest, to sleep, to sleep for a million years. Cold, tired, weak, he used the warped spear as a crutch.

And this betrayed him. He planted the butt end of the spear on a slippery patch. The support he relied on so heavily squirted from under him. He fell headlong, his heavy IR goggles flying from his head. As the archaeology professor stood, he realized he had gone farther than he'd intended.

Another projector beam touched his mind and imprinted its eons-old message.

". . . Dial," said Querno, "this place is as dangerous as our Far Home."

Ralston-Dial looked at his friend. How could an intelligent person such as Querno not realize the awful truth?

"Querno," Ralston-Dial said, heart heavy with what he must say, "you do not understand. This planet was clean before we came to it. It is *our* presence that tainted a virgin world. We've carried the diabolical gases with us."

"The trip was costly," admitted Querno. Scores of the refugees had died during the long, long sublight speed journey. Fennalt had pushed the ship to ever higher speeds, but the barrier of light speed eluded them, as Dial had worried that it might. Barely had they reached ninety-percent light speed. But the void of interstellar space provided them with the molecular hydrogen fuel needed for their scoop. They had accelerated for twenty years.

Ralston-Dial knew that they had been in space for almost eighty years, even though, for Dial and Fennalt and Querno and the others fleeing Alpha 3, it had seemed little more than half that.

For the Alphans, this concept of time dilation lay far in their physical and mathematical future—a future they would be denied because of the chaos device.

"Costly, yes," Dial went on, "and we carried the seed of destruction with us. We planted it on this world."

Ralston shook all over, wanting to call out to the avian scientist, to tell him how wrong he was, how the chaos device had already passed through the Beta system and left its swath of wrongness. The telepathic projector strengthened its hold on him; Ralston was forced even more into the scene, assumed Dial's persona even more.

"We've tried all the ancient purification rites. They failed," said Querno.

"This is not a matter of spiritual belief," said Dial,

exhausted from his research. "I have failed to detect the gas. I wonder if the others might not have been right. Perhaps it was an electromagnetic field that has somehow infected us." Dial shook his head, tears welling up to run down his hard nose.

"Our two cities are distant enough so that one might survive if the other perishes," Querno said. "Fennalt leads the other well. He finds new rooms daily."

"Has he discovered who built that city?" asked Dial.

"No. But the buildings are useful. Fennalt will flourish. He is a proud and honorable man."

Dial shook himself all over and made mock-preening gestures, a remnant of times long past. "It will do no good dividing our forces. We have journeyed so far and so long only to die. Look around, Querno. Can't you see this is so?"

Querno squawked and protested. "We fight, Dial. We will not surrender to these alien influences."

"Yes, yes, we fight. But it is in vain. Look and you see only men and women of honor disgracing themselves in increasing numbers. They flop and thrash about and there is nothing we can do to bring them back to their senses. Just as before, just as it did on Far Home, this curse works on us in the most degrading way possible."

Dial looked from the roof of the one-story building. The world appeared so invitingly gentle. But he knew the raw fury the capricious weather brought with it. One day they enjoyed peaceful summer, the next brought ice storms. As soon as the arctic weather turned, they might experience autumn or summer—all at random. The true miracle lay in how the world's wildlife coped with such virulent change.

But it did, as they did. Life refused to give up even a tenuous grasp. Dial saw that as both a blessing and a curse.

"We've got to get him out," exclaimed Nels Bernssen. "We can't leave him locked up in there. Look! He's bleeding. That damned animal clawed him badly."

"No, Nels." Leonore Disa held the physicist back. "We've never pulled him from one of the dioramas before it had run its full message. I'm not sure what might happen to him if we tried it now."

"He's bleeding to death! There's no telling what internal damage there might be. *Madre de Dios*, Leonore!"

"Nels, please." The woman held him back. "If you go into the diorama, you'll be caught up in it, too, and be no good to Michael. It's a risk leaving him there, but less a physical one than the mental ruin we risk pulling him out."

"*Hijo de puta*," Bernssen grumbled, caught on the horns of the dilemma. "What possessed him to go into one of those damnable scenes in his condition?"

Leonore had no answer. The evidence on that point was less than clear. Ralston had killed the beast with the spear, then mysteriously gone into the diorama on the left. The sniffer showed definite and lingering human body pheromones there. Leonore adjusted the quartz light they'd brought.

Ralston had crossed the floor, then entered the diorama directly across from the first one. The professor now stood within, locked with the peculiar muscle rigidity characteristic of the telepathic projector's operation.

Leonore wanted to take the chance, to drag him out before the lesson had run its course. But she stood and watched and waited. Better to turn Ralston over to the automedic for a long stay than to do damage to his brain.

"How long do they usually run?" asked Bernssen.

"We know so little about them. I suspect that these aren't designed to run long. They are museum exhibits—at least, the ones on Alpha 3 were."

"So the crowd wanders in, gets a short lecture, then moves on?"

"Something like that. But these might be different. These might be—probably are—left to tell the history of their travel and all that happened to them once they landed on Beta 5."

"You're saying he might die of starvation before the field releases him?"

"I doubt that," said Leonore. "After all, the Alphans were physically similar to us. They must have eaten on a regular basis. They wouldn't want to kill themselves by going for days or weeks inside a diorama. Nothing indicates their mental makeup was too divergent, either. That means their attention span wouldn't exceed a human's by much. He . . . he should be out of the scene soon."

She hoped that were true. Ralston had been locked within this one for at least an hour. It had been that long since she and Nels had ventured down the crevice after returning to the camp and getting the portable light. They had blundered into the room and found the creature dead of stab wounds—and Ralston already within the diorama.

"The one next to him. He shows up in all the scenes," said Nels. "He must be the leader."

Leonore had to agree. And Ralston had assumed a pose next to the leader, which probably meant that he had to endure the longest lesson of any within the diorama.

Leonore wandered around the small chamber, impatiently waiting for something to happen. She was peering at the scene next to Ralston's when Bernssen yelled, "He's coming out. I saw his eyes blink. And look. His color's changing."

"He's turning white. What's wrong?" Leonore took a step forward but Bernssen held her back. She stopped, her hand on his. If she'd entered as she'd impulsively tried, she might be caught up alongside Ralston. They both might be trapped and helpless.

Her professor stumbled out and dropped to his knees just outside the diorama. He looked up with haunted gray eyes. His lips moved as if he tried to speak.

Then the epileptic fit seized him.

EIGHT

MICHAEL RALSTON'S ENTIRE body stiffened, then he began snaking about on the floor with a series of uncontrollable convulsions. For him the world turned into a white glare; for those watching, it became a nightmare of helplessness.

"Don't let him bite his tongue," cried Leonore Disa. She tried to hold the thrashing Ralston and failed. Even the much stronger Nels Bernssen had difficulty. By the time the large physicist had gotten his knees onto Ralston's shoulders in a schoolboy pin, and Leonore held the man's legs, the worst had passed.

Ralston blinked and opened his eyes, not seeing.

"Are you all right?" Bernssen asked nervously. One hand went to Ralston's forehead and came away sweaty. The archaeology professor's eyes focused now.

"Can't breathe too well with you sitting on me like that. And something seems wrong with my legs. Can't move them at all. It's dark, too."

Leonore and Bernssen slowly released their grips. Ralston stirred weakly. If he had been mauled repeatedly by the creature whose lair they'd invaded, he couldn't have felt much worse. The claw marks throbbed, but it was the rest of his body that suffered even more. Every joint, every muscle, everything refused to function—except to send out a signal of dull, aching pain.

Bernssen helped him sit up. "Why did you go into the diorama? The dioramas," he amended, the proof of Ralston going from one to the other visible on the floor from the disturbed debris.

"Didn't mean to," Ralston said. His throat barely worked; he knew how the ancient criminals felt during a hanging. He spat, took a few deep breaths, and decided against trying to stand yet. "The resident of this fine suite of rooms didn't take kindly to me invading its lair. It came for me, I killed it, then staggered back. It was an accident that I fell into that scene." He pointed to the one showing Dial, Querno, and Captain Fennalt preparing for takeoff.

"Then you came stumbling out and fell into this one?" asked Leonore, hardly believing such an incredible story.

"I wouldn't have dared it," said Ralston. "Not in my condition." He squinted into the quartz lamp. "How long has it been? For me it seems like about fifteen years."

"A little longer than an hour. We were afraid to come crashing in on you, so I went back to the compound and got the lamp while Nels stood guard. When I got back we decided to come down to see what had happened to you."

"Wish you'd come sooner. I could have used the help." Ralston's gray eyes darted to the fallen animal. He regretted having to kill it. With some luck, they might decide how the creature had come to hunt by sending out its telepathic bait. If nothing else, the xenobiologists at the University would have gotten a thousand publishable research papers from studying it.

"You scared us when you came reeling out of the diorama," said Bernssen. "That fit looked just like the ones that took my researchers back on Alpha 3."

Ralston frowned. "I had a fit? I don't remember—wait! I *do* remember. But I didn't have it. The seizure was Dial's. He—" Ralston stopped, trying to sort out the confusing array of facts, half memories, and telepathically infused knowledge.

He went pale when he figured out what had happened. "The convulsions *are* projected," he said. "We're going to have to be extremely careful examining the later scenes. After de la Cruz's death, I suspected it, but this is certain."

"Salazar would shut down their project to duplicate the machine if he knew," said Leonore with some glee. "And Daddy will be horrified. He's so conscious of IC's reputation. Any hint that mental disorders can be projected will kill all their research."

"That's be the wrong thing to do," said Bernssen. "We need the knowledge. If anything, such a projection technique might help psychologists correct their patients' problems."

Ralston said nothing. He knew how the telepathic projector would be used. With crime a constant and increasing problem, the government psychologists would first try it as a new method for criminal rehabilitation. Rather than burn out their victim's brain with chemicals and electricity, they'd use the Alphan projector to impress the new, "normal" behavior patterns.

Ralston had just seen firsthand how effective it might become. He shook himself. To dwell on such negative aspects of a new technology hid what good might actually come from it.

Still . . . to be rehabbed that way was a new form of mind death. And what of the newsers? They always sought fresh ways of enhancing their news-report ratings. A trivid screen coupled with such a projector might prove the unraveling of society. No matter what the newser said, the audience would believe it absolutely.

"This is dangerous," he said. "We've got to try to learn how it works." He made a gargantuan effort and heaved himself to his feet. "If for no other reason, we need to protect our minds from it. The Alphans had the same problems, I'm sure. We're supposed to be archaeologists. We can find out how they really used the dioramas."

Ralston looked around the chamber in wonder. The refugees had crossed, for them, infinite light years of space to flee the effects of the chaos device. They had only run into the jaws of the chaos, landing on a planet already in the throes of ruin.

"Let's get out of here. I need some repair work done." Ralston touched his injured side and winced, a wave of nausea breaking over him. "And I want to make notes of all I've discovered. There's something I can't quite remember that seems significant. But it's hard for me to concentrate."

He slumped forward. Leonore caught him as he fell face forward, unconscious. She and Bernssen dragged Ralston through the small tunnel leading to the forest. A full-blown winter storm pelted them with sleet all the way back to the compound.

"How's excavation coming?" Ralston asked.

"That's not the usual question," said Leonore Disa. "You're supposed to ask, 'Where am I?' or even 'How did I get here?' "

"I know where I am," Ralston said. The plastic walls and the partially emptied equipment crates told him that much. They had brought him back to his shelter. The other question seemed equally amenable to logic, even in his weakened condition. Leonore and Nels had been responsible for returning him to camp. His side had been expertly mended: the automed's work. The only thing bothering him was the chilly air. He commented on it.

"We're in the midst of a heavy winter storm," said Leonore. "It hit while we were in the creature's lair."

"But it was autumn. Or spring." Ralston experienced a moment's dizziness. Parts of his memory had become blocked. The seizure had a greater adverse effect than he cared to admit.

"Westcott says it's a product of the chaos field. His dynamical variables are all being altered, sometimes on a second to second basis. That's why we're getting winter now."

"Snow?"

Leonore nodded.

Ralston sank back onto his cot and silently cursed. "The diggers aren't having any problem, are they? I've found it hard keeping them going when the temperature dips down too low. Something about moisture and their block circuits. The manufacturer denies it, but they start going off course, sometimes by as much as a radian per hour. When I worked the Transients' site on Icefloe 6, I had to chase one that had decided to run off. Got it just before it tumbled off a cliff into a lake of freezing water."

"The supervisor is taking care of all the corrections. It's a good machine." Leonore chuckled. "After all, it's made by IC."

Ralston's mind spun and whirred as it struggled to put into order all the things he needed to say.

"Westcott. Get him. I've got some information he might be able to use."

"Getting him away from his computer is hard. His IR link doesn't work outside his shelter. In rain or snow it's even harder for him to keep an interference-free link. Absorption on the transmission frequency, he says."

"Can Nels rig him up a relay?"

"Verd, but IR absorption in a snowstorm will still make it a futile project."

"Dammit, I *need* to talk to Westcott." Ralston forced himself to sit up. The world oscillated in crazy arcs.

"Don't, Michael. Please. I'll see if I can appeal to Westcott's sense of decency." She snorted derisively. "And when that fails, I'll grab him by his implanted sensor and drag the hijo over here. Is that verd with you?"

"Do it." Ralston sank back, his thoughts already on what he had discovered in the dioramas.

In less than ten minutes a wet, cold, and angry mathematician blundered into the shelter. Westcott sat down, crossed his arms and glowered at Ralston.

"Good to see you, too, Westcott," Ralston said. The sarcasm failed to penetrate Westcott's ire at being separated from his precious computer. Ralston fleetingly wondered if Westcott had ever considered a portable unit. The idea died as quickly as it had been born. Such a unit would be too feeble for the mathematician, he decided. Nothing but supercomputer power appealed to the direct-linked researcher.

"Work on this for me," said Ralston, the snap of command in his voice. Westcott sat straighter, ready to protest. The coldness in Ralston's gray eyes silenced any such outburst. "When in the second diorama, I experienced a seizure—or rather, the character whose identity I'd assumed did. This projected convulsion must be prevented if we're to continue. How do we prevent the seizures from happening?"

Westcott shrugged. "Drugs. Chaotic dynamics seems an appropriate method for calculating which ones, what dosages, their effective durations. It seems little more to me than a parameter resetting. A boundary condition here and there . . ." Westcott shrugged.

"What do you mean?"

"Any reliable mathematician should be able to calculate how to prevent the chaotic bifurcation. See," said Westcott, beginning to warm to his lecture, "a tiny change in just one parameter throws the entire system into random behavior."

"The leaf falling causes the tornado," said Ralston, remembering that part of Westcott's theory.

"Verd, this abrupt change in the system characteristics comes in response to a single parameter alteration. Normal behavior in humans must change to chaotic as a result of neurons and neural networks shifting due to the telepathic projection."

"To prevent bifurcation, some dosage of a drug will suffice?"

"That seems plausible to me." Westcott closed his eyes. His lips moved silently. He finally gave a half smile. "Yes, it is plausible. What drug, I cannot say. You'd need a medical doctor to advise you, but this procedure is possible."

"And?" Ralston prodded.

"The implications go beyond preventing these mal seizures." Westcott hugged himself and rocked back and forth as he spoke, his eyes lit by an inner fever now. "Heartbeat irregularity. That's a product of chaotic behavior. Bifurcation occurs and fibrillation destroys the normal rhythms. And there must be some cellular mechanism that—"

"Causes cancer," Ralston finished for him.

"Why, yes, yes!"

Ralston licked dried lips and burrowed down into his cot. Dial had never admitted it—his culture denied any public show of physical weakness—but there had been the subtle fears of cancer. A word crept upward, one he only barely understood, "Neuroblastoma."

"That seems a distinct probability," said Westcott. "Coupled with the neural and network instability, cancers of the nervous system would be the most likely to be transmitted by your telepathic projector. The oncogene might be triggered." Westcott sat back, pleased with himself. Ralston had to admit that, even without the direct-link to a computer, Westcott seemed a formidable intellect.

"The Alphans might have been dying of cancer as well as the more obvious epileptic effects," he said. "And it can be transmitted through the dioramas?"

"High probability," agreed Westcott. His eyes focused on the wall and he muttered something. "The equations governing all this . . . what degree of reproducibility can I obtain in the calculations? A tricky set of pseudolinked nonlinear differential equations."

"Work on calculating the dosage to prevent the convulsions," ordered Ralston. "Hook your computer directly into the automedic. Use its pharmacy library."

"Yes, good, very good." Westcott rose and walked from the shelter, not bothering to close the door behind him. A steady blast of wintry air threatened to freeze Ralston. He staggered to the door just as Leonore returned.

"I'll get it," she said.

Ralston pulled the thin insulating blanket around him. It

trapped all his body heat and should have made him unbearably hot by now; he was still cold.

"You get what you needed out of . . . him?"

"Westcott's peculiar," agreed Ralston to his graduate assistant's unspoken appraisal, "but he might be the one who lets us explore with impunity." He quickly outlined Westcott's search for the precise equations governing the bifurcation.

"We use the automed, then go in? That's all?"

"I hope so. If we'd brought along a more powerful automedic, I'd be happier about trying it."

"You need your rest. I'll go into the next diorama." Ralston started to deny her permission, then stopped. She was a researcher, just as he was. Leonore knew the dangers and, as much as he hated to admit it, she was the better choice. She had a med-port imbedded in her stomach. With a supervisor hooked into a network with the automedic and Westcott's computer, Leonore's condition could be monitored continuously and any needed drug administered swiftly. Even more to the point, Ralston knew he wasn't able to withstand another session in one of the scenes. Not soon, at any rate. He healed rapidly, but the automed hadn't been able to manufacture much synthetic blood to replace what he'd lost. The small field unit was intended to be used as a first-aid robot, not as a full-fledged hospital doctorobot.

"I can do it, can't I?" Leonore asked.

"I want full recording. If Nels can be there, I want him. And I'll be there, too, even if I can't participate directly." Ralston thought on it. "I wonder if the scene varies if two people enter. Would Nels be willing to try?"

"You must have hit your head," Leonore said, brown eyes wide in surprise. "Where's the stuffy old prof who won't let anyone take a risk, except himself?"

She sobered when she read his expression. "You think it's that serious a problem?"

"More than the chaos device causing normally stable

stars to explode. More than the entire race of Alpha 3 perishing. More than weather disturbances.''

''You're trying to tell me we've got to solve the question of where the chaos field came from?''

''More. We've got to track it and stop it. Look at the . . . well, the chaos it's created. And while talking with Westcott, the idea came up that it might trigger oncogenes.''

''We'll get cancer?'' Leonore shrugged. ''Unfortunate, but that's hardly much of a problem. Not with our medical technology. If a gene toggles on, we can toggle it off.''

''The types of cancer the chaos field might cause are swift acting. We might be dead before we even detected it.''

''I'll order weekly automed tests. Or should we do it daily?'' Leonore cocked her head to one side and listened. The mournful howl of the winter wind had died. She opened the shelter door to syrupy warm sunshine. ''Daily,'' she said with conviction.

Ralston drifted back to a fitful sleep, dreams of oncogenes and bifurcation and randomly changing seasons troubling him.

''The digger froze,'' said Nels Bernssen. ''I tore it apart and looked at the guts. The heavy rains had soaked in around its seals, then the cold snap froze the water. Part of a block circuit cracked. The rest of the damage is minor.''

''Can you reprogram?'' asked Ralston.

''Hard to make the time to read out the old circuit and burn a new one,'' the physicist said. ''My own research is reaching a critical stage. We finally got enough satellites up and working to do a good study of the primary. Solar activity is increasing, just as it did back in the Alpha system.''

''Any immediate danger?''

The tall blond smiled. ''Are you asking if the Bernssen Condition has been achieved yet? The answer's no. The Beta sun won't go nova for some time yet. My new best estimate is a minimum of a standard year—two planetary years. We've got time to study it.''

"It's hard for Leonore and me to keep up the excavations by ourselves,'' Ralston said. He looked out over the partially cleared field where the ultrasonic digger had been working. About a quarter of the structural foundations poked up nakedly above the muddy, half-frozen ground. "We've got to make plans for exploiting the dioramas, too. Full spectrum photos, surface acoustic wave, a dozen other things. The information gleaned there might be more important than learning how the refugees lived here.''

"You're trying to say that because I have a staff of researchers with me, and you've only got Leonore, that I ought to help you?'' Nels made a wry expression. "Get Westcott into the field. He's pasty-faced. The air will do him good.''

"I know your work's important,'' said Ralston, "but we're unlocking the effects of the chaos field on people. The avians were similar enough to humans to put them in a parallel taxonomic branch.''

"Xenobiologists would dispute that.''

"Let them,'' said Ralston. "An entire world was destroyed due to the effect of that chaos device. I'm wondering if it wasn't a weapon that got out of hand.''

"It wasn't the product of the Alphans,'' said Bernssen. "That much is apparent.''

"All the more reason to study the problems and learn to cope with them—and then find the chaos device and stop it.''

"Go starring off in some random direction to hunt for a comet-sized gadget that'll scramble our circuits and brains? You archaeology researchers aim high.''

"What if the chaos field passed by Novo Terra? What if there're several orbiting around the galaxy? What if it's a natural phenomenon that might spring up anywhere at any time?''

"Work on studying the induced solar nonperiodic behavior is as important,'' said Bernssen.

Before Ralston could shift the argument in an attempt to persuade Bernssen to devote more time to the archaeological side of the expedition, a heartrending shriek tore the crisp, cold air.

"What in the name of the Trinity was that?" demanded Bernssen. He craned around, seeking the source of the piteous outcry. "It wasn't human."

Ralston went into the equipment shelter and worked for a few minutes on the supervisor. He had programmed in a signal response to everyone wearing a wristcom. All those in the field sent back satisfactory responses.

"No one's in trouble," Ralston said. "It must be another animal."

"We haven't seen any since you killed that mind-baiting creature."

"That worries me, too," said Ralston. "How can a solitary creature survive? The biome requires a certain population for species propagation—about three percent predators and the balance prey, which live off vegetation. The herbivorous animals keep down the foliage, the predators keep down the grazing animals, and lack of prey keeps the predators' numbers in check."

"The residual effects of chaos?" asked Bernssen. "That's what governs this planet?"

"The weather tells us that much." Ralston rummaged about until he found the battered spear he'd used on the animal making its lair in the dioramas. He replaced the battery and tested the tip. A satisfying spark leaped off the steel tip.

He and Bernssen went back outside in time to see a hunched over creature stalking the broken ultrasonic digger.

"What is it?" whispered Bernssen.

"Whatever it is, it thinks the digger will be dinner."

Ralston moved forward to frighten off the creature, when it pounced. Strong claws ripped open the metallic siding of the digger, spilling wiring and circuitry to the cold ground.

"Damn!" roared Ralston, outraged. Without thinking,

he ran forward, spear in hand. The animal looked up. One emerald eye blazed with hatred. The other had been malformed, only a patch of fur where the socket should have been.

"Stop, Michael. Don't!" called Bernssen.

Ralston saw a precious piece of equipment being destroyed. While still recovering from his bout underground, he wasn't going to let this creature bring valuable work to a halt due to his own weakness. The creature swiveled about, one hind leg shorter than the other. Forepaws with glistening talons raked the air to hold Ralston at bay.

The professor feinted to the left, moved right and lunged. Just as the steel tip passed the creature's defending talons, Ralston hit the contact at the base of his spear. A jolt powerful enough to kill most animals this size jerked the creature back.

The potent shock hadn't even stunned it. If anything, it enraged the beast.

"Here, over here!" yelled Bernssen, waving his arms and trying to distract the creature. Only when the physicist threw a stone that bounced off the animal's misshapen skull did it turn.

Ralston saw his chance and acted. The spear flashed forward once more, this time finding a vulnerable throat. He didn't waste time with the switch. The nicked steel blade severed arteries. Blood spurting, the creature spun back to face Ralston.

On impulse, Ralston closed the contacts once more. This electrical surge flopped the creature onto its side. It lay there, feebly pawing the air. Bernssen came up, breathing hard and said, "Never saw anything like it."

"Look at its claws. They're metallic—naturally metallic. And the musculature. Such a powerful creature, but twisted out of shape."

"What spawned such a monster?" asked Bernssen.

"It's a mutant," said Ralston. "A mutant spawned by chaos."

Bernssen looked from the dead creature to Ralston and

back. The physicist swallowed hard. "We might be able to spare some extra time for you and Leonore," he said. And then, in a voice so low that Ralston barely heard it, Bernssen said, "I don't want my mother and sisters to *ever* see anything like that back on Novo Terra. Not ever!"

NINE

MICHAEL RALSTON SAT in his shelter, head cradled in his hands. For all the progress he'd made in finding the final refuge of the natives from Alpha 3, it had come undone. A dead end. There just wasn't anything more for him to find.

The excavation had been finished, in spite of the foul weather, in spite of the destruction wrought on the one digger, in spite of a dozen other vexing problems. Increasingly, they had been plagued with catastrophic equipment failures that Westcott attributed to the residual chaotic effect. The mathematician spoke of strange attractors and four-dimensional phase portraits and other terms so esoteric, Ralston followed not even the faintest of threads of the explanations given with such loving attention to rigorous detail.

"Michael?" came Leonore Disa's soft voice. "Are you all right?"

"No, dammit, I'm not," he snapped. "Why should I be? I've been mauled and beaten up and put through convulsions, and for what? Nothing. There's nothing here!"

"That's not so. We still haven't finished with the dioramas yet. There might be something in the few we haven't tried. Nels and I will start again early tomorrow morning." No conviction rang in her voice. She sounded as downcast as he felt.

"I know the contents of the last scene. I lived through it."

"We're gaining much more data," she said. "The anti-convulsant drug works well. Neither Nels nor I have experienced any ill effects from the scenes we've studied." She tried to put a bit of humor into her words. "It does make us a little sick to our stomachs, but that comes from my medport more than anything else."

"There's got to be something I'm missing. There must be. I *feel* it!" Ralston stood and began nervously pacing, hands clasped behind his back. "I'm not thinking this through. But what can be wrong? What is it I'm missing?"

"The city is completely excavated. Not much left, I'm afraid. The few artifacts don't give us any clearer picture of the Alpha 3 society than we'd already gotten."

"They lasted almost a hundred years. Dial and the others landed, and at least one generation of Alphans followed. But the chaos destroyed them, just as it had their planet. It must have worked on the embryo Alphans, and this decimated their birthrate. If only their culture had been more inclined to leave debris, garbage, something for us to study. All the Alphans seemed to have left of any consequence was their telepathic museum."

"Nels says the primary has quieted down. That's typical, though. Long stretches of intense solar storms followed by shorter plateaus of relative inactivity."

"The epilepsy," said Ralston, not listening to her. "There's that. Cancers. I'm sure their entire population was rife with it. The chaos field triggers oncogenes. Look at the hideously deformed creatures we've found. Those must have been native to Beta 5."

"You think they've mutated this rapidly?"

"Leonore, evolution is a rapid process, at least in a geologic sense. We're not talking millions of years to form those beasts, but a handful of thousands. The chaos device sowed its seeds of change all too well, I think."

"We're still likely to figure out how to duplicate the

telepathic projector,'' Leonore said. ''That'll make the expedition seem better to Salazar, at least for us.''

"This is really Bernssen's expedition. We just rode along. I need *more*. And there's something I've overlooked. Not the city. That was a dead end. The dioramas aren't giving us any more information than we either had or had guessed. What have I overlooked?''

Leonore shook her head. "Those seem to be the pertinent points, at least from an archaeology standpoint. Dial tried to leave as complete a record as possible, but they seemed to struggle too much just to survive. Querno died of an epileptic convulsion soon after they landed. Fennalt scavenged their spaceship to—''

"Fennalt!" cried Ralston. "That's it. I . . . I remember it now. In the last diorama. Dial detailed their troubles. He said that Captain Fennalt had settled on the far side of the planet hoping that this isolation would keep the chaotic plague from spreading.''

"It obviously didn't.''

"Get the satellite photos of the spot. Do it. Now!'' he yelled. Leonore jumped at his tone. She took the hardcopy photos out and spread them on the table.

"So?" she asked.

"How extensive is the city on the far side of the planet? The one Fennalt settled?''

"Big,'' Leonore said, not sure what Ralston meant.

"Much bigger than this one, yet how many Alphans did Fennalt have with him? Only the ones they thought were untouched by the chaos—less than a hundred.''

"You're saying they prospered and built the city? Verd, they may have lasted a generation or two longer, but they're gone, too. No trace of survivors anywhere.''

"They weren't untouched. We know that. All who escaped Alpha 3 carried with them the kernel for their eventual destruction, whether it was fast from epileptic seizure or slow from cancer. And they certainly found no relief on Beta 5—not with the chaotic effects running rampant among the animal population.''

"I don't understand."

"Fennalt's group had no better chance to survive. And I don't think it did. Something Dial said—something in the diorama—went by me until now. I can't remember the exact words but the thought was that Fennalt had gone to colonize a city already constructed."

"Not by natives of Beta 5," said Leonore. She frowned. "We haven't found any trace of intelligent life anywhere else. Just those two spots. That's stretching logic to think that any natives would concentrate in one city, then just leave it for the Alphans."

"What if they weren't native to Beta 5? What if that was only a colony?"

"You mean another race colonized Beta 5, left, and then Fennalt moved in?"

"I have to start excavation at the other site. We've documented this one well enough. We can get our equipment crated and ready to move in a few days."

"But what about the dioramas we haven't activated!" Leonore protested.

"They're interesting, but only for details. *This* is new science. This is another find. Imagine, Leonore. We've found a planet that boasts *two* colonies. And the first ones to Beta 5 had to have space travel. Where else would they come from?"

"Inside the system or from outside?"

"How can we tell unless we work the site?" asked Ralston, smiling. Hope again rose within his breast. More of the Alphan culture might be revealed.

Ralston could hardly hold back the irrational hope at the idea that some of the Alphan refugees might have left Beta 5 with the builders of the colony. To speak directly to any survivor of Alpha 3 would prove invaluable. Not only could he check his guesses about their society, he might be able to learn exact details of the disaster that had befallen them.

He might learn everything about the chaos device.

●   ●   ●

"I don't like it, Leonore," Nels Bernssen said. The tall physicist slumped forward, a dour look on his face. "There's no way I can break off now and go with you. And changing our site is impossible. We've too much time and effort invested here." He straightened and almost shouted, "Dammit, why couldn't you have begun on the other site! Why change your mind now?"

Leonore hugged him tight and burrowed her face into his chest. "I don't want to go, Nels, but I have to. Michael can't work alone. Even with the cargo robots, one person can't set up a functioning dig."

"I can't let you take the supervisor. I need it to . . . to monitor the others." Nels' voice almost broke. Two of his team had developed cancers, one of the thyroid and another of the spleen. The automedic had painstakingly cured both, but Bernssen feared a virulent cancer might be beyond the small machine's capability. An undiagnosed pancreatic cancer might end a promising career and rob him overnight of a friend and colleague.

Even worse, from Bernssen's standpoint, was the potential for convulsive seizures.

"Keep the supervisor. We can get along without it. If there's just Michael and me—and maybe Westcott, if he decides to go—we won't need it. We can run one digger more efficiently using manual controls. The other equipment we can take out as needed."

"I don't want you to go," the man said simply.

"It's what I want to do. There's a good chance Michael is right. This might be another major find, a new alien site. Our job is to research other cultures by digging through their abandoned cities. I can't ask you to give up your work. Don't ask me to give up mine."

"I didn't say I wanted you to," Bernssen said. "I just meant that I'll miss you. With solar activity increasing the way it is, we might not be able to talk much, even using satellites."

"Set up one to relay microbursts. I can beam up as much as I want, the satellite will store it until it's overhead here, then you can retrieve it. The proton storms won't affect that much, will it?''

''I prefer holding you when I'm talking to you.''

''I know.'' Leonore Disa snuggled closer, but it soon came time to leave. Ralston waited impatiently for her. The pilot had returned with the landing pod to shuttle them halfway around the planet. This concession from the reclusive pilot wasn't to be dismissed lightly. Anger him and he might return to the starship still in orbit and not ground again on Beta 5 until they wanted to return to Novo Terra.

Leonore broke away and hurried outside, not daring to look back at her lover.

''This the place? Doesn't look like anything.'' The pilot's nimble fingers worked over the computer console. Ralston knew that the man had already programmed everything in; this was simply a show for the passengers.

''Mostly desert,'' said Ralston. ''Land anywhere beyond the red rock upjuts. We want to stake out the site on the alkali plains.''

''Hard to call them plains. Look at the way the water's eroded them. Damn crazy weather on this planet. Can't tell from minute to minute what it's going to do.''

''This is unusual,'' pointed out Leonore. ''The Alphans chose gently rolling land with grass and wooded areas nearby for their other cities. This is so . . . so different.''

''It reinforces the idea that someone else built it, doesn't it?'' said Ralston, peering into the viewscreen. His words abruptly cut off when the pilot touched down. The roar of rockets and the intense vibration jarred Ralston's teeth, and a momentary stab of pain went through his side. The automed had done a good job repairing the wounds inflicted by the mutant creature but deeper mending needed to be finished.

''We're down. I already got the laborobots working to uncrate for you. You want me to stick around for a while or get back into orbit?'' The pilot's tone made it obvious which he desired. Ralston made it easy on the man.

"Get us unloaded, then go on up. I want you to be able to pick either group of us up at a moment's notice."

"With the solar storms as bad as they are, you might be safer down here," said the pilot. But Ralston saw that the man preferred his lofty perch, no matter what the danger. "But all you need to do is call and I'll be here. Or give a flash if the radio transmission is out. You got the lasercom, don't you?"

Ralston looked to Leonore, who nodded. The cargo robot had unpacked their emergency communication unit first and had already checked it out.

"We're on our way. Thanks."

Ralston and Leonore clumsily left the shuttle and made their way through the slowly growing forest of crates. They had left most of their equipment at their first site with Nels Bernssen, but they still carried a great deal of mass.

"There's as good a site for camp as any," said Ralston, eyeing the terrain. A low sand dune would partially protect them when the shuttle launched; he might have chosen a spot farther away, but Ralston didn't want to take the time required to move the equipment.

"Mighty close," said the pilot, eyeing the choice critically. The man shrugged and turned back to the shuttle, not waiting for Ralston's answer. The pilot assumed Ralston knew the dangers—and like any other scientist, was absolutely insane.

Two hours later the shuttle launched. Ralston and Leonore Disa crouched behind a makeshift blast deflector. They hardly noticed the added heat from the shuttle pod's exhaust gases. The incessant winds blowing across the desert provided a natural kiln-hot environment. Shaking the dust and sand from their clothes, the two archaeologists stood and watched the contrail forming high above them in the clear azure sky.

"Makes you feel alone, doesn't it?" said Ralston.

"Verd," agreed Leonore. She shook herself again and

sent up a cloud of dust. "I hate this place. Let's get the digger going. The sooner we start, the sooner we leave."

"That's not the proper spirit," said Ralston, even though he shared her distaste for the desert. Like the Alphans, he preferred greener lands. Staying in the desert too long might even make him homesick for Novo Terra.

"I know. We go where the ruins are."

"You could have specialized," he told her. "The underwater excavation teams never have to deal with sand."

"No, just exterior pressures high enough to crush titanium hulls like paper. Funny air mixtures that make you squeak when you talk. Never being able to go for a nice long walk alone. I know all about the undersea people. They're crazy."

"They say the same about us," Ralston said. He bent to the task of pulling open the crates containing their digger while the laborobots put up plastic shelters to house them and the manually operated controllers. Four hours of work in the sun completed their camp.

"I've had it, Michael. I feel drained." Leonore collapsed onto her cot and hiked up her feet. She closed her eyes.

"We've done enough for the day. I wanted to get everything established. We'll work at night. Even with the sun only about half as bright as home, this heat is killing me." Ralston sighed and took a long, tepid drink of water already distilled by their precipitator. "Should have landed at dusk and worked in the evening to set up," he said. "Hindsight's always better."

"Not as good as sleep," murmured Leonore. In minutes, Ralston heard the woman's slow, even breathing.

The professor stared at her, wondering what drove her. She came from one of the richest families on Novo Terra. Why expose yourself to dirt, grit, and discomfort when you could be dining elegantly at the finest restaurants?

Ralston's thoughts turned to what drove him. He found this as unexplored an area of motivation in himself as in Leonore. The discovery of small pieces of information no one else had uncovered thrilled him, but was this the only reason he risked his life on a half-dozen different planets? It hardly seemed enough. Curiosity? Was it that simple? Ralston rolled it over and over in his tired brain, seeking the answer. Did he run from something or to it? The way he felt, he couldn't even walk.

He left Leonore's tiny plastic shelter and went to his own. He stretched out, tried to sleep, and couldn't; tiredness prevented it. His mind kept turning over and over what he hoped to find in these ruins. Dial *had* mentioned another race already here, but the Alphan had spoken so briefly of it that Ralston knew the ruins were ancient when the refugees landed on Beta 5.

The thought turned repeatedly in his head that the chance existed for some of the Alphans to be alive on some other world, that he might get closer to the mystery of the chaos device. It had ruined worlds, exploded stars, killed races, and hideously deformed creatures on Beta 5. As he drifted off into a sleep that was more like a coma, Ralston realized that he was interested in the refugee Alphans, he was interested in what might prove to be Betans, but his real desire for knowledge lay with the chaos field.

Was it a natural occurrence? A weapon? An accident? Had some race tried to contact others using it as a communication device? Why did it exist? Why?

"Over to your left. More, more, that's it." Michael Ralston signaled to Leonore to put the digger on a straight course. The ultrasonic broom spewed forth a miniature tornado of dust and white clay as it revealed the buried ruins.

The synthetic aperture radar had shown the buried structures, but it had failed to indicate their depth. It had taken a week of intense work to even reach the ruins. Ralston and Leonore worked in a pit almost four meters deep. The first meter had been the worst. Sand without anything to hold it poured into their excavation as fast as the digger removed it. Ralston had finally resorted to fusing the sand into glassy slag with a plasma torch.

After the first meter, work went faster until they struck a white caliche layer that continually overheated their digger. Water refused to soften the hard clay. Only patience worked. The final two meters had been relatively uneventful.

"We need a couple dozen others working with us," complained Leonore. Ralston saw that her nose was peeling from sunburn in spite of the medications she applied. Leonore had long ago turned off her jewelry plates; the water loss and sun-hardening of her skin, in spite of working at night, caused the plates' soft outlines to become more prominent. "Or a supervisor and a dozen diggers."

"We're getting there," said Ralston. He was hardly in better condition than his student. "But it is too bad Westcott didn't want to leave his computer. Imagine what he'd look like out here scrabbling through debris with his fingers."

The image of the mathematician doing anything but sitting in a chair and gazing glassy-eyed at infinity amused them both.

Ralson stayed on hands and knees following the digger as it unearthed the top of a building. The archaeology professor took photos of every trinket found, carefully tagged and boxed them, and kept on with the dreary work. The acquisition stage always dragged on interminably for him. He preferred the work of piecing together what they'd found, figuring out how the society had functioned, what the recovered oddiments were used for, *who* the people were.

"We need a sonic prober," he said. "This is a dome for a large building. From the curvature, it must be a good twenty meters in diameter."

"At least," agreed Leonore, standing to get a better look at the dome appearing under the digger's snout. "We'll have to put lights up higher to get a better look at it."

''What worries me is having to excavate over it if we want to expose it all. That's, hmmm, four meters deep and twenty diameter . . . almost twelve hundred fifty cubic meters.''

"We might as well give up on that notion," said Leonore. She stared at the thirty-meter long, three-meter wide trench they'd dug. That had taken a week. The excavation Ralston threatened would require another month of hard work. Even then, they had no guarantee the effort would be rewarded.

"Can't figure out what this material is," said Ralston. "I'm actually considering using the torch to cut through it."

"That's sloppy archaeology. Do you really want to destroy what you've found?"

"Hardly, but we both know there won't be time for a real expedition. We don't have the equipment now, and the University isn't likely to send another group within a year. Nels said the sun's going to go nova some time after that, which would discourage most reputable University archaeologists.''

"It didn't discourage us, either here or on Alpha 3."

"It'd discourage any *sane* archaeologist," he amended. Ralston continued to brush away the grit and the white clay with his hands while the digger worked ahead, removing the bulk of the sand. "Dammit! I'm so far gone I refuse to be stopped, by Chancellor Salazar or good sense or even chaos.''

"And I'm with you!"

Ralston looked up. He had his answer. Leonore Disa had left Novo Terra for the same reasons he had. Unlocking the past held a lure more potent than any drug. To know things that others didn't, to present those facts, *that* was the addiction they shared.

"You're going to get committee approval on your thesis before long," he said. "If you ever finish it. You been working on it?''

"Michael!" she protested. "I've been spending every spare minute going over Beta material."

He shook his head in mock disapproval. "That's no way for a student to behave. The degree, that's the important thing."

"The work is," Leonore said flatly.

Ralston nodded, happy to hear her say it. She might be his graduate student, and he might be a political pariah at the University of Ilium, but he'd fight for her degree with the rest of her committee, with the entire department, if necessary. Leonore Disa was a good researcher and one of the best field investigators he'd ever seen.

"We're in luck," he said. "Look at this."

Leonore left the digger controls and stood above Ralston, looking over his shoulder. "What is it?"

"Don't know. It might be a hatch or a door. It seems to open by dropping down and then sliding to the side. Do you see any lock or opening mechanisms?"

"I'll direct the digger over and clear off a larger area. Maybe we can find the door bell."

A cracking sound echoed like thunder along their excavated trench. Ralston and Leonore exchanged glances.

"What was that?" she asked.

"It sounded like something breaking. Glass or . . ." Ralston's voice trailed off as he looked up at the sides of their trench. The areas where he'd fused the walls were starred with cracks.

"The trench is falling in. Get the—"

Ralson's words were cut off as an even louder crack sounded. The sandy walls of the trench collapsed, sending up dust clouds—and bringing down four meters of sand on top of them.

TEN

SHARDS FROM THE plasma torch-slagged trench walls shot past Michael Ralston's head like vitreous bullets. He ducked and felt himself being surrounded by the sand. Somehow, Leonore grabbed his arm. He pulled her close.

"Climb," he shouted. The rush of sand almost drowned out his command. But even as Ralston spoke, he knew that it wouldn't be possible. They were being swamped. The weight of the sand crushed him down to his knees, Leonore beside him.

Instinct for survival took over. He arched his back and strained mightily to keep from being driven flat onto the domed structure. With his arms outspread, Ralston managed to form a small cavity under his chest. But he found it increasingly difficult to maintain even this small breathing space as more and more of the sand piled on top of him and found its insidious way around his body.

"Michael!" cried Leonore. He sensed her wiggling around under him. "Hold on!"

"Trying," he panted.

Already the air turned stale. Less than a cubic meter of free space remained underneath his torso. Even as he panted and strained, sand poured around him, filling up this small space that gave them both a small hope for escape. Ralston began to black out. The pressure on his back and shoulders overwhelmed him. His side began to ache, muscles ripping within his chest cavity. He tried to gasp in a lungful of air and got only sand. He choked. His strength began to fade, slowly at first, then with mounting speed.

"Leonore," he gasped, trying to tell her to get out from under him. She didn't hear; his voice failed. He crumpled onto her, the weight of the sand driving him down with manic fury.

For a moment, Ralston hung suspended in time and infinite space. His entire world had turned dark and sandy. His lungs strained and life ebbed from him.

He shrieked in surprise as he suddenly plummeted, the dome and Leonore no longer beneath him. Arms flailing as if he were a bird trying to fly, he fell through the air. He smashed hard into Leonore, his body atop hers.

Ralson lay stunned, not knowing what had happened. A tiny trickle of sand from above annoyed him. Then he laughed in delight. He could be annoyed. The compression of sand on his back had vanished. His lungs pulled in stale but breathable air. What was an hourglass trickle compared to that?

"Get off me, dammit," he heard Leonore say. The floor wiggled: Leonore.

"Sorry." Ralston moved slowly, painfully. The muscles in his side refused to give him anything but stabbing agony whenever he twisted. The professor tried to remain upright and not torque the damaged area. "What happened? We were trapped, then . . ."

Probing around with his hand, Ralston paused when he touched Leonore. They had fallen into the dome. That was the only possible answer. But if they'd found the front door, they had yet to discover the light switch.

"It's too dark to see anything," she said. "There must be lights, if we can find them."

"Let me catch my breath," he said, wincing at this small exertion. "What happened? How'd we get inside?"

"I found a depression in the dome just as the trench

walls caved in on us. I pressed down hard and the door worked. I didn't expect to fall so far, though. I think I broke my arm.''

"That makes me in better shape," lied Ralston. Every breath, now that he had sufficient oxygen, proved a trial. Knives of pain lanced into him each time he breathed in or out—and he wasn't up to holding his breath yet. Not after escaping a premature burial.

"You don't sound it.''

"Help me up. We're going to have to explore. There's still sand coming down on my face. I don't think the door shut.''

"It must have," she pointed out. "The entire dome would have been filled by now. Maybe the door only partially closed. That gives us time.''

Ralston didn't ask time for what. He wanted to believe they could escape, but how they'd accomplish this miracle wasn't clear. Even if they turned on the lights, they were still in a dome buried under almost four meters of heavy sand. With his side injured again, and Leonore's arm broken, digging out using their hands didn't appear too attractive an option.

Edging slowly in the direction he faced, Ralston began his blind exploration. Several times he tripped over debris scattered on the floor, and once he took a nasty fall over a railing that caught him just below waist level.

"We can go on like this for years," complained Leonore. "We can starve to death doing it.''

"I know. I'm hoping that we'll reach a wall soon. We can go around the entire circumference and get some idea what we have in the way of resources.''

"After almost ten thousand years, you don't think the Alphans left anything useful, do you? Like a nice salad or even a few dried-out chocolate bars?''

"I just want to see where I am," he said. The mention of food caused his belly to grumble. For all his careful movement, Ralston slammed hard into the dome wall. The curvature had become more acute, allowing him to hit his head even though his probing foot and groping hand had found nothing.

"The wall?" Leonore asked eagerly. She tugged on his free hand as she worked around. In less than a minute they both squinted under the harsh light filling the huge dome.

Ralston held up a hand to protect his eyes until they adjusted. He realized that the light level was very low, far lower than an Alphan would find comfortable—and it was even dimmer than a Beta 5 twilight.

"I seem to have the knack for finding their controls," Leonore said proudly.

She had moved in precisely the right direction along the wall to find the lighting control panel. If they had gone in the opposite direction, they would have traversed over half the circumference before finding another switch. At least a dozen circular openings radiated from the dome, two of them between the archaeologists and the other light control. They might have blundered down one of those passages before finding the switch. Leonore's success almost made Ralston believe in luck.

"Let me look at your arm."

"What are you, an automed?" She winced as he gently probed. The simple fracture had to be set. Leonore gasped and almost fainted on him when he firmly grasped her wrist and elbow and exerted a steady pressure. He felt the bone snap into place just as the woman began to fight to get away from him.

"We'll find a splint for it somewhere, and you'll be all right again."

Tears ran down her cheeks and left dusty trails. "All right? How can you say that after you almost killed me?"

She looked up to the dome entrance, where sand still sifted past the door, then laughed. For a moment, Ralston looked at her, then he joined in until they clung to one another, laughing hysterically. Finally, sore and exhausted, the need for nervous release past, they sank to the floor of the dome and leaned awkwardly against the wall.

"What do you think this place was?" Leonore asked.

Ralston shook his head. "A storage area. A warehouse. Mostly, it looks unused by the Alphans. And the Betans didn't leave much."

He studied the sloping wall and the blister-shaped surface arching above them. The material appeared to be a tough plastic, but it had a metallic sheen to it that spoke of a different, otherworldly origin. The hatchway in the top of the dome wasn't intended to open into space as it had. Ralston saw points where a walkway had once been attached to the inner surface around the hatchway. For some reason, it had been taken down and the framework stored on the opposite side of the dome. Of a ladder or other way up he saw no trace.

"There's a corridor going into the rest of the complex," Leonore said. She cradled her right arm in her lap and used her left to point out the dark circular doorway.

"We're not going to find a way out sitting here."

They helped one another to their feet and started off, picking their way through the alien debris. Repeatedly, Ralston fought the urge to stop and study it. This wasn't merely garbage, it constituted an artifact left by an alien culture. As such, it held information. But he kept moving. While they were better off now than a short while ago, their lives still hinged on quickly finding a way out from under the crushing thousands of kilograms of sand.

"No lights," Leonore said. "We'll have to go slowly."

They edged down the tunnel. Ralston ran his hand along the sharply curved, smooth ceiling just a few centimeters above his head. The width didn't exceed two meters. The faint available light dimmed quickly. Luckily, they found the end of the tunnel before they floundered about in total dark.

"These are strange doors," Ralston remarked. "It's as if they pressurized the inside of the dome and connecting tunnels."

"Designed for a being used to living in a higher-pressure atmosphere?" Leonore asked.

"I can't think of any other reason for choosing the

interior designs. It gives me the sensation of being in a spaceship, the walls between me and a vacuum. But the atmosphere is a normal pressure for us, and very close for the Alphans.''

The door to an airlock slid open slowly, its mechanism still functional after almost ten thousand years. Inside the chamber, Leonore found another light-control panel. Like the airlock and the other mechanisms, it, too, functioned perfectly. They entered a second, smaller dome. Ignoring the stale, dead air, the archaeologists looked around. This one had been outfitted with bars parallel to the floor and mounted just above eye level.

"The Alphans?" she asked. "They were avian. I'd never gotten any indication that they hung from perches, though.''

"I never did, either, but most of what we know has been gathered in the dioramas. Those were intended to give specific history lessons, not an account of their day-to-day lives. We don't even know for sure what they ate.''

Leonore looked around, shaking her head. "Whoever built the structure built it to last. Imagine buying anything on Novo Terra that'd last ten months, much less ten thousand years.''

Ralston looked at the light source. "No filaments. No gas inside to leak out. I'm not sure how the light's produced, but it's a good guess that the light level and frequency hasn't changed much since it was installed. If we find out how the Betans did this, Salazar will jump through hoops again. Especially since it's an immediately marketable theft.'' His scorn for archaeology placed on such a basis was obvious, yet Ralston had a pragmatic side. He might not be liked or appreciated at the University of Ilium, but if he kept returning with profitable geegaws, his position, if not his often-denied tenure, was assured.

"Any culture that builds so solidly and well must be long-lived,'' said Leonore. "Even if we had the proper equipment, how would we determine the age? Take a chunk of the dome itself and check it out for radioactive decay?''

"That'd be one way," said Ralston. "But carbon dating is good for only about seventy or eighty thousand years. We might have to use fission-track dating, if we can find any uranium in the shell."

"You think this structure is *that* old? That technique will date back for billions of years."

"It's all guesswork. I doubt we'll be able to accurately date the structure, even if we had the time. We don't have any of the equipment for thorium-lead or potassium-argon series. We'd have to send it back to the University labs."

"And the entire system will be superheated plasma in a year or two," Leonore said dejectedly. "Why is it you can't make a discovery on a planet not at jeopardy?"

"It happens that way," Ralston said. "Live life at the edge and you're bound to fall off. My acquaintance with the chaos device has made it all the more likely I'm going to fail."

"The thought just occurred to me: Since the chaos field passed through this system, would *any* of the radioactive dating methods be accurate?"

"I'll have to ask Westcott," said Ralston. "It seems likely that decay mechanisms would change if subjected to an enforced randomness." He let out a long sigh. "It might even make elements not normally radioactive begin to kick out gamma rays."

Ralston fell silent as they examined the chamber. All that speculation might die with them unless they found a way to the surface. But in spite of the danger, Ralston found himself more and more engrossed in what they discovered about the Alphans' living arrangements in the Betans' abandoned colony.

Ralston had to call a break when his side began throbbing with pain strong enough to bend him over.

"Your ribs might be broken," Leonore said, a hint of sadism in her voice. She hadn't forgotten the way he'd jerked on her arm to reset the ulna. "Is there some way of bandaging you?"

"I'll be all right, if we can just get out of here. This looks more and more like a prison to me. Let's hope it doesn't begin to look like a coffin."

"They must have had ways out. The beings that build so sturdily wouldn't risk being trapped by a sandstorm."

"That doesn't follow," he pointed out, his mind working on the problem. "If they were higher pressure beings, they wouldn't venture outside much. It wouldn't matter to them if they were buried under a kilometer of sand or sat on the surface." Ralston moved to a more comfortable position. "They had to have built on the surface, though. The four meters we dug through are the result of chaotic storms over the years since the Alphans came."

"The Alphans wouldn't have wanted to be buried."

"The storm patterns might not have been the same then. Or they might have excavated. . . ." Ralston paused and thought for a moment. He and Leonore exchanged glances.

"No, I didn't shut it off. I didn't have time," Leonore said.

"Then the ultrasonic digger is still working above us." Hope flared. "It had been programmed to clean off the stretch of dome around the hatchway, and it doesn't care if it's buried or not. It burrows as well as it sweeps."

"Then all we have to do is get back up to the hatchway and get the digger as it comes across. We can direct it upward."

"That's a lot of digging—and don't forget, the sand will come rushing in when we open the hatch."

"We can figure out something," Leonore said, dismissing this. "It might be harder for us to get back to the hatch. The ladder's gone and the walkway has been junked."

Ralston remembered the drop; they had fallen almost six meters.

"We can stack up debris," he said, looking around. It would be hard, but he thought they had enough to make a tottering mountain. "We might have to scavenge the entire complex, but I want to look through it, anyway."

"There must be ladders or climbing apparatus stored somewhere," Leonore agreed.

The two left the chamber where they thought the Alphans had slept. A tunnel leading to another, smaller dome, seemed to be the pattern followed throughout the buried complex. The central dome through which they'd tumbled provided a hub for the outstretched tunnels, the body of an octopus throwing out its tentacles.

Hours later, after they had separated and explored independently, they reunited. Ralston and Leonore sank to a low uncushioned bench made from the same material as the dome.

"No dioramas," Leonore said in disgust. "I'd hoped to find one telling all about this place."

"The Alphans were desperate and under immense strain when they established this outpost. Most of their equipment and expertise remained at the other site."

"It didn't do them any good. There aren't even any bodies."

"I gathered some dust that might be organic. I put it in a specimen envelope. When we get back, we can run some tests on it to determine the source." He looked at a small bag Leonore dragged behind her. "What's in that?"

"I don't know. I found it in a small room at the far end of the third tentacle-corridor. The room looked like an office, but it didn't have any furniture in it. Hardly any furniture anywhere, for that matter."

Ralston rummaged through the bag and came out with a stack of shiny disks. He held one up to the wan light and studied it.

"This might be a primitive laser recording," he said. "You didn't see any equipment?"

Leonore shook her head tiredly.

"I didn't, either. There's no hint to the original owners of this fine property," he said. "But I did find a room filled with stanchions and spare paneling. If we can get it up to the hatchway, we might be able to build a dam to keep the sand from pouring in.''

"And from there we can get the digger and burrow for the surface." Leonore's face had a pinched, drained, white look to it. Ralston realized the strain she was under—the strain they both felt so acutely. He was in charge of this expedition and he had let down his student, endangering her life in unprofessional ways. Worse, he had to continually fight to keep from rubbing his stomach to quell the growls of hunger.

But Ralston had one advantage over Leonore. He had been hungry before, many times before. Back on a burned-out Earth he had often gone days without any food and only a thin, dirty trickle of water to provide a small measure of liquid. And again, during the Nex-P'torra war, he had almost starved until he found which of the Nex foods suited him and which didn't. None of their warships had been equipped for aliens.

Ralston chuckled when he thought of the food he'd managed to get aboard to supplement the Nex rations. To this day he shuddered at the memory of peanut butter eaten to the exclusion of all else. But even this wouldn't go down badly, he thought.

"Let's get to work," he said. "The sooner we get out of here, the sooner we can eat." He watched in concern as Leonore got to her feet and wobbled. She caught herself and pretended it hadn't happened. Ralston tried to remember how long it had been since they'd eaten.

A day? Even if it had only been a few hours, they'd been through much. The strain of survival burned calories quickly.

"Bring that bag with you. It's got about all this place has to offer in the way of artifacts.''

·Leonore listlessly dragged it behind her into the main dome.

Ralston, in spite of his injured side, did more of the heavy work. Leonore's right arm lacked strength. It took only a few minutes for him to see how much it still pained her. He dragged the panels and beams into the room while she worked out a system for getting them the necessary distance to the overhead hatchway.

"It'll be shaky, but bracing one beam there, lifting and bracing another against it like this, and then dragging the panels up one sloping side is the easiest," she said, sketching out the blueprint in the sand beneath the still-leaking hatch.

"Let's do it."

Ralston started and, with Leonore's help, they built the rickety structure in less than an hour. It took him another two to get the panels up and in place.

"I can hear the digger working," he said, shouldering a panel into position. The cofferdam seemed ready.

They looked at one another. In their weakened condition, they had done all they could. If only they'd had their full excavation equipment with them!

"Ready?" asked Ralston.

Leonore nodded. She edged along the beam and found the inner lock mechanism. Ralston readied himself to force the paneling through the hatchway when it slid open.

"Now!" she cried.

The hatchway slid open, and Ralston shoved with all his strength to lift the cofferdam into the imprisoning sand.

He knew instantly that he'd misjudged both the weight of the sand and his own strength. The makeshift wedge shifted to one side and Ralston was unable to hold it. The rush of sand drove him backward along the narrow platform they'd constructed.

Torrents of choking sand rushed to fill the dome.

ELEVEN

"No!" SHRIEKED LEONORE DISA. "Stop it! Don't let it come in!"

Michael Ralston had no way of stopping the torrent of crushing sand. It bowled him over, sending the pitifully inadequate cofferdam in one direction and him in another. He clung onto the platform brace and watched as the cascading sand took his laboriously constructed panels to the floor of the dome and immediately covered it. He spat and fought to get the sand from his eyes. Side hurting terribly, he got back to his feet and joined Leonore.

Less than two meters away the sand rushed noisily into the dome in a torrent so powerful that the best excavation equipment couldn't have halted it.

"We're going to die," Leonore said in a voice totally calm. "The sand will fill the dome and we'll die. We can't even reach any of the branching corridors."

Ralston shielded her with his body, but the choking sand flew everywhere. He pulled off his shirt and tore it into strips. He and Leonore breathed through the sweat-stiff fabric, but this did little to furnish clean air to his lungs or to stop the polar coldness in his gut from spreading. He had heard the woman's dire words; he knew they were true.

All they could do was stand on the rickety platform and wait for death.

"What's that?" Leonore asked. "Something's wrong."

Ralston almost laughed at this. Everything had gone wrong. Then he heard the curious, unexpected sound, too. It was almost as if the deafening rush of sand diminished. Squinting, he turned and peered into the dust.

"It's stopping. I don't know why, but it's stopping!"

In less than a minute the torrent had reduced to a trickle. Ralston, curious, edged over. Leonore followed closely. He peered up through the hatchway and saw the ultrasonic digger humming away as it cleared a spot on the dome's surface.

"The digger?" asked Leonore, incredulous.

"No, not entirely," said Ralston, suddenly realizing what had happened. "When the hatchway opened, the loose sand that had collapsed on us came rushing in. When a cone shape formed, the edges of the sand cone poured through, but soon after an equilibrium was formed. Getting out will be hard since we have to climb the sloping walls of a sandpit, but we can breathe! And the sky!"

"I'd thought Nels had come to see why we hadn't reported in," she said in a low voice. Then, brighter, "I never thought such dry desert air and hot sun would look good."

"You first," Ralston said. He boosted her up, wincing at the sharp pain in his side. He stood wobbling as Leonore kicked her way through the hatch and onto the small area the digger worked persistently to keep free of sand.

"We can make it, Michael. The climb won't even be that hard. Do you need help?"

"Get some rope and tie it around the digger's frame. Let it pull me out," he said. Ralston didn't want to admit to her that he wasn't able to follow.

"That'd mean going back to camp. I'm not sure I can make it up the slope without help. Here."

He heard ripping noises. In a few minutes a tattered rope made from her blouse dropped in front of him. He hefted the bag containing the disks Leonore had found, secured them to his belt, tied a bowline in the cloth rope, and fitted himself inside the loop.

"Pull away!" he shouted.

The digger almost didn't have enough power to lift him. But with Leonore's one-handed aid, he managed to get free of the dome without fainting from the pain. He lay on the sandy surface and shook. They had cheated death too often since arriving. This alien structure had almost become their tomb.

"I don't want to stay here. I want to get back to camp, where I can take a bath. It doesn't even matter that it's a chemical one." Leonore stood bare to the waist.

"You're going to sunburn," Ralston said. He sat and stared at her. She wasn't beautiful, but Ralston wasn't sure he had ever seen anyone more attractive.

"Do you gawk or do you climb?" she asked indignantly.

"Climb, but the gawking isn't such a bad choice."

Together they made their way up the shifting, treacherously yielding slope of the land. They finally flopped flat on the sunbaked surface and looked down into the cavity.

"I'd heard about insects on Earth that trap their prey using this arrangement," he said. "Ant lions, I think they're called. The ant slips down the side. When it tries to climb out, the ant lion begins digging under the ant's feet. When it tires, it slides all the way to the bottom, where the predator eats it."

"I'm glad you told me about that now," Leonore said, looking at the bottom, where the digger worked to hold back the inevitable cascades of sand.

They helped one another back to their shelters. Ralston wanted nothing more than to collapse. Without undressing he fell onto his cot. Nearby, he heard Leonore cursing as she clumsily worked to take a chemical bath. Ralston fell asleep, happy to be alive.

"You didn't make yourself look very clever," said Nels Bernssen, looking over Ralston's shoulder as the archaeology professor finished his weekly report. "In fact, when Salazar gets this, he'll have you up on charges."

"That'd be nothing new," said Ralston. He leaned back, free of pain at last. The automedic had worked on him for three days, then given him sedation for another three. Even though he hadn't broken any ribs, Ralston wondered if it might not have been better if he had. The muscle tears refused to heal quickly. Long after Leonore's broken arm had been returned to use, he had still moved with some difficulty and often considerable pain.

"You don't have to be so . . . frank."

Ralston looked up at the physicist. "This is what happened. I'm not going to alter the truth just to make myself look better. I know others do it." Ralston's mind produced a list of a half dozen just in the archaeology department at the University who had been overly creative in their reports to avoid problems with both University officials and protective parents. "Who knows? This might give us a real clue to the Betans. If I tried to make myself look less like an idiot, that might hide the facts we need."

"Still, Michael, there're ways of telling the truth without it being so masochistic. What's wrong with saying you thought about it, then logically figured out how to escape from the dome, rather than saying what happened was both accidental and unplanned and that you hadn't intended to get out that way?"

"Nothing, but it didn't happen that way. 'Hard are the ways of truth, and rough to walk.' "

"What?"

"A friend of mine is a medieval lit prof. Some of it must have rubbed off. That's from Milton."

"Milton who?"

"What's going on with the primary? How're your experiments coming along?" Ralston asked, changing the subject. Bernssen's expression turned to one of concentration.

"Good. We're able to find more pronounced pre-nova conditions in the Beta star than we did in the Alpha. My theory is working out well. The only trouble is equipment failure. Westcott says it's due to the chaos field's residual effects.''

"I want to fission-track date the dome and other artifacts we found, but I'm afraid that the chaos field might have affected the rate of radioactive decay. Did Westcott say anything about being able to correct for this?"

"We've been talking a great deal about the fusion process in the primary. I can't say I like him much, but I'll give the hijo this—he knows his math. That question came up. He showed me how a rapid passing of the chaos field wouldn't affect radioactive decay.''

"Why not?" Ralston frowned. He wasn't a physicist but it seemed logical to him that if people developed neural problems and computer components failed, the radioactive decay process would be similarly afflicted.

"All nuclear processes are reversible. If the field forced an alpha decay, for instance, it also changed the probabililty for an alpha collision into the stripped nuclei.''

"So we're getting as much change in decay as we are in creation?" Ralston worried over this. It didn't seem right.

"We'd never be able to observe the difference," Bernssen said with confidence. "It's like the Doppler shifting on stars. We talk about red shift if the object's moving away and blue if it's coming toward the observer, but the human eye still sees the star as its original color. *All* the spectrum is shifted, so the components that were in either IR or UV are brought into the visual, depending on the direction of the shift. Instruments can pick it up because the characteristic spectral lines are shifted, but the eye is happy.''

Ralston had trouble even figuring out the operational theory behind his automated excavation equipment. This had the ring of truth to it but lay beyond his expertise.

Leonore interrupted before he could work out the logic.

"Michael, Westcott wants to see you. It's about the disks.''

"Disks? Oh, the artifacts you found in the dome. What about them?" Ralston had another page to write before the weekly report was finished. And, although he didn't want to tell her, the luxury of simply sitting and not moving seemed more valuable than finding what the computer-connected mathematician had to say.

"It's important. You might want to come, too, Nels."

Ralston heaved himself up and switched off his recorder. No pain. He appreciated that more than he had in the past. Maybe he should try to placate Salazar and the others and stay at a nice, safe, injury-free teaching post. As quickly as the thought crossed his mind, he rejected it. Ralston wouldn't become like Pieter Nordon, content to lecture and live off past glories. Nordon only put in time until retirement; he no longer did research.

As far as Ralston was concerned, Nordon had already retired—died—and didn't know it.

The trio went to Westcott's shelter. From inside the plastic shell came the dull, almost infrared glow that Westcott preferred when he linked to his computer. In a way, it reminded Ralston of the illumination inside the alien dome.

"Close the damned door," Westcott grumbled. "Too much light confuses my sensory link."

The three said nothing. Westcott would get to his discovery when it suited him and not a second before. The mathematician swung around on his hard chair and pointed.

"Those are recording disks. A form of laser disk, but very primitive. We must leave the surface of this planet immediately."

Ralston recovered first and asked, "Why? Are those the records of their last days? What happened to them?"

"What? They left. They got bored. I can understand that. They didn't seem to have computers, at least not good ones. No, they had none at all. None. Odd." Westcott shivered at the very idea of a culture not using the device he found so vital to his research.

"You're referring to the Betans?"

"Call them what you will. They colonized, put down the remote post in the desert, then decided against maintaining it, so they went back home."

"Where?" demanded Bernssen. "In this system? If it

is, we've got to locate them soon and warn them about the sun. A year or two is little enough time to leave a research facility. For an entire planet's population—"

"Wait, Nels," cut in Leonore. "We didn't detect radio transmission from any of the four sunward planets. And the three outer ones are gas giants."

"They left for the outer moon," said Westcott, ignoring the debate raging around him. "They had used it as a stepping-stone. Their main base was located there. The one you found in the desert," he said, looking at Leonore with some scorn, "was only a minor outpost. A trifle, a curiosity and nothing more."

"Moon?" asked Bernssen. "The moon orbiting this planet?"

"Where else?" the mathematician said, irritated. "These disks hint that they hollowed it out, then lived within it."

Bernssen muttered to himself and left without another word.

"There might be artifacts left on the moon—in the moon," Ralston corrected. His heart beat faster as the possibilities came to him. Digging out the dome on the far side of the planet constituted a chore he didn't want to think about. Even with full-scale equipment and enough personnel to do the work, it'd be a tedious process and one hardly worth the effort.

Deep down, he thought he and Leonore had scoured the inside of the dome complex as well as if they'd taken their time, used proper archaeological procedures, and had photographed everything in detail as they went. The recording disks had been the true find—and the light source for the interior of the dome provided a possible cash return for the expedition that would suit the bureaucrats back on Novo Terra. Ralston knew they could always burrow back into the dome to study the lighting system and the metallo-plastic walls.

The idea of a new base inside the moon orbiting Beta 5 excited him more. Such an outpost might hold more artifacts, perhaps even star charts to indicate the home planet of those he called Betans. And Ralston couldn't deny the fervent hope on his part that the Betans had observed the passage of the chaos device. They had to be more experienced and sophisticated space travelers than the Alphans to establish such a durable base on another planet. The Alpha 3 refugees had fled their home world through necessity. The Betans were explorers, and probably disciplined, accomplished scientists.

Ralston glanced at Leonore, who nodded and smiled broadly. Her thoughts paralleled his.

"We're going to check out the moon. What else did you find in the disks?"

"They said nothing useful. Meanderings on shuttle schedules, manifests, things like that." The mathematician carelessly tossed one of the disks onto his cot.

Ralston didn't quite dive after it, but the urge proved hard to deny. They had blundered across an archaeologist's dream. To know the daily schedules and concerns of the Betans could be as significant as finding the Domesday Book.

"It did set me off on another, rather elegant proof, however," continued Westcott. "This is the first opportunity I've had to see alien records. Their lack of computer encoding interested me, even though the data were entered in a binary code." Westcott sat with eyes closed, hands crossed over his belly. The IR sensor atop his head pulsed slowly as it linked with the computer across the room.

"What's your problem?" asked Leonore. Ralston shot her a sharp look. The mathematician failed to understand or take offense at the double entendre.

"It's been shown repeatedly that all computer languages are equivalent, that none is in any way ultimately superior to another. These trinkets suggest to me another proof that is more universal than the others presented. This will create a stir, yes, it definitely will. And it is so elegant, so brilliant."

"The disks," pressed Ralston. "What about them?"

"I don't need them any longer. They've served their

purpose. But I do want to accompany you when you explore the moon. That can present all manner of new problems to solve." Westcott actually cackled and rubbed his hands together. "This expedition is providing me with data that'll take years to work through. What a bonanza!"

"We feel the same way, Dr. Westcott," Leonore solemnly assured the mathematician. Before she could say anything more, Bernssen opened the door of the shelter and motioned silently. Both archaeologists left to join Bernssen outside.

"This son of a bitch is right. *Madre de Dios!*" Muttered Bernssen. "I ran a quick check on the orbital dynamics of the outer moon. It couldn't possibly be solid. It's nothing more than a hollow shell. We should have discovered that, not him!"

Leonore laid her hand on Bernssen's shoulder. This didn't seem to soothe him.

"Westcott expects us to go check out the moon. For once, I have to admit he has a good point." Ralston shook his head. "There might be more than a little scientific curiosity lurking within him, in spite of the computer linkage."

"I used the lasercom to get a beam up to the pilot. Even though he's not too happy with us—claims we're using him as a taxi service, first to one side of the world, then back—he'll be landing at dawn tomorrow. We're going to have to consider conserving fuel on the shuttle now, after all these up and down trips. I don't think there's need for more than the three of us to go."

"And Westcott," added Ralston. "He's proving himself useful, even if getting information out of him is like drawing blood."

"We just don't talk the same language," said Bernssen. He smiled wryly. "And I thought I was good at math. Westcott lives in a different geometry from this universe."

"The four of us will go. Some equipment, but not much. I don't want to spend the rest of my life packing and unpacking. Cameras, some analysis equipment, a few robot probes.''

''Michael,'' Leonore said gently, ''I know what we'll need.''

Ralston nodded absently and left, walking off into the newly forming rainstorm to think about all that Westcott had discovered. He might not like the less-than-human mathematician, but he couldn't deny that he'd done a considerable amount of good work for the expedition.

An entire moon filled with artifacts! A new chance to find the source and destination of the chaos device awaited him. The fate of the Alphans, the home of the Betans, those were promised him, too.

Michael Ralston could hardly restrain himself until take-off the next morning.

TWELVE

"IT CAN'T BE done. I refuse to commit suicide for you fools." The pilot grumbled even more under his breath, only faint static noises reaching Ralston and the others in the passenger compartment of the starship.

"Can we use the shuttle to land on the moon?" asked Nels Bernssen. "The maneuver won't be too hard, and it's similar to landing on the surface of Beta 5."

"No, it's not," snapped the pilot. "You can't orbit this son-of-a-bitch moon. Too small for that. Too small for any of the damned things you plan to do."

"It's not too small," said Westcott. "Why is he saying that? I can show mathematically that we have ample room to maneuver, and of course it is always possible, if not desirable, to orbit another celestial body. The diameter of this particular moon is, of course, smaller than either of the moons circling Novo Terra, but this has nothing to do with the shuttle landing on the surface."

"He's mad at us," said Ralston. "We've disturbed him for a third time."

"It's his business to move us from one spot to another," Westcott said, almost primly. The sensor mounted on top of the mathematician's head winked on and off slowly. Ralston decided it must have been put on standby

Robert E. Vardeman

since they were out of line-of-sight for any of the on-board computers or linkups.

"We'll handle it," said Leonore. She flipped around neatly in free fall and faced the vidscreen. "Please, we do so need to land. It's *very* important for us."

Bernssen snorted in disgust. To Ralston he said in a low voice that didn't carry any farther, due to the low air pressure in the ship, "She always gets what she wants when she uses that tone of voice. Works every time on her father." The physicist snorted again. "Works every time on me."

Ralston smiled when he felt the steering jets on the ship kick in. The starship rolled slightly as it oriented itself in orbit. In the vidscreen he saw the pilot beginning the maneuver that would place them in position to launch the shuttle.

"I'm putting the ship into a figure-eight orbit around the moon and the planet," the pilot said with ill grace. "That means I can only rendezvous with you every third day."

"Not so," said Westcott. "The actual calculations show that—"

Bernssen shut up the mathematician before he angered the pilot further. "Let's get into the shuttle, why don't we, Dr. Westcott?" Bernssen asked, pulling the man along like a captive balloon. Ralston saw that the physicist had to restrain himself from grabbing the IR sensor unit and using that as a convenient handle.

Ralston no longer cared about the petty squabbles between mathematician and pilot. Pilots were notoriously difficult to deal with, and Westcott's unnatural direct linkage with a computer had turned him into something other than human. Ralston's real interest focused on the second vidscreen and its telescopic display of the outer moon's dusty surface. Some medium-size cratering was evident, but not as much as Ralston would have thought.

"The moon rotates slowly, once every 448 hours," said Bernssen as they drifted along the narrow access corridor toward the shuttle airlock. "When I checked my figures, it became apparent that it isn't as massive as it should be if it were solid. Moments of inertia and all that. Should have been more careful. With that sort of information you and Leonore could have explored here first.''

"Now is as good a time as any. If we find the proper location, do you think you would want to set up an observatory? It'd be clear of Beta 5's atmosphere.''

"Actually, that's been proving helpful, having an atmosphere,'' Bernssen said. "It filters out the worst of the solar storms. The planet's magnetosphere captures the ionized particles, and I've always found it easier to work with a near-normal gravity. Some of the men, though, prefer zero-g or near-g. The moon'll only give us about ten percent what we're used to.''

"Would those solar storms have damaged anything inside?'' Ralston asked, the possibility of finding nothing but fried artifacts not suiting him at all. He'd come too far to lose out again. Alpha 3 had been ripped away from him in the cataclysmic explosion of a nova. Beta 5 would be taken sooner or later, too, before he could mount a proper expedition and carefully document the most significant of his finds. To not even have the opportunity of digging through meaningful debris of this unknown alien culture irritated him.

"Getting radar returns from the moon,'' came the pilot's voice. He sounded almost cheerful.

Leonore looked questioningly at Ralston, who only shook his head. He had no idea what amused the pilot about standard procedures.

"Buckle up. We're going down,'' said Bernssen. Leonore slid into the co-pilot's seat beside him. He frowned but said nothing as he began to look over the instruments. The pilot had programmed the on-board guidance computer. All they had to do was sit inside the shuttle and go along for the ride.

Ralston watched as Bernssen made a few minor adjustments. Leonore waited for the physicist to finish, then changed the controls back to their original reading. Ralston wondered at the relationship between his graduate assistant and Bernssen. He suspected Leonore was a competent enough pilot, but Bernssen obviously didn't know. Why hadn't she told him?

To pass the time while he awaited the sharp acceleration from the shuttle rockets, Ralston worked over the problem as if it were one of archaeological importance. Leonore Disa came from a very wealthy family; Ralston knew nothing of Nels Bernssen's background, but he didn't seem to be rich. Everyone on Novo Terra was well enough off so that no one starved, but most lacked the substantial wealth of a Disa family. Was Leonore holding back some of her talents to keep from hurting Bernssen's ego? Ralston considered this and decided it might be true. Bernssen had found fame with the chaos-induced nova of the Alpha primary, but researchers seldom got wealth along with their notoriety. Leonore might be keeping back some of her skills—such as piloting a starship or shuttle—because that accentuated the differences in their backgrounds. Most people never left Novo Terra, much less had the money or opportunity to use a private starship.

Such deception, or at least lack of honesty, on Leonore's part surprised Ralston. He had to consider that she worked conscientiously and well in the field when it came to scientific matters but operated under a different set of rules in her personal life. Leonore was no tri-vid beauty, but Ralston had always heard it said that money was the perfect aphrodisiac. What did the woman have to contend with as she grew up? Fortune seekers?

Whatever else Nels Bernssen was, Ralston got no hint of avariciousness in the man. His dedication to his work was foremost. In fact, that dedication almost amounted to monomania, something with which Ralston could identify. Nothing thrilled Ralston more than the beginning of a dig, the first find, the piecing together of the information to create a coherent whole culture. Bernssen's excitement over the chaos field and its effects rivaled his own.

It was good that Leonore shared such devotion. They

wouldn't have much common ground otherwise, Ralston decided. And the woman wouldn't have anything in common with Bernssen, either.

"Any way we can make a few circuits around the moon before grounding?" asked Ralston. "I'd like to get a close-up view of it. Take a few photos and—"

The acceleration shoved him back into his couch. Over the vibration of the rockets, Leonore called out, "We can't. We're going straight in. We have to conserve fuel for the shuttle. Too many trips back and forth to Beta 5 already."

Ralston cursed. He knew she was probably right. The pilot hadn't been speaking out of irritation over the extra work when he said they were getting low on shuttle rocket fuel. Without the laser launchers used on Novo Terra and other planets, fuel mass became a real economic consideration.

"Picking up extraneous signals on the radar," said Bernssen. "Leonore, do you recognize the pattern?"

Ralston saw her shake her head. Short brown hair flew in all directions as the rockets momentarily cut off and let them coast. As suddenly as the free fall had come, the acceleration again seized him. The shuttle touched down on the surface of the moon. On the screen Ralston saw huge clouds of grey-brown dust rising around them. The computer instantly cut rocket blast, but the cloaking veil continued to rise. In the moon's low gravity, it might be hours before it settled again and allowed them a clear view of the surface.

"I don't know what to make of it," Leonore said. "We're picking up a radar signal. Not a return but a new signal."

"Not from the starship?" asked Ralston.

"From the horizon. That's in the wrong direction for the pilot to reach us," she said.

Ralston looked at her, thought about their situation, then felt a momentary pang of guilt. His excitement at what this meant was undeniable. A radar pulse meant that the Betans had left a beacon, and their approach had somehow activated it after all these millennia. New sites to sift through, a new culture to bring from the depths of time to the bright light of scientific scrutiny. Ralston's guilt came from this selfishness on his part.

Leonore Disa was his student, and he was responsible for her advancement. She had applied for a doctorate, and every new discovery put her that much further away from fulfillment of the requirements. How could anyone keep from following the intriguing threads of Beta culture? Yet Leonore needed to concentrate on one aspect—of the Alpha 3 society—and do a thesis. Without direction, without narrowing her sights to a single topic, she might drift along, forever doing research and not finishing her degree requirements.

And Ralston was responsible for her lack of diligence in pursuing her degree. He continually dangled new and ever more enticing puzzles before her. Anyone with scientific curiosity had to follow. It was his academic responsibility to stop her from going in all directions, get her oriented properly, complete the degree and *then* explore the new clues to a different alien society.

But time! Ralston cursed the arrow of time piercing his schedules. The chaos device had shaken up all Ralston's perspectives. The Alpha primary had gone nova. Bernssen said the Beta sun would follow soon. Time crushed in from all sides.

"Michael, are you all right?" she asked.

"Oh, verd, yes, fine, fine." Ralston shook himself and swung out of the acceleration couch. He tottered for a moment as he adjusted to the slight gravity. "Let's find that radar beacon," he said, picking up a camera and a half-dozen floater probes.

"From the first contact and the one now," said Bernssen, "it must be about four kilometers toward the low hills." He pointed, but the direction made no difference to Ralston. He had no sense of a north or any other direction.

Westcott sat on the edge of his couch with a distant look

in his eyes. The slow blinking of the red indicator light on his IR sensor gave the only hint that the man still lived. Even his breathing seemed to have ended.

"What's wrong?" asked Ralston, knowing how the mathematician hated to be disturbed, and not caring. If Westcott's been injured in the descent, Ralston wanted to see him attended to before they left.

"Signals. The entire moon comes . . . alive. We have set off a chain reaction. I can't understand it. Any of it. The computer senses, yet it doesn't. There is too little to compute properly. I don't understand." Westcott put his head in his hands. Ralston thought for a moment that the mathematician had begun to cry, but Westcott looked up with dry, wide eyes. "I'm frightened," he said in a low voice that chilled Ralston more than if Westcott had screamed it.

"Of what, Dr. Westcott? The radar beacon signal? Something was activated?" Leonore obviously didn't share Westcott's fear. She already worked to don her spacesuit.

Westcott couldn't answer. Ralston helped the mathematician to his feet and started getting into his own suit. In less than fifteen minutes they had fastened the last of the web straps and collected the equipment they'd need. Ralston nodded to Bernssen, who cycled open the airlock. Only a tiny hiss sounded in Ralston's ears, then nothing. They looked out across the dust-shrouded surface of the moon.

The four of them unloaded the remainder of the equipment they needed for a preliminary reconnaissance and started toward the low hills and the radar beacon. Ralston alone of the four felt comfortable in the spacesuit. He led the way through the tumbled, jagged rocks and heavy dust. In less than twenty minutes they emerged from the cloud of dust stirred by their landing. In another twenty they had reached the base of the hills.

Ralston turned up the volume on his suit com and spoke to Bernssen. "Where do we go up?"

Bernssen looked back at the stubby shuttle sitting in the middle of the plain, checked his inertial tracker, then pointed off at an angle. Bernssen and Ralston looked up the slope, and Leonore might have, too. But not Westcott.

From the mathematician came a choked sound. He stumbled forward, still unused to moving in low gravity and spacesuit. "Here. It's here. But what is it? I can't think fast enough to find out. What is it? Oh, why can't I be faster, like my computers?"

The moan of frustration and fear brought the other three around. Ralston saw the source of Westcott's reaction. A small circular cut of decidedly artificial origin opened into the hillside. The four advanced slowly. Ralston photographed as he went, and Leonore took one of the robot probes from his pack. She moved it around so that he could see the settings she made.

"Think this is too far?" she asked. She had set it to fly five hundred meters down the dark corridor, then return.

"Let's try it and see what happens."

She triggered the probe. It vanished silently, to return in less than five minutes. Leonore plugged in the reader and studied the abbreviated output, telling what the probe had discovered.

"Well?" demanded Bernssen, obviously uneasy now. Ralston saw that Westcott's barely controlled panic affected them all, the astrophysicist most.

"Nothing. Just a smooth-walled tunnel. There's some indication of a door another hundred meters deeper. Nothing to indicate weak walls or ceiling, no pits, side tunnels or . . ."

"No traps," finished Westcott. "This is a dangerous place. I . . . I feel it. They did not build this for us. No, not for us."

"You don't have to go with us," said Ralston. "It might be better if you stayed behind. We'll want to be able to relay back to the shuttle and to the pilot if anything happens. If we all went into the tunnel, it might cut off radio transmission."

"I can't stay here and simply wait," said Westcott, almost in a panic. "I have to go in. Don't you see,

Ralston? This might hold the key to it all. All of it! I can't let it frighten me off. I couldn't live with myself if I did!''

"The key to what, Dr. Westcott?" asked Leonore.

"The chaos equations. I *see* them in my head all the time. Their solution is so close. If I can only get the key, the one elegant masterstroke that will allow it to fall into place. What causes the bifurcation in the parameters? I need to know that or nothing makes sense.''

"The answer is inside?" asked Bernssen. He stood a pace away, as if afraid that Westcott's insanity might be contagious, even through the spacesuits. He dealt with men and women whose genius placed them perilously close to insanity. From the way the physicist stood, he had decided Westcott had passed the boundary and now existed in his own psychotically dominated personal universe.

"I don't know what's inside. But it frightens me."

Ralston saw Westcott's IR sensor blazing its brightest red. A signal from some line-of-sight source impinged on the sensor element and caused Westcott's upset. He moved to place his gloved hand in front of the sensors. Westcott pushed him away.

"Don't. I . . . I'll lose it if you do that."

Leonore muttered, "He's already lost it and doesn't even know it."

Ralston looked from Westcott to the dark circle that marked the tunnel entrance. He remembered the octopus tentacle arrangement of the dome they'd found on the surface of Beta 5. There had been nothing intentionally hazardous within the dome. Their problems came from their own rush to explore rather than perverse traps set by the Betans. He saw no reason to suppose the aliens would substantially alter their planetary colonizing design on this tiny moon, even if this proved to be their main base.

"Send a probe ahead of us, fifty meters a minute max," ordered Ralston. He waited for Leonore to launch the robot sensor, then started after it. If any danger presented itself to the probe, they'd have several seconds to prepare. How, Ralston couldn't say. They carried no weapons and, he thought uneasily, no excavation equipment. If the tunnel collapsed, they'd never be able to dig out with their hands.

The four crowded close together as they made their way down the dark tunnel. Ralston switched on a headlamp and cast a sharply defined beam around the airless corridor. Westcott muttered in protest, but Ralston refused to walk in darkness, no matter how this might interfere with the mathematician's damned computer-link sensor. He thought Westcott must have picked up a com beam from an alien communication source. The IR frequency used for Westcott's computer-mind link was too useful for other purposes not to be encountered exploring an advanced culture's base.

But Ralston knew he again violated not only strict archaeological rules, but common sense as well. Having Westcott or Leonore or Bernssen remain outside to relay transmission from inside the tunnel was safe; having them pressing close, however, was comforting. Every step Ralston took, his excitement mounted. The walls nearest the dusty plain were featureless and bare. A hundred meters into the tunnel he found cryptic hieroglyphics.

Instructions? Decorations? Graffiti? Warning symbols? Ralston had no way of telling, and photographed them as he walked.

Three hundred meters brought more vivid writings on the walls, many in color and all of definite information intent.

"That one," said Bernssen. "That means don't spit on the floor."

Ralston and Leonore laughed harder than the slight joke merited, but it provided nervous release.

Ralston said, "It's more likely to tell them to slow down, that they're approaching the terminus."

"Air," muttered Westcott. "I hear it."

Leonore turned to the mathematician to tell him to be quiet, when it hit her, too. She experienced a definite pressure against the front of her suit. She said, "He's right. There's air pressure here. But where's the airlock? What holds it in?"

"I don't know," answered Bernssen, checking one of his instruments, "but don't try breathing it. Heavy on ammonia. Enough to choke you to death in a few seconds."

"I wasn't planning on it," said Leonore.

Ralston stopped and shined his light against the end of the tunnel. A simple sliding door ahead was all that barred them from entering the alien base. He hesitated, took a deep breath to relax, then reached out and pulled the door aside.

"An elevator?" Leonore asked, craning her neck to look around the cage. "If it is, they weren't big people. This isn't large enough for more than a dozen humans."

"No controls," said Ralston. He kept his camera working constantly. When he got the block recorder out and ran hardcopies of the prints, he wanted to be able to study every detail of their journey.

"There are controls," said Westcott. The sensor mounted atop his head flashed once. The door closed silently, and the sudden descent caused the other three to grab one another for support. The cage stopped as abruptly as it had started, sending all four to their knees.

Ralston pulled back the simple door and shined his lamp into the corridor beyond. Dozens of tunnels radiated from it, confirming the theory that the moon had been hollowed extensively.

"Where do we start?" asked Leonore, eager now to begin.

Before Ralston could lay out a plan for exploration, Westcott walked forward, as if under intense compulsion. He went a short way down the tunnel, then turned to the left.

"Wait, dammit, don't go off like that!" shouted Ralston. The echo within his suit helmet almost deafened him. He cursed more quietly, and motioned for Bernssen and Leonore to come with him. He reset his wristcom so that they could return to this point, no matter what turnings and twistings they encountered.

But Ralston worried. The wristcom's inertial tracker worked only on a two-dimensional surface. He'd seen no reason to bring a more expensive three-dimensional unit from Novo Terra. The archaeology professor cursed the need for such cost-cutting on any expedition, and cursed Chancellor Salazar, the Alpha 3 refugees, the Betans, and his own stupidity for not planning better.

"Stop, Westcott, come back here!" he called when he reached the juncture where the mathematician had turned. Ralston shined his lamp along the corridor and saw nothing of Westcott.

"Where'd he get off to so fast?" asked Bernssen. "Do you think we're out of contact with him?"

Ralston stepped into the corridor Westcott had taken and motioned for Leonore to go back to the elevator cage. "How do you read?" he asked.

"Just fine, Michael. No signal loss."

"Come back. Westcott can hear us; he just doesn't want to admit it."

"He's acted strangely ever since we found the entrance on the surface," said Leonore. She made an ugly noise and said, "But then, he's always strange."

Ralston didn't bother pointing out that the mathematician probably overheard. He even dared to hope the insult might bring Westcott rushing back to complain. It produced no such reaction. Of the mathematician he saw no trace.

Ralston dropped to hands and knees and studied the floor.

"What're you looking for?" asked Bernssen.

"Dust. A base abandoned on a moon like this for thousands of years should be filthy with dust. There's not a speck on the floor." Ralston stood and shook his head. "I can't even find scratches showing where Westcott went by."

"Here," said Leonore, handing Ralston the four robot

probes they'd brought along. "We might as well send them out to find him. They can travel faster than Westcott, and it'll keep us from wandering around aimlessly."

Ralston silently launched the probes. They hissed in the ammonia-laced atmosphere, then vanished down the corridor the mathematician had taken. Ralston put one down each branching tunnel, until all four had left the main hallway.

"When I find him, I'm going to rip out that damned sensor by its platinum wires," Ralston grumbled. "He's going to have one chinger of a headache."

Leonore looked at her professor and shook her head. She'd seldom seen him this angry, even when he'd been dealing with Salazar and the other University bureaucrats. Ralston took off, and Leonore and Bernssen followed closely, flashing their lamps down each corridor and finding nothing but emptiness stretching as far as the headlamp's beam was capable of illuminating.

"Damn!" swore Ralston. "The probe's died on me."

"Getting some fluctuation in the ammonia level," said Bernssen, tapping the side of his analyzer. "I think it must be coming from the walls—the ammonia, I mean. Outgassing over the years."

"For ten thousand years?" Leonore sounded skeptical.

"It can happen. Especially if the atmosphere originally here had been put in under very high pressure. The porous rock walls adsorbed huge quantities, then released it slowly over the years as the pressure declined."

"I don't care about that," snapped Ralston, still angry at Westcott and his behavior. "I just want to find Westcott."

"The compression waves in the ammonia tell of something moving ahead of us," said Bernssen, growing irritated at Ralston. "It must be Westcott, verd?"

Ralston said nothing as he worked on the control for the second probe. The robot eye returned from its wanderings, hovered beside the impatient archaeologist, then took off with a faint whine to find Westcott.

"Damnation, it's gone, too," exclaimed Ralston within seconds. "What's destroying my probes?"

The words had barely left his lips when a deep virbration came up through the soles of his feet. Something ponderous and powerful operated within the corridor.

Leonore and Bernssen added the power of their headlamps to Ralston's. The three beams converged on a low-slung robot with six metallic tentacles waving in front of it. The mechanism drifted forward; due to a broad protecting skirt that brushed the floor as it moved, Ralston couldn't see if it hovered or ran on wheels. In two of the six flexing tentacles it held Ralston's robot probes, crushed and spilling their block circuits out as the robot came forward inexorably.

"I don't think it's friendly," said Bernssen, backing away. He reached out and tugged at Leonore's arm to urge her to get out of the robot's path. She tried to shake him off but the physicist was insistent. She, too, began to retreat.

"Look at the power in each of the articulated tentacle tips," muttered Ralston. "Those probes are supposed to be invulnerable to anything less than—"

"We'll sue the manufacturer," cut in Bernssen. "Let's regroup and consider what we're going to do. I don't want to end up like those probes."

Ralston hesitated. One of the tentacles took a swipe at him. The sudden electric jolt from even the close passage sent him reeling backward, arms akimbo. Leonore and Bernssen held him upright until he regained his senses.

"It looks like the night watchman," said Leonore. "I've been running my analyzer and haven't gotten any hint of motive power, age, composition, anything!"

"Wrong equipment," said Bernssen. "We aren't ready to fight it out with this one. Come on!"

Ralston disliked running from the robot, yet he saw no alternative. Westcott might be dying just on the other side of this ponderous guardian. As he edged back, Ralston cursed volubly. Nothing had gone right with this expedition. He needed time to analyze and correlate the data he gathered. Events had moved too fast for him to reflect on exactly what everything meant, where it all fit together in a grander pattern.

The Betans were the enigma that bothered him the most. The refugees from Alpha 3 had acted from necessity. Stay on their home planet and die from the random, chaotic destruction of body and culture, or else flee. Those had been their only options. Their escape had only prolonged their eventual demise.

But what of the alien Betans? Ralston hadn't a clue as to physical shape, origin, or their reason for putting an outpost on Beta 5. All he knew was what he, Leonore, and Bernssen had pieced together: the Betans probably breathed high-pressure ammonia, indicating they might be native to a gas giant. Which one? This system? Another? Was this robot slowly moving after them intentionally dangerous, or had time and the chaos device altered its programming to something less benign?

"Here, Michael. Down here," urged Leonore.

He looked and saw that the corridor she indicated narrowed substantially from the one they were in. Ralston ducked down it just a few centimeters in front of a probing robotic tentacle. The robot strained to drive its bulk after them but the rocky walls prevented it. As if caught up in a fit of human pique, the robot threw both of Ralston's probes at him. The archaeology professor easily avoided the clumsy toss.

"What now?" he asked. "We've still got to find Westcott. He might have run afoul of that automated watchdog."

"We might be able to get back into the corridor behind it, using some of the adjoining halls," said Leonore. "Send out a probe and let's see what it finds."

Ralston spent a few minutes recalling the last two probes, bringing them in high and fast over the still-raging robot guard's top. A few more minutes work had the probes exploring the depths of this auxiliary corridor.

"Its programming is obviously faulty," said Bernssen.

He frowned. "Didn't you tell me Westcott had said the Betans didn't have computers? How did they keep this monster running for so long? Or at all?"

"Westcott had only the laser disk records to work with," said Ralston. "No matter how much information he found there, he couldn't have known everything about the Betans. After all, they were obviously alien, and Westcott isn't trained to decipher hints left by alien cultures."

"Not like we are," said Leonore, with more than a hint of biting sarcasm in her voice. "Did we ever walk into this mess with our eyes wide open. We should have left someone outside to relay back—or to help us."

"The rock would have eaten our radio signals," said Bernssen.

"A fiber-optic com circuit, then," the woman said. "A few kilometers of that stuff wouldn't weigh much. We could have unrolled it as we came and—"

"There wasn't any in the supplies we brought," said Ralston, distracted. He kept track of both roaming probes and the signals they returned. What Bernssen said about absorption of signal by the rock appeared true. Less than five hundred meters dropped reception strength to a quarter of maximum.

"Who'd ever think I'd end up like this?" said Bernssen, with a small hint of humor to his words. "Mama raised me to be a physicist, and here I end up on Beta 5's moon after letting alien telepathic messages be forced onto my brain, traveling around dusty moons, being chased by a sentry robot." He shook his head in mock despair.

"That's my Nels," said Leonore. "Always looking on the bright side."

"The probe's found secondary corridors leading to Westcott," said Ralston, still worried about the weakness of his probe signals. "I'm checking to make certain one is smaller in width than our unfriendly host." He gestured obscenely in the direction of the still-straining robot. Bits of rock and dust accumulated at its base, where it ground hard against the unyielding wall.

The trio started down the corridor, and found the intersection indicated by the probe. Leonore said, "The robot's left. It must be trying to head us off."

Ralston stopped to consider their chances of returning to the main corridor and following in the robot's wake. He decided to continue along the course mapped out by his probe. Until they confronted a small guard robot, they were relatively safe.

Ralston swallowed hard when he remembered that only broad corridors led back to the elevator. If they had blundered over some activating switch and brought the robot guards to life, they'd have to run for the only way they knew back to the surface. He didn't look forward to that prospect. Ralston's arm still tingled from the electric charge the robot had given him. He wondered if the creature he'd killed with his primitive spear had felt the same before it died in its lair.

"Down there!" warned Bernssen.

To the left down a corridor meeting theirs at an acute angle, rushed the large guard robot. Ralston urged his friends on, herding them like cattle. They barely got through the intersection and into their smaller corridor when the robot began grinding against the rock and probing for them with its tentacles.

"Persistent chinger, isn't it?" said Bernssen.

"I'd like to dismantle it," said Ralston.

"We both would."

"I meant so that we could find out something about the Betans. Computer architecture can tell much about a society's thought processes. Find out what makes them design in the way they do, and you've gone a ways toward understanding them."

"All I understand is that it wants to fry my neurons," said Bernssen, in this instance not sharing Ralston's devotion to science.

Ralston stopped abruptly and pointed to a wall inset. The metal plate contained a dozen large buttons. A few of the wiggly hieroglyphs they'd noticed earlier paraded along the side of the plate; instructions for operation, Ralston guessed.

"Any idea what these do?" he asked the physicist. Bernssen shook his head. "Leonore, any ideas?"

"I don't see any of their light tubes. This segment of the tunnel doesn't appear any different from the others." Leonore shrugged. "We might press one to see."

"Too dangerous," Ralston decided. "It might call smaller guard robots."

"A fifty-fifty chance that it'd disable the big one," pointed out Bernssen.

"Too dangerous. We need a supervisor and circuit probe equipment to decipher what this controls." He glanced down at the readings from his probes. His mouth turned to cotton. Another probe had been destroyed. With only one left, they'd have to exercise even more caution—and do much of the scouting on their own.

Continuing cautiously, Ralston peered around the intersection of another large corridor with the one they traversed. He saw the battered remains of his probe on the floor. He couldn't find any trace of the cause for its destruction.

He hurried on, Leonore and Bernssen behind. As they entered the far corridor, his remaining probe gave a strong signal burst.

"Westcott!" cried Leonore. "It's found him!"

"Let's hurry. The vital signs off him don't look good. It might only be signal disruption, but I don't think so," said Ralston.

At a run, they made their way down the corridor, along a still smaller side tunnel, then into a broad corridor three times as large as the guard robot that had chased them earlier.

"No compression waves in the ammonia," announced Bernssen. "But the robot might be on idle. I can't detect that."

"The door," said Leonore, pointing. "Is Westcott behind it?"

"Definitely." Ralston saw that the door had been opened a half meter—large enough for both the mathematician and the probe to enter. "Wait here. I'll keep you posted."

"And we'll warn you if we see the robot," Leonore said anxiously. She reached out and gripped his suit sleeve. Ralston smiled weakly and patted her hand. "Be careful, Michael."

Ralston swung out into the broad expanse of the corridor and ran awkwardly for the opened door. He paused, cast his headlamp beam inside and saw nothing menacing. Here and there his bright cone of light reflected off silvered buttons and meter panels of unknown function. Not wanting to present a target for the prowling guard robot, he slipped into the room.

Ralston glanced over his shoulder and saw a familiar sight. The light switch beside the door looked identical to those in the dome on Beta 5. "I'm going to turn on the lights to get a better idea of what this room is."

"Careful," cautioned Leonore Disa.

"Here we go." He winced as he touched the switch. Only the familiar dim red lights came up. Ralston slowly turned, stopped, and shouted, "No, don't!"

But it was too late for any warning the archaeologist might give.

THIRTEEN

"DON'T, WESTCOTT, DON'T do that!" Michael Ralston shouted. The echoes inside his helmet made him instantly regret the warning. Some reactions came instinctively—even in a spacesuit. Ears ringing, he rushed forward, weight farther forward than usual in the low gravity, and grabbed for Westcott. He missed.

Westcott turned his head in such a way that the sensor unit mounted there made connection with a small red light burning on a huge instrument panel. The infrared beam from Westcott's sensor and the alien one touched, linked. The mathematician stiffened and stood with an expression of stark pain on his face.

Ralston stopped and tried to decide what to do. Through the ringing in his ears he heard Leonore's frantic voice. "Michael, what happened? Are you all right? Please answer!"

"It's Westcott. He's allowed himself to plug into the control console. At least, I think it must be the alien's central controller. It extends along an entire wall. His IR sensor locked onto the signal from an equivalent one on the panel. I don't want to break the contact because I'm not sure what it'll do to him. He said it gave him a headache when he was linked to his own computer. With this one, it might do permanent damage."

"We're coming in," came Nels Bernssen's words.

"Hurry. I need you to look over this damned panel to see if you can make anything out of it. To me it's just a hectare of meters and switches."

Ralston took Westcott's shoulders and gently shook the mathematician to see if he might get a positive response. None. The man's eyes had turned to translucent glass. His mouth hung slack and a string of drool came out one corner. All the blood had rushed from Westcott's face, giving him the look of a corpse. Ralston started to twist him around to break the IR beam when Bernssen stopped him.

"Give it a few more seconds," Bernssen said. "Can't hurt anymore, verd?"

Ralston didn't know. He might be expert at unearthing ruins thousands of years old and piecing together the day-to-day life of the former inhabitants, but in matters such as these he felt like a complete tyro. He knew enough about block computers and electronics to help him do his research and no more. There was always too much to learn, too many things to know for anyone to command it all. He had to let the physicist decide this.

"Better be quick, Nels," Leonore said. "There seems to be uncontrollable twitching in his extremities. I wonder how he can still stand."

"The beam linking him to the console," said Ralston, horror growing inside him like an ugly, crawling beast. "That's holding him in an iron grip." His concern mounted even more when he saw that Leonore's appraisal of Westcott's condition was only too accurate. The shakes spread from hands and feet through the mathematician's limbs.

"Nels, we've got to act. He's going into convulsions."

"Wait, just wait a second," the physicist said. He stood in front of the panel, hands resting on two buttons. "Here goes nothing." He leaned forward, his weight depressing both buttons.

Nothing happened.

Ralston didn't wait for Bernssen to try another possibility on the alien controller. He took Westcott by the shoulders and jerked as hard as he could. It might have been his imagination, but he thought the sensor atop Westcott's head actually tried to turn to maintain contact with the alien computer's signal. But when Westcott broke free, the muscles that had been held in rictus suddenly relaxed. The man fell in slow motion to the floor.

Ralston tried to support him and failed, forgetting that mass and inertia counted more than weight. Together, the two of them sank down in the low gravity. Ralston got to his knees and turned the mathematician onto his back. The eyes continued to stare vacantly.

"It might be bad. I get no response from his suit's life com." Just inside the faceplate of the helmet Ralston saw the vital signs readout. All stayed on neutral, as if no one wore the suit—or the occupant was dead.

"He's still breathing," said Leonore, working with Westcott's air mixture. "I've cooled off the suit by bleeding in a quick charge of oxygen. See the condensation on the inner surface of the faceplate from his breathing?"

"Still no vitals," said Ralston. He checked his remaining floater probe, silently hovering a meter away. The response from it differed from Westcott's suit reading. Definite but feeble life readings came over the broadcast circuit. "His suit might be damaged. Probably is."

Ralston turned icy at the idea that not only the suit but Westcott may have become electrically overloaded because of the connection. The man may have been rehabbed inadvertently by his reckless behavior.

"Why'd the hijo do it?" wondered Bernssen. "That's the damnedest, stupidest thing I've ever seen."

"He didn't seem to be in control. Not after we entered the complex," said Ralston. "He might have been receiving a low intensity IR input ever since we entered the exterior tunnel. Who knows how it might scramble his senses?"

Westcott's eyes focused and he began blinking and squinting, as if the dull red illumination proved too much for him. With Ralston and Leonore rubbing his arms through his suit, Westcott recovered enough to speak in a low, cracked voice.

"So vast. I . . . I was wrong. They have computers. But so strange. Not like mine. The input is wrong, so strange."

"Don't try to speak," said Ralston. "Just rest. We'll get out of here soon. You can sleep aboard the shuttle."

"I don't think so," said Bernssen. "I'm hardly an expert at what all this means, but since the only light flashing is that one—" he pointed to a dull red pulsation on the far right of the console—"and all we know for sure is that the guard robot is activated, we've got a dangerous trip ahead just reaching the surface."

"Nels, look!" Leonore took her lover's arm and moved closer.

A second light began flashing, and a third and fourth and fifth. Soon an entire army of lights glowed with an intensity matching the room's overhead illumination.

"I can't tell if Westcott activated them or this is in response to our brush with the first guardbot," said Bernssen, "but it looks as if we've got dozens of the damned things to sneak past now. I don't think we can do it. I doubt the aliens manufactured only one size of guard. Those tunnels we followed must have their own patrols by now."

"Try pressing the buttons under the lights," said Ralston. "That might turn them off."

"No!" cried Westcott. "That puts them on alert status. We'll never get free if you do that."

"You're the expert," said Bernssen, settling down on his heels near the mathematician. "What did you learn from their computer?"

"It's vast, bigger than anything I'd believed possible. But it's different, slower. As a computer it's worthless for just about every useful application." Westcott laughed harshly. "It's so slow my thought speed exceeds its cycle time."

"What caused you to go into shock?" asked Ralston.

"Its size! Never have I been inside such a large memory. I got lost. I tried to follow the usual limited pathways, but they went on to infinity. The harder I tried to return, the more confused I became. My thought speed matched the computer's, but I needed a . . . a schematic. I got lost!"

"Great," muttered Leonore. "He gets lost in the computer's memory, and we're trapped."

"Did you learn anything about the Betans? Or the condition they left this base in?" asked Ralston. "Those guard robots will kill us unless we can shut them off."

"The far side of the console, there, verd, higher, that button. Press it." Bernssen did as instructed. Westcott said, "It'll take a *wah* for them to shut down automatically."

"What?" asked Ralston.

Westcott looked sheepish. "It's a Betan time unit. I don't know how long it is. There wasn't any conversion factor, any common denominator for calculation."

"So your *wah* might last ten seconds or five thousand years?" asked Bernssen. "Still, it's better than not having the robots turned off at all. I just don't like the idea of a rescue party finding our skeletons guarded by an army of robots."

"Nels, there's not going to be any rescue party," said Leonore. "The pilot can't reach us without the shuttle." The woman clamped her jaw firmly shut and a look of pure horror crossed her face. "If we can't get back to the shuttle, the rest of the expedition on the surface of 5 is stranded! We've got the only transport up to the starship!"

"And we're pinned down for the moment," said Ralston. He took a deep breath. "The one good thing is that our suits are in full working condition." He checked his readouts. Air for another thirty hours remained. Nutrients and water in nippled tubes were close to his mouth, and the energy packs showed a virtually full charge.

"My suit's not in such good shape," said Westcott.

"Your vital signs readout? I noticed. We get a better reading off the probe," said Ralston.

"When you broke me free of the circuit," said Westcott, "all my muscles relaxed. *All* of them. The inside of my suit is quite a mess. The waste recycler came loose."

"Live with it," Bernssen said, thinking Westcott had finally received poetic justice. "It looks as if we're going to have to do something more than wait for the robots to shut down." All the indicator lights still glowed palely.

Ralston paced around the room, trying to get a feel for the architecture, the way the Betans built and thought and worked. Without any idea as to their body form, he found himself at a loss. The panels were lower than waist level, indicating they had been short. It meant nothing that there were no stools or chairs in the room. They could have been removed—or the Betans might not have used them. The controls were mostly push buttons the size of Ralston's fist. The Betans might not have good manual dexterity or, from all Ralston had seen of their robots, any digital dexterity at all. They might have been possessed of only tentacles. He finally gave up on the futile guessing game and stood next to Westcott.

"They won't come in here," said the mathematician. "The robots. This is a . . . safe area. The Betans didn't want their guards blundering about. They aren't very precisely controlled."

"Never mind that," said Ralston. "Tell us about the Betans. This base, the outpost, anything you gleaned from your connection with their computer."

Westcott frowned. "That's the odd part. I got—am still getting—this sense of dread. It has something to do with the computer. How did they keep it powered up for so many years? I got no feel for that. Only the anxiety. It might be *its* anxiety."

"That's a good point, Michael," said Bernssen. "What power source is keeping everything going? Find it, turn it off, the robots go to sleep. We don't need the lights to get out."

"If you cut all the power, though," said Leonore, "won't that kill the elevator?"

"She's right," said Ralston. "We're better off doing as little as possible since we don't know what we are doing. We're trapped for the moment. Until that off-switch returns them to standby."

"In a damned *wah*, whatever that is," grumbled Bernssen. The physicist began studying the console with as much success as Ralston had achieved deciding on the Betans' body size and shape.

"This entire complex, the computer, everything," said Westcott, "is a prototype. That I did learn for certain. None of this had ever been done before."

"This and the outpost on 5 were their first?" Leonore let out a low whistle. "I'm impressed. As impressed as I am with Dial and the other refugees from Alpha 3. Did necessity push the Betans? Did they know of the chaos device and try to escape it, too?"

"They knew," said Westcott. "There's so much stored within the computer. It's so huge."

"I know, you got lost," Ralston said impatiently. "What of the Betans? Their detection of the chaos device? Did you happen to get a hint of what they looked like?"

"Or how to operate this console," cut in Nels Bernssen. "There doesn't seem to be any simple order to it." Bernssen dropped flat onto his back and kicked under the console to begin tracing wiring. Ralston considered this a fruitless pursuit, but it kept the physicist busy. And Ralston would be the first to admit that any information would aid them. Any at all.

Westcott moved closer to the panel, his face haunted. "It's so hard for me to keep from reestablishing a linkup. Keep me away. It frightens me."

"But it also intrigues you, doesn't it?" asked Leonore. "You're afraid, but you're also afraid you'll miss something important."

"It's all in there. I know it. But it'd take so long to find it. And the entire computer's a prototype, too. Just like the rest of the base.''

Ralston went to the console and gripped the IR sensor there. With a mighty jerk, he broke it free and turned the sensing element toward the wall, where it wouldn't interfere with Westcott.

''Thank you,'' the mathematician said, sounding sincere. ''It truly draws me, just like a Siren's call.''

The classical allusion startled Ralston. He hadn't thought Westcott read anything but mathematical treatises, then realized the man had access to everything within a computer, not just its computational capabilities. Some of the other stored bytes must have registered on his wired brain as he haunted the circuits of the University computer.

''Now, Dr. Westcott,'' said Leonore, settling onto the floor next to the mathematician, ''we need to know what you discovered. If you don't begin soon, we might have to turn that sensor back around and do some checking on our own.''

Ralston started to protest his assistant's behavior. He checked his outburst. Westcott was uncooperative at the best of times—and these were far from that. If Leonore's thinly veiled threat produced results, he wasn't going to say a word.

Westcott began babbling to the point that Leonore had to stop him several times and gently calm him.

''The Betans,'' she prompted. ''What of them?''

''They came from this system. Beta 7. It's a gas giant. They breathe a standard CH_4 and NH_3 mixture under high pressure. You already know that. There was something different about the leader of the expedition that established this base and the outpost on Beta 5.''

''Different in what way?'' asked Ralston, finding himself engrossed more and more in Westcott's telling. He checked twice to be certain his recorder caught every syllable of the descriptions.

''Unusual, different, psychotic. He wasn't like the rest of them. I can't say how. There's so much lost in the depths of that computer. It's so huge! Not even the University computer has—''

"The Betans," urged Leonore.

"Yes, yes," Westcott said irritably. "There's another base similar to this one on the outermost moon circling Beta 7. It was from there that—they don't seem to have names—the one who established this base made the observations of the chaos field as it entered the system.''

"How close did it pass the primary?" asked Bernssen, still buried under the control console. "Within a dozen A.U.'s?''

"Less than an eleventh of an A.U. The . . . observer noted it pass through the photosphere. I have no idea what equipment he used to record it, if he even did. There is a lack of curiosity about the universe that borders on the obscene.''

"Are those laser disks likely to hold the information about the chaos device?" asked Ralston.

"Not the ones you gave me. I've already told you about them. But there might be more on the Beta 7 moon. Not here. This base was stripped of all but the heaviest equipment when the chaos effects began manifesting themselves.''

"What happened to the Betan?''

"He wasn't affected, but the equipment began malfunctioning. The computer shows signs of failure throughout due to the chaos field's effects. The solution to the chaos equations lies within this machine. I know it.''

"The other moon. The one circling Beta 7. Would it have a better functioning computer? One you might get better information from?" Ralston began worrying about this expedition.

The chaos effects closed in around them. Ralston closed his eyes and tried not to worry. The sun prepared itself for explosion, the animals on Beta 5 exhibited nonviable mutations that had to be a result of a continuing chaotic influence, the Alphan dioramas had induced an epileptic fit in him—but both Bernssen and Leonore escaped through proper medication—the alien base had been abandoned, all because of the roving chaos field.

The chaos field.

Ralston itched inside over that unseen alien enigma. Who had created it? Why did it exist? It both gave him the opportunity of a lifetime and robbed him of those same fabulous archaeological sites. He had to know.

And the answer lay on a distant moon.

Before Ralston could ask Westcott any further questions, Leonore said, "The lights! They're going out. Does that mean the robots are turned off?"

Bernssen scooted from under the console. "I think it does. I traced some of the circuits to a single black box. When the lights started going out, I felt the box vibrate as if mechanical relays were closing. I'll give the Betans one thing—they knew how to build to last. It doesn't seem that this place is a prototype. They did some good work." He shook his head at Westcott's contention that this was the first—and possibly the only—base ever built.

Ralston peered out the door and cast his lamp beam down the broad corridor. He saw nothing.

"Do you think it's really safe?" asked Leonore. Her eyes never strayed from the indicator lights, as if she expected them to flash on again in mockery of her hope.

"It looks like the best chance we've had," said Ralston. "I'll send the probe out to backtrack our course here."

"No," said Westcott, his voice almost breaking with strain. "Map out and scout the most direct route to the elevator. I don't want to stay here any longer than I must."

Ralston silently sent the probe flashing into the darkness. He adjusted his controls, made a few corrections to peak the signal, and waited. For long minutes the probe floated through the long corridors. Twice it noted inert robots. Then came the slow flash of a green lamp on Ralston's control unit.

"It's waiting for us at the elevator," Ralston said. He heard three sets of lungs release pent-up breath.

While the probe had cleared the path, Ralston still pro-
ceeded cautiously. They passed the silent guard robots,
their tentacles dangling loosely at their sides. No other
evidence of habitation presented itself to them before they,
too, stood in front of the elevator door.

"I'm glad, now, that we didn't try to kill all the power,"
said Leonore. "Passing through here is scary enough. To
be trapped here . . ."

They entered the elevator. As the door closed, Ralston
couldn't help taking a quick peek around the edge and
giving a slight shudder. He had violated every tenet of
good xenoarchaeology and had lived to tell about it. He
almost came to believe in luck. Almost.

"This chaos thing you're always talking about—that's
what's scrambled your brains, isn't it?" The pilot floated a
meter away, arms crossed, legs twined together in a knot
that belied bones. His expression matched his tone.

"We need to go to Beta 7," insisted Ralston. "Can the
shuttle make it?"

"Impossible. Unless you want to strand those men on 5.
Go on, do that. See if they won't complain."

"Not enough fuel left," Bernssen said, all energy gone
from his voice. "That's the problem. We need what fuel's
left to land the shuttle and retrieve the expedition."

"One trip for the men, two for men and equipment,"
said the pilot. "And that's depending on everything going
without a problem. The way you people operate, I wouldn't
count on anything happening the way you planned."

Ralston ignored the sarcasm. The pilot had every right
to be upset with them. They had exited the Betan base on
the outer moon and immediately signaled for rendezvous.
The pilot had expertly matched with them on his first
figure-eight orbit around Beta 5 and the moon, then began
shouting that he should have abandoned them when Ralston
told of their need to go to the gas giant.

The pilot had done more than required every time they'd

asked. To take such a foolish risk now violated the pilot's code, not to mention going past the bounds of rationality.

"Can't you get us a low energy Hohmann orbit?" asked Bernssen.

"Sure, punch it up yourselves. Take a look at it."

"No need," said Westcott, eyes slightly glassy and his mouth slack. The sensor atop his freshly shaved head blinked balefully. "We'd be eleven months to arrive, and a seven-month stay allows us a fourteen-month return."

"That's almost three years!" blurted Leonore Disa. "We might not have that long. The sun's going nova in a year or two."

"We don't have the supplies, either," pointed out Ralston. "We need to blast directly."

"Can't be done. No fuel. Figures don't lie. Ask that one, the freak computer man with the hardware head." The pilot lifted his chin in Westcott's direction.

"What if we didn't take the shuttle," said Ralston, thinking out loud. "If we used the starship, we could—"

"*No!*" The pilot's denial was both immediate and emphatic. "That's dangerous!"

"The stardrive interaction with gravity wells around planets is unpredictable," said Westcott. "An interesting effect in the theory I'm working on."

"The chaos equations?" asked Ralston, confused.

"Before that, before you brought such a fine problem to my attention, I spent my time deriving a new quantum gravity theory. Very difficult geometry involved."

They each floated in midair, surrounded by a tiny shell of silence in the central chamber's low atmospheric pressure. Ralston's mind worked over their dilemma. The shuttle was out of the question; only the starship could be used, but that posed problems of a nature they wouldn't be able to overcome.

"We might be getting ahead of ourselves on this," said Ralston. "The Betans might not have survived. We're talking about their abandonment of this base almost ten thousand years ago. Westcott wasn't sure about their motives in founding the outpost. They might have been refugees from cataclysm on their planet.''

"Odd choice, isn't it?" asked Leonore. "If they're native to a gas giant, why would they flee to a stony planet? There's another gas giant in the system almost identical to 7.''

"What I'm saying is that we don't know if there's anything to find on Beta 7. Let's rig a probe and send it. If it finds evidence of the Betans, we can return to the problem of reaching them. If it doesn't, we've saved ourselves a lot of work.''

"A probe we can arrange," grumbled the pilot. "Too bad you all can't be stuffed into it.'' He expertly rolled in midair, caught an elastic strap, and levered himself across the room, hitting the shaft leading to the cockpit with contemptuous ease.

"It's off," said Leonore, watching the radar screen. A tiny green dot crept away from them, looping once around Beta 5 to pick up speed and then be slung from the gravity well on its way to Beta 7.

"With constant acceleration we won't have long to wait. By the end of the week we'll check it for midcourse corrections," said Bernssen. "In two we'll be nearing 7.''

"Any idea about a radiation field around the destination?" asked Ralston. "I don't want the instrumentation fried. That won't tell us anything.''

"We're taking a chance, as is," said Bernssen. "I've got the probe protected, more against solar flares than planetary radiation belts, but it'll be verd all the way.''

Ralston still worried for the entire three weeks until it arrived in orbit around Beta 7.

Then they all started worrying in earnest. The probe found definite indications of life on the surface of the gas giant. The race that had built the outposts on Beta 5 and its moon still lived—and might still have detailed knowledge of the chaos device and its passage through their solar system.

═════════ FOURTEEN ═════════

"THE SIGNALS COME back too slowly," complained Michael Ralston. He spun slowly in the starship's passenger compartment, irritated at the need to be inactive.

"The speed of light is the best I can do," said Bernssen. Turning to Leonore Disa, the physicist said jokingly, "You ought to find an alien dig with ftl communication gear for your professor. That'd get you a degree in nothing flat."

"If I ever found anything like that," Leonore said, "I'd go into business for myself and put Daddy and IC out of business." She chuckled, adding, "That'd drive him *crazy*!"

"The signal quality isn't very good, either. Can't you boost the gain?" Ralston found himself becoming as singleminded as Westcott about this project. The data from the surface of Beta 5 continued to come in as the ultrasonic digger continued its work on the Alphan refugees' city, but nothing as exciting as the information gathered by Bernssen and Leonore—and himself—from the diorama.

He shook his head as he thought about those messages. How far he'd come since blundering into the diorama and experiencing the Alphans' warning to generations then unborn. He'd discovered Fennalt's attempt to create a new city out of the Betans' abandoned outpost and the intricate maze of tunnels in the hollowed-out moon, with its still functional equipment, and now he had found a living alien race on Beta 7's ammonia-cloaked surface.

And Ralston hated it. He hadn't followed correct procedures at any stage. He had lost valuable information. He knew he missed a great deal, lost it for all time due to the pressures of exploration. He felt more like Bishop de Landa destroying the Mayan codices than he did a preserver of ancient lore.

Ralston almost cried, thinking of their blundering through the moon's tunnels. Activating guard robots alone had been a major sin for any archaeologist, but he had allowed Westcott to tap into the Betans' computer without the necessary months of study and discussion of precautions. He could have restrained the mathematician, kept him from wandering off once they had entered the elevator. He should have realized the danger in exploring the alien base. Ralston had only himself to blame, yet if Westcott hadn't resurrected the long-slumbering computer memory, they wouldn't have known about the Betans' existence on the gas giant.

"It's all going too fast for me to analyze," he said. "I feel as if I'd been run back in time to the Nex-P'torra war. There was never time to relax and reflect then. Always, we dashed from star to star, fought on one planet after another, then hurried on until I didn't know or care where we were." He looked at Leonore, who nodded slowly. "I feel that way now," Ralston said.

"I understand," said Leonore. "Any of the sites we've found deserve major funding and intensive work—years of work. We've skimmed the top, and possibly done more harm than good."

"That probe circling Beta 7 will be the determination of whether we succeed or fail miserably," said Ralston. "The Betans might not know their star is pre-nova. We can warn them, though what good that'll do, I can't say. If Nels is right, they'd have only a handful of years to build ships and escape."

"You don't think the government would be willing to send rescue ships for them?" asked Bernssen.

"For ammonia and methane breathers used to living beneath a kilobar of atmosphere? The Church would raise the issue of whether they possessed a soul and cloud the issue. By the time any of the bureaucrats could see how a rescue would benefit their careers, the Beta primary would have exploded."

"Don't sound so bitter, Michael," chided Leonore. "There are others who might help in a rescue mission."

"The P'torra? Hardly. The Nex were too devastated by the war to do more than hold their own boundaries. None of the other races I can think of have any major starfaring capability."

"It hardly seems moral for us to interrogate them for information on the chaos field and then let them die from its effects," said Bernssen. 'But what other choice do we have?"

"I can't see any," Ralston said bleakly.

"You, back there," came the pilot's annoyed voice over the intercom. "New signals from your probe. Check them and clear the channel. I need to talk to the poor chingers you left on the ground. We're overdue for their progress reports."

Bernssen twisted around and went to his makeshift control panel. He worked for a few minutes, then frowned.

"What's wrong, Nels?" asked Leonore.

"I didn't collect the entire message. Wait a second and let me decode."

The physicist started clumsy console work. Westcott pushed him aside. Bernssen started to react angrily, then subsided and let the mathematician direct-connect to the computer. In seconds, Westcott's face turned flaccid, all humanity gone. When he blinked and turned from the console, he smirked.

"You have no luck whatsoever," he said. "The probe reports a retrograde satellite, the one farthest out."

"What of it?" demanded Ralston, anxious to cut through Westcott's gloating.

"It's outfitted similar to the one around 5. Hollow, heavily instrumented, abandoned." Westcott's smirk grew into a grin that split his face. "Then the probe died."

"Died?" Ralston echoed.

"No more. *Pop!*" Westcott made a small exploding gesture with his hands.

"There goes any chance of contacting the Betans," said Bernssen. "A constant monitoring of the usual radio frequencies hasn't turned up which they use, if any."

"They might not radiate," said Leonore. "Look at Earth's com development. It took less than a hundred years to use microburst pulses relayed through communication satellites. And fiber optics were very common for ground communication. Almost no leakage to space with either of those technologies."

"The probe didn't find any artificial satellites," said Bernssen. "But that doesn't mean anything. It made fewer than a dozen orbits before it died."

"No chance of reviving it? A chance burst of radiation might have blanked out the rest of the signal," suggested Ralston.

Westcott shook his head and smiled until the corners of his mouth must have hurt from the strain. "The probe failed permanently and irretrievably," the mathematician said smugly. "You neglected to plan for all possible contingencies."

"Go plug yourself back into the Betans' computer and see if I care," snapped Ralston. He shoved himself away from the control console and came to rest at the far side of the compartment. Leonore drifted over to join him.

"Michael, don't let him upset you. He's not human. He spends all his time with computers. This might be Westcott's first real contact with others in years."

"He doesn't teach that many classes at the University," Ralston conceded. "But there's no reason for such childish behavior. He *delights* in my failure!"

"Westcott may not know any better." She glanced over her shoulder at Westcott and Bernssen, who still argued. "He may never learn, either. But we can use him."

"What? How?"

"I've been discussing this with the pilot. If Westcott hooked directly into the starship's computer and controlled a shift, we might be able to hop out to Beta 7. Nels and I discussed it, we've talked with the pilot and with the others down below at Nels' observatory, and there's no other chance."

"Why can Westcott do something the on-board computer can't?"

"The programming. The pilot is good but Westcott is better. He knows the computer intimately in ways no one unlinked can. For such a precise shift, Westcott is perfect. His field of expertise is quantum gravity theory. He said so. Remember? He can negotiate the gravity wells and calculate well enough to drop us within a thousand kilometers of the satellite the probe found."

"And then we could examine *that* outpost and maybe contact the Betans directly," Ralston said, his enthusiasm for the attempt waxing. "They must have left some equipment linking the outpost with their surface launch site."

"There's no way we could ever land on the surface of Beta 7," pointed out Leonore. "This is a chance to warn them, if they don't already know of the nova, and also to find out what they learned about the chaos field. You know what I think? I think that the chaos field might be what drove them off Beta 5. If it is, they have detailed observations. Nels needs that; so do we."

"Will Westcott do it?" asked Ralston.

"He'll do it," the woman solemnly assured him. "Or I'll promise him a long walk home."

For a split second, Ralston wasn't certain which he'd rather see. Then scientific necessity reasserted itself over personal antipathy. They were starring to Beta 7!

•   •   •

"I don't like it. Not at all. You chingers haven't shown yourselves to be any good at this. Damn! Wish I'd drawn Velasquez and that Proteus assignment. But no, I get . . ."

The pilot's acid words trailed off as Westcott positioned himself before the ship's main control panel. The small sensor recently installed on the console flashed its baleful infrared message. Westcott tipped his head forward until his sensor locked with the output beam. The mathematician's body went rigid.

"I'll never get over seeing him like that," said Ralston.

"You'll never get used to it if the chinger wrecks us," warned the pilot. As caustic as the man sounded, he was drawn to the ease with which Westcott worked in conjunction with the computer's intricate starfaring programs. Lights flashed and indicators began giving readings in agreement with the pilot's laboriously planned shift. "Damn, but he controls the ship better than I could."

Ralston could never find it in his heart to envy Westcott. Pitying the mathematician took all his surplus emotion.

"Here we goooo!" cried the pilot.

Acceleration slammed them back into their couches. As abruptly as it had come, the invisible hand changed position and pushed forward against the restraining webs.

"Exact position to the tenth decimal place," the pilot said, awe tinging his voice. "Damn, but I wish I could do that." He eyed Westcott's sensor, then shook his head.

"I've got the probe on visual," came Bernssen's excited voice. The vidscreen flickered, then formed into the image of Ralston's twisted and broken probe, its electronic guts spilled onto the dusty plain of the retrograde moon.

"No sign of weaponry," Ralston muttered, more to himself than to the others. "What brought it down like that?"

"Chaos," came Westcott's reply.

Ralston spun and almost collided with the mathematician. "Any sign of life on the moon?" he asked, to cover his surprise at Westcott's nearness. He had been so engrossed in the problem, he'd ignored everything around him.

"None. The pilot says we can descend using the shuttle. There will be very little fuel usage."

"Can we make more than one trip?" asked Leonore, obviously interested in exploring, then doing real archaeology.

"One trip only," said Westcott. "The fuel is at a lower limit now for a one-shot safe retrieval of those back on 5."

Ralston motioned for them to get into their suits. He wanted to get started as soon as possible.

'I protest!'' Leonore Disa shouted. "You can't do this!"

"Explain it to her, Nels," Ralston said.

"*Madre de Dios*, you do it," said the physicist, fastening the last strap of his suit.

"I want to go. You can't keep me back." Leonore floated with arms crossed just a few centimeters away.

"Fuel limitations," said Ralston. "One less to go, less mass to boost back, even against four-percent gravity. Bernssen is needed to study the equipment, Westcott is willing to connect to any computer we find, and I'm in charge." Ralston took a deep breath. "We violated every law of xenoarchaeology and good sense before. Not this time. You'll stay aloft with the starship and monitor our every communication."

"Which will be nil when you go into the tunnels to get to the Betans' computers," raged Leonore.

"This time, we're setting up a com-link to relay out our signal," said Bernssen.

"You just don't want me to go because you think it's dangerous. You can't do this, Michael. And you, Nels. You're not even arguing with him!"

"It *is* dangerous," said Ralston. "And there's no one else I'd rather have along than you. We've been through too much for me to not know your abilities, Leonore. This is a pragmatic decision." He smiled slowly. "Only one archaeologist is needed. And you don't expect *me* to stay behind, do you?''

"Yes," she said, not meaning it. Her anger faded. "You'd better bring back everything we need, Dr. Ralston. If you don't, I'll go fetch it myself!''

"Agreed." Ralston buttoned up the last fasteners on his suit and made sure that both Westcott and Bernssen checked his seals; he did the same for them. Even triple-checking sometimes afforded room for mistakes. On this quick in-and-out expedition there could be no mistakes at all. Ralston knew they'd been inordinately lucky before. A second time they couldn't count on luck.

They slipped into the shuttle, with Bernssen again at the controls. The pilot had programmed exactly, and the physicist's minimal skills weren't required. Ralston heaved a sigh of relief when the rockets died under them. As before, the vidscreens showed immense clouds of soft dust billowing around. This moon was half the size of the other they'd explored; the major difference, as Ralston saw it, was the presence of Beta 7 in the sky. The giant filled the sky with an awesome sight of colorful gas bands and raging storms.

Ralston shook himself from the view. He was no mere tourist. He had left Leonore behind to lead this expedition—and with leadership came worry. He swallowed harder, thinking that anything might happen to Westcott. Without the mathematician's direct-link to the ship's computer, shifting back to the inner planet would be difficult for the pilot.

Without the shuttle, it might not matter. The pilot wouldn't be able to pick up the scientists still on 5's surface doing their astronomical observations.

"Got the equipment?" asked Bernssen, settling his own load. They had scavenged much from ship's stores. In addition to the transmitter relays they'd place every time they turned a corner within the tunnel system they expected to find, Ralston had pulled free almost a kilometer of fiber optic from the starship's guts. With a small crawler robot and a dust-grain camera, he hoped to bypass the guard robots and not awaken them from their centuries of downtime.

"All set," said Ralston. He cast a quick glance at Westcott, who weaved off-balance under his load, in spite of the low gravity. Together they left the shuttle and started across the dusty plain for an infrared source they'd detected from orbit.

"That's it," said Bernssen with some satisfaction. "I didn't think anything natural would have a thermal portrait like that." The tunnel mouth had been hewn in a perfectly circular pattern.

Reaching it, Ralston dropped the most powerful of the transmitter relays. "Leonore, you read?"

"Reading verd," came her immediate answer. "We're almost directly overhead."

Ralston craned his neck and saw a bright spot moving across the airless sky. Behind loomed Beta 7, majestic behind its cloak of swirling gases and typical Jupiter storms. His muscles began to knot. Ralston turned back to the job, setting the microburst relay. Every time the transmitter received a signal from Leonore in the starship, it would spew forth the entire conversation recorded since the last pulse. With the triggering signal, Leonore could send any information she thought they'd need.

"Start the crawler," Ralston told Westcott, "while I finish with this."

The mathematician pulled out a robot hardly larger than his hand. Tracks ran on either side, and a large spiked wheel could be lowered for terrain requiring more traction than that afforded by the treads. Westcott attached the miniature camera, its optics system no larger than a dust mote. Bernssen set up a reel with the fiber-optic cable and attached one end to the crawler and the dust-grain camera. The other end he fixed to the transmitter.

"Good visual," came Leonore's acknowledgment. "Good hunting. Damn you all!"

Ralston waited nervously as the crawler started off on its

slow exploration of the entry tunnel, down a spiraling ramp, and through a variety of rooms. Twice it passed an inert guard robot without activating it.

"Good choice of equipment," said Westcott, with unexpected praise. "Finding a ramp was lucky, too. Saves losing the fiber in a closing door." The mathematician beamed unexpectedly. "I have a good idea how to reach the main computer console. An analysis of the geometry used in designing the tunnels shows a central hub—turn left! Yes, down that direction." Westcott stood and peered at the tiny monitor screen.

Ralston guided the crawler in the direction indicated. After less than a hundred meters he saw a door similar to the one on the moon half a solar system away.

"How do we get there?" asked Bernssen. "The crawler went by a pair of the robots. We'd activate them."

"Use the wheel to enter the room," said Westcott. Ralston sweated freely by the time he lowered the large geared wheel and worked open the control-room door. Inside he sent the crawler directly for the right side of the console. The faint IR imaging failed to pick up the buttons that disabled the robots.

Westcott took over. How he managed to become so adroit using remotes, Ralston could only guess. Perhaps the mathematician considered this a primitive extension of his linkup with a computer. Maybe he'd practiced for some other chore at some other time. Ralston cared only that Westcott got the crawler onto the control console and ran the spiked wheel over the appropriate large control buttons.

"What do we do, wait a *wah* for them to turn off?" asked Bernssen.

"They were never activated. This ensures they won't come on," said Westcott. "And I timed the *wah* duration to be four seconds longer than four minutes."

"Maybe they'll rename it after you," Bernssen said sarcastically.

Bernssen hefted a pack and started into the tunnel,

Ralston and Westcott following. At every turn they dropped a relay transmitter and checked its operation. Ralston wanted their every move recorded.

He jumped when Leonore's voice boomed in his helmet, "How's it going?"

"No problems yet," he answered. "Have you orbited once already?"

"Verd. The pilot doesn't want to change altitude. Once around every sixty-one minutes."

"I'm putting the crawler on random walk through the tunnels to record as much as possible before we have to leave."

"The pilot wanted me to tell you to bring back as much of the fiber optic as possible. He doesn't like not being in contact with all the hull sensors."

"Verd."

Ralston and the others stopped just short of the first guard robot. The archaeologist pointed to his helmet. They pressed their helmets together and shouted at one another to keep from broadcasting on a band that would arouse the guard.

"How sure are you that the robot is disabled?" he shouted at Westcott.

The mathematician, looking irritated that Ralston challenged his judgment in such matters, swung off past the robot guard without hesitation. As if he walked on ice, Ralston slipped past the robot, sure that it would blink once and start reaching for him with its electrified tentacles.

Nothing of the sort happened. They passed the second robot, and only then did Ralston start to breathe more easily. By the time they'd entered the control room, Ralston's apprehension had turned once more to excitement. He was a field xenoarchaeologist with an entire site to explore!

"Don't touch those buttons," Ralston warned Bernssen, as the physicist started toward the controls for the robots. "I don't want to fight my way out this time."

"With what? Your bare hands? We don't have any more weapons now than we did before." Bernssen snorted and dived under the control console to begin mapping out the circuits in an effort to determine how the Betans controlled their equipment.

Ralston touched a bulge in his pack. He hadn't told the others, but he had spent the better part of four hours assembling a laser capable of burning through a robot's metallic body. It had been several years since he'd fought beside the Nex, but their training had stayed with him. Given time, Ralston felt confident he could assemble a device capable of destroying the entire complex.

But destruction wasn't what brought him here. He needed data. On the Betans. On their artifacts. On the chaos device.

"I'm recalling the crawler to make a more systematic search," he told the others. Bernssen grunted acknowledgement; Westcott simply stood and stared at the console. Ralston had the image of a high diver in mind. Westcott looked as if he summoned the courage to make the first step that would send him plummeting toward a distant patch of water.

The crawler returned and Ralston sent it back along a nearby corridor. As it rolled, he stayed well back and photographed every room he came to. Once, the crawler detected a robot sentry; Ralston backed up the tiny probe and the camera it carried and sent them exploring down another tunnel.

One room in particular fascinated him. Nowhere in the complex weavings of tunnels had he seen anything he'd label as art. In this small rock-walled room he found paints squirted across the walls in patterns he took to be representational.

"I'm getting a good photo," came Leonore's voice. Again Ralston jumped. He hadn't realized they'd been in the base this long. "Are they decent depictions?" she asked.

"Who can say without actually meeting one of the Betans?" he answered. "There's something peculiar about this room, other than the art. It seems familiar, like I've been here, but I know that's not possible.''

Ralston hesitated, thinking hard. Instinct often gave him a better idea than rigidly following procedures outlined by scholars a hundred light years distant.

"What's wrong, Michael?" Leonore sounded worried.

"Nothing. Nothing's wrong. I have the oddest feeling of having entered one of the Alphan dioramas. I don't feel the beginning of the telepathic projection, though." Ralston bent forward and examined one wall. What he'd first thought to be part of the picture turned out to be a smaller metallic panel with two large buttons. Designs had been scrawled across the surfaces, making them blend into those on the wall.

"Don't press it. Get Nels. Let him examine it."

"I'm not touching it, Leonore," he said. Dropping to his knees, Ralston shone his headlamp directly onto the buttons. Of the circuits behind, he saw nothing. "This is frustrating. Maybe it only activates some art display."

"Michael," she warned.

Caution forgotten, Ralston brushed across the righthand button. Pale light came up in the room and the images began to flow sluggishly. He rocked back and simply stared in fascination as the blurred images began to take on more distinct form.

"It's like an ancient moving picture," he said. "I wonder if it's telling a story? Without a slight ammonia atmosphere in here, I can't pick up any vibrations. I'd think any high pressure being would be especially sensitive to sound."

"You shouldn't have done that, Michael," Leonore scolded. "Nels is on his way. Westcott, too."

"No need. I haven't done anything." Ralston got no reply. He guessed that the starship had passed beyond line-of-sight with the transmitter again. All he said would be recorded for the next flyover burst transmission.

The figures continued to move, but were still vague. "I think these may be exact replicas of the Betans. They have no rigid shape, but flow amorphously, like a jellyfish. I have no idea what the red currents that seem to flow in and out of the creatures represents. Nutrients? Exhaust heat?''

''Michael, there you are!'' Bernssen almost collided with the rock wall, misjudging the low gravity in his haste. ''How'd you find this place?''

''Just happened across it. It must be a vidscreen for tri-dee programming, though it is primitive.''

''It's the communication center.''

''What do you mean?'' Ralston stared at the physicist.

''Westcott tapped into the computer once more. I gave him a one-minute jaunt, then blanked his sensor. Together with the way the leads from the console ran in this direction, we decided this is what we've been looking for.''

''This is a com center? Ridiculous. Those are . . . real?''

Westcott came to stand near the dual button controls. ''As close as we can determine, this is a live picture beamed up from the surface of Beta 7.''

''What's the other button do?''

''Try it,'' urged Bernssen. ''Westcott hit a dead end trying to find information on the chaos field.''

''The history left in their computer memory only confused me,'' the mathematician said. ''Dr. Bernssen and I mutually discovered that this studio existed.''

''A broadcast studio,'' murmured Ralston. He shook his head in disbelief.

Westcott reached past and touched the left-hand button. For several minutes, nothing seemed to happen. Then Ralston tried to cover his ears. The sudden ear-splitting roar coming through the suit speakers rivaled a rocket blast.

Westcott twitched uncomfortably and touched the button again. By this time Bernssen had removed the metallic panel, to expose a wrist-thick band of wires. He took a sensor similar to the one Westcott had mounted on his skull and placed it near the bundle.

''Which ones?'' Bernssen asked the mathematician, with

some distaste. Westcott pointed, and Bernssen severed the wires and placed the sensor into the circuit.

"What are you doing?"

"Linking to the computer again," said Westcott. He turned his head so that the IR beams intersected. His body stiffened but he forced himself to keep talking. "I now have a linkup that allows communication. How well this works is unknown."

"Put out a general call," urged Ralston. He crowded close and stared at the images flowing around the room. One of the images stopped and seemed to peer in. "There, direct your request to that one."

"I . . . I have. He-she-it is not interested." Even as Westcott spoke, the creature faded away. "Their life is unusual. There is no . . . threat."

"The chaos field. Tell them about the danger from the chaos field!" cried Ralston, agitated now. He refused to allow such an opportunity to slip past him.

"They do not care. They have no predators on Beta 7."

"That's not possible," said Bernssen. "Where's the goad to advance?"

"They absorb nutrients from the atmosphere. Not osmosis. A different process. But how?" Westcott's voice rose to a wail. "Curiosity. An aberration. Not allowed, scorned by truly civilized beings. Why have we come?"

Ralston jerked around and saw another fuzzy shape peering in, as if they were specimens in a cage. His eyes darted to the open doorway before returning to the creature who somehow addressed them through Westcott's mind-computer linkage.

"Why are you here?" repeated Westcott, his voice cracking under the strain of input from the alien computer.

"We seek information, to give you information," said Ralston, trying to keep calm. Few of even the most successful scouts ever discovered another life form. One in a million found intelligent life.

"Why? That is sick. They all tell me this is so."

"Give information on this outpost," requested West-cott. "And the one on Beta 5's moon."

"Those? I built them. I am sick and unwanted by others."

"You?" asked Ralston. "Ask it to explain, Westcott. Ask it!"

The creature flowed and changed shape as an unseen and unfelt breeze gusted past. "I left the surface of this planet many rotations ago because I am unwell in my thoughts and pursuits. Passage of a peculiar cometary object unreasonably excited me."

"The chaos device?" Ralston asked.

"The peculiar cometary object," the gaseous creature went on, using Westcott as its voice, "displayed none of the attributes I had calculated. We do much of a theoretical nature, little of a substantive. Except for I, who am forever sick."

"The cometary object," said Ralston. "Tell us about it."

"I have that data," cut in Westcott, his voice lower. Tears ran down the mathematician's cheeks. "The strain of maintaining this contact is too much for me. I can't keep it much longer."

Ralston found himself caught between his desire to learn as much about the Betans as possible and the need to warn them of the impending solar explosion.

"Tell him about the nova and how it was caused by the chaos device—what he calls the cometary object."

"Verd, but it'll be the last I can send," said Westcott, his entire body trembling with exertion.

Ralston slipped closer and peered into the mathemati-cian's helmet to read the vital signs. For once, Westcott wasn't acting willfully. His blood pressure was at a dan-gerous level, and blood electrolytes had fallen mysteri-ously to a danger point.

"Warn them," urged Ralston.

Westcott gasped and fell forward, breaking the sensors' IR beam. Ralston cradled the quaking man in his arms.

The gas creature to whom they'd spoken shifted and moved away, becoming increasingly blurred as it left.

"Did you warn them?" asked Bernssen, helping Ralston support Westcott.

"I did. He . . . he said I was sick, too. They have no fear of death, no reason to live except that is what they've always done. He wasn't even interested!"

"We're leaving," said Ralston. "Now. We're getting Westcott back to the starship. He's been through enough."

But as Ralston left the communication room, a pang of guilt assailed him. He knew they did the proper thing in returning Westcott to the medical facilities aboard the ship, but now he wanted to explore just a little longer!

FIFTEEN

"HE'S RESTING COMFORTABLY," said Leonore Disa, "but the pilot is threatening to toss him out the airlock." She settled into a half huddle in midair, one leg hooked around an elastic cord. "Frankly, I'm inclined to help the pilot."

Ralston inwardly groaned. Ever since leaving the treasure trove on Beta 7's moon, Westcott had caused nothing but trouble. He hadn't wanted to be treated by the ship's automedic. When they forced him, he didn't want the injections prescribed. By then the automed had already performed its duty. Westcott fought the administered sedative to the point of hooking himself into the ship's computer and ordering a stimulant. Only the pilot's quick thinking had prevented the automed from obeying the larger computer's command.

"What's he doing now?" Ralston asked, not wanting to know.

"He insists that he must work on the data accumulated. He refuses to do anything else, even eat. The man's gaunt to the point of starvation when he's in his usual condition. Now?" Leonore shook her head. "I don't understand how sheer stubbornness can keep him going. But it is, verd, it is!"

"What data did he get?" asked Bernssen. "I didn't

think he got anything significant from the Betan he contacted.''

"I didn't, either," said Ralston, curious. "We need Westcott in top shape to shift back to Beta 5. Let me go talk to him."

"Take a wrench with you," called Leonore. "You'll need to bash him over the head a few times just to get his attention." Disgusted, she drifted away, to where she and Nels Bernssen could talk in private.

Ralston hurried along the central shaft of the starship and found the medical cabin. Inside, the distinction between walls and ceiling proved even more elusive than in other portions of the ship. Equipment sprang from every available flat surface. In the center of what appeared to be a clumsy spider's web, hung the mathematician.

Westcott grumbled constantly and tried to reach the sensor mounted on his head. Someone had taped over it, then used the webbing material to bind his hands so he couldn't remove the tape. Ralston had to laugh at the man's predicament. Then he sobered. What was it like for Westcott to lose that computer contact? Could it be similar to Ralston losing human contact? The P'torra had broken many human fighters using isolation techniques. Was Westcott suffering as a result of his inability to link with the ship's computer?

"Get me out of here, dammit!" raged Westcott. "I will not submit to this indignity!"

"You need rest," said Ralston.

"I need to work!"

"On what?" asked Ralston. "You said you got nothing of importance from the being who claimed to have built the outposts."

"He did. They are immortal and don't experience death in the manner we do."

"You need to rest so that you can safely make the shift to Beta 5 for us. We can't leave the others stranded on the planet while we swing in orbit about a gas giant and watch the Jupiter storms."

"Pah, they mean nothing. There is little on this planet of merit, though they do good theoretical work."

Ralston sized up the mathematician. He phrased his words carefully. "You learned a great deal from the exchange, didn't you? Perhaps not direct knowledge, but some—shall we call them sidebands—crept over, and you saw much you haven't bothered to mention to the rest of us."

"I won't share it. I know how all you other scientists are. If I told you what I learned, you'd demand that I put your name on the research paper. I won't do it. I got this all by myself!"

"What would you do if I told you there wouldn't be any paper, yours or anyone's?"

"Censorship!"

"Death," Ralston said flatly. "We are stranded here. We can't simply shift away. Only you, in direct-connect with the ship's computer, are accurate enough to return us to 5."

"Ching all those fools!" Westcott shouted.

"No," said Ralston, "what'll happen is that the pilot shifts out of the system for a week or two—enough to give him a chance to shift back."

"That's dangerous."

"Possibly fatal," agreed Ralston. "But we have to try—to rescue the others." Ralston didn't like being so overly dramatic. No direct or immediate danger manifested itself to threaten those on Beta 5. Bernssen's observations showed relative quiet in the chaos-induced storms raging on the primary's surface, but Westcott in his self-centered way wouldn't consider anything but his own work as important. Ralston hoped this would shock him into compliance.

"Not fatal. The pilot, even though he is such a clumsy oaf, is competent enough at programming."

"But not as good as you are," said Ralston.

"Of course not."

"We'll be shifting out a small distance within the hour. It'll be necessary to keep you sedated for the entire time."

"My mind! I can't *think* with the chemicals dulling my mind!"

Ralston did the best he could to shrug in the zero-gravity.

"Wait! Damn you, wait! If I get us back to Beta 5, will you promise not to pump me full of drugs?" The desperation in Westcott's voice convinced Ralston that the mathematician would do anything to keep from being sedated.

"Yes."

"Get me out of here. Why waste weeks and weeks starring to some unmapped point when we can go directly to 5? Damned waste of time and effort." Westcott kept grumbling the entire time Ralston pulled him free of his medical webbing. The first thing Westcott did was rip off the tape over his sensor. Ralston saw the relief flood over the man's features.

Westcott's piloting dropped them less than five light seconds from Beta 5.

"Don't let it eat you up inside, Michael," said Leonore Disa. "You knew there would have to be a compromise somewhere along the way. It wasn't that bad a one, all things considered."

"I didn't think it'd mean we'd be stuck in orbit."

"You did, too," she chided. "Using the shuttle as much as we did, had to mean no more jaunts down to Beta 5. Nels' men are finishing up their observations and powering down. Do you think they want to leave their equipment?"

"It is expensive," granted Ralston, "but there's so much to do there that we haven't touched."

"It's given me the chance to complete the reports on the Alphans' diorama."

"I want Nels to do the same. The two of you experienced more in those scenes than I did." Ralston shuddered, thinking of the seizure he'd suffered. Leonore and Bernssen had taken a great chance entering the telepathic dioramas and experiencing their messages, even with the medication to prevent what Westcott called bifurcation.

The one good thing about it was Leonore's accumulation of enough data to finish a detailed and unusual thesis. Too many Ralston saw researched trivial topics. Not this one. Leonore Disa's would make archaeological history. Deservedly.

"He's so busy. You know that, too." Leonore heaved a deep sigh. "Michael, you've got to stop torturing yourself. We can't do it all—*you* can't do it all, even though it's what you want."

He admitted his graduate assistant was right. And that galled him all the more. He'd found not one but two alien cultures touched by the chaos field—and he still knew nothing about the device, its origin, operation, and purpose. Westcott grumbled constantly but appeared to be making some headway in describing mathematically the effects of the field. Given such a beginning, it might be possible to duplicate the chaos device.

Ralston didn't mind Chancellor Salazar and Leonore's father working with the Alphans' telepathic projector. Such a breakthrough meant major advances in treating mental illnesses, teaching at all levels, myriad other applications he only dimly sensed. And the odd glowing tube used by the Betan, which appeared to function without filament or gaseous element, intrigued him, even though this lay beyond his expertise. The lighting tubes had lasted for thousands of years. He and Bernssen had taken several from the base above Beta 7 for study. These would benefit the University financially and give something to society.

It troubled Ralston deeply, thinking how Salazar and the other would use the technology of the chaos device if Westcott successfully unlocked its secrets. Unchecked, it produced instability in stars and eventual novas, epilepsy in humans, catastrophic equipment failure and, from all he'd seen on Beta 5, mutation of the worst kind. Ralston didn't trust Salazar with that kind of power.

He trusted no one with it.

He shuddered when he thought of the uses to which such a weapon might be put by the P'Torra. They devastated entire planets with their biological weapons. Ruin an inhabited planet with chaos? They'd never hesitate. Destroy an entire solar system? The weapon would be launched without a second thought.

"I just wish I could do my job," Ralston said.

"So do it. You don't have to be present on the surface. We've got adequate remote sensing equipment, even if it is starting to show traces of chaotic failure." Leonore chewed her lower lip as she studied her professor. "Michael?"

"I know. We've got to leave soon. That's part of what's worrying me. Even giving those still on the planet anticonvulsives, some are developing symptoms of epilepsy."

"Nels said that a couple are beginning to forget. They start to say something and it's just . . . gone. The chaos effects are erasing their minds."

"I still want to excavate there. The clues we're missing! Think of it, Leonore."

"And the Betan outposts, too. Those are finds that deserve more attention than we've given them."

"We'll never return," Ralston said dejectedly. "This expedition hasn't produced enough to make it worthwhile. Any expedition that has to star longer than a week isn't worth it to the University unless the returns are substancial—or the professor's reputation is such that they feel obligated." Ralston snorted and shook his head. "My reputation's not going to grow with this one."

"It was really Nels' expedition—and Westcott's," she pointed out.

"That makes it even worse," he said. "I can't even mount my own trips. And with what we've discovered, they ought to be *begging* me to form new digs. Think of it, two cultures—one dead, one in peril from the chaos field. We've made huge strides. And just barely started the journey." He folded his arms across his chest and floated away. Leonore started after him, then stopped. She let him simmer in his own misery.

Seventeen days later, they retrieved Nels Bernssen's expedition from the surface of Beta 5 and starred for Novo Terra.

No newsers awaited them when the shuttle touched down on the isolated landing pad. The University of Ilium hadn't even bothered to send transportation to get them back to the campus. Disheartened, Ralston saw to what little he'd salvaged from Beta 5, made sure all his photographic equipment and the precious block circuits recording all he'd done were properly stored for later transport, then called Druanna Thorkkin and asked for a lift.

"Hail the returning heroes, is that it?" she asked.

"Several of us will need rides. Leonore and Nels. Probably Westcott, if you don't mind. If I don't see him safely back in his lab, he'll wander the streets aimlessly for years, hooking into anything using a computer. Kitchen appliances, floaters, streetlamps."

"If I didn't know what a brain-case burnout he was, I'd think you were joking."

"You don't mind?" asked Ralston.

"I'll be out in a half hour. See you then."

Ralston sat on a crate and stared off into the distance, wondering if this actually was the life he wanted to lead.

"Cheer up, Michael," said Leonore. "When you show the chancellor those photos, he'll put in the request for funding. We can get back to the Beta system and finish off those ruins in a proper manner."

"It'll never happen. Salazar might send someone back to strip the Beta dome of anything they can find, but research it? Hardly. With any luck, a few xenosociologists might get a chance to talk with the Betans. But we won't be back in that system again."

"You're such a pessimist. Salazar can't deny the significance of all we've uncovered."

Ralston said nothing more. He knew Leonore might be

trying to dispel his depression. Or she might be that much of a starry-eyed optimist. Either way, he didn't want to dampen her obvious good spirits on having returned safely to Novo Terra.

When Druanna came to take them back to campus, Ralston pumped her for any gossip. He saw it as a good excuse not to have to talk about the expedition.

"Dr. Ralston, we've gone over your findings. To say that you've exhibited shoddy technique is an understatement."

"Chancellor Salazar," Ralston answered, knowing how those who'd endured the Spanish Inquisition had felt just prior to the physical torture. Ralston cleared his throat and started again. "Dr. Salazar, my techniques may have lacked scientific rigor but they were necessary, under the circumstances."

"This lighting element seems interesting," another on the Committee for Academics said. "We might be able to exploit such technology to University advantage."

"The winds of chaos are blowing through the Beta system," Ralston said, ignoring the comment. "Weather patterns are disrupted. Mutations of an awful variety occur. Dr. Bernssen has already related the instability in this system's star. It will go nova soon."

"Yes, we've discussed his work. Sound technique, good results."

"I discovered an alien race," Ralston said, frustrated. No matter what he said, Salazar and the others on the committee ignored him. "They require immediate aid. Their sun's going to explode and destroy them if we don't do something."

"There's nothing we can do about this nova business," said Salazar.

"Evacuation! Aid to build ships. The Betans need to leave!"

"And go where, Dr. Ralston?" asked Salazar. "Here? I am sure they'd enjoy an oxygen atmosphere. Your report states that they are ammonia and methane breathers.'' Salazar ran his fingers over a console and read parts of Ralston's report on the monitor. "Yes, and high-pressure beings, too.''

"It's their lighting element you're salivating over.''

"You forget yourself, Doctor,'' snapped Salazar.

"You're not going to help the Betans? You're going to sit by and allow an entire race to be snuffed out in a nova?''

"Such aid is beyond the scope of the University of Ilium,'' Salazar said pointedly. "A report will be forwarded to the government, but their decision is likely to be one of neutrality. What do we know of these creatures?''

"They're intelligent and have a complex society. They established colonies on another planet in their system. They have advanced communications capability. They—''

"Irrelevant, Dr. Ralston. It pains me to say this, but intelligent races litter the starways.'' Salazar made a gesture of distaste. "Several insist on educating their young at our school.''

"You won't have to worry about the Betans,'' Ralston said nastily. "They'll be snuffed out in less time than it takes to file an application for admission.''

"Good. Now that the matter is settled, we can continue to other points barely touched upon in your report.''

Ralston sat in stunned silence. Salazar had dismissed an entire race with that simple statement. It mattered nothing to him that the Betans would die. Ralston barely comprehended how the Betans themselves could be indifferent to their fate. Not only were they alien, their body structures and chemistry were alien in the extreme. The one who'd called himself an aberrant implied that they were immortal, that they had no natural enemies or need to fight for sustenance. Ralston understood such a race wouldn't think like a human.

But what race did Salazar come from? Ralston sat and listened in silence as the Committee on Academics concluded their meeting. Salazar was human. Maybe all too human in the way he wrapped himself in his work to the extent of forgetting his humanity.

". . . in conclusion, we will again review Dr. Ralston's work in, hmm, one month. At that time we shall make recommendations for change in his field techniques and ways to improve the overall quality of his work. Dismissed, Dr. Ralston."

Michael Ralston stood without a word. In a daze, he left the meeting room. Of all those present, only he realized that Chancellor Salazar, by deciding on inaction, had killed an entire race.

Even worse, Ralston worried about the chaos field. It still traveled from star to star, leaving behind its random legacy of confusion and death. The Alphans had died. The Betans were next. How many others had there been? How many more would there be?

Chancellor Salazar might not care, but Ralston did.

SIXTEEN

"I'VE FAILED." RALSTON told Leonore Disa. "Every time I get in the same room with Salazar, I start losing my temper. I can't help it. It's just the way that man strikes me."

"It didn't sound that bad," Leonore said without much conviction.

"Salazar is holding another hearing in a month or two and will decide then what to do about me. He suggested I needed some remedial work. Sloppy archaeology, he called the expedition. And it was. Dammit, he's right. That makes me madder than anything else!"

"The time pressure prevented us from doing more than we did. He ought to know that. So should you," she said, brushing back her short brown hair and peering up at him. "You might be an archaeology professor but that doesn't make you a god."

"It doesn't make me good at politics, either," said Ralston. "Salazar refuses to listen to me about the importance of finding the chaos field. We've got to track it, go to it, investigate it. This is the ultimate artifact, Leonore. Think. A device that challenges the basic parameters of the universe itself. What race designed it? Why? Did it get away from them or was it intentionally sent on its course? Why this particular trajectory? The questions!"

"I know, I know, Michael. But just because Salazar doesn't agree that it's worth investigating doesn't mean you don't have some allies. Nels is at a seminar at the University of Novo Terra. Interest is incredible among the astrophysicists. They see the chaos field as an opportunity of a lifetime."

"It is!"

"They don't care if it's natural or constructed, though."

"It's artificial. It had to be. I feel it in my bones."

"Very scientific," Leonore said, laughing. She reached out and lightly touched his arm. "But I agree. Look, I'm flying over to Novo City to meet Nels. Want to come?"

He shook his head. He had no business being with them.

"Suit yourself. We'll be back before midnight. Nels might want to talk to you then about the seminar's outcome. Will you be at home?"

"Try my office. I've got a hundred years worth of data to sort before I can get down and do any real thinking about what it all means."

"Your office. Midnight. Bye." With that, Leonore took off, almost skipping with happiness.

Ralston wished he could share even a gram of that cheerfulness. But he couldn't. All the expedition had done for him was to reinforce his opinions. Opinions—nothing more.

Ralston found himself walking across the quiet campus toward Westcott's laboratory. He didn't want to confront the mathematician, but he found this less disagreeable than being alone. Druanna Thorkkin had classes for the rest of the afternoon and into the early evening, and he had no one else to occupy his time or take his mind off his considerable concerns.

Ralston paused at the door into Westcott's lab, took a deep breath, knocked and went in, eyes closed. He remembered all too vividly the last time he'd barged in. Slowly, Ralston opened his eyes. Again he spun through space, odd music ringing in his ears. Whatever there was about this tri-dee screen and the musical patterns that soothed Westcott, it only disoriented Ralston.

"Westcott?" he called softly. Through the darkness he saw the mathematician hunched over the computer console. The IR sensor on his head blazed a pure red light. A blink, then solid beaming again. Whatever held Westcott's attention, he used the mind-computer link to its fullest capacity.

"Ralston!" Westcott spun and had a smile as broad as any Ralston had ever seen. "I've done it. This is the most elegant work I have ever done!"

"What's that? Something with your quantum gravity theory?"

"That? No, no, why bother with that? I'm talking about the chaos equations. I've found a solution."

Ralston felt as if he'd stepped into an empty elevator shaft and plummeted for the core of the planet. Should he kill Westcott? The man was unique on the campus. No one else could have derived the solution to such complex mathematical structures. Ralston didn't want the University—and Salazar—in possession of such a potent secret.

Weapons? Salazar would have no qualms about licensing the technology that would come from the theoretical solution to the highest bidder. Ralston wouldn't tolerate the P'torra ever obtaining the secret. To prevent the misuse, Ralston would gladly kill Westcott.

"It's not a general solution, but that'll come. Oh, yes, that'll follow. I used a simplified set of assumptions to begin with, then predicted radioactive decay in uranium. I used one of deCastro's fourteen atom specimens, that being the smallest he had on hand. I applied the boundary conditions, determined which of the fourteen atoms would show decay—and it did!"

"You predicted only one decay?"

"I predicted seventy-four consecutive decays. I need a larger universe, a larger sample. DeCastro said he could manufacture a thirty-atom sample for me. I see no trouble in predicting the decay there, either."

"I didn't think the chaos field caused noticeable radioactive decay."

"The residual effects can't cause decay because of reversal, but my equations can *predict*. The other effects of the field—the weather and component failure and the rest—will fall into place when I have a better handle on the system."

"So this is only a small step?"

"Small, but significant." Westcott cackled and rubbed his hands together. "I'll go down in history with Gauss and Lobatchevsky and Minkowsky. When I find a general solution to the system, *then* they'll notice me!"

Ralston blinked in surprise. He'd never heard Westcott talk in such a fashion before. Fame seemed an unlikely pursuit for the mathematician, yet the need must well from deep within him, driving him onward.

"It's only a simple set of nonlinear equations, but I've learned so much. The Betan gave me so much. Just knowing the chaos field was artificial told me so much."

"It is!" Ralston sank to the floor, sitting cross-legged and staring at Westcott. "Why didn't you tell me before?"

"You knew it." Westcott frowned. "Or you seemed to know. The observations made by the Betans—or the aberrant one with curiosity—verified it. There were large metallic projections on the body that radiated in the ultraviolet. The Betan's instruments weren't good enough to pick up the exact frequencies, but I don't think that matters. No, not at all, not at all." Westcott began chuckling again.

"Why not?" Ralston asked, intrigued in spite of himself. He ought to be angry at the mathematician for withholding this from him for purely selfish reasons, but the sheer impact of the information robbed him of any emotion other than interest.

"It is not a physical device in the strict sense, in the way we'd mean. This is a conceptual machine."

"I don't understand."

"I don't either, not exactly. But I will. The mathematics is so intricate, so elegant!"

"We need to study it in ways other than just document-ing its effects," said Ralston, more to himself than to Westcott. "Direct observation. If there are artificial struc-tures, these might tell us something of the race that built it."

Ralston fell into deep depression at the thought of being forced to remain at the University of Ilium and never again go starring. Salazar wouldn't authorize any expedition headed by Ralston—ever. Ralston had ridden along on Nels Bernssen's good luck to excavate in the Beta system, but he couldn't count on the physicist's and his own interests to converge again in the future.

But to examine such a relic!

"I need to see it," said Westcott. "Nothing else will suffice. If it is more concept than physical, only by wit-nessing it in action can I get a handle on the mathematics involved. Boundary conditions are everything in the chaos equations. Parameters varying by infinitesimals produce radical changes."

Ralston smiled. He might not be able to mount the needed expedition, but Westcott could. Ralston chuckled. He had chided Bernssen about astronomy becoming an experimental science. What would the academic commu-nity say about pure mathematics similarly changing?

"Are you interested in tracking the chaos device down?" Ralston asked, trying to keep the eagerness from his voice.

"I know the trajectory with some exactitude. Simple calculations give me the volume of space where it is likely to be. Yes, definitely, I must go."

"You arrange the funding, I'll put together the equip-ment."

"Equipment? I don't need much. A few cameras. A spectroscope, possibly. Definitely I need monitoring of the local gravity fields to determine the proper tensor strength. But a single ship and one or two people to assist will be sufficient. I don't want more. Too confusing and distract-ing for me."

"You don't want to be bothered by details. I'll take care of that in exchange for the chance to go along."

"Don't bother with him," came Leonore's voice. She and Nels Bernssen walked into Westcott's lab. "Nels has a better proposition."

Ralston dared to hope again.

He turned to see Leonore and Bernssen in the doorway. "You weren't in your office so we decided to stop here," said the woman. "Nels got back early, saving me a trip. Go on, Nels, tell him."

"I've just finished one of the most incredible meetings of my life," the physicist said. "Can't believe it, even now. They almost thrust money at me and begged me to take it. The Bernssen Condition has moved up from theory to reality in most of their minds—and I haven't even written the definitive paper yet!"

"Trivial," said Westcott, annoyed at the crowd in his laboratory. "Compared to the solution of the chaos equations, this is nothing."

"You might be right," said Leonore, "but Nels is already planning an expedition to follow the chaos device. He needs measurements to determine the forces that alter the nuclear chain in stars. With this, he might be able to formulate a more accurate theory of conditions inside a normal star."

"I—" began Ralston.

"We can go, Michael," said Leonore. "We might not have much of a role to play with so many physicists running loose, but we can go."

"I'll resign my position with the University, if necessary," said Ralston. "I know the discovery of the century—of all time!—when I see it."

"See what I meant, Nels?" the woman said. "I told you he'd be hard to convince."

Ralston didn't care who commanded the expedition. The knowledge this would yield would be priceless, beyond money, beyond even ego. He had to share in the exploration process, not for fame or glory, but for the *need* to know. No other archaeological discovery in history was as significant—or deadly.

He was through following the wake of destruction left by the chaos device. The time had come to study it directly.

"When do we leave?" Michael Ralston asked.

3: COLORS OF CHAOS

For Geo. and Lana,
good friends
on "the never-ending flight
of future days."

ONE

THE MAGNESIUM FLARES boiled away lakes of frozen ammonia and sent hot winds gusting through the forest of ragged lava spires. The spawn of Beq surged before the wavefront, screaming in agony as the intense heat ripped away life and thought from his vaporous body. It rose and twisted in midair riding the concussion, vainly seeking escape.

The last thought before it dissipated totally in temperatures exceeding those of melting water ice was of its spawn partner. Then came a burning followed by a darkness so total that it defied even the spawn of Beq's philosophy to define.

Deep within the sheltering bulk of the planet, the other product of Beq's fission-spawning coalesced into a tight ball and rolled with the shuddering impacts of the bombs on the planetary surface.

"Will it never end?" Beq's spawn moaned. It tightened even more and sank to the floor of the chamber. Warmth spread into its body and provided sustenance—and a small measure of courage. Pressed into the lava-fed warmth of the floor, it remembered nostalgically the moments before Beq's fission and the joy of that reproduction. When it had been fully Beq, the spawn had felt the need for renewed vigor, added mental capacity, new curiosity to fuel intellectual search.

The spawn of Beq reveled in that comforting memory. Knowing that its spawn-twin had been trapped on the surface when the enemy began bombardment filled it with a void that refused to yield to explanation. It was no longer the spawn of

Beq, it knew. Not with its fission-twin gone. It now assumed the full name of Beq.

The burden of this sudden and unexpected solitude made the gaseous body quiver and ripple with self-pity. Alone again. It would require at least a hundred planetary revolutions around the distant, pale star before spawn time came and allowed it to produce another partner. Life proved so unfair.

"Damn this war!" Beq cried.

"We failed to detect their war vessels when they entered our system," said another in the council chamber. The advisors had gathered in this safe underground vault hewn from solid obsidian for a routine meeting, only to be told of the devastating raid within minutes of convening. "The mechanicians who allowed this outrage will be thrown into the plasma torch!"

Beq composed itself, sending out feathery tendrils to brush across the surface of feeding pillars. The warmth from the planetary core fed it, giving the creature the energy necessary for more complex thought. Beq sighed, gusting out a thin current of ammonia that immediately cooled and turned to crystalline splinters in the air. It preferred drifting on the surface winds, scattering its body into a transparent veil, and returning—almost—to the most primitive state possible. Only in this animalistic condition did Beq get its most innovative ideas.

"Our surface defenses have prevailed," said this day's head of the ruling committee. The creature floated to the top of the vaulted chamber and thickened its tendrils to gain the others' attention. "Twelve enemy war vessels are no more. Another ten have been driven off. The planet is again safe."

Beq pondered this. Safe? How was it possible that the enemy penetrated planetary defenses so easily? Beq tried not to think of its lost spawn-twin. The toll had been heavy, indeed, because of laxness in detecting the attacking fleet until the sizzling magnesium bombs superheated the surface and brought death and destruction to any creature unfortunate enough to be exposed. The ruling committee needed to prevent future tactical forays against their planet.

"Our mechanicians are at fault," Beq said, after considering the issue for a full planetary rotation. "They allowed the enemy to elude our far-flung observation web."

"Impossible," flared another creature. Its anger showed in the vibrant color of its tendrils circling a lava column. Reds and yellows glowed to an unhealthy level, then cooled to a more controlled green and blue. "I personally oversee the detection system. It functions perfectly. How dare Beq make such allegations without proof?"

"Proof?" asked Beq. Why did the others always insist on physical proof when mentation provided the answer to any question? Beq saw in them the failing of the race. Empirical concerns should never overwhelm the philosophical. Beq formulated its response carefully, knowing that no one else on the ruling committee took the joy it did on soaring on the high-velocity, upper atmospheric winds, defying death by dissipation, returning to a level where ideas boiled without the restrictions of civilized behavior. It was in such a state that Beq—or Beq before fissioning—first conceived of the chaos equations. And it was in such a carefree euphoric state that Beq solved those equations and allowed the lesser mentality mechanicians to build the ultimate weapon.

Those mechanicians to whom it revealed the weapon design had been careless in releasing the weapon, more a concept than a physical entity. Beq had fought long to gain the ruling committee's approval for the project, but it had prevailed when the enemy had countered every other weapon directed against both planetary stronghold and space-borne fleet. Beq had seen that the enemy—fixed form beings with eerily warm bodies—commanded vast resources from a hot world and cunningly avoided most attacks directed against them.

It had floated on ammonia winds until the notion of a chaotic weapon came to it. Beq had watched the chaos field being launched, a space-warping field that changed nature's laws in ways seemingly random but controlled by Beq's mathematics and the elaborate command center at its heart. That field would drift through space, intrude on the enemy home world, and create havoc unparalleled in the history of Beq's race. The enemy's sun going nova was the least of the disruption—but it would be the most emphatic.

Working its unfelt, unseen chaos, the device would visit upon the enemy's world unpredictable storms. Familiar chemical reactions would no longer proceed. And worse for the fixed form enemy, their biologic systems would begin to fail. The laws of heredity would be violated, producing sports and mutations of obscene proportions.

Beq's body elongated as it twisted into a figure-eight pattern around two warm rock posts. There might be more, Beq thought. Here it envied those empiricists who floated and observed rather than working through every conceivable outcome mathematically. Beq's unfamiliarity with solid body life forms prevented it from making a positive estimate of other effects induced by the chaos field. Beq's surface rippled as it considered the possibility of its weapon disrupting thought processes by changing axon and neuron potentials, altering the effect of brain chemical transmitters, and causing random convulsions.

Such power, such a weapon. And because of the subtle influence of the field, those chaotic effects could not be measured directly. The chaos device traveled past the enemy worlds, leaving behind a legacy of corruption both physical and spiritual.

Beq addressed the problem presented by the enemy invasion and bombardment. "Proof is not required in this matter. The evidence is everywhere. Consider the firestorms produced by their falling bombs. Consider the flares of their rocket exhausts boiling away sacred spawning lakes. These point to failure. If not in our mechanicians, then who is at fault?"

"I stake my life on the effectiveness of our detection system. The enemy has produced a new countermeasure that thwarts our most sophisticated equipment. It is you, Beq, you who rank as our leading theoretician, who has failed. You neglected work to float on your ammonia currents and return to a bestial state."

"I have not failed. The enemy need not have contrived new and more diabolical evasion measures." Beq uncurled and rose to the top of the vault. It spread out its body mass to maintain elevation and studied the ruling committee scattered about the rocky chamber. So many of them, so few of any capacity. Beq knew that they *did* blame it.

And perhaps such blame was well directed. Its intellect outclassed theirs. None stood in its rank. Beq pondered how it should have predicted the mechanicians' failure—for it was not possible to come to any other conclusion save that the mechanicians were at fault.

None of the ruling committee understood. And Beq did not understand or appreciate this eons-long war with the enemy. The two cultures did not strive for the same planets. Those worlds favored by the hot-blooded enemy constituted Beq's notion of eternal damnation. It thought that the enemy considered its own fair ammonia wind-wracked planet to be equally unappealing.

So why the war?

Beq did not know. Perhaps a member of the ruling committee had once known, but Beq doubted this. Too many spawnings had passed for that knowledge to be absolute now. Although each division presented added room for mental development, not all knowledge from the parent was carried by each of the spawn-twins. Beq knew that its spawn-twin had certain knowledge of their parent-Beq that it did not possess, but both had inherited the original Beq's mathematical talent— and the oddness that set them apart from all others of their race.

Beq wanted nothing more than to leave this enclosed, constraining chamber and soar on the high-velocity winds far above the surface. When it thinned and let those breezes whip it about the planet, ineffable emotions welled within and promised knowledge unattainable by any other means.

But Beq knew that such comforting thought and stark delight could not occur until this matter of unrestricted bombardment came to a successful conclusion. If the enemy, even at high odds, raided their surface at will, it would be less than a dozen revolutions of the primary before all meaningful life vanished.

Beq tried to imagine the surface heating to the point that water ice melted and those bizarre green things called plants by the enemy began growing. It shrugged off such fantasy. Heat the surface their enemy might. But to actually begin the photosynthesis process that had been discovered in the laboratories? Never. The primary swung through space at such a great distance that the solar constant at the planet's surface was minuscule.

"I will examine the launch area and prove my contention," said Beq. "There has been a serious and vexing mistake made by careless mechanicians."

Beq watched as several others of the ruling committee began their protests. Pride prevented them from analyzing the information available and coming to the same conclusion. It wished it might present the symbolic logic to prove the hypothesis of error but Beq knew this would mean nothing to most of the ruling committee. They lived in another world, and it was not a better one, Beq decided.

It pulled in tentacles finer than mist, solidified, and found an updraft at the side of the cavern. Whistling upward to the frigid surface through a lava chimney, Beq thrilled at the motion. But the instant it erupted into the atmosphere above the surface, Beq's mood turned somber.

Magnesium still burned and an odor both cloying and ugly hung in the air. Beq tried to moderate its gaseous intake from the surrounding contaminated air and failed. It felt sick to the core of its being.

Thinning to an arrow, Beq allowed the wind to take it on a roundabout path to the launch area where it—the parent-Beq—had watched the launching of the first chaos field weapon.

Past the areas melted to slag Beq flew; it knew intense sorrow. What destruction had been wrought on the rugged lava flows that nourished it! Beq did not understand the purpose of this conflict, but it felt no emotion concerning its unleashing of chaos on the fixed form enemy. Any creature who burned and left behind such destruction was not worthy of its pity—or mercy.

Beq tightened its gaseous body into a sphere and plunged downward. Finding a sudden cross current, Beq surged around and through black lava arches ammonia winds had eroded over the centuries. A particularly warm pillar drew it. Beq turned more bulletlike and shot through a tight entry port and into a small cavern populated by a dozen of its kind.

"Beq," greeted a mechanician. "Your spawn-twin . . ."

"Perished," Beq said, cutting off the mechanician's words. It had no desire to linger on personal tragedy. If its questioning uncovered the facts, the ruling committee could correct these mechanicians' errors and such space bombardment would cease. No more of their precious population need die.

"Condolences," said the mechanician.

"Accepted. I wish to study records of the launching."

"Of the chaos field? Or the defense system?"

"The former. The ruling committee already knows of the defense system's failure. It has been thrust upon me to determine why you have not carried out your duties."

"Not so!" protested the mechanician. "We toil diligently!"

"You fail. No other explanation is possible for the enemy's penetration of our system."

"They have new countermeasures that bypass our equipment's detection spectrum," said the mechanician. The sullenness in its voice convinced Beq that the mechanician did not truly believe this.

"The records."

Beq drifted behind the mechanician to a large metal data plate etched with acid. A quick glance satisfied Beq.

"This is incomplete. There are other records. Bring them."

"The other plates have been lost. During the attack. Magnesium has eaten through some and . . ."

The mechanician's voice trailed off. Silence descended on the chamber, leaving only the mournful whine of the ammonia wind whipping in from outside to fill the void. The mechanician knew how feeble this excuse sounded. Both it and Beq knew what had really occurred. No record had been kept—or the records had been purposefully destroyed to prevent punishment for inefficiency.

"Send for *all* records," ordered Beq. It had no desire to serve on the ruling committee, but it would perform its duties well as long as it remained in that position.

The mechanician hurried off so quickly that it left portions of its body behind. Beq rippled and pressurized at such unseemly haste. To weaken the body by such a maneuver usually indicated that a new spawn struggled to recover full control of its functions. For this ancient and unspawned mechanician to do so betold more than inefficiency. Beq began to consider the possibility of severe physical and mental dysfunction in the mechanician.

Beq spent the two planetary revolutions that the mechanician was gone thinking. Its mind manipulated esoteric mathematical concepts, worked on more profound philosophical levels, then erased all from its brain and tried the most simplistic solutions available.

Beq did not like the answer that recurred. No matter what level it tackled the question, an approximation of the same answer provided full explanation.

"Here," said the mechanician, returning with two large plates. It dropped the data into Beq's shadow, a definite breach of etiquette. Beq started to chastise the mechanician, then subsided. A member of the ruling committee might be merciful—and Beq had to admit that the mechanician might not be responsible for its behavior.

Another major ripple, this time accompanied by both pressurization and a flash of reds and greens. Not to be responsible. Beq barely comprehended the enormity of such a concept, yet it was mathematically probable.

It turned to the data plates, computing, comparing the data against its own inherited memory of the chaos field launching, then indulged in wilder speculation. Beq settled around a warm lava pillar made radioactively unstable by application of the chaos field, then began intense calculation.

Beq reconstructed even the most minute detail of the launch. Its own calculations had shown how it was possible for radioactive isotopes to be formed; the direct interaction of field with certain elements produced artificial warmth no less nourishing than that seeping through the crustal plates from the planet's core. But something more now surfaced in Beq's computation.

"The radioactivity cannot be generated indefinitely," it decided. The action of the field with itself produced instability, uncertainty—chaos. The symmetry of radioactive decay and formation could not be supported by the moving field. The probabilities being altered in one direction were also altered in the other. The chance for radioactive decay was changed in precisely the same way that radioactive formation was.

"This violates the concept of chaos," mused Beq. Its equations predicted much. But it had erred in this matter, overlooking higher order solutions to the nonlinear equations. "The field decays because of its own action on space around it," concluded Beq.

It shuddered at this. The launching of the chaos weapon had ruined the surveillance system put into space to defend their planet—and the system had been installed *after* the chaos field had been launched and sent toward the enemy's home world. Residual chaotic effects lingered, ones Beq had not considered.

"I am responsible," it said.

"What? You are the one who allowed the enemy to attack?" demanded the mechanician. "You sabotaged our defenses?"

"No, not directly." Beq still worried over the mechanician's instability of personality and body. Hazy wisps swirled from the mechanician's hintermost tendril. "Were you present at the launching of the field weapon?"

"I was in charge." The mechanician looked like a spawn-parent, almost splitting entirely in half. Only great concentration forced the halves into a coherent whole.

"Are you well?" asked Beq. "Your substance appears thin, as if you require rest and sustenance." How the mechanician could lack for nourishment with the chaotically created radioactive pillar in its workshop was more than Beq could understand—unless the chaos field had worked on the mechanician, turning it into something not quite sane.

"Do you often leave your workshop?" asked Beq.

"I never leave," came the expected answer.

Beq settled and began calculating the residual field effect and how this would translate into erratic behavior in the mechanician. When the results fell out of the intricate and esoteric mathematics, Beq almost turned and caught an updraft to flee.

"This is a dangerous place. The residual chaotic effects are causing great damage, not only to you and your staff, but to everything you manufacture in this chamber."

"The weapon has ruined my defense system?" The mechanician's voice came out thin, high-pitched, unbelieving. "That's not possible. I built well. I am responsible for failure! *I* certified the system. I did. I did!''

Before Beq could issue the words to calm the mechanician, the creature spun through its workshop, whirling about faster and faster until it formed a vortex. Never had Beq seen this, though it had always believed the act possible.

The mechanician killed itself by spinning faster and faster until the radial acceleration overcame the weak intermolecular binding forces holding it in a coherent, thinking, living being. Veils of the creature's being spun away from the core to spread moisture-thin on the chamber's rocky walls.

Beq watched in horror, then calmed. The spectrum of emotion flashing along its gaseous shell faded. Beq realized that death had become commonplace on this world. If the enemy did not kill instantly, then madness did slowly.

Madness Beq had created using the chaos field. Something had altered the flow of energy in the mechanician and caused it to perform aberrant acts. The suicide Beq had just witnessed was only the finale.

What else had the mechanician done? Beq began to study the data plates more intently, trying to understand from what was omitted as much as what had actually been inscribed.

As if liquid helium had been pumped along its ventral side, Beq found what it had feared. The mechanician had made mistake after mistake, then altered the records to hide it. Society had been served when the mechanician had died, Beq realized. But the effects of the chaos field lingered and contaminated planet and population.

Beq finished within four revolutions of the planet about its distant primary, a quick study for the seriousness of the matter. It left the workshop, with the other mechanicians drifting aimlessly, all upset at the loss of their master. Beq neither knew nor cared if those others had been tainted by its creation. The damage had been done. It had loosed a weapon against their enemy—and that weapon had changed like a thing alive, evolving, mutating.

The chaos field did not live, Beq knew. But it changed because of its own nature. It had been constructed and launched to slowly destroy the enemy. It now destroyed itself as it spun through space, changing its internal structure, randomly altering the equations that governed it. Beq no longer predicted the weapon's course or its function. Whatever it did, it did with the full power of chaos behind it.

Beq soared on the ammonia winds, thrilling to the feel. Duty lay in reporting to the ruling committee, but for a moment it could float and soar and experience this animalistic delight.

For a moment. Then Beq, the most able mathematician of an entire race, worked through the intricate symbolic logic that provided answers to profound questions.

Beq understood the mechanician's suicide in that instant of surfacing knowledge. Beq surged higher, body becoming increasingly tenuous and mental responses more primitive. By the time Beq's substance dissipated totally on the upper winds and it joined the mechanician in a newer, higher plane, it had forgotten—almost—about the chaotic horror it had unleashed on the galaxy.

TWO

MICHAEL RALSTON SPUN around in his chair and stared out the small window behind his desk. The peace of the University of Ilium seemed limitless, but Ralston knew that increasingly vicious riots had been raging for days. This lush, green campus only rested before a new bout of unrest seized it.

Ralston reached over and tugged at the mechanical latch on the window, an anachronism that branded him as strange among his peers. Every other professor in the archaeology department had scenic views of mountains or oceans or special displays of far-off worlds to stare at when they daydreamed. Many ordered the scene changed on a daily or weekly basis to duplicate extensive travel. One even insisted that his primary off-world dig sites be displayed so that he could enter his office and be "inspired" anew.

Ralston snorted as he thought of Velasquez and the discoveries he'd made on Proteus. A ancient post-spaceflight culture on that planet, yes, but nothing that special. But Velasquez carried the discovery to absurd and pointless heights. To hear him talk, anyone would think that Proteus was *the* discovery of the century.

Ralston fought with the latch and worried the window open on aluminum tracks that galled with every movement and resisted his desire for clean air not from an air conditioner. A soft breeze holding the promise of a mild winter blew in, caught up a miniature tornado of papers on his desk, and further scrambled their order. Ralston ignored this natural refiling. He hiked his feet to the windowsill and tried to relax.

"Dammit," he muttered. "Velasquez *hasn't* made the discovery of the century. *I* have!" Ralston folded arms across his broad chest and tossed back his head, moving an annoying lock of hair from his eyes. The work he'd done under time pressures in the Alpha system constituted major discoveries on a dozen different fronts. The Alphans had been a pre-space culture propelled into sublight star travel to escape the plague of chaos that had touched their planet.

Either the Alphans' escape to the Beta system *or* the disruption of their culture due to the passage of the chaos device should have firmly established Ralston's career. The death of a graduate student on Alpha had brought only notoriety and censure—and no fame. By the time Ralston had smoothed over the trouble with the University and the student's influential family and returned to Alpha, the pre-nova condition in the system's primary had progressed too far.

The star exploded, Ralston and his students and the solar observers escaping only hours before. Nels Bernssen had become a shining light in astrophysics because of his observations. Ralston had been ignored, even though his work had uncovered an Alphan telepathic device used in their museums for teaching purposes. His most promising graduate student's father now controlled development and marketing of the device for the University. Dr. Michael Ralston did not figure in Leonid Disa's plans, academically or otherwise.

Ralston sighed. As for his graduate student, Leonore Disa, she and Nels Bernssen would soon be married. She had successfully written and defended her thesis and had earned her doctorate, in spite of the sorry reputation of her advisor.

For that, Ralston was happy. Leonore deserved her degree and the stature due her in archaeology. Her work had been exemplary. Her advisor's problems with the University chancellor, the others in the archaeology department, and the campus in general shouldn't reflect badly on her.

Still, Ralston felt cheated. Everyone prospered and he languished in disgrace. Leonore had her degree. Bernssen had become a celebrity from formulating his Bernssen Condition for Stellar Instability. And a university mathematician, Westcott, had more data from the chaos device than he could analyze in a lifetime of work.

The chaos device.

"Dammit!" shouted Ralston. His feet fell to the floor and he bent forward, chin on crossed arms as he stared across the campus Quadrangle. The chaos device had been his discovery— and it was the most significant archaeological discovery of all time. Was it a weapon gone awry? Was it an attempt to communicate that had proven more dangerous than informative? What was it?

What?

Every chance for investigation of the device had been ripped away from him. The Alpha primary had gone nova, destroying all evidence of the device's passage through that system. The Beta system's primary showed Bernssen Condition Instability; that sun would soon explode and erase all evidence of the device's passage.

"Hell and damnation, I can't even convince Chancellor Salazar that the University ought to help the people on Beta 7." Ralston had found not only the remains of the Alphan refugees on Beta 5 but also evidence of other colonization. The gas giant Beta 7 had proved the home for those creatures, more fluid than material—and of truly alien concerns. They knew that their star's lifetime was measured in short years. And they did not care. The being responsible for the colonization was considered insane for unsocial activities of experimentation, inquiry and exploration of other planets, construction of satellite bases.

"Too many alien races to aid, Salazar says," grumbled Ralston. "Can't afford it now. Hell, let him take one percent of what he and Disa make off the telepathic projector and they could finance the start of an evacuation program."

Ralston stopped mumbling, knowing that this wasn't possible. Evacuating an entire culture—and one so physically and mentally alien—proved beyond the resources of any world, much less a single university. But Ralston hated the callous attitude shown by Salazar and the others. In part it came from their dislike for him. Repeatedly, they had denied him tenure. With Velasquez back from his easy excavation on Proteus 4, the chancellor would see to removing Ralston permanently from the faculty. The only thing that had stopped Salazar previously was the lack of qualified personnel to teach.

"Cancel even one class," said Ralston to himself in a mocking, sarcastic tone, "and the department loses precious grant money. And that casts a bad light on everyone in the University community." Keeping Ralston on had proven financially advantageous. Firing him immediately and cancelling the three courses, he taught would have cost the archaeology department grants equal to a full third of their trivial annual budget for research.

Ralston jerked around when his message terminal beeped that mail awaited his attention. He reached over and began digging in the stacks of old books and papers that hadn't been moved by the wind gusting through the window. He located the computer terminal and quickly scanned the message flashing on the screen.

"About time," he said. Ralston had submitted a survey paper to the *Novo Terra Journal of Field Archaeology* covering the impact of the chaos device on the Alphan culture, how it had induced a mass insanity and brought about epileptic seizures. With it accepted, Ralston felt confident that a series on the Alphans could be run.

Only now did he have the time to sift through the photos of their ruins, the computer data about the artifacts found, their distribution and importance—and the all-important telepathic projection equipment discovered in the subterranean museum. Ralston had a lifetime of papers to write and had just scratched the surface.

"Let's see when they'll publish." With the *Journal*'s reputation for promptness, he hoped to see it on the network before the end of the month. Ralston smiled as he pressed the "accept" button to signal willingness to read the message.

The smile faded as Ralston scanned the rejection. At first, he thought it was a terrible joke. Bernssen had been known to play pranks. Maybe Leonore had helped him with access codes. Ralston read the message again and found the verification number. No matter how elaborate Bernssen got with his sophomoric practical jokes, he'd be hard-pressed to fake one of this magnitude.

Ralston knew that the journal rejection was real long sec-

onds before the computer verified transmission from the publication office. Ralston swept some of the books from the
keyboard and began tapping in an angry response. Almost
instantly came the reply.

Ralston didn't know which he hated worse. The speed of
the answer told him that someone gleefully awaited his protest. That was bad. What Ralston came to realize was the
ultimate in professional assassination was a refereed journal
refusing his work, not because of anything wrong with his
paper but because it had been Michael Ralston submitting it.

"Go on, give me a hearing," he said savagely as he filled
in the exception request on the computer. Ralston snapped the
terminal off when the exception was noted and rejected, again
almost instantaneously.

They had cut him off in all directions, and there was
nothing he could do about it. Chancellor Salazar didn't have
to grant tenure, especially if no one spoke strongly in Ralston's
favor. The journal didn't have to accept his paper unless the
"impartial" referee approved it as being original work of a
professional quality.

Ralston's finest discoveries were being reburied because no
one approved of him personally.

Ralston spun around and glowered at the peaceful campus,
as if accusing it of originating his problems. In a way, it only
reflected the world Ralston had come to hate so much. He
enjoyed teaching; he hated the petty bureaucrats in administration. Nothing thrilled Ralston more than digging at a site,
finding secrets of civilizations long dead, and returning their
glory to the full sight of interested scholars. But the delight he
took in such discovery dimmed when he dealt with the politics of tenure and publication.

He could protest. The system allowed that. But Ralston
knew it'd do him little good. The very people listening to his
complaints were the ones responsible for them.

Ralston knew it would be a long, long time until he headed
another expedition. And he had to! The chaos device swung
through the galaxy on a trajectory calculated by Westcott
from the archaeological information. That device had to be
studied. It had destroyed countless suns through induced chaotic instability. Ralston knew of two cultures it had either

destroyed or soon would. The Alphans had died out to the last being. The Betans on their gas giant world, so different from Alphan or human, would soon follow.

Had there already been Gammas and Deltas and Epsilons? More? How many intelligent beings had perished because of the synaptic disruption that was the chaos device's illegitimate legacy?

Ralston chafed that he'd not get the opportunity to study the device for information about the race that had constructed it—and Betan observations had confirmed that it was, indeed, artificial. Why would any society build such a device?

Ralston had to know. He had to.

Ralston walked across the deserted Quadrangle, hands jammed deep into pockets. In the distance he heard the loudspeakers at work whipping student radicals into a frenzy. He shook his head. He knew the source of that unrest. It wasn't the students' fault as much as it was the single P'torra who always lurked near the edge of those riots, impulse driver in hand. The constantly striving P'torra used the computer device to assay the emotions and emotional potential of a crowd, then carefully manipulated the factors feeding the unrest. A deft P'torra might be able to bring an entire city to the point of anarchy—and most humans refused to believe this.

Ralston knew. Only too well, he knew. He had fought in the Nex-P'torra war on the side of the reptilian Nex rather than with the humanoid P'torra. That was another bone of contention on campus. For all their vaunted open-mindedness, few of the professors were willing to be seen with non-humanoid aliens. Ralston had tried to assure them that the Nex were more like humans psychologically than the P'torra, but outward shape mattered more to those bigots.

Ralston had seen the planets laid waste by the P'torra bio-weapons. He could never align himself with a race capable of such emotionless genocide.

The sound of speeches reached a crescendo, then faded. Ralston tried not to strain to hear what was being said. He knew most of it by heart. The lone P'torra on campus had directed more than one crowd against Ralston in the past months, more for practice than out of true malice. Ralston wasn't even sure the P'torra had emotions—certainly they lacked compassion and love and other feelings Ralston counted as necessary for a human to be truly human.

He pushed the thought of the humanoid aliens from his mind and found that he kept returning to the rejected scientific paper. Ralston wasn't sure which he preferred to seethe about the most. The journal rejecting his work simply because it had been Dr. Michael Ralston who had submitted it cut deep into pride and ego and the need to inform others of the danger brought by the chaos device.

But the P'torra had been more active and it would only be a matter of time before the alien turned the rioting against him personally, if for no other reason just because he was here and a known opponent from a war long declared a stalemate.

"What's the old saying?" he wondered aloud, trying to remember what a medieval literature professor friend of his sometimes said. "Nuking fish in a pond. That's how hard it will be to get rid of me. If Salazar doesn't do it first, the P'torra definitely will."

Ralston stopped and stared at the building he had unconsciously walked toward. The laboratory building stood silent, classes over for most students who actually attended the University to use the expensive lab equipment. Ralston sighed. Most of his students had chosen the transmission option, preferring to stay at their homes and watch his lectures via satellite link. Only those in lab courses routinely attended now, even though Ralston wished all would physically attend. Something about the actual bodily presence of students inspired him to put more into his lectures than if he simply spoke to a flat, cold, gray electroceramic camera eye.

But this building housed Westcott's lab. Ralston didn't like Westcott—that understated his feelings. He disliked the man intensely and, if Ralston had an honest instant, admitted to fearing him. Ralston went inside and climbed the stairs to Westcott's second-floor lab. He paused uncertainly outside the battered wood door with the red sign ordering everyone away.

He didn't want to talk to Westcott. If he never saw the man

again it'd be a century too soon, but Ralston recognized within him the need for some human contact.

If talking with Westcott could be called human contact. If Westcott could be called human, he mused.

Ralston took a long, deep, calming breath and found it did nothing to still his racing pulse. The last time he had barged into Westcott's lab, he had found himself floating endlessly between the stars, cut off from gravity and sight and all reality. Westcott had reduced unwanted sensory input so that he could listen to data turned into musical tones, seeking the proper relationship aurally rather than visually. Ralston opened the door, peered in, and saw a dim light, which was all Westcott ever tolerated, but no fantastic stellar display.

He went in, still cautious.

Westcott sat hunched over a table, arms thrown limply on the surface. Three different computer screens were turned so that Westcott sat in the center of this electronic spiderweb. Ralston's eyes immediately traced across the room to a large computer with a single infrared communications link atop it. The baleful red of the com-link told that Westcott was connected directly to the computer, the artificial circuitry imbedded in his head translating the superspeed input into slower terms Westcott's brain could handle.

Ralston held back the shudder of distaste. Few people were given permits authorizing the surgery that directly linked them to a computer. Westcott's framed license hung on the wall, the only decoration visible in the dreary lab.

Ralston avoided walking through the IR linkage. Westcott always complained that interruption of data flow gave him a headache. Ralston stood and waited for the mathematician to notice him; something that might take hours if Westcott was engaged in complex equations.

Almost immediately, though, Westcott looked up, his eyes slightly glazed as if he'd been taking drugs. Ralston knew better. The only reason Westcott would ever indulge was to speed up the computer-mind communication, and Westcott had said repeatedly that drugs dulled the edge, not sharpened it. The cause turning Westcott's face slack lay within the total isolation from reality. Westcott forgot the world around him and lived only within the speed-of-light constraints of the computer's immense memory.

"Pretty," said Ralston, indicating all three screens. "I don't recognize the patterns. Did you create them?"

"Chaos," murmured Westcott. "Those are the colors of chaos."

"What?"

"I needed some method for watching how the equations vary when I make small changes in a single parameter. The colors change, making the effect obvious."

"Oh." Ralston knew that the intricate chaos equations Westcott had mastered permitted no deviation in boundary conditions. The slightest change might bring about catastrophic results—hence the name "chaotic." A system of nonlinear differential equations could be set up deterministically describing a thundercloud—and the beating of a single butterfly's wing at the edge could produce lightning by introducing a new parameter.

What Westcott studied was the flap of such a wing.

"The colors tell you how fast the equations go to infinity?" asked Ralston.

"Yes, hmm, yes," said Westcott, his eyes focusing on Ralston. The archaeologist wished the man would turn his attention elsewhere. Those eyes carried more than the seeds of madness within their depths.

"I use complex numbers in my equations, then take the sine of the number. Then I take the sine of that and plot it, then take sine of the result and if it is different, assign another color."

"If not?"

"The same color. It is possible for entire planes to be equivalent in my mapping schemes. But these, these are the ones of interest. The speed at which they diverge to infinity—or converge—tells me much."

Ralston knew that Westcott had made a reputation for himself in both physics and mathematics circles by accurately predicting which nucleus of a forty atom sample of uranium would decay. With this specific solution of the chaos equations, Westcott never missed. Radioactive decay had become predictable under stringent laboratory conditions. Ralston only vaguely understood the furor in quantum physics this created. Indeterminancy was being questioned, but Westcott had gone beyond this, ignoring critics, ignoring supporters, concentrating on newer and more intricate solutions to the equations.

Westcott mastered chaos slowly, turning it into a slave for the first time.

"For the second time," Ralston said to himself. "Whoever launched the chaos device knew how to . . ."

"The builders might have been lucky. It might be accidental."

"Do your equations prove this?"

"No, not really. Just a guess, a speculation. Too much has been happening. Look, look at this plot. I alternately take the sine and tangent of the complex number $z = 1 + 7i$ and plot those colors. It reveals much about the internal working of the device that has wrecked the stellar fusion mechanisms in the stars."

"It does?" Ralston stared at the pretty colors marching across the screen. They reminded him of Rorschach patterns more than anything else, but to Westcott they provided answers.

"Can you build a chaos device of your own?"

"No, that's beyond me, but the mathematics of it are becoming accessible. I understand more. A bit here, a bit there. I will soon understand it all."

Ralston didn't ask what happened when he did. Westcott's mind would turn to even stranger paths of knowledge, paths never imagined just a few short years earlier. Just a few hours earlier than Ralston's discoveries in the Alpha system of the chaos field and its effect on an entire society.

His anger mounted once more. Bernssen prospered. Leonore Disa got her degree. Westcott became even more renown in his field. The University got the use of the telepathic projector. Everyone but Michael Ralston profited from his discoveries!

Even worse, Ralston had to make them understand that the danger presented by the chaos device might transcend anything that had ever confronted mankind before.

Suns going nova, people developing epilepsy, brains malfunctioning, DNA patterns becoming confused and creating uncontrollable mutations—what else? The dangers screamed at him and no one listened. The others were too caught up in their fame and good fortune to listen to an intellectual pariah.

"Keep me informed of your progress," Ralston said. He could no longer stand the sight of Westcott and his shaved head with the IR probe obscenely protruding from the pate. He wasn't even sure he could stand himself. He had tried to touch some humanity in Westcott and failed, as he always had. Whether the failure rested on Westcott or himself, Ralston wasn't sure.

He wasn't even sure he cared.

Not with the universe in danger from the chaos device orbiting through the Orion spiral arm—where all known civilizations were clustered.

THREE

MICHAEL RALSTON CLOSED the lab door behind him with a click that sounded like a thunderclap of doom. He leaned back against the cool, varnished wood surface, sweat running in cold, itching rivers down his spine.

"Why?" he wondered out loud. Ralston had no easy answer for that question—no answer at all. He had been through so much and had profited little from it. What rewards that had come his way turned out to be insubstantial and even philosophical. Leonore Disa did well and prospered. Seeing a student succeed made him glow with achievement of a job well done. But Ralston couldn't deny that Leonore would have done well in any field she'd chosen. The daughter of one of the richest men on Novo Terra would never end up begging over the charity broadcasts.

Ralston heaved himself forward and took a deep, steadying breath. Feeling sorry for himself accomplished nothing. He wanted to rewrite the article he'd sent in to the *Journal* and see if another might take it. Salazar and the others couldn't have blacklisted him everywhere. If nothing else, a popularization might be good for the tri-vid. It had all the elements that amused the masses. Dying races, peril, derring-do. Ralston smiled as he thought of casting himself as the intrepid professor leading his stalwart band of investigators into the dangers found in the Alpha and Beta systems.

"If I don't stand a chance as professor, why not give acting a try?" The outrageous idea amused him so much that he whistled a bawdy song off-key by the time he descended the stairs and reached the side entrance to the laboratory building.

The whistling stopped when he heard the chants of the crowd. Ralston slipped behind a large pillar and looked around it cautiously. Some distance away a student stood on a makeshift dais and harangued his peers. The words rang clear and brittle. The hatred never stopped, even after the war had sputtered to an indecisive halt. Ralston considered this the major problem in the Nex-P'torra conflict's outcome. Neither side had won decisively. This left uncertainty in both the combatants and curious onlookers about who was "right," and it planted a seed of hatred to blossom again over the same issues.

Ralston had fought beside the reptilian Nex. He'd do so again, for the same reasons.

He felt the hairs on the back of his neck begin to rise at an unwanted presence behind him. Ralston turned and saw a P'torra standing a hundred meters away, stubby fingers working swiftly over the keys of the impulse driver resting in the broad palm of his hand. The professor didn't think the alien had seen him. The P'torra concentrated too hard on the input to his miniature psychological evaluator. The alien came to a decision, reached up, and spoke softly into the microphone concealed under a wrinkled lapel.

Ralston jerked around, eyes narrowed and intense. The leader of the demonstration continued his harangue but the mood of the crowd changed subtly. If Ralston hadn't known of the P'torra's prompting, he would have thought that the students had simply reached the boiling point on their own. That the P'torra had signaled the speaker told Ralston more. The P'torra had found the precise trigger to incite violence.

Ralston watched it erupt before his eyes. Captivated, almost hypnotized by the intensity of the riot, Ralston found himself following the mob of students across the Quadrangle and toward the administration building. Seeing their destination, Ralston hurried ahead, taking a shortcut that brought him into the long hallway leading to Chancellor Salazar's office.

Ralston skidded to a halt on the highly polished floor when he saw that he hadn't acted swiftly enough to warn the chancellor of the danger coming through his front doors. The students burst inside and smashed through the double doors leading to Salazar's office. Ralston slid into a doorway and watched.

There was nothing he could do, and in any case, he saw no reason to risk his life for Salazar's. If anything, his sentiments matched those of the students chanting for Salazar's resignation. The only drawback lay in the source of their desire. Ralston knew it came not from within themselves or out of shock and indignation at Salazar's policies but from the P'torra and his damnable computer.

Ralston recognized Salazar's secretary as the crowd tossed him from side to side. The man tried to escape but too many hands groped for him, each seeking another drop of blood, a tiny scratch of skin, a piece of clothing. Sobbing, the man fell to his knees. Ralston saw in that act a mistake that could mean his life.

The leader harshly commanded a small group to take the secretary away. They kicked and pommeled him before jerking him to his feet. The man stumbled a few paces; not wanting to wait for him to rise, they dragged him away, not caring that he bled from a dozen minor wounds or held his arm as if it had been severely injured.

Ralston heard the student leader's demands.

"Deal with us, Dr. Salazar, or you'll deal with history! We demand redress for all the evils committed by the University."

Ralston had no idea what evils these might be—probably imagined or even created by the P'torra. The University of Ilium had a reputation of being conservative and not a little cowardly when it came to facing difficult political decisions. His own problems with Salazar showed that the preferred solution was flight or subterfuge.

The professor slipped along the corridor, his click-click steps drowned out by the students' angry cries. Outside the administration building once more, Ralston circled and found the group of four students bullying Salazar's secretary. The four took turns beating the man. Ralston knew what good sense dictated. He should walk away, find a com unit, and summon the campus security force.

If he wanted to feel he was in some way getting back at

Salazar for sabotaging his career, he could let the pompous ass of a secretary take his licks and find some consolation in this.

Ralston did neither. Salazar ran from his problems or tried to get rid of them, never squarely facing anything of a complex moral nature. Ralston was of a different bent. He *had* to act.

One student's balled fist rose to descend on the side of the secretary's bloodied face. Ralston acted instinctively. His fingers closed around the young man's wrist, went along with the force of the blow, redirecting it only at the last possible instant. The fist missed the secretary's head—and sent the student stumbling facedown to the ground. Ralston didn't bother warning the other three.

He spun and kicked at a kneecap. The sudden yielding under his feet told him he'd broken the cartilage and need worry no more about this opponent. A short punch to the belly doubled over another. The remaining student came in from behind. Ralston drove his elbow back as hard as he could and impacted hard on the man's lowest rib. The jolt rocked Ralston forward even as it stunned the student.

Ralston recovered first. A fist driven into an exposed throat ended the fight.

Ralston looked around, a faint smile on his lips. He took no pleasure in fighting, especially when the others presented no real challenge. But they had shown no honor in ganging up on the secretary. The man lay on the ground, crying piteously.

"Are you all right?" Ralston asked. He turned the man over and probed with merciless fingers. The secretary winced but his reaction was one of anger, not pain. Nothing except for his right arm had been broken or even much damaged.

"Verd, I'm alive. Not much more." The man straightened painfully, then saw his rescuer. "You, I might have known," the secretary gasped between split lips. Blood trickled down his chin. He wiped it away, cringing at the pain this caused. "You're responsible. You sent them in to get me!"

Arguing would do no good. The man was Salazar's lackey. Let him think what he wanted. Ralston hadn't rescued him intending to get into Salazar's good graces. The secretary had been in trouble and for that reason alone Ralston had risked his own safety to aid him. Honor didn't require any more of Ralston.

He stood and peered down at the battered man. "The campus security will be here soon. I'm sure Salazar has alerted them, unless the crowd's managed to disrupt the com system."

Ralston didn't think that an impulsive riot would show such planning. After all, the P'torra merely flexed his muscles to see how far he could manipulate. The success or failure of the students and their protest meant nothing to him.

"I'll have you in remand for this, Ralston. I swear it! You're the one responsible for them doing this to me. They're only doing what you ordered them to do!"

Ralston walked away without turning back. Let the man think what he wanted. To Ralston it made no difference. His tenure at the University had been denied and they could dismiss him for any reason. Even with tenure, he wasn't sure that Salazar couldn't come up with adequate rationale to fire him.

"You need not have intruded into this exercise," came a soft voice that made Ralston spin about. The P'torra stood behind a waist-high bush of late-flowering thorny pyracantha. Ralston considered reaching out and grabbing the P'torra by the lapel— the one concealing the microphone—and pulling him face-first into the sharp spines. The P'torra seemed to understand the risk and stepped back.

"I shouldn't have meddled," Ralston agreed. "But some-times a man has to make a stand. This was a minor one."

"He is not worth your effort."

Again Ralston had to agree. "However, any effort against you is worthwhile."

"Your attitude is one I find hard to fathom." The P'torra pulled his impulse driver from a pouch at his belt. Fat, stubby fingers flew across the keys. What data went in or what results flashed on the tiny screen Ralston didn't know.

"How much longer are you going to incite the riots? I'd think burning down a building or two would be enough. Or must you kill a few administrators before your 'exercise' is finished?"

"Such bitterness, but then this is to be expected from you." The P'torra widened his stance and settled into what Ralston considered a defensive posture. To physically attack a P'torra required more than bare hands. The thick layer of subcutaneous fat insulated them from both temperature extremes and assault. A long, thin knife blade such as he'd carried as a soldier for the Nex would have worked nicely. Or even a more sophisticated sidearm.

"Interesting," said the P'torra, blunt fingers still working on the keys. "There seems to be no convenient verbal lever to employ against you."

Ralston started to agree, then bit back the words. The P'torra played on the sense of moral superiority Ralston felt over the alien. Any advantage for exploitation would be used. Any.

"There are levers in every human," said Ralston.

The P'torra smiled, thick lips rippling. He replaced the impulse driver in its pouch and said, "You are correct. All humans have emotions, and those emotions can be molded into patterns more in keeping with P'torra goals. It is difficult to maintain the level of involvement, however. You creatures have such a transient attention span."

"You mean we don't stay brainwashed."

"I am unfamiliar with this term, 'brainwashed.' "

"An old one from Earth describing what you're attempting." Ralston tried to decide if the P'torra had given him worthwhile information. Was he saying that the P'torra, once swayed, could not easily revert to their prior belief? It had always perplexed Ralston why the P'torra expended so much effort briefly altering human opinion. The P'torra might not be able to understand why their procedures worked for only short periods. Playing on emotion worked—until the emotion changed.

"What are you going to do with Chancellor Salazar?"

"I? I will do nothing with him. In fact, I have nothing against the man, in the sense you imply. It might surprise you to know that I have seen only pictures of him and have done nothing in the way of research about his policies. My project depends on isolated responses. Can I generate appropriate action from a limited number of stimuli. Actually patterning my programs on Dr. Salazar's record would introduce a variable I have no wish to correct for."

"Then all the rioting is purely academic?"

The P'torra's shoulders weren't designed for shrugging. He shuddered all over in a gesture Ralston equated with a shrug. "What else? I have no true desire to be on this filthy world of yours. Only to seek knowledge do I come here."

"When will the P'torra start a war against us?"

"Again, such bitterness. It comes from associating with slime creatures. They have affected your outlook on the universe, Dr. Ralston. You should choose your comrades more carefully."

The tone made Ralston even more cautious. He read into it a warning that had nothing to do with his past association with the Nex.

"You have nothing to fear from us," the P'torra went on. "We come only in peace." The smile this time revealed twin rows of needle-sharp teeth. The P'torra relaxed his defensive posture and waddled off in the direction of the administration building. The sound of security sirens filled the air, and the P'torra had work to do, things to learn, humans to manipulate.

Ralston idly rubbed a skinned knuckle across his shirt as he watched the P'torra cross the grassy area in front of the administration building. The veiled threat made little sense. Ralston shrugged it off. This might be nothing more than another verbal assault dictated by the P'torra's impulse driver, though Ralston had a deep-down feeling it was something more. He had no time to worry over such things.

He had classes to prepare for. A paper to rewrite. People to contact. If Salazar wanted rid of him, somewhere else on Novo Terra there must be a position that would allow him to continue his study of the chaos device.

More than the immediate threat posed by the P'torra, the chaos field or device or weapon—no matter how he thought of it—presented a world threat unparalleled in history. It had destroyed the Alphans, bringing about epileptic seizures in the people and stellar instability in an otherwise ordinary star.

The Betans would soon follow, dying in the hot embrace of their sun's explosion. Who else? How many other races had already died? How many more would perish because Ralston couldn't get anyone at the University to believe that this was a significant menace, something worthy of intense study?

The feelings of impotence returned.

Hands thrust into his pockets, Ralston walked aimlessly, unconsciously turning away from the loud noises of the crowd and the whine of security force sirens. He no longer had the morbid curiosity about the fate of Salazar and the others. If anything, he might find himself brought up on criminal charges when the beaten secretary gave his statement. Ralston had passed the point of caring.

All he wanted was to do archaeology. He had made the most significant finds of the century—perhaps of all time— and had garnered no recognition for it. He had to live off what sense of achievement he had inside. Worst of all, there was more work to do, exciting, fulfilling work.

The threat of the chaos device aside, who had built it? When? What was its purpose? What sort of being sent such a machine among the stars? Ralston wondered if it might be a mode of communication rather than a weapon of war. Different cultures saw menace in different things, communication in still others.

The Onslong culture of Gamma Triangulus 3 declared war by spraying scent into the air. The first human ambassadors had inadvertently started a war by wearing the wrong perfumes. One chameleon race Ralston had read about attached great importance to skin color. No human had been able to negotiate trade treaties with them because the coloration was wrong; however, scientific information was freely exchanged because the coloration was acceptable for this purpose.

Perhaps the chaos device wasn't even intended as a communique. It might have been built for some other purpose. But Ralston would never be able to study it and the machinery powering it without a fully funded expedition.

He heaved a deep sigh thinking that Leonid Disa might be the only available source of money for such a trip. Ralston hated dealing with the man. Interstellar Computronics hadn't become one of the largest corporations on Novo Terra without a sharp eye kept on profits. Anything funded by Disa through IC would become the company's property. The joint venture with the University on the telepathic projector showed Disa's astuteness in such matters. Ralston wondered how badly Salazar had lost out on that deal.

The very nature of the physical law-confusing properties of the chaos field made it dangerous to anyone contemptuous of its power. Leonid Disa was contemptuous of any power other than his own. Ralston had seen enough of the man to know this. It amazed the professor that the magnate's daughter had turned out to be so earnest and forthright in pursuing knowledge for its own sake. Leonore's need to unravel the mysteries of the past for the sheer job of *knowing* elevated her far above her father, as far as Ralston was concerned.

He'd ask Disa to fund the expedition only if there was no other way. And then Ralston would begin to make plans to destroy any information that might be exploited before it became dangerous.

Any device altering the chance properties of weather or radioactive decay or the stellar fusion process or even the way a human's mind functioned was not to be taken lightly.

Ralston stopped on a low hill and looked out over the campus. It had again become deceptively calm in the twilight. The riot had been successfully quelled, from the chancellor's viewpoint, Ralston guessed, in that no students were to be seen. This unrest could only lend impetus to those on the Committee on Academics wanting to conduct all classes via tri-vid and keep students off campus entirely.

Ralston shook his head. Lab courses were pale and second-rate when conducted for the students. Even with clever placement of the cameras, having the professor perform the experiments wasn't the same as hands-on experience for the student. Beyond this, Ralston preferred his students to be physically present in a classroom. It might be archaic but the interaction seemed more intense. The mere act of coming to the classroom also showed a modicum of dedication that wasn't there when a student need only turn on his set and watch from a tiny cubicle, perhaps halfway around the planet.

The professor knew all this was moot, at least as far as he was concerned. His career teaching at the University of Ilium had ended on a sour note.

Ralston sat down on the grass, noting how it had begun turning brown as winter's first breezes touched it. The sunset was particularly vivid, the high cirrus clouds catching the pink and purple along their feathery ice crystals.

The sunlight faded rapidly. Ralston decided he had much in common with it. His star was setting, too, and chilly winter was coming on. It would be a harsh battle from now on, away from the comforting cloister of academe.

But it was a battle that had to be fought. Michael Ralston had never turned away before from a fight for what he considered right. He wouldn't now.

He stood and brushed off the dried grass before starting down the hill. Less than halfway down, he paused, head cocked to one side. Something or someone moved through the bushes less then ten meters away.

He sniffed the air, trying to pick up the P'torra scent. Only crisp autumn smells found their way to his nose. More curious than apprehensive, Ralston moved along the path until he came to a tree with large overhanging branches. He never broke stride as he reached up and caught the thick lower limb and pulled himself upward. Many of the leaves had already fallen; this proved both a boon and a hindrance.

Although the leaves rustled dryly and gave scant protection from probing eyes, the sparseness allowed him to make his way along the limb without much noise. Ralston came to the end of the limb and dropped to his belly, arms and legs dangling. He waited.

For a few minutes, Ralston thought his senses had betrayed him, that he'd become too nervous over the encounter with the P'torra and the rioting students. Then came small slithering noises that told him something did follow.

Closely.

Ralston prepared to drop from the limb as the sound came ever closer in the darkness.

FOUR

A HISSING NOISE, hardly louder than the wind blowing through the upper leaves of the tree, reached Michael Ralston's ears. He tensed. The sound was a familiar one to him.

Ralston swung off the tree limb and dropped lightly to the ground, staying in a crouch. "Where are you?" he whispered.

The hissing came from his right. Ralston pivoted and stared directly into two peculiarly irised yellow eyes that burned with fanatical intensity. Ralston reached out slowly, his right hand palm up and fingers spread wide. A long black, forked tongue flicked out and damply touched each of his fingertips, then stroked roughly across his palm, sampling, scenting.

"Much time it has been, Ralston doctor."

Ralston stood slowly. A dark figure shot forward with incredible speed, brushed over his legs, and rose until the reptilian face behind those eyes was only a centimeter from his.

"Commander Slenth," greeted Ralston. "It's been over five years since I've seen you."

Ralston realized how much he had become reintegrated into human society when he recoiled slightly from the Nex when Slenth thrust out his own hand, palm up and slender, taloned fingers spread wide. Ralston swallowed hard and covered his surprise as he bent down and repeated the greeting given him. The alien's hand tasted slightly alkaline, but it was a flavor Ralston had come to tolerate during his tenure with the Nex fighting forces.

"Your tongue is wet and your courage high," Ralston said ritualistically.

"Danger leaps every spot about here," said Slenth. Ralston had expected an equally formal reply. That he didn't receive it constituted a major breach of Nex honor—unless Slenth's appraisal of the danger was accurate.

"What? The P'torra?"

"P'torra fish," the Nex agreed, adding the insult with some enthusiasm.

"We can go to my office and talk."

The Nex hesitated, then bobbed his slender head rapidly. Ralston swallowed again, realizing how comfortable he had become teaching at Ilium, seeing only his own species. Everything about the Nex struck him as odd now, alien and— evil. The thin-boned skull and close-set yellow eyes reminded him of desert lizards on burned-out Earth. Although the Nex stood less than shoulder high on Ralston, a long tail swished restlessly behind the muscled body. Taking that powerful appendage into account, the Nex would stretch longer than any two men of normal height. Slender arms almost laughably weak waved about wildly to show the true level of the reptile's consternation and the strong legs set Slenth to bouncing up and down.

Ralston wasn't sure how even a mother could love this brown-scaled reptilian nightmare. The dread and even fear inspired in most humans at the sight of the Nex were understandable and their inability to learn human syntax as well as the P'torra made the differences between the two races even more apparent.

Ralston paused for a moment. The Nex weren't as vocal as the P'torra because they depended on more primitive senses and their thought processes were markedly different. The greeting ritual was based more on scent and taste—virtually the same for a reptile—than word inflection and tone. The thrill of fear that had coursed through Ralston died down as he remembered the other things about the Nex, the reasons he had fought beside them.

Shape and sensory input had nothing to do with kindness and caring and, in spite of their outward appearance, true humanity. In the ways that counted most, the Nex were more human and humane than the diabolical P'torra.

"All places, the P'torra travel here. Must danger look out always," Slenth said.

"We're safe enough," said Ralston. "The P'torra spent the day causing riots. He'll be safely in his tank analyzing the results." Still, the professor kept a wary eye on any student he saw. Luckily, the campus security force had swept through and chased off most of the students. The Quadrangle lay cloaked in shadow and a silence both palpable and intimidating.

"Much more danger to me. To us," Slenth insisted. The reptile shrugged sloping shoulders to get his harness into place. Ralston noticed for the first time that Slenth's clothing concealed several flat energy packs. He failed to find the nozzles for the energy weapons those modules powered.

For Slenth to come into human society armed in this fashion told Ralston much. Slenth, like all Nex, observed human laws and mores scrupulously. No matter what indignities were heaped on him, the Nex stoically endured them, realizing that not everyone could accept him or his race easily. Unless Slenth had changed drastically in the years since Ralston had served with him, the Nex would never consider violence a way to settle a dispute with a human.

"Do you plan to use the weapon?" Ralston asked.

"If necessary. Many occurrences strangely happen often and dangerous to us recently."

Ralston wished he could speak Nex and eliminate the problems with deciphering all Slenth said, but two long years of attempts had availed him little. Only the most rudimentary Nex speech sounds could be reproduced by the clumsy human solid tongue. Slenth's delicate forked tongue darted out and both tips vibrated to produce a buzzing noise that Ralston recognized as one of intense impatience. Whatever bothered Slenth was not trivial in nature.

"In here." Ralston motioned toward the side door that led to a broad marble stairway spiraling around to the second floor where his office looked out over the Quad. Slenth tested the air with his sensitive tongue again, garnering scents and checking for danger. Only when his thin head bobbed quickly did Ralston go up the stairs. He trusted Slenth with his life. If the Nex sensed no danger, none would be waiting at the top of the stairs.

And none was. Each of Ralston's footsteps echoed hollowly down the deserted corridor. Slenth came behind, his footfalls gliding, making only small scratching noises as talons tapped into the hard flooring. Ralston went into his office and said, "Lights, minimum."

The computer obediently turned on the lights and kept them at a level that barely cast shadows. Ralston closed down the polarizer on the window to prevent anyone from across the Quad from seeing Slenth.

"Well?" asked Ralston. "You've come to ask a favor of me. What is it?"

"Humans eager worst to think of Nex. Cannot friends of old seek out others of same time?"

"That's not so, at least in my case, Slenth. You know that. Didn't we fight alongside each other in dozens of battles as comrades?" Ralston leaned back in his chair, eyes half closed as he remembered. The Nex preferred physical confrontation while the P'torra were more devious. The P'torra might infect an entire planet's population with their bio-weapons, but the Nex mind concentrated on frontal assaults, definite battles with precisely defined strategic outcomes. The Nex fleet had landed shock troops on many planets, and on scores of battlefields he and Slenth had fought side by side, sometimes victorious, many times not.

The P'torra had been successful in their use of impulse drivers to turn the very populations they slowly destroyed against the Nex, who might have saved them. This irony had never been lost on Ralston.

"We are friends," Ralston agreed, "but we were more. You were a surrogate for my brother."

"Must we pay respect to dead?" asked Slenth.

"My brother's long dead back on Earth. I meant that I think of you as a brother now." Ralston saw that such a concept meant nothing to Slenth. It never had. Slenth had forty brothers and sisters, all hatched in the same egg-laying season. The Nex shared no familial ties but were strongly bonded to their race. Ralston considered doing a social anthropology paper on this, then discarded the notion as a harmless fantasy. Field archaeology mattered more to him; he had devoted his life to learning what he could of ancient cultures and the process of uncovering the tiny hints that would make those lost races come alive once more, even if only in the pages of some scholarly archaeology journal.

"It's been a long time since we spoke, Slenth. Only a matter of some importance could bring you to Novo Terra. I know how the others treat you. There's no reason to endure that simply to visit me."

Ralston said nothing about skulking around in the dark—armed with the most deadly portable weapons available to modern science.

"Much there is to your work, Ralston. We must never the P'torra allow possession of it."

"You don't want the P'torra to get my work? You've heard of the telepathic projector?"

Slenth rocked his head from side to side indicating Ralston has missed the point.

"It'll be a great benefit. You can train troops even more quickly," said Ralston, remembering the long months he'd spent with Nex psychologists when they hypnotically condition-ed him to endure the rigors of interstellar battle. "You can teach your young in a fraction of the time. There is even . . ."

Ralston's words trailed off when he saw Slenth's expres-sion. The burning yellow eyes blazed behind a nictitating membrane. Slenth tensed for battle.

Wordlessly, the Nex drew a small aluminum box from under a cloth covering. A single red light shone. Slenth's taloned finger stroked the side of the box and the light went out. In a gesture he borrowed from his human comrade, Slenth placed that same finger upright across his lips to caution Ralston to silence.

Mouthing the words, Ralston said, "Someone is eaves-dropping?"

Slenth nodded vigorously.

Ralston turned to his computer console and began tapping in a sequence of numbers. Over the years, he'd had students barely able to pass his course. He'd exchanged long hours of personal tutoring to get them through his class with minimal passing grades for their expertise in other areas. Mostly,

Ralston had been interested in the University computer system and more than a few of his trouble students had been geniuses when dealing with the network.

One had set up a special account for him that dipped into strange places. Ralston now examined the campus security force's use of the computer system. A parade of numbers dashed across the console. Ralston had to turn to a reference book on the shelf next to his desk and spend several minutes searching until he found matching sequences.

He indicated to Slenth that they should leave. In the hall outside his office, Ralston said, "Security has Chancellor Salazar's permission to spy on me. That was their authorization code. Do you know how they were listening in?"

"Most smaller devices, both sound and looking. They know I and you talked."

"Why didn't you pick up their cameras when we went in?" Ralston had no idea what the small box was that Slenth carried, but he knew it must contain elaborate counterelectronic equipment. The Nex had always been masters at miniaturization and computer technology.

"Microburst reports only sometimes sent. Uncontinual makes difficult to detect."

Ralston thought about the situation. Salazar had violated his rights by authorizing the security force to spy on his office, but this wasn't a matter of any interest to Slenth. It was peripheral to the Nex's purpose for visiting.

"If not the telepathic projector, then what?" asked Ralston.

Slenth cast a quick look at his detector; the red light stayed dark. "The destructor for planets and stars found by you."

"I found nothing of the sort," started Ralston. Then he knew that Slenth meant the chaos device.

The archaeology professor went cold inside. He had wanted to keep the secrets locked within the chaos field away from Salazar and the University because of how they might be misused. He had not thought in broad enough terms, though. He had been too wrapped up in academic politics to remember what the universe did with real weapons. What would the P'torra give for a weapon that could cause a sun to go nova? Or that induced epilepsy in an entire population?

What would the Nex do with that same weapon?

The Nex-P'torra war had petered out and the resolution had been unsatisfactory to both sides, but it had seemed better to cease hostility rather than continue the world-draining interstellar battles. The expense had been great, both in lives and resources. The war had continued, but without casualties that could be tallied and buried. The Nex and the P'torra engaged in trade fights and sabotage that stopped short of sparking another round of open fighting.

Would the Nex use the chaos field against the P'torra home planet?

"Some too fearsome weapons better much to kept away from P'torra," said Slenth, answering Ralston's unspoken question. "That is only Nex goal."

"You're proposing yourselves as caretaker for it?"

Slenth rocked his head in negation. "We need knowledge to prevent P'torra from gaining knowledge. They never against any to use it if Nex hold secret, too."

"A balance of terror is what you're saying. If both sides have the weapon, then neither will use it for fear that the other will retaliate." Ralston watched as Slenth bobbed his head in agreement. "That won't work. It never has."

Ralston closed his eyes and pictured the blackened cinder of Earth. Most of the northern hemisphere had been burned away in short, vicious exchanges. Much of the southern hemisphere and the points just within the arctic circle had been spared. Ralston had been lucky, escaping death through a quirk of fate, but the rest of his family had perished in the first blasts.

"Of Earth history we know well. What else dare we seek to pursue? If P'torra gain use of your device, how many hours go by until against us they use it?"

In that Slenth spoke the truth. The P'torra would never be content to sit on a weapon that potent. If they saw the chance to dominate totally, they would never hesitate.

"It may not even *be* a weapon," protested Ralston. He fell silent when he realized that the race's motive for constructing the chaos field did not enter the argument. No matter what the builders had intended for their device, it could be used as a weapon. Ralston felt more confident with it in Nex hands than in the control of the P'torra, but he wanted neither to use it for destruction.

It brought death and ruin wherever its field touched, but the knowledge to be gained from it was immense. Westcott had spoken of more accurate weather control through predictions based on the equations governing the chaos field. Ralston hoped that epileptic seizures might become predictable using the same mathematics. Hadn't Westcott already successfully predicted which atoms in a radioactive source would decay? What power lay within that? Ralston didn't know, but it couldn't be strictly destructive. The knowledge that threatened destruction could also promise life and a better world.

It had to, or Ralston had no idea what the true purpose of science was.

"This Salazar you as a swimming fish treats you," pointed out Slenth. "P'torra roam at will trouble to cause everywhere. All your peers are scorn filled of you. Give us the knowledge!"

Ralston rubbed his hand over dried lips. He began pacing in the hallway, worrying about the spy devices in his office, Chancellor Salazar, the University and its student unrest, his own career, what unwanted power he controlled. Even the Archbishop agitated against him for his past alliances with the Nex. No matter where Ralston turned in the niche of society he had wanted to call his own, people denounced him. Given enough time, the P'torra would turn the small crowds against him. What had happened to Salazar's secretary would be only the beginning.

Ralston shivered lightly at the thought of being ripped apart by a mob while the P'torra tapped in statistical analyses of the death into his impulse driver.

"I fought alongside the Nex because few other humans would. But I fought as much for them as I did for you. No matter how they behave, I'm not turning my back on them."

"They in the back give you a deadly shot," said Slenth.

"Possibly. Probably. But I can't give you the information you want." Ralston smiled without humor. "I can't give it to the P'torra, either. I simply don't have it. The University would have to fund a considerable expedition to gain such knowledge. Perhaps it's for the best that Salazar denied me funding. Let's leave the chaos device orbiting through space, its secrets untouched.''

"Nex will for you give money funds to examine.''

The light shiver became a cold shudder of dread. Ralston had gone from having no source of funding to one posing a difficult moral dilemma. The Nex were an honorable race but Ralston didn't want the chaos artifact to be turned into a weapon, even by those he had fought alongside. Better to let it continue through space untouched.

"Many know of this exact orbit chaos machine through space?'' asked Slenth.

Ralston stared into the reptile's unblinking yellow eyes. Slenth knew as much about the chaos device as any of those on the expeditions, Ralston saw. Was this the source of the P'torra's veiled warning about choosing companions? The P'torra would want the weapon as much as the Nex. Perhaps more.

Michael Ralston couldn't give it to either.

"Not many,'' said Ralston. "I've made no attempt to keep it a secret, but the chancellor saw fit to ignore much of my report. Nels Bernssen must have mentioned it in his papers and seminars. Leonore Disa has, also, though her thesis did not specifically refer to it.''

"P'torra must not possess secret of randomness,'' said Slenth. The reptile's talons clicked on the floor to emphasize his concern. "Must *never* learn of its nature.''

Ralston struggled to find the words to tell his friend and comrade in arms that the Nex weren't likely to get it from him when a soft click alerted him. He swung around. In the shadows at the far end of the hall he saw a darker figure. A glint of light caught the focusing magnetic muzzle of an energy weapon.

Without thinking, Ralston threw his arms around Slenth and drove forward as hard as he could. The two of them smashed hard into the wall just as a sizzling blue torrent of energy ripped through the space where Ralston had been.

Slenth's reaction time far exceeded that of Ralston. The Nex slithered out of the grip, dropped to the floor, and had his own weapon in action before Ralston could recover his senses. The acrid tang of ozone from the heavy electrical discharges filled the corridor. Ralston stayed low and wiggled toward his office door, pushing it open and getting into the office. The once sturdy-seeming walls of academe would provide no protection against the energy weapon trained on him, but Ralston still felt safer out of sight inside his office.

The computer console blinked slowly, numbers still solemnly marching across the screen. Whoever had put the spy devices in his office now alerted campus security about the brief firefight in progress. Would this save them—or doom them?

"P'torra!" came Slenth's voice. The Nex spit out the name as if it were a curse.

"I thought so. I only caught a glance of him, and he was in the shadows. The focusing muzzle was distinctive, though."

Ralston ventured a quick look around the doorjamb. Slenth had taken cover across the hall behind an uncollected trash receptacle. Down the hall in the shadows came no hint of movement or sound. Ralston waited a few seconds while Slenth's tongue flicked into the air, sampling for the odor of a P'torra.

"Gone," said the Nex. "We must, too. Come and go let us now. Trouble all about."

"Campus security's on its way," said Ralston. "We should wait for them."

"Wait and be ambushed?"

"What do you mean? They won't harm either of us." Ralston's irritation rose to protest such an absurd notion on his friend's part. Salazar and his campus security force might not approve of his archaeology professor and none would like the Nex, but the security force wouldn't harm them.

"What with us will they require?"

"Nothing. We'll have to fill out endless forms but . . ."

"Where to fill such forms out will we go?"

"The main office for security. Across the Quad."

"In wait will P'torra lie to kill us dead. From ambush the fish egg spawn will shoot."

Ralston couldn't answer that, but he did know that no human on the campus force would allow Slenth to keep his energy weapon. Removing it from a dead Nex would be preferable to Slenth simply surrendering it, Ralston knew.

And with all the campus rioting, he had no doubt that the security force would come well armed and ready for a fight. The message flashing on his screen to the University computer would definitely have reported energy weapons discharge—that might incite the campus force to request militia backup.

"Do you want to track down the P'torra?" Ralston asked.

"We must. It kills from back shooting positions. Try to stop P'torra is only course of real logic."

"I don't know how much help I can give you. I don't have a weapon." Ralston remembered his thoughts earlier about attacking the P'torra with his bare hands. The thick blubbery hide would protect the P'torra from any bare-hands attack he might launch.

Ralston blinked when Slenth reached under the harness he wore and pulled free a small energy pack. Ralston took it. The Nex continued to delve into his clothing until he produced the power lead and a small fixed-focus nozzle. Ralston saw that the weapon wasn't much good over ten meters, but that might be enough.

"Just as in old times," said Slenth. The reptile reached out a thin-fingered hand and lightly raked his talons over Ralston's shoulder in a gesture of comradeship.

"Just like old times," Ralston said, feeling dead inside. He'd thought escape into academe relieved him of the old responsibilities, the old duties, the still older fears and doubts.

He'd been wrong.

He and Slenth jogged down the corridor, following the fleeing P'torra's spoor. They'd have only minutes to make the kill before the security force arrived.

FIVE

MICHAEL RALSTON SETTLED the energy weapon in his hand. Old habits returned, as if they had never been broken. He slid the battery pack into his back pocket where it made an uncomfortable lump. Ralston glanced to his right. Slenth glided down the stairs with a silence that Ralston found eerie. They reached the shadowy bottom of the stairs and paused, every sense alert.

Ralston used his vision, which was keener than Slenth's. The reptilian Nex's tongue flicked in and out, sampling, touching the airborne particles for a taste of their prey. In the distance, Ralston heard the whine of sirens as the campus security rushed to the building. For them it had been a long day and one likely to get even longer. Ralston made an impatient gesture to tell Slenth that they'd have to hurry. Once the campus security deployed, they'd have little chance to find and eliminate the P'torra.

Slenth shot toward a door, skidding most of the distance on his belly. Strong back legs propelled him forward, as if this were more a natural mode of movement. For all Ralston knew of the Nex, he was unsure about their preferred posture. They seemed equally suited to slithering on their bellies or walking upright.

"There," said Slenth. His tongue darted in and out. Ralston watched in fascination as both branches of the split tongue vibrated and snapped independently like tiny black leather whips. "P'torra goes without real caution."

"Why'd he try to kill us?" asked Ralston. "He had every-thing going his way." Ralston lengthened his stride to keep pace with Slenth. The Nex covered vast distances without seeming to expend any effort. Ralston found himself panting and in a sweat by the time they reached the crest of a low hill.

"Us? Or you? Many often times the P'torra think in crooked ways. You possess knowledge better dead than given to Nex."

Ralston sucked in a long, deep breath and released it slowly. It had never occurred to him that the P'torra would resort to such overt violence against him. They had always approached the University of Ilium and all those within its system covertly, using their impulse drivers, manipulating and then stepping away to watch. The solitary P'torra now study-ing at the school must have received specific orders from his superiors to dare lose his position by murdering a professor.

Even one like Michael Ralston who was in abject disfavor with the administration.

"Never thought of myself as having such valuable infor-mation."

"Dangerous information," corrected Slenth. "If P'torra their advantage goes away by Nex gaining from you the chaos weapon, they can no more plan sneak attack."

"Sneak attack? Where?"

Slenth looked at him, no hint of his alien nature apparent. He might have been completely human, so poignant and real was the displayed emotion. The membrane covered his yel-low eyes and muted their fire, but the hatred burning there told Ralston that P'torra strategy had not changed since the end of the war. Given the chance, they would launch a sneak attack to wipe out both Nex and humans.

"You need nothing in this to know details of, my good friend," said Slenth.

"They can't find out from me what you know if I fall into their clutches, is that it?" asked Ralston, trying to keep his voice light. He failed. After all this time he again became embroiled in intrigue—and sudden death.

He had almost forgotten their purpose for coming to the top of the quiet, grassy hill. The wavering line of blue-white

energy that sought to rob them of their lives painfully reminded him of the deadly nature of their hunt.

Slenth's strong tail knocked his feet from under him even
as the Nex dived for cover behind a small boulder. The shrub
above his head exploded into flames as the deadly energy
beam shifted and cut through a small arc. The continuous
burn of the weapon had to use up its energy pack quickly.
Ralston tried to decide if the P'torra had more than a few
seconds worth of fire-time left.

He was enough out of practice in such matters not to trust
his own judgment. Long ago during the war, Ralston would
have charged, confident that his enemy had briefly exhausted
his weapon. But only when Slenth shot forward, did Ralston
strike. The Nex still showed great expertise in the ways of
death.

They ran forward a few meters, then split, one going left
and the other right to bracket the P'torra with their fire. The
rustling in the bushes ahead betrayed their enemy's position.
Ralston knew that Slenth's eager tongue had already scented
the P'torra, too.

As one, their energy weapons spat death. Ralston's weapon
guttered and went out after only one long release of fire.
Slenth's continued to surge and seethe for another five seconds.

Ralston and Slenth looked at one another. Ralston nodded.
Even his more feeble sense of smell picked up the charred
flesh odor. They advanced cautiously, both unarmed now
until they could replace their energy packs. Ralston saw that
the caution wasn't needed. A mound of sizzling blubber
stretched a quarter of the way down the hillside. Their beams
had converged directly on target—in the P'torra's face. They
had blown the top quarter of the P'torra apart.

Ralston stood and looked at the gory smear down the softly
grassed hill and felt . . . nothing. It had been this way during
battle. The first time his gorge had risen and he'd thought
he'd be sick. The Nex hypnotic commands had prevented the
horror from impacting too much; getting sick inside a pressure suit helmet could be fatal.

"You remember that first time?" asked Slenth.

Ralston nodded. "We weren't fighting in a poisonous atmosphere this time, but otherwise, no difference." He handed

the useless energy weapon back to Slenth. The Nex slipped it back into the maze of harnesses crisscrossing his slender, scaled body.

"Our really most good fine techniques of mind conditioning hold you yet?"

Ralston found himself unable to speak now. He nodded again, his head feeling as if it would split apart at the seams. The headache started low at the neck, moved up the back of his head, and then burst like some black, evil flower spreading its pollen over his skull.

"Go we must soon," urged Slenth. "Your security forces track carelessly but in this way do finally come."

Ralston turned and went back to the top of the hill. Slenth's appraisal of the University security force's skill proved accurate. A real soldier could have taken them all out with a few quick blasts. But Ralston felt nothing toward them. They assumed duties beyond their training. Even the riots inspired by the P'torra lay beyond most of the security force's coping ability. They patrolled the grassy hills and issued traffic citations and occasionally turned off lights carelessly left on. To deal with this . . ."

"That way," Ralston said, finding his voice. "We can walk down the hill, circle, and come up behind them. There'll be no indication that we were ever here."

Even as he sketched out their retreat, he studied the ground to be certain that they hadn't left behind damning evidence. The grassy ground didn't take good footprints. Neither of them had dropped incriminating clues. Even with sophisticated forensics equipment, there would be nothing to tie them to the P'torra's death.

They walked away, not hurrying. The mild exercise brought Ralston back to a more normal condition; his battle training once more sank beneath the waves of his mind. But he knew it could resurface anytime he needed it.

"I must not with you be seen," said Slenth. "The questions to be then asked are difficult to answer with properness."

"I'm not sure I'd give you the information about the chaos device, even if I had it," Ralston said suddenly.

"With the Nex you are more safe. With the P'torra . . ."

Slenth pointed back to where they'd killed the humanoid alien.

"Personal safety isn't as important as the possible death of entire planets," said Ralston. "I never thought of myself as an idealist, but maybe I am."

"They can make you die and still the information use. What use of it is this? Allow Nex to furnish expedition. We will not misuse the weapon as would do the P'torra."

"I know, Slenth, I know. But can you promise that the P'torra wouldn't be able to *steal* it from you? Protecting such data might prove impossible."

"Is it the better to let it cast all through space randomly destroying for unknowing any to find and die from?" asked Slenth.

The Nex had a point—and one Ralston had considered. The chaos device had to be neutralized before systems other than the Alpha and Beta died. How many other races had perished over the eons due to its pernicious effects? Ralston didn't know, but if he could only examine its mechanism, determine something of the nature of those beings sending it forth and guess at their purpose, he felt confident that he could dismantle it—or destroy it totally.

"The ways to determine its position are to us also very open," said Slenth. Ralston had no doubt that Westcott or Bernssen or someone else had the same information—better information—concerning the chaos field's current location. One would let the information out, knowingly or otherwise. To stop the information's spread seemed as impossible as returning glue to a tube.

Ralston had to examine the chaos device personally. Soon. And without being obligated to the Nex or the University or anyone else to reveal all the details. If they somehow learned how to control the awesome power generated by the field because of Westcott's work or Bernssen's, at least Ralston would have the small consolation that he had not been the one to unleash it on humans, Nex, or P'torra.

Study it. Destroy it. That seemed the only course open for him. But how?

He started to say something more to Slenth, but the Nex soldier had slipped tracelessly into the night. Ralston wiped sweat from his forehead as a cool breeze turned it to ice. He began shaking in reaction to all that had happened. Feet like lead, he walked slowly to his office, went in, locked the door, and flopped down hard in his chair.

"To hell with whoever's listening," he said. He lounged back and hiked his feet to the cluttered desktop. Eyes closed, he began mentally working through his problems. Ralston hadn't been in his office five minutes when the door slammed open and crashed hard into the wall. One book precariously balanced on a shelf gave up its fight against gravity and fell noisily.

"The door was locked," Ralston said, eyeing the small, dark man framed in the doorway. "How'd you open it so fast?" He'd heard no fumbling outside to alert him to the intruder.

"Captain Estevez, campus security."

"Captain?" asked Ralston, one eyebrow raised. "Why, you're just the man I needed to call."

"What?" Estevez was taken off guard.

"Someone's planted spy devices in my office. That's a direct violation of some law or another, I'm sure. Certainly it's a violation of my privacy and that of any student who visits me with a problem, academic or otherwise."

"The Nex. What did you say to him?"

"Now that you've confirmed who planted the devices, Captain, would you answer why? And who ordered you to do it? Chancellor Salazar must have better things to do than spy on me."

"You know that Salazar ordered security to monitor those most likely to be endangered by the rioters."

"I knew no such thing. Interesting that the chancellor is so solicitous of my safety after all he's said and done. Perhaps hell will freeze over yet."

"The Nex. His name is Slenth and he's a high-ranking officer in their military force. What did you talk about?"

Captain Estevez had a single-minded determination that Ralston would have appreciated more in a student's devotion to learning. He studied the man and didn't especially like what he saw. The razor-tight lips, the narrowed dark eyes, the set of the body, all spoke of tension and mistrust. Estevez obviously wished he was elsewhere rather than in the presence of a dangerous campus radical like Ralston.

"Slenth is 'high-ranking'? Good for him. Always was ambitious, even among the Nex."

"You're avoiding the question."

"Captain Estevez of the campus security force gets top marks for an astute observation," said Ralston. He had begun to like this. Estevez could do nothing to him, even if he suspected Ralston's involvement in the P'torra's murder. Estevez would have to call in outside criminal authorities before any arrest could be made. All he wanted was to exercise what little power he had and puff up his self-importance.

Ralston wasn't having any of it.

"You already know everything that went on in this room," said Ralston. "You *are* responsible for the spy devices, after all. Anything I'd add would only be my impression of it."

"You left the room."

"Look around. Do you see any sanitary facilities? No? It might come as a surprise to you, but even professors require such a break now and again."

"The Nex went with you?"

"Strange how biological systems on all planets produce bodily waste that requires evacuation. You might inquire about that with some of the staff in the xenobiology department."

Estevez started to speak, then bit back the words. Barely controlling his anger, he said, "A student was killed tonight."

"I tried to warn Chancellor Salazar about the riots some weeks back. A pity he didn't attach more importance to the events going on outside his office walls."

"He wasn't killed during a riot."

Ralston said nothing.

"He was murdered not two hundred meters from here," Estevez went on.

"In the Quad? I saw nothing. I've had the polarizer on all evening. As you know, I usually enjoy looking out at Bacon's statue, but not tonight. Too much on my mind."

"He wasn't killed on the Quad."

"The only other conclusion I can think of for such questioning, then," said Ralston, "is that he was killed in the faculty restroom and you suspect me."

"Oh, yes, I suspect you. And the Nex." Estevez spat out the last word. "When we have enough evidence, you will not mock us. You will beg for mercy. We know you for what you are, Ralston. You are a murderer and will get no mercy from us!"

"You accuse me of this evening's death? Remember that you're being recorded, Estevez. We have slander laws on Novo Terra. Charge me or apologize."

"I referred to your graduate student. The one you killed on the field expedition."

"De la Cruz died from misadventure. That was the official ruling. I had nothing to do with it." Ralston wanted to add that de la Cruz had died from his own stupidity and avarice but held back.

"We will speak again, Ralston."

"Dr. Ralston to those who spy on me and burst into my office unannounced, Captain." Ralston put as much inflection on the word "captain" as possible to show his contempt.

Estevez spun and stalked off. Ralston waited a few seconds, then crumbled inside. He wasn't cut out for such confrontations. All he wanted to do was archaeology, to dig and think and reconstruct lost cultures and to teach what he knew to eager young students.

When had it all turned to dust?

"We consider this conduct unbecoming to a member of our faculty." The Chancellor of the University of Ilium sat back and folded his hands across his broad chest. Ralston thought Salazar looked like an ancient king back in Earthly Spain's heyday. All Salazar had to say was, "To the dungeons with him!" to make the picture complete.

But the academic world wasn't that blatant. Salazar would find a way to issue the command without it sounding like an intellectual death sentence.

"Are you suggesting that I should have let the students beat your secretary to death? They were well on the way to doing just that when I intervened."

"The four students in question decided not to press assault charges against you, Dr. Ralston."

"Good of them," he said sarcastically. "They aren't going

to press charges against your secretary either, I hope? Especially since he kept throwing himself in front of their fists and feet."

"Your sarcasm only clouds the issue and prejudices this committee against you, Doctor."

"Nothing I could say will prejudice this committee," said Ralston. Under his breath he added, "More than you are now."

"Thank you for the vote of confidence in our objectivity," said Salazar in a neutral tone. "However, we feel that your record of violence is adequate reason to examine your future as professor at this institution."

"Record of violence? You can't be referring to the de la Cruz matter again."

"No, no, nothing of the sort," Salazar said, looking embarrassed. Salazar and Leonid Disa had come to terms over this. Disa had paid off the de la Cruz family in exchange for rights to the telepathic projector Ralston had found. This bartering would not look good on the record for Salazar and he sought to avoid mention of it.

Salazar cleared his throat and hurried on. "I referred to your enlistment with the so-called Nex Planetary Defense Force in that unfortunate war. Further, you have been the target of many of the campus demonstrations because of your past Nex alliances. We are not accusing you of unwonted violence, Dr. Ralston, but you seem to act as a lightning rod for it."

"That's none of my doing."

"But you are still the proximate cause. To allow you to teach the classes already agreed upon for this semester will only incite further unrest among the students."

"I *do* have a contract with the University," Ralston pointed out.

"But no tenure. We can remove you for cause."

"You admitted that I wasn't responsible, Dr. Salazar. Can you dismiss an astronomy professor because the sun comes up and gives everyone sunburn? The University should be committed to a free exchange of ideas, no matter how unpopular."

"We cannot tolerate civil disorder. As you have been

informed by Captain Estevez of our security force, a student
was brutally slain last night.''

"Citizen Estevez did allude to it," Ralston said cautiously.
The feeling he got from the others on the Committee on
Academics and Freedom was one of increasing uneasiness.
They were not happy with the notion of firing a professor
innocent of anything but irritating the chancellor. But they
were also astute political animals seeking their own survival.
To cross Salazar in this matter would put them next on his
list. One or two would be up for tenure hearing soon, Ralston
knew. A wrong vote might jeopardize their position.

Better to oust a rebel like Michael Ralston than to lose their
own positions. Ralston read this clearly on several faces.

But the uneasiness remained—and grew. All thought the
same thing: If Salazar did this to Ralston, he could do it to
any of them. For any reason.

"Dr. Salazar," spoke up a man at the far end of the long
table. "My esteemed colleague has a point about his culpabil-
ity in this distasteful unrest among some of our more imma-
ture students." Ralston almost choked when he followed the
line of Velasquez's thinking. The man had successfully plun-
dered Proteus of several technological gadgets and had con-
solidated his position. To him Ralston presented no challenge,
but one never knew.

Ralston knew what Velasquez would propose as clearly as
if he could read the other archaeologist's mind.

"However," Jaime Velasquez went on smoothly, "this
unrest is not to be lightly dismissed. The death of our only
P'torra student points this out.''

"What are you saying, Dr. Velasquez?" asked Salazar,
irritated at having his line of thought interrupted.

"Dr. Ralston is a valued and capable member of the University community and it would be ridiculous to penalize him
for events beyond his control. We can use his talents, both in
the field and in the classroom.'' Jaime Velasquez smiled
winningly. "However, his presence only causes more unrest.
Perhaps he should consider taking a year's sabbatical. It has
been some time since he sampled other teaching methods in
other institutions. Many schools on other planets would welcome him for his ability.''

"An excellent idea, Dr. Velasquez," said Salazar. The quick, nervous nods up and down the table showed that the committee favored this easy way out.

"But, Chancellor!" protested Ralston. "I'd need several months to arrange everything. I've not checked at other schools for available positions."

"I'm placing you on immediate sabbatical, Dr. Ralston. I realize that this might constitute a vacation without pay for you until you can find another university position, but it is necessary. Ilium's budget has come under fire from the Regents and we simply cannot afford the luxury of a non-teaching professor on our payroll. I'm sure a man of your academic caliber and superior standing will readily find another school for your sabbatical."

Salazar raised and dropped his small gavel, signifying the matter had been closed, that justice had been served, and embarrassment for the University again avoided. Ralston started to protest, to demand a hearing of the full faculty, then turned and left without speaking. They hadn't had the courage to fire him outright, but they had gotten rid of him just as surely as if they had.

Damn Salazar! Damn them all!

Michael Ralston had no idea what he was going to do. Accepting Slenth's offer still carried the seeds of universal destruction with it, yet he had no other way of reaching the chaos device without some source of financing now that the school's field research funds were totally closed to him.

What was he to do? Ralston walked aimlessly, in a vain attempt to find an answer.

SIX

MICHAEL RALSTON DROPPED the last of his archaic reference books into a box, then reached over and began working on his computer console—his former console, he mentally corrected. Within a few minutes, he had permanently locked his records onto the University files. If he ever returned, he'd be able to pick up the work where he had left it. But the most important component of his work wasn't inside any computer data bank but in his head.

He sighed and looked around the tiny cubicle that had been his sanctuary for the past three years. He knew it'd be for the last time. No other university would take him on sabbatical on such short notice. No off-planet school would consider a request now, unless his luck improved and he managed to coordinate well with a starting time slightly different from those on Novo Terra.

Offhand, Michael Ralston didn't know of any he'd care to teach at. And with no funds available, he wouldn't be able to simply do research. His field work was expensive. Even old proton magnetometers cost a young fortune.

"Michael?" came a familiar voice. He looked up to see a brown-haired, somewhat plain woman in the door. Ralston noted that Leonore Disa was about the same height as the captain of University security; their heads cast a shadow at about the same point on the door.

"You can either come in and watch me finish packing, or you can help me. Take your pick."

"Always the latter," she said, smiling. He'd seldom seen her happier. But then, Leonore had good reason to be happy. Finishing off her doctorate had been a milestone in her life. Soon, she and Nels Bernssen would be married. Another happy event.

"You're the only one who hasn't come by to gloat. Velasquez is particularly vicious."

"I'd heard it was his idea to send you off to limbo. What'd you ever do to him?"

"Rivalry over Proteus. He knew that dig should have been mine. And I'm sure he's gone over my data from Alpha. *That's* the real find, and he knows it. This is his way of increasing the importance of his work and decimating mine."

Leonore perched on the edge of his desk, silently noting the dull computer screen and the filled boxes. She swung her leg back and forth in a nervous pattern that made Ralston want to reach down and grab it to still the pendulum motion.

"Nels is finishing a seminar," she said. "He can't work hard enough to fight off the recruiters." Leonore wrinkled her pug nose and made a wry face. "I really *don't* like the one from the University of New Salamanca. She's pretty and she knows it."

"Trying to lure him away using sex, eh?"

"Worse than that. She knows her physics better than any of the others going after Nels. *That's* the part that worries me."

Ralston had to laugh. "Makes me consider changing fields. Think she'd like to recruit a former archaeologist?"

"Why former?" asked Leonore. "That is, unless you just want to hang around campus."

"You've heard of the offers, then?" he asked. "I can't get caught between the Nex and the P'torra over the chaos field. I just can't. I'd prefer it in Nex hands, but trusting them—even Slenth—isn't easy. You know what Lord Acton said."

" 'Power corrupts, absolute power corrupts absolutely,' " Leonore answered.

Ralston smiled. His best students knew more than the narrow field of archaeology. But then the best in any field always knew more than just their subject. That was part of what made them so special.

"Getting back to what you were saying, Michael, no, I hadn't heard about the Nex offering you anything. I suspect Daddy would make an offer, but he's been off planet for a month now and can't know anything about this."

Ralston perked up. He looked squarely at his former student. "There's another offer?"

"Nels is turning down all the offers to speak. And he's already turned down five teaching positions, one of them an endowed chair with the promise of tenure after one year. He's put together a half-dozen grants that'll fund a really good expedition this time."

"But it'll be his expedition," said Ralston, his hope fading. What an astrophysicist would want from the chaos device differed mightily from what an archaeologist needed.

"Of course it will, mostly."

"Mostly? What part won't?"

"Mine. I got a pair of unlimited-scope research grants, no restrictions, no reports required, nothing but field study. *I* want to study the device as badly as you do, Michael. Come with us. Please. We need your expertise."

"The only reason you didn't hear a sonic boom as I accept and race to the shuttle launcher is that I'm weighed down with all these books. Help me get them home, then let's sign some papers."

"You don't mind working for me, rather than the other way around? That's the way it'll have to be."

Ralston swallowed his pride. He wanted all his students to do well on their own. Leonore Disa had certainly succeeded beyond his expectations for a new Ph.D. But to work under such a recently former student might be seen as degrading.

He didn't care. He'd be in space and on the track of that damned elusive chaos field!

"I'll scrub the decks to study the device," he said, meaning every word of it.

"No contracts, then. Your word is good enough." Leonore thrust out her hand. Ralston engulfed the small hand in his larger one and shook vigorously.

He almost glowed from the anticipation of again being in space on the chaos device's trail as he carried his boxes out and loaded them onto a truck. Ralston didn't even notice the watchful eyes of Captain Estevez on him as he worked.

He was going back to space to unlock the most perplexing, the most dangerous, the most significant puzzle of a lifetime!

"It hardly seems enough," Ralston said, studying the pile of their equipment. For every small box he and Leonore had been allowed, Nels Bernssen and his crew of fourteen astrophysicists had a score of large ones. "But it is his expedition. We're going to have to discuss what it is he wants when we find the device, and how to best get it without interfering with our work."

"I want to check out the markings," said Leonore. "The Betan reported curious hieroglyphic characters that sounded similar to those on a couple of other planets. We might be dealing with a race that has visited other worlds, then left messages."

Ralston shook his head. It was a pity only one creature had seen the chaos device passing through the Beta system. The Betan had not been a reliable observer. By the creature's own admission, it was regarded as insane by its peers. Ralston couldn't pass judgments like that, but he knew that a creature living under ten atmospheres of ammonia and methane pressure didn't have the same perceptions of the universe that warm-blooded mammals did.

Ralston looked over the shuttle launch area. Here and there concrete depressions dotted the tarmac, immensely powerful pulsed lasers at the bottom of the pits. The stubby shuttles would be launched by the action of the laser against splash plates until orbit, then tiny steering jets would move the shuttle to their starship. Ralston had gone this route many times, but still a sense of eagerness lingered and kept him on edge. Out among the stars lay the traces of cultures long dead. He would put all the pieces together and discover what had been lost for eons. The anticipation of actually seeing the chaos device made him forget all that had gone on at the University.

Almost.

"Ready to do science?" came Nels Bernssen's deep voice. Ralston looked over his shoulder. Nels hadn't been speaking to him but to Leonore. A pang caught at Ralston's throat. The expedition leader spoke to the secondary leader—and it wasn't him. It was his former student. Former, recent student.

Michael Ralston pushed such feelings away with some difficulty and went to where Bernssen checked off the masses of Leonore's equipment on a manifest.

"Looks like you made the limit. Even came in a microgram or two under."

"Does that mean we can pack something else?" asked Ralston.

Bernssen laughed at this. "Hell no, it means I don't have to throw out something I might need when we get there. I wish we were all traveling as light as Westcott." He gestured in the mathematician's direction. Westcott sat silently on a plastic crate, eyes glazed and his head-mounted IR sensor covered by a knit hood. It made him appear even less human than he was.

Leonore saw Ralston eyeing the sensor covering and said, "I knitted it for him. I couldn't stand staring at the hardware gleaming on the top of his head. It still gives me the cold shudders."

"I know what you mean," said Ralston.

"Has Westcott shown you the plots for his equations?" asked Bernssen. "The more I think about the color scheme the more I like it. I think there might be other applications for the technique."

"The colors are lovely," said Ralston, not caring that much about mathematical processes. He wanted to be aboard the shuttle and lifting for orbit, away from Novo Terra and the University. Only then could they star out and find the alien chaos device.

Bernssen slapped Ralston on the shoulder and said, "We'll be on our way soon. Try to relax. Enjoy the trip, Michael. Let Leonore do the work." Nels smiled broadly. "After all, it is her first expedition where she's in charge of worrying."

Nels had meant the comment to be light and reassuring. Ralston couldn't take it that way. He flashed a fake smile and let Bernssen get on with the final loading and stowing of their equipment. Reluctantly, Ralston went and sat beside Westcott. The mathematician acknowledged his presence with a quick dart of his eyes. Other than this small movement, the man didn't stir.

"The basins of attraction are diminished in the latest plot," said Westcott.

"What?" Taken aback, Ralston turned and stared at the mathematician. He had no idea what he meant.

"In my plot. The dark areas are always stable and tend toward the strange attractors, points that are either fixed or periodic."

"So?"

"The colored areas of the graph are unstable." Westcott's eyes seemed to focus on his color plots rather than anything at the shuttle site. "The colors are expanding, taking over all the graph. The instability is increasing."

"What were you plotting?" Ralston asked, suddenly worried at Westcott's tone.

"The equation governing the device itself. I believe I've found the underlying equation that creates the field. I did a time progression on it. And it's decaying. It's becoming more chaotic."

"And less predictable?"

"It was never predictable, not in the sense you mean. But my mathematics is unable to deal with it."

"What does this mean?" asked Ralston. "Put it in words I can understand."

"The field is intensifying and creating more and more chaos as it travels. It might not last another year."

"But you can't be sure of that, can you? This is all speculation. You can't know." Cold panic clutched at Ralston's throat. The chaos device had triggered novas that destroyed his greatest finds. It couldn't be so unstable that it'd self-destruct before he had a chance to determine its planet of origin and something about its builders. It just couldn't do that to him! Not after all he'd been through.

"No, I'm not sure. But the mathematics is precise enough to describe the general trend of the equations. How fast the chaotic effect spreads, when and if it become self-destructive, those I can't say with any certainty."

Ralston relaxed.

"It might not be a year. It might be a month." Westcott spoke with such confidence that Ralston wilted.

"The only problem I see," Westcott went on, "is in my not being able to record directly the effects on the appropriate tensors surrounding it. Can't study what's no longer there."

Westcott rubbed his chin slowly. "In this case, it might be possible. The equations go to infinity at different speeds. The colors show that."

Westcott hopped off the crate and wandered away, muttering to himself. Ralston wanted to call out and warn him not to blunder into a laser pit, then stopped. It might be better if the mathematician did something like that. He had no right depressing Ralston even more by telling him the chaos device was unstable and would soon blow up or fall apart or whatever its particular course of destruction was.

"Launch in one hour!" called out Nels Bernssen. "Get aboard and let's button up. I want to get to orbit and star out of here as soon as possible."

Ralston went toward the squat shuttle, no longer excited about the prospects ahead. The future would repeat the past. His greatest achievement would be ripped away by chaos and he'd be left with nothing. Nothing at all.

Ralston lay in the acceleration couch staring at a gray carbon composite bulkhead. He imagined he could almost see the individual whiskers that made the light plate so strong. He began to twitch and stir against the web harness, then shucked off the straps and sat up to look around.

On the other side of the small compartment Westcott lay with his eyes closed. He might have been sleeping or lost in his mathematical fantasy world. Ralston didn't know and wasn't going to disturb him to find out. His restlessness increased when he failed to hear the usual whine of servomotors getting the shuttle ready to launch. If anything, the ship was too quiet.

It sat as if deserted.

Ralston swung out of the couch and made his way to the tube running the length of the shuttle. Upward lay the cockpit where the pilot balanced the ship on the vicious end of the laser. Ralston craned around but saw no one above. He deftly spun about and caught the rungs in the tube and descended a level. Leonore Disa slept quietly in one couch. Bernssen's was empty beside hers.

Ralston frowned. Going lower he found the rest of the expedition either dozing or idly chatting, most of them bored and wishing to get into space. Ralston talked with the two nearest the tube but they had no idea what the delay was.

Coldness formed in Ralston's guts. In earlier, happier days he would have shrugged it off and decided that something minor held them back, something of no real importance. Now he feared the worst. He dropped down the long access tube and landed in a crouch just inside the airlock. Both doors stood open, indicating that pressurization for launch hadn't even begun.

He crept forward and almost fearfully looked out. Nels Bernssen and the shuttle pilot stood at the edge of the launch pit arguing with three men. Ralston frowned. Those three looked familiar but he couldn't place them.

When Captain Estevez came up and joined the group, he recognized them as campus security.

Ralston was too far away to hear over the clanking and pounding and electrical crackling that came from the field, but their stance gave him a good idea what was going on. Another man came up and spoke quickly with Estevez, then turned and spoke to Bernssen. The disgusted expression on the newcomer's face and the way he dismissed Estevez told of authority exceeding any mere campus policeman.

Ralston held back from descending to ground level and seeing what the officers wanted. He could guess. Estevez had followed him for days after their confrontation, no doubt looking for some minor violation. When Ralston had been sent packing from the University, that should have ended Estevez's interest.

It hadn't.

The peace warden turned and pointed toward the open airlock. Ralston wasn't able to slip back inside quickly enough. Over the noise on the field he heard a bull-throated yell, "Get down here, Ralston. Now!"

Bernssen and the pilot huddled together, then Bernssen motioned for Ralston to come down. Whatever happened, Bernssen was his friend, but the physicist wasn't going to jeopardize the expedition for that friendship. To him, finding the chaos device was more important than any single member of the team.

Perhaps even more important than Leonore Disa, though

Ralston wouldn't want to go that far in judging Bernssen's devotion to his work. But he could definitely say that Nels would throw him to the dogs rather than delay much longer.

Ralston saw no reason to not obey. He went down the ladder slowly, his mind racing. Estevez and the peace warden could want any number of things from him, but the one that lodged firmly in his head was the death of the P'torra. That was the only capital crime he'd committed that would be worth the time of so many enforcement officers.

After all, Salazar had successfully rid himself of a problem by sending Ralston on an enforced year-long sabbatical. He had no reason to detain him.

"Dr. Ralston?" said the man with Estevez. "Warden Kolkoff, assigned to investigate the student's death."

"They're going to hold up launch until they talk with you," cut in Bernssen. "Make it quick. We have a launch window to meet or we have to lay over an extra day." Bernssen referred to the starship in orbit. Departures and arrivals were carefully regulated. It might even be necessary to cancel the departure from orbit and wait for another week or more.

Ralston felt as if time crushed down around him. He couldn't get Westcott's comments out of his mind. The chaos device had reached a point of instability where it might destroy itself at any time. After hundreds of thousands, perhaps millions, of years, it had chosen this particular year to chaotically fall apart.

Not for the first time, Ralston wanted to scream, "It's not fair!"

"I've already told Estevez all I know about the death. A P'torra, wasn't it? I think I saw that on the news."

"That's what makes the matter so delicate," said Kolkoff. "The P'torra ambassador is understandably upset. That makes my superiors upset and, well . . ." The peace warden spread his hands and tried to smile winningly. He failed.

"I understand all that," said Ralston. "I don't understand why you're delaying us."

"We feel you know more about the P'torra's death than you told Captain Estevez. A lot more." Kolkoff ran a finger under his nose, as if wiping away sweat or trying to keep from sneezing. "I just looked over his preliminary report and, well, sir, I must agree. You should come with us for questioning."

"Nels!" Ralston looked to the tall blond. Ralston saw the pale eyes harden. Quick calculations went through both his and the pilot's mind. Ralston preferred those that Nels worked on. If they reached orbit in time to transfer, they could star out before the authorities on planet stopped them.

Even as the thought flashed across Nels' mind, it vanished. A simple radio message to starship control would stop them.

Nels Bernssen wouldn't halt his expedition for Ralston. Never. Help if he could, yes, but not stop the expedition. Too much rode on the man's shoulders for that.

"Nels," Ralston said quickly, "if we got up without being stopped, could we make it out of orbit within a few hours?"

"Within an hour," spoke up the pilot. "We've been delayed enough. We're damn close to the launch time. I'd barely have time to unload the equipment and secure it in the starship's hold before you'd be on your way. I need to get free of the ship's drive field before it shifts. That means another hour. You'd need a minimum of three hours after we hit orbit, just to be sure."

"Dr. Ralston, this isn't a smart course of action on your part," said Kolkoff. "Resisting only makes it appear that you *do* know more than you've said. Perhaps you're involved in a more significant way."

Peace Warden Kolkoff stepped back and reached into a pocket. Although he didn't reveal what lay inside, Ralston guessed it was a stun weapon and it was aimed directly at him. Any attempt to resist and he'd end up flopping about on the ground in extreme pain, his nervous system jumbled for hours.

Ralston, Kolkoff, Estevez, and the three campus security men with him turned to go back to a low shed where their aircars were parked when the archaeology professor saw something that returned hope.

Over his shoulder, he called, "I'll be up in a minute, Nels. Get everything ready, but don't close up till the last possible instant."

"Dr. Ralston," said Kolkoff in a tired voice. "The only place you're going is—"

Ralston dropped forward, catching himself on his hands. His right foot swung out and back in a short, vicious arc that caught Kolkoff behind the knee. The peace warden yelped and lost his balance, falling backward. As Estevez and the others turned, an energy beam crackled just above their heads.

They, too, dropped to the ground.

"Run into your ship at the launch," came Slenth's command. "These five are not to move about too soon until you can go."

"I'll need at least three hours, maybe more."

"They will my company enjoy for this and even more so time," said the Nex. "All are sane and not wanting to be fried in the energetic beam of my weapon."

"Thanks. Thank you." Ralston clapped Slenth on the Nex's slender shoulder, then turned and ran for the ladder.

"You won't get away with this!" called Kolkoff.

Ralston saved his breath for running. He jumped and caught the fifth rung up and climbed like his distant ancestors must have when they swung in the trees. Ralston somersaulted through the airlock and cycled it shut.

"Who was that?" asked Bernssen. "Never mind. I recognized him as a Nex. I don't think I want to know any more about what you're involved in."

"We've got four hours. Can we really get our equipment transferred and star in that time?"

"We'll have to, won't we?" said Bernssen.

Ralston barely made it to his acceleration couch before the pulsed laser fired and slammed them up into the sky and toward the waiting starship.

SEVEN

RALSTON JERKED AND sent himself spinning away into an elastic protector mounted on the starship bulkhead when Nels Bernssen called out, "We're ready to go!"

The others gathered in the starship's main lounge spun around to anchor themselves down for the gentle rocket shove that would take them out of orbit around Novo Terra and send them flying faster than light toward the Beta system.

"Any contact from planetside?" Ralston asked anxiously. Bernssen's head hardly moved as he shook it. Ralston didn't know whether to relax now and assume all was well or to keep worrying. Slenth might even confess to the murder to free Ralston of suspicion. The Nex might enjoy some form of diplomatic immunity; Ralston didn't know. Whatever happened with Kolkoff and Estevez, once the stardrive engaged, they were beyond the reach of any planetary authority.

Ralston closed his eyes and hung weightlessly. Although it might not be true, after his escape from Kolkoff, he had to reckon himself a fugitive from justice. The entire Novo Terra peace staff would be seeking him for murdering the P'torra. At best, he would be considered Slenth's accessory, a crime carrying only slightly less penalty than the actual commission of the murder itself.

But in his own mind, Ralston had killed the P'torra. His finger twitched, the same finger that had curled around the energy weapon's trigger and sent the blast of energy blazing out to cinder the alien. The P'torra wasn't the first he had killed in such a fashion. Michael Ralston could only hope that this one would be the last. He didn't like the gut-chilling sensation of taking another being's life, even a P'torra's.

A fugitive. He ran like a coward. All that Salazar had said about him would be believed without question now. Michael Ralston, former University of Ilium professor, had murdered a student and then fled with the aid of his accomplice, the dastardly Nex mercenary and murderer, Slenth.

He *had* killed the P'torra, but it had been in self-defense, although a jury would find this difficult to believe. He and Slenth had hunted the blubbery alien creature down and ambushed him. It wouldn't matter that the P'torra had attacked first. They had followed and killed him. That was the hinge point of the law. His and Slenth's lives were no longer in danger and yet they'd chosen to find the P'torra and kill, kill, kill.

Ralston's head felt as if it would explode from the tension. He jumped when hands touched the back of his neck.

"Relax," Leonore Disa said softly. "You're too tense. When we star, you're going to be turned inside out."

"You know what happened planetside?"

"Nels told me. I don't for an instant believe you had anything to do with the P'torra's death."

"But you'd believe Slenth responsible."

Leonore frowned, not understanding. "You mean the Nex who took the peace warden prisoner?"

"That's Commander Slenth, of the Nex Planetary Defense Force. The best friend any soldier in the field can have."

Leonore's fingers worked at the tight knots on his shoulders. Ralston couldn't keep from wincing. He'd reacted more strongly to his problems than he'd thought; even with Leonore's expert kneading, the muscles refused to relax.

She said nothing for a few minutes, then pushed back. Ralston half turned and hung suspended so that he could look into her brown eyes. What he read there did not surprise him.

"Yes," he said, knowing that the truth would be better than a lie, even if it did change the way she thought of him. "Slenth and I did kill the P'torra. It was in self-defense, but no human jury would believe that. They'd be too quick to condemn a Nex.'' Ralston laughed bitterly. ''And if Salazar could add a vexing problem professor to the murderer's indictment, he'd do it.''

''You're selling yourself short, Michael,'' she said. ''I don't pretend to approve of killing the P'torra, but if you say it was self-defense, it was. I just wish you'd have told the authorities. They'd not condemn you without examining the evidence.''

''There wasn't much evidence left,'' he said. ''Slenth and I are good with energy pistols.''

''There's the signal,'' Leonore said. ''We're ready to blast out of orbit.''

Only then did Ralston begin to let the tension drain from him. Once free of Novo Terra's gravity well, return wouldn't be easy. At a few AU's, the star shift would occur and they'd be past any planetary control.

The rockets gently forced him into the restraining pad. The red indicator light flashed faster and faster until it became a steady glow. At one-tenth of a gee, the ship accelerated from its parking orbit. Two midcourse corrections later, their heavy gyroscope spun to hold their axis steady and the pilot lined them up precisely for the light years-distant Beta system.

A green light began flashing to indicate the approaching shift. When it went solid green, Ralston gasped involuntarily, his heart stopping, his lungs freezing, and the universe turning into a maelstrom of swirling colors more intense than anything Westcott had plotted using his chaos equations.

For an infinite time, Ralston swam through the colors, tasting them, letting them coolly caress his cheeks, his eyelids, the inside of his skin. Only slowly did the colors fade and his senses return to normal.

Many of the others had recovered from the drive's unpredictable side effects but he had asked and no one else experienced the disorienting sensory shifts. A few times Ralston experienced no sensory confusion. But the last three or four shifts had been particularly devastating to his equilibrium.

''You look pale. Are you all right?'' Bernssen asked anxiously. The big blond drifted nearby, one long arm curled around Leonore's slender waist.

"I . . . I'm fine," answered Ralston. "The shifts are getting harder for me."

"Ever since you used the telepathic projector on Beta 5," said Leonore. "You touched on the chaos-induced epilepsy of the Alphans then."

"I did?" Ralston still felt disoriented, confused. He remembered nothing about that.

"You did," Leonore said, concern for Ralston mounting. "You went into a seizure. It wasn't a grand mal seizure, but it was strong enough to frighten me. You became the Alphan scientist and you endured what he had—an epileptic seizure."

"A chaotic event," cut in Westcott. The mathematician drifted by, his infrared sensor unit blinking. Across the large lounge he had mounted a receiver onto a linking unit that put him into contact with the ship's main computer. Once again, Westcott was whole.

"Call it what you want," Leonore said, "but it might have permanently affected him." Leonore rotated and faced Ralston again. "You did get a complete physical when you got back to the University?"

"The doctor couldn't find anything wrong. Gave me an unconditional pass. But how could he check for shift-related problems without putting me through the dimensional changes?"

"Doesn't matter," said Westcott in his smug tone. "A chaotic event isn't going to be obvious. The residual effects might linger for years. Perhaps forever."

"I don't remember this seizure," Ralston said.

"Part of it." Westcott nodded sagely, a smirk on his lips. "You might have patches of memory loss similar to a stroke. Pinpoint losses you'd never notice unless a complete brain map has been made and a comparison can be done."

"I've never had it done," said Ralston. "There didn't seem to be any reason."

"He won't suddenly forget or have another seizure, will he?" Leonore put Ralston's fears into words.

"We're dealing with randomness induced mathematically. It is wonderful, isn't it?" gloated Westcott. "We have the chance to observe the results of chaos on otherwise orderly systems."

"The system you're talking about is *me!*" Ralston shouted. Several others in the lounge turned to see what caused the commotion. The lowered air pressure saved Ralston from complete embarrassment. Only those closest heard his outburst. The others continued their private conversations undisturbed.

"How can I be sure I'm not carrying the seeds of chaos within me?" he asked in a more controlled tone.

"There's no way to know," said Westcott. "I suspect you are. I suspect all who were on either Alpha 3 or Beta 5 and were touched by the residual effects of the field are tainted. Yes, tainted is a good way of putting it. Very good. Nothing major wrong with us, but small parts no longer function properly."

"You mean my liver might give out because of the chaos field?" asked Leonore.

"I doubt that, unless we come into direct contact with the fully functioning field. However, your hormone balance might be subtly different. Or a gene might have toggled. Probably nothing significant is wrong inside your head. Possibly you have triggered an oncogene and cancer is even now beginning to devour your body. Who can say? It's all random, after all."

"You're able to determine mathematically what's going on!" cried Ralston, still upset.

"Only in special cases. The radioactive decay calculation is a phenomenal breakthrough. But to predict, say, weather patterns? Not yet. My computations need more sophistication, more elegance. These are nonlinear differential equations we're dealing with. The slightest parameter change results in a wild fluctuation. I showed you the mapping I did."

"The colored plots?"

"The black is stable, the red is most unstable, the most chaotic. The greens and blues show a slower trending toward the unstable. This is how I determined that the chaos field generating device is quickly becoming unstable. It has acted upon itself long enough to begin to introduce increasing random behavior."

Ralston couldn't bring himself to carry on with the conversation. He kicked against an elastic band and began slowly drifting into the center of the chamber. Already most of Bernssen's colleagues had left, gone to attend to their various duties. Boredom destroyed more expeditions than any danger among the stars and Bernssen wanted his researchers busy from the first minutes of the trip.

Ralston felt strong fingers circle his ankle. Nels Bernssen pulled alongside until the two of them floated eye to eye. By speaking quietly, they were effectively isolated from the few who remained.

"Are you all right, Michael? You're looking worse every time I see you."

"I'm fine. Really."

"You don't sound it. And that business back on Novo Terra is going to be difficult to sort out when you return. You know that, I hope."

"I know." Bleakness filled Ralston. Westcott said the chaos device fell apart daily and might vanish totally before they tracked it down and a murder charge hung over his head like the Sword of Damocles. He had no job and had been allowed to accompany this expedition only through Leonore's influence with Bernssen.

"I'm going to need you, Michael. A great deal, when we find the chaos device. You'll have to do all the preliminary work."

"What?" This brought Ralston back. "I thought all you wanted to do was measure the physical fields around it."

"Westcott says the device might be more conceptual than physical. Whatever that means, we're going to need someone to decipher the motives of the race constructing it. If my crew can tear it apart and find out how it works, they will. But there might not be much to rip into. We'll need all the information we can get on the race building it, what they looked like, how they thought, how their civilization functioned. We'll need it all to even begin to understand."

"Leonore's idea about the markings might not be far off, but I've got a few other notions of my own. We can . . ."

"Good," said Bernssen, smiling broadly. "That's your area, not mine. You don't need to know about proton-proton cycles or any of the rest of the subatomic particle jungle. And you need only give me the results of your work. A deal?''

"Done!''

Bernssen waved to Leonore, then kicked off and drifted to join her. Ralston wasn't sorry to see the physicist go. He wanted a little time alone to think this through. Perhaps he wasn't as useless as he'd thought. A good picture of the society building the chaos device *would* help Bernssen. Ralston hadn't thought that the physicist recognized that. But he did and Ralston wanted to do everything possible to help.

Ralston left the lounge and made his way down the shaft running the length of the starship. When he came to the storage area, he found himself waiting in line to get to his equipment crates. A half dozen of Bernssen's expedition wanted access to their equipment, too, to calibrate, to study, to prepare.

"Give me a hand, will you?'' asked one earnest young man. He sweated as he wrestled with a heavy crate.

"You'll never get it out that way. Inertia,'' Ralston reminded the physicist. The idea that he, as a seasoned space hand, could tell the youngster about his own field bolstered his confidence even more. Together, they fastened down a few crates and used a block and tackle arrangement to gently pull the needed equipment crate free. Storage had been done haphazardly due to the lack of time before leaving Novo Terra orbit. Ralston made a mental note to tell the pilot that they should rearrange everything before shifting back into normal space. It wouldn't help the handling of the starship but it would protect valuable equipment from possible damage.

"Thanks,'' the man said, once they'd retrieved the desired instruments. "Calibration's going to take me a couple weeks. Then I have to set up in the lounge or on these walls.'' He looked around, sizing up potential mounting spots. "Dr. Bernssen wants everything ready to go the instant we shift into the Beta system.''

"First expedition?'' Ralston asked. He knew the answer before the man answered.

"That it is. I read about Dr. Bernssen and his successes with predicting the nova conditions and knew I had to be on his next trip. I just *had* to. This is where science is being done and I want to be a part of it." The young man looked at Ralston more carefully, recognition slowly dawning on him.

"You're one of the grave robbers, aren't you?" The man clamped his mouth shut quickly when he realized he must have insulted Ralston.

"I've been called worse."

"Sorry. We were told to keep the jokes to a minimum since Dr. Bernssen's marrying one of you."

"You make us sound like aliens. We're just plain folks who enjoy digging around in lost garbage to find out why it was discarded, who did it, and something about why it should be left."

"Sounds dirty to me. I prefer something clean. I do spectrographic work in solar coronas, specializing in iron sublimations."

Ralston had no idea what the young man meant.

"Good luck," said Ralston, beginning his hunt through the piles for his own crates. "Hope all your lines come out nice and sharp."

"Thanks. And thanks for helping me. No matter what the others say, you're all right." He thrust out his hand and said, "My name's McGhee. Glad to meet you, Dr. Ralston."

Ralston laughed at this. He knew the physicists under Bernssen might gossip a little, but they had no time to discuss the likes of an archaeologist. They'd be more inclined to talk about Leonore and Nels. For the first time since boarding the research ship, Ralston felt a part of this expedition, accepted by Nels and Leonore and now by one junior member.

He searched until he found their small cache. Leonore Disa had arranged for a pair of "supervisors," sophisticated controllers that would keep track simultaneously of more than a hundred different automated probes. If time proved to be of the essence—and Ralston knew it would because of the chaotic effects induced into electronic circuitry by the field—they might have only a few seconds before everything failed. All needed data had to be gathered in those precious instants.

His equipment crates had been better designed than those used by the physicists. Side panels snapped off to allow easy entry without moving the crate from its stack. Ralston burrowed into one to find the first set of probes. He needed to calibrate their spectral responses to view everything from hard x-ray through soft infrared. This covered any possible visual input.

Ralston peered up from his work when he heard loud clanging. To his surprise he saw the pilot working hard to pull off an access hatch to the ship's electronics.

"Need help?" he called out. Pilots were notorious loners, having as little to do with their passengers as possible. Ralston didn't want to irritate the man a single hour into a journey of over six weeks.

"Can use it," the pilot grunted. "Damn ship's falling apart already."

"What's wrong?" Ralston knew pilots were as close to perfectionists as anyone in the galaxy. Few starships failed to return because of malfunction.

"Not much," the pilot grumbled. He was a smallish man with Leonore Disa's coloration. His light brown hair flew in a wild disarray that made Ralston wonder if the man had already touched a live circuit and electrocuted himself. Powerful hands with thick, short fingers pried open the hinged hatch and revealed a mind-numbing array of block circuits and other electronic paraphenalia. Ralston had no idea what this panel controlled.

"Here, put your finger here. Press hard. Harder, dammit," the pilot snapped. Ralston did as he was told. The block circuit he shoved against sank a few centimeters, then began to heat.

"What's supposed to happen?"

"Nothing. That's what's wrong. St. Christopher, why does this happen to me? I ask you, why?" The man swung around to brace his feet against the bulkhead above Ralston, then began inputing a string of numbers into the control console.

"It's getting hotter," Ralston said. "And I think it's sinking even farther into the board."

"Don't let go. Whatever you do, don't let go!" The panic in the pilot's voice worried Ralston.

"This controls our shift mechanism, doesn't it?"

"Damn right it does. Lose this baby and we're dead in space. Noticed that the redundant circuits had blown. All three of them. God in space, why isn't this working?"

Ralston yelped in pain when the block circuit heated up to the point where he couldn't bear it. Reflexively, he jerked his hand away, allowing the block to rise back from its depression.

Instantly, alarm bells throughout the ship began their strident message of disaster. The lights in the cargo hold dimmed and Ralston fought to see even the pilot less than a meter distant.

But the pilot's words rang all too loudly. "Mother of God, don't let me die!"

The starship gave a convulsive shudder and the lights failed completely, plunging the cargo bay into total darkness.

EIGHT

MICHAEL RALSTON OVERCAME his panic almost immediately. He had been in situations like this before, mostly during combat. He remembered the time he had blundered into Westcott's lab, only to find himself tumbling helplessly among the stars because of a bizarre data analysis method the mathematician used.

Ralston's priority lay in finding a bulkhead. Cautiously reaching out to prevent himself from hitting something and beginning an uncontrollable spin, he found the soothing coolness of the composite bulkhead. His groping fingertips lightly brushed along the surface until he came to the ubiquitous elastic cords used for anchoring and propulsion in the zero-gee ship. Ralston tugged and came up against the bulkhead, orienting himself the best he could.

All the while he worked, he heard the pilot cursing volubly.

"I'm anchored. What do I do?" Ralston called out.

"You by the godforsaken control panel?" the pilot demanded.

"Yes, I've got it. What happened?"

"When the alarms went off, I jerked and sent myself off into the hold like some green kid. Dammit!"

"With the ship," said Ralston, trying to keep his anger down. Their lives might be forfeit and all the pilot wanted to do was cover up his embarrassment at drifting in the center of the hold.

The pilot cursed again. Ralston heard a solid *thwack!* that meant the man had finally drifted into a crate. Scratching noises sounded over the still-ringing alarms.

"Talk me in."

"What happened?" Ralston asked again. "You said the redundant systems had gone out. We're not lost between shifts, are we?"

"Got it!" cried the pilot. Ralston felt the pilot pressing close beside him. The man's instinct in the absolute darkness of the hold proved accurate. Ralston heard the pilot working on the panel.

"How serious is it?"

"Serious enough. There." The lights came up slowly. Even so, Ralston squinted and shielded his eyes with a free hand. The pilot continued to work with studied efficiency. The lights returned to their normal level. He finally plucked out the offending block circuit that had burned Ralston's fingers.

"Can you replace it?"

"No problem with that. The problem's in what caused everything to go haywire in the first place." With a casual disregard for the safety of others, the pilot tossed the fused circuit over his shoulder. Ralston watched it tumble away, catching light and reflecting it in rainbows off now-rippled plastic casing. "But we're not."

"Not what?"

"In danger of being lost in mid-shift. We'll exit just fine. I promised we'd come out within ten planetary diameters of Beta 7, and we will. But this . . ." The pilot mumbled again as he worked on the panel. More block circuits followed, to be replaced from a box of spare circuits the pilot pulled from a cache in the wall.

Ralston had begun to relax and watch the man at work when a sizzling sounded. The pilot floated back a meter and stared at his handiwork in disbelief.

"Something's badly wrong with the circuitry. Bet that burned their toast in the galley. Be a while getting this fixed. You want to drift around and watch or do you have something else to be doing?"

Ralston knew when he was being dismissed. He muttered

something and left the cargo hold, taking with him the block circuits from his supervisor to program them. Halfway up the tube he saw Leonore Disa.

"What's wrong, Michael?" she asked. "The lights came back on in parts of the ship. The rest is still dark."

"The pilot's working on it." Ralston didn't try to hide the worry in his voice. "He seems competent enough but the ship acts as if it's on its last legs."

"Nels wasn't able to get any better on such short notice. The pilot came highly recommended, though."

"They're all tinkerers. He'll get the lighting and the rest into shape soon." Ralston had only minimal faith in the pilot's abilities. Over the next week, the lights or the air circulation fans or the heat radiators periodically went out. Only into the third week did the pilot seem to have the problems under control. By the eighth week Ralston had forgotten their early troubles and concentrated on the notes he'd taken during the prior meeting with the Beta 7 native. Once more they would speak with it in an attempt to gain information and to give the warning about the Beta primary going nova.

The senses-ripping transition back into normal space left Michael Ralston stunned for several minutes. Again he experienced the mingling of one sense with another. For a few seconds he thought that he had gone blind, but it proved only a momentary dimming of the ship's lights. The pilot's careful work hadn't been as perfect as he'd bragged. But the lights came back on strongly.

"Everyone in good shape?" called out Nels Bernssen. The blond man drifted to the center of the lounge and slowly rotated, studying those in his expedition. Leonore Disa he knew had come through the shift. The only two requiring assistance were Ralston and Westcott.

The mathematician had struck his head against a wall and damaged the IR sensor. He complained of headaches from this and a ragged flow of information from the ship's computer. Bernssen motioned for one of his technicians to fix the damage.

"Now that we've got our big problem fixed," Bernssen said, looking Ralston over, "how's the minor one? You're pale and your hands are shaking like a bistable vibrator. Want to plug into the automedic and let it check you out?"

"I'm all right," said Ralston, wishing he meant it. "Each transition is a bit harder than the last. I don't believe Westcott's explanation that I'm more susceptible because of the chaos field's residual effects, but what's going on in my head *is* chaotic." Ralston managed a smile that fooled no one.

"The pilot's as good as his word," said Leonore. "He dropped us within ten diameters of Beta 7."

"I wish his repair work was as good as his navigating. The entire ship's going to fall apart at any second," said Ralston.

"I've had some of my people working with him. The pilot wasn't happy about it but we had a long discussion on this point. There were some problems in the control block circuit programming but we've worked through them. The redundant systems are functioning and there's no cause for worry."

Ralston still worried. He'd seen the lights dim at the shift. What else might go wrong?

"I've got the outer moon sighted in, Michael," said Leonore. "We won't be able to land there again, even for a short while, but I'm sending down a dozen automated probes to collect data. Have you looked over their programming?"

"Checked it out a few hours ago. Not what I'd have the probes looking for, but it'll do."

"Any way we can retrieve the probes when they're done? I hate losing this many before we even find the chaos device." Leonore pushed a strand of her lank hair back under a headband. The concentration on her face made her appear years older. Ralston's mind wandered as he remembered the first expedition he'd commanded. Had he looked this intense? Probably. The responsibility for equipment and personnel— and success—was great. Not having this pressure on his shoulders made the trip more enjoyable for him, but still Ralston envied Leonore.

The head of the expedition chose the study topics. Leonore's interest lay more in calligraphy and visual communication than did his. She had done wonders analyzing the records left by the Alphans, but Ralston thought this missed the true grandeur of that sad, lost race. The telepathic projector was the Alphans' true accomplishment. What factors had gone into the discovery and invention of that process? Although Ralston was no physicist, he needed to know to get a better idea of how the Alphans worked and built and what they expected from their lives.

Of the Betans, they had even sketchier information. A quick landing on the outer moon of Beta 7 had allowed them to use a native-built communication station for a few minutes. The contact had been maddening in its brevity. A xenobiologist would have wanted intimate contact with the Betans; that wasn't possible under ten atmospheres of pressure. A xeno-sociologist needed more data about the beings and their inter-action; Ralston had discovered one self-proclaimed insane individual. None of the other Betans would even speak with them. So much about these people would go unexamined.

The entire Beta system would disappear in the fiery flash from their primary going nova in less than a year.

"I've got everyone hard at work," said Bernssen. "The ship's hull is positively bristling with equipment. Although it would be nice to get much closer to the star, I think we can get good data on the instability and its progress."

"Is the Bernssen Condition fully met yet?" asked Ralston, referring to the theoretical conditions at which the primary would explode. Bernssen had been the first to identify the chaotically induced process in main sequence stars. The passing chaos device had altered the stellar furnace's normal functioning subtly—and enough to cause a nova within a few hundred years.

This star had progressed enough toward destruction that Bernssen estimated only months of life left it as a stable G-class star.

"We're picking up enough instability to set a date," said Bernssen. "Westcott's working on it now."

"Forty-seven standard days, fourteen hours, and a few minutes," came the mathematician's cold answer. "I am unable to determine the time more precisely. The equations diverge more slowly and produce more uncertainty than those for radioactive decay. If you can obtain more precise boundary conditions . . .''

Ralston turned away and left Bernssen and Westcott together. He had little interest in the details. Knowing that this entire solar system would be superheated gas in only forty-seven days depressed him. Not only would countless lives on Beta 7 be lost, but the final refuge of the fleeing Alphans on Beta 5 would also be destroyed. Nothing of the Alphan culture would remain in the universe. An entire world with living, breathing, feeling creatures had been snuffed out. Now the final vestige of that intelligence would disappear completely.

All that was known of the avian Alphans had been collected by his pitiful expeditions.

''There they go,'' said Leonore. She pointed to a small viewscreen showing a radar return. The tiny blip sank toward the surface of the moon and landed. She turned to the supervisor and began making needless minute adjustments on the controls.

''The programming is fine. Let it work. We can get a readout as the probes spread out to explore,'' said Ralston. He understood her nervousness. This was the first time she was in command, and she wanted everything to go smoothly.

''Here comes the first signal. I'm putting most of the effort into visual. Those walls with the murals? Remember them? I want closer examination.''

Ralston floated away until the lower air pressure in the lounge built a tiny bubble of silence around him. Throughout the large room men and women worked feverishly. Their time here would be limited. The astrophysicists watched the last days of a star before its fiery death. None wanted to miss a single clue to the chaos device's effect on the fusion process.

Westcott correlated data and worked through his intricate equations governing chaos. Ralston felt alone, adrift at the thought. Equations that predicted random behavior. That seemed to be a contradiction, but then he didn't understand the mathematics at all. He'd been told that quantum level effects were statistically predictable, but that wasn't the same thing. Not in his mind, it wasn't.

He rotated to look at the ship's viewscreen. The pilot had shifted the camera to Beta 7 itself. The gas giant showed the typical green, red, and brown bands across its surface. No major cyclonic storms wracked the planet, but Ralston guessed that one or more would become visible if they watched long enough.

"Any contact with their computer yet?" asked Ralston. He hovered close to Leonore's shoulder again. The last time they had been on this moon, Westcott had linked himself directly to an alien machine that allowed the communication and translation with the single being below willing to speak with them.

"Probe 9 looks like it's got contact. Verd, there it is!" Leonore's voice almost cracked with excitement. "We've got a patch through now to the supervisor." She looked over her shoulder at Ralston and said in a low voice, "Do you think Westcott will link up again? It might be our only way of contacting them."

"I'll ask."

Ralston cursed himself for not having thought of this earlier. Westcott had not liked the linkage before and Ralston saw no reason for the man to seek out another bout of brain-searing contact. He should have been cajoling Westcott throughout the trip. There'd been ample time. Ralston sighed and resigned himself to simply not caring for Westcott's company. The computer-brain linkage made the mathematician too strange for Ralston's liking.

"Westcott," he said, hardly wanting to disturb the man now. He had no idea what Nels and the others fed into Westcott's brain for computation. Watery eyes opened and fixed on Ralston.

"I wondered if you would ask."

This startled Ralston. He had thought Westcott lived in his own world, a world distant from reality. That the man understood showed more sensitivity than Ralston had given him credit for.

"I have to. We can get information from the machinery— and we are—but only you can reach the inhabitants again. We need more information. Both Nels and us."

"Bernssen mentioned this. He wants full data on what the Betan called the 'cometary object.' That is how he-she-it saw the chaos field as it passed through the system."

"Then you'll link minds with their computer? I don't know how to thank you."

"I'll find a way," said Westcott in his smug, superior tone. The mathematician kicked free and awkwardly swam to where Leonore worked at the supervisor console. All twelve probes returned a full information stream; she barely kept up with monitoring it.

"He's ready, Leonore," said Ralston.

Her face brightened. "We've used the probe arm to press what we think is the summons button." Huge buttons constituted the major control switches on the alien computer. "If I'm reading our reports correctly, the Betan is trying to respond."

Hesitantly, Leonore moved from the console and allowed Westcott to plug his remote IR sensor into one side. He spent a few minutes adjusting, then said, "I'm ready. Be sure to record everything that is said and done."

"Do you want the automedic standing by?" asked Ralston. He remembered how Westcott had gone into shock on the prior contact.

"Not needed. This time I've built in a filter circuit. I'm not rooting about like some primitive this time. I have the resources of the ship at my command, even if the onboard computer isn't of a significant size."

Westcott touched the toggle switch, hesitated for dramatic effect, then flipped it. Ralston thought the man had accidentally run a killing current through his body. Westcott stiffened and jerked so hard that he began to rotate away. Both Ralston and Leonore grabbed him to maintain the infrared linkage. Westcott's body trembled and his lips moved. No words came out.

"Tell us about it, Westcott. Don't forget that you're safe," said Leonore. "Everything's working out fine." Even as she spoke, she motioned to Bernssen to get the small medical unit. Several of Bernssen's technicians would have to bring it from its storage room since it wasn't mobile in freefall.

"I recognize you," Westcott said in a voice totally unlike his normal tone. "Aberrants! You are the alien aberrants who visited my moon before."

Ralston fought to hold Westcott in position to maintain the infrared link. He hadn't thought it necessary to strap the man down. Leonore lent what help she could but her attention turned more and more to the supervisor controlling the probes exploring the alien base on the moon.

Westcott made choking noises and began frothing at the mouth. Ralston almost reached up to block the beam and cut the mathematician off from this brain-computer-alien linkage, but Westcott batted his hand away. Through lips turned bloody from biting, the man's curt words stopped Ralston. "It's all right. Verd, it's all right. I *need* this creature's information for the equations."

As he spoke, Westcott stiffened even more and alien words spewed from his lips. "The cometary object? Again you ask. I know so little of it. Only a few thousand years ago it came. Or was it a few hundred? It passed by, of that I am certain. Of that and the fact that I am insane. Those I know well. Everyone tells me."

Ralston and Leonore both spoke at the same time. Ralston reluctantly allowed Leonore to ask the questions.

"You have no natural predators?"

"Do we die? Yes, of course. Sometimes a fissioning fails and both parts perish. But only rarely does anyone attempt to fission. Why? Nutrients abound. The air is filled with them."

"Cities?" asked Ralston. "Do you have cities? Buildings to live inside. Machines? What of them?"

"We protect some of our equipment with buildings. But to live? We absorb the air and the food within it. Why hide from it, unless you want to starve to death? Once I tried to kill myself in such a manner. No one cared that I tried, so I gave up on the pursuit. I am quite mad, you realize."

Ralston ran the automedic's probe over Westcott's face and neck, holding it firmly at the base of his skull. The readings on the small auto-doc showed abnormal brainwave activity— nothing Ralston hadn't guessed. How much of this conversation came from the creature on the surface of Beta 7 and how much did Westcott supply? Many concepts had no common ground between things of such diverse bodily forms. Did Westcott interpolate and supply what should be said or what he *thought* should be said?

Only careful analysis afterward would give a clue.

"We need the data on the chaos machine, Michael," came Bernssen's urgent request. "You couldn't maintain contact long before. We dare not miss this chance."

"Westcott," Ralston whispered into the man's ear, "get all the data on the chaos device—the 'cometary object.' All of it! Now!"

Westcott drooled a mixture of blood and saliva down his chin. Ralston wiped it away. When the mathematician attempted to jerk free, both Leonore and Nels held him in place. Ralston regretted this; what torture built in the man's head? Did his body seek to escape while they held him? Was there a brain left after this forced contact?

"They are taking me away. They have decided I am a disruptive influence. Curiosity is aberrant behavior and I am curious. I seek to know everything. The cometary object was only a part of it. I am lost, oh, I am lost to their sanity!"

Westcott sagged.

"Kill the connection," Ralston snapped. Bernssen flicked the toggle while Leonore brought the automedic up to work on Westcott. They guided the unconscious mathematician to a bulkhead and fastened him down. Beside him they attached the auto-doc. Its lights flashed in brilliant, marching sequences as it worked to sedate and cure a condition that might lie beyond its capacity.

"Do you think he was hurt? Permanently, I mean?" asked Leonore. "The last time might have prepared him for this."

"Does he look prepared?" asked Bernssen, his words critical. "He'd better have gotten the data we need. How long before he'll be able to talk?"

Ralston looked at the readouts on the automedic and shook his head. "Can't tell for certain. Nothing here looks familiar. It's working overtime to help him."

"Can we get the information through his IR link?" asked Bernssen.

"Why the rush?" asked Ralston, angry at the physicist for his callousness toward Westcott. Westcott might do little to inspire friendship but what Bernssen proposed might actually damage the man's brain permanently.

"McGhee just finished the first pass on the spectrometer. Your genius made a mistake with his forty-seven days. We might be lucky to have forty-seven hours. If he didn't get the information this time, we might never get it."

Ralston and Leonore exchanged bleak looks. Again the nova would rob them of their find—and again it would destroy an entire planet of intelligent beings.

NINE

"There is little time left before the sun explodes," said Nels Bernssen. "The changes in the spectrum show it. No doubt," he added, cutting off Ralston's protest.

"What went wrong with Westcott's calculations? We were supposed to have more than a month." Ralston had slipped both arms through elastic bands and looked as if he wore the entire starship as a knapsack. "How could he be so wrong?"

Bernssen shrugged. "You'll have to ask him. My guess is that he didn't use the proper parameters for the boundary conditions. We're dealing with minute quantities, Michael. The slightest change can upset everything."

Ralston remembered Westcott telling of the absurdly delicate balance in nature, how a butterfly's minute wingbeat might produce a severe thunderstorm. The chaos equations allowed for tiny effects to cause immense results.

"How is Westcott?" Ralston asked. Leonore looked worried.

"He's worse than he was before. This time we have the auto-doc handy. I'm not sure what it can really do, though, since the trouble is mental and not physical. The shock of linking brain to brain with the alien has driven him into a coma. The auto-doc keeps his body running but there's no way I can tell when he'll come out."

"We should have brought a medical doctor to handle this. We knew it'd happen."

Even as he complained, Ralston knew this wasn't possible. Every member of this expedition was a specialist, an expert in a narrow field. The automated medical unit was capable of handling almost all accidents and injuries that might occur. The more complex problems might not be handled by a human doctor, either. The human doctor would have been a needless luxury on a flight requiring tight controls on weight and membership.

What Westcott needed more than anything else was a good clinically trained psychologist.

"We're looking at hours, not months," said Bernssen. "I've alerted the pilot to be ready to star out."

"Where?" asked Ralston. "Unless we confirm the data we got before, where do we shift to find the chaos device? Westcott was wrong about the nova's timetable for explosion. He might be wrong about the device's trajectory, too."

"We can't stay here," Bernssen pointed out.

"We might have to. For a while," said the pilot. The man had drifted up and came to a halt in midair without seeming to touch anything. Ralston marveled at his control—and felt his heart almost stop when the pilot's words sank into his churning mind.

"What do you mean we're going to be here for a while?" demanded Ralston. "Didn't you hear Nels? The star's going to blow up at any instant."

"More trouble with the electrical system. We can probably shift with it not working to one hundred percent, but I don't want to try it. This time we might not come out of the shift." The pilot got a pensive look and said, "Wonder what it's like being caught permanently between shifts? Had a math prof in school who tried to figure it out. The math is strange; infinite speed over infinite distance, but the infinities don't match, so that's why we get anywhere. Imagine traveling at infinite speed for infinite time and never going anywhere."

"This is not funny," snapped Leonore. "Are you trying to scare us?"

"Scare you? Why should I? You people seem to do enough scary things to yourselves." He glanced at Westcott, who hung like a bug in a spiderweb. A tiny bead of blood hung at the corner of a bitten lip. Westcott looked more dead than alive.

"If you're not ready to shift away from the Beta system within two days, it might not matter," said Ralston.

"Verd, you told me. The sun's going to go *pop!* at any instant. Puts a bit of pressure on me to fix the old ship, doesn't it?" The man's tone didn't tell of any pressure. If anything, he seemed to be enjoying the prospect of becoming a nova-generated plasma floating outward from this system at sublight speed.

"Talking about it won't get it done," said Leonore. "Do you need help? I'm sure I could find fifteen people in Nels' group to help and two in ours." She exchanged glances with Ralston, who nodded.

"What if I need him?" The pilot pointed at Westcott. The mathematician continued to drool.

"We can use some stimulants to see if this brings him out of shock," suggested Ralston.

"You'd do that just to help? Touching, very touching. You people really are nice, no matter what the other pilots say. Don't bother with him. I'll see what can be done on my own. You just keep peering at the sun and let me know if anything changes."

With that, the pilot drifted off, unconcerned about their fate.

"Why is he like that?" asked Leonore. "He doesn't care if he lives or dies—and he doesn't care if we do, either!"

"Pilots think it's courageous to act like damn fools," said Bernssen. "Never saw one who'd admit to being afraid in any situation. I'm going to send all my technicians to help him. We need this ship in good condition, whether we chase the chaos device or simply go back to Novo Terra." Bernssen licked his lips and ran a quick, nervous hand through a shock of unruly blond hair. Ralston saw that the idea of being trapped in mid-shift didn't appeal to the physicist any more than it did to anyone, except for their pilot.

"Can you plot a trajectory for us, using the data we obtained last time?" asked Ralston. "That way we might be heading in the general direction of the chaos device when we leave this system. We can fine-tune our shift later."

"In spite of Westcott's protests to the contrary, I don't know which way the field traveled. Did it orbit in—for reference let's call it the left—and exit on the right side of the system? Or did it come from the right and go left?''

"I thought he'd established the course from the path of novas it left behind." Ralston uncovered lost civilizations. This type of argument was more alien to him than the cultures he pieced together from physical evidence.

"There's evidence it might have been either. Complete symmetry. Reversal." Bernssen began mumbling. Then, louder, he said, "I talked with Dr. Chen about the survey probes he lost in the Crab Nebula—the 1056 'guest star' he was investigating. The time frame is wrong if the chaos device left this system and then triggered instability in the 1056. It might not be any better if we assume the field passed in the opposite manner."

"You're saying that we don't know whether to go left or right when we leave the Beta system," said Ralston, despair clutching at him. Again, he felt as if he lost everything that he'd worked so long and hard to achieve.

"Westcott might have the information. Or he might not have gained any more than we knew previously. Only he can answer that." Bernssen and Ralston turned to the mathematician. He hung limply in the safety harness, appearing more dead than alive.

"Unless the pilot fixes the ship, we might not be able to go in any direction," said Leonore.

Each floated away in a different direction, cloaked in their own dark thoughts. Fourteen hours later, McGhee gave the warning of intense solar flares. In sixteen, Bernssen warned that they had only minutes before the star exploded. In twenty, the pilot shifted them along the orbit followed by the chaos device, choosing direction at random.

In forty hours, Michael Ralston knew they were in serious trouble.

"Never seen anything like it," the pilot said. The man appeared unruffled by the catastrophe that had stranded them between shifts. "It's almost as if God's hand reached out and squeezed down. The gyroscope just blew itself apart."

The starship's gyroscope provided a vital function in the precision alignment needed for the ship to precisely span light years. The slightest quaver in the ship at the time of starring magnified into huge errors in arrival.

"What happened to it?" asked Ralston. "The 'scope's encased, isn't it?"

"Nothing happened to it, as far as I can see. I've been a pilot for almost eight years and never heard of this happening. The circuitry failed and the gyroscope wobbled. I can't tell you how that's possible. At the speed it rotates, it should have taken a year to slow down enough to wobble like it did." The pilot scratched himself, then smiled. "I guess I'd better get to work figuring out how to fix it. Without a machine shop aboard, I don't see much way. You folks don't happen to have a complete set of machine tools I can use, do you? I didn't think so."

The pilot kicked free and headed down toward the storage area. All Ralston could do was numbly watch him go.

"Happy son of a bitch, isn't he? Does he think God will pluck us out of shift and drop us where we want?" Leonore Disa's bitterness hid her fright.

"He might think that very thing." said Bernssen. "Pilots aren't ordinarily logical, and this one's more gregarious than any of the others I've met."

"Without the 'scope, we might not be able to reenter," said Ralston. "There's no way for the shift engine to perform accurately if we're not lined up right."

"We can get out," said Bernssen. "That's not the problem. Where we end up is. All that talk about varying sizes of infinities is an imprecise way of stating it. Westcott can do better." Ralston, Nels, and Leonore all turned to look at the mathematician. He still hung in his harness, oblivious to the disaster unfolding around him.

"You're saying we can get out, but we won't know where. Is that it?" asked Ralston.

"We might end up a million light years away—or we might drop out of shift in the center of a sun. That's never happened. I doubt we'd do much to the sun. The best that can be said is that we'd never know what happened."

"So we'd be no better off than if we stayed in the Beta system and let the nova take us." Leonore's bitterness carried an even harsher brittle edge now.

"We're still alive," said Bernssen. He made it sound like a curse.

"Can the pilot fix the gyroscope?" asked Ralston.

Bernssen shook his head. "From the sound of it, there's no way of making one precise enough, even if we had the equipment. It takes a carefully programmed lathe just to rough out the body for the spinning mass. Lasers hone it down to within a thousandth of a micron. Even the mass of a partial fingerprint on the surface would throw it out of balance— that's why the disks are sealed in a vacuum a hundred times harder than interstellar space." Bernssen closed his eyes. "A vacuum of less than one atom per hundred cubic centimeters. How do we duplicate that, even if we had the rest of the equipment?"

"The presence of any more atoms would throw off the spinning?" asked Ralston.

"Probably."

"We're dead," Leonore said in a monotone. "We're not going to survive this, are we, Nels?"

"I don't see how," the man answered. He swam to her. They left the lounge. Ralston watched them go, heavy of heart. Their lives should have been ahead.

Anger replaced the self-pity. *His* life still lay ahead! He refused to quietly die. He had been robbed too many times of real fame. The chaos device had taken entire systems in the wink of a nova's eruption. He had lived aboard weightless starships, taking the dozens of foul-tasting drugs that kept the calcium from leaching from his bones, his muscles from atrophying, his vision from fogging, his cells from surrendering to the radiations from the shift engines. He had suffered through all this and for what?

To die without trace between the stars? No!

Ralston knew nothing of the mechanisms involved in running the starship or the physics governing them, but he knew who did. With a deft midair twist, he faced Westcott. The automedic purred quietly as it kept a steady stream of nutrients flowing through the comatose mathematician's body.

Ralston tapped in a new regimen of drugs. Red lights protested this drastic change in therapy. He pushed the override button, then threw two safety toggles and for a final time hit the override. What he did to Westcott he did with full knowledge. Westcott might die from the stimulants surging through his bloodstream, but so what if he did? Would he be any worse off than the others aboard? His death would be a quick, peaceful one.

"To never know," muttered Ralston. Westcott's death might be for the best. He wouldn't spend long weeks anticipating death.

But Michael Ralston could never see Westcott doing such a thing, even if he knew. Westcott was scarcely human. What emotions he still possessed were egocentric. Seldom had Ralston seen a man so totally self-involved and isolated from those around him.

Perhaps that was what made Westcott such a phenomenal theoretician. Ralston didn't care to delve into epistemology.

"Come on, Westcott, snap out of it." Ralston restrained himself from shaking the man or banging his head against the ship's hull. The reward for his control came almost immediately. Westcott's eyelids fluttered and pale, watery eyes struggled to focus.

"They know and they don't care," Westcott said, his voice weak and distant. "They don't care that the primary is going to explode. Danger is an alien concept to them."

"Westcott, we're in trouble. We left the Beta system almost two days ago. Our ship's gyroscopic control is out. We can't accurately shift back."

"Such precision," Westcott went on, as if he hadn't heard. "The creature I spoke with had plotted the chaos field's progression through the system with incredible precision. Such a masterwork. And even he doesn't care that they'll die!"

"The 'scope, Westcott, we've lost our gyroscope."

Westcott's eyes focused and he took in more of the world around him and thought less of what had been burned into his brain by the alien contact.

"The pilot shifted with a bad gyro?" he asked.

"It blew apart after the shift."

"Impossible. It can't happen." Westcott frowned. "Why did we shift? Only I have the precise information needed to find the chaos device."

"The star went nova ahead of schedule. Your calculations

were off." Ralston took a savage glee in revealing this to the mathematician. "We had less than—"

"Uncertainty," cried Westcott. "We returned to the system and introduced a new element of uncertainty by our presence."

"I know, I know. The butterfly causing the thunderstorm," said Ralston.

"It doesn't *cause* anything. It adds a new parameter to the system and creates nonlinear change. The equations change, the result diverges or converges at a new and different rate. I must study this."

"Go on, since it'll be the last work you ever do."

"The gyroscope," said Westcott, forcing himself back to more practical concerns. "That fool of a pilot ruined the gyroscope." Westcott blinked and fought against the restraining harness. Ralston checked the readout on the auto-doc and decided that Westcott, although still not functioning at optimal, was out of danger and no longer required the chemicals pumping into his body.

As Ralston unhooked the IVs, Westcott said excitedly, "The residual chaotic effect! It must be that. In rapidly rotating systems the effect might be more pronounced."

"It didn't affect the other ships in earlier expeditions," pointed out Ralston.

"Do you know? Who thought to check? This gyroscope might—never mind all that. Is the gyro completely destroyed?"

Ralston couldn't force the words from his lips. He nodded.

"Leave," said Westcott. "I need to be alone. No, no, you idiot. Don't turn off my IR link with the computer. There's something I can—almost—remember. It must be in the data banks. It must!"

Westcott got the glassy stare when he linked fully with the ship's computer. Ralston wondered at the direct-connect so soon after coming out of shock, but he pushed the thought away. Nothing Westcott could do to himself was worse than what would happen if he didn't come up with something.

Ralston even allowed himself a ray of hope to shine through the bleakness. Westcott was a genius. He might not like the mathematician, but Westcott worked at a level few in the universe did.

"Wait!" called out Westcott. "I have it. Yes, it's there. Obscure, very obscure, but it is so elegant!"

"You can repair the gyroscope?" Ralston hardly believed his ears.

"Repair it? Who wants to? I can design a better one. Why hasn't anyone done this before?"

"So you design a new one," said Ralston, hope fading again. "We don't have the machining tools to manufacture it."

"This requires only simple electronics. Yes, an electronic gyroscope at least a full order of magnitude more accurate. It's possible. It *is* possible!"

"Let me get the pilot. And Nels. And some of his technicians!" Ralston hit a call button and assembled them within a few minutes. The pilot was the last to arrive, indolently floating in, as if this meant little to him.

"What do you need from me?" the pilot asked.

"Your attention. Listen to what Westcott's come up with."

The mathematician hardly noticed the others. He warmed to his topic, thinking aloud. "The Sagnac effect. I knew it but had forgotten. Why remember when the computer stores everything perfectly? The computer has only sketchy information, but we can use its information to build a new gyroscope. And one with true elegance."

"Never heard of this Sagnac effect," said Bernssen. He looked around. Ralston's heart turned to ice when he saw that none of the physicists had heard of it, either. In such an assembly of talent, Ralston thought, at least one should know what Westcott hinted at.

"We need a length of birefringent fiber optic," said Westcott.

"I've got a kilometer or more in the hold," said one scientist. "Want me to get it?"

Westcott motioned him on his way. "And lasers. Several tuned to different frequencies."

"We've got enough tunable continuous wave lasers onboard to open a secondhand store," said Bernssen.

"I use one to heat my meals," said the pilot, still not interested in Westcott. "I don't see what all this is leading to."

"In the birefringent fiber, the light is polarized in different directions and travels at different speeds to produce an interference effect.''

"So?" asked the pilot. But Ralston noticed that the man's eyes had hardened. Westcott now had undivided attention.

"Change the birefringence and the interference pattern changes,'' said Westcott. "Make loops of the fiber, send laser beams both clockwise and counterclockwise. Any rotation of the loop will change the relationship between the two beams and . . .''

"And change the interference pattern. So all we do is put an interferometer on the pattern, hook this into the computer, and let it align the ship. No more need of doing it mechanically. We can do it all electronically. I got to say that this is a righteous scheme. I do hope it works.''

"You think it won't?'' asked Ralston.

"I didn't say that. I think it sounds good, but one thing I've learned, nothing ever works quite right.''

"Take a look at the way you've maintained this ship and you can come to that conclusion,'' muttered Bernssen.

"You can walk home,'' the pilot said without animosity. "I got to do some rigging. You got the fiber optic? Then I want to get to work. I figure it'll take a week or two of programming to get this into the computer.''

"I can do it in only a few hours,'' said Westcott. The sensor atop his skull gleamed a dull silver like a badge of honor.

"I won't argue that. Get to it, Doctor. And the rest of you want to build the new gyro? That looks like it's more in your field than in mine. But I insist on doing the connections for the actual control. This ship is mine.''

Ralston watched the assembled scientists go off in tight knots of two and three to discuss what had to be done. Hollow inside from the strain, Ralston relaxed and floated in mid-room.

Leonore came over to join him. "Not much we can do, is there?'' she said.

"Makes you feel useless,'' Ralston agreed. "I don't know anything about optics or Sagnac effects or any of what they're talking over.''

"Nels does. We're lucky to be aboard a research ship

where the people know instrumentation, lasers, optics, all that."

"Who knows?" said Ralston. "We might get the chance to pay them back using *our* specialty. When we find the chaos device, all their rules are gone. We're used to putting together puzzle pieces in ways no one's ever considered."

"Do you think we'll get the chance?" asked Leonore.

He took her hand and squeezed. Ralston didn't know the answer to that. The laser-optic gyroscope might work and save them.

Or it might fail and leave them stranded forever.

TEN

"CAN'T WE TEST it first, before trusting it too much?" asked Michael Ralston. "It's risky simply . . . trusting it." He looked at the pile of equipment with growing skepticism. Bernssen had attached an interferometer—this was the only portion of the equipment that Ralston recognized. The rest appeared to be hidden by coils of the fiber optic cable, leads running to the lasers and ship's computer and other devices Ralston couldn't begin to identify.

"How do you propose to test it, Doctor?" Westcott asked acerbically. "It will work. I see nothing wrong with the principle or construction."

"And you were the one who said we'd have almost two months to study Beta 7 and its inhabitants," snapped Ralston.

"I've explained that. Our return to the system changed the boundary conditions. This is different."

Ralston didn't see that, but he kept his peace. Nels Bernssen and the others waited nervously to see if this solid state gyroscope worked. Ralston prayed that it would. For all their sakes.

And for the sake of those who might be touched by the chaos device unless they found and stopped it. Westcott might say it was decaying, falling apart under its own effects, but Ralston had no confidence in the mathematician's predictions now. More variables entered the equations daily, possibly changing the lifetime of the chaos device to centuries or even millennia—or perhaps Westcott had ignored one tiny factor.

When minutiae magnified into star-killing, world-wrecking ability, a small parameter could mean a great deal.

"It's got to work," said Nels. "What choice do we have?" The physicist's arm circled Leonore Disa's waist and drew the small woman close.

Ralston agreed reluctantly. They had no option other than to trust this untried device with their lives. Bernssen had said the shift back into normal space wouldn't be difficult. Where they might end up presented the true problem. And if the gyroscopic alignment system failed in any way, they might be thousands of light years from human-inhabited systems with no way to find their way home.

Ralston screamed as the shift grabbed his senses and shook. Reds burned his tongue and yellows screamed in his ears. Smell turned into a spectrum of color and the tang of ozone from the electrical equipment could be heard ringing throughout the ship.

Tucked into a fetal ball, Ralston rolled over and over in the middle of the chamber. Only when hands reached out and slowed his rotation, did he uncurl to see everything around him appearing normal. His eyes shot toward the viewscreen, but he couldn't tell anything from the star patterns.

"Looks strange," murmured Bernssen. "I don't think this is where we intended to go, but we're not lost. Look," he said to one of his team. "That's a portion of the open star cluster we checked out a year or so back. And over there's Albierio, only slightly distorted. I recognize the gold and blue stars."

"We dropped into real space just fine, ladies and gentleman," came the pilot's cheerful voice over the intercom. "We missed our target but landed at the edge of Nex-controlled space. Blind luck, I call it, but we're less than a week's ordinary travel from Upsilon Hydra 3, or Tosoll as the snakes call it."

Ralston didn't even react when the pilot called the Nex snakes. The relief he felt was too great to take offense at any racial slur. He had been to Tosoll before; he had fought on Tosoll no fewer than three times. Part of the Nex-P'torra settlement had been to allow the Nex full colonization rights to the world. They would be able to find a replacement for their gyroscope and do complete repairs.

"Tosoll's a major base for the Nex," he told Leonore. "Everything's all right now."

Even as he spoke, the pilot increased magnification on the viewscreen and he saw that luck had given them a nearby planet—and luck had also placed them in the center of an invasion fleet.

A P'torra invasion fleet.

"They still haven't detected us," said Ralston. He studied the readouts in the cockpit. It had been many years since he'd worried over such things, but he was the only one aboard the research ship with any military experience. "When they shifted to the Tosoll system, they came out in disarray. Just enough to lose formation. If they keep com silence, we can cruise along with them to Tosoll."

"And then what do we do?" asked the pilot. "By all the saints, I haven't got a clue why you didn't want me contacting the P'torra fleet commander. They're like we are. They'd lend us the equipment we need. I'm sure of it."

Ralston didn't want to start the old argument anew. He had convinced Bernssen that an invasion fleet would destroy without question anyone appearing in the center of their battle cluster. But the pilot had a good point. Should they try to warn the Nex on Tosoll and risk immediate destruction by the warships surrounding them, or should they continue as they were?

When the fleet reached Tosoll, they'd assume preplanned positions and it would become obvious that an extraneous ship toured in the middle where it didn't belong. Any unknown ship had to be the enemy. Ralston could see the P'torra opening fire instantly. Yet trying to hold back while they were still some distance from Tosoll presented problems of its own. What if a P'torra ship pulled alongside to see if they could lend aid to another they thought to be one of their own?

"We're living on borrowed time," said the pilot. "This bollixed together gyro is still working, but we can't hope to go tearing off without replacing it. The St. Dismas-damned thing has to be replaced. I *will* see it replaced, too, or I don't pilot another centimeter after this space gadget of yours.''

"We could send a message rocket down to Tosoll," suggested Leonore. "If the Nex knew the danger coming in on them, the P'torra might break off and leave."

"How likely does that sound?" asked Ralston. "The P'torra have assembled a war fleet. They'd simply accelerate their attack. As it stands, they're spiraling down slowly. We're on the opposite side of the sun from Tosoll right now and the Nex aren't likely to see us until it's too late. Even with a continuous-drive rocket we're not going to get it to Tosoll in time for any meaningful response."

"Do you suppose they're at war again? The Nex and the P'torra?" asked Bernssen.

"It looks that way. Or perhaps the P'torra decided on a sneak attack. A quick thrust, take Tosoll, then consolidate before word can get out. They might be able to take several Nex planets that way before anyone realizes the war has heated up again."

"Michael, you make it sound as if the P'torra are evil." Leonore stared at him. He had to keep reminding himself that the others didn't necessarily share his pro-Nex views. As he'd learned on campus, most of the students and faculty openly opposed him on this issue. Leonore had believed him when he said he killed the P'torra student in self-defense. That didn't mean she accepted his views about them generally with an open mind.

"Those are old questions I've answered for myself. You'll have to do it for yourself." Ralston gestured, taking in all the space around their ship with the arm motion.

"What *are* they doing here?" asked Bernssen. "I can't come up with any answer other than the one Michael's proposed. It looks as if the P'torra are attacking."

"Unprovoked?" asked the pilot. "None of us can say. How do we know that the slimy Nex didn't do something to bring all this down on their pointy heads? By all the saints and Mother Mary, *they're* the ones we can't trust."

"Whoever started it—or will start the war again—we're agreed that alerting the P'torra ships englobing us is suicidal," said Ralston. He watched the pilot's reaction. The pilot had resigned himself to obeying the orders given by Bernssen. And Nels had made it clear to the pilot that they were not to communicate with anyone until he decided.

Ralston motioned for Bernssen and Leonore to talk privately. The three hung in the center of the lounge, isolated from the others.

"Any bright ideas?" asked Bernssen. "I'm tapped out. There doesn't seem any good way for us to declare ourselves neutral."

"We might not be able to, even if we wanted," said Ralston. Seeing the others' expression, he said grimly, "The P'torra threatened me about revealing all I'd discovered about the chaos device. And Slenth offered to finance an expedition. The Nex want control of it."

"It is an interesting—" began Leonore. She covered her mouth with a hand and gasped when the real reason came to her. "They want it as a weapon. They want to turn each other's sun into a nova."

"The Nex would be happy with that," agreed Ralston. "The P'torra might find the notion of giving everyone on a Nex-held planet incurable epilepsy interesting scientifically. Or mutations in the germ plasma. They'd enjoy watching a Nex-inhabited world destroyed by genetic mutation over a hundred years. The P'torra time sense is considerably different from ours. A century of planning to them is about the same as a month is to us."

"I feel I'm hearing only one side of a propaganda broadcast," said Bernssen. "No disrespect meant, Michael, but we know you're prejudiced in this. The P'torra might not be the vile backstabbing bastards you make them out to be."

"We don't have to worry about Michael," spoke up Leonore. "He's here, with us, in an expedition where he's not primary investigator. Doesn't that tell you something, Nels?"

"What?" The blond man frowned, not seeing what Leonore was getting at.

"Michael turned down the Nex offer to finance his own expedition. He doesn't want them to have the secrets locked in the chaos device, either."

Ralston had seldom felt more desolate and lost. "Leonore's

right. Whatever happens, we can't afford to let either side have the information we gather.''

"Keeping it from them is going to be hard, especially when my people start publishing papers on the field. Westcott's got a start on solving the equations. When the theoretical work is done—and put with the direct observation of the device—we might be able to build one ourselves. And anyone reading our papers can duplicate our work.''

"You're not asking us not to publish, are you, Michael?'' Leonore's eyes blazed in anger at this notion.

"We've got some responsibility, not only to science but to civilization.''

"Keeping this knowledge to ourselves won't serve any purpose,'' said Bernssen. "It will come out. A hint here, a solid clue there. Both the Nex and the P'torra are highly advanced. There's no real difference in the level of their science and ours. We can't be responsible for how they'd use—or misuse—what we find.''

"We're going back a couple centuries with these arguments, Nels,'' said Ralston. "Rather than talk them to death again, let's agree on what we can do. Foremost is to stay alive. Agreed on that point?''

"You make it sound difficult, Michael,'' said Leonore. "I'm not convinced that we can't simply contact the P'torra commander and declare ourselves neutral and in trouble. Put out a distress signal and then talk.''

Ralston wanted to scream in frustration. All around them rocketed warships armed with interceptor missiles capable of laying waste to a planetary area equal to half the island on which the University of Ilium stood. Call it fifty thousand hectares. Call it a million. To Ralston it didn't matter; one of those missiles could destroy their ship as surely as the nova that had taken both the Alpha and Beta systems.

Getting Leonore to understand this wouldn't be easy.

"Let's approach this question in a different way,'' Ralston said. "Imagine yourself the commander of a P'torra warship. Like the ones all around. You're keyed up, aren't you? No matter what's gone on—either the Nex started this or they didn't—you know that the Nex will destroy you if they get the chance. Verd?''

"Verd," agreed Leonore.

"You're approaching an enemy-held planet and a strange signal blasts across your com unit. Enemy? It might be since you're under com silence. Or is it a neutral ship? Does it matter? It's endangering your approach and might alert the Nex. Solution: destroy the problem."

"All right, all right, I see the problem. With reservation, I'll go along with doing nothing to contact the P'torra. Where does that leave us?"

"We're scientists. We're used to finding solutions to knotty problems. What are our resources? What can we do in the time we have?" Ralston had answers of his own dealing with contacting the Nex, but the others wouldn't accept them.

"Our equipment," said Bernssen. "We've got a large amount of equipment for studying solar activity."

"Putting together the fiber optic-laser gyroscope shows we can put it together in different ways," said Leonore. "A weapon?"

"No weapons," said Ralston. Both stared at him.

"Why not? I'd have thought you would be the first to advocate firing on the P'torra," said Bernssen.

"No suicide, remember. We're noncombatants and I want to keep it that way, if possible. They outnumber us fifty to one. It's going to be hard enough not being in the middle when the battle starts."

"The point is well taken about them outnumbering us. They're experienced, too, unless I miss a guess," said Nels. "So, no weapons. Studying them isn't going to help us."

"We have something else," said Ralston, not knowing where he went with the idea. "We have knowledge. Both the P'torra and the Nex want what we've found out about the chaos device. How can we use that data to our benefit?"

"As trade?" suggested Leonore. "No, we're agreed that neither side should have that information." The woman's statement surprised Ralston. They hadn't decided that. When Nels tacitly went along, Ralston mentally scored a major victory for himself. "How can we use the knowledge of the chaos device to extricate ourselves?"

"That's a question we should pose to Westcott," Ralston

said. "He's the one with the most intimate knowledge of the chaos equations and potential solutions."

"We can't expect to put together a super-drive and simply leave," said Bernssen. "Likewise, we can't expect some miracle weapon or gadget that'll solve everything for us."

"Why not? Westcott's been working overtime to redeem himself for the mistake in his calculations back in the Beta system."

"That wasn't his fault," said Leonore.

Ralston knew this was true, but an entire planet filled with intelligent beings had perished. Nothing Westcott could have done would have prevented their destruction, but of all those in the expedition, Westcott felt the closest to the inhabitants of Beta 7. Only he had communicated directly with them. He had to feel the loss of untold millions of thinking, if alien, creatures. And he had miscalculated. Although it wasn't logical, Ralston believed that Westcott felt responsible for the Betans' earlier than expected deaths. Just the way the mathematician drove himself hinted at that guilt. Ralston found himself smiling. Westcott might retain more humanity than he had given the man credit for.

"I'll go see what he has to say," offered Ralston. "Why don't you two start asking the others if they have any ideas? It'll be helpful to know where we stand with them."

Nels and Leonore silently left. Ralston heaved a deep sigh. He found himself hoping again, pinning all his faith on Westcott. Saving the expedition might be more than even his genius could deliver.

He found Westcott curled up near the sensor unit mounted on the computer. The slack expression on Westcott's face told Ralston that the mathematician worked constantly with the computer. For a fleeting instant Ralston wondered what it would be like to have instant access to all that information, to be able to retrieve any detail, no matter how obscure and have it a part of you, to calculate faster than any other human, to become more machine than man.

Revulsion replaced curiosity.

"Westcott," Ralston said, shaking the man gently. In freefall this didn't work too well. Ralston planted his feet under conveniently placed braces on the bulkhead and tried again. This time he aroused Westcott from his meditations.

"What?" Westcott's irritability indicated that Ralston might have caused a headache by precipitously breaking the brain-computer infrared link.

"We need you," Ralston said simply.

Westcott blinked. His shaved head reflected light from a nearby lamp. His eyes narrowed, as if expecting this to be a trick. "What do you mean, 'you need me'?"

"Just that." Ralston quickly explained their dilemma. "We need the facilities on Tosoll. If the P'torra fleet continues on course, those facilities might be destroyed or captured. But we can't fight their entire force, nor can we warn the Nex. Doing so would mean sure destruction for us."

"Mathematics does not lend itself to matters of war," said Westcott. "I fail to see how I can aid you."

"The chaos equations," said Ralston, inspiration flowing. "You mentioned once that the equations might describe how wars occur. The dynamics of randomness sets off fights."

"It's possible to develop such a system of equations, but it'd take years to find the proper parameters. What matters? What doesn't? It'd be easier to figure out how the chaos device worked, using the same nonlinear equations."

"It would?" Ralston brightened. "How long would that take?" He had visions of a chaos ray totally destroying the P'torra fleet.

"Couldn't take longer than, say, two years of dedicated work. I would have to be alone, though. No more interruptions."

"Two years!" Ralston exploded. "We need answers *now*."

Westcott only shrugged.

Ralston's mind raced. He refused to let loose of the idea that within this science ship's hull someone had the solution to their survival. Over and over, the thread of his tangled thoughts returned to Westcott.

"You have the system defined for radioactive decay, don't you?" asked Ralston. Westcott nodded. "What happens if you consider the ships around us as atoms, their missiles as, say, alpha particles? Could you decide which was most likely to shoot at us?"

"The answer to that doesn't require complex matrices,"

said Westcott. "The nearest one would fire and destroy us."
Westcott's eyes glazed as he drifted off on a mental tangent. Ralston almost shook the man again but for some reason he couldn't understand allowed the mathematician to continue his thought.

It proved worthwhile.

"There is something, though," said Westcott. "Intriguing idea. Of course the chaos equations describe conditions leading to war. Radioactive decay is another random event. What if I analyzed the trajectory away from the fleet that afforded us the maximum chance for escape and also resulted in maximum confusion among the P'torra? Is there an optimal course that will ram one of their ships into another—several into each other—and let us reach Tosoll before them?"

"Is there?" asked Ralston.

The computer began working hard as Westcott turned to it, his IR sensor linking again with the larger machine. For long minutes, Westcott hung immobile and then turned, a faint smile on his lips.

"There is such a course. We must be able to make corrections constantly, according to the shifting patterns of the P'torra vessels and the probability of destruction from each. However, we must embark soon. And I would need to connect directly with the ship's controls to control the dodging we will undoubtedly need to do."

Ralston slammed his hand against the intercom call button. Reluctance etched in every line of his body, the pilot came from the cockpit to listen to Westcott's scheme.

"By Mother Mary, no!" he roared. "I won't turn over my ship to anyone."

"Even if it means we'll all be killed—and your ship blown out of space." With the last statement Ralston knew he'd caught the pilot's full attention.

"You'll guarantee us getting through?" the pilot asked. "With no damage to the ship?"

"Does it matter what Ralston agreed to?" asked Westcott. "If we are destroyed, it will be after considerable effort. As it stands, we have no hope."

"Do it," said the pilot. "But I'll be at the controls. The first time it looks as if you're chinging it up, I take control and we blast hard for Tosoll."

"Agreed," said Westcott. The pilot left, muttering to himself.

"You'll keep total control, through the computer?" asked Ralston.

"Of course," Westcott said smugly. "Our course will be illogical, contrary to everything he has learned about piloting. We will have to be chaotic in our effort."

Westcott turned and anchored himself firmly, head and IR sensor just centimeters from the receptor unit on the computer. The ship jumped almost instantly. Ralston heard the pilot over the intercom ordering all hands to secure for rapid maneuvering.

Ralston slammed hard into the bulkhead as Westcott turned the ship on its axis, then accelerated all out.

And this was only the beginning of their race.

"Missiles launched," came the pilot's anxious voice. "Mother Mary, here they come. Four of the chinging whoresons!"

Ralston braced for the impact. P'torra missiles never missed their targets. Never.

ELEVEN

WITH EVERY SHARP movement of the ship, Michael Ralston thought they'd been hit by the P'torra missiles. But as far as he could tell, they escaped unscathed. Westcott's precipitous turnings and dodgings produced all the motion within.

"Inertial system," muttered Westcott, hunched close to the IR sensor and the computer. "We can turn quickly enough."

Even as he spoke, Ralston felt as if he'd spun about wildly. The ship lurched under him and slammed him hard into a bulkhead. He struggled to put on a harness and get into the nearest acceleration couch. Even this didn't keep him from bruising shoulders and waist. The couch had been designed for acceleration in one direction. Westcott had the ship dancing and sidestepping to a chaotic tune.

"Pilot's trying to regain control. Won't let him. Won't!" Westcott cackled. Ralston closed his eyes and found this worse than staring at the viewscreen.

A field of stars dotted the screen. None of them appeared to be moving, but Ralston knew this was deceptive. He blinked when two tiny dots moved slowly from left to right across the screen. As suddenly as they appeared, the star field abruptly changed and the dots disappeared. Westcott had accelerated along a new vector to leave behind the deadly missiles.

"We can't outrun their weapons," called Ralston. "Maybe we should surrender."

"No!" bellowed Westcott. Ralston had no idea if the

mathematician was denying the suggestion or responding to some condition picked up by the ship's radar.

From over the intercom came the pilot's frenzied voice. "You've blown out two rockets. We can't make it on the three remaining. Give it up, by all the saints, give it up!"

Westcott had become a part of the ship and its computer. Ralston studied the man and saw no vestige of humanity remaining. Westcott might have been a component plugged into the circuit.

The component performed flawlessly. In the viewscreen came a tiny dot that grew larger with breathtaking rapidity: Tosoll.

"The planet. There's Tosoll! We've gotten through to the planet!" cried Ralston. Even as he recognized the outlines of the continents through the gauzy white cotton of clouds, he knew they'd only succeeded halfway. By now the Nex battle command had been alerted and waited for the invasion fleet.

What ship came blasting down first? The one that had escaped the P'torra fleet. Them.

"Westcott, listen," Ralston cried out. "The Nex will try to blow us apart, too. Evade. Evade anything coming up from the planet!"

"Surveillance units," muttered Westcott. "New variables. New matrix required. Need time. Need time to compute."

Ralston jerked free of the straps which had held him together during the maneuvering. He kicked out and fell heavily. Westcott maintained a steady acceleration now, giving them almost the full Novo Terra gravity. Legs unused to such strain, Ralston fought toward the cockpit. The pilot seemed unaffected by the acceleration—Ralston guessed he was more consistent in taking the medication designed to prevent muscle atrophy caused by prolonged weightlessness.

"I need the com unit. I've got to get in touch with them before they blast us out of space."

"The P'torra or the Nex?" asked the pilot. His eyes had gone as round and glazed as saucers. "Both are turning everything they can on us."

Ralston doubted that. A full planetary defense system would ignore a single ship and let only a few units cope with it. And the P'torra wouldn't have more than one or two ships dispatched to eliminate them. Their primary targets lay below on Tosoll's surface.

"Static, can you get rid of the static?" Ralston demanded of the pilot.

The man shook his head. "I've never seen such intense jamming. Both sides are preventing us from talking."

Ralston understood all too well. The P'torra thought they were a Nex reconnaissance ship. To prevent them from reporting back on fleet strength required sophisticated jamming of all the communication channels. The Nex also tried to prevent them from communicating, because they thought this might be a P'torra advance scout determined to trigger defenses and pinpoint strengths and weaknesses.

"Can we get a lasercom unit working?" Ralston asked.

"There are a dozen still mounted on the hull," said the pilot. "They belong to your team—or to Dr. Bernssen's."

Ralston remembered that Bernssen and the others had monitored the Beta primary across a full electromagnetic spectrum. He left the pilot vainly trying to regain control of his ship. Staggering, Ralston made his way below and found Leonore Disa and Nels Bernssen.

"Nels, I need to use a lasercom. You have one mounted outside that'll go in the right frequency?"

"To contact the Nex?"

"Both sides are jamming the usual channels. We're going to have to punch through the static and find one of their commercial stations and try to overload its pickup with our signal. Both sides will blow us into dust if I don't."

"Don't know how much good this will do, but give it a try." Bernssen painfully worked his way across the cargo hold to where instruments had been shock-mounted on the bulkhead. Only this had saved them from being smashed during Westcott's violent course changes.

Bernssen sighed as he saw the minor damage done. "Have to recalibrate all this. No good for scientific work, but it should give you what you need."

Ralston saw an immediate problem. "How do I hold it on target, should I get lucky enough to find one?"

"Controls are there, but they're for fine-tuning. No gross

movements are allowed. No need when we sight in, it's usually on a star.''

Ralston struggled with the equipment, swinging the lasercom beam back and forth desperately seeking a carrier signal. He found one but the abrupt turnings of the ship prevented him from locking on.

''Want me to see if Westcott can slow down the dodging?'' asked Leonore.

''No!'' Ralston had some idea of the armament turned against them. To stay on any single vector now without chaotically determined variation meant instant death. ''I'll try to do better.''

Sweat blinded Ralston as he worked on the lasercom unit. Finally, he found a carrier signal—or it found him.

He didn't care which it was. Ralston began pulsing the laser in the code he had learned while with the Nex. In the intervening years, he was sure they'd changed the code, but Ralston hoped that someone recognized- it and would be curious enough to cease firing long enough to establish hard communication.

''Lost it. Damnation!''

The ship rolled, then went into a wild spin that threw Ralston hard into the bulkhead, stunning him. It took long minutes for him to realize that he was still alive and that the most violent of the maneuvers had passed. Ralston picked himself up and wiped away the bloody smear from his forehead where he'd connected with the edge of a crate.

''Nels, Leonore?'' he called out. They had been thrown together behind another crate. They lay together, still groggy. He checked to be sure that they hadn't sustained serious injuries, then turned back to the lasercom.

The rapid fluctuations on the power meter indicated complex signals coming along the beam—signals Ralston had no hope of translating without the needed codes.

He slammed his hand against the intercom call button and shouted to the pilot, ''Anything on the regular com channels?''

''Orders for a parking orbit,'' the pilot responded. ''Should we trust those snakes?''

''Westcott!'' called Ralston, ignoring the pilot. ''Follow the Nex instructions. Do you understand?''

"Safety behind their orbiting fortress, yes, yes," said West-cott, his voice distant and strained.

Ralston didn't know what the mathematician muttered about, but he knew any relief from the dangerous maneuvering could only benefit them. Ralston fought his way up the central passageway, being driven to his knees once when Westcott accelerated abruptly. Fighting the black tide of rising uncon-sciousness, Ralston made his way back into the lounge area where Westcott had established his computer link.

A few others had come into the lounge to watch. All had wisely strapped themselves down in acceleration couches.

"What's happening?" he demanded.

"Nex orders to go to a base. A satellite fortress, from the description." Westcott's face had turned gaunt and haggard. No color remained and the man's clothing hung wetly on his skinny frame. His eyes peered at Ralston, with recognition and infinite tiredness. "I didn't think I could do it. But I did!"

"You got us through in one piece," agreed Ralston.

"No, no, not that. The piloting was secondary. The com-putation, man, the computation! The chaos equation matrix had to be solved several times a minute. At one point, I had to solve it every fifteen seconds. So complex. The computing power." Westcott closed his eyes and put his hands on his shaved skull, as if trying to hold in his brains. He stroked the IR sensor as if it were a loved one.

"You did it," repeated Ralston, not understanding but still approving.

"I treated the P'torra ships as if they were atoms trying to decay. I considered this ship as a particle traveling through the lattice structure and sought a path for us that caused maximum interaction." Westcott chuckled. "Four P'torra ships rammed into one another."

"And one shot the other out of the sky," chimed in the pilot. "I saw it on the screen. By the saints, we may not have been armed, but we eliminated a full ten percent of their fleet."

"How badly damaged are we?" asked Ralston.

"The rockets are shot. Try to fire them again and we all go up, *poof!* But the damnedest thing's happened. That Sagnac gyroscope gadget you people put together is still working. Working better than it has any right to. The saints smiled on us this time." The pilot glanced over at the viewscreen. "They smiled then and must be laughing now. We got *them* to deal with. Imagine a snake ordering me to spin the ship so they can come aboard in comfort. Imagine them ordering me to do anything!"

The viewscreen showed small tugs fastening probes to the ship's hull. Ralston knew that the Nex would monitor the internal workings of the ship and be warned if they tried to escape.

"Let their representatives in," ordered Ralston. "I'll talk to them."

"Not unless you can hiss," said the pilot. "Those scale-faces don't speak our language."

Ralston again marveled at the lack of knowledge and the extent of prejudice against the Nex. He waited for the pilot to say something about the Nex looking like expensive luggage, but the comment never came. The man sank down into a silent sulk when the Nex commander and two assistants came through to the lounge.

The scientists noted the heavy energy weapons the Nex carried.

Before any of them could create a problem, Ralston went forward, arms extended and palms upward in the traditional Nex greeting.

"You are to know well of us?" asked their leader. He had thrown back the fragile-appearing hood of his spacesuit. Unlike Slenth, this Nex was gray-scaled. Ralston knew that some status was attached to scale coloration, but he had never determined exactly what it was.

"I wish you long life and victory over your enemies, may they fall from space!"

"Sentiments of goodwill ring nice," said the Nex. "Humans?" The reptile glanced around, but his hard black eyes never strayed far from Ralston.

"We come only in peace. We inadvertently shifted into the middle of the P'torra invasion fleet. We are no allies of the P'torra. We're damaged and need your assistance."

"You are neither of the Nex," snapped the commander.

"I fought with Commander Slenth," said Ralston. "Before that, I fought three campaigns on the surface below. I was there when Tosoll returned to Nex control."

The commander dropped to all fours and scurried around, tasting the air with his long, forked tongue. He rose in front of Ralston, that leathery black tongue whipping about. Ralston didn't stir. He held out his hand again, palm up. The Nex lightly sampled.

"There has talk of you before this."

"I'm Michael Ralston. I've resigned my commission in the Nex Planetary Defense Force and am now a professor at the University of Ilium on Novo Terra. The others are also researchers. We're neutral, not involved in any new dispute with the P'torra."

The Nex whipped about and hissed loudly. Ralston tried to follow the orders flung at the reptile's subordinate but failed. The words came too rapidly and in a dialect with which he wasn't familiar.

"Peaceful mission of seeking?" asked the Nex commander.

"We had our shift alignment gyroscope go out. We tried to replace it and we ended up here by accident. We had no idea that the P'torra were attacking Nex outposts."

"P'torra attack constantly. Vigilance needs always watching for those fish."

"We have no desire to take sides. We wish to remain neutral," said Ralston.

"You, neutral? When is this?"

Ralston struggled with what the Nex meant. "Ever since the war officially ended, I have been neutral in such matters. Politics has lost its appeal."

"You meet Slenth only time short while ago," accused the commander.

"I hadn't seen him in over five years."

"Come with me." When Nels and Leonore started to follow, the commander snapped, "This one only. You stay and be neutral. No danger will harm you."

At the airlock Ralston said, "I'll get my suit on."

"No need. We move through quick-tube."

Ralston uneasily trailed behind the reptile. He noted that the commander had fastened his spacesuit hood against emergencies. The Nex quick-tube connectors between ships were notoriously leaky, but Ralston saw he had little choice. The Nex treated them all as prisoners of war rather than neutral civilians. He couldn't blame them, yet it frustrated him mightily.

The tube creaked and groaned as it flexed to make up the small differences in rotation between the research ship and the small scout docked and orbiting around. Ralston admired the Nex piloting ability, but if they hadn't ordered the ship spun for artificial gravity, there'd have been no need for such fancy work. That was the Nex way. Ralston had never fully understood their desire to do things the hard way when simpler ones were just as good. In a sense, this had been their major obstacle in the war against the P'torra. The Nex chose methods of attack that were needlessly complicated and often did not succeed fully.

In the scout ship, Ralston found an acceleration pad against the rear bulkhead. He fixed himself to it without being told. The Nex drove like wild men. In a combat situation such as this, their maneuvering would be even more spectacular.

Ralston wasn't disappointed. The rapid dodging that took them to the surface of the armored moon left bruises on Ralston's arms, legs, and body where the broad web straps stretched taut.

On shaky legs, Ralston went through the airlock once more. The difference in gravity was all that kept him from falling on his face. This moon's pull amounted to less than ten percent of Novo Terra's. He held himself as erect as possible. To show weakness meant a major breach of etiquette and made it more difficult to successfully present his case of neutrality.

"There," said the commander. "Sit."

Ralston gratefully sank into a cushioned chair that had never been built for the human frame. The sides came in too severely and squeezed at Ralston's hips. His shoulders and upper body found no support, but the way the chair stretched back almost parallel to the floor gave him the chance to lounge enough to rest.

Another gray-scaled Nex entered. Ralston did not stand. He had been offered the chair and, as a guest, he had the right to remain in it. The Nex came over without introduction.

Ralston held out his palm and endured the light, damp flicks of tongue against his flesh.

"Slenth is told me of you." The Nex shook his head slightly, then said, "Slenth *has* told me of you."

"You know Commander Slenth?" asked Ralston.

"His mission to your planet world is of vital importance. You are Ralston doctor." The way the reptile said it left no doubt that they had identified him. Ralston wondered if Slenth had marked him in some fashion. The Nex tongues were incredibly sensitive organs. In spite of scrubbing for space, heavy disinfectants, and almost two months since he'd seen Slenth, some trace of Slenth must remain on his skin.

"I know nothing of his mission. I am neutral now. The P'torra fleet was—"

"This has been explained," said the Nex. "Coincidence occurs. We are glad you arrived."

"The battle," said Ralston. "How is it going? The P'torra seemed to have launched a sneak attack."

"We prepare for any treachery. Your cleverness destroyed five of their vessels. You must tell us of your evasion plan. It will serve us well."

"Luck," insisted Ralston. "Only luck. We are severely damaged and our course proved too erratic for the P'torra to track accurately. Our maneuvering rockets are burned out and we need a new gyroscope before we can continue."

"Continue to what location?" The Nex hunkered down, tiny hands fluttering in front of him like captive birds. Ralston knew this indicated strict attention. The Nex missed nothing in what Ralston said. The archaeologist had to admit that he'd never met a Nex with such a good command of the human language, either.

"We're following a . . . cometary object that passed through a system we've noted as Beta. Most of the expedition staff are astrophysicists interested in examining it."

"What of you? An archaeologist of such fame would not share the physicists' goals. Slenth tells of a discovery of important meaning that you seek."

Excitement caused the Nex to revert to, for him, more natural speech patterns.

"In the Beta system we found ruins that gave some indication about the trajectory of the cometary object. Further, we contacted intelligent beings who lived on a gas giant who had directly observed the object. For this research, I and a former student of mine are required."

"Slenth hints at greatness in your work. No details have come to such distant outposts, but this maybe might give Nex superior edge over the P'torra?"

"Knowledge is its own reward. We are scientists. We don't look for weapons of war."

"But this maybe can be changed for this?" the Nex pressed.

"How knowledge is used is beyond my realm. I am interested only in the civilization that constructed the object we follow."

"What share might we obtain of your knowledge—in exchange for rocket repair and new gyroscope?"

Ralston had no immediate answer for this. He couldn't promise to reveal to the Nex any information obtained from the chaos device. But they were obviously in the middle of a war situation; the Nex might refuse to give them the equipment or even imprison them until the P'torra had broken off their attack.

Ralston didn't like the idea of being in a Nex jail for years.

"You put me in a bad position," Ralston said. "I don't believe I know your name or title."

"Excuse such bad manners on this one's part. I am Chosinth, Regent of Tosoll."

"Chosinth, it is my honor. Your fame precedes you." Ralston tried to hide his fear. Chosinth had a reputation for viciousness when it came to dealing with the P'torra that even exceeded that of the rest of his cold-blooded race. Ralston had never seen a Nex offer the slightest mercy to a captive P'torra. Chosinth had built a reputation on being even more ruthless.

"I have killed many P'torra, and I will kill many more." The Nex ruler of Tosoll opened his mouth and revealed the sharp teeth within in a mocking smile. "With your aid, I will kill many more."

"How does the battle go?" Ralston had been straining to hear the defensive arms responding to any attack. No sound of them had come while he'd been with Chosinth.

"They arrived in great disarray. Although we had not expected them, we rallied quickly to defense. Your appearance in their fleet aided us greatly and hindered them. The warning we thank you for. It saved many Nex lives."

"Is this not payment enough for the repairs we need?"

Chosinth hissed in approval. "Your displayed courage in barter confirms Slenth's opinion of you. He spoke well of your battle courage. Your current bravery reflects well on him and you."

"Many lives were saved," Ralston mused. "No one can place a value on a life. A gyroscope? A rocket tube? Who can say?"

"Such might be available, now that the P'torra have run like cravens once again."

"But you want more."

"The chaos weapon you seek. We want it. It will save many, many Nex lives." Chosinth rocked slowly on his powerful hind legs. Ralston read determination in every line of the Nex's body.

"For the reasons I gave Slenth, I can't turn over such data to you."

"I know nothing of what you said to Slenth."

"We will publish scientific papers on our discoveries."

"All can read these. Even the P'torra. We need this weapon before they have it."

"It's impossible for you to send along an observer," Ralston said. "Human feelings against the Nex run high. Even the pilot would refuse to continue in such a case."

"It would place immense burden on the observer, also," said Chosinth. "Your return to Tosoll is impossible to force. You do not command this expedition." The way Chosinth inflected the words told Ralston that the Nex knew just about everything about the organization of the expedition. "Would it be wrong to see before the publication any of your research papers? It is my belief that such practice is not of unusual nature."

"You want a prepublication look at my results?"

"All results. This is price of gyroscope and rockets."

"I could promise and then ignore it later. Or there might

never be a publication. Nothing might work out for the expedition.''

Chosinth again smiled. ''Another human might lie. You have true honor. Your word is sufficient.''

''I can't promise for Bernssen and the others.''

''Ask of them. We will trust in your honor. If you vouch for them, we will trust in theirs, too.''

Ralston worried over the dilemma. They might not find anything of value when they got to the chaos device—they might never even find it. On the other hand, if they unlocked the deadly secrets of chaos it held, giving these to the Nex might be the start of a new and infinitely more deadly war with the P'torra.

He didn't know what to say because Chosinth had him estimated well. Once he gave his word, he wouldn't go back on it. Salazar and the others at the University had stripped him of almost everything he'd spent a lifetime working for. No tenure, no position, cut off from deserved publications. All he had left was his honor.

Damn Chosinth! Damn them all!

TWELVE

"THEY LIED," EXCLAIMED the pilot. "By all the saints, those slimy snakes lied!"

He crossed himself as an explosion caused the ship to shudder. The pilot turned back to the control panel and punched in viewscreen coordinates that showed part of the P'torra battle fleet coming around the bright crescent of Tosoll.

"The Nex said they'd driven off the P'torra. They didn't say they'd stopped the attacks." Even as Michael Ralston watched, trails of two P'torra missiles appeared on the screen. Nex interceptors destroyed both in silent fury.

"The P'torra are dropping most of the missiles in from a dozen A.U.s," said the pilot. "Then there are the ones in orbit around Tosoll. They seem to bombard the surface as much as they bombard us. Really turning the surface to hash." The man's voice carried distaste at the destruction done by the marauding P'torra.

The research ship still clung to the Nex moon base, more dismantled than put together. The pilot agonized over every bolt removed, every piece of delicately calibrated equipment replaced, every slither and hiss made by the efficient Nex workers.

"You don't think they enjoy having the P'torra bomb their planet, do you? If they could, they'd get rid of them in an instant." Ralston fell silent at his own words. The reptiles would destroy the P'torra home world completely, given the chance—given the deadly power of the star-altering chaos weapon. And how could Ralston deny their cause? The P'torra laid waste to hundreds of thousands of hectares on Tosoll's surface. Of the fifty ships in the P'torra invasion fleet, all but a dozen had been destroyed or run off.

But those dozen still made a hell out of the surface. And occasionally they directed a few missiles at the armored moon base to keep Chosinth and the others occupied.

"I'd enjoy bombing the snakes' planet," grumbled the pilot. "Slimy reptiles." He crossed himself again and found another saint to invoke when a new round of P'torra shelling rocked them. The only cheer Ralston found in the man's words was the weakness of his cursing against the Nex. The P'torra ferocity in destroying the planetary surface worked on the pilot's sympathy.

"How much longer before they finish all the repairs on the ship?" asked Ralston.

"If they finished four days ago, it wouldn't be soon enough for me." The pilot turned and studied a readout on the panel, then said, "I think they'll have most of the important work done within ten hours. I want to be out of here in eleven. You have Dr. Bernssen and the others ready for liftoff then. I don't care if anyone gets hurt or not, we're flaming out of here!"

"I'll warn them about your intentions," promised Ralston. He had much more on his mind. He had given Chosinth his word that everyone in the expedition would send preliminary drafts of their scientific papers to a Nex representative before publication. He had promised. Now he had to convince Bernssen to agree. And Westcott. And Leonore. And all the others.

Ralston made his way down the central passage and found Nels and Leonore in the large lounge area. They talked quietly and intensely. Ralston didn't want to disturb them but had no choice. Time pressed in on him and required immediate decisions.

Nels Bernssen looked up. He was obviously not pleased to be interrupted.

"Wait, Nels, please," said Ralston, cutting the other man off before he could protest. "I've got something important that's got to be said right now."

"How are the repairs coming?" Nels asked.

"Fine. We'll be shifting in eleven hours. I don't think the pilot wants to stay to even test the Nex equipment."

"Understandable," murmured Leonore.

"I haven't told you what I promised to get the work done. It involves you and the others."

Leonore's eyes went wide as she imagined the horrors perpetrated on Ralston—and that which would be visited on the rest of them by the non-human Nex.

"It's not all that bad, but it *is* galling."

"We won't turn over the chaos weapon to them," Bernssen flatly said. "We're agreed on that point. No one race gets it."

"Agreed," said Ralston. "I'm not sure I want even our people to have control of it." He heaved a deep breath, then plunged into the explanation. "So," he finished, "they want first peek at our work before it's published. They'd get it after publication. This just gives them a few weeks or maybe less head start on the P'torra."

"You agreed to this?"

"We needed the gyroscope and new rocket tubes. Without the one we don't star accurately and without the tubes we can't even get into position for a shift."

"I don't like it," said Nels.

"I don't, either. How could you ever agree to this, Michael?" asked Leonore.

"What other choice did I have? We can't buy the equipment from them at any price. Chosinth made it clear that Tosoll is on a war footing. The P'torra attacks show that the regent's not exaggerating the danger they face daily. And there's nowhere else to turn. We fell into their base. Without this agreement we'd be virtual prisoners until they decided to get rid of us."

Leonore shuddered at the way he'd worded it.

"They wouldn't kill us," Ralston said. "But the Nex have no incentive to let us go, either, unless I agreed. This isn't *that* bad."

"The precedent it sets is bad," said Bernssen.

"I know, I know. Can you think of any other way around this? We have to pursue the chaos device. If Westcott is right, it is falling apart even as we sit here."

"He might not be right," said Leonore. "He was wrong about the Beta primary and when it'd go nova."

"But he was right in how he used the chaos equations to get us through the middle of the P'torra fleet. Do you know anyone else who could have done that?" countered Ralston.

"It might have been luck—or stark insanity." Nels Bernssen slumped down, arms crossed tightly across his chest and his face clouded with emotion. He thought hard for a few minutes, then said, "The Nex don't have to see every paper. Yours and Leonore's will be innocuous enough. Even mine might be, since it deals with stellar mechanisms. Explaining how the fusion process proceeds is different from telling how to build a machine to disrupt it. There's always the chance we won't be publishing anything at all, that the trip will turn out different from what we expect.

"But Westcott," Nels went on. "He's another story. If we're successful, he'll be able to spell out in mathematical detail how the chaos equations can be used. The maneuvering he did would be a small part. He might be able to give ways of predicting how to topple a society or all the rest we've talked about. His papers will be important."

"Withholding them from the Nex isn't possible," said Ralston.

"Because you promised?"

"Because they know everyone aboard ship. And no, I didn't tell Chosinth. He already knew. The Nex have effective intelligence-gathering networks."

"Slenth had shown an interest in this expedition," finished Leonore. "Their communication network must be extraordinary for Chosinth to hear about us—and the chaos field—less than two months after we leave Novo Terra."

"We must continue," said Ralston. "We need to find the chaos device as quickly as possible. Whether Westcott is right in his calculations or the device will last a million years, we *must* find it."

"I agree," said Bernssen. "Better us than either the Nex or the P'torra."

"Do we keep silent after we've found it?" asked Leonore.

"Let's worry about that when we finish. Right now, do you agree to the Nex condition?"

"All right, Michael, I agree," said Leonore. "It really rankles. There should never be such conditions placed on research. It's not fair putting us under such pressure."

"They don't want to censor our findings, after all," said Ralston. "They just want a head start on the P'torra."

"They know better than to ask for us to hold back important details," said Bernssen. "We'd never agree. I'd hate to spend the rest of my life in remand, but I'd do it rather than give in to censorship or publishing false data. Better not to publish anything."

"What of Westcott?"

"His interests are so varied, there's no telling what he would want to publish. Remember how enthused he was about his quantum gravity theory? As far as I can tell," said Bernssen, "he's dropped all work on it in favor of the chaos equations solution. He might decide that the chaos device isn't important and go off on still another tangent."

"We've got to ask him."

"Let's get on our way, then worry about it," suggested Lenore.

Ralston didn't like this but his heart wasn't in confronting Westcott on the matter. What worried him the most was Chosinth's reaction to this cowardice on his part. The Nex regent had to know everything that went on inside the ship. Those probes attached to the hull were sensitive spy devices.

"I've got to ask him," Ralston decided. "Besides, we need a course to follow. We ended up at Tosoll by accident. Westcott must have a trajectory plotted by now."

Both Nels and Leonore nodded. They seemed restrained, possibly because of those Nex spy probes.

Ralston found Westcott hunched over the computer. He reached out to break the infrared beam but the mathematician's hand shot up to grab his wrist.

"That gives me a headache. I've told you that before. Do you want me to write it down for you so you won't forget?"

"Sorry, but we have a major problem."

"About the Nex demand to see our papers before publication? There is no dilemma involved. We must track the field. Therefore, any agreement allowing us to do so is in everyone's best interest."

"How'd you . . ." Ralston's question trailed off. Westcott was hooked into the computer and must have sophisticated sensing equipment of his own monitoring the Nex spy probes. After all, everything ran through the ship's computer—and in a sense because of his direct-link, Westcott *was* the ship's computer. Ralston held back a broad smile.

"Here. Take this to the pilot. It's a course input for the navigation computer." Westcott's watery eyes locked with Ralston's. The silent message was apparent: Do not allow the Nex access to the course information.

"I'll see that he gets it. How near completion are the repairs?"

"The gyroscope is installed and checks out. The one we built is more accurate. We should consider contacting the father of that assistant of yours—what's his name?"

"Leonid Disa?"

"He's the one. Interstellar Computronics can make a fortune off a precision instrument like this. We can get enough in royalties to finance a hundred new expeditions."

"What about the rockets?"

"Almost done. Testing them will be more difficult. Must blast for at least five minutes to burn off the protective layers of graphite and get down to the boron-fiber ceramic throats. Always dangerous since slightly less than two percent are defective. A tiny crack or chipped area means a blown rocket."

Ralston started to ask how Westcott had become such an authority, then stopped. The mathematician had full access to the ship's data banks. Such information had to be there for the pilot's benefit in any foreseeable emergency situation.

"Eleven hours?" asked Ralston. "Is that a good estimate for completion and launch?"

"I've done the calculations for such a time." Westcott turned away and hunched back toward the IR sensor on the computer console. Ralston took this as dismissal.

He left, almost cheerful again. Dealing with Westcott over the Nex demand had proven easier than he'd thought. Maybe the other rough spots would prove equally smooth once they came to them. Ralston hoped so, but he didn't believe it. The chaos device lay ahead somewhere in uncharted space—and he had seen how it had destroyed untold billions of people and two entire solar systems.

What other destruction did it hold in store for them? Ralston knew they'd find out soon.

"We are an escort for you until there is no more orbit," said the commander of the Nex military force.

"We won't need it," said the pilot. He crossed himself, then vanished toward the cockpit, not waiting to hear the answer.

"Are there still P'torra ships in orbit around Tosoll?" asked Ralston.

"Some. One," admitted the commander. "Regent Chosinth wants none of the wrong mistakes to be made. You are many valuables to us, he orders me."

"Damn right, we're valuable," grumbled one researcher. Ralston motioned him to silence. The scientist moved away to find an acceleration couch and strap down.

"We've given you our course heading," said Ralston, wondering how far off it really was. Probably not by much. Westcott had calculated it, possibly using the chaos equations to provide an added degree of randomness to the trip. They had all agreed that the Nex would be unable to follow, even knowing their precise heading. The length of their shift mattered as much as the heading, but Ralston had agreed that even this small bit of information should be hidden from the Nex, if possible.

Considering the Nex intelligence network and how efficiently it had operated so far, he doubted they hid much from the beady black serpents' eyes.

"Thank Chosinth for the hospitality. We won't forget it."

"He knows *you* will not forget, Dr. Ralston," said the military commander. The Nex turned and looked from Westcott to Bernssen and then to Leonore. His tongue flashed forth and quivered, then vanished between scaly lips. The Nex left quickly, motioning to his guard. In less than a minute, the reptiles had dropped to all fours and slithered from the research ship.

"I'm ready to blast," came the pilot's terse words over the

intercom. "Let's hope I catch a few of those snakes in the rocket wash."

Ralston hopped into a couch next to Nels. On the blond scientist's other side rested Leonore, her hand in his.

"We'll be all right," said Ralston. "But after we make the shift, we'll have to examine every part of the ship. I don't want to be carrying any recording equipment that's not ours."

"Do you think they'd do something that blatant?" asked Bernssen.

"Not really." Ralston settled into the couch when he felt vibrations from the rockets shake the entire ship. "But it can't hurt."

"We're off!" cried the pilot.

Ralston closed his eyes as the abrupt acceleration rammed him deep into the couch cushions. Nothing had gone right recently, but still he felt a curious hope warming him inside. Their deal with the Nex meant little. They would only receive information a bit ahead of the P'torra this way—and Ralston couldn't know in advance what that information might be.

This expedition might unleash a Pandora's box of nameless chaotic horror. Radioactive decay of once-stable elements. Mutation. Epilepsy. Devastating weather patterns. Stellar imbalances. Others that he couldn't even guess at.

But this hadn't happened yet. He screwed his eyes even tighter when a new fist of acceleration pounded at his chest. Whatever happened, he knew he couldn't go back on his word to Chosinth. Without personal honor, nothing mattered. Nothing.

"I got us lining up just fine," said the pilot. "We'll be shifting in about ten minutes. Everything's working great."

Ralston turned toward Westcott. He forced his eyelids open to see that the mathematician lay on his couch, sensor in a special brace so that the infrared beam wouldn't deviate from its receptor atop the computer console.

"What's the status, Westcott?" he called. The mathematician grunted against the force of their blast.

"Gyroscope is functional and on our star target. Tubes have burned through their protective layer. No cracks. No holes in the throat liner. We're going to shift without problem."

"Let the pilot do it," ordered Bernssen. "No need to upset him further."

"I . . . have computation to do before shift," said Westcott. "He is welcome to his ship."

Barely three minutes had passed before the pilot bellowed, "I'm picking up a radar trace. I think we have company. Mother of God, we do! It's one of those damned P'torra ships dogging us!"

Ralston fought to lift his hand to the intercom call button. He failed. He had to listen to the pilot without being able to respond.

". . . the snake ship's vectoring in to protect us. I didn't believe they'd risk their scaly skins to help us, but they are. St. Francis, yes, there they go!"

On the viewscreen Ralston saw tiny blips appear. The perspective distorted what actually happened in space. Even smaller blips began curving back and forth, some colliding, others slipping by: These were deadly missiles.

"The Nex got a hit in on the P'torra. Three minutes to our shift. Everything still functioning to optimal. Shift timer's on. We're going, no matter what."

"Westcott!" called Leonore. "Can you tell us what's going on out there?"

The mathematician grunted again. His voice came muffled and indistinct. "Want to work. No time for this. No time."

"Westcott!"

"The P'torra ship is not destroyed. It is launching all its missiles, hoping one will penetrate the Nex defenses."

"Are we behind the Nex ship?" asked Ralston. From the viewscreen he thought they might be in the direct line of fire if the Nex warship was destroyed. Another two minutes and it would no longer matter; they'd have starred out after the chaos device.

But until that instant, they were vulnerable.

"The Nex stopped all the missiles. No, wait, one penetrated its defenses."

Ralston didn't need Westcott to tell him that the Nex ship was in serious trouble. The sudden flare on the screen told of a hit. How serious he couldn't say. They'd need special radar to tell that. At these distances they watched the results of a battle that had occurred thirty seconds earlier. The speed of light was insufficient for learning the outcome.

"Westcott, is that a P'torra missile? Did one miss the Nex and come on after us?"

"The Nex ship is destroyed. It blew apart trying to protect us, according to my analysis of their maneuvers."

"Oh, my God, no!" cried Ralston. He had seen this happen before. The Nex made no provision for surrender on their warships. If this ship had been destroyed, it might have cast all its unspent missiles into space. Any differential motion each missile sensed would activate it and send it on its deadly mission.

The Nex warship itself might trigger a response; so would the P'torra ship. And so would the research ship.

"Four missiles abandoned, then launched spontaneously," came the pilot's voice. A quick prayer, then, "We've got twenty seconds until we star away from Tosoll."

"Westcott," asked Ralston, not wanting to know but having to ask. "How long before those missiles reach us?"

"Ten seconds," came the mathematician's answer. "Only ten seconds. We'll never have time to escape!"

Ralston gritted his teeth and began the death count.

Ten, nine, eight . . .

THIRTEEN

MICHAEL RALSTON FOUND himself unable to take his eyes off the viewscreen. The sight of the missiles coming for them—Nex missiles—hypnotized him.

". . . four, three . . ." He wished he could stop counting the seconds until their deaths.

The shift took him by surprise. At first he thought the sudden disorientation and sensory confusion he had come to experience at starring out and death were identical. He tasted the sounds and smelled the colors and screamed and saw the voiceless cry hang suspended before him. Ralston forced himself to relax. Slowly, the scrambled sensation loosened its grip in him and sounds became sounds, sights became sight.

"We did it!" he crowed when he was able. Ralston looked around the lounge area. Westcott still lay on his acceleration couch, head fastened down so that he wouldn't lose contact with the computer. Nels Bernssen had unfastened his restraining straps and held Leonore Disa tightly, rocking her back and forth as if she were a small child. The others in Bernssen's expedition moaned and moved slowly, barely understanding how they had escaped.

Ralston hit the call button and yelled at the pilot, "What happened? How did we avoid the missiles?"

"The Nex," the pilot mumbled. "By the saints, they gave their lives to protect us."

"What happened?" Ralston demanded a second time.

"They cast out their missiles to get the P'torra. Two of

them did. But one missile came for us because we were in motion. But, St. Jude be praised, we were accelerating too hard for it to catch us. We had enough of a start. We shifted just as it reached us.''

"Is the ship all right?"

"Verd," said the pilot. "Everything shows green here. The missile might have exploded, but it couldn't touch us once we folded space around ourselves. Both St. Francises, thank you!''

The pilot started thanking a pantheon of saints. Ralston slumped and rested his head against the cool composite bulkhead of the ship. His feet rose and went over his head with the motion. They had, indeed, achieved stardrive. The weightlessness told of that.

Ralston heaved a deep breath, spun adroitly, and kicked over to where Westcott still lay unmoving. The infrared sensor blinked on and off slowly, showing most of Westcott's time was spent thinking rather than computing.

"The pilot says we made it. Did the shift come precisely on our target?"

"There is something wrong," said Westcott in a slow, almost drugged voice. "I cannot see what it is. There are strange attractors in this area that have never existed before.''

"Strange attractors?"

"Mathematical points on an imaginary plot like nodes in real space. We seem to be lodged in one.''

"We can't get out?" Ralston refused to feel panic. They had just escaped one of the most efficient and deadly weapons ever built. The Nex missiles seldom missed their targets and had destroyed one another. Luck had been a part of it, but they had survived.

Perhaps, reflected Ralston, luck mattered more when it came to survival than skill. The Alphans had been adroit, successful—and the chaos weapon had destroyed their culture, their population, their solar system. The Betans had been vastly more alien, but the passage of the chaos field had tainted them, also. Ralston screwed his eyes shut and tried to imagine the cleansing flame from the nova turning the monstrous gas giant planet into superheated vapor. What had the Betans done to deserve such a fate?

What had he and the others on this expedition done to deserve escape from death?

"It must be the result of the shift mathematics," said Westcott.

"What must?" Ralston came back to his senses and tried to pay more attention to what Westcott said.

"When we star out, all the distance is traveled in the first split second. The rest of the time is spent forcing our way back into space. The longer the shift, the harder it is to get free and the longer it takes."

Ralston blinked. He had never heard this. All the months he'd spent in space, he'd naively assumed that the distance was covered in some linear fashion, that every day's travel got them that much farther along toward their destination.

"If anything disturbs the shift space, we can find ourselves thrown out, not at the point we intended but at some other spot on a sphere with the same shift-distance radius."

"If we star for ten light years, you mean, and something disturbs us, we won't end up at the spot we intended but at another point on a ten light-year sphere?"

"It's more complex than that, but it's verd. We must be close to the chaos field. It has produced the attractor."

"What does this mean? We won't be able to leave shift space?" This frightened Ralston more than anything else about travel. To be forever doomed to weightlessness and the meaningless jumble shown on the viewscreen was a hell he wanted to avoid.

"I don't know what it means. The strange attractors are points of utter stability in a sea of chaos. This is the product of the equations' solution. What can it mean?"

Westcott closed his eyes and the dim red light on his head-mounted sensor began to glow constantly. Ralston pushed himself away to let the mathematician work through this problem.

It sounded as if they were trapped, but Westcott hadn't seemed concerned on this point. But the man had been worried. Ralston saw this. He forced himself to laugh ruefully. Westcott's concerns were not those of ordinary mortals. He might be worrying over an abstruse solution rather than their plight. If it could even be called that.

They were alive! In that Ralston rejoiced.

What did it mean to be in a well of stability during a shift?

"We will shift free and find what we want," said West-cott. The mathematician lounged back on the acceleration couch as if barely able to hold himself erect. In the weight-lessness of the ship, this made Westcott appear even more enervated.

"Is he all right?" asked Leonore, whispering to Ralston.

"I can't say. He hasn't eaten, he doesn't sleep, he just works."

"How can you tell?"

"The sensor has been glowing a brighter red than normal. I think he must be forcing hundreds of hours of work into just a few."

"I don't want to be caught in mid-shift," said Leonore. Her brown eyes welled with tears. Ralston thought that this expedition had been hard on her—and on Bernssen. They had left under the stigma of Ralston's problems at the University, had found mistakes in Westcott's calculations that robbed them of precious months of research, had fallen into the middle of a renewed Nex–P'torra conflict and now they had finally tracked the chaos device and found themselves caught in a spacial anomaly created by the chaos field's passage.

"We won't get lost. Westcott's assured me that won't happen." Ralston went on to explain how they might end up at some unknown point on an imaginary sphere with the radius of their shift, but that would be better than coming out of the shift in some distant galaxy, lost beyond all hope of return.

"I always knew starring was more of a mathematical con-cept than something definite," the woman said, "but I'd never realized it was that abstract."

"The attractor!" cried Westcott. His eyes blazed as brightly as the infrared sensor mounted on his shaved head. "We have reached the proper point."

Ralston cried in surprise when the ship lurched. He fell heavily, hitting his knees on the floor. It took Ralston several seconds to realize that they had regained gravity and that this was the source of his problems. He straightened painfully, rubbing his skinned knees and a banged elbow.

"Are we out of the shift?" he asked. Something deep within him told him that the danger—whatever it might be—wasn't past.

"Yes. No. I can't say where we are," said Westcott. "We have entered a new type of space, one with a physical reality different from what we've known."

"Physical laws still operate?" demanded Bernssen. "Space is still isotropic, isn't it?"

"I don't think so. We . . . it's difficult to say how this space operates. We have fallen into a special type of well. Not a gravity well. This isn't a topological quantity in the same sense that gravity is. It's *different*."

Ralston looked up at the viewscreen and thought that his eyes had been affected by the shift.

The silence that fell when the others looked made Ralston even more uncomfortable.

"Are those all starships?" Leonore asked, her voice cracking with strain. "It's as if they were sucked into this hole and . . ."

"And couldn't get out," finished Ralston.

Nels Bernssen began snapping orders. "I want a full scan of whatever's there. Entire spectrum. Photos. Find out if there's any hard radiation. Do it now!"

A dozen of the researchers jumped and ran down toward the cargo hold to unlimber their equipment.

"All different shapes and designs," said Ralston. "It's like an old Earth legend. What was it? I remember. The Sargasso Sea. Legend held that ships blundering in were trapped for all eternity."

"It's no illusion," came McGhee's voice from across the room. The scientist pressed himself close to a control panel he'd mounted on the bulkhead. Outside the ship ran his probes. "Solid."

"It's a treasure trove!" cried Leonore, coming out of her shock. "There must be a half-dozen different kinds of ships. And each is unlike anything I've ever seen."

"I agree," said Ralston. "Any one of those ships constitutes a major find. If we can trace their origins back to a home planet, we can be listed as discoverer." Ralston rocked back and held down the bitterness that welled up within him. "Dammit, listen to me. I'm starting to sound like Jaime Velasquez. It's *knowledge* I should be thinking about, not gain."

Ralston's mind still lovingly cherished the idea of being the primary discoverer of a new humanoid race. One percent of any trade, any scientific exchange, any gain whatsoever from that planet's society, went to the discoverer. One such find made men wealthy beyond the dreams of avarice. Presented for Ralston were a minimum of six different types of ship, any one of which might be enough.

"Salazar would let you back into his good graces," said Nels. "Imagine being able to buy the entire University. You could—we all could. Even splitting the take among us all, each of us could buy a dozen Universities of Ilium."

"As if we'd want it," said Leonore.

Ralston wasn't sure that this wasn't exactly what he wanted.

"We're missing something," he said. "Those ships are here because they couldn't get out. We might be trapped, too."

All eyes turned to Westcott. The mathematician sat with glazed eyes. Spittle ran from the corner of his mouth. Seldom had Ralston seen a man so oblivious to the world around him. Or was Westcott more aware than any of them? The sensor glowed brilliantly now. Whatever the man worked on, it had to be of solid, significant importance to them all.

"Westcott? What is it?" asked Nels. The physicist shook the mathematician's shoulder slightly. "What readings are you getting from the ship's external sensors?"

"We are the only life in the attractor pocket," Westcott said. "Dead ships. All are dead ships—and all failed in precisely the same manner. This spot draws a particular dysfunction."

"Did it cause the problem?" asked Ralston.

"No, not at all. Those ships. All have a stardrive significantly different from ours. The mathematics of their operation is not ours. The chaos field passed by, disrupted their spacial manifold, and jerked the ships to this stability point."

"We're in no danger, are we?" asked Leonore.

"Our drive was interrupted, not destroyed as theirs was. We . . . we can continue on our course in a few hours. We must build up speed again, as if we were accelerating to a shift. But it'll seem that we're stationary. This is not the space we came from, nor is it the space we normally occupy during a shift."

"If he says we're in good shape, I'll believe him," said Leonore. The woman's face glowed with excitement. "We've got a chance to do some archaeology, Michael. Do you want to go with me?"

"Which one?" asked Ralston. His heart beat faster. The idea of discovering not one race, but six thrilled him. He had been cheated out of full research on the Alphans and the Betans, but not now. He'd find these aliens' star charts and track them down. If they still lived and prospered, fine. If only ruins remained, he'd have a lifetime of work ahead of him picking and choosing the best sites to explore and reconstruct.

"The nearest one. We can work across from it. I'll want a supervisor, ten—no, make that twenty!—probes, enough block circuits to record everything a dozen times over."

Leonore's enthusiasm for the unexpected find was contagious. The others in Bernssen's expedition began chiming in with their findings. No hard radiation. No reason for the gravity field; it was simply there. Fourteen ships within observation range, only two of them with similar design. Measurements were being made at a frantic pace.

Ralston and Leonore walked quickly to the airlock, gathering their equipment as they went, arguing over the best way of examining their lucky find.

"Nothing but probes first," insisted Ralston. "We'll want a gas-content probe, all the visual spectrum on another, hard UV and IR on another, one to drill for samples of the hull, at least five for any bodies we find."

"We can go in ourselves," said Leonore, "and save a lot of time."

"Too dangerous," said Ralston. "We're expecting to find no one alive. How do we know they're not all waiting for us?"

"Better and better."

"They might have died from something not inherent in this." Ralston gestured vaguely, indicating the attractor well.

"Westcott said this is only a mathematical concept. How can that kill anyone?"

"How can it hold so many ships? And we'll want a couple probes to begin work on dismantling their drive system. If it's different, we'll want to know how."

"That's low priority, Michael."

"High priority," he contradicted. "We're still looking for the chaos device, remember? We need all the data we can for Westcott to determine how it affected the drives. Might give him a clue to the workings of the chaos device."

"Well, all right," Leonore agreed reluctantly. "We certainly need a probe for photographing their charts and for worming around in their computer. And their communications gear. We need—"

"Everything," Ralston cut in, laughing. He felt the same ebullience. So much to do and so little time to do it. He sobered when he considered how little time they might have. Lingering in this anomaly wasn't much to his liking, even if it did present such a wide variety of fascinating discoveries.

"Can we send at least one probe to each of the other ships within range?" he asked.

"There's no need. We can go through the others one by one, when we finish with the first." Leonore started to say something more, then clamped her mouth shut and looked like a fish out of water. "We can't examine them all, can we? We'll have to leave sometime. Nels and the others will want to get on."

"The chaos device. That's what we're all agreed on finding." Too many times interesting but tangential topics presented themselves. It took real discipline to let those avenues pass by untouched while pursuing the main topic. If this rule wasn't strictly adhered to, nothing would ever get done.

"It's not fair," grumbled Leonore. "How do we mark this spot in space so we can come back—or at least give the coordinates to another researcher?"

"I don't know. We'll have to ask either Westcott or the pilot and find out." Ralston didn't want to consider the chance that they'd never be able to return, that this trip had been caused by the chaos field and duplicating its random effect would be impossible.

"Where are you two going?" came Bernssen's stern voice as they were suiting up for the trip to the nearest of the alien vessels. "You can't personally go to one of those ships."

"Why not?"

"We're getting ready to leave. Westcott says it's now or never."

"No!" protested Ralston. "We need the information locked in those ships. We do! We need to find out how they failed so that Westcott can prevent the same thing from happening to us when we get to the chaos device."

Bernssen shuffled his feet, then shook his head. "I'm primary researcher on the expedition, Michael. I'm in charge. I can't let you go—either of you."

"How long?" demanded Ralston. "Long enough to send over a few probes?"

"You'll probably lose them."

"Send them. Now!" snapped Ralston. Softer, he said, "Sorry, I'm used to being in charge."

"You're not in charge," Leonore reminded him. "If Nels says we might lose the probes, we've got to consider if it's worth saving them for later." She smiled wickedly.

As one, she and Ralston said, "Launch the probes!"

"I'd help," said Bernssen, "but I've got to keep a close watch on my own monitoring equipment. Make it quick and don't interfere with any of my readings."

"How long do we have?" asked Ralston, already programming the supervisor to handle ten probes, each capable of measuring and sending back different data.

"Less than you need. So hurry."

Ralston and Leonore were sweat-soaked by the time they finished their programming. The master computer controlled the probes perfectly; the ten small, silver fish-shaped probes darted across the short distance to the nearest ship.

"Definitely alien design," said Ralston, checking the visual readouts. "I've got photos of the exterior hull and the equipment hanging on it. Going around to the stern. You search for their airlock and try to get in that way. I may try burrowing through their hull to record the composition."

"That's dangerous, Michael, especially if any of them are still alive."

"Do you think any of them are?"

"We go in through the airlock or not at all," Leonore decided.

Ralston wanted information, not safety, but he acquiesced. Leonore Disa was, after all, in command. He had agreed to this before leaving Novo Terra, and he wasn't going back on his word. He had ceased being the instructor and was now the associate of a former student.

"No rocket nozzles," he said. "Wonder how they maneuver when they're not under stardrive?" The supervisor began to hum as its block circuits recorded everything sent back by the ten probes.

"Got it!" cried Leonore. "Their airlock. But I don't see the activator mechanism."

"There. There it is. But there's no power on it." Ralston bounced the probe off what he thought was the opening mechanism and finally gave up. "This might be a mechanical assist," he said. Ralston guided one probe in against a large, circular plate in the center of the door, applied the probe's magnetic snout, had some difficulty in getting it to grip, found a hold, then used side jets to rotate the probe. The rotary motion spun the plate and the airlock slid open soundlessly.

"Can't keep all the probes going manually," said Leonore. "Put three on automatic and let them scour the ship's outer hull. The others we put inside. You take four, I'll take three. You go for the engines. I'll find the cockpit."

Sweat poured into Ralston's eyes as he worked his four probes back through the winding maze of the alien starship's corridors. Using the infrared did little to aid him. The interior of the ship had long since cooled to a point where everything had come to thermal equilibrium. Cursing, Ralston took a chance. He reached across Leonore and flipped a switch.

"Michael, stop! You're going to destroy a probe!"

"Going to blow it apart to give some heat. I need to see where I'm going."

"Not much in the spectrum, is there?" she admitted. "We should have outfitted one probe with a headlamp."

"Didn't think it'd be needed. My fault. I'm used to exploring warmer ruins, though."

"I'm in charge. It's my oversight."

"There!" cried Ralston. The probe exploded nicely and sent heat radiating down the long corridor. The afterglow where it warmed the walls allowed Ralston to drive forward quickly and find the engine compartment. One probe he set to burrowing. The other two he put on automatic, but he quickly ran into the same problem. The heat from the destroyed probe had not penetrated the engine room.

"Got a couple bodies," said Leonore. "Can't think what else they'd be."

"Any power sources at all?"

"Nothing. No radioactivity, nothing."

"Here goes another probe," he said, flipping the toggle that sent the destruct message through the supervisor to the probe. The remaining two probes processed information at a furious clip.

But it wasn't fast enough.

"We're getting up to speed," came Bernssen's words from the cargo hold. "Westcott says it's now or never. The entire attractor is sucking up our energy and driving everything to zero point. Radioactivity, our power plant, our bodies, everything. If we don't start now, we're going to be sapped and trapped."

"Sapped and trapped?" exploded Leonore. "Did you come up with that on your own?"

"Westcott's words," Nels said almost sheepishly. "But they fit. A couple reports of batteries being drained have already come in. Equipment's failing, as a result. We've got to leave."

"Just a few more minutes," begged Ralston.

"Now. It's now or never."

Ralston looked over to the supervisor's panel. It took in prodigious amounts of information from his two working probes and the three Leonore had roaming the starship's cockpit, but it wasn't enough. Not by days, months, perhaps years, was it enough.

Robbed again. Michael Ralston once more had a career-making discovery ripped from his grasp.

The research ship shuddered and strained, as if it were chained down. They had begun their flight back into normal space.

FOURTEEN

"WE NEED MORE time!" cried Michael Ralston. "We can't leave yet. Please!"

Even as he spoke the research ship shuddered harder, struggling against unseen bonds.

"Give it up, Michael," said Leonore Disa. "The probes are dead. We don't seem to have moved a micron, yet the indicators show we've gone beyond their effective transmission range."

Ralston worked at the supervisor's console for several minutes before coming to the same conclusion. The ship had somehow gone beyond the considerable transmission range of their probes, yet visually the alien derelict lay exactly where it had before. The laws of physics in the attractor well had been redefined in ways Ralston couldn't begin to comprehend.

"All our equipment has gone dead, too," said Nels Bernssen. The blond physicist stood with his arm around Leonore's shoulders. "It's best we get out of this spacial backwater as quickly as possible. It's draining all our stored energy."

Ralston sat down heavily, disconsolate. He shivered, wrapped his arms around himself, and asked peevishly, "Is that why it's getting so cold in here?"

"Ship's temperature hasn't changed but a degree or so. It's you, Michael," said Nels. "The attractor is sucking away your vitality." Bernssen rubbed one hand up and down his arm. "It's working that way on us all. There's a leveling or neutralizing process at work I don't begin to understand.

Nothing but gravity—the weakest of the forces, oddly enough—seems to have survived by the way the ships cluster together. Barranquilla was working on magnetic moment measurement of the ship, and she found it to be decreasing rapidly. Almost nothing of a magnetic nature can last longer than a week inside this field. Electrical is going at a measurable rate.''

"A vampire sucking its prey,'' muttered Ralston.

"What's a vampire?'' asked Bernssen.

"Are we getting free?'' asked Ralston. "Freezing to death isn't too cheerful a prospect.''

"We might not even freeze,'' said Nels. "Chances looked good that our bodies would simply stop converting food into energy for us. That's the least efficient of any of the chemical processes.''

"But to leave it all. We needed more time. We hardly have one block circuit of information about that alien ship. I'm not sure we can figure out how its engines worked, either. The two probes had only begun scanning the control equipment.''

"One probe of mine scanned what may be the aliens' star charts. We'll have to analyze the data to see.''

"That's something, but not too much. I wanted to give Westcott the complete design of the alien stardrive so he could determine how this attractor worked.''

"It must be an important part of the chaos field's effect,'' said Nels Bernssen. "Everything works in reverse here due to the chaos induced by the device.''

"What do you mean?'' asked Leonore.

"The field causes random events to happen, creating its own cause and effect relationship in real space. But here, just the reverse occurs. Everything smooths out, falls into one energy level. In a way, what the attractor holds is the ultimate fate of the universe. Entropy has increased to the point where everything is homogeneous. This is the exact opposite of chaos. This is sameness. Forever.''

"The ships hadn't fallen apart,'' said Ralston. "That means the binding forces holding the metallic lattices together hadn't given up and turned into soup.''

"In time,'' said Bernssen. "That's my first guess, at least. Any idea how long those ships had been inside?''

Ralston shook his head. They had nothing to use as a

measure. If they'd found a radioactive material aboard, this might have given some clue. Or perhaps not, if what Bernssen said was true. The radioactive isotopes might have decayed far faster than their "natural" half-lives demanded.

"The alien bodies were in good condition," said Leonore. "No decomposition that I saw."

"What's to decay the bodies?" asked Nels. "All the microbes likely to cause the decomposition are dead, too. Only the dissolving of the electronic bonds in the bodies themselves would cause the flesh to fall off the bones."

"We—" Ralston stood and took a step toward Leonore. The abrupt cessation of gravity sent him cartwheeling through the air, to smash hard against a bulkhead. He tried to grab a conveniently located elastic band and missed; he rebounded and sailed back into the room. Nels had been luckier. He and Leonore still stood with their arms around one another. Inertia held them for the brief instant it took for their space instincts to return and allow them to react by grabbing at the supervisor for anchoring.

"What happened?" cried Ralston, still struggling to control his spin. He hit the far bulkhead and succeeded in tangling one foot in an elastic band. Slamming hard against the wall produced a few bruises but he stopped his uncontrolled trip.

"We made it!" cried Nels Bernssen. "We shifted out of the attractor well!"

Ralston worried that they might have blundered into worse trouble. He had experienced none of the phenomena he'd come to associate with beginning a shift. He worked his way around, then kicked accurately and caught the edge of the supervisor on his way across the room. With deft movements, Ralston secured the computer equipment and vented a deep sigh at the lost probes. He could only hope that they had found something of interest before destruction.

Leonore popped the block circuit from the side of the supervisor and tucked it away in a special carrying case.

"For Westcott," she said.

"I want to talk with him to see what our progress is," said Ralston. Together, the three made their way up the central shaft and to the lounge where Westcott remained motionless, unchanged from when they'd last seen him. If Westcott's narrow chest wasn't rising and falling slowly, Ralston might have pronounced him dead. As it was, Ralston merely considered him not alive.

"The pilot needs someone to talk with," said Westcott. "He is frantic. I have control of the ship and cannot relinquish it for some time yet. Perhaps another hour."

"What happens then?" asked Ralston.

"We return to normal space."

"How's this possible? We can't be anywhere near ready to exit. We just began the shift." Ralston rubbed the bruised spots that gave mute testimony to how suddenly the shift had started.

"The strange attractor is a product of the chaos field. We were pulled along behind the field by the attractor. Yet we remained where we were, stationary in space."

"You're talking riddles."

"All this is one giant puzzle," said Westcott. "The mathematics are complex and not amenable to simple words." Westcott ran a pallid hand across his sweaty forehead. "They might not be amenable to even the force of my intellect. The chaos equations hold even more suprises than I'd thought at first."

"When we come out, will we be close to the device?"

"There is no other conclusion," said the mathematician. "The attractors are formed by the passage of the field. A symmetry *does* exist in the universe."

"How can there be symmetry," asked Bernssen, "when the chaos field is spreading randomness?"

Westcott chuckled. "The dice play God with the universe."

"We have the data from the alien ship," spoke up Leonore, not wanting to get into a theological argument with a mathematician. "You said the other ships used a different form of stardrive, one that quit when it came into contact with the chaos device's sphere of influence. Michael thinks a schematic of their engines might help you in working on a new solution to the chaos equations."

"It might, it might. If I can determine why their engines failed, it gives new perspective on how the chaos field interacts with and destroys classical mechanisms."

Westcott took the block circuit and slipped it into the side of the ship's computer. Westcott stiffened as the thundering assault of information flooded his brain and turned him into more of a computer than a human being. Settling back, he began forming theories and testing them mathematically.

"He's lost to us for a while," said Ralston. "I'll go calm the pilot."

"I . . . I'm tired," said Leonore, looking over at Nels. "I think I'll go to my cabin and get some rest."

"Remember what Westcott said. We come out of the shift in about an hour. Be sure you're strapped in for it," warned Ralston.

"We will be." Together Leonore and Nels floated away. Their soft voices vanished in the low-pressure bubble around them. Ralston closed his eyes for a moment, envying them. He'd been in love like that once, a long time ago. Old warmths rose within, along with the memories. Ralston pushed it all away, forced it down into the depths of his soul once again. There wasn't time for nostalgia—or was it better described as reveling in maudlin emotions?

He made his way to the cockpit where the pilot lit one votive candle after another on the small altar he had at the side of the controls. A small circulating fan kept the combustive gases from snuffing out the flames.

"Isn't it dangerous having all that open flame?" asked Ralston. "One good oxygen leak and you'd be fried."

"The saints won't permit it," said the man. "With all that's happened on this trip, I need to know that someone's listening to me. If not the saints, then who?"

He crossed himself and swung in a quick movement that deposited him directly in his command chair. Legs curled around the stanchions under it, the pilot seemed to be sitting down with the pull of gravity working on him.

"Has Westcott told you that we'll be reentering normal space in less than an hour?"

"That chinging son of a bitch has told me nada of what he does to my ship!" the pilot almost shouted. "*I* command this ship. I, Juan Jose Gonzales y Vega!"

Ralston blinked in surprise. Pilots normally kept to themselves and never had he heard a pilot reveal his name to a passenger. The pilots had their own superstitions and mores. Consorting with passengers seldom occurred because of the need for concentration when on duty—or so they claimed. Had Gonzales snapped under the extreme pressure of their expedition?

"Why don't you go to your quarters and relax? Take a short nap."

"Take drugs to calm me?" snapped Gonzales. "Pilots do not drug themselves under any circumstances. Never have I heard of a pilot taking even a painkiller!"

"The beta endorphins are natural painkillers," said Ralston before he realized that the pilot only raged because of West-cott assuming control of the starship.

"Look," said Ralston, trying to calm the man. "We're in grave danger because of our choice of investigation topics. The chaos field we pursue does things to people, to machines, even to stars."

"One of the physicists—the cute one with the nice ass—"

"Barranquilla," supplied Ralston, without even thinking.

"Verd, Dr. Barranquilla mentioned this to me that the chaos weapon reset the Beta star's inner mechanisms and caused it to go nova."

"There's much more. It can affect people by changing chemicals and electrical potentials in the brain. Epilepsy, even mutation, is a possible result of contact with the field."

Gonzales snorted in contempt at that. "I take all the precautions against radiation."

"This is a different type of radiation. It might even be different, not a radiation at all. Westcott calls it a concept rather than a physical reality, but it *does* interact with stars and biological organisms and most everything else."

"What do you tell me, Dr. Ralston?"

"Burn a few more candles for me. Implore the saints for help. But let Westcott run the ship for a little longer. He's the only one among us who can begin to understand what we're up against."

"Such is the nature of research, verd?"

"Verd," Ralston agreed.

"But it is accepted that *I* am pilot and in command? If a situation occurs where we are all in danger, I must act as pilot."

Ralston said nothing. He slapped the pilot on the shoulder and knew instantly that this was a mistake. Gonzales flinched back, not wanting any physical contact with his passenger. Ralston left the cockpit with its burning candles and upset pilot, knowing that the pilot didn't understand the magnitude of the chaos field's importance.

Michael Ralston wasn't sure that he understood.

The shift into normal space came with a jolt. Ralston strained against the straps on the couch and then sagged down, forcing his tensed muscles to relax. Across from him Westcott's eyelids fluttered and the mathematician came out of his trance.

"The pilot can have control back," said Westcott. "We have starred to a point within twenty light minutes of the chaos field."

"What?"

Ralston surged against the straps in an attempt to lift his head enough to see the viewscreen. Nothing appeared on it other than a star pattern similar to hundreds of others he'd seen over the years he'd spent in space.

"You cannot see it yet on the viewscreen," said Westcott. "It is a small planetoid, hardly two kilometers in diameter." The man shook his head slowly, the silver sensor mounted atop his bald pate gleaming brightly as his head turned. "Such a small device to bring such havoc to the universe."

"We'll get to monitoring it right away," said Ralston. He pulled the straps away from his body and swung out of the couch, kicking hard enough to send himself down the central shaft toward the cargo bay where much of their equipment had been set up.

Leonore and Nels already worked on a variety of instruments.

"Nels wanted to start the spectrographic photos right away," said Leonore, almost apologetically. "And I wanted to see if I could get another set of probes ready to go."

"Let me help." Ralston began working with Leonore, but soon stopped and stared at the cases. "These don't seem to respond when I press their test circuits. See?"

"Some of my equipment is malfunctioning, too," spoke up

Bernssen. "We're near the chaos weapon. We can't expect to have everything one hundred percent from now on."

Ralston swallowed hard. He had been touched by the chaos field's residual effects back in the Beta system. Using the telepathic projector left by the Alphans to learn about the travails in reaching Beta 5, he had shared the epileptic condition with the avian scientist making the recording. Ralston didn't remember the seizure, but the others had told him about it.

He had been touched by chaos. He felt an itching sensation up and down his spine and fear rose to the point where he wondered if he could contain it. Being this close to the source of so much chaotic misery might trigger a new and more dangerous seizure.

"It might not, Michael. We don't know enough," said Leonore, as if she'd read his mind.

"Am I that easy to read?" he asked.

"What else could you be thinking about?" she asked. Leonore rested her hand on his arm to reassure him. It helped, but not too much.

"Let's try to fix what we can in the probes. We'll want as many going out as possible when we get within range."

"Damn," complained Bernssen. "The block circuit for the spectrometer's gone haywire. Everything is beginning to fall apart randomly."

"Better have the automatic sedate everyone," Ralston suggested. "That helped back on Beta 5 to keep down the incidence of severe epileptic seizures."

"All right," said Bernssen. "I'll order it. But you're going first."

Ralston had no argument with that. They left Leonore to work on the equipment while they both returned to the lounge area. There, Ralston saw almost half of the expedition working on equipment mounted around the walls. He couldn't help but notice Barranquilla. The pilot was right. She did have a nice ass.

"What is it?" she asked, glancing back over her shoulder at Ralston. "Can I do something for you, Dr. Ralston?"

"Maybe later. Any trouble with your equipment?"

"None," the physicist said. "The computer failed to record properly while we were trapped inside the attractor, but now I'm getting strong magnetic moment measurement from the chaos field.'' Barranquilla sounded happy at the randomness flowing all around, but then she hadn't experienced its effects personally. She had readings now and, because of that, she was content.

"Everyone, listen up," called Bernssen. "Light sedation is required. We found it worked to lessen the chaos field's effect when we were exploring the ruins left on Beta 5."

"Those were residual effects," said a scientist. "We're dealing with primary sources now. I don't want to go around groggy because you've got me drugged to the ears. I'd prefer to take my chances."

"Everyone," insisted Bernssen. "This isn't open to debate. The auto-doc will be set for the lightest dosage possible. Ralston and I will go first, then the rest of you will let it inject you. I'll be back in an hour. I expect the auto-doc to register administering a dose to each of you. No exceptions."

Ralston rubbed his arm after the vapor injection from the automedic. It had broken blood vessels just under the skin, something that happened only with poorly calibrated automedics.

"We'd better run a check on its block circuit," said Ralston. "It's no more immune to the chaos field than we are."

"Good point. In fact," Nels said, "we'd better swoop in, collect our data, then get the hell away." He slammed a fist against the call button and roused the pilot from his work. "We want a hyperbolic trajectory past the planetoid. Navigate so that we'll spend a minimum of time within ten light seconds."

"That'll require hard acceleration."

"Do it. We've got our equipment lashed down."

"No close-in approach, no exploration, nothing? You come all this way and do nothing? What's with you people?"

"Do it," said Bernssen. He released the call button and turned to Ralston. "I think our pilot's not going to be able to stand the strain. It might be the chaos effects or it might just be losing control to Westcott."

At the mention of the mathematician, Ralston rotated slowly and faced the man. Westcott's eyes were open but unfocused.

A thin hand lifted and motioned to Bernssen and Ralston. The two swam over.

"The pilot's course is adequate. You've chosen well on course and duration. But I must be fully connected to the computer for maximum efficiency. The sedative you've ordered for the others will dull my senses and slow interfacing."

"I ordered everyone to get the sedative," said Bernssen. "It's for everyone's safety."

"It will prevent me from functioning to the fullest." Westcott sounded adamant about not taking the drug.

Ralston saw that the expedition leader wrestled with this problem. Allowing Westcott to avoid taking the calming drug could only cause dissension among those others who resented being sedated. What the mathematician said made sense. Speed of interaction with the computer was slowed by drugs.

"No sedative," Nels Bernssen decided. "But the automedic stays beside you. The first sign of trouble and it goes into action. And then it'll be everything, sedatives, whatever."

Westcott dismissed them with the wave of a hand, just as a Spanish king might have dismissed peasants from his court.

Leonore Disa returned to the lounge, eyes bright with anticipation. "Every probe we have is ready for launch. The supervisors will handle them."

"How many probes did you get working?" asked Ralston.

"Fifteen. Not as many as I'd've liked, but it should be enough." Leonore reached out when the ship vibrated. The rockets had cut in, positioning the research ship for its rapid hyperbola down and past the chaos device—and away.

"Here we go!" cried Ralston. The acceleration brought them to the floor of the lounge. He swung around and watched as Bernssen's researchers began flipping switches. All the equipment went to automatic. Nothing would be done manually; there wouldn't be time.

"He looks terrible," Leonore said. "Westcott. Look at him. I've seen corpses that looked healthier."

Ralston swallowed hard when he saw the gaunt, pallid face begin to contort as if in intense pain. Westcott screamed then and thrashed about. When his silver, shiny sensor lost line-of-sight contact with the infrared receptor mounted on the computer console, Ralston knew something had gone wrong.

"He's having a seizure. A big one, too," Ralston called. "Help me with him."

Westcott had been strapped down securely, but this hadn't saved him from injury. His powerful muscle contractions had broken one strap and left behind a bloody streak on the mathematician's thrashing legs. Ralston grabbed the auto-doc's probe and thrust it against Westcott's arm. Sedatives sprayed out and into the man's bloodstream but did little to quiet him.

"He's still linked to the computer," cried Leonore. "See? How's that affecting him?"

The sensor on Westcott's head gleamed as if it connected to the ship's computer. But they blocked it. It was as if Westcott had linked himself with a bigger machine, one vastly more potent—and couldn't handle the input.

"The chaos device's got him!"

Westcott jerked even harder, completely out of control, dominated by the enforced randomness of the chaos field.

FIFTEEN

MICHAEL RALSTON'S ARMS twitched and a curious sensation of falling came over him. The research ship accelerated and drove at the chaos device with such speed that the pull inside amounted to more than Novo Terra's gravity. Why should he feel as if he fell?

"The chaos field is affecting me, too," Ralston said to reassure himself that he hadn't gone insane. "Everything seems so strange." He blinked and saw a rainbow of colors. The whine from the rocket engines almost deafened him, and the heavy odor of ozone clung so tenaciously to the air that even the hard-working circulating fans and filters couldn't remove it.

Ralston sat down heavily at the edge of one couch and tried to control his fear. This was unlike the shift that hurled the ship to the stars. No sensory scrambling occurred now. Every sense reported accurately—but why did the colors still paint his vision like an artist's drop cloth? That came from somewhere.

It had to be induced by the chaos device.

"Michael, please. Help us with Westcott." Leonore's voice cut through the heavy fog of his thoughts. With some reluctance, he turned back to the mathematician. Westcott's condition hadn't changed, nor had it worsened.

"If the chaos field is holding him, only getting away from it will help. Where are we on the trajectory?"

Nels Bernssen moved heavily to a wall-mounted radar-ranging unit his team had installed. "We're less than a hundred thousand kilometers from the planetoid's surface. Most of the instruments seem to be functional and reporting accurately. We'll be swinging away from the device in another few seconds."

Even as he spoke, the ship shuddered and the acceleration vector changed, violently throwing them to the floor. Ralston got to hands and knees. One restraining strap across Westcott's chest had held the mathematician into his couch. Some of the others hadn't fared as well. Barranquilla moaned, her arm dangling at a crazy angle from being banged against the edge of her couch. McGhee wheezed noisily, as if he might have a punctured lung. A half-dozen others appeared in better shape. Of those in the cargo hold, Ralston had no clue about their condition. Ralston crawled to the automedic and punched in the command to do triage, then begin work patching up the researchers.

The machine whirred happily and set about its task. For long minutes it stood next to Westcott. Ralston finally hit the cancel command on it and sent the auto-doc on its rounds. Determining what had gone wrong in the mathematician's head would require facilities far beyond those available to a portable medical unit.

"You're so pale, Michael. If you're all right, can you help us check the equipment?" Leonore Disa bent over him. Ralston hadn't even realized that he still sat on the edge of the acceleration couch, staring at a blank bulkhead. He slowly nodded, wondering if his head would tumble from his shoulders. When this didn't happen, he decided that he might really survive.

"Come on." Leonore put an arm around his shoulders and helped him stand. The acceleration still pulled heavily at him, but he found himself enjoying its feel more than he'd have thought possible. Floating weightless for weeks and months took its toll on him, not just physically but mentally. He was a planet born and bred creature and he needed the reassurance of gravity's pull.

"You did well setting the automedic," said Nels. "McGhee was in bad shape. Hit the side of his head. Looks like it might be hemorrhage in the brain."

Ralston went to the auto-doc and tapped the keys on its report screen. "Code 2-23. That's, let me look it up, that's a subdermal hematoma. Guess you were right. He'll be the first one the automedic tends to when it's finished looking at the others."

"No one is dead," said Bernssen without any indication of triumph at this. "Let's see how the recording went."

They made a quick circuit around the lounge area and studied the readings on Bernssen's equipment. Half had failed. The other half had performed well. Going down to the cargo hold where the bulk of their equipment had been set up showed similar results.

"We have enough data to keep us busy for a dozen years," said Bernssen, satisfaction finally showing in face and tone. "The price wasn't too bad, either. McGhee's the worst injured. We can always get more equipment, especially after this trip."

"Westcott is badly hurt," said Ralston. "There may not be any way out of that coma for him. Not unless we can figure out the chaos device's true nature."

"Why do you say that?" asked Nels. "That damned direct-link he uses malfunctioned and that's what put him into the trance. The auto-doc can snap him out of it."

"No," said Ralston. "I have a gut-level feeling it's more complicated than that. You know how I get my senses mixed up at the beginning of a shift?"

"You're the only one I ever heard of who had that problem. Me, I just get a headache," said Nels.

"As we passed by the chaos device—at perigee—everything around me seemed more intense, more vibrant, more colorful. But there wasn't any sensory confusion. I saw and heard and smelled a thousand times better than I ever had."

Leonore wrinkled her nose. "You most certainly *don't* smell better than you ever did. The chemical showers make us all smell like dead goats."

"You know what I mean. I came alive, truly alive. It was the reverse of entering a shift."

"You thrive on chaos?" asked Nels.

"Maybe, in a way. Maybe the touch I got before has attuned me to it. We've got to get to work to see what data we've collected. There might be a clue in it that'll help both Westcott and me." Ralston turned to the supervisor. Of the fifteen probes sent out, only two had penetrated to the surface of the chaos planetoid. But these had sent back such a wealth of data that it stunned Ralston with the implications.

"It's all here," he said softly. "Look, Leonore, look. Markings on the lava upjuts. Those have to be writing. Instructions for operation? Warnings?"

"It might be a stellar return address. Sort of a 'if lost, return, compensation guaranteed.' "

"We'll need the ship's computer for detailed analysis," said Ralston. Adrenaline flowed through his body now. He had data to work with. They had found the chaos device and had accumulated much of what they sought. Now came the long, laborious—and, for Ralston, exciting—process of sifting through it and puzzling together the pieces to learn all they could about those beings who had built the device.

"We got good readings, too," said Bernssen, after checking with several others of his expedition in the cargo bay. "It might even be possible to analyze the field generation itself. We have enough different readings to give good guesses now. Somehow, all those have to correlate. With it, we can fit it into the way the field functions, why it seems to disrupt the laws of physics." Bernssen's eyes glowed. "We can even find out what initiates the instability that causes novas. When we do that, we'll have a better idea what causes natural ones. This is the find of a lifetime."

"No one's ever discovered anything like it, Nels," said Ralston. "In physics, in mathematics, in archaeology, we're all winners because of that thing."

Ralston's left arm twitched seriously, causing him to knock over a block circuit he'd set on top of the supervisor. Only Leonore's quick reflexes saved it before it hit the floor. Although such a fall wouldn't have damaged it, they were all tensed and acutely aware of anything out of the ordinary. Ralston grabbed his left arm with his right hand and held it down. The jerking ceased, but he felt sweat soaking his body.

"Would more sedative help?" asked Leonore, worried about him.

"Much more and I might pass out. There's too much to do for me to take a nap now."

The pilot interrupted them. "Do you want me to shut down the rockets or keep going? I'm getting indications of system failure throughout the ship. I need to tend to this before we shift."

"No shift," said Bernssen, hitting the call button. "We need to set up an orbit around the planetoid and continue surveillance."

"Orbit it? I'm not a genius like Westcott. I can't see how to do that. The godforsaken rock is accelerating and decelerating, although I don't see any rocket exhaust. I'd recommend just trying to parallel its course and watching carefully. I read us as being about eighty light seconds away from it."

"Maintain a parallel course at one hundred seconds," decided Bernssen. "And report immediately any major system failure."

"I'll do that," Gonzales said. "You can count on me doing that—and no closer." The pilot clicked off. Only irritating static remained on the intercom.

"We might be unable to do more than limp away from the planetoid, if we sustained too much chaotic damage," said Bernssen. "But it seems that we're in good enough shape to keep going for a while longer."

The uncontrollable twitching in his arm abated, and Ralston settled in to analyzing the prodigious amounts of data collected during their frenzied fly-by of the chaos planetoid. Ralston was fascinated by the rock spires and the obviously crafted caves visible in many of the probe photos. None of the probes had penetrated into those caverns, but Ralston thought they held the real chaotic secrets. In those dark holes lay the controls to the chaos device, its programming, its generating mechanism, everything about it that he wanted to know.

And behind the controls lay the intelligence that had formed them. What of the builders? Ralston hoped for photos of the creators but knew that wasn't likely. If this had been built as a weapon, those building it weren't likely to send photos. But it didn't have to be a weapon. It might be another race's attempt to contact others. If they were truly alien, what passed for speech with them might be totally different with a human.

Ralston leaned back, a cool crate along his spine, and considered how lucky they had been in speaking with the natives on Beta 7 about the chaos device. Without Westcott and his direct-connect to the computer, it would have been impossible. He had linked with their computer, then had his computer speak with the Betan one. Somewhere Ralston had seen a proof that all computer programs were, at the most elementary level, identical. Nothing could be done in one programming language that couldn't be done in another.

Certainly for computers with a binary orientation this was intuitively clear. For those based on the ternary system, it wasn't. But Ralston had asked and Westcott had told him the Betan computer was binary. On-off. True-false. Open-closed.

"Is it computer controlled?" Ralston asked aloud. "The planetoid. Is it controlled by a computer? If it is, we can get Westcott to link with it and find out all we need about the beings building it, just as we did on Beta 7."

"Might be," said Nels. "There are some interesting power-level readings. Heavy radioactivity from some of the lava spires. Unnatural, definitely chaos-induced. I think the chaos field is being generated deep inside the planetoid."

"No, Nels," said Leonore. "One probe shows strong surface forces but just inside one of the caves is nothing. If it radiated from within, the cave wouldn't give any protection. But the probe acted like a point inside a sphere with a surface charge—no charge inside. I take this to mean that inside the cavern is the chaos field source."

"Westcott," muttered Ralston. He had become so engrossed in the data collected that he had forgotten the mathematician's comatose condition. While Leonore and Nels argued over where the chaos generator was located, he rose and went back to the lounge.

Barranquilla rested quietly, her arm in a carbon composite sheath. The automedic hovered over McGhee, just as an attentive nurse might. Slim silver and plastic tubes ran to the man's arms and neck, multicolored fluids pumping in and out of his body. The bruise to the brain was serious, but Ralston felt confident that McGhee wouldn't suffer any long-term effects. The auto-doc was efficient and effective.

But for Westcott, there seemed to be no real hope. Ralston dropped beside the comatose mathematician and gently prodded him, hoping for signs of stirring. Nothing.

"Let's give you a headache," Ralston said, the idea of speaking to Westcott seeming more important than what he said. Ralston placed his hand over the infrared sensor and shut off all possible input. Westcott didn't move.

Looking over his shoulder, Ralston saw that the ship's computer was in full use. The receptor unit on the console had been turned off. Only a dull, blank gray electroceramic eye peered at him, useless without power. Three of Bernssen's team crowded close to the console and worked feverishly, discussing the toothsome tidbits of information they'd gleaned from the chaos planetoid.

Ralston moved his hand back and forth in front of Westcott's eyes. The pupils dilated slightly. Other than this, there was no response. The mathematician was trapped within his body and lacked any way of communicating with the rest of them.

"Hey," yelled Ralston as the idea struck him. "Let me use the computer. Just for a few minutes. This is important." He looked down at Westcott. "It might mean his life."

The two doing the computer analysis grumbled but relinquished the console. "For five minutes. No more, Dr. Ralston, or we have to ask Nels to get us the time."

"I'll only be a few seconds. This'll either work or it'll fail fast." Ralston turned on the computer receptor. The electroceramic eye glowed a dull red. Ralston went and positioned Westcott so that the beams matched, fixed the mathematician's head firmly with a strap, then returned to the console. There he slowly put in his request for information—directly from Westcott's brain.

"It works!" he yelped. "I've gotten through to him. Something shorted out the rest of his body's motor functions, but this works."

The others crowded close. "You're talking directly to Westcott?" asked one.

"Verd. I'm bypassing his vocal chords and going directly to his brain. We did this before in a slightly different way when we contacted the Betan."

"You are slow, so slow to understand," came Westcott's reply via the computer readout. "But I have learned so much while out of contact. I need to communicate it to you."

"Send it directly to the data bank. Code it into a block circuit so that I can pull it and examine it at length," Ralston tapped in.

"Must tell you this now. I am dying in my present state. The chaos field seized me and changed neural connections. I am permanently linked to it unless you deactivate the device. Stop it, save me."

"Deactivate it? But how? We can't even get close to it. And we don't have any missiles. This isn't a Nex warship."

"Destruction by that method isn't possible. The device must be turned off."

"How?"

"I . . . I don't know." Westcott's words wobbled across the screen, as if he were stuttering. "On the surface is the answer. You must disconnect me from it. Please, I beg you!"

"We need all the information you've gathered. Anything, Westcott. Give us all the data and your conclusions. Can you maintain contact with the computer?"

"Difficult now. So painful, but the pain is reassuring. It tells me I still have a body. I am so cut off. The chaos device has done it. My brain is alone, so alone . . ."

"The trajectory," Ralston typed into the computer. "Feed us all your work on the chaos device's trajectory. We need to know how to predict where it'll be if we're going to land on the planetoid."

"What are you saying, Ralston?" demanded a researcher who had been watching over his shoulder. "To land on the planetoid is suicide. No question about that. You'd die in minutes. Didn't the chaos field destroy the Alphans?"

"It did," said Ralston in a low voice. "But we may not have any other choice, if we want to save Westcott's life."

"Is he so bad off?" asked another. "Look at him. He's not much different than he usually is. What's he need a body for? He's pure intellect. He's certainly not human the way he direct-links with the computer."

"What would you say if it were you that needed rescuing?" Ralston shot back.

"Leave me. For the good of the team, leave me. No one person's worth risking everyone for."

"Westcott knows so much about the chaos device and perhaps even the beings who built it."

"We can find all that out—if we survive," said Barranquilla. The woman had struggled to her feet and had joined the group. Her sentiments were echoed by the ten others who had formed a tight ring around the computer console.

Ralston wasn't sure she was right. Westcott's unique skills at mathematics were necessary for full understanding of all they'd found. They might never truly know the purpose or how the chaos field functioned without Westcott.

"Is he worth risking your life for?" asked another.

To this, Ralston didn't have a good answer.

"We're not going to allow you to swoop down on the planetoid again," said Barranquilla. "We sustained enough damage the first time. And I'm not just talking about my arm. Ask the pilot. A full quarter of all ship circuits are intermittent. Try to star back to Novo Terra in this condition and we're dead."

"I know," said Ralston. "But Westcott is important."

Someone made a comment about the unimportance of a blob of protoplasm more machine than human.

Ralston wondered at his own motives for wanting to save Westcott from this living hell. Ralston could hardly stand the idea of Westcott being alive in the brain but a slave to the chaos device, with no body control, no way of communicating except through the computer—and this only sporadically. He had never even liked the mathematician. Admired his talent, yes. Loathed him, yes. Feared him, yes, that, also. Why should he risk his life to save Westcott's?

The archaeologist had no real answer for that. His emotions answered rather than his intellect. Westcott had to be saved. Even if the man didn't hold so much valuable information about the chaos device stored within his head, Ralston knew he'd try to save him. The two of them were cut off in different ways from society.

Westcott had chosen his path. For Ralston, it had come about through no fault of his own. His teaching position at the University was gone. He might be listed as being on sabbatical, but Salazar was still chancellor and would try everything possible to remove Ralston permanently from Ilium's faculty. His papers were rejected, not for content but because of Salazar's enmity.

And the Nex. Ralston couldn't forget how Slenth and
Chosinth had come to him. He had promised the Nex first
look at any results he obtained—that anyone on the expedition obtained. Such could only mean increased conflict between the Nex and the P'torra.

Ralston had fought on the side of the Nex. Now he viewed
them as much an adversary as he did the P'torra or Chancellor
Salazar.

He and Westcott shared aloneness. They drifted through
space wrapped up in their own concerns. The only difference
lay in the demands placed upon them. Westcott had none.
Ralston carried the burden of the promise to the Nex.

Dying in the name of rescuing Westcott from imprisonment
looked like a more noble way of suicide than any other
Ralston might devise.

"No!" he shouted. The others stepped back, staring at him.
"I won't let him die. And I won't die, either. By damn, I
won't. It's not right to die like this. Too many others' lives have
been taken by the chaos field. It's time to stop it right now!"

He shoved himself away from the computer and rushed to
the cargo hold where Nels and Leonore worked at an almost
frantic pace to get their data in some semblance of order.

"Westcott's locked in to the chaos device," he said. "The
only way he knows to get free is for someone to go to the
planetoid's surface, find the controls, and turn off the device."

"That's not possible," said Bernssen. "There's every reason to believe that this is a weapon of war. Why build such a
weapon if the enemy could land and turn it off whenever they
pleased? They'd redirect and send it back at you."

"Westcott claims that the controls exist. We're dealing
with alien thought processes," said Ralston. "And we don't
know that it was a weapon."

"I think we have evidence now, Michael," said Leonore.
"The markings. I've had the computer working on them.
Perhaps they tied in with something Westcott had left in the
data banks. I don't know, but the probability that this is a
weapon is 0.9 with a confidence level of ninety-five percent.
It might be other things, even a paper weight for some
immense and ancient desktop, but it looks good to state that it
is a weapon of war."

Sweat beaded Ralston's forehead. "Have they protected the surface with armament?"

"Do they even have to?" asked Nels Bernssen. "The chaos field itself disrupts most attempts to reach it. Only two of fifteen probes reached the surface. That tells a great deal, doesn't it?"

Ralston's mind raced, then rolled over and over covering the same arguments repeatedly. Why save the mathematician? Did he dare risk his own life when he knew he'd been touched by the residual field on both Alpha 3 and Beta 5?

Intellect told him to stay safely aboard the research ship and content himself with data reduction and trying to build a picture of the race that constructed the chaos device.

Emotion told him to take a shuttle and land on the planetoid's surface, find the controls, learn to operate them, and turn it off.

"I've got to do it," Ralston said. "I'll take the shuttle. Cram in all the spare equipment you can find, Leonore. I'll relay everything possible back as I descend to the surface. Once there, I doubt if much will continue working."

"You may not last longer than a few minutes," said Bernssen. "Remember your seizure? Being this near the source of the chaos may kill you outright. This *is* a weapon."

"I know. I'll land near the caverns where the markings are. They must be a 'Keep Out' sign. That's exactly the spot I want. With luck, I can be in, look around, and see what needs to be done before I keel over."

"Flop over like a fish out of water, you mean," Leonore said sourly. "I don't want you going, Michael. As head of the expedition, I can order you to stay."

"You can," Ralston said. "But you won't. I know what I'm doing. And I'm going down."

The words had barely come from Michael Ralston's mouth when he realized that he had just committed himself to a course that could end only in death—his own death.

SIXTEEN

"BOTH SUPERVISORS?" ASKED Michael Ralston, eyebrows rising in surprise. "Shouldn't you keep one, just to be sure that you can monitor the working probes?"

Leonore laughed. "Michael, Michael, we want to get back in one piece. Equipment doesn't matter. People do."

For a moment, Ralston started to thank her for the kind thought, then understood what she'd said.

"*We* want to get back? What's this 'we' you're talking about? I'm going alone."

"Sorry, Michael, that's too dangerous." Leonore Disa glowed with excitement. "As head of this part of the expedition, you don't think I'd let you go alone and have all the fun, do you?"

"There's not going to be any fun," he said, grimness in his voice. "I'll probably not make it back alive. One suicide per expedition is enough. Keep one supervisor and monitor me closely. That might tell more than a random walk route for a probe across the planetoid's surface."

"Here," said Nels Bernssen, heaving the second supervisor into the shuttle. He pushed Ralston aside and began installing it. When he finished, he flopped into a tiny acceleration couch that barely held his bulky body. "You going to pilot or am I?"

"You, too? No, absolutely not," Ralston said forcefully. "You're not going, too."

"As the one responsible for how the funds are spent, I'm

in charge of the expedition. Leonore's in charge of her part of it. You're the hired help. Want us to leave you behind?''

"Leonore, Nels, please!"

"Stop whining or we *will* leave you behind. We've got to launch in less than ten minutes if we want an optimum time trajectory to the planetoid's surface. The pilot's worked out the round trip for us and I've got it on four block circuits.'' Leonore patted a small bag hanging at her waist. "Each of us will take one. The fourth will go into the steering computer. If anything chaotic happens to it, each of us has a chance of getting back with their spare.''

Ralston's head spun. Everything moved too quickly around him. He had intended this to be a solo mission, quick in and even quicker to find the chaos weapon's controls. Nothing else mattered, if he wanted to free Westcott from his domination by the field.

"Maybe we should call it off. One of the others said that no single life is worth risking everyone's for.''

"Locked inside Westcott's head is a phenomenal amount of data,'' said Bernssen. "We need it. No one else can duplicate what he's learned about the strange attractor, the chaos field, the history of it, the people who built it. He's unique in that.'' Nels had hit Ralston's weakness: the race that constructed the chaos device.

"Three of us needn't go.''

"I'm going because Leonore is. Since I'm the primary investigator for the expedition and supposed to make decisions, no one overturns me in these matters.''

"And I'm going because you are, Michael,'' said Leonore. She smiled wickedly. "Even if you backed out, I might still go. This is an opportunity no one else has ever had and I'm not going to miss it.'' She clasped his upper arms and squeezed hard. "Knowledge isn't always advanced safely. We know the risks and have prepared for them the best we can. We might lose our lives.''

"Chances are damned good we will,'' said Ralston.

"But there's a chance also that we won't, that we'll learn even more about the chaos field and its generation and its builders. We all know this opportunity might not happen again.''

"You're right. We still haven't disproved Westcott's notion that the field will self-destruct due to its own nature. Who knows what would happen to him if that happened. We've got to take this chance, no matter how slim it seems,'' Ralston said, resigned to having the others along. Out loud, he tried to dissuade them, but deep down he was happy for their courage and company. He might need that more than any technical expertise on their parts.

Ralston reached over and hit the call button to connect him with Gonzales. "We're going airtight now. Launch window still open?'' he asked the pilot.

"That crazy set of coordinates Westcott put into the computer is proving damned accurate,'' came the pilot's voice. "The planetoid is surging and decelerating till the saints won't have it. I can maintain a parallel course for another ten hours, if Westcott's numbers stay accurate.''

"We'll be back before then,'' said Ralston. He silently added, *Or we won't be back at all.*

Ralston settled into the couch. The tingling in his arms had stopped for the moment. The lightheadedness he experienced might be due to nerves and not the effect of the chaos field. He didn't know, but it would bear watching.

"All set?'' he called out to Leonore and Nels.

"We're strapped in. Kick us free whenever you want,'' said Bernssen.

"Good-bye it is, then!'' Ralston rammed home the throttle and sent the shuttle leaping from its bay in the side of the starship. The acceleration crushed him down like a giant invisible fist until he turned over the course control to the precomputed trajectory locked within the block circuit.

Lateral blasts threw him to one side, then the shuttle corrected its course and they settled into a more sedate trip.

"We'll be down in less than an hour,'' Ralston said. "The ship's flying a braid pattern orbit around the planetoid, dipping in, then surging out.''

"Ten hours?'' asked Leonore. "We're down in one, have eight, and then one back. Not much time to look around.''

"One down, five to look,'' corrected Ralston. "And maybe faster, if I can get to the controls and shut down the field.''

"But . . .''

"But nothing,'' cut in Ralston. "We're already dying. We may not feel it, but we are. What took centuries to affect the

Alphans will be happening to us in minutes. We're not passing near the field, we'll be as close to it as possible—in it."

"I'm still getting reports back from the two probes, Michael," said Leonore, not arguing with him over the time for exploration. "Every tiny glitch is being recorded and backed up. So far, neither supervisor is showing any trouble. I'm running the internal self-check every five minutes."

"Good. Nels? Your equipment still functioning?"

"Verd. Fantastic readings I'm getting. The field strength indications show that it varies randomly. We're in a period of low intensity now."

"Let's hope we stay there," said Ralston.

He worried for the duration of their flight, fidgeting and nervously tapping his fingers across the controls. He wanted to stand and pace, but the shuttle had been laden so heavily with equipment that little room had been left for such a show of nerves.

"Here it comes," Ralston finally called. "Got visual on the front viewscreen."

"Also got malfunction on the steering," chimed in Leonore. "Need any help?"

"Take over for me," ordered Ralston. Leonore was a better pilot than he was—and his arms had begun twitching hard enough to make it difficult to pilot. Ralston slipped his hands under a restraining strap and tried unsuccessfully to control his spastic movements.

"Here we go, then," said Leonore. Deft, small, strong hands worked on the controls, fine-tuning, adjusting, giving instructions to the computer to land them less than a hundred meters from a tiny cluster of lava upjuts covered with the markings a probe had photographed and relayed back before going dead.

"There. Touchdown," she said.

"You pilot better than Ralston," said Nels in admiration. "Hell, you pilot better than I do."

"One advantage to growing up rich. I've always had my own ship to dart around in." Leonore swung free and began to fasten up her helmet for the preliminary exploration.

The only exploration, Ralston corrected. There would be no methodical, painstaking examination of the ground, of the lava pillars, of their immediate surroundings for artifacts or other remnants of the civilization constructing the device. As he'd been forced to do so many times before, this would be more hit-and-run archaeology. Land, photograph wildly in all directions, take what wasn't too large to carry, then leave in a hurry.

He hated it but there was nothing else he could do. Better to obtain a few bits of data than none.

"I never knew you could pilot, much less do it this well," said Bernssen.

"We can talk about it later," Leonore said. She ran her fingers around the edge of her helmet, fastening it down expertly. "How's the suit radio doing?"

"Fine," said Ralston. He glanced down at his arms. The muscle contractions had stopped. To Nels he said, "Keep me posted on the field strength."

"Still at a minimum, though we went through a small increase coming in."

Ralston had feared this. The field strength determined how much—or how little—control he had over his own body.

"What are you measuring when you say 'field strength'?"

"Magnetic field," said Bernssen.

"Can we use it to find the generator?"

"Maybe. I'm not sure exactly what we're supposed to be doing," said Bernssen.

"Nobody's sure," said Ralston. "So let's do whatever it is we're supposed to do but don't know about yet."

He got his feet under him and gingerly put his weight down. His legs held. No quivering in them. With more confidence, Ralston fastened the hood of his spacesuit and checked out the radio. Nels did likewise.

"We're all set to do some archaeology," said Leonore. "But first, here're the block circuits with our programmed course." She handed each of them a precious block of yttrium aluminum garnet ceramic. "Keep 'em safe and let's hope we don't have to use any but the one that's in the board."

"Send out the probes," Ralston ordered. "We want a quick check for radiation, poison gases, loose dust, and pits."

"All the probes are gone," said Leonore.

"Do you mean sent out or *gone*?"

"Not working. Out of commission. *Muerto*."

"I get the picture. We're on our own. Carry what you can and let's get going." Ralston checked his chronometer. "We've been down almost eight minutes."

"Field strength rising," said Bernssen.

Ralston knew. His hands shook so hard that he dropped the IR camera he'd taken from an overhead rack. The shakes passed and Ralston indicated that they should leave.

They descended to the base of the shuttle. The lava had flowed near the rocket exhausts and left tiny puddles of bubbling rock. They skirted the minor destruction their landing had caused and went directly to the lava pillars. Leonore chuckled to herself as she began photographing. She soon quieted down and started recording a long verbal description of the markings they found.

Ralston had insisted that they use technology as primitive as possible. The fewer sophisticated parts, the less likely their records were of being destroyed. He mistrusted the block circuits; one small magnetic domain realigned might destroy huge segments of information. Audio recording was old-fashioned but durable. Ralston hated having to use the block circuit camera but they hadn't brought along an old silver halide film camera and there hadn't been time to make one and the film it required.

Nels Bernssen crouched down on the surface and took readings of anything and everything with his hand-held analyzer.

While they worked, Ralston wandered. The markings were bright yellow against the dark black of the jagged lava. He didn't attempt to interpret; he allowed himself to drift. The markings appeared to indicate one particular cave opening.

Ralston went inside.

Barely had he entered when a seizure grabbed total control of his body. Ralston flopped about, knowing what happened and feeling degraded, embarrassed, outraged. Clenching his teeth tightly to keep from biting his tongue, Ralston slammed hard against the cavern wall. Arms reached out and closed on a small boulder. He rolled over and over, clinging to the rock as if his life depended on it. When the seizure passed, Ralston lay panting.

"Michael! What's wrong?" came Leonore's cry in his ears.

"I had a seizure. My mind didn't go blank but I couldn't do much more than flop around. I'm all right now."

"Nels, come on. We'll go with him."

"No!" called Ralston. Too late. Both Leonore and Nels stepped inside the cavern, but for them the experience was different. Wildly different.

"It's so pretty!" cried Nels. "I never imagined anything like this. I can smell colors. And hear taste."

Ralston stared at them. They experienced the sensory confusion he did during star shifts.

"I can hear the darkness," said Leonore. "It's singing such a mournful song. How it hurts. Oh, I want to help it, but I can't. I don't know how."

"Stay where you are, please," pleaded Ralston. "I'm not confused the way you are. Stay outside and monitor my signals." He stood and forced calm on his trembling hands. This time his shaking came from fear rather than chaos-induced epilepsy.

"You don't see this? Oh, I'm sorry for you, Michael."

Ralston shoved both Leonore and Nels from the mouth of the cavern. They fell heavily, lying on the stony ground for a few minutes, shaken and unable to move.

"I have no idea how I know it, but this is the control center," Ralston said. "What was a hindrance for me before looks like an asset now. I experienced the sensory disorientation during shifts and you didn't. This is scrambling your senses and not touching mine." He dropped to his knees, intense pain shooting through his head, turning the world red before his eyes.

"The chaos field is working on me. I feel it," he said. "We won't even have five hours. I've got to find the controls and turn them off. I've got to."

He spoke more to convince himself that he could fight than to inform the others of his intentions. Ralston stumbled forward, going deeper into the darkness of the cavern. The walls turned into liquid-smooth obsidian beneath his fingers; he ran one hand along to hold himself upright. A hundred meters into the cave, Ralston remembered the IR camera dangling around his neck.

Lifting it to his eye, he peered through the sights. The darkness vanished, replaced by the eerie infrared world of heat. Brilliant plumes rose from the floor of a chamber he hadn't even realized existed. Not five paces away Ralston saw a steep precipice, dropping two meters to a rocky pit. In the center of the circular pit stood a solid column.

"The colors," he muttered. "The colors! Around the column of lava are all the colors of the rainbow—more! I've never seen such beauty. It can't be natural. It's too . . . too fantastic!"

"Michael, are you experiencing the scrambling we did? That you do during a shift?"

"No," he said. "I can see heat rising around the spire through the camera. But the colors are there. They shift and dance and change. They're like electronic veils of aurora, some type of coronal discharge."

"I'm not picking up any electrical disturbances," came Bernssen's voice, much weaker now than Ralston would have thought. He'd traveled less than two hundred meters from the cave mouth to this point. "Are you all right?"

"Fine, fine," said Ralston, distracted. He slid down the slope, taking care not to tear his spacesuit on the sharp lava rock edges. Staring up at the gauzy veils glittering around him, he walked to the central spire and laid his hand on it.

Warmth flowed through the glove and into his hand—and a convulsion struck him so hard that it sent him tumbling head over heels. Ralston moaned as the sharp rocks jabbed into his side. He carefully rolled to hands and knees, trying not to puncture his suit. The fabric was impervious to any but the most insistent attempts to breach it, but Ralston wanted to take as few chances as possible.

One epileptic seizure could unlock the ferocious power in his muscles and cast him hard enough against a rock to puncture the suit.

He looked up and saw the rainbows of delicate colors fluttering about his head, as if caught on gentle summer breezes. In the airlessness of the chaos-wracked planetoid, that wasn't possible. Ralston stood and returned to the spire.

"I've found the controls," he said with certainty. "I have no idea how they reached them, unless they flew. The spire holding the controls might be climbed, if I'm lucky."

Intense sizzling static reached his ears. Through it, he made out Nels' voice. "... Leonore's had a seizure ..." were the only words he caught.

"Get back to the ship. I'll follow when I can," he ordered. But Ralston had no confidence that his words weren't similarly garbled by the rise in static. If that meant the electrical field changed abruptly, the magnetic field—the only indicator they had—might be changing, too. And that meant a new bout of chaotic troubles.

Ralston brushed his fingers across the rocky spire. No sensation. The archaeologist took a deep breath, found hand- and footholds, and began his way up.

"I hope these *are* the controls," he said, more to himself than to Bernssen. He had blundered into this spot simply because of the yellow markings on the rock. This might be anything—it might be an exhaust or a projector for a death beam or any of a thousand other things.

But something deep within Ralston told him these were the controls for the chaos field.

Scampering as fast as he could, he got to the top of the spire. His heart sank. He had expected to find a box with neat rows of switches and readouts. He found nothing but the rocky tip of the lava pillar.

All around him floated veils of color, changing from red to blue to yellow and through every possible hue between.

"The colors," he said reverently. "The real colors of chaos."

Ralston clutched at himself when the colors flowed into a crimson curtain. His arms flopped as if he tried to take to wing and fly. As the color changed slowly to a more sedate olive green, control of his limbs returned.

"They must act as an indicator of what's happening," he said. Ralston took pictures, changing the spectral sensitivity of the block camera. He had no idea if he recorded anything at all. He could only try.

"The colors of chaos," he mused. He remembered—so long ago!—back on Novo Terra in Westcott's lab how the mathematician had plotted the chaos equations visually. The blacks were stable points, the strange attractors. The brightest reds were the most unstable points, the ones going to infinity in the complex plane the most rapidly.

Ralston looked around and saw the dazzling display as an immense imaginary number graph. He had no idea of the equation being plotted, but it resembled the one Westcott had generated. Nodes and peaks formed, sharp singularities and entire stable areas stretched out.

"All the chaos equations are being generated," he said softly, almost as if the builders might hear and appreciate his understanding, "and this shows what damage is being caused!"

The colors swirled in sharp, saw-toothed patterns, then worked through every conceivable shade and shape.

"That's exactly like the one Westcott plotted," Ralston said, noting a particular pattern forming. "The one for the radioactive decay." Ralston felt stirrings deep within his skull. He held at bay the panic and tried to guess how the colors would progress.

They followed the exact pattern he'd predicted!

Through the static came Bernssen's voice, much clearer now. "Heavy radiation. The surface is turning hot, Michael. We've got to get away."

Ralston began thinking of the colors as deepening, turning darker—more stable.

"Is the radiation level decreasing?" he asked.

"Yes, but how'd you know that?"

"I've got the controls. I don't know what to do with them exactly, but I am at the controls."

"Turn off the field. Don't worry about learning the controls," cried Bernssen, "just turn it off! I've got to get Leonore back to the ship. She hasn't come out of the seizure."

"We're more susceptible than you are. We were touched by the residual effects on Beta 5 and on Alpha 3 through the telepathic projectors," said Ralston, more interested in how to shift the colors and their patterns than in Bernssen's problems.

"Turn it off!" pleaded Nels Bernssen.

Ralston saw a new shape forming in the space around him. Marching black "S" shapes moved to a jerky beat. The colorful iteration repeated as far as Ralston could see.

"Got contact from the ship," came Bernssen's voice over the spacesuit speakers. "The sun's preparing to go nova. It's been here long enough to cause the sun to explode. We've got to leave *now*, Michael."

"It's the pattern," Ralston said. "This pattern induces novas. The other conformal mapping causes or suppresses radioactivity. Which one causes the epilepsy?"

He played with the colors, changing them by his thoughts to a brown and finally finding true blackness. Ralston wondered if the Bernssen Condition for novas had vanished. He thought it had gone with the colorful pattern.

New and disturbing patterns appeared, almost flashing past him before he could see them. Ralston closed his eyes and concentrated on the color black. Only in blackness was there stability. The attractors were black; those were stable points.

If all turned black and stable, that meant the chaos device was inactivated. It had to.

Ticklings at the fringes of his mind told Ralston that he skirted at the edge of real control. Much of the spacial plotting of the chaos equations turned black, but enough didn't to let Ralston know some randomness still occurred.

"There, there, more black, less pattern and more stability," he almost chanted. "Darkness, darkness, be my guide. Stability!"

The patterns moderated, turned quiescent and dark. Whatever generated the field calmed and began to sleep.

Then came the random shift to an exploding fountain of colors, bright yellows and greens and blues and oranges and reds, that Ralston couldn't control.

The froth of color shot upward, heading for infinity. And along with it, Ralston felt control slipping from his body. This was the pattern he'd dreaded most.

This was the pattern of personal destruction. Ralston lost consciousness and flopped off the rocky spire, muscles locked in the rictus of epileptic seizure.

SEVENTEEN

"So COLD, TOO cold," mumbled Michael Ralston. He felt as if he floated, drifting disembodied in a sea of ice. He kicked feebly, his legs finding only the rough-edged shards of lava. "Arms. Can't move my arms." He struggled until strong hands shook him.

"Stop that. I'm trying to get you out of here. We've got to return to the shuttle right away."

Ralston thought that his senses had been scrambled by the chaos field. He reached out with his mind, as he'd done before, to adjust the flow, to change the mathematical progression of the colors, to alter their confusing multitudes of infinities. Only glaring white light struck his eyes. He squinted and one hand rose to shield his eyes.

"Nels?"

"Stand up. I can't drag you any farther. I thought I could, but this has taken too much out of me."

Ralston's eyes adjusted to Bernssen's brilliant headlamp beams. He sat up and reached for his face, only to find the spacesuit helmet in the way. Memories returned in disconnected trickles, a little here, more there. But it confused him so.

"We're still in the cavern?"

"About fifty meters out. I got Leonore back to the shuttle when she had the seizure, strapped her down and sedated her, then went after you. By the time I'd reached the cave entrance the field had died down and I didn't get the sensory confusion.''

"I turned it off," Ralston said in a low voice. Louder, "I turned it off. *I shut down the chaos field!*"

"Verd, of course you did," said Nels. No hint of belief carried in his words.

"But I did! I stood on that spire. You saw the lava spire? I got to the top of it and saw the colors dancing around me like veils and sprites and exotic figures. Somehow, I managed to attune myself with it, and I *controlled* it."

"It's not going to come back on unexpectedly?"

"I don't know. I don't think it will, but if it does, I can turn it off again."

"Fine, fine, but we've got to get to the shuttle. The launch window is closing rapidly on us. We've got to blast off within twenty minutes or we won't have enough fuel to return to the ship."

"But there's plenty of time. We had ten hours . . ." Ralston glanced at his chronometer. "This can't be right. The chaos field changed it, speeded it up."

"It's right," confirmed Bernssen. "You were inside the cavern for almost the full ten hours. Leonore and I waited outside for almost six before she had the seizure."

"Time flowed differently for me. I spent only a few minutes on the spire." Ralston heaved himself to his feet, wobbled, and then took a few tentative steps. When he didn't fall over, he began walking slowly, each step a major accomplishment.

By the time they exited the cave, Ralston had regained much of his strength. He stopped and looked around the barren planetoid. So many secrets were locked away under this rocky surface. He had turned off the field but he hadn't seen the mechanism creating it. Westcott had claimed it was a concept rather than an actual device. Ralston didn't know— and couldn't speak authoritatively even though he'd experienced the field's effects at their source.

There hadn't been time to explore, to photograph, to learn. Never enough time!

"I know, Michael," said Nels. "What we did in the six

hours you were inside wasn't complete. Leonore complained bitterly about how inadequate our exploration was."

"Did any of the probes come back to life when I turned off the chaos field?"

Bernssen shrugged. "I wasn't interested in that. Only in seeing that Leonore was resting comfortably."

They reached the shuttle. At the top of the ladder, Ralston stopped and looked back over his shoulder. A tear formed in the corners of his eyes. What secrets the race that built this planetoid-sized weapon had. And they could have been his!

He tumbled into the airlock and then helped Nels struggle inside. They impatiently waited for air to pump in. Their helmets zipped off and stored, the two men hurried to the cramped cockpit. Leonore lay on the rear couch, snoring softly. Almost hesitantly, Ralston took her pulse: steady and slow.

"She seems all right. We'll have to hook her up to the automedic to be certain."

"I had nightmares of brain aneurisms and strokes from the exposure to the chaos field," said Nels. He stood beside her, shifting back and forth uncertainly.

Ralston dropped into his couch and reached over to check the supervisor. Dead, a victim of chaos. Its electronic circuits had suffered the equivalent fate that Leonore's biologic system had. He turned and looked at the second supervisor. It had fared better and still functioned. A self-check of its circuits showed most to be operational—and four probes had reactivated after the chaos field had been turned off. Ralston hit the control toggle that stored the information in the supervisor's block circuits, then made spare copies.

"Let's get out of here," he said. His fingers seemed numb on the controls, but he fought to keep his concentration on the work and not his personal condition.

"What's wrong, Michael?"

"It's the block circuit with our programmed escape course. It's dead." Ralston reached up to the shuttle's control panel and popped out the destroyed block and tossed it aside. He pulled out the one Leonore had given him and inserted it.

It was dead, too.

"Here's mine," said Bernssen, handing over the tiny ceramic computer block.

The engines vented throaty roars and lights began flashing, but it took only seconds for Ralston to see that Bernssen's block circuit had also been a fatality to the chaos-induced randomness.

"We can wing it," said Nels. "You fly, I'll compute."

"We're too close to the edge of the window," said Ralston. He held back the panic rising within. He had turned off the most fearsome weapon the galaxy had ever seen and now a broken block circuit might kill him. He refused to die because of it. He wouldn't die!

"Fuel level is critical," said Nels, looking at the readout. "But if we can get near enough to the ship, they can maneuver and pick us up."

"Oxygen is critical, too. Look at the indicators."

"That's impossible. We have full tanks. Enough for weeks."

"Sniff." Ralston opened a valve and jerked away when the gas spewed forth.

"Smells like garlic."

"The chaos field turned the oxygen into ozone. Must have done the same to the fuel blocks. We'll be running short on both oxygen and fuel if we don't make rendezvous the first time."

"Can you do it?"

"No." Ralston knew his limits as a pilot. Leonore might be able to, but he couldn't, not now that their block circuits had fallen prey to chaos. Ralston leaned back when he thought of the woman, then laughed. "What idiots we are. There's one more chance. Leonore's block. Get it."

Nels fumbled in his haste to pull the block circuit from the sleeping woman's carrying pouch. With a comic reverence, he carried it in cupped hands to Ralston.

It slid into the control panel. Lights again blossomed. And the navigation computer chuckled merrily to itself, finding acceptable data to guide the ship.

Ralston almost fainted with relief. He sat up and began to prepare for the launch. "All set," he called to Nels. "Make sure you're both fastened down tight. This is going to be a rough trip. We're just past the last computed launch window."

"Can you contact the ship and let them know we're coming?"

The red light on the control panel told Ralston that most of their communications circuitry had died in the chaos field.

"We'll be all right," he assured the physicist. Ralston kept repeating the same words over and over to convince himself. It didn't help.

The kick from the rockets drove him back into the couch. Ralston fought to keep from passing out. Although the acceleration wasn't that intense, his battered body wanted to quit. Only force of will kept him going. Ralston watched the readouts through half-hooded eyes. The block circuit had them on the proper course.

He hoped it was the right course. He couldn't know the details, but it seemed right. Only when Ralston thought they were safely en route did he relax and let the waves of blackness wash over him. He passed out.

"How long has it been?" he asked. Ralston forced his eyes to open and focus on Nels Bernssen. The physicist huddled over the control panel and ran his fingers almost lovingly over the switches that determined their fate.

"Too long. We boosted for almost an hour and then ran out of fuel."

Ralston felt an icy spike driving hard into his guts. They'd left the research ship with enough fuel for a dozen trips to the planetoid and back.

"The effects of the chaos," Nels confirmed. "Something happened to the chemical makeup of the fuel blocks. Some fired, most didn't. Engines shut down to keep from uneven burns."

"The same as what happened to our oxygen." Ralston's nose wrinkled at the harsh ozone odor lingering from the brief venting while we were still on the planetoid's surface.

"It must be. We're drifting without rockets, and we have less than an hour's worth of oxygen."

"And we can't contact the ship," Ralston finished the litany of despair. "Most of the equipment on the shuttle's not working and we're drifting now." He leaned back, eyes closed. It seemed anticlimactic for his life to end in this way.

Of all the archaeologists working in the field, he had made the most astounding discoveries, had discovered lost worlds and cultures, watched them snuffed out in a blast of chaos-fueled nova, and had capped his career with finding the source of the most devastating weapon in the universe.

"There is a bright side to all this," said Nels.

"You might as well tell me. I can use it."

"We don't have to write any papers or reveal what we've discovered about the chaos weapon to the Nex."

"Bright spot," muttered Ralston. Maybe this *was* the best they could hope for. Keeping the awesome power of the chaos field from Nex, P'torra, and human war fleets might rank as his major accomplishment.

Only no one would ever know. Ralston glanced around the shuttle cockpit that would be his eternal tomb. He'd hoped for more.

"How's Leonore?"

"Still in a coma," said Nels, worry in his voice. "But she's resting comfortably and doesn't seem to be in pain."

"She'll come out of this all right. We all will," Ralston said.

Even as he spoke, the air clogged his nose and throat with its staleness. He coughed and rubbed his watering eyes. Every muscle in his body ached horribly.

"Want something to eat?" asked Nels. "We have enough, unless it's been chaotically changed into poison."

"Might be a boon, if it has," said Ralston. "The air's getting close, isn't it?" He coughed again.

"While you were out, I checked all the tanks. The main tank's more ozone than oxygen. The secondary tanks are exhausted. What's in the shuttle now is all we have."

"Spacesuits?"

"Another few hours each, but without maneuvering rockets, what's the difference?"

Ralston closed his eyes, temples pounding hard and his heart feeling as if it would leap from his chest.

"Fire," he said. "A torch. Can you put together a plasma torch?"

"We have a couple welding lasers aboard." For a few seconds Nels Bernssen didn't understand, then a big grin spread across his face. "I'll get it. Want to open the oxygen valve?"

"How dangerous is this going to be?"

"What's the difference?" asked the physicist. He returned with a welding laser, adjusted the twin beams to intersect at the precise point where the ozone would exhaust from its tank.

Ralston opened the valve slowly and let a small stream out. The laser superheated the ozone and broke it down into oxygen. What other combustion products were formed would be removed by the shuttle's efficient filtering system.

"Enough for the moment," Nels said. "We've got enough to last a day or two before it gets stuffy again."

"The mechanical filter's not likely to quit on us," said Ralston. The air tasted metallic on his tongue, but it carried none of the choking ozone vapor.

"We've got food, air, and all the time in the world. What should we do with it?" asked Nels. The man's tone was light, but Ralston noticed that he kept glancing toward Leonore, worried for her.

"Data reduction? We've got enough to work on for a lifetime." Ralston instantly regretted his choice of words.

"I think I'll take some more data," said Nels. "I never did like the dogwork of actually sifting through all the numbers to find the one or two gems."

The physicist settled in front of a spectrometer and aimed its optics at the solar system's primary. Ralston lay back on the couch, eyes closed, mind racing. They couldn't contact the research ship because they had no idea where it was—and with their rockets useless, reaching the ship would be impossible. How could they skirt all those impossibles and survive? He worked over one scheme after another, each more implausible than the one before.

"Michael, I've just finished with the first pictures of the star."

"And?" asked Ralston.

"The Bernssen condition is present. This sun's going nova soon. I'd say within a few months."

Ralston accepted the news calmly. They'd be dead long

before the cleansing plumes of superheated plasma licked outward in the star's death throes.

"That means the chaos weapon will be destroyed. There's no way it can orbit free of the system in time, not at sublight speeds."

"I never had the impression that it traveled faster than light," said Ralston. "It might have, but there's so much we will never know about it." He lay back, quiet now, reflecting on fate. The chaos weapon might be decaying, as Westcott had calculated, but it didn't matter. It had sent such a jolt of chaos into this star's stellar furnace that it couldn't escape the system before being destroyed.

It would die in fires of its own creation. A fitting end, thought Ralston.

"There's not any chance to make a primitive radio and contact the ship," said Nels.

"What?" Ralston's chain of thought had been broken by this unexpected comment.

"I'd considered bollixing together a radio and trying to set up an interference field that the ship might find, but with the sun's instability at such a level, it'd drown out any noise we might make."

"It might not have been powerful enough, in any case. There's not much laying around loose in the way of equipment." Almost all equipment aboard the shuttle came in prepackaged modular form. Tearing it apart would avail them only broken equipment, not valuable parts to be reconstructed into life-saving gadgets.

"Most of it isn't working right, anyway," said Nels. The man slumped back in a couch, tiredness permanently etched on his face. "But we can't give up, can we?"

"I can't," said Ralston. "I'll keep thinking about it until something occurs to me. I don't believe the pilot would abandon us."

"They might decide to leave if they've noticed the increasing instability in the stellar furnace," Nels said.

"We're supposed to find ways out, not invent new problems. But that's an easy one to get around. Would you leave a newly formed nova unless you had to immediately? No, you'd stay as long as you could to study it. So will McGhee and Barranquilla and the others."

"Barranquilla's in charge since I'm gone," he said. "She wouldn't want to leave until the first hard gamma and x-rays struck the hull of the ship. Nothing's more important to her than her magnetic moment measurements."

They talked idly, occasionally drifting up to check the few readouts still functioning.

Time ceased to have meaning, although Ralston frequently checked his chronometer. Sometimes only a few minutes had passed. Other times showed long hours. Both intervals seemed identical to him. And always he worried over how to contact the research ship. He'd insisted that Bernssen set up monitoring equipment to automatically alert them if the ship neared, but even Ralston had to admit the chances of this happening accidentally were close to zero.

The shuttle had started for a rendezvous point with the research ship, but when the engines had quit, their course was directly out of the system. No planets orbited nearby, they detected no asteroids or small bits of matter, and the chaos planetoid hurled itself away, far away from any chance of returning.

Four days of drifting. Five. Eight. Ralston and Bernssen spent most of their time asleep. Leonore's condition did not improve, but it did not worsen. Of the three Ralston envied her the most. She knew nothing of their peril—or the initial boredom followed by increasing realization that they would die.

Ralston awakened, nose clogged and the shuttle cockpit wavering behind his watery eyes. He'd managed to get a cold. Without the auto-doc he had no real chance of getting over it before they all died.

Ralston laughed hard at this, then laughed to the point of hysteria. He had reconciled himself to dying, or lied to himself well enough that he believed he had. But to die with a head cold? That was an indignity he wouldn't tolerate.

Nels had tried to put together any number of communication devices. None worked. Ralston knew he had no chance of succeeding where the physicist had failed, but checking the instruments now and then made him feel he was doing something useful.

"I'm not going to die with a cold. I'm not!"

He wiped his eyes and stared into the eyepiece of Bernssen's spectrometer. It showed a band pattern unlike any he'd ever seen before. Nels had been watching the star and Ralston had accustomed himself to the light and dark bands. This was different, more intense.

"Nels?" he called. "What do you make of this? Is the sun going to explode?"

The physicist heaved himself up from the couch beside Leonore and stared at the spectral pattern. His mouth opened, then snapped shut hard.

"What is it?"

"That's the spectrum for a rocket exhaust."

"The research ship? But how?"

"I don't know. I just don't know. Even if they were hunting for us, they'd have no way of finding where we'd gone."

But they had been found. An hour later, magnetic docking lines from the research ship slammed into the airlock and slowly pulled the shuttle into its docking bay.

EIGHTEEN

"WESTCOTT!" CRIED MICHAEL RALSTON, seeing the mathematician waiting for them inside the research ship's airlock. "You're all right! You came out of the coma!"

"Verd, I am well again." Westcott looked curiously uneasy. His watery eyes refused to meet Ralston's. "I want to thank you. You saved my life."

"What? Oh, turning off the chaos field? That did it?"

"It did. Once the power of the chaos faded, I was able to fight against the residual bonds holding me. It took almost a week, but after that, I returned to normal."

Ralston refused to comment about what was normal for the computer-linked mathematician. Instead, he said, "You're the one who started looking for us, aren't you? It looks as if we all owe *you* a debt of thanks."

Westcott watched emotionlessly as Leonore Disa was carried from the shuttle, Nels Bernssen following closely. "It posed a problem requiring considerable thought and computation. No one else is capable of solving such a complex set of equations."

"How did you know where to look for us? Or even that we wouldn't be able to contact you? You could have assumed we were dead on the planetoid."

"Barranquilla and the others noted the Bernssen Condition and the incipient nova. I, naturally, knew that the chaos field had collapsed because of the skewed time between chaos introduction and the ultimate effect. The onslaught of this nova had to mean success on your part. The collapse of the chaos field would result in a sudden burst, then nothing. Because of this burst, the nova was initiated and I knew that your equipment would, in the main, have failed. That would include the most chaotically 'fragile,' all the communication and computer equipment.

"Further reflection told of potential problems with your solid fuel blocks. Chemical reactions would not proceed properly near the center of the chaos field."

"But how did you find us?"

Westcott smiled. Ralston wasn't sure he liked the cadaverous expression.

"The chaos equations. I simply added in equipment failure to possible courses and random direction of takeoff from the planetoid to get the most volumes of space."

"And you sailed straight to us, just like that." Ralston marveled at what he had to rate as luck, in spite of knowing the mathematics—and Westcott's genius—behind their rescue.

"Not exactly. We searched seven different volumes of space before finding you."

Ralston laughed, then stepped forward to shake Westcott's hand. He reached out and collapsed, the strain finally taking its toll on him.

"Leonore is up and around?" he asked Nels Bernssen. The tall blond's head bobbed up and down, his smile almost dazzling.

"The auto-doc had her fixed up in less than a day. She'd suffered a series of strokes on the planetoid, nothing too dangerous. She still lisps a little, but that will go away after a bit more therapy. But how are you feeling? You look a world better."

"Feel it," said Ralston. He stretched and sat up in the bunk. He knew he had to be on the mend. Already, his cabin seemed constricting to him, too small, too plain. "In spite of being in the center of the chaos field, not much happened to me physically. The automedic has been whirring away. What problems remain are the ones I've always had."

Ralston saw Bernssen's worried expression and asked, "What's wrong?"

"Nothing, actually. It's just that you were unconscious for so long."

"Long? But it's only been a few hours."

"It's been close to two weeks. We've held off starring back to Novo Terra because of your condition."

"Starring back? Why?"

"The sun. You remember it was going nova? Westcott's calculated that we have less than four days left before it explodes." Bernssen held up his hand to forestall Ralston's objection. "He was wrong before, but then he didn't have the data from the planetoid. He's been refining his solution sets. This time we have physical evidence that he's right. And he measured the chaotic burst that set off the Bernssen Condition."

"Why worry about me?"

"We didn't want to shift and have your senses scrambled. The auto-doc thought it might kill you, in light of what happened on the planetoid."

Ralston snorted in disgust. He felt great. Nothing could harm him now. He'd fought chaos and won!

"Have you been studying the planetoid?" Ralston asked.

"It's been difficult. Its course took it almost directly across the disk of the star. Solar activity blotted out most of our sensitive measurements."

"Then it'll be destroyed in the nova?"

"It would have been destroyed within a week, anyway. We were lucky to reach it when we did. Westcott is sure that it was already decaying, fading to nothing all by itself."

Ralston sank back on his bunk, a curious mixture of feelings fighting for supremacy within. The opportunity to study it for archaeological evidence had passed. For that, he mourned. But the chaos weapon would never again threaten entire solar systems and bring about the woe that it had for untold millennia.

But the knowledge that was being destroyed in the blink of an eye!

Ralston reconsidered this lost knowledge. What they hadn't learned, they couldn't pass along to the Nex. And if the Nex didn't have it, then neither did the P'torra. That didn't reduce the chance for war, but it removed a weapon from both sides' arsenals that neither could control, much less understand.

"How much has Westcott learned?"

"That's hard to say," said Bernssen. "A great deal. We've all got mountains of data to sift through, and it will be career making for us all. Epoch making for science, too. Every field of endeavor will be affected. Biology, physics, mathematics." Bernssen smiled. "Archaeology. Leonore's been working on a computer simulation of the planetoid and has learned a great deal about the race that constructed the chaos weapon."

Ralston's heart pounded with excitement and a flush rose to his cheeks.

"I've got to see what she's done."

Bernssen pushed him gently back into the bunk. "Later. I'm going to tell the pilot to star for home."

"Home," Ralston said. He couldn't keep the bitterness from his voice.

"Home," insisted Nels Bernssen. "Not the University. *Home.*"

"You'll be there. Leonore will, too. But I've—what did you mean?" The inflection of Bernssen's words meant more than what he'd said.

"Neither Leonore nor I will be returning to Ilium. I don't think Westcott will, either. We've discussed this, the three of us—and the others, too. We're establishing a private research foundation devoted entirely to further study of the chaos weapon, its cause, effect, origins, everything about it."

"And?" prompted Ralston.

"We want you to be a director. In charge of researching the planetoid's origins, the race that built it, things of that nature."

"Where will the funding come from?" asked Ralston.

"We won't have any trouble finding it," said Bernssen. "Putting together what we know about chaos gives us a fantastic spectrum of products to market. Westcott can predict weather, or so he claims, given enough parameters for his equations."

"What about the Nex? We promised them a first look at the information in our research papers."

"I don't know about you, Dr. Ralston, but I don't intend publishing for free anything that might bring us enough money to do as we please for the rest of our lives. We might consider selling the Nex some of our predictions for bargain rates. But papers? Why publish trade secrets? We don't have to publish any longer. Unless we want. I called the shots when I took the money to fund this expedition and didn't guarantee anything to anyone. In fairness, I suppose we'll give the sponsors first grab at some of the things we produce—the predictions— but we don't have to dance to anyone's tune but our own."

"This is so big, Nels."

"I know. And we're lucky to have Leonore in it with us. She has incredible skills she's hidden away." He smiled sheepishly. "She didn't want to frighten me away with her brilliance, I suppose. But she was raised by one of the foremost entrepreneurs on Nova Terra. If she can't handle the business for us, she knows the people who can—and can hire them away from her father. The man's not well liked."

"But this affects so much," said Ralston. "If Westcott can predict weather, we can do sociological dynamics studies to predict wars. Maybe even determine how to stop them."

"There's that," agreed Bernssen. "And more. So much more we'll still be figuring them out a hundred years from now."

"Director of Archaeology?" asked Ralston.

"Or whatever title suits you. Results are what we need at first, to establish credentials and start the money flowing. Then we can funnel a limitless flood of funding into pure research. And we will!"

"Get the pilot started for Novo Terra," said Ralston. "I can't wait to return!"

Nels Bernssen slapped Ralston on the shoulder, then left. The archaeologist settled back in his bunk, mind unable to seize on any single fact and think about just that. So much had happened.

The chaos weapon was destroyed by its own existence, but it had taken with it countless lives. Ralston thought it was only fitting that some good come from the destruction it had wrought.

He smiled at the thought of Salazar's reaction. The man would be livid at losing Nels, Leonore, and especially Westcott, not to mention the others in the expedition. As Francis Bacon had written, "Revenge is a wild kind of justice." At last Ralston would get justice from the school. The University of Ilium's faculty would be banging on their doors, begging for research positions.

The Chaos Foundation? Ralston liked the sound of it.

He pulled taut the restraining straps when the pilot announced the shift. The sensory scrambling that had proven so beneficial in dealing with controlling the chaos field now sent him spinning in dizzying circles, tasting sound and hearing the touch of the bunk against his body. But Michael Ralston didn't care.

A universe lay beyond such momentary confusion, a universe defined by chaos controlled!

THE JADE DEMON QUARTET

ROBERT E. VARDEMAN

Kesira, beautiful, last survivor of the sacred Order of Gelya, looked about her. Demon-destroyed, all her past, all learning and companionship lay blasted into nothingness by the liquid jade fire that had lanced down from the apocalyptic skies.

A terrible understanding grew and flared in her mind. She knew now that the time for her Quest had come. Accompanied only by the magical, future-seeing bird Zolkan and Molimo the changeling man-wolf, she must challenge the Jade Demons.

Gigantic, fearful creatures, they loomed and battled in the skies, destroying the land and the people, as they fought for final supremacy.

Kesira, votive maiden turned she-warrior, set forth on her fate-ordained path . . .

Never before published in the UK, THE JADE DEMON QUARTET comprises *The Quaking Lands*, *The Frozen Waves*, *The Crystal Clouds* and *The White Fire* in one volume.

A Royal Mail service in association with the Book Marketing Council & The Booksellers Association.
Post-A-Book is a Post Office trademark.

MORE SCIENCE FICTION AND FANTASY
AVAILABLE FROM HODDER AND STOUGHTON
PAPERBACKS